Harlequin
Omnibus

3 Great Novels by

Roumelia Lane

Harlequin Books

TORONTO • LONDON • NEW YORK
AMSTERDAM • SYDNEY • WINNIPEG

These books by Roumelia Lane were formerly published as follows:

HOUSE OF THE WINDS
Copyright © 1968 by Roumelia Lane
First published in 1968 by Mills & Boon Limited
Harlequin edition (#1262) published December 1968

A SUMMER TO LOVE
Copyright © 1968 by Roumelia Lane
First published in 1968 by Mills & Boon Limited
Harlequin edition (#1290) published April 1969

SEA OF ZANJ
Copyright © 1969 by Roumelia Lane
First published in 1969 by Mills & Boon Limited
Harlequin edition (#1338) published October 1969

ISBN 0-373-70321-X

First **Harlequin Omnibus** edition published January 1976
Second printing July 1976
Third printing October 1976
Fourth printing February 1977

Contents

HOUSE OF THE WINDS

Don Sinclair

Laurie experienced a feeling of dismay. Was that how Ryan Holt was going to regard her from now on? As a little sister? A playmate for his younger brother?

As she looked at the swaying palms and blazing jacarandas, Laurie knew she should be overjoyed at the opportunity to remain in Africa, but somehow her heart wasn't in it.

Not on those terms!

CHAPTER ONE

THE red earth road veered suddenly as though bored with the endless thorny scrub and distant lilac hills. It loped eagerly towards a line of spreading acacias and then widened expansively to take in white thatched huts, open-fronted stores and a petrol station. Now its edges sprouted spindly palms that strained away from each other at awkward angles, giving a criss-cross view of sprawling one-storied blocks and tin-roofed bungalows.

So this was Mbinga?

Laurie cast a dubious glance towards a drab buff-coloured building coming up on the left, which boasted 'Safaritrek Hotel' in chipped black letters. Somewhere near there must be the Safaritrek office and its director, Ryan Holt. She swallowed hard and suppressed a desire to instruct the driver to turn round and go back, not sure whether it was this first sight of her destination that taxed her nerves or the thoughts of a subsequent meeting with Tanzania's famed big-game hunter. Shivering slightly, she clutched her cameras to her and half closed her eyes. She might as well admit it. She wasn't looking forward to the meeting at all.

With a title like that, he had to be big, aggressive and full of his own importance. Imagine having to ask such a man a favour!

As the car crunched to a stop, she realized she must have been slightly mad to have landed herself in such a position. It was one thing to dream up all sorts of wild and marvellous schemes wrapped in the security of an armchair in a London flat, but when it came to putting them into practice . . . oh, how they lost their sparkle! The driver opened the door and she threw a quick look over a town prostrate with heat and dust, the only signs of life, a green lizard snaking its way over a wall, a fat toad pulsing sleepily in the shadows. Well, all she could do now was to hope that this Ryan Holt man wasn't as terrible as he sounded and that it wouldn't prove too much of an ordeal asking him to take her deep into the African bush. Reaching down inside herself for a steadying

9

breath, she stepped out of the car and deliberately averted her gaze from the way they had come. Too late now to turn round and run. This was Mbinga. She had arrived.

The driver took her bag to the entrance of the hotel, nodded briefly and returned to take his place behind the wheel. Trance-like, she watched the vehicle turn round, take off in a cloud of red dust and disappear mistily between the palms. Only when the dust had dispersed and the noise of the engine had faded out in the distance did Laurie make an anxious grab for her case. She swung it wildly through the double doors of the hotel to land almost on top of a recumbent figure immediately behind. There was the flash of white teeth in polished ebony features, a heavy-lidded blink and then a gentle snore. She stepped over the sleeping form to find a dull red floor dotted with plain tables and armchairs.

The heads of horned animals stared down glassy-eyed from the walls, and a fan whirred lazily over a reception desk opposite.

Beyond was an alcove leading through into a succession of other rooms. There was no bell to push and Laurie was wondering if she ought to touch one of the other two sleeping figures on a rush matting near the desk when a sound caught her ears.

She listened, puzzled. The click of stiletto heels? Surely not? Out here? She turned to see a slim, lilac-clad shape approaching through the alcove. The next moment there was the sharp clapping of hands and the figures on the floor stretched up with good-natured grins and padded to their various stations.

The woman, who looked probably twenty-eight to thirty, flicked a bored glance in Laurie's direction and moved towards the reception desk.

'You must excuse the boys—' she sounded cold '—they're not exactly at their best at this time of day.'

As the other woman thumbed over the book on the desk Laurie noticed the beautifully kept hands and coral spear-shaped nails. There was a thick band of gold on her third left hand finger topped by a stunning outsize diamond.

'Have we got your booking?' She didn't raise the ash-blonde head.

'Well . . . er . . . no.' Laurie drew her case nearer. 'I'm

10

Laurie Weldon. I won't be staying more than three or four nights. I didn't think there would be any need to . . .'

'You should always reserve your accommodation well in advance, Miss Weldon. You'll find our safari hotels are very popular and often booked to the hilt.' There was a slight pause and then, 'Luckily I think I can fit you in.'

Laurie smiled her relief and signed the book eagerly.

'You're very kind. I'm rather new to this sort of thing. You see I only flew out from England the day before yesterday. It was silly of me not to . . .'

The smooth head was nodding abruptly.

'I'm Mrs. Lewis, the hotel proprietress. I hope you will be comfortable. The boy will show you to your rondavel.' She tossed a key to the white-clad figure who was stooping over the case. 'Meals are in the hotel. Three a day. We do a packed lunch for those who prefer it.'

Laurie had to draw in a smile. A few minutes ago she had been near to a state of panic at the wildness of her surroundings and what she had let herself in for. Now the atmosphere had the distinct ring of an English seaside hotel where one was immediately acquainted with the service, and the landlady's offer of sandwiches for would-be picnickers. A very elegant landlady in this case, Laurie mused, noting the expensive cut of the linen suit, the slender winged eyebrows. Perhaps Mbinga wasn't so frighteningly far away from civilization after all? But there was still the safari master to contend with. She made to follow the luggage and then turned back thoughtfully.

'Oh, Mrs. Lewis. Perhaps you could help me? I was wondering where I might find the Safaritrek offices?'

The smooth head tilted upwards and Laurie had her first clear view of fine-boned features and a pale flawless complexion.

Hyacinth blue eyes dropped down the length of her, slowly, thoughtfully.

'To the right at the end of the road. Any special reason for asking?'

Laurie fidgeted beneath the sweeping gaze, suddenly acutely conscious of her crumpled dress and dust-covered hair. She blurted nervously, 'Ryan Holt is the safari master, isn't he? I'm hoping he'll be free to take me on a trip.'

11

Mrs. Lewis closed the book and came round the side of the reception desk, the suggestion of an amused smile playing around the coral lips. 'I'm afraid you've had a wasted journey, my dear. Ryan would never go big-game hunting with a woman.'

'I don't want to hunt—' Laurie cringed a smile. 'At least . . . well, only to take pictures. I'm an animal photographer. Mr. Holt was recommended to me by the agent in Dar es Salaam.'

'Of course he would be,' Mrs. Lewis drawled. 'He's recommended to everyone, but Ryan picks his clients, and you can take it from me they've never included our sex.'

'Oh . . . I see.'

There was a silence and then Mrs. Lewis shrugged her reassurance.

'There are plenty of guides, my dear. You'll find enough animals in the immediate locality to fill a couple of reels.'

But not the kind *I* want, Laurie thought.

'I think I'll go and see him anyway,' she said down to her shoes.

'You'll have quite a journey—' The sultry voice seemed to hold a note of subdued satisfaction. 'He's over at Lake Shimo taking a breather. It's a considerable distance from here.'

Laurie drew in her lower lip. 'How can I get in touch with him?'

'Telegraph is about the only thing we have.' Mrs. Lewis turned back towards the alcove. 'But I'd advise you not to waste your time. He won't come.'

Dejectedly Laurie followed the boy out of the side door. She had prepared herself for all manner of difficulties in the shape of the safari master, except to find he had no time for women! That was a bit of a blow. Especially as she was entirely dependent on his help.

A rondavel, it seemed, was a hut similar to the ones she had seen coming into town. Pointed, thatched roofs topped sturdy bamboo struts, while the lower half circled round in neat cement.

There were plenty of windows, a cool stone floor and the same items of furniture that one might find in a small hotel room.

Laurie didn't bother to explore the bathroom some forty yards away from her hut, for the hotel boy had offered, with a wide smile and in attractive sing-song English, to take her message to the post office for a small fee. There was time to be rid of the coating of red dust later. She rummaged for a pencil and paper and sat down to compose the message. It wasn't easy, and was probably a waste of time anyway. Mrs. Lewis had said he wouldn't come and she looked as if she knew what Ryan Holt would or wouldn't do.

After some thought, Laurie pencilled a half-hearted note stating her interest in a safari and where she could be reached. It was only when she was signing the message that the idea came to her. Laurie Weldon. She looked at the name. It didn't sound so feminine, in fact it could be taken as . . . Before her conscience could rebuke her, she wrote out a fresh note signing herself merely 'L. Weldon' and handed it to the boy.

The bathroom proved to be adequate, though Laurie didn't care for the journey back to her rondavel in the gathering shadows. The trees rustled ominously, and the ground seemed to move beyond the bushes. It occurred to her that most of the other huts, about a dozen in all, seemed unoccupied. Either the occupants were all late-nighters or Mrs. Lewis wasn't as fully booked as she liked to make out. The weird calls and shrieks in the night put paid to any further speculation. She hurried towards her own tiny home and bed.

At breakfast there was little evidence of other guests, but the long room, which was dining room, bar, reception and lounge progressively, began to fill up during the morning. From their conversation Laurie gathered that the men were mostly from the nearby coffee plantations, or government workers on their leisurely way to some even remoter destination. She would have preferred to remain a little aloof, to continue her watch along the road, but it was difficult to ignore the curious, appraising glances and more than occasional friendly nods. Almost before she knew it, she had been warmly drawn into the men's midst. There were offers of drinks and advice on all topics and amidst the general conversation and laughter Laurie relaxed a little and laughed too.

This was all new to her, but it certainly did wonders for the morale, being the centre of attraction.

She didn't pay much attention when a tall khaki-clad figure stooped through the swing doors and threw a distasteful glance up the room. Another planter, though obviously not in the best of spirits, she mused, vaguely aware that he had moved towards the reception desk. It was only when she heard a vibrant enquiry for a 'Mr. Weldon' that her knees started to tremble. The boy at the desk looked vacant under the piercing gaze and took refuge in the visitor's book. Laurie moved away from the crowd and down the room as the man swung round to survey the occupants impatiently.

'Mr. Holt?' Her voice sounded suddenly faint. Raising her eyes, she caught a glimpse of powerful shoulders and a glitter of green as his glance flickered over her. He returned to studying the talkative men at the bar. She moved nearer.

'You . . . er . . . had a message? A request for a safari?'

'That's right. From a Mr. Weldon. You with him?' He didn't alter his gaze.

'No, I'm . . . I'm here alone, but . . .' she stepped up eagerly, 'I *would* like to talk to you about that safari. You see I'm Laurie Weldon and . . .' She gulped as narrowed eyes swung suddenly round her way. The longish copper-tanned features took their time in tightening until the mouth was no more than a forbidding line beneath the flaring aquiline nose.

'So you're Weldon?' He let a derogatory gaze slide down the length of the slight figure in sleeveless lemon dress and up again to the swatch of corn-silk hair curling up from one shoulder.

The already deep voice dropped an octave lower to take on something of a growl. 'You missed out an important piece of information in your message, Weldon. The bit that would have told me I was wasting my time!'

He pushed his back away from the desk, but Laurie hurried to step in front of him.

'Mr. Holt, I'm sorry I had to deceive you to get you here, but I'd heard about this ridiculous rule of yours of not taking women on safari and . . .'

14

'That's right. I don't take women. Too much trouble. Children even more so.'

With a meaning half-sneer, he almost lifted her out of his path and strode away towards the door.

Children! Breathing rapidly, Laurie followed him outside.

'It must be a long time since you've seen any children, Mr. Holt,' she snapped. 'I'm almost nineteen and I probably know nearly as much about the wild animals in these parts as you do, that's why I wanted . . .'

'Look,' he slid into a dusty estate car and, after tossing his gaze in the direction of the hotel and the sound of men's laughter, turned an icy green glance her way, 'I know all about the kids of today being bored to distraction, but if you're looking for kicks my advice is to find them elsewhere. This is the African bush, not open day at Whipsnade.'

He slammed the door and roared away in a cloud of dust. Laurie stared after him, her grey eyes bright with tears of fury. Of all the unreasonable, bigoted . . .! She closed her eyes and breathed hard to disperse her anger. Well, at least she could congratulate herself on one thing – she had been right in her own private assessment of Mbinga's safari master. Big, aggressive and definitely hateful!

CHAPTER TWO

LAURIE was still looking after the car, hands clenched, when Mrs. Lewis's voice floated lightly along the road:

'You ought to have taken my advice, Miss Weldon. Ryan can be quite churlish when he's annoyed.' She stepped daintily along the road as though it were some select suburban avenue, a fine chiffon scarf caught at her throat and a shopping basket on one arm. Of course she must have seen the whole performance, Laurie thought, wishing now she had hurried inside instead of standing there, nursing her anger. The older woman drew level and held out the basket.

'Take this for me, would you, my dear? It gets heavier with every step in this heat.'

Laurie didn't think the heat was particularly overpowering at this time of day, but she had no option but to take the basket.

She saw it was filled with hair shampoos, nail lacquers and lotions, and weighed hardly anything at all. Seeing Laurie's downard glance, Mrs. Lewis drooped a smile.

'I have all the good brands specially ordered by the local store. Heaven knows what I'd look like stuck out here without them!' She guided Laurie away from the swing-doors and round to the side of the hotel. 'We needn't go in by the main entrance. Through here, my dear.'

Through a door towards the back of the block Laurie saw a large airy room shabbily furnished, with huge tapestry armchairs and faded carpets. One of the boys from the hotel was bending over a flower-bed beneath the window and a yellowish lawn rolled down to a cluster of trees. Laurie placed the basket inside the door and with a brief smile turned to go.

'I must say it was a clever idea of yours not signing your full name on the telegraph yesterday.'

As Laurie shot a startled glance upwards, Mrs. Lewis was swinging the tan jacket away from her shoulders. She opened a silver box and hung a cigarette on the drooped smile. 'You mustn't mind the boys, my dear. They speak quite freely

16

amongst themselves and one can't help overhearing at times.'

And if the boy who had taken her message, no more than a folded note, could speak English, he could read it too, Laurie reflected, feeling a warm flush surge along her cheeks.

'I thought it was worth a try.' Laurie wanted to smile, but somehow her lower lip got caught between her teeth. One sandalled foot scuffed against the other.

'And it worked!' Mrs. Lewis breathed throatily. 'But, of course, I knew the minute Ryan set eyes on you. . . .' She dropped a hooded glance down the slight, pony-tailed figure and blew out a gust of smoke contentedly. A flicker of irritation prompted Laurie to return, 'You seem to know all there is to know about Mr. Holt. Your husband and he must be very close.'

'My husband is dead, Miss Weldon, but you're right about Ryan and me. We are very close, and of course I couldn't manage without his help in running this place.'

And welcome to it, Laurie thought, still prickling from her first, and what was probably her last, brush with the big-game boss. She stepped outside, curiously reluctant to have a prolonged conversation with the hotel proprietress.

'If you'll excuse me, Mrs. Lewis, I think I'll go and have a look at the town.'

'One street!' The widow tilted an eyebrow quizzically. 'What about the animal photography? If you require a guide I could . . .'

'That won't be necessary, thank you, Mrs. Lewis. I won't be staying after today.'

The older woman shrugged, drawing on the cigarette lazily. 'You'll pay for the full four days, of course,' she murmured.

'Naturally—' As Laurie turned away, Mrs. Lewis's voice drifted from an armchair: 'Sorry we couldn't have been more help, my dear, and do see that your rondavel is dusted and swept, won't you? The boys create so when there is extra work.'

Mbinga looked vastly different when not stupefied by the afternoon heat. The stores were doing a lively trade and the wide road was thronged by smiling natives in multi-coloured shirts and skirts of green and gold. Laurie strolled on, a tremor of excitement coursing through her. This was Africa! She was really here. Yesterday she had been too keyed up to sense its magic, but who could turn a blind eye to a morning that was blossoming flame-trees, swift-winged birds and endless caressing sunshine?

Africa, the unpredictable, the brochures said, the land of intense beauty and strange excitement, the charmer that could hold one for ever in its spell. She closed her eyes to breathe deeply of its hundred tantalising perfumes, its hot earth and crackling bush, and opened them to come up against the Safaritrek office.

Some of her elation fell away. It looked as though Africa wasn't going to get a chance to work its spell on Laurie Weldon. Her stay was destined to be short-lived and all too predictable.

No safari and no breathtaking reels of film to flaunt at Desmond when he got back to England. Her plan had gone all wrong, but how could she have known there would be such a despot to wreck it? Ryan Holt with his stuffy outmoded ideas on women and . . .

The anger started to boil up again and, to suppress it, Laurie fixed her gaze on the mauve-tinted flower of a jacaranda that dazzled against the duster-blue sky. This was still Africa, and Ryan Holt or no Ryan Holt she had today at least. Why should she run away with tail down just because he had barked? Why indeed!

She swung her camera jauntily, and looked round for possible sitters. She could get some pictures, at any rate, and if she liked the life she might stay on another day just to annoy him. Not that she was likely to see him again, thank heaven. The longer he stayed at this Lake Shimo place, the better she would like it.

A plush-faced monkey pushed its head through the tropical foliage and stopped to gaze down at her thoughtfully. Excitedly Laurie grabbed for her camera, but after the dip of an indifferent eyelid, the head receded, to be replaced by a thin swishing tail that seemed to say 'Do not disturb'. She laughed lightly and passed on. Time enough to coax the camera-shy monkeys. Right now there might be far more thrilling things to record. She wondered what kind of animals would be likely to show themselves around here, and racked her brain to try and bring to mind some of the names she had seen in the books on the library shelves. After all her boasting to Ryan Holt (and he had asked for it anyway) it was disgraceful to think she could only come up with three or four, and these not very exciting.

Impala she knew about, and hyenas, but they weren't very nice. There might be zebra or giraffe. Now that would be something worth while! The road had narrowed down considerably and she hadn't realised that there had been no thatched huts or bungalows for some time. The town had receded quite noticeably in the distance.

Looking back at it now, it seemed no more than a cloud of trees in a world of yellow plains and stunted vegetation. She heard the sharp cry of a bird wheeling above. A high-pitched chuckling bark was followed by the distant thud of hooves. Some of Laurie's nerve went. Perhaps it wasn't terribly wise to be out here on foot. Didn't people usually take their photographs of wild animals from the safe confines of a car?

She turned and walked back thoughtfully. Mrs. Lewis had mentioned a guide. Perhaps, Laurie considered, she would hire one after all – anything to prove to Desmond that her photography was as good as the next man's . . . or woman's. Even a docile giraffe would do right now, she half-smiled, scanning the plain. The smile faded. Her heart lurched. Something, and certainly not a docile giraffe, was moving towards her. On the shimmering heat haze a wave of tossing heads and flying legs was rolling steadily nearer. Laurie stood alarmed yet intrigued, her camera poised. If only she could make out what the animals were, then she could decide whether it was worth hanging on for a shot before getting out of the way. But a quick move apparently wasn't going to be necessary, for although they were getting closer it looked as if they were slowing down. The dust settled and the thunder receded. They came to a snorting halt only a few yards from the road. Two dozen or more perfectly beautiful zebras! Ecstatically Laurie took a breath. Now if only they would stay still long enough for her to get a couple of pictures and not take it into their heads to go dashing off again. Drat it! Wasn't that a car engine? The noise of it would be bound to upset them.

Hurriedly she edged in, but the hum of the machine was

now a roar and several of the younger animals were tossing their heads. Of course she hadn't expected that when the zebras started up again they would make straight for the road . . . and her! And with that idiotic car driver coming up behind, the situation was, to say the least, tricky. Nor was she prepared for the crazy route the car seemed to be taking. It tore up the road, screeched out in a curve, and slewed to a shuddering halt between her and the oncoming zebras.

Amidst the dust and thud of flying hooves she had a hazy recollection of a door opening, a steel clamp fastening on her wrist, and then she was yanked back against the metalwork of the car with a force that knocked the breath from her body. It was some minutes before she regained it, and by that time the zebras were no more than a black line on the horizon. She hadn't got one single picture. Not one! Thanks to this moron who couldn't drive for. . . . Oh, *no*!

Her eyes had drawn level with a heaving chest. There was something vaguely familiar about the pull of the bush jacket, the way the lapels curved out against the strain of the wide shoulders — She raised her eyes quickly to get the worst over with. It was Ryan Holt all right, and his temper seemed little improved on this second meeting.

'What in heaven's name do you think you're doing?' he thundered.

'Taking pictures,' Laurie replied, shaking inside but hoping she sounded annoyingly innocent.

'What for? You want them hung over your epitaph? Do you realise if I hadn't seen you from up the road you . . .' he hissed a breath between white even teeth. 'Who are you with? How did you get here?'

'I'm not with anyone, and I walked,' Laurie said, counteracting the green scowl with a bland grey stare.

'You walked!' His hand was still wringing her wrist. 'Hell's teeth! What will you come out with next?' He swung her towards the open door. 'Get in!'

'Mr. Holt, I don't see why . . .'

'In! I'm taking you back to Mbinga, and you'd better see about arranging your transport back to wherever you came from and those responsible for you.'

'I'm responsible for myself.' Laurie dragged her wrist away angrily. 'And since you've refused to take me on a safari you have no right to be ordering me about this way. You not only ruined a perfectly good shot just now, but you have the cheek to blame me for the zebras' stampede.'

'And how did you expect them to behave with you rushing about waving a camera all over the place?'

'I like that! If you hadn't come tearing up . . .'

'Lucky for you I did!'

Laurie had run out of retorts. She stood there, breathing rapidly, while a sea-green glance dipped over her and came to rest on the quivering pony-tail. He pushed the wide-brimmed hat back and shook his head disbelievingly.

'What's a little thing like you doing out here anyway?' he asked.

Little thing indeed! Just because *he* was immense. Laurie drew herself up. 'I'm taking a walk. You don't own the whole of Tanzania, do you?'

'No, not all of it.' His tones were less harsh and there might have been the glimmer of a smile, but Laurie was having none of that. 'Are you trying to tell me I'm trespassing?' she asked coldly.

He pondered for a moment on the thick-fringed lashes and small, straight nose; the smile was almost in evidence and then it disappeared, and he swung away and into the driving seat.

'No, but the animals have right of way here. I intend to see that they get it.'

As if *I* could stop them, Laurie thought wryly, stepping into the back seat. The car was a furnace of heat and smelled vaguely of old leather and tobacco. She stared at the berry-brown neck and now hatless head with its thick, neatly-styled hair. It started as a dark fuzz just below the collar and rose with the merest suggestion of a curl to lie in slight waves on top. None of it seemed more than an inch long. She heard herself saying absently, 'I thought you had gone back to Lake Shimo?'

The car was doing above average speed. He didn't speak until the huts of Mbinga came into view and then only to reply cuttingly, 'You'd be better employed in making arrangements to leave than trying to keep tabs on me, Weldon. I presume you can get back the way you came?'

He had pulled up near the path that led to the rondavels

and Laurie struggled out, slamming the door behind her. 'Yes, I can, thank you – and don't worry, Mr. Holt.' She crammed the straw hat further down over the long-suffering pony-tail and stretched the rose-pink mouth tight. 'Nothing would induce me to stay now that I know *you're* going to be around!'

She didn't hear the engine start up until she was well on the way down the path, but she didn't care. Let him think what he liked, and if all safari masters were as rude and as arrogant as *he* was, then thank heaven he was the only one in these parts!

'Hey there!'

In her hurry to get back to the rondavel where she could fume in private, Laurie didn't see the thick-set form until it reared up inches from her nose. Suddenly the world became a wall of striped shirt and outstretched arms, and then jerking hands were trying to steady her. They didn't succeed. She landed with a dull thud on the ground and her camera came down just in time to take an unbalanced boot squarely across its middle.

She shuddered at the crackling impact, but there was nothing she could do except perhaps say goodbye to an old friend that had taken all the pictures it was ever likely to take.

'Now that's a shame. A real shame!'

She was helped to her feet to the sound of a deep American drawl. Her splintered camera was retrieved in a pair of square-shaped hands while an equally square face topped by sandy hair nodded apologetically over it. 'Arnold Cape never did know where to put his feet!'

Taking this as an introduction, Laurie smiled wanly. 'I'm Laurie Weldon. Please don't blame yourself. It was my own fault.'

The middle-aged man gave a throaty chuckle.

'Young woman in a hurry, huh? Even out here. You must be real go-ahead.'

'Not really. Just an animal photographer, I'm afraid.'

'Well, I guess you've taken your last picture with this,' he sighed.

Laurie took the camera with a rueful nod. 'That should teach me to look where I'm going. I hope I didn't give you too much of a jolt?'

He patted his protruding bulk lovingly. 'Take more than a breath of wind to get through this. I'm Arnold Cape,' he said again, taking her hand as though it were eggshell. 'Come on over and meet the rest of my party. Maybe we can fix you up with another of these things.'

'Oh no, I couldn't let you do that!' Laurie clutched the dismembered camera to her. 'And please don't worry. I've got two more besides this.'

'But this was the favourite, I bet.' The pink features looked puckishly downcast as he added, 'You know, I'm going to feel awful bad if you don't let me make a replacement. Me and my big feet and all.'

Laurie shook her head. 'I couldn't let you pay for something that was obviously my fault. But thank you for your offer—' She moved off towards her rondavel with a backward smile.

Lunch was a succession of indifferently cooked dishes that left Laurie wishing she had taken up the alternative of sandwiches. Apart from the boys drooping at their posts, the hotel was empty.

It would have been a better idea, she thought, to sit in the shade of one of the big umbrella-shaped acacias and watch the life of the town. Perhaps she still could. Later she must pack what few things she had taken out of her case and sweep and dust the rondavel. Then it would only be a matter of hiring a car to take her back to the coast, but right now the task was managing at least two or three mouthfuls of this pale lumpy substance that came under the title of sweet.

She had taken only one when the sleepy museum-like stillness of the hotel was assailed by the sound of loud laughter and the tramp of heavy feet. A party of middle-aged men, pink-faced and jovial, pushed through the doors. Their hunting outfits looked spanking new. Their hats were gigantic and gaudily decorated with bands of animal skin. Laurie was just thinking there was something reminiscent of Mr. Cape about the men when she saw him in their midst.

He had something in his hands and came clumping over with a rumbling laugh as though caught up with the light-hearted mood of his friends.

'The boys'll never miss this one. Reckon you can handle it?'

23

Laurie almost sprang to her feet at the sight of the camera before her. It had several attachments and there was a couple of reels of film in a box.

'Mr. Cape, I couldn't!' she gasped. 'Why, it's far more expensive than the one you stepped on.'

'Don't worry, I've got its exact replica in my store back home to make good my giving you this one. And right now its one less under our feet.'

As though to put an end to the camera episode, he pulled down the front of his tunic with a questioning grin. 'We just fitted out down the road. How do we look? All set for safari?'

Safari! Laurie felt like a dog who had pricked his ears up at the magic word. 'You look just the part.' She smiled to cover up the sudden acceleration of her senses, and then asked slowly in case she had been mistaken, 'Did you say . . . I mean, are you really going on a safari?'

'Uh-huh. When you're doing Africa it's all part of the business,' Mr. Cape rumbled happily. His new outfit creaked, and the well-worn features had a look of amused bewilderment. The other men drifted in to be introduced and then back-slapped their way down to the bar. Mr. Cape seemed aware suddenly that he was in the dining section.

'Didn't disturb your meal, did we?' he asked.

'No, I'd just about finished.'

She saw him nod a grin towards the half-eaten sweet.

'Food not too good?'

Laurie shrugged a smile. 'You don't get much appetite in this heat.'

He nodded, mopping his brow. 'Kinda slows you down. How about a drink?'

'I don't think I will just now, Mr. Cape.'

'Well, we've got a whole load of fresh fruit down at the rondavel if you care to go and help yourself.' He moved off in the direction of the bar and Laurie watched him insist on buying the round of drinks. Now she knew what typical American generosity was all about or, in her case, what it must feel like to have an indulgent uncle. She pondered dreamily on the description, and then came a thread of excitement, blended with the murmurings of an idea. An indulgent uncle! But how indulgent? And was she going to get the chance to find out?

Luckily the Americans seemed determined to make the most of their stay in Mbinga. During the afternoon their rondavels reverberated with the sound of transistors and the clattering of tin trunks, and in the evening everyone who could come was invited to the sundowners they had ordered on the back veranda.

Laurie didn't need to seek out Mr. Cape. He came sweeping up behind her as she strolled over the lawn.

'Now this little lady's with me! What are you drinking, my dear?' he beamed.

'Oh, just a lime, I think.' In the gathering shadows Laurie found herself a chair, and Mr. Cape came over, a glass in each hand. He sat down beside her, taking a deep breath of warm air.

'Say, this is quite something, isn't it?'

She nodded. Out there, beyond the hum of men's voices, trees were arranging themselves in black silhouette against a violet sky. Grey clouds drifted over faintly forming stars and a night alive with the throb and click of nocturnal insects. Laurie lay back. Behind the pretence of still absorbing the night she was trying to think of an opening for what she wanted to say.

'Mr. Cape—' she took a breath.

'Honey, if my store assistants call me Arnold I reckon you can.' She was temporarily put off her stroke by his suggestion, although on second thoughts christian names were not out of place on indulgent uncles, she considered.

'Well . . . er . . . Arnold,' somehow 'Mr. Cape' sounded better for what she wanted to say, 'this safari that you're going on. As you know, I'm an animal photographer. I work for a magazine in London and I came out here to . . .' she swallowed. 'Well, I have the safari fee and you see I . . .'

'And you'd like to hitch up with us?'

She held her breath as he threw back his drink. He clapped it down with a hearty flourish. 'Why, sure. Me and the boys would be glad to have you. No sense in you heading off on your own when there's a whole party of us going.'

Laurie blinked as he swept on.

'Of course, this safari feller tells me that it's quite a ride to the big stuff and there's not much killing, but then I don't suppose the shooting side would bother you none, except

25

with a camera, huh?' He laughed at his own joke and the bulky chest expanded agreeably. 'All in all, I reckon it should be quite a fun trip.'

Laurie blinked again. It couldn't be as easy as that, could it? No, perhaps not. The worst part was still to come. She took an apparently leisurely drink, and then: 'This safari man, Ryan Holt — They say he's against taking women on his trips.'

'Is that a fact?' Mr. Cape answered absently and then rolled a twinkling chuckle her way. 'I guess we've got no worries on that score, you being only knee-high an' all—'

She pushed on uncomfortably. 'Well, I believe it's females in general. You know - this rule of his.'

'You don't say?' Mr. Cape was fumbling with a lighter and some kind of cheroot. He didn't seem seriously concerned and Laurie asked quickly, 'Mr. Cape, what if he refused to take your safari now that I'm with you? I mean . . . could he?'

From what she had seen of Ryan Holt, nothing would surprise her.

'Nope.' The American puffed contentedly. 'This trip was all tied up long ago. There are no conditions about who we do and don't take.'

'I see—' Something inside her relaxed a little. She murmured slowly: 'So my going wouldn't alter anything? The safari would still be his responsibility?'

'One hundred per cent. Say, you're all drunk up! How about another?' He pushed himself up, obviously bored with the subject, but Laurie wanted to savour it to the full. She was actually going on safari, after all! That was thrilling news in itself, but there was another reason for this private little glow.

Could it have something to do with the fact that for once Laurie Weldon was one up on Ryan Holt?

Preparations for the trip began almost at first light when the Safaritrek hotel became the centre of much comings and goings.

Laurie hung around helplessly, listening to talk of guns and permits, medical equipment and food supplies, between the men and the safari assistants. Vaguely she supposed that some preparations were needed for her own trip, but she wasn't quite sure what.

Mr. Cape was too busy to pin down and looked as if he had forgotten all about her in the excitement of things, though he did stop to raise his hat to her one time, and another to tell her that all was going fine.

During the afternoon, things were slightly better. After a considerable effort, she managed to get herself caught up in the stream of journeys to and from the Land Rover and lorry outside.

The first part of the trip would be done by road, and it looked as though the Americans planned to take everything including the proverbial kitchen sink, which was actually a plastic wash basin complete with stand and chrome plug.

Laurie was allotted the lighter tasks of carrying knapsacks and cardboard boxes. She enjoyed herself immensely and the men were in high spirits, like boy scouts preparing for annual camp.

Perhaps if she had stopped to think about it she might have realised that things were going just a little too well . . . and deep down inside her she had this peculiar little niggle.

The reason for it came striding over the road from the direction of the Safaritrek office just as she was about to make her sixth successive trip to the Land Rover. She caught a glimpse of ramrod shoulders and jutting chin, and though her heart dipped she carried on to hand over her load with apparent unconcern.

It would have been easier to hold the pose if the men had kept up their bantering and jovial good spirits, but they chose that particular moment to question an unlabelled crate in the back of the Land Rover and hurried off to the hotel to check.

Laurie was left standing, without any visible means of protection. She had a wild desire to crawl under the vehicle, but judging by the force of the step coming up behind, that wouldn't help her now.

She waited, tense, but the onslaught wasn't half so violent as she had expected.

'Well done, Weldon. I hear you got what you wanted.'

The tones were almost light, but her relief was short-lived, for it took only one look at the face to see that the safari master wasn't a man given to displays of temper. It was all

27

there, though, in the dilating nostrils and ice-flecked gaze. There were no wildly waving arms, no flow of abuse, but the Ryan Holt brand of steel-lined control looked none the less dangerous for all that. She tried desperately to match his coolness with a little of her own.

'I did come out here with the purpose of going on a safari, you know.' The way it came out she sounded anything but cool.

'Let's say by now I've gathered that.'

She swallowed. 'But you weren't prepared to do anything about it.'

'So you turned the "little girl lost" charm on old man Cape?'

'I didn't have to. Mr. Cape doesn't have any petty biases.'

'Maybe you're going to wish he had.' Tight-lipped, he walked round her, and then pushing his hat back, rocked back on his heels.

He had this irritating habit of surveying her as though she was some kind of oddity. His scowl did nothing to bolster her control.

'For heaven's sake, I *am* one of the human species, you know. Seems to me you've lived so long in the jungle you . . .'

A flash of green told her she would be wiser not to finish the sentence. She changed track jerkily. 'Mr. Cape doesn't seem to mind my going.'

'Let's hope he knows what he's letting himself in for. Where's your gear?'

'What gear? My case is packed, if that's what you mean.'

He sighed, and sent a glance down the nylon blouse and froth of skirt.

'How far do you think you're going to get, dressed like that? And this—' He gave a derisive flick to the saffron pony-tail. 'You'll be strung up at the first tree we meet.'

She whipped her hair away from the brown hand. 'That wouldn't be wishful thinking, would it?'

'It's coming to that.' He took her arm roughly, and with another intake of breath at the flimsy attire. 'We'd better see about getting you something a little more hard-wearing. The outfitters is at the other end of the town.'

At first, Laurie thought she was going to have to do the whole trip at a steady trot, his strides were so long, but think-fully there were many hold-ups along the way. Judging by the babbled greetings and wide grins, half the population of Mbinga knew Ryan Holt. She watched him take a dark hand firmly in his own and exchange a few words in a language he spoke with ease, or toss a brief smile into a dim doorway. Obviously, these people hadn't had the kind of dealings with him that she had. She turned her head away from the gleam of white teeth. Nothing would induce *her* to change her dislike of him!

They came to the trading area where many of the shops had tin roofs. There were one or two cars about today and girls moved along the road carrying baskets of fruit on their heads. Watching one turn off along a path towards a thatched hut, Laurie thought she had never seen a more graceful walk or as many jingling bracelets on one wrist. The safari outfitters was a surprisingly derelict-looking store. Inside were crude shelves holding haphazard piles of folded garments, and around the walls various types of bush shirts and trousers hung limply from makeshift coathangers.

Laurie's heart sank. The whole lot seemed to have been tailored for heavyweights. She turned away distastefully, to come up against a wide chest.

'Not exactly Carnaby Street, but there ought to be something.'

She watched the safari master finger through the size tabs. Was that a hint of humour in the piercing green eyes? He turned them down on her suddenly, catching her off balance. She jerked a smile. 'Imagine you knowing about the with-it fashions of Carnaby Street!'

'Surprised?'

'Well, you don't exactly enthuse over the younger generation.'

'I've a kid brother studying in England. He's about all I can cope with.' The gleam faded and he thrust into her arms a couple of pale khaki garments. 'These should do. There's a changing booth at the back.'

Laurie followed his finger meekly. It might be wiser to try them on before she committed herself. A few minutes later she emerged, the light of alarm in her eyes.

'You're not serious! I couldn't possibly wear these. They don't fit anywhere.'

'Nearest thing to your size. They'll have to do.' He turned to pay and she flapped after him angrily.

'I won't wear them! You're deliberately trying to make me look grotesque so I won't go on your safari!'

'Can I be of any assistance?'

For a minute Laurie thought she was back at her own local store, so helpful and solicitous was the enquiry, but as soon as she turned, the illusion died. For one thing she had never seen an English shop assistant with chestnut red side-whiskers and such a huge impressive moustache. Another, they didn't go round in knee-length khaki shorts and carpet slippers. The man ran a pair of sharp blue eyes down the wide-legged trousers and drooping shirt.

He grinned lazily and bent down to take a handful of surplus material. 'We could lop a couple of inches off here,' he suggested. 'And maybe you'd like the trousers tapered?'

'Oh, could you?' Laurie shot a relieved smile his way. 'I'd be very grateful if you could.'

'Take a couple of hours.' He stretched, sending a blue twinkle towards the other man and back to Laurie. 'Did I hear the word "safari"?'

Ryan Holt took out a pipe and filled it. He made the intro-ductions without expression. 'Bill Alexander. He owns the store. This is Miss Weldon. She's with the Cape party.'

'Ah yes, the jovial chap. He was in here yesterday. Didn't say anything about a girl, though.' A freckled hand went up to the side-whiskers as he studied the other man humorously. 'I never thought I'd see the day when Ryan . . .'

'I think you've got a customer, Bill,' the safari master inter-jected smoothly. 'We'll pick up the things later. Make it two of each.'

Laurie felt an iron grip around her arm and she was led roughly back towards the changing booth. The voice, harsher now, added:

'Better put a topee in, and some boots.'

Boots! She changed, fuming silently. Ryan Holt might not be able to prevent her going on the safari, but he was deter-mined to make her suffer in other ways. She took her time fastening the buttons of her blouse, thinking he might leave without her, but that was too much to hope for. When she came back into the shop, he was puffing darkly over a

30

pile of shirts. He stood aside at the door to let her through.

Outside, the town looked about to settle down to its usual doze. Much of the traffic had departed and there was a somnolent air about the hot tin roofs and dusty road. They walked along in silence and Laurie wished more than ever that she had been able to make the journey back to the hotel alone. Of course, it was quite ridiculous to feel this sudden knot of shyness. Ryan Holt was only the safari master, after all. Maybe it would help a little to talk, but what about? She wouldn't know the first thing to say to a man whose world was totally different from her own.

They were halfway between the outfitters and the hotel when Laurie thought her eyes must be playing tricks on her. She looked again along the road. Surely that little dark patch to the left moved just then? She blinked. No, it must be the sun. The Mbinga road was not a tidy sight. There were often cocoons of dry grass rolling in the breeze and rattling palm leaves. More than likely it was something like this that had attracted her attention. Unconvinced, she kept her eyes on the dark heap. There it was again. A slight rise of . . . yes, a furry body. It was moving painfully slow and straight into the middle of the road.

The rumble of heavy wheels from behind made her hurry forward. There was a sharp intake of breath and a hand gripped her shoulder.

'I don't think this is the time to cross, child,' the safari master snapped.

'Let me go!' She broke free. 'There's an animal out there – injured, I'm sure of it!'

The green eyes crinkled along the road. He said beneath his breath, 'He'll have to take his chances now.'

'How can you be so callous!' Ignoring the oncoming lorry, she hurried forward to scoop up the bedraggled animal and in turn was swept against a hard body. In the cloud of dust she saw heavy rubber tyres turn over the mark where she had stood only seconds before. A dazed, dark-skinned driver stared back along the road. She sensed rather than saw the thunder above her, but when the words came they were laced with sarcasm.

'I should play the humane acts down a little if you intend leaving here in one piece.'

31

Pink with embarrassment, she drew away from the closeness of his embrace. 'How was I to know the lorry would come along at such speed?' With one hand she made a brisk effort to brush the dust from her clothes and then raised the grey eyes slowly:

'I suppose I should say thank you?'

He nodded to the heap in her arms. 'I doubt whether he would say it even if he could.'

'You mean he's really badly hurt?'

The animal quivering against her was about the size of a small dog. Its fur was a tawny gold and there were tufts of white inside the enormous ears. A pair of beige-coloured eyes stared up at her impassively.

'Back legs are gone.' The man beside her ran a hand expertly over the limp body. There were smears of blood in the fur. 'Been mauled, by the look of it,' he added thoughtfully.

'Is it some kind of dog?' She looked at the sharp nose encircled with white. It was the only place she could rest her eyes comfortably, for forest green ones were but inches away.

She waited, palpitating, for the wide shoulders to recede, but they didn't, at least not until he had turned a sardonic smile down her way.

'I thought you might be able to tell me,' he commented dryly. 'You're the authority on wild animals around here, remember?'

'He doesn't look very wild to me,' she countered quickly, and then, fondling the soft ears, 'He's such a darling. Couldn't we do something? I'm sure with proper care he could pull through.'

'After the risk you took just now I'd say it was the least we could do.' The smile was grim, but he took the limp form gently in both hands.

She hurried along at his side. 'I'd like to take care of him. Could I?'

'I'm not sure that would be wise.'

'Why? He's not dangerous, is he?'

He shook his head, looking down at the small furry animal.

'Bat-eared foxes are quite harmless. They make good pets. The trouble is, people take them on and then lose interest. This little chap looks as if he's been on the road a long time.'

'Oh, but I wouldn't lose interest.' She fondled the small

head and turned a pair of soft grey eyes upwards. 'Please. I'd like to keep him.'

A green gaze held hers for some considerable time and then suddenly the safari master's strides lengthened. He said in harsh, matter-of-fact tones, 'Let's just say it's up to the vet, shall we?'

With a brief nod he left her at the entrance to the hotel. She watched him stride away, a red-gold bushy tail hanging down from one arm.

Life at the hotel seemed somewhat mediocre after the events of the last hour. Laurie wandered amongst the empty armchairs and tables aimlessly and then turned out again into the brassy glare of an African afternoon. Mrs. Lewis was on the lawn talking in authoritative tones to a white-clad boy. Round the corner the Americans sat, drinking, in the inky shade of a huge spreading tree. The talk, on the best way to confront an elephant, was light-hearted and punctuated with gusts of laughter.

Laurie carried on towards the rondavel. The stone floor was blissfully cool after the scorching earth. She padded around in bare feet, removing things from her case. As there was no sign of the safari getting under way today, she thought that she might as well spread a little. There was a fair-sized mirror on the wall. She took out a comb and swished the pony-tail thoughtfully in front of it, then gathered the hair up in her hands. The grey eyes stared back at her, larger than ever. Honey-tanned cheeks looked fuller and rounder against the cloud of fair hair. She dropped her hands irritably and swung away. Good heavens, she'd always had a pony-tail. Why should she want to be altering things now?

Vibrant tones rich in sarcasm came floating along her mind: *Little girl lost . . . So you turned the little girl lost charm on Old Man Cape . . .*

Of course, she couldn't stand this Ryan Holt, but just the same, it might be nice to be looked upon as a woman, instead of a tiresome child. Turning to other things, she noticed there were streaks of blood on her blouse, and thankfully set about changing.

She searched amongst her clothes for a suitably cool garment and smiled a little to herself at Ryan Holt's 'Carnaby

...reet' remark. Did he think her clothes were terribly Mod? If he did, he hadn't been to England for some time. She liked the shorter skirts and trendy outfits, but never followed any fashion slavishly.

The blue glazed cotton she slipped into now was at least two years old, yet she felt herself in it.

She hurried off to the bathroom to rinse the soiled blouse. It would dry in a minute in the sun and needed no ironing, thank goodness, she thought. Some time later, when it was neatly folded and in with the rest of her things, she turned to notice a long shadow on the ground in front of the doorway. It doubled up and she saw Ryan Holt crouching over a somewhat livelier bat-eared fox, though half his body was strapped and he hadn't got used to the strip of leather collar around his neck.

'Looks like young Kanzu here is on the mend. Reckon you can cope?' The tanned brow he turned up her way was furrowed, but the white teeth clenched over the pipe gleamed in a kind of half-smile.

Laurie dropped down with slightly parted lips and a look of misty wonder. 'Is he really going to be all right? What did the vet say?'

The safari master shrugged. 'He's out of town. I had his assistant look the injuries over. Nothing internally gone, apparently. A couple more injections should set him right.'

The fox sniffed around carelessly and then cast a bright-eyed stare up at Laurie. He made a peculiar, half-circle trot to her feet, bringing up the back legs in heart-rending jerks. She scooped him up, laughing, and yet swallowing painfully.

'What was that you called him just now?' she asked, puzzled. 'I thought a Kanzu was something they wore out here?'

'That's right. His is a little tighter, may be.' Ryan Holt nodded towards the white-bandaged body. Laurie laughed and nuzzled her cheek in the soft fur. It smelled strongly of disinfectant.

'Little Kanzu,' she murmured. 'Or Can Do! That might inspire him to get well quickly.' She turned towards her rondavel. 'I'll make him some kind of a bed in here with me.'

'No, he stays out here. We're not sure yet whether he's okay, and he'll be fine in the shade of the hut.' He looked around, biting on the stem of his pipe. 'There must be something he could curl up in.' He strode off in the direction of the hotel and Laurie wandered amongst the other huts, looking for stray tufts of reasonably soft grass or moss.

She had retraced her steps almost back to the rondavel when a footfall, lighter than she was used to hearing out here, came long the path. Mrs. Lewis, exquisite in grey cotton satin, cast a sharp-eyed glance beyond her.

'I thought I saw Mr. Holt down this way.'

'He was,' Laurie smiled, 'but I think he went to find some kind of box for our friend here.' She held the furry form high and Mrs. Lewis eyed it with unemotional disdain. The smile when it came was curiously off-slant.

'I hear you are going on safari after all, Miss Weldon?'

'Yes, Mr. Cape has agreed to take me.'

Mrs. Lewis stretched the smile wider. 'I must say, my dear, you don't seem to be short of initiative when it comes to getting your own way.'

Laurie held on to her smile with difficulty.

'I have a job to do, Mrs. Lewis. I just want to get on with it.'

'Of course. You're only interested in the animals round here.' The words were wrapped in honeyed tones, yet Laurie had the feeling they could be razor-sharp. They reached the rondavel and she knelt to place Cando gently on the ground. The other woman drooped a dark-fringed glance over him.

'I hope you weren't thinking of taking charge of this one personally?' she asked stiffly.

Laurie looked up quickly. 'Why, yes, I was. He needs care.'

'Of course. But you understand I can't have him here. One must have rules, my dear, otherwise the guests would have half the African bush tethered to stakes outside the huts.'

'Yes, of course,' Laurie gulped. 'But I won't be here long, and he's very small.'

Mrs. Lewis shrugged a bored sigh. 'I should drop him back where you found him. He'll probably make out.'

A familiar voice interrupted: 'Not this one, Gayna. He won't be properly mobile for some time.' Ryan Holt strode up with a sawn-off tea chest. Smiling, he dropped it in the shade of the hut and snapped his fingers at Cando.

'Come and try this for size, young feller.'

35

Laurie spread the handfuls of grass she had gathered and the little animal stretched out blissfully as though he would rest an aching body. She heard a slow intake of breath from behind her.

'Ryan! You know my rules about animals!'

'I know, Gayna, but I think we can bend it a little in this case. Don't worry, he wouldn't get five yards in this condition.'

There was a pause until the quick breathing had subsided and then Laurie turned to see Mrs. Lewis beaming a smile in his direction. 'Well, if it's attention the animal needs I'll take him into my apartments. One of the boys can keep an eye on him.'

The safari master looked thoughtful. 'No, I think we'll leave him with Miss Weldon. She's the one who got him this far and I think he knows it.'

There was a silence and then, 'Of course—' Mrs. Lewis went to drape a slender arm across Laurie's shoulders. 'See you take good care of him, my dear, and don't forget, I'm here to help if you want me.' She swung round to gaze up at the safari master.

'Ryan, I wish you'd come over and look at the books. I can't make anything add up as it should this week.'

'Sure, Gayna. I'll be along when I can. Right now I've a considerable amount of my own work to catch up on.' With the cryptic lift of an eyebrow at Laurie and her small charge he turned and strode off.

Mrs. Lewis didn't leave immediately. She seemed in no hurry. She strolled into the rondavel and, after casting a lazy gaze over Laurie's possessions, draped herself in a chair with, 'Have you a cigarette?'

'I'm sorry, Mrs. Lewis, I don't smoke.' Laurie perched herself on the end of the bed, although her churned-up feelings at the moment made it feel more like a raft on tossing waves. 'Can I go and get you one?' she offered politely.

Ignoring the offer, the other woman stood up and strolled again. Laurie couldn't help marvelling at the superb figure and carriage, though the small chin seemed just a little too thrust forward. She stopped to drop a supercilious glance outside the window.

'You may have manoeuvred the safari, Miss Weldon, but

if you're hoping *that* will pave the way for a smoother passage I should forget it.'

Laurie followed her gaze to the sleeping Cando.

'I'm not sure I know what you mean.'

'Just that Ryan never wanted you in on the trip, and he's a tough man to cross. I've no doubt he means to let you find out just how tough.'

Laurie shrugged. 'I suppose I'll have to meet it when it comes.' Her lighthearted tones seemed to cause some irritation. A slight frown flickered across Mrs. Lewis's smooth brow, though her tones were almost as lighthearted as she replied, 'Just remember I warned you, my dear.' She left to swing her hand over the odd flower along the path like someone just off for a carefree walk.

The safari was scheduled to start at sundown the next day. Laurie wanted no part of the rifle practice due to take place in the morning, so after breakfast she made Cando a fresh bed of grass, fed him on the tit-bits he seemed most fond of and then hurried off to the safari outfitters. Bill Alexander was just going over her safari clothes with his order book. He held up her slacks proudly.

'How's that for high fashion?'

Laurie's eyes shone. 'Oh, they look marvellous! Can I try them on?'

He handed her the shirt which looked little more than doll-size but fitted her perfectly, as did the slacks. She came out of the changing booth rolling the sleeves up high above her elbows, thrilling at the slim-line picture she made in the full-length mirror. She hadn't noticed before that the material had a silky sheen about it. The creamy shade of khaki was definitely flattering to the honey-gold tan of her arms and throat.

She preened shamelessly in front of the mirror and Bill Alexander folded his arms comfortably.

'Reckon I got just the right effect, eh?'

'Don't tell me you do the alterations yourself?' She tried on a topee, feeling a little like one of the jungle heroines in an old television film.

'We bachelors become quite adept at handling sewing machines and things. How about a hat?' He dropped a soft felt trilby style with slightly wider brim on her head.

'Perfect,' she smiled. 'And I'll leave the boots.'

He looked at his book, totting up the cost with one breath, chatting with the other.

'Comfortable at the Safaritrek?'

'Very,' Laurie nodded.

'Find it odd bedding down in a rondavel?'

'I did at first, but I'm getting to like it now.'

He smiled. 'The hotel had rooms on the premises one time, and then the Lewises got the idea of building the rondavels. Thought they'd give their guests a little more atmosphere.'

There was plenty of that, Laurie thought, remembering the dark shape she had seen in the bushes beyond the bathroom. She asked conversationally, 'Have you lived in Mbinga a long time?'

He stopped to check off the goods and then nodded. 'Fair while. Came out here with a suitcase and stayed on to open this place.'

Laurie turned a polite smile around the jumble and he laughed.

'Got that unsettled look about it, eh? Maybe that's because every week I tell myself I'm going, but somehow I never quite make it.'

As he scribbled in his order book, Laurie studied him. She thought he might be about forty, although the side-whiskers and moustache gave him a definite middle-aged look.

'That's it, then, without the boots,' he finished. 'I threw in the hat. I never did get round to trading stamps.' He gave her a wicked smile and Laurie laughed.

'Trading stamps! All this talk about darkest Africa. I'm beginning to wonder if there *is* such a place!'

He shrugged with a blue twinkle. 'You might find it when you go on safari with Ryan Holt.' He gave her the receipt when she had changed back into her dress. 'I'll have the lot delivered to your rondavel this afternoon.'

She thanked him for the hat and walked to the door. She was almost through it when a kind of tacked-on enquiry reached her ears.

'By the way, how's Mrs. Lewis?'

Laurie stopped to look round. Bill Alexander was idly sorting through a pile of dusty boots.

'Mrs. Lewis?' she echoed. 'She's fine, I think.' There was no further comment, and she left feeling slightly puzzled.

Obviously Bill Alexander didn't go out much. The hotel proprietress lived no more than half a mile up the road, yet he asked after her as though she lived in another town.

Laurie had no idea where the men had gone to carry out their rifle practice, but she was glad there was no sign of them when she retraced her steps back to the hotel. She had seen the rifles. Apart from being big they were reputed to have a kick nearly as strong as the animals they were supposed to bring down.

She wished rather wistfully that the men had been content to go along just for the trip instead of hoping to shoot to kill. And as for Ryan Holt – going by his gentle handling of Cando yesterday, he didn't seem the kind who would enjoy a heartless chase, yet she had seen some of his gruesome trophies on the hotel walls.

After lunch she made some enquiries concerning the vet's whereabouts, and found him, or at least his assistant, in a long hut at the side of a barbed wire clearing. He was not much older than the boys at the hotel, yet he handled Cando with expert tenderness and a slow smile of affection. It was difficult to know how the little fox was progressing, for the boy only spoke Swahili.

Things looked good, however, for the bandages were thrown into the waste receptacle and after an injection Cando was lowered gently to the floor. He gave himself a wobbly shake as though to show off his beautiful coat and then trotted endearingly at Laurie's heels. She resisted the temptation to pick him up. Now that he was walking reasonably well she thought she had better encourage him all she could.

After a tour of the wire netting where one or two small animals were in various stages of convalescence they crossed the road back to the hotel. Laurie was struck by the silence. Come to think of it now, she thought, there hadn't been much life about the place all day. The stillness reminded her of the afternoon of her arrival when there had been nothing but the snores of the hotel staff to greet her. She looked at her watch. It couldn't be more than two or three hours to the start of the trip, but knowing the Americans they would come rushing

39

in just before it was time to go, with no shortage of energy for last-minute preparations.

She went to the rondavel and listened to Cando snuffling in the grass as she lay drowsing on the bed. An hour later her safari clothes arrived and she rose with a ripple of excitement to prepare for the trip. There were still almost two hours to go, but an idea had been circling in her mind for some time. She was eager to put it into practice. Luckily the scissors she had brought with her were of a reasonable size and sharpness, and untying the ribbon on her pony-tail, she settled herself in front of the mirror.

At first the dreadful sound of blades against hair was almost too much and the slick of cornsilk at her feet enough to induce a state of cold panic, but she steeled herself and soon the back was cut in layers to the nape of her neck. Stiffly she lifted her head and proceeded with the top. Now for the shampoo.

Fortunately she had bought one on the way back from the outfitters this morning, and happily too her hair had sufficient wave in it to disguise the cut ends. Once the set was dry the front shone in high springy waves, while the back nestled close to her head, with just a wisp to curl forward under each small ear. She changed into the shirt and slacks, added a brush of lipstick and stood back to ponder on the reflection. Not too drastic, was it? she considered. The face that stared back at her didn't seem to think so. The mouth looked softer and wider somehow. The full round cheeks showed a clearness of skin that had never seemed to be there before.

She had swept the rondavel immediately after cutting her hair, so there was nothing left to do now except dust around and sort out just the clothes she would need for the safari. She could take the rest over to the hotel. The men ought to be back by now.

She listened. The only sound was the heavy drone of an insect, and Cando scratching outside the door. She picked him up and wandered down to Mr. Cape's rondavel. The door was shut tight. In fact, none of the huts seemed to have any signs of life about them. She took a breath and then relaxed. No doubt all the men were having a last drink at the hotel. She fastened Cando lightly to his stake at the side of the hut and strolled thoughtfully towards the main building. It was something of a shock to find it completely empty. She paced the dull red floor, glancing worriedly at her watch. What could have happened? Surely somebody should have been here by this time? It was less than twenty minutes to sunset and the start of the safari.

She heard the familiar sound of stilettos coming through the alcove and turned eagerly. Mrs. Lewis ought to be able to tell her something. But the hotel proprietress seemed in no hurry to impart any·information. She came round the side of the reception desk and let her eyes roll slowly down Laurie, from the top of her shining hair to the bottom of her tapered slacks.

'I'd no idea,' she said with an unusually pleasant smile, 'that we had a hairdresser in town.'

'I did it myself.' Laurie jerked a hand to her hair self-consciously.

'And the outfit!' The other woman wandered around her, one elbow in her hand, the fingers on the other hand caressing the smile at the corners of her mouth.

'You . . . you think it's all right?' Laurie queried uncertainly.

'All right? My dear, you look perfect!' She did another trip round, stroking the smile. 'No need to ask who would have stolen the show on safari.'

'Would—?' Laurie looked blank. For the first time the empty hotel and locked-up rondavels were beginning to mean something.

'Ah well, these things happen, I suppose,' Mrs. Lewis sighed lightly. 'I do hope you managed to get enough pictures to warrant your trip out here? And of course you'll be settling your bill before you go.'

Laurie swallowed. 'I'm not sure I . . .'

'What? Oh, you mean you haven't heard?' Mrs. Lewis's smile was drawn in slowly and pleasurably as though she was sucking on some delicious sweet. 'The safari is off, Miss Weldon. Mr. Cape broke his collarbone with his first shot this morning. The whole party have flown home.'

CHAPTER THREE

LIKE most African towns Mbinga came alive in the evening. The lights along the road were sparse yet sufficient to attract many from their homes. There was also the pull of the local cinema, which unfortunately for Laurie was in the opposite direction to her destination. She picked her way through a steady stream of laughing youths in vividly patterned shirts and girls whose dresses were brilliant flashes of crimson, green and gold. Normally the carnival-like colouring of the scene would have made her reach for her camera, but tonight her only objective was to get to the Safaritrek office as quickly as possible.

Thankfully, she saw that the light in the building was still burning.

She pushed on for the last few yards and lifted her foot to take in the dim blur of the first step to the veranda. Possibly because she had her head lowered she didn't see the big black shape about to step down. Suddenly she was knocked back with a force that would have sent her spinning to the ground had not an arm whipped out to save her. She was held roughly for several seconds after she had regained her balance. It was some time before her breathing settled down, for she was gazing up into shadowy brown features and the familiar glint of green.

'Weldon! What the devil are you doing out alone?' the safari master barked.

'I . . . I wanted to see you.'

The tight mouth slanted down into a peculiar smile. 'I thought you might. Come on in.' He helped her up the dim stairway and along the veranda to a painted door. Inside was a huge desk and a leather swivel chair. Three of the walls were covered with maps, while the fourth had a bookshelf and chairs against it.

The fragrance of pipe smoke and something like the masculine tang of after-shave lotion hung on the warm air. Ryan Holt draped himself back against the desk, arms folded, long legs stretched.

'Have a seat,' he offered levelly.

'I don't want to sit down,' Laurie blurted. 'What I wanted to . . .'

'Well, well! What's this?'

She had come under the light, and eyes a darker shade of green were taking in the gleam of corn silk waves, the slim khaki-clad figure.

'Mr. Holt—' Laurie had other things to think of at the moment besides her appearance. 'What exactly is my position now?'

He dropped his hands to press them palms down on the desk. He seemed in no hurry to move his gaze.

'Well, with the American party gone and no one else likely to come along that you can twist round your little finger, I'd say that puts you back at square one.' He lifted the powerful shoulders. 'I believe that's the phrase you're using nowadays?'

His smile had a coolness that suggested that her youth offended him.

She gauged *her* smile at an even lower temperature.

'I get the feeling you don't think much of our generation, Mr. Holt?'

He shrugged mildly. 'Too much money, and not enough to occupy their time – that's the impression I got when I was over in England last.'

'I can't think where you were looking. I can assure you most of us have to work very hard for our living.'

The features chiselled in teak nodded annoyingly. 'I suppose you could call it hard work soft-soaping wealthy Americans.'

Laurie stepped forward angrily and then bit back her temper. Any display of emotion here would simply be put down to teenage tantrums. She could see by the gleam in his eye that he expected such an outburst. Well, too bad. She had no intention of playing into his hands. No matter what *he* thought, she was a full-grown woman and quite definitely intended to act like one. She took a deep clean breath and exhaled smoothly with, 'I suppose one would have to be at least thirty to soft-soap you?'

He drew the hard mouth into a smile. That wasn't a flicker of admiration showing beneath the hooded eyelids, was it?

'I'm not in the market,' he drawled.

She lowered her gaze, then because something made her want to try anyway, she said slowly, 'Square one was when I sent you the telegram. I don't suppose you've altered your views since then?'

'Not in the least.'

She took a step forward, the grey eyes pleading. 'But you don't understand. I've just got to go on some kind of safari.'

He let out a patient breath and dropped his hands on her shoulders. 'Weldon, tonight you look every inch a woman, but you're still playing childish games. The safaris out here are not afternoon picnics.'

'I know, and I'm glad they're not. I want to photograph real wild animals, dangerous too. How else am I going to prove to Desmond . . .' She stopped, slightly shocked to realise that she hadn't thought of that name since after her arrival at Mbinga.

'Desmond?' A dark eyebrow arrowed upwards. The hands dropped.

'Desmond Lester. He's the man I work with. He thinks more of a good photographer than he does anything else. That's why I want to show him I'm capable of any assignment, not just the local cat and dog shows which is all he ever gives me.'

Ryan Holt had dropped back on the desk. He crossed one leg over the other, stating lazily, 'Chap seems to have some sense.'

'Well, he has usually,' Laurie replied, ignoring the mocking tones. 'Yet he never lets me take any of the tricky jobs. He'd rather get someone else or go himself.'

'So you decided to take on your own tricky assignment?'

'Well, it should convince him, shouldn't it? I mean it's not exactly child's play photographing your kind of animals.'

'That's just it.' His lip curled as a deprecating glance swung over her. 'It isn't.'

She kept control of her tongue. She was getting adept at ignoring the sarcastic thrusts. After a silence, he added, 'This is tough country. You could have gone to one of the big national parks where everything is laid on.'

'But that would have been too easy, wouldn't it? I wanted something with a challenge, that's why I chose this part of the country.'

He nodded. 'And what does friend Desmond think you're doing out here?'

'He doesn't know about this trip. He's gone after moose in Canada. It's the third time he has refused to take me along.'

The safari master got up to reach for his pipe and stood by the window, packing it. 'Seems to me your partner has all the say,' he returned.

'He owns the magazine I work for.'

'I see.' There was a long pause while he lit his pipe and drew on it and then, 'And does he own anything else?'

She felt a suffuse of colour as a derisive glance slid over the fingers of her left hand. 'We're not exactly engaged,' she explained tremulously, 'but . . .'

'But you're hoping the pictures will clinch it?'

She looked at him quickly. 'I merely want to be good at my job.'

'Of course.' His sarcastic tones had lapsed, and he had become suddenly cool. She stepped forward eagerly. 'Please, I know I could get some worthwhile pictures of the wild life if you would take me. I still have three weeks' holiday due to me and I can easily pay.'

'Pay?' He scowled. 'I thought you were a working girl. I suppose you know a safari can cost from anything up to forty pounds a day?'

She gulped. 'I have a little money put by. The agent said if I didn't insist on too many luxuries . . .'

'I'd like to get hold of the agent that sent a kid like you out here.'

She thrust her chin higher. 'I'm really very good at taking care of myself.'

'You could have fooled me,' he snapped disagreeably.

Laurie felt her temper rising at his unexplainable change of mood. She took a deep breath before asking, 'I take it there's no chance of you changing your rule for me?'

His smile was more of a sneer. 'From what I've seen I'm fully convinced you'd be a menace both to yourself and whoever was fool enough to take you.'

'Really! Well, somebody *will* take me.' She swung round to the door, the slight shoulders square. 'I haven't come all this way to go back empty-handed.'

'Now wait a minute.' He came up swiftly behind her. 'The guides around here may be all very well for monkeys and impala, but when it comes to the big stuff they haven't a clue.'

She turned. 'I've only your word for that, haven't I? After all, you're the only safari master in these parts. How do I know you're not just saying that because you're afraid of a little professional competition?'

He swung her angrily towards him. 'That's something else you'll have to take my word for, seeing you're not likely to be giving me any.'

'Oh no! You mean to see to that, don't you?' Her eyes bright with tears of frustration, she would have spun away, but his hands were steel. She felt the green eyes searching her face and bit back a tear. After all her good intentions here, she was going all teenage again.

She heard him take a deep breath and then he was saying in gentler tones, 'You really want those pictures, don't you?'

Laurie stared up at him. Well, yes, she supposed she did. It was just that . . . It was crazy, of course, but the battle between this big obstinate man and herself seemed to be putting everything else in the shade, even the photography and Desmond.

'Had all the necessary injections?' he was asking thoughtfully.

She nodded, her heart hardly daring to beat. He gazed down at her for some time and then swung suddenly away.

'Looks like I'm about to take over where Arnold Cape left off.'

'You mean you'll take me?' She stepped forward eagerly, but he put up a hand.

'Don't get carried away. I'll see you get the pictures you want. A few action shots and that's all. It will be the shortest safari on record.'

'I don't mind as long as you help me to get some good photographs.'

As he turned, the gleam of teeth didn't quite make a smile.

'Anything to impress the boy-friend,' he drawled, dropping his pipe down on the desk with a clatter. 'It will be something to do until my next client comes along.'

Well, he might sound a little more enthusiastic, Laurie

thought soberly, even though he did consider her nothing but a nuisance.

'When do we start?' she asked quickly, afraid he might be going to change his mind at any moment.

'Right now.'

She blinked. 'Now?'

'Why not? Everything's prepared.'

'But it's dark!'

He went to scoop up a sheaf of papers in a businesslike gesture.

'There'll be quite a few dark nights. Do you mind?'

Her heart felt as though something had been tugged from under it, but she managed to answer evenly enough, 'No, why should I?'

He replied with a rough grip on her arm and a flint-eyed smile, 'Right, then. Let's go!'

It took slightly longer than 'Right now' to complete the last-minute arrangements for the journey, but for Laurie it entailed no more than sitting next to the driving seat in the Land Rover.

She heard Ryan Holt giving clipped orders for a quantity of supplies to be taken from the lorry and re-loaded into a smaller sturdier vehicle behind, and just before the job was completed a slim figure immaculate in khaki drill came hurrying along the road to take his seat at the wheel.

'My cook boy,' the safari master nodded towards the other vehicle and then dropped Cando on her knee and dumped her case noisily in the back. 'That's all your luggage, I believe?'

She glanced over her shoulder. 'Why, yes, but I was only going to bring the things I needed for the trip. I thought I'd leave the rest at the hotel.'

'Well, you've got the lot now. Classifying feminine fripperies is not exactly my line!'

She felt herself blushing furiously as he climbed into the seat beside her, but as they jerked forward into the night her embarrassment turned to annoyance. Why did he have to be so tense and moody about everything? Was he already regretting his decision to take her? She had thought for a moment in the office tonight that he had softened, been almost human, but it must have been the African night that had gone to her head. Ryan Holt would never be anything but rock.

They ploughed along something that barely resembled a road. She could see the dark humps of boulders strewn at the side.

Mbinga was no more than a fuzz of light receding in the distance. She gritted her teeth as the car flew over another ridge of earth, and the man at her side turned to give her a drawn smile.

'There's talk of making this whole area into a game reserve. You can bet we'll have some better roads then.'

'What's the difference,' she asked, trying to take her mind off the bumps, 'between the national parks and a game reserve?'

'The game is protected in a reserve, but it has to share its living space with local tribes and cattle,' he explained. 'In the national parks the interests of wild life are paramount.'

'Are there no restrictions on the killing of animals around here?' she queried, thinking of the Americans and their guns.

'Hardly.' He swung the car round a bend. 'But all that's coming to an end. The conservationists will see to that.'

'Conservationists?'

'People who believe in the conservation of nature. The idea is to protect the animals.'

Laurie nodded thoughtfully. 'I think it's a good idea, don't you?'

'Very good.' He gave the ghost of a grin and she realised with a little jolt that the talk had been almost friendly for about sixty seconds.

After a while, the going became easier and Laurie was able to look out of the window in comfort. She felt a stab of excitement at the sight of ambling black shapes silhouetted against a ghostly plain and caught her breath as a furry tail that lay in the headlights of the car whipped up just seconds before the wheel arrived.

She wanted to point out and exclaim her delight, but instead she sat rock still on her seat. She had been told that women on safari were too much trouble. She was out to prove different.

Nothing could have annoyed her more than when the chill night air induced a shiver to run through her.

'Cold?' The safari master turned.

She gave the briefest of nods. Now he would say she was fussing. 'Perhaps if I could get a cardigan from my case . . .' she ventured.

'It wouldn't be wise to stop out here. Take this.' He handed her a khaki zip-up windcheater that had been draped over the back of his seat.

'I couldn't take that. You may need it.'

'Put it on,' he said firmly. When the wrists were flapping some three inches from her hands and the waist in the vicinity of her hips, he added with the hint of a smile, 'And if you can manage to look like that all the time, Weldon, you and I should get along fine.'

Now what kind of a remark was that? To hide her confusion, she replied primly, 'You mean you'd like me to look as unfeminine as possible?'

'Exactly. I don't want to be reminded too often that I've been fool enough to bring a girl out here.' The smile was no more in evidence and Laurie turned to stare dejectedly out of the window. What it was to be unpopular, and what a pity it had to be with the one man she had asked to help her.

She had almost nodded off when the rhythm of the car engine changed. They were slowing down and just out of the headlights she could see a dim shape. The Land Rover drew up and the vehicle following pulled up close behind. The cook boy leaped down and hurried towards the door of a wooden building. Ryan Holt had gone round and was opening the door at her side.

'Nabu will make up your bed. Is there anything you want before you turn in?'

Laurie shook her head. 'Only bed,' she murmured wearily, clutching Cando to her and staring around. 'Where are we? It looks a lonely kind of house.'

'It's one of a handful of bungalows dotted around these parts. They're attached to the Rongo safari lodge, a kind of bush hotel,' he explained. 'We'll be staying the night here.'

Laurie wandered nearer dubiously. 'It doesn't look very big.'

'Big enough. There's a kitchen, bathroom, living room and bedroom.'

As she turned, he added dryly, 'Nabu and I will be camping out.'

'Will you be all right? I mean . . . is it safe?'

'Reasonably,' he replied with a sardonic twinkle. 'No need for you to worry. If you hear noises in the night just remember this isn't Mbinga. Don't get any big ideas about wielding a camera.'

'Daylight shots will do me fine,' she shuddered, circling her gaze over the bowl of midnight sky and eerie bushes. 'I suppose all this looks fine in the daytime,' she added uncertainly.

'Relax, I haven't lost a client yet.' With a grin, he took Cando from her and rubbed his fingers in the silky fur before placing him down. His mood seemed considerably softer. She could see the gleam of his teeth as he came close to unzip the windcheater at her throat. Something made her jerk out of it quickly and step inside the door. 'I expect . . . I'll get used to it,' she laughed shakily.

'I expect you will, if only for the boy-friend's sake.'

Nabu passed by and out into the night, nodding her a grin as he went. He returned with her suitcase and after he had left she was just about to shut the door when wide shoulders came through the opening. 'Cando will be okay in the car seat.' He nodded to the bolts on the door, 'Make sure you push them both home.'

'Don't worry.' With a determined smile she shut the door and bolted it. She needed no coaxing on that score. Nothing could give her greater peace of mind at this moment than to have a closed door between herself and the unfathomable Ryan Holt.

He made her feel unsure of herself. One minute he was impatient and cold with her, the next . . . well, anyway, thank heaven for the bungalow!

Later, when she lay in bed, she was glad she had ·pushed the bolts home for several other reasons. The weird calls and shrieks in the night were not exactly conducive to sleep, the snuffling and rustling around the hut definitely nerve-racking. It ought to have been some comfort to know she had the presence of Tanzania's skilled safari master on her doorstep. She stared up at the clouds of mosquito netting. Somehow thatknowledge was a lot more disturbing than it was soothing.

The African sun was rising in fingers of gold when Laurie

pulled back the bolts the next morning. Ryan Holt was shaving in a mirror hung from a tree. Nabu had something delicious sizzling in a frying-pan on an open fire. The safari master turned.

'We didn't want to disturb you for the kitchen. Like to have breakfast out here?'

'Love it!' Laurie spun round to take in the breathtaking scenery. Was all this here last night? If she had known such a view encircled her, she wouldn't have been quite so shaky.

Tiny yellow flowers dotted the trees around, and an endless plain was washed with the pink sheen of a new day. A brilliantly coloured bird quivered expectantly on a thorn bush and, beyond him, blue hills tapered up to an ice-topped mountain, and a pearly cream sky.

Laurie drew in a sigh. Something in the dawn-spangled air made her want to run everywhere at once. It had even put the suggestion of a friendly light in Ryan Holt's eyes. She felt the green glance running over her as she scooped up Cando and nuzzled her cheek in his fur. She was glad she had washed and spruced up before venturing out. The little fox was on a lead now and when placed down he trotted sedately at her side. She knew it wasn't wise to get too attached to a pet she would have to leave behind when she returned to England, but there was something endearing about the sharp little features and great silken ears, and the way he turned a frequent golden brown glance in her direction as though he understood every word she said to him. Well, at least she wasn't due to return to England yet for a while.

A sudden burst of happiness sent her running off into the trees. She picked a flower to slip through Cando's collar and laughed as he tried to lick it out with a slender pink tongue. Ryan Holt came up behind her.

'Better stay out in the open,' he advised. 'That way you can see what's coming.'

She swung wide grey eyes up his way. 'You mean there might be something as close as this?' And then with an eager light, 'I must go and get my camera.'

'Save it.' He dropped a hand on her arm. 'There's only time for a preview before breakfast.'

He swung a pair of field-glasses from his shoulder and

focused them on something on the plain. She noticed the lean, smooth-shaven features and freshly combed hair, sensed a kind of restrained vitality in the powerful physique.

'There—' He pointed to a spot straight ahead and handed her the field-glasses. They were a considerable size and she held them with some difficulty. He went behind her, and put an arm round each side to hold them.

'See it? A cheetah.'

Laurie didn't know whether she trembled at the idea of a real live cheetah out there or the close proximity of a certain cool-mannered safari master. She tried to ignore the fragrance of shaving soap and freshly-laundered khaki drill and concentrate more on the view in front. Suddenly she had the picture in focus and gave a gasp of delight.

'I've got him! Oh, he's beautiful!'

She gazed avidly at the superb lithe body and small spotted head and then the cheetah was off again, long legs flying over flat ground. Laurie waited carefully until the arms lowered before she turned round. 'Couldn't I get a picture of him?' she asked.

The man beside her shook his head. 'Too fast,' and then, as she turned a disappointed glance back towards the plain, he drawled, 'Relax. There's plenty out here to make Desmond sit up.'

'When do we start taking pictures?' she asked, not sure whether that was a smile playing about the taut lips or a sneer.

'As soon as we've picked up the necessary trackers. The village is about ten miles from here.'

'Trackers?' She looked blank. 'Can't we just keep going till we find something?'

He allowed her the gleam of a grin.

'Tanzania's a big country, Weldon. We could walk and ride all day and not spot a thing.' He took her arm. 'Just what kind of something did you have in mind to photograph?'

'Well—' She took a deep breath, hoping she sounded knowledgeable, though the little she knew of Tanzania's animals was what she had gleaned from Mr. Cape and his friends. 'I was thinking the most impressive would be the Big Five.' She felt him slant a glance down her way and stumbled, 'That *is* what you call them, isn't it? . . . The ones that . . .'

'The ones that bite back?' he nodded. 'That's right, the Big Five. Lion, leopard, elephant, rhino and buffalo.'

She felt the fingers tighten imperceptibly on her arm and had to look up to see what he was thinking. She thought the green eyes looked slightly metallic. The smile a trifle thin.

'Really aiming high, aren't we, Weldon? Still, if you reckon that should do the trick with Desmond it's okay by me.' He dropped his arm and walked on ahead.

Immediately after breakfast the equipment was re-packed and Laurie's suitcase was brought from the bedroom. Cando had worn himself out straining after his own shadow and was happy to curl up in the cool at the back of the Land Rover. Once again they were on the road, and this time Laurie had hardly a thought for anything save the country they were travelling through.

The plain was a desert of bright yellow grass deepening where it curved upwards in the distance to brackish browns, greys, and purples, similar, Laurie thought, to the moors at home. The steep rising hills were a deep jungle green. What secrets did they hide? she wondered, perching expectantly on the edge of her seat.

The warm grey eyes were alight with interest, she gripped Mr. Cape's camera in one small hand. Looking down at it now she thought of the big-hearted American. What ghastly luck to break his collarbone just a few hours before the safari! She had never had time to thank him properly for his kindnesses, but she doubted whether she would ever forget him and his jovial friends.

The Land Rover was topless this morning. She could feel the warm breeze brushing over the top of the windscreen and lifting strands of her hair. She felt no pangs for the vanished pony-tail, nor as yet any need of Bill Alexander's hat. She cast a quick glance at the big man draped at the wheel. She might have picked the most trying safari master in Tanzania, she thought wryly, but at least she had had better luck with the climate.

Apart from a couple of exhausting hours in the afternoon, the sun was no more overpowering than it was on a hot summer's day in England. The change from the stickiness she had experienced at the coast was no doubt due to the fact that this area was on considerably higher ground.

As Ryan Holt had said the country was big and the animals widely scattered, but later on there were plenty of the smaller variety to keep her happily clicking her camera. She had her pick of creamy fawn gazelle with a gorgeous brown stripe along their sides, and of course the graceful impala ballet dancing all over the road. They seemed to want to cross at the exact moment the Land Rover drew level and then it was a matter of floating high in the air to avoid disaster. A lonely warthog was even more ambitious. He trotted obligingly alongside until Laurie had captured his ugly portrait and then he swerved like a racehorse out into the middle of the road. With a gentle curse the safari master dug his foot on the brake, and Laurie, caught unawares, was jerked off balance. She saw a brown arm shoot out to rail her from the windscreen, and then she was being firmly pushed back against the leather.

'You'll find it a lot more comfortable,' he breathed, 'if you sit back and enjoy the ride.'

She sank back away from his arm irritably. Did he have to talk to her as though she were some fidgety child on a bus? There was no time to fume, for over to the left something else had caught her eye. Something that brought her slithering to the edge of her seat again. She had heard about the majesty of the giraffe, but nothing could come up to actually seeing one. Well, not one, in fact, but possibly thirty. It was ridiculous to feel this overwhelming flood of emotion at such a number, but she blinked back the shine of happy tears, knowing it wasn't just the fact that here were splendid subjects for photography. No, it was something else.

A new and deeper feeling of actually coming face to face with Africa. The real Africa, not the one they rambled on about in the brochures. She swallowed, wondering what had taken hold of her.

Her heart had an excited beat. Was this the magic? Was she really falling under its spell? She gazed at the sun-drenched terrain and bluebell sky, the ragged wildness of distant mountains and the green of the flat-topped trees that was almost hypnotic . . . and then her eyes clashed head on with another shade of green.

At the sudden realisation that the Land Rover had stopped and that she was gazing into the mocking gleam of jade, she clamped the slightly parted lips shut and shrugged off what must have been a ridiculously dreamy expression. If only she could stay sophisticated and cool instead of just melting at the views, and so providing constant amusement to one hard-bitten safari master!

He surprised her by waving Nabu and his vehicle on and then turning off the track. He drove lazily over towards the giraffes and Laurie held her breath, sure that they would be offended by the intrusion. If they were, their only sign of displeasure was a swishing tail, the flick of a small ear. The pattern of their black and orange coat reminded Laurie of crazy paving. They gazed down into the lens of the camera with a total lack of curiosity and she wondered if she ought to try for a little more animation.

'May I get out to take pictures?' she asked politely.

The safari master lay back and drooped an indolent smile. 'You'll do okay from here.'

'But surely it wouldn't do any harm to . . .'

As she half opened the door the leader of the group of giraffes threw up his head. Several long legs bent restlessly.

Ryan Holt jerked up and pushed her roughly back into her seat. He closed the door across her, remarking coldly, 'It would do a great deal of harm to my reputation if I put a green kid like you out there. Now take your pick, and make it quick – it's time we were moving.'

Laurie took a few shots, quietly seething. Green kid indeed! If he thought she was going to take all her pictures from a car seat he was in for a surprise.

The village where the trackers were to be hired was a circle of huts inside a high stockade, although much of the life seemed to be going on outside. Laurie gathered the enclosure must be for night-time use, possibly to house the livestock that was scattered now over the surrounding land. She had a picture of pale yellow dogs, laughing children, and villagers gossiping beneath tall spiky trees. Nabu was standing with a group of eager-looking young men. The safari master strode over to have a few words and then the cook boy came away to lead Laurie to one of the largest huts. She was nodded into its shadows by a plump-hipped woman, and was amazed to find so much comfort in what had looked no more than a hollowed-out mud pie.

Sisal mats were spread out on the smooth beaten earth. There were skin-covered divans, and rough-shaped furniture. She accepted a crescent-shaped stool and was handed a small gourd to drink from. Whatever the liquid was it was cool and delicious. Nabu told her that the safari master was talking to the men in Swahili.

When she showed an interest he said that if she liked he would teach her some of the simpler words. She learned *mbaya* for 'bad,' and *mazuri* for 'well done' on the spot, but then the conversation between the men became too rapid to follow and the cook boy chatted on about other things. This was the first conversation she had had with him since starting out from Mbinga, but she had liked him on sight. His open friendliness made up a little for a certain amount of hostility from other quarters.

She noticed that much of Nabu's English and mannerisms were pure Ryan Holt, but you couldn't hold that against him, Laurie thought wryly – nor the fact that he obviously thought a great deal of his boss. He was a good-looking young man, twenty-fiveish with milk-chocolate-coloured skin, eyes a flash of dark brown and the most perfect even teeth she had ever seen. She thought he might be of Indian extraction, for he referred to the safari master as Sahib. As soon as he was sure she had everything for her comfort he hurried back eagerly towards the group of men, and later five of them were hired for the safari. They swung up into the back of the small truck and Nabu left the village in a cloud of dust. Ryan Holt came over to the hut and accepted a drink from eager hands and after passing the time of day pleasantly with the group of villagers he turned to Laurie.

'All set?' he enquired.

She nodded and waved her goodbyes and thanks as she left.

The safari master led her over to the Land Rover and looked down with a hard smile.

'Looks like you're in luck, Weldon. The first of your Big Five has been spotted not far from here.'

She licked her lips excitedly, meeting his gaze.

'Really? Which one?'

'Lion. There's a pride of them over the next ridge. We'll make camp at this side and move off at dawn.'

For the first time since starting out from Mbinga Laurie felt she was really on safari. On the banks of the wide stream she was allocated a mosquito-proofed tent with a veranda, and a metal bed with a foam rubber mattress. Nabu brought her a canvas bath which she accepted tentatively. All these luxuries were bound to be putting up the cost of the trip, but one couldn't dare question the authority of the big man at the back of the truck, giving the orders. All the men, or safari boys as Nabu called them, seemed to know just what tasks were expected of them. They moved methodically about the camp, arranging equipment and helping Nabu to build his kitchen. Laurie was amazed to find he had a refrigerator, stove and long metal table for serving. By the time she had arranged a bed for Cando at the entrance to her tent, several of the pans were jumping in a businesslike manner.

It was just a little bit nerve-racking having to eat in the close confines of a netted dining booth with only the safari master and herself at the table. But Nabu's delicious cooking, and the surprise of having such things as sweet potatoes and chicken and iced wine out here in the wilds, took some of the strain away. She saw a large insect hit the netting and bounce away again, and realised the reason for the drape. Their soup would have been littered with bodies in seconds. With a half smile she picked up the carefully placed napkin to dab at her mouth. The safari was turning out to be something of a picnic after all. Quite a high-class one too!

Ryan Holt lay back to fill his pipe.

'Something funny?' he queried.

She gazed at him above the top of her wine glass. 'Not really. I was just thinking, all this must be costing me something like forty pounds a day.'

'Reckon it's worth it?'

'It all depends on the kind of pictures I take back,' she countered carefully, and then because he hadn't taken his gaze away, 'I'd no idea safaris could be so . . . so civilised.'

'Mine are not usually.'

'You mean you had all these extras laid on for me?'

He hung the pipe on a half smile. 'I couldn't somehow see you bedding down under the truck like the rest of the boys!'

Laurie couldn't think of any reply to this. Certainly she found the present arrangements much more acceptable than sleeping out in the open, but was her bank balance going to stand it?

She had never had cause to draw on her aunt's legacy until this trip to Africa; now it looked as though the whole lot was going to be swallowed up in one go. Well, at least she would have something to show for it. The photographs would prove a lot to Desmond, and she wasn't likely to forget in a hurry the experience of being on safari with a man like Ryan Holt. Not that she really knew what he was like, apart from being autocratic and cool, of course. She lifted a glance up to his face to see if she could learn anything. He was pulling on his pipe and eyeing her from under lowered lids. She had forgotten they had been talking about the camp until he said, 'Don't let the amenities worry you. Most of this stuff was ordered by the Cape party. You might as well take advantage.' He stood up. 'If you're finished I'll show you how to rig the mosquito net over your bed.'

She passed through the flap as he held it for her. 'I thought Nabu said my tent was mosquito-proof?' she commented.

'It is,' she had got used to him holding her arm now wherever they went, 'but let's say I believe in taking extra precautions.'

Night dropped like a blanket thrown abruptly over the world and with it came the familiar sounds of Africa let loose. It was as though the animals waited for the cover of night to voice their noisy opinions or settle outstanding arguments. Laurie was glad of the bright winking lamp hanging from her tent. She could see the huge shadow of the safari master moving about and knew a ridiculous comfort at having his tent only yards away from her own. Cando was behaving boisterously, no doubt beginning to feel the benefit of having a whole body once again. He had twice been in to rush clumsily round the space of the tent, now he gambolled away past the fire where Nabu and the safari boys sat chattering softly, and on towards the stream.

Laurie supposed she ought to go after him. He might get carried away and lose sight of the camp, and there was no telling what might be out there. She strolled over the coarse grassy bank.

It would be chilly later, but for the moment strands of warm air draped about her bare arms and throat. After the luxury of a bath she had succumbed to the desire for something a little more feminine than slacks and shirt; now she secretly revelled in the delicious swish of flouncing nylon. The firelight played on the clearing through the trees, picking out Cando in his scurrying circles. He was very young and had the antics of a puppy, and sometimes, Laurie thought, watching with a vexed smile, he could be just as troublesome. He finally came to rest at the water's edge and thankfully she snapped the lead on him, staring down pensively.

It was only a stream, but even so, one never knew what might be lurking in its depths.

Almost before she had turned there was a soft footfall behind her.

'You seem to have a taste for wandering off, Weldon. Maybe I should have brought a lead for you too?' The safari master's tones were laced with lazy inflection, but she didn't miss the sharpness of his glance over the surrounding undergrowth nor the fact that there was a small bulky holster resting on one lean hip.

She gave him a nervous smile, unable to come up with anything more than,

'It might be a bit uncomfortable.'

She saw his eyes drop down to her bare throat and then over the rest of the white nylon. She half expected a clipped remark about the change of attire, but there was nothing except a murmured,

'It might at that.'

No reprimand? She half lifted her gaze. He had taken out his pipe and was gently tapping it against a rock.

'Looking forward to the lion shoot tomorrow? Camera-wise, of course.' The white teeth gleamed a smile in the shadows, and Laurie's heart crept cautiously from its hiding place. He wasn't actually attempting a pleasant conversation?

'Tremendously,' she heard herself blurt like an eager schoolgirl. 'Will there be any difficulties?'

'Not if we stick to the rules. The animals are rarely dangerous unless wounded or threatened. They sometimes get a bit irritable at being photographed. That's the time to pull out.'

'What happens when you come out to shoot them? Really shoot, I mean?'

'I don't.' He bit on the stem of the unlit pipe. 'If my clients insist on going in for the kill I merely stand behind with a rifle in case of trouble.'

'But you *have* shot the animals,' she accused. 'I've seen your trophies on the walls of the Safaritrek hotel. Mrs. Lewis told me they were yours.'

He shrugged, twinkling slightly at the small adamant features.

'I make a habit of shooting only when there's a danger to life and limb. Without the animals I have no business.'

She gave a light laugh of relief. It was true, of course. If these men went around shooting everything on sight there would be nothing left to bring people like her to Africa.

She looked at him thoughtfully to ask,

'Do you come from England?'

'Originally. I came out here on an engineering job and got caught up in the safari business.'

'It's an exciting life.'

'It has its moments.' He slanted her a downward mocking gleam and with galloping heart Laurie found herself wanting to hold on to that gaze. She did for some time until a breathlessness compelled her to jerk laughingly,

'You're not barking at me tonight. And you didn't last night at the bungalow,' she swept a quick glance up and away again. 'In future I'll prefer my safari masters in the evening. They're more mellow then . . . and almost friendly!'

'Imagination.' He spread the wide shoulders against the rock to fill his pipe. His smile was slightly lopsided. 'Or maybe you've been reading too many romantic stories about white hunters.'

'That's not true!' Laurie felt herself colouring furiously. 'Why, I've never read a thing about Africa until . . . until . . .' she pressed her lips together. Perhaps it wouldn't be over wise to continue.

'Until you got the notion to take pictures and flew out here on a crazy impulse?' he had finished the sentence for her.

She turned a glance up from lowered lids and then bent down to fidget with Cando's lead. She heard Ryan push away from the rock with a mild sigh to say,

'It's no surprise. You kids are doing it all the time these days. The first tin-pot idea that comes into your heads . . .'

'I suppose you never had a tin-pot idea?' she protested. 'Yours would be all master strokes, of course!'

'Of course.' He took her arm with an infuriating smile. 'Apart from this one. Bringing you out here.'

Laurie jerked away to walk on her own.

'I wish you'd make up your mind whether you can stand the sight of me or not!' she retorted.

'I'm trying, Weldon.' His arm came across her shoulders with a firmness that said it was going to stay. 'I'm trying.'

CHAPTER FOUR

TAKING photographs of the lions next day proved to be too easy. The family, a lion, lioness, and three half-grown cubs, stretched obligingly at the side of the track, drowsily oblivious of the Land Rover and the click of the camera going on from within. The elephants proved a different matter, for it was three days before any were tracked down, and Laurie had her own ideas on how she would go about getting their likenesses. Every shot of the lions she had been compelled to take across the bulk of Ryan Holt, and though she had a healthy respect for the big cats, she did feel that the safari master might have arranged for them to be on her side of the car or at least to have had the top down so that she could stand up.

As it was she had felt rigidly confined. The lions hadn't moved, nor had she, for any eagerness on her part to encourage them into different postures would have meant brushing across Ryan Holt, and that was out of the question. Thanks to him she had a feeling her lions were going to turn out about as lifelike as the ones in Trafalgar Square!

Luckily the elephants were in the forest, so it was possible to drive in only so far. The rest of the journey had to be done on foot. Nabu was close at her side now as they followed the trackers. Ryan Holt carried a rifle, but he was well up in front and this time, she thought, with any luck she would get her pictures without his interference. She had seen a picture of an elephant in a magazine at the hotel; its trunk had been raised, its huge ears flapping angrily. She felt tense with excitement. Maybe she wouldn't get anything as dramatic as that, but at least she could tell Desmond she had actually gone off on her own to take the shot.

The men ahead had fanned out and the safari master was striding back. He spoke in low tones.

'There's a sizeable group just ahead through the trees. Wait here and I'll give you the all-clear when to come up.'

He left them again and Laurie watched him disappear; then she cast a glance over to her right. She could see a heavy lumbering movement through the bushes and guessed that these would be the stragglers of the group of elephants ahead. She bit her lip. Perhaps, if she hurried . . .? She hadn't taken two steps before a light hand dropped on her arm.

'Memsahib would do better to wait here,' Nabu advised solemnly. Laurie turned quickly to the cook boy. Although looking now at his bush clothes and experienced air, she was beginning to think that title covered a variety of duties. 'Listen, Nabu,' she whispered, 'I have an idea I can get just the pictures I want if I go through here. I'll be back in a minute.' She hurried off before he could argue.

'Sahib will be very angry,' he replied, loping beside her, his eyes staring worriedly ahead.

'We'll be back before he's had time to miss me.' She turned a conspiratorial smile and forged ahead.

The view was well worth the detour, for apart from several breathtakingly big elephants there was also one which was half-size and another but a few feet high. They were all foraging lazily with their trunks in the long grass and Laurie had a first-hand impression of brownish-grey, wrinkled bodies and great canopied ears framing gently benign expressions. She moved round the group to get a clearer view of the very tiny baby. For some reason the elephant nearby swung his ears forward. She saw a large trunk suddenly snake into the air and hang there searching the breeze.

'He knows we are here,' Nabu whispered close to her ear. 'Better to come away now.'

'I will, I will,' Laurie replied excitedly. 'Just one more shot – the baby. Isn't he adorable?'

She parted the bushes again and had all but lined up her subject, when the big elephant, his trunk in the air, suddenly lurched across the clearing. Laurie raised her camera. She couldn't afford to miss such an action shot. Though the huge animal was quite a few yards away she could see white lashes framing a tiny red-rimmed eye. It swivelled a curious stare as though trying to focus on something ahead.

'Please, memsahib. We dare not stay,' Nabu called urgently.

Laurie was beginning to get the feeling he knew what he was talking about, for though the other elephants had drifted off, the curious one continued to search the air with his trunk. His expression looked anything but benign at the moment.

She backed away steadily, but in doing so one of the branches on the bush caught at her shirt and catapulted back with a noisy crash. After that, she had no clear recollection of what happened. It seemed that the elephant's trumpeting and Nabu's running started at the same time. She felt his hand slip from her arm and then she was alone, rooted to the spot, her camera at her feet. The only thing that struck her at that moment was Nabu's crazy route. Instead of retreating back out of the beast's way as fast as possible, he was merely taking a wide circle away from her. She stood paralysed.

Didn't he know the irate elephant had sensed him and was following? She struggled to stay upright as great feet came down only inches from her and crackled on through the undergrowth. Her camera winked up at her, polished and untouched. She wanted to run to retrieve it, but a sudden bout of shakes took control of her body.

She could do nothing but lean weakly against the trunk of a tree, shuddering to think what had happened to Nabu. She heard the sound of crashing undergrowth and thought for one appalling moment that the elephant had come back to have it out with the real culprit, and then a pair of hands swung her roughly round and she was gazing into strained grey features and a pair of molten green eyes.

'Of all the hare-brained . . .'

She thought the safari master was going to shake her, and set her teeth against the iron grip. Whatever he had been going to say seemed to dissolve in a long harsh sigh. He let it out slowly through clenched teeth and drew her jerkily towards him. How long she stood there leaning against the wide chest she couldn't be sure, but the rough embrace did more for her trembling limbs than the tree trunk had done. After a while, she pushed shyly away and ran a hand through dishevelled hair.

'Where's Nabu?' she asked shakily. 'Is he all right?'

'Apart from a few scratches. He took to a tree and left the beast heading for the plain.' He went to pick up her camera, his face grim. 'If you'd stayed down wind you would have been okay. The elephant goes mainly on scent. Once he's on to something he has a habit of investigating.'

Laurie looked sheepish. 'I thought Nabu was running away,' she murmured weakly.

'He's had plenty of experience when it comes to thinking fast,' the safari master nodded. 'He knew that, with a split scent, the elephant would be too confused to understand what he was about.'

'I ought never to have put Nabu in such a dangerous position.' She looked up. Threads of colour were finding their way back into her pale cheeks. 'Would you tell him I'm sorry?'

'You can make your own apologies.'

As he led her back to the Land Rover, she had a feeling she hadn't heard the last of the matter. She was right. As they turned back towards the camp he gave her a tight-lipped scowl, swinging the driving wheel viciously.

'What in heaven's name possessed you to make a crazy move like that back there?' he demanded. Laurie stared carefully ahead. Now that the peril of the moment had passed, she was secretly congratulating herself on the new batch of shots.

'I thought I'd like to get something to make my trip to Africa worth while,' she said airily. 'So far, I've had nothing that I couldn't have taken in the zoo back home.'

'You consider it worth the risk, I suppose?'

She drew on her lower lip, knowing that he was brooding on his pet adage – *women on safari are too much trouble* – and hating herself for proving him right in this case.

'These are the first decent shots I've taken since I came on the trip,' she replied coolly.

'Well, you'd better hang on to them. They may be the last you'll get.'

Her mouth dropped slightly apart at his words. She swung a questioning gaze up to his face. What was he saying? That they were returning to Mbinga because she had been a naughty child and disobeyed? She couldn't bring herself to ask the question and turned to gaze miserably ahead. He flickered a glance over her.

'From now on you'll take your shots from up a tree,' he stated. 'I'm having a platform built at a water-hole a few miles from here.'

'Up a tree?' Laurie was aghast. 'But that will be worse than taking them from in here!' She turned to give him the full force of her anger. 'I wish now I *had* gone to the national park! At least they would have let me step outside the cotton-wool long enough to get something other than cardboard animals. You're just trying to make things difficult because you never wanted to bring me on this trip in the first place!'

'I don't have to *try* to make things difficult with you, child; you're just naturally troublesome. You've been aching to come face to face with something you couldn't handle ever since we started.' He swung the wheel round a pot-hole with a steely smile. 'This Desmond guy must be quite something. You think nothing of risking your neck for him.'

'It's my job to get good pictures,' she snapped.

'And it's mine to send you back to him in one piece. Now what's it to be? The tree-platform or back to town? Take your pick. The water-hole serves most of the animals around here. You could do worse.'

Not much, Laurie fumed, but it was obvious that, when Ryan Holt made his mind up, there was no arguing. She nodded coldly. 'I suppose the tree platform would be better than nothing at all.'

She couldn't know then that, after it, life would never be quite the same again.

The term water-hole was something of a misnomer, for it turned out to be a fair-sized pool. It was a considerable distance away from the camp, but Laurie was pleasantly surprised at the situation and design of her photographic stand. The tree was a huge spreading affair with massive branches and a thick cover of foliage.

There was a rope ladder to pull up once they were on the platform, which was only about the size of a small room, but with such luxuries as flasks of iced water, rugs for reclining, and telephoto lenses, life didn't seem too bad. Cando would have made it perfect, but he was too fidgety and the safari master had him packed off back to camp.

She hadn't expected much help from him with her pictures, but surprisingly he didn't stay rattled over the elephant incident for long, and by the end of the week she had learned to recognise every animal that passed beneath the tree. None of the 'big five' came to the water-hole, but strangely enough it didn't seem important, when there was a broad khaki-clad shoulder just behind hers, a finely shaped brown hand to point out the distant blur of pink flamingoes, the rainbow slant of mist on the hills.

It could have been that the silent leafy surroundings of their temporary quarters, or the splash of African dawns and sunsets, were more conducive to friendly feelings. Whatever the reason, the days drifted by in quite bearable harmony. She had learned that the best time to come to see the animals congregate at the pool was daybreak, and again just before sundown, when the air had cooled, although this wasn't the ideal time for clever photography because of fading light. Laurie spent her time then watching with an amused smile the antics of the young, and also Ryan Holt, draped back against the trunk of the tree, a rifle across his knees, the gleam of biting teeth on an unlit pipe.

Sometimes she wondered if he was interested in photography, for often, when lining up a shot, she sensed him watching her through half-lowered lids. Perhaps he was, for one afternoon he drawled,

'You handle that thing pretty expertly for a girl.'

She smiled. 'I ought to. I took a two-year course at college.'

'The magazine your first job?'

She nodded, watching a gazelle trip daintily by below.

'Someone gave a party to celebrate our release from exams. I'm not sure how Desmond came to be there, but he offered me a job with his firm.'

'Sounds like he happened at just the right time?'

'Well, I might still be looking for a position,' she twinkled. 'There's a glut of photographers on, you know.'

'He must have thought you had something.' The safari master let a long lazy glance linger over her.

'I can't think what—' she jerked a laugh '—except perhaps a zany desire to get on.'

'It's zany all right.' He crossed the long legs. 'But you should feel good. You've almost made it.'

She stared down at the buff-coloured earth. She had almost made it, hadn't she? She was the next best photographer to Desmond. She had the chance now to go on the more adventurous trips instead of the same old dreary rounds searching for new slants on local colour.

That was of course if Desmond was pleased with the results of her trip out here. He had been vague and absent-minded about her work lately, and they hadn't been out together in the evenings quite so often, but things would be different when he got back from Canada. He might even bring up the subject of their engagement again. She dropped gold-tipped lashes thoughtfully. They were going to have to get round to the idea of a ring some time. When she lifted her gaze, it was to catch a narrow-eyed smile.

'Not doubting our success at this stage, are we?' he asked with a twinge of sarcasm.

'No.' She raised her chin a little. 'I think Desmond will be impressed with what I have to show him.'

'Enough to propose, of course.'

'I expect we'll talk of marriage.'

'Which is what all girls talk about.'

She didn't miss the mocking spears of light in the sea-green eyes. Even so, her pulses fluttered queerly. She heard herself murmuring casually, 'Have you got something against it?'

'Just enough to steer clear.'

'I suppose that's why you don't accept women clients?'

'Could be. Conditions out here make for fairly rapid pairing up.'

They make for fairly rapid something, Laurie thought, noticing the acceleration of her heart whenever she looked at certain copper-tanned features.

'That's why you insist that all your women dress like zombies,' she said a little breathlessly.

'For their protection, not mine.'

His height was such that he could never stretch fully on the platform. As he helped her to her feet now she found his face too close, crooked lips slanted in a lazy smile only inches from her own. There was no hope of getting by until he moved, and he seemed in no hurry to do that. She stammered unevenly to a khaki breast pocket,

'I . . . I think Nabu is waiting.'

He turned to throw the rope ladder down negligently.

'Good old Nabu.'

It was the night after when the cook boy lost his reputation for reliability, or rather the Land Rover did. Neither turned up at the arranged time, although it wasn't until much later that Laurie suspected disaster. She had been watching intently the winged performance of two flamboyantly coloured cranes and looked round with surprise to find that the daylight had almost gone.

The snuffling and grunting below suggested that the wild life had started its nightly trek to the pool in earnest and soon the sun would be no more than a red disc rushing towards the skyline.

Strange. She turned her head listening for the familiar throb of an engine. Where was Nabu? He had never been this late before. The safari master was obviously wondering the same thing.

He trained his field-glasses on the distant terrain, but as far as Laurie could make out in the pearly light there was no sign of anything that remotely resembled a Land Rover.

The drill had always been for Nabu to drive out from the camp about dusk, cruise over the last few yards, and pull in under the tree when the track was clear. He had done it every night for a week, so why not tonight? She shivered slightly as a cool wind heralded the darkness. Ryan scowled at his watch and then at Laurie,

'Something must be holding Nabu up. We'll have to take a chance.'

She couldn't imagine what sort of chance it was that was going to get them some three miles back to camp in complete darkness.

She was spared the experience of finding out, for no sooner had the dark head disappeared over the side than it was back again.

He swung himself on to the platform.

'Looks like we'll have to stay put for a while. There's a couple of rhino heading for the pool.'

'Rhino?' Laurie hurried to the edge of the platform. 'Just my luck! The first time something really worthwhile comes along and it has to be dark!'

She felt an arm draw her firmly inside. 'Take it easy or you'll be meeting those jokers sooner than you think.'

She saw a lean jaw working in chiselled features and looked up to whisper worriedly,

'Are they as bad as that?'

He nodded. 'The rhino is one of the most dangerous animals. Bad-tempered, short-sighted, and with a grudge against anything that moves. He'll charge another rhino, a safari car, or even an elephant.'

She stared nervously. 'But . . . surely not a tree?'

'We're safe enough up here.' He drew her close and there was something rather nice about being reassured by two muscular arms, until she heard him remark absently,

'It's my guess that something has happened to the transport between here and camp. If I'm right, Nabu will be in a similar position to ourselves. It's never safe to investigate car trouble at night, and it wouldn't be advisable to walk back alone to camp for help, unless the breakdown occurred practically on the doorstep.'

She took a quick breath. 'What on earth will he do?' she asked.

'I've taught him all I know, and that includes staying put inside a car till it's light enough to see what's coming. By that time the safari boys will be on to something. They'll probably meet him half-way.'

She took another, deeper, jerkier breath. 'Does that mean . . . we might end up . . . staying the night here?'

He nodded. 'With rhino down below and probably more in the vicinity, I'd say it's the wisest bet.' He went to spread the rugs. 'Better get comfortable.'

Laurie stepped back a pace. 'I'm really quite comfortable, thank you,' she said stiffly.

'Suit yourself.' He dropped down on the rug with a half-smile. 'You don't mind if I stretch, do you? My neck's breaking.'

She turned her back on him and stared up at the stars, folding her arms against the cold. Their stay on the platform hadn't as yet been very long, but she had the strangest feeling that there had never been a life before it, and that now it would go on forever up in this tree. Afraid that her thoughts might be taking a dangerous trend, she tried to pace, but her legs were so set with cold they refused to move. Above the annoying chatter of her teeth, she heard the voice drifting up lazily from behind,

'Better come and sit down before you drop down.'

In the starlight the warmth of the rug looked inviting.

She sank down almost before she reached it. Another rug was being draped around her shoulders and then she felt the firmness of the tree trunk at her back.

'Try and get some sleep,' the safari master was saying. 'It will be light almost before you know it.'

Laurie lay back obediently, but she felt as though she would never sleep again. She gazed up pensively at the foliage.

'I suppose,' she said carefully, 'that this is where women on safari turn out to be a nuisance? You would have risked the walk back to camp if you'd been on your own, wouldn't you?'

'It's quite on the cards I would have made it to the stranded Land Rover, yes.'

'You still could.'

'Minus my client?'

'I wouldn't be afraid to try it.' She turned.

He shrugged eloquently, training his gaze on hers. 'You might find it more of an ordeal than spending the night up here with me.'

Her heart thumped in her throat. She returned, too lightly:

'It's no ordeal.'

There was a long pause before he murmured, 'But you'd rather I was Desmond?'

Laurie smiled to herself. If Desmond were here he would probably be scheming out ways and means of getting some artificial light so he could grab a scoop picture of the rhino down there.

The voice close to her ear drawled perceptively, 'Don't tell me you hadn't thought of swopping me, in your imagination, for Desmond?'

'It wouldn't help much if I did.'

'It might.'

She felt as though she were walking across stretched tissue paper. It wouldn't be safe to go on, yet she couldn't go back. In her desire to stay exactly where she was, she retorted somewhat unwisely,

'No, I'd rather spend the time brooding on the action shots you promised me. The ones I never got, remember?'

She hadn't realised he was quite so close until she saw the

gleam of his smile. There was a queer light in the green eyes as he drawled vibrantly,

'Don't ask for action, Weldon. You might get it!'

For one panic-stricken moment, her gaze locked with his and then she was murmuring in stifled tones,

'On second thoughts I think I *will* keep my mind on Desmond.'

'A good idea.'

She felt his warm breath on her throat. A strange new weakness prevented her from drawing away. He was saying in gravel-like tones,

'I think Desmond would handle the present situation . . . maybe something like this . . .'

She never quite knew how she came to be in his arms, only that the rug had slipped from her shoulders and she was being caught roughly against him. She felt a hard mouth descend upon her own and then she was swept along on the wild surging tide of his kiss. A kiss that seemed to kindle a frightening spark within her. At first, she drew back, startled, and then the flame flared gently in an all-consuming warmth, and her lips wanted to give something of it to the ones above.

As suddenly as she had been swept forward, she was thrust back. The trunk of the tree was once again supporting her trembling body, wide shoulders had receded, disappeared completely. She saw them loom up with the rest of Ryan's bulk near a branch at the edge of the platform. The profile seemed hewn out of granite as he stared out into the night. The unlit pipe held rigidly between clenched teeth. He didn't turn as he spoke.

'Get between the rugs. Sleep will make the time pass quicker.'

Laurie swallowed chokily. His voice had a brittle quality about it. Obviously the time couldn't pass quick enough for *him*!

Nabu came at first light full of apologies and long explanations about the Land Rover's flat tyre. The safari master showed little inclination for detail, he merely gave an understanding nod, and helped Laurie down the rope ladder. Stiffly she took her place beside him at the wheel and with Nabu still apologising in the back they sped over the red earth back to camp.

72

A warm bath eased the ache in her bones, but it couldn't do anything for the tightness around her heart. There wasn't likely to be any remedy for that. Certainly not another of those brutal kisses from Ryan Holt. He must have enjoyed teaching her the dangers of taking women on safari!

She slipped into a cotton negligée and moved into the main part of the tent just as the flap was being raised. The safari master flicked a green glance over her and let it linger for a moment at a point just below her chin. He spoke almost curtly.

'I was just going to suggest you spend a few hours in bed. I'll have some food sent in. Nabu will give you a call at noon.'

Suggest! It sounded more like an order. She nodded, watching him leave. He had spent most of the night on his feet. That would account for the pale, slightly-drawn features.

When Nabu came to call her at noon, she rose, drowsily aware of a certain change in the atmosphere of the camp. Perhaps it was that the cook boy had deserted his shorts and shirt for the more immaculate khaki drill, or the fact that she couldn't now hear any sounds of the safari boys. Puzzled, she washed and dressed and stepped out of the tent to find that hers was the only one standing.

Everything else had been re-packed into the truck. She hurried to where the cook boy was pushing a bolt home at the back.

'What's happened, Nabu?' she queried. 'Are we moving camp?'

She was given a white smile and the shake of a raven-black head.

'Sahib says to make ready to return to Mbinga.'

CHAPTER FIVE

'BACK to Mbinga? I don't believe it!' Laurie stared as the safari master snapped the lead on Cando's collar. 'What about the Big Five? So far I've only managed to photograph two of them. I thought you said . . .'

'The Big Five was your idea, child, not mine. If you're all set, we'll get going.'

She watched him help Nabu to dismantle the tent, and then he was holding the door of the Land Rover. She scooped up Cando and raised her eyes to his. 'Couldn't we just go back to the water-hole? The rhinos might still be around.'

He took an impatient breath. 'If the boy-friend can't take you on the strength of what you've got, I doubt whether the rhino would make much difference.'

Laurie swallowed miserably. She supposed she couldn't blame him for being bored with a trip he had never wanted to make in the first place. He closed the door after she had stepped in and strode round to his side. She stared silently ahead as he switched on the ignition. Within minutes the stream and the grassy banks where she had strolled in the evenings with this man at her side were no more than a precious image in her mind.

The odd tree, rock, and startled animal zipped by as the Land Rover ate up the miles, and Laurie knew she might as well face it. The safari had come to an end. Plans for her return journey to England and Desmond were just beginning. She supposed she ought to start by paying her bill to Safari-trek. She said to the windscreen, 'If you'll let me know what I owe you I'll call in at your office in the morning.'

'Skip it. It'll do as a wedding present.'

She raised her chin a little. 'If you're thinking, as a working girl, I can't afford it, perhaps I ought to tell you I had a little money left me on my eighteenth birthday. My fare and hotel fees have taken quite a bit, but there should be enough left over to cover what I owe you for booking this trip.'

'You didn't book anything. I offered. Let's leave it at that.'

Who could argue with Ryan Holt? She would just have to forward the money when she returned to England. There was no time to ponder over any other plans, for Cando was in high spirits and insisted on attracting her attention. She smiled at him in spite of herself and, after lightly pecking the sharp little features with her lips, placed him in the back of the car. He scrabbled happily around for some time and eventually flopped down on a box, with his nose resting on her shoulder. The safari master nodded briefly towards him.

'What's going to happen to the little feller? Taking him back with you?'

She considered a moment, turning her gaze over the sun-washed plains and mountains. 'I don't somehow think he would be happy away from all this,' she said.

With a dry gleam, he looked at the furry nose and drooping eyelids resting close to her throat.

'I can't see him settling down with anyone else now, and he wouldn't make it in the bush.'

After a silence in which the Land Rover swallowed up the track, he added, 'If you like I'll take him over to my place. He knows Nabu.'

'Your place?' she echoed. 'A house, you mean?'

He sloped a smile, the first one she had seen since just before the kiss last night. 'I don't spend all my time in a tent, you know.'

She blinked. 'No, of course not.' Her smile was slightly tremulous. How could she say she had never imagined him anywhere else but out of doors? Was there a doorway big enough to take that physique? A room to match it? What would he look like reclining in an armchair, tapping out his pipe at the fireplace? She pulled herself up sharply. Why waste time asking herself questions she would never know the answers to? Some arrangements had to be made for the bundle sleeping on her shoulder.

She turned to give him her answer. 'I'd like you to take care of Cando if you would.'

He nodded, turning the wheel and taking them over a small bridge and on to a tarmac road. She had thought the subject was closed until he drawled, 'Like to come and see him settled in before you go?'

Laurie hesitated, though her pulses quickened. There was

75

the chance to have those questions answered, after all. Should she take it?

Better not. The less she knew about this man at her side, the easier it would be later. Even now she was going to have quite a bit to push to the back of her mind when she got back home.

Not that she intended to dwell on cool sea-green eyes, teak-tanned, slightly hawk-like features. It was just that the less she put into her last hours here the quicker the memory would fade. Her mind made up, she shook her head firmly. 'No, I think I'll just leave Cando with you.'

There was the merest pause before he answered,

'Not curious to see his future home?'

'Very, but . . .'

He darted a dark eyebrow upwards and suddenly increased speed. She didn't get the full benefit of the slightly twisted smile, only the low clipped tones.

'I employ quite a few people. You needn't worry about being alone with me.'

She felt the blush tingling up to her hair roots, but thank heaven he was still staring at the road. He closed the subject with a terse,

'I'll pick you up in the morning.'

Mbinga looked deserted as they drove through in the middle of the afternoon. Laurie amused herself by thinking that everyone must have a hole to go down while the sun was at its zenith.

She had never yet seen any signs of life at this time of day. As usual, the boys at the hotel were drowsing, but Mrs. Lewis, surprisingly very wide awake, was totting figures up at the desk.

She looked cool and poised in pastel pink. A pair of deep turquoise drop ear-rings drew out the sheen of her ash-blonde hair, the silky curl of dark lashes.

After the wildness of the bush, Laurie thought she had ever seen anything look so close to perfection. Maybe those were Ryan Holt's thoughts too, for he drew Gayna near and dropped a light kiss on her cheek.

'Hello, Gayna. Anything new in Mbinga?' he greeted her.

She slanted him a bored smile. 'Is there ever?' and then with a slight bite, 'And by the way, thanks for coming in to

76

help me with the books. I don't know what I'd have done without you.'

He grinned down at her, running a hand quickly through his hair.

'Sorry, my dear. We took off in a bit of a hurry, I'm afraid,' he said.

'And came back the same way.' One perfect eyebrow rose and fell as she draped a smiling glance over Laurie. 'Don't be surprised, Miss Weldon. We have our grapevine, or should I say bush telegraph?'

Laurie found she wasn't too surprised. It was obvious that Mrs. Lewis had been expecting them.

'I hope,' the hotel proprietress was saying lightly and swinging her back to Ryan, 'the safari was a huge success?'

Did she? Laurie wondered. There was a brittle light in the hyacinth blue eyes now. The skin on the high cheekbones and around the coral mouth had paled slightly as though drawn tight by some inner emotion.

Laurie found a smile and countered evenly:

'And *I* hope you can put me up for one more night, Mrs. Lewis? I shall be leaving tomorrow.'

'Of course.' The sultry tones had lost none of their smoothness. 'Your own rondavel is vacant. Help yourself to the key, my dear.'

Ryan came round the desk and dropped the key in her hand. Without looking up, she murmured, 'If you'll excuse me – I think Cando would like a drink.'

The next day, Laurie went to the small car-hire firm at the back of the cinema and found she could book a reasonably held together vehicle for the journey back to Dar-es-Salaam. The driver said he would call for her some time in the afternoon, and she had to be content with that, for no self-respecting Mbingan would pin himself down to a time. She retraced her steps back to the hotel with a half-smile. In a fast and furious world, where people were keen to get on, it was refreshing to find there were still some who felt that tomorrow would do just as well as today. She hoped though it wouldn't be so in the case of the hired car.

With something of an aching heart, she waited for Ryan Holt to come and pick up Cando. The little fox was particularly bright-eyed this morning. All unsuspecting, he sat at her feet, pink tongue hanging sideways from slightly pointed teeth. But for his big ears and rather slant-eyed looks, he could have been a small eager puppy waiting to be taken for a walk. She hoped she didn't give a similar impression. It wouldn't do to let a certain person know just how much she was looking forward to this trip.

She gazed down at her rainbow mini-tented dress and patent button-over shoes and wondered why she had chosen anything so madly up-to-date for these last few hours. Perhaps it was some kind of last-minute defiance? She smiled wryly to herself. During the last few days she had become well versed in Ryan Holt's views of the modern teenager. It seemed funny now that she wanted to hide behind that pose when in actual fact she felt considerably older than her years.

When had she grown up? It was hard to say, but the transition had definitely taken place since, or during, the safari.

Her heart leapt as a familiar-looking estate car glided along the road, but sank when she saw Nabu at the wheel. She liked the friendly cook boy, but the realisation that Ryan hadn't thought her important enough to come for her himself dropped her in the throes of a deep dejection. She stepped into the car, and struggled to take an interest in the scenery out of Mbinga. Why should he care? she asked herself. He might have taken her on a half-hearted safari, but he was under no obligation to say goodbye.

They must have covered endless miles and she was wondering if they would ever reach their destination when suddenly the car took a turn and she was gazing on a view that took her breath away. A shallow valley, dark and rich in colour, dipped and rose and finally came to rest at the foot of a towering purple mountain.

To the left, a circle of lake mirrored the deep blue of the sky and its necklace of lacy cloud, and beyond, blinking up through the trees, was a solitary red-tiled roof. The car carried on for some time, and then, when it seemed they must almost run into the lake, it turned off along an avenue of cypresses and through a pair of ornamental iron gates.

Laurie felt herself being drawn to the edge of her seat, intrigued at the name of the house, Nyumbaya. As the car wound its way up the curving drive, she saw the rich red-

78

tiled roof hanging over white-arched balconies and magnolia-tinted walls. There were jutting porches drawing in the sunlight and cool creepers trailed the oriental-style windows and covered verandas. Built dashingly at different levels, following the natural rise and fall of the ground, the whole house looked down on cascading flower beds and smooth, terraced lawns. A garden-boy was spraying the roses as Laurie stepped from the car, a white-clad servant padded along the terrace. Nabu came round to her side and she asked with a lightness she did not feel, 'Am I to leave Cando in your care?'

The cook boy smiled and spread an arm. 'I have built a small enclosure where he can run during the day. Come, I will show you, it is just beyond the . . .'

Laurie shook her head and blinked down at the furry bundle in her embrace.

'If you don't mind, Nabu, I think I'll just leave him with you.' She dumped the fox into his arms and turned quickly away. 'I really ought to be getting back,' she laughed jerkily.

'But you will take a drink first?' He nodded towards the house. 'It is cool inside. I will return soon.'

He moved off over the lawns and along a path through the trees, and after watching his slim back recede, Laurie took the steps that were placed at intervals towards the shady veranda. There were comfortable-looking canework chairs up there, and a drink would be welcome before she returned to Mbinga. Once on the veranda, she was seized with a desire to hurry back to the car, even though the view through the trees clamoured for her attention.

What if Ryan Holt should come along now? Wouldn't he think she had an awful nerve, sprawling in his chairs? Too jittery to sit, she wandered erratically towards the front of the house. As soon as Nabu returned, she decided, she would ask him to take her straight to Mbinga.

Against her will, she looked through the wide-arched doorway of the house. The interior looked cool and restful. She could see a room with white walls and black leather armchairs. The curtains and carpets were in a deep rich flame and there was a bowl of white blossom on a polished table . . . and there too, reflected in its gleaming surface, was a well-worn ivory-stemmed pipe. She turned quickly away. It would definitely be a better idea to go and wait in the car.

She hadn't got two steps back along the veranda when another figure appeared round the opposite corner. Laurie saw a slightly-built young man about her own age. He wore a gaily-striped shirt and tight-fitting white trousers, and as he strolled towards her she noticed the slim hips swung lazily as though walking was too much of an effort.

There was something vaguely familiar about the face. She had a feeling that the eyes that slid down the length of her should have been green, yet they were in fact a light hazel. And that dark hair – it wasn't just slightly wavy, the finely-shaped head was covered in tight curls. The jawline had nothing of that clenched, set look, but everything else told her that this was Ryan Holt's brother. As he grinned, she saw the teeth were just as white. He swung an appraising glance over her outfit and murmured reverently, 'A slick chick from the Great Outside? I don't believe it! I must be looking at a mirage.'

He prodded a finger into her shoulder and jumped back dramatically as she laughed.

'I'm quite real,' Laurie twinkled.

'You are!' His eyes were laughing now, and with that lazy proprietorial air she had seen so often in the boys at the college, he turned an arm tightly about her waist, relaxed his knees and drawled, 'Well, what are we doing out here, girl?'

Laurie spun out of his hold and smiled, 'I'm Laurie Weldon. I'm staying in Mbinga. I think Nabu was going to get me a drink.'

The young man turned his lips down expressively before replying, 'Things are looking up in Mbinga!'

He dug his hands deep in his pockets, apparently abandoning for the moment his young Romeo act, and grinned, 'I'm Dave Holt. I can order you a tray of drinks if you like. Where shall we sit?'

He led her indoors towards the white and flame room, yelling for drinks to some unknown body. Almost before they had each dropped into an armchair, a white-clad servant, slightly older than Nabu, appeared with a tray of refreshing-looking liquids. Dave Holt sprang to his feet again and opened a hand towards the tray expansively. 'What's it to be?' he asked.

'Anything long and cool will do.'

He made a show of dropping in the ice and pouring on the liquid, and watching his nonchalant floppy air, Laurie was reminded again of the boys of her student days. He handed her the drink with a slow smile.

'If I'd known you were over here, I'd have got suspended sooner,' he said blithely.

'Suspended?' Laurie stared back from her drink. 'From college?'

He gave a loose-jointed shrug. 'I'm supposed to be a law student, but the whole thing's a drag.'

Laurie took a long drink. What could she say? She had found her own schooling tedious, but she had never had a suspension! That was serious, wasn't it? He strolled the room, swishing his drink round in his glass, and when she had drained hers, she asked, 'What happened – I mean, why did they suspend you?'

'Oh, the usual thing. We were having a rave and some old nut . . . still, that's history.' He grinned down at her. 'It's what's happening now that counts. You've had your drink, how about you and me going out to burn up the tyres some?' He nodded towards the estate car and Laurie rose to place her glass on the tray.

'Well, you can take me back to Mbinga if you like,' she replied. 'Nabu seems to have got held up somewhere.'

'Mbinga?' He raised a raffish eyebrow. 'Okay, it will do for a start.'

His arm was back again round her waist and she laughed up at him, about to say mischievously that it would have to do for the finish too, as she was leaving for England that afternoon, but no words passed her lips. She was suddenly acutely aware of another presence in the room, and turned to see Ryan standing only a few feet away on the thick-piled carpet. Cool, green eyes were raking her outfit. They swung slowly over his brother.

'Shades of the with-it kids!' He slanted a dry smile and went to pour himself a drink. Laurie thought he looked hot and slightly dishevelled, as though he had been moving.

'Cando settled in okay?' he asked. 'I wasn't sure I'd make it back. There was an enquiry into Mr. Cape's accident.'

'Who or what is Cando?' Dave fell into a chair and clapped his hands on the arms.

'He's a little bat-eared fox we found in Mbinga,' Laurie explained. 'He was trying to cross the road, you see, and . . .'

'Oh, gosh, is *that* all?' Dave sank lower in the chair. 'And whose idea was the crummy name?'

'Well, it was mine.' Laurie smiled. 'I thought that . . .'

He took a breath and then sprang up impatiently. 'Ry, is it okay if we go for a drive? There's just nothing to do around here.'

'You can eat,' his brother said sardonically. 'It's almost lunch. Perhaps Miss Weldon would care to stay?'

'Sure she'll stay, won't you, Laurie?' Dave moved to her side eagerly, and took it for granted she would, for he led her across a hall with polished red lozenge tiles, saying, 'I'll show you where to wash.'

Laurie ate a tremulous meal, with Ryan sat silently opposite, and Dave talking about everything that was happening in England, from the latest craze in neckties to the price of tickets at the next Albert Hall pop show. He was evidently a keen follower of the pop groups and could impersonate any one of the stars with ease. She laughed when he made a show of grabbing hold of an imaginary microphone, and almost clapped when he did a perfect take-off of a top disc jockey.

Looking at Laurie's flushed features, Ryan drawled, 'Let's get the meal over, shall we, Dave? You're enough to give anybody indigestion.'

Later, when they were drinking coffee on the veranda, he said casually, 'I'll drive you back to Mbinga, Miss Weldon. I have a few things to pick up.'

Dave, not terribly interested in his coffee, flung away the pebble he had been tossing and jumped up.

'But, Ry, I told Laurie I . . .'

'Hardly worth while your going, Dave.' Ryan got up to knock his pipe out pointedly. 'I believe Miss Weldon leaves for England today.'

'Oh no!' Dave sank down with a grunt of disappointment, 'Just when things were beginning to look good.' He turned towards her. 'Do you have to leave, Laurie? I mean, couldn't you hang on for a bit?'

'Afraid not,' Laurie smiled. 'I've a hired car waiting to take me to the coast.'

Dave got up again and drove his hands deep into his pockets in slack-limbed dejection. 'Just my luck! Suspended till next term, and I've got to stick in this crummy dump. You know what's going to happen?' he brooded almost to himself. 'I'm going to go clean out of my mind, that's what, no decent pop music, not even a telly.'

'You can always study,' Ryan put in evenly. 'Maybe if you'd given a bit more attention to that and less to the other stuff, you wouldn't be stuck in this crummy dump.'

Ryan took the estate car back along the road to Mbinga at a leisurely speed. He seemed preoccupied and Laurie guessed he had much of his brother on his mind. She didn't mind the silence. It gave her a chance to cast her mind back over the morning's happenings. She could still see Ryan standing on the thick flame carpet. He had looked shatteringly different in fawn slacks and silk shirt. The smile had been the same, but she hadn't been able to fathom that look. Had there been a flicker of pleasure in the green eyes? Perhaps because he had managed to get back before she left? Or had it been only derision at her outfit and her obvious success with Dave?

She looked at him now without noticeably turning her head and quickly swung her glance back to the front again. How easy it was to delude oneself into thinking what one wanted to think! It was obvious by the set features and steely green eyes that he didn't even know she was in the car. He must have done, though, for he said suddenly, abruptly, 'Know how to handle a car, Weldon?'

She looked at him and replied, slightly puzzled, 'I passed my driving test just before I came out here.'

'I seem to recall you telling me in my office your holiday had some three weeks to run. Taking in the safari, I make it about ten days you've got left.'

'That would be about right,' Laurie nodded, wondering what was coming next. She didn't have to wonder long, for his next question told her exactly what he was thinking.

'Would you consider spending them with Dave?'

So that was it! Dave! For one moment, her heart had been flexing its wings like a butterfly in the sun. Now, it slumped in the shadows of disappointment. She hadn't been able to find a reply, and Ryan was continuing evenly, 'Dave needs time to sort himself out. He's been keeping pretty wild company of late. I think a level head for a change might help to tone him down a little.'

She turned to give him a sly look.

'You can't be meaning me. I'm the one with the tin-pot ideas, remember?'

He twinkled down at her, 'And no doubt you'll have a few more yet, but compared to Dave you're a paragon of stability.' He held her gaze. 'Well, what do you say? You could drive out to Dave most days. There's the lake. It's free from hippos and crocodiles and safe for swimming, and there's some quite passable scenery. You'd be doing me a favour, so I'd expect you to charge the hotel bill to me.'

'What would I do for a car?' she asked.

'You and Dave could have this one. I'd use the Rover.'

She looked at him, considering for a moment.

'Talking of level heads for Dave, what about you? Surely his own brother . . .?'

'Dave doesn't want to take anything from me.' Ryan swung the car round towards the acacias and palms of Mbinga. 'I'm fifteen years his senior, and age is the one drawback to giving any kind of advice.'

'I hope you wouldn't want me to give any?'

He shook his head. 'You wouldn't have to. You've made a pretty decent start on a career. It won't take him long to catch on which one of you is making the most use of their abilities.'

'You've given him everything he wants, haven't you?' she said perceptively.

He shrugged. 'Plus a little of what he doesn't want – a good education. Dave has a near brilliant mind. He could have his degree in half the time it took me to get mine, but he seems to have lost his taste for hard work.'

Ryan drew in outside the Safaritrek Hotel and draped an arm across the back of her seat. 'You haven't said yet whether I can count on your help,' he pointed out, and then, watching her face: 'Don't worry about Desmond. I wouldn't want Dave to get any romantic ideas anyway. He hasn't got the time.'

She looked down at her hands.

'He might wonder about my stay out here – Desmond, I mean. If he gets back to England before I do.'

'I'll square it for you if he does.'

'You would even do that?'

She raised her head to see his smile as he opened the door across her.

'It's all part of the big brother role,' he said lazily.

She stepped out of the car with a slightly sinking feeling. Was that how Ryan was going to look upon her from now on? she wondered. As a younger sister? A playmate for his younger brother? She caught a glimpse of the swaying palms and blazing jacarandas and knew she ought to be overjoyed at this opportunity to stay on in Africa, but somehow her heart wasn't in staying.

Not on those terms.

CHAPTER SIX

SHE heard the door slam shut smartly and sensed a ripple of impatience in the action. Ryan was saying harshly, 'If staying on is going to be as tough as all that, maybe we'd better forget it. Dave will make out, I guess.'

'No! Wait a minute.' Laurie hadn't realised her dejection had shown so clearly in her face. She put a hand on the window before he had started up. Wasn't a younger brother better than nothing at all?

'I was just thinking of the hired car,' she lied. 'It's ordered for this afternoon.'

'No problem.' The teak brow cleared rapidly. 'I'll cancel it on my way through. Is it Mahmoud's?'

Laurie nodded. She saw the gleam of his smile, and eyes a sunny green, as he let in the clutch.

'Get Gayna to book you in for as long as we said,' he called. 'I'll be seeing her later. Right now I want to get back pronto to give Dave the news.' He gave her a salute and put the car in motion.

Laurie watched it shoot away and turned towards the hotel with an apprehensive bite of her lower lip. Somehow she had a feeling that Gayna Lewis wasn't going to take too kindly to the idea of her extended stay.

The hotel proprietress didn't look in the best of moods. She stood in front of the reception desk, arms folded and a frown directed towards a figure wobbling on a pair of wooden steps. The frown lifted slightly as she saw Laurie.

'Mahmoud's been looking for you, my dear,' she remarked. 'I believe he's waiting for you at the garage. I put your luggage out at the side entrance.'

So she had even packed for her? Laurie opened her mouth to speak, but the sound of a hammer on wood drowned her words. She turned to see Bill Alexander nailing a splintered section of the window aperture. Mrs. Lewis dropped the silken lashes witheringly:

'Take no notice of him, child,' she said irritably. 'He's got some crazy idea that I can't attend to my own repairs.'

A bewhiskered face turned to smile mildly.

'A jagged edge like this could do somebody an injury. Luckily I spotted it on my way by this morning.' He tapped thoughtfully for a while and then spun a blue glance across the room. 'Have a fight in here last night?' he asked.

'How perfectly ridiculous!' Mrs. Lewis waved a hand. 'You know as well as I do this place is falling to bits.'

'Maybe if you spent the profit on doing something else up beside yourself?' he suggested with sly humour, and then, ignoring her compressed lips, he tapped the splintered wood cheerfully. 'I should tell the customers to leave their pangas outside in future.'

Mrs. Lewis gave an impatient sigh.

'The boys sometimes get a little boisterous when they're cleaning up,' she said acidly.

'Seems to me the boys could do with a little discipline.' He put a nail in his mouth and tightened his lips over it.

Mrs. Lewis shrugged before turning away. 'You know Ryan attends to all these matters for me. Forgive me, Miss Weldon. If you're just waiting to say goodbye . . .' She put a slim hand out slackly. 'Nice to have met you. I don't suppose we'll see you around these parts again.'

'Er . . . Mrs. Lewis . . .' Laurie felt that now was the time to interrupt. 'Actually I haven't come to say goodbye. What I wanted to ask is if you could put me up for about another ten days?'

The smooth head shot up and Laurie, confronted by a wide hyacinth-blue stare, stumbled giddily. 'Mr. Holt has asked me to stay on for a while,' she went on.

There was a silence then in which Laurie noticed Bill Alexander watching Mrs. Lewis with interest. He said with the suggestion of a wink at Laurie, 'How was the safari, Miss Weldon? Did you find darkest Africa?'

Laurie didn't know why she should think of Ryan's kiss just then, but she immediately wished she hadn't. The feeling that humorous blue eyes could see straight through to the picture in her mind brought a surge of wild colour to her cheeks.

'About ten days more?' Mrs. Lewis was echoing crisply. 'That's right.'

Laurie saw the safari outfitter cup his chin in his hand.

The copper eyebrows had dropped into an amused slant.

Mrs. Lewis flicked him an irritated glance and then replied in peculiarly high-pitched tones, 'Well, it looks like we don't have to say goodbye after all, my dear. You'll let me know if you intend to make a permanent home in my rondavel, won't you?' Her laughter sounded like the rattle of ice cubes. She turned to open the book on the desk.

Laurie left, to the clatter of intensified hammering. Perhaps it was her imagination, but she could have sworn the blows were spurred on by some kind of elation. Some time later, when they had died away completely and she saw Bill Alexander moving off along the road, another sound came to her ears – the familiar click of high heels. They came gradually nearer and Laurie realised that Mrs. Lewis was making for her rondavel. She moved curiously to the door, one dress half-way on its hanger.

'Ah, Miss Weldon—' Smooth features were raised upwards. There was a smile. 'Something entirely slipped my mind when we were talking just now. It means, I'm afraid, you won't be able to take the rondavel, after all.'

Laurie felt the dress slip from her fingers and drop with a tiny clap to the floor.

'Silly of me not to remember, of course,' the hotel proprietress was saying as she paced leisurely, 'but repairs and maintenance of the rondavels must be carried out during the off season. That's the only time we get.'

Laurie looked round. Compared to the hotel, the rondavels looked in remarkably good repair. She bent to pick up the dress, saying, 'Couldn't I move into the hotel?'

Perhaps the smile on the other woman's face was meant to be apologetic? To Laurie, it looked more like one of satisfaction.

'I'm afraid we go right through the place, my dear,' she shrugged. 'As I'm the only hotel in town you can appreciate that I have to be ready for the hunting season.'

'Of course.' Laurie gave a weak smile and turned back inside the rondavel. Mrs. Lewis came in and started to re-fold the dresses on the bed.

'I shouldn't worry too much, my dear,' she said chattily. 'Mbinga's a dead-and-alive hole anyway. You'll have much more fun at the coast. With such a pretty hair-do I bet you'll have an escort in no time. Now—' she snapped the case shut breezily, 'would you like me to get hold of Mahmoud for you?'

'Well, I think I ought to . . .'

'Oh, it's no trouble!' The hotel proprietress put up an insistent hand. 'I'll get one of the boys to run down the road. It will only take a few minutes.'

Some time later, Laurie heard the crunch of car wheels as she sat, still in a daze, on the end of the bed. There was nowhere else for her to stay in Mbinga, so it was obvious she would have to forget the idea of spending her holiday with Dave, but oughtn't she to get a message through to Ryan, telling him she was returning to the coast? It did seem awfully bad manners just leaving without a word.

Her suitcase disappeared from the doorway and then Mrs. Lewis was helping her along the path.

'I've arranged everything, my dear,' she purred. 'I knew you wouldn't want to be bothered with tiresome formalities,' and then gaily. 'Lucky you, living it up in Dar-es-Salaam! I wish I was going.'

The door was slammed shut and now the wheels were in motion. Mrs. Lewis was waving vigorously. 'Bye-bye, my dear. Bye-bye!'

Laurie was conscious of the palms flashing by at an alarming rate. She wondered just what instructions the driver had been given and then heaved a sigh. What difference did it make? She was leaving Mbinga, and something told her that was the wisest move.

She could write a letter of explanation to Ryan once she got to the coast. Maybe it wouldn't reach him until she was well on her way back to England, but he would get it some time.

They had left the town and were on the long, red-dust road. The driver thrust his back into his seat as though settling down for the long ride. Laurie supposed she should try a similar form of relaxation. If she sat as tense as this all the way, she would be no more than a limp rag at the other end. With an effort she lay back and stared at the scratched and pitted roof of the interior.

That was when she heard the sound of a car passing them on the road. There might not be another one for the next hundred miles or more. She thought she heard a screeching of brakes and a crashing of gears, but as most of the car owners took the roads that way, she didn't put any special importance on the sound . . . but they didn't all deafen the surrounding brush with long, loud blasts on their horns, and now another car was drawing level with theirs.

She looked out to see Ryan waving her driver over.

As the two cars stopped, he sprang out and strode towards her window. She couldn't tell what he was thinking, for his face was a mask of inscrutability, but the green eyes looked as bright and as hard as beach pebbles washed by the waves. Flickering them over her suitcase, he said sourly, 'So the idea of staying on didn't appeal, after all?'

Laurie sat more erect. 'I was going to write and explain when I got to Dar-es-Salaam,' she murmured.

'Explain what? Why you found it necessary to slip out the back way?' He stood back to give the rickety machine a searing glance. 'For heaven's sake, why didn't you say you couldn't wait to get out? I would have driven you to the coast myself.'

Laurie took a breath. 'I wish you'd stop trying to make out that I was sneaking away! I certainly never intended to leave like this. It was just that things started to move very quickly, and when Mrs. Lewis said she couldn't put me up I thought . . .'

He turned his head sideways as though not sure he had caught the words right.

'Gayna couldn't put you up?'

Laurie nodded. 'Something about repairs and maintenance of the rondavels during the slack season.'

Ryan opened the car door thoughtfully. 'That's right. With no guests, it's the ideal time to get all the odd jobs done.'

He raised his head and gazed at her for a long and palpitating moment. She saw the white teeth show in a slow-formed smile, and then he was saying humorously, 'To use an old and worn out phrase, it looks like I owe you an apology.'

Laurie didn't know why he was helping her out of the car. She still had to get to Dar-es-Salaam. Unless of course he intended to drive her there himself. That must be it, for he had removed the case and was paying off the car driver. He tossed her luggage in the back of the estate car and held the front door for her.

'I really came back to see how you were at handling a car on these roads but it's not important now.' He closed the door and went round to step in beside her.

'What do you mean *now*?' Laurie looked puzzled as he swung the car out on the road.

'With you staying up at Nyumbaya no doubt Dave will be doing most of the driving.'

'Oh, but . . .' she gulped. Surely he didn't mean she was to stay at *his* house? Hadn't she just been telling herself that the wisest move would be to leave Mbinga?

He nosed the car out over the plain with an absent nod.

'I was going to suggest your moving in with us from the first, but thought you might welcome an occasional breather from that wild young brother of mine. Needless to say, Dave didn't see it like that. He's expecting you anyway.' As she still hadn't found her tongue, he continued lazily, 'You needn't worry about me, by the way. I don't intend to make myself too obvious.'

Laurie digested this with mixed feelings, and then she said carefully, choosing another track, 'I'll see Cando again.'

'And spoil him no end.' He tossed her a tolerant smile. 'He's not getting on too well with the enclosure. I reckon we'll have to put up with him flapping at your heels.'

Laurie laughed her relief. Cando was a far safer subject than Ryan Holt. She said with a happy sigh, 'I can't wait to hold him in my arms again.'

Ryan shot the car forward. 'Just remember you have Desmond to go back to, child.'

She wasn't sure whether he had been speaking to her or whether he preferred the words to be whipped away on the passing breeze.

It was late afternoon when the car slid in through the ornamental gates. Almost before it had come to a halt, Dave was loping over the lawns to swing open the car door.

'This is great,' he glowed, helping her from her seat and up towards the house. 'Your room's all fixed. It's the one at the end. Got a fab view of the lake and a balcony too if you want to use it.' Laurie smiled as he curled an arm about her waist. He drew her close happily. 'Am I glad you decided to stay on!'

She was conscious of Ryan looming up behind, and then Dave was having her suitcase thrown playfully towards him.

As he caught it, Ryan said dryly, 'No need for greased lightning tactics, Dave. This is Africa. We do things a little slower out here.'

Dave grasped the case with a grin and went off, whistling tunefully. Laurie looked up at Ryan, but before she could ask the question, he was saying laconically, 'One bat-eared fox coming up!'

He led her over the lawns towards the path Nabu had taken earlier. Laurie took a deep and tremulous breath. She had seen all this once before today, and yet now her whole being throbbed with an awareness, a sweet consciousness of every blade of grass, every exotic flower. Through the bleached trunks of the eucalyptus trees, she could see the lake, a sheet of pale gold, in the fading light. The purple-black mountain looked like a paper cut-out against the peach-tinted sky. In the garden, chattering parrots and blue and scarlet birds dipped and swooped over thick clouds of white frangipani, and blazing hibiscus.

They wandered along the path, past tall cypresses and rustling jacaranda, and Laurie moved, enthralled by the shade and perfume of blossoming shrubs, the breathless perfection of waxen canna lilies. She must have given an involuntary sigh of pleasure, for Ryan dropped a negligent arm across her shoulder, murmuring softly, 'It's a good time to see the garden.'

They walked for a while and then he asked easily, 'Like the house?'

'Like it?' Laurie gave an incredulous smile. 'I'm still trying to get over it! Such a house in such an idyllic spot. It's like living on the edge of the world.' She looked up at him. 'I thought everything was bush around here and the architecture limited to tin-roofed bungalows and bamboo huts.'

He smiled. 'The colonial type who had this built was slightly more ambitious. The only thing it needed was the electric light engine.'

'What does it mean, the name Nyumbaya?' she asked dreamily.

'It was originally "Nyumba ya Upepo," Swahili for "House of the Winds." The old boy was something of an Indian romantic, though I preferred the local translation, and that got whittled down to "Nyumbaya".'

Laurie studied. 'There is a Palace of the Winds in India, isn't there?'

He nodded with a grin. 'You've been doing your homework! Built mainly of windows and arches, it's positioned, they say, to catch the breezes.'

She turned eagerly to look back at the house with its many windows and surrounding rustling trees. 'Do you suppose he was after the same effect here?'

'No.' He drooped a cynical smile over her. 'I think he was just looking for an excuse to hang the name.'

'Ouch!' She gave him a cool grimace. 'I can see there's no danger of the present owner being a romantic.'

'I wouldn't go so far as to say that.' The imperceptible tightening of his fingers on her shoulder sent Laurie's heart spinning along in a series of uneven bumps. She clutched drowningly at the edge of the subject, 'Where is he now, this . . . this romantic?'

'Got homesick for India,' he grinned. 'Nabu and the servants elected to stay.'

'So you took it over, just as it was?'

'More or less, apart from a few changes inside.'

Laurie nodded. The solid colours, huge armchairs and bold design of the rooms had something of Ryan's personality about them.

They had come out on the edge of the valley where a sizeable stretch of ground had been given over to various types of stockades and enclosures. Laurie saw the long neck of a giraffe poking over one, and a pair of curly horns over another. She stepped forward, intrigued.

'I thought you hunted animals, not kept them as pets,' she breathed.

'These are not exactly pets,' he explained. 'I suppose you could call it an animal orphanage. For some reason or other, a number of them become orphans, and when that happens their chances of survival are practically nil.'

'But don't they grow up troublesome?'

'Occasionally. Some of them go to the zoos.'

Laurie saw a man exercising a gangling, fluffy-haired ostrich, and a dark-skinned boy fondled a velvety-looking gazelle. When she could drag herself away, Ryan led her to where Cando was lying with his nose between his paws, staring into space. She called him, and at first there was no response, then the bushy tail began to quiver. He pushed to his feet and padded over to give her a cautious slant-eyed gaze, before thrusting his nose excitedly into her hand.

Laurie picked him up with a small laugh and held the palpitating body close. The fox would have licked her face in his joy, but Ryan slid a hand between and took the lick instead.

'A pity he's not a dog,' he said, as they made their way back to the house. 'You could have taken him back with you.'

Laurie nodded with a fanciful smile.

'I never in my whole life owned a dog,' she said softly.

'Parents not having any, I suppose?' He looked down at her.

'Not parents,' she sighed. 'Brothers. Three of them.'

'I thought boys were keen on dogs?'

'They are, I suppose, but my brothers are so much older than I am. They were grown up and married before I was eight and took it in turns to look after me when our parents died.' She smiled up at him. 'I couldn't very well expect them to take a pet in too, could I?'

'Maybe not.' His lips tightened as he asked, 'What exactly did "taking it in turns" mean for you?'

'Well,' she explained, 'I used to go and stay with my oldest brother for six months, and then on to the the middle one, then after six months with the youngest I was ready to . . .'

'To start all over again.' He reached for his pipe with a slight frown. 'That was a pretty disrupted kind of a life for a child, wasn't it?'

'I soon got used to it,' she shrugged. 'All my brothers live in the same district in Folkestone, so I didn't have to change schools or anything like that, and they didn't object when I wanted to get my own flat,' she added defensively.

'I don't suppose they would,' he commented dryly, 'but in my opinion you're too young to be living alone.'

There was a rustling amongst the shadows and Laurie drew unconsciously closer to him. He took her in an encircling arm and smiled, 'You're quite safe here. Fortunately we're at the end of the valley with the mountain behind us. The lake forms a convenient barrier between the wild life and the house. That old romantic knew what he was about,' he twinkled. Laurie felt her pulses quicken at his smile.

94

Taking up the conversation again, she heard herself saying airily, 'You're always on about how young I am, yet I'm almost nineteen.'

He turned his lips down and raised the dark eyebrows mockingly, 'Almost as old as Dave,' he said.

'But girls mature much quicker than boys,' she parried. 'If you're going to compare me with Dave I could be about twenty-two.'

He gazed down at her in the violet glow of the evening, a tolerant smile playing about the tanned features. Laurie felt suddenly irritated. She wanted to swing out of the strong curve of his arm, but couldn't bear to. She heard herself asking slowly, breathlessly, 'Ryan, why do you always think of me as a child?'

'Because, kitten—' He paused, and a heart-stopping silence seemed to drop over the world. They had come to the end of the path. He finished in thick tones slightly reminiscent of the night on the tree-platform, 'It's safer that way.'

She might have dreamt hard fingers gripping her shoulders, the sudden flame in glowing green eyes, for already they were crossing the lawns and Dave was taking the steps down two at a time. 'Hey, guess what?' he laughed. 'I've just found out Nabu has one of those old wind-up gramophone things. And that's not all—' He took her arm importantly. 'He's actually got some decent records. Nothing that you or I would recognize, of course, but it's noise – and man, what a noise!' With a wide grin he swivelled his eyes expressively and Laurie tried to whip up enough enthusiasm for a similar show of excitement, but all she could think of was Ryan's arm about her shoulder. She went over his last words again and again in her mind. *Because it's safer that way.* What had he meant by that?

Safer for whom? For her? Was he thinking of Desmond or was he afraid of his own thoughts?

For one brief and fleeting moment she seemed to be walking on a golden cloud, and then the hardness of the cool grey terrace came under her feet with a sickening jolt, for Ryan was saying, 'I'm off to change now. Don't wait dinner for me, Dave. I'll be having a meal with Gayna.' He bowed lazily. 'Have a good time, you two, and don't stay up too late.'

Of course, that was it. Laurie had to suppress a small

95

hysterical laugh. Ryan Holt meant it would be safer for Dave! It was obvious he preferred to look on the two of them as mere children with no thoughts other than enjoying a brief holiday together.

And now that he had got his younger brother sorted out, she watched him stride away with something like a stone in her throat. He was free now to get on with living his own life – one that seemed to have close connections with the Safaritrek Hotel.

Dave jolted her out of her gloom with an impatient, 'Well, come on, girl! You can't dance hugging that thing.' He whipped Cando out of her arms and dropped him roughly on all fours. 'I don't know about you,' the swivel-eyed grin was back, 'but I like the music loud enough to scrape the paint off the ceiling.'

'I do too.' Laurie nodded her head vigorously, determined to enter into the spirit of the evening. Perhaps the music would help brush away this mist of unhappiness forming around her heart?

For the best part of the evening her head throbbed in rhythm to Nabu's choice of African records. She hadn't realised how out of touch she had become with the latest dance movements, but Dave was a marvellous teacher and she had to admit he was certainly fun to be with. In a long room flanking the veranda and obviously set aside for music and dancing, they moved over the polished tiled floor, through record after record, stopping only occasionally to swallow a cool drink. Laurie didn't mind how tired she got, she wanted to go to bed tonight to sleep, not to think.

Happily there wasn't much time to think with Dave around. His car rides were nightmare excursions, with the speedometer needle swinging gaily round to ninety and Dave whooping to the heavens as they went. She didn't know whether to be relieved or sorry when Ryan put a stop to it.

'I saw you bucketing along at close on a hundred,' he said sternly to Dave one day. 'Cut it out. I don't want to find the two of you in a heap.'

It was fun at the lake, though Laurie only splashed about while Dave went in for serious swimming. She was constantly being drawn to the bird life that frequented the waters. It wasn't long before she was packing her camera along with the picnic lunches, and taking feverish shots of scarlet ibises, snowy white storks and multi-coloured ducks. When they roamed the acacia woodland, she saw kingfishers, larks, and wagtails, but Dave found photography and the click of the camera too tame. He preferred the thumping beat of the transistor that Ryan had ordered through Bill Alexander. It was bouncing now just inches from her ear, as they stretched out on open grassland at the back of the house. Nabu was sitting half a dozen yards away, with a rifle slung carelessly over his knee as was his practice. Laurie wondered why Ryan had ordered the cook boy to accompany them everywhere. Hadn't he told her the area was more or less free from wild animals? She shrugged mentally. Perhaps he was being ultra-cautious.

Her thoughts were interrupted by the sudden silence that had descended. Dave had reached out to switch off the transistor. He said with a lazy grin, 'One can have too much of the rave sound.'

Laurie smiled. 'Perhaps you were lying a little too close?'

Dave said, watching her with interest, 'I bet you like all that soft dreamy stuff really. The kind that went out with Grandma.'

Laurie laughed. 'I do like waltzes and things, but I'm very fond of good pop music too.'

He nodded, the hazel eyes tinted with green now under the brightness of the sky. She saw them swing over her shorts and shirt and then he was asking, 'What happened to the gear clothes? That first day you looked real mod, now.' He gave a roguish grin. 'Strictly from freaksville.'

Laurie cast her mind back to the first day at Nyumbaya. It seemed an eternity away, yet was less than a week. She nodded reflectively. 'That's the only mini-dress I have, I'm afraid. I bought it as an experiment.' She looked at him. 'Are you very interested in modern fashion?'

'Up to a point, though the latest "in" craze is a bit too go-go even for me.' He raised himself on an elbow to give her a bemused smile. 'You're not like the girls I'm used to going around with, Laurie,' he said. 'You're different somehow, more . . . well, subdued.'

She smiled. 'I suppose being a working girl has made me old and staid.'

He sat up. 'What's it like going out to work? Better than polishing your elbows on a desk, I bet.'

Laurie leaned forward to hug her knees. 'It has its compensations, but I wouldn't have said no to a fuller education if I'd had the brains.'

'Who needs brains these days? There are a dozen and one ways of making money. Nobody cares about degrees.'

Laurie raised a fair eyebrow. 'That's not what I heard.' She looked at him. 'Are you going to throw up your studies?'

He nodded. 'I've fluffed enough exams lately. One more should do it.'

He waited with a proud light in his eye for her comments. When she made none, he added, 'You're on your own. You seem to be doing okay.'

She smiled. 'I can't grumble, but with a man it's different, isn't it? I mean, when you're married, perhaps with a family, you might find qualifications can guarantee a certain amount of security.'

He shrugged blithely. 'There are short cuts to everything.'

After a silence, she asked, 'What will you do? Work with Ryan on the safaris?'

'You must be joking!'

He tossed her a disbelieving glance and then swung his eyes humorously round the landscape. 'They say you can never say goodbye to Africa once you've been. Me, I can never wait to get away fast enough. I don't know where I'll end up.'

Laurie followed his gaze around with a wistful smile.

'Funny how we're all different. I fell in love with Africa almost the minute I set foot in it.'

Dave reached out for the transistor and switched it on, jumping to his feet. He said above the racket, 'You're like Ryan. The further you are away from civilisation, the better you like it.'

Laurie had never thought of it quite like that, but she was inclined to agree that Dave had something. She had never felt more alive than she did now out here in this wild and beautiful corner of Africa. The prospect of returning to the pace and clamour of London filled her with a bleakness she couldn't describe.

Still, there was quite a while to go, yet why spoil things with the thoughts of London and work. She picked herself up and followed Nabu and Dave back to the house. The tune she had been humming stopped in her throat when she saw the scene in the garden.

Gay rattan chairs and a table had been set out on the crown of the lawn, and Mrs. Lewis stretched languidly in a long chair, a cigarette between tapered fingers, a tall glass near her hand.

Ryan was bending close to her, glass in hand, and Laurie heard a ripple of deep-throated laughter as Dave led her over the lawn.

He gave a resigned sigh and murmured close to her ear, 'Mrs. Lewis! That's all we need.'

Ryan turned lazily as they approached, and Laurie saw sea-green eyes drift towards her hand held in Dave's. Mrs. Lewis, cool and flawless in apricot silk, crossed one sheer-stockinged leg over the other and let a navy blue gaze roll over small, flushed features, faded blue blouse, and brief white shorts. The wide coral smile drooped just a little at the edges, as the glance lowered towards slender sun-tanned legs and small neat sandals. After a pause, taking Dave in her glance, she gave a tiny laugh to the sky and exclaimed effusively, 'Why, Ryan! They make a darling pair!'

The flicker of a frown ran across a tanned brow, and Laurie surreptitiously removed her hand from Dave's. If her assumptions were correct, his brother was thinking they weren't supposed to be making a delightful pair, just holiday companions. No doubt he was thinking too of Desmond and her consequent return to him.

'Good afternoon, Mrs. Lewis.' Laurie smiled politely, hoping, as she knew Dave was, that they might be able to pass on into the house, but Ryan was already holding a chair for her, and Dave, sensing the inevitable, flopped down in the chair on her other side. They all drank in silence for a while, and then, much to Laurie's surprise, a familiar thick-set figure with chestnut side-whiskers came round the side of the house. Bill Alexander, looking unusually smart for Bill Alexander, in a well-pressed linen suit, and ox-red sandals, held Cando high in the air.

'Handsome little blighter, Ryan,' he growled. 'Make a fine ornament about the shop. I'll take him off your hands if the price is right.'

Ryan shook his head with a lazy smile.

'Not for sale, Bill,' he drawled. 'He's Miss Weldon's pet. She's had him ever since she came to Mbinga.'

'Ah, but what happens when she goes again?' Bill bounced the fox optimistically, and winked at Laurie. 'You'll want him to have a good home then, sweetheart, won't you? He'll get none better at my place, you know. Huge meals and lots of company.'

'He's doing okay here, Bill. I reckon he'll be staying on.'

Laurie thought Ryan's voice sounded faintly tinged with impatience.

Mrs. Lewis drank daintily from her glass and sighed languidly. 'I don't know what all the fuss is about,' she murmured. 'There are dozens of the little beasts at the back of the hotel.'

'Ah, but this chap's rather special.' A shaggy copper eyebrow quivered unmistakably. Blue eyes lit with sly humour, danced between Laurie and Ryan. He said with mock innocence, 'I mean you've only got to look at his coat. They're usually a mousy grey. This one's got a deep, solid red-gold sheen. Reminds me of . . .' With another twinkling glance towards the chairs, he said to Gayna, 'Have you never heard the story of the enchanted fox? There was this prince, you see, and the girl he . . .'

'Really, Bill, your imagination sometimes is quite comic!' Gayna Lewis looked slightly short of breath. Her bosom was rising and falling quite noticeably. She finished acidly, 'We'd rather not listen to your brand of fairy tales, if you don't mind.'

Bill shrugged humorously. 'It's a good story.' He lowered the fox gently to the ground and watched him pad off over the grass. 'And I wouldn't mind having a part share in young what's-his-name.'

Gayna dropped silken lashes as though she would dismiss the subject. 'So many dogs and only one bone,' she said idly.

'Well, of course I know you would rather we were wrestling over you, darling, but . . .'

'I don't care for wrestling myself.' Gayna returned smoothly, quite in control now. 'Nor hangers-on. Ryan invites me up here for a few days, and what do I find? You nosing your way behind in your car.' She puffed out a breathful of cigarette smoke disgustedly and Bill smiled undisturbed in his glass.

'Well, you know how it is, old girl. Town's dead just now, till the hunting season breaks. I thought it was the ideal time for a change of scenery, and providing Ryan doesn't kick me out . . .'

'Well, I for one . . .'

Ryan leaned forward to tap his pipe out with a slow smile.

'If you two can let go of each other's throats long enough, we might be able to sort out the rooms.'

Laurie breathed an inward sigh of relief. Everyone else seemed to take Bill and Gayna's bickering as a matter of course. Personally she didn't care for it. She had an idea that Bill would get the worst of it in the end.

Ryan rose unhurriedly to say, 'Gayna, my dear, Miss Weldon is in the room you usually occupy, so you'd better have the one across the hall from mine.'

Mrs. Lewis turned misty blue eyes up his way.

'That will do splendidly, Ryan,' she replied, in sultry tones. 'I wouldn't want to put Miss Weldon out in any way.'

'And you, Bill. How about the room next to Dave's? You have my permission to jump on the transistor if it interferes with your sleep.'

Ryan turned and led Mrs. Lewis inside.

Laurie felt that his last remark had been meant as something of a joke, but it seemed to have fallen curiously flat. Dave remained in his chair, staring thoughtfully into space, and Bill watched the couple turn into the house with a hard light in the sky blue eyes. As for Laurie, she felt as if a sharp instrument had been thrust and turned in her heart.

With an attempt at casualness, she sauntered into the house and up to her room. She stared around at the leaf green carpet, matching armchairs, and padded head-board of the bed; its white cover and the yellow and white curtains draped at the windows. So this was really Gayna's room. Ryan had invited her to his home before; often by the sound of it.

Laurie took herself sharply to task. What possible difference could it make to her, and wasn't it perfectly natural anyway?

When she first came to Mbinga, Mrs. Lewis had told her that Ryan and she were very close. Now there was no mistaking how close!

101

CHAPTER SEVEN

LAURIE wondered if she was going to be able to stay out her full ten days at Nyumbaya as she had promised. She was supposed to be here on holiday, but emotionally the days were turning out to be anything but restful. Minute passed on agonising minute as she watched Ryan and Gayna together, talking over drinks in the garden, smiling at one another across the dining table, or strolling side by side towards the car for a day's outing.

Laurie had to admit bleakly that they looked perfect together: Ryan, tall and bronzed with his lazy stride and sharp white smile, and Gayna, fair-haired and faultless, and breathtakingly feminine in her gossamer fine pastel-shaded silks, with perhaps a flutter of silken embroidery at the hem, or a whisper of lace between neat uplifted breasts.

What man could resist such a woman? Laurie asked herself more than once, and each time she felt as though the question had been hammered out word for word with every beat of her heart. And why should Ryan resist anyway? It was obvious by the tilt of silken lashes, the glow of hyacinth eyes turned frequently up in his direction, that Gayna Lewis was his any time he said the word. They must have been fairly close to marriage when Laurie had arrived in Mbinga. No wonder Mrs. Lewis had been showing a little frustration at not having Ryan to herself!

Laurie decided to p it these kind of thoughts out of her head by entering into a full programme of riotous living with Dave. They danced endlessly to the transistor, both inside the house and out, drove madly over the country unknown to Ryan, and even visited the cinema in Mbinga and talked through the whole length of the film.

When Laurie actually had Dave dropping hints about doing something a little more restful, they splashed in the lake, wandered through the acacia woodland, watching fantastically-coloured birds, and spent long sessions down at the animal enclosures.

Whatever Dave suggested, Laurie offered no objection to

it. She was here strictly as a holiday companion, and for the last few days of her stay she resolved to throw everything she had into being a success at that, whatever she achieved in other directions.

Bill Alexander seemed to be throwing everything he had into making a nuisance of himself. A rather endearing nuisance, in Laurie's opinion, though she was a little ashamed of herself for having such thoughts. He had a habit of making out that there was something wrong with his rather outdated Chevrolet in order to cadge a ride in the estate car. Sometimes his ruse would work, and Gayna would train a cool glance in the region of the back seat before staring rigidly ahead. When the ruse didn't work, he would toss a rueful smile across the garden, swing into his own car and zoom flamboyantly away. He also seemed to derive a kind of quiet satisfaction from stopping a dreamy dance tune slap in the middle and replacing it with a noisy brassy sound that defied twitching to, let alone dancing. He would turn and carry on with his conversation with Dave, apparently unaware that he had left a couple stranded between notes, in the middle of the polished tile floor.

On these occasions, Gayna's face would take on a marble-like mask of suppressed annoyance, but Ryan would shrug good-naturedly, slant a half smile down the room and drop into a chair with his pipe.

One morning Dave and Laurie sat in the garden discussing plans on what to do for the day. Sunbirds flitted over the poinsettias and the vivid blaze of the shrubs. Everywhere there was the hot insidious perfume of frangipani. Out of the corner of her eye Laurie saw Ryan and Gayna strolling across the lawn. Probably going off for the day again, she thought heavily. She searched inside herself for the smile that would be needed as they passed her chair, but either it was keeping itself fairly well hidden or she was running out of smiles completely. Nothing came from within and she could only stretch her lips tightly into something that felt like a grimace. She decided it might be better to appear intensely interested in the buckle of Cando's collar, but when she raised her head they hadn't passed by. Gayna was standing with her smile pasted on and Ryan was drawling, 'How about you two coming along with us today? I thought a trip over to the Zikiwe Ruins might be interesting.'

'Ruins?' Dave lay back in his chair with a look that said 'spare me' or something to that effect, and Bill Alexander strolled up apparently from nowhere, wisecracking,

'Probably thinks he's seen enough of those these last few days. That so, old chap?'

Dave struggled to suppress a grin and said with an attempt at politeness, 'If it's all the same to you, Ry, I don't think I'll bother. Nabu's been telling me about the fish at the north side of the lake. There's black bass and Nile perch there. I thought we'd take the Land Rover.'

'The north side?' Ryan rubbed his chin. 'It's reasonably safe up there. You'd better tell Nabu to take the rifle just in case, and remember to stick close to the Land Rover.'

'Okay. Will do.' Dave stretched his legs and got up. 'Coming, Laurie?' He took her hand and Mrs. Lewis draped an arm through Ryan's with a serene smile.

'Well, bye-bye, children. Have a good day.' She must have wondered why Ryan didn't fall into step with her. She looked up to see him, shaking his head.

'No place for a girl up there, Dave,' he pointed out. 'The mud's at least a foot thick. You and Nabu will have enough to do watching the fish and yourselves.' He turned to Laurie lazily. 'Fancy a trip to our ruins, Weldon?' he asked.

'I think I'd rather go with Dave,' Laurie replied, loathing the idea of all that mud, but hating even more the possibility of being a third party in Ryan's car. 'I can take care of myself,' she smiled.

'I've no doubt you can,' came the cool reply. 'But I think this is one adventure you're best out of.'

There was a silence then in which Laurie took care to look everywhere but at a certain pair of green eyes, and then Bill Alexander stepped into the middle of the discussion with a jaunty, 'Well, I'm game for the ruins!'

Gayna answered him with a bored sweep of her lashes which said all too plainly, I expect *you* are.

But Ryan was saying matter-of-factly, 'That settles it, then. I don't suppose Miss Weldon will mind going in your car, Bill. I'll lead the way.'

'Well, don't lead too fast, old man. Wouldn't want to lose track of the main party.'

There was something that looked like a smile beneath the chestnut whiskers. The gaze trained on Gayna was ablaze with flint-eyed humour.

In the half-hour that Laurie was given to get ready, she took Cando to his enclosure and fastened him in. He watched her depart forlornly, but she knew he would be happier there than tossing about in the car on a long journey.

Not sure what to wear, she exchanged her shirt for a cool ice-blue chiffon blouse. A tailored linen skirt in pale cream took the place of her shorts, and then she added a light dusting of make-up and a brush of peach lipstick. Her hair, only recently washed, had plenty of bounce. It gleamed high on top and hugged her head in soft waves. She stepped into medium-heeled cream sandals, picked up her handbag and stood back from the mirror with a sigh.

She was conscious that the result came nowhere near the sophistication of Gayna Lewis, but it was the best Laurie Weldon could come up with. Perhaps, though, she didn't look too bad, for Bill rubbed his hands as she came over to the car. Ryan watched her beneath hooded lids as he stood lighting his pipe.

'I say! I say! This can't be the little tomboy I saw lounging in the chair just now,' Bill growled. He raised a roguish eyebrow in Ryan's direction. 'Maybe we don't mind losing sight of the main party, after all!'

Laurie smiled shyly as Bill helped her into her seat. Ryan opened the door of the estate car to step in beside Gayna. He replied with some irritation, 'Just keep your attention on the road, Bill. You're too old for games.'

He started the car and shot away without warning, leaving Bill to start up leisurely and murmur with a peculiar smile, 'He's touchy sometimes, our Ryan, isn't he?'

Not sure whether he was talking to her or himself, Laurie decided to let the question go and concentrate on the scenery. At first, she thought they were going to arrive at their destination caked in red dust, but after a while they were on to tarmac and from then on the trip was pure enjoyment. The intense beauty of Africa never failed to excite her. She gazed avidly over corn-coloured plains, scattered with humps of rock.

There were patches of thorn bush, the occasional small river, woodlands and meadows, reed-beds and soda flats and masses of brilliantly-coloured flowers.

The man at the wheel relaxed into an easy gentle-mannered urbanity, pointing out items of interest along the way, and taking each dip and turn in the road with a shrewd blue gaze. This, Laurie felt, was the real Bill Alexander, the one she had met and liked on sight that day in his shop. She didn't know why Bill had acted so completely unlike himself these last few days, but she was almost sure it had something to do with the woman sitting beside Ryan in the preceding car.

The Zikiwe ruins proved to be just as exciting as Laurie had expected them to be. After refreshments along the way, they stopped at a huge grey mottled dome with something resembling a stone chimney rising from its middle. All around, pitted into the building, were great tunnel-like doorways which seemed to bore endlessly within. Laurie penetrated a few yards into one but hadn't the nerve to proceed further. She was annoyed with herself for having forgotten her camera. The animals during the drive had been varied and exciting. The ruins would have been good for a few shots too, but in the excitement of preparing for the trip – and she might as well admit there had been a certain feeling of butterflies in the stomach at the thought of coming here with Ryan – the camera had been left on her dressing-table.

She looked along the path to where Gayna kept Ryan just that little way ahead of Bill and herself. She couldn't imagine now why she should have been so keyed up. Ryan had been with Gayna all day, and they would be heading back to Nyumbaya any time now.

She was mildly surprised when he suggested that they all go on to the Lake Shimo Hotel. Laurie was hoping that Bill would offer a polite refusal and return to the house immediately, leaving Ryan and Gayna to themselves, but he jumped at the idea and everyone assumed that Laurie would want to go too.

Bill didn't say much on the run over to the hotel. He seemed preoccupied and every now and again would burst out into a fierce bout of whistling through his teeth. By the gleam in his eye, she gathered he was pleased about something, but she couldn't imagine what. They reached the hotel at apparently just about the right time, for long expensive-looking cars were just gliding into the drive. There was much slamming of doors and the general route seemed to be towards the bar, but after the men had gone off to park their cars Ryan led the way straight in to dinner. It was a wise decision, for there were very few tables left unreserved.

Once the booking had been arranged with a smart African waiter in bottle green tarboosh and tailored evening wear, Ryan turned to say suavely, 'The ladies will no doubt want to powder their noses, Bill. How about you and me going to wash some of the dust off?'

Gayna, obviously well acquainted with the layout of the hotel, was already clicking her way out of the double glass doors. She disappeared out of sight, and Laurie, unable to guess her direction, floundered helplessly along a corridor thick with laughing elegantly-dressed females, and their pushing male companions. She felt a light touch on her shoulder and swung round almost into Ryan's chest. He placed a steadying arm around her waist, and noticing the wide-eyed apprehensive look, he murmured dryly, 'You haven't been deserted, child. The ladies' room is the next door on your left.'

Laurie smiled her relief and wondered why they didn't part immediately. Perhaps Ryan was waiting until there was more room to move in the corridor and perhaps that was why he was holding her so close now. That *must* have been the reason, for suddenly the way was clear and he had dragged jade green eyes away from hers and disappeared.

Laurie found Gayna already half-way through a fresh application of make-up. The other woman raised a perfectly pencilled eyebrow through the mirror. 'Ah, there you are!' she exclaimed with a half-smile, pouting her lips towards a rod of coral lipstick, 'Where on earth did you get to? I thought you were right behind.'

'I got caught up in the crowd,' Laurie smiled feebly, and went to wash her face. Mrs. Lewis had completed her make-up almost before Laurie had finished drying, but this time the other woman seemed in no hurry to leave. She draped herself in a chair beside the mirror and watched through half-closed eyes as Laurie finished her toilet. Seeing the comb slide through high corn silk waves, she murmured throatily,

'You should never have cut off that marvellous length of hair, you know, you're nowhere near ready for sophisticated hair-do's yet.'

Laurie applied her lipstick silently, thinking it wasn't very long ago that the hotel proprietress had congratulated her on her pretty hair-do. But that had been the day when Laurie had been presumably leaving Mbinga for good. Mrs. Lewis, still watching, relaxed her mouth into a faint smile. 'There's nothing more delightfully amusing than a child too eager to grow up,' she breathed.

'And yet tonight I feel quite ancient,' Laurie smiled, picking up her bag. 'It must be all this sophistication I'm mixing with.'

'Must be.' The other woman lowered a tolerant glance over Laurie's skirt and blouse. 'Pity you didn't think to ask my advice before we started out, my dear. I would certainly have advised against wearing a skirt and blouse.'

'Too late to do anything about it now.' Laurie forced a carefree laugh, feeling her self-confidence plummeting down to zero. 'Shall we go, Mrs. Lewis?' she suggested.

'You must call me Gayna, and I shall call you Laurie.' The hotel proprietress took her arm, showing small white teeth. 'I know you will be leaving quite soon now, but I don't see why we shouldn't use each other's christian names, do you?'

When they got back to the double glass doors, Ryan and Bill were talking over their wine glasses. They turned as Laurie and Gayna walked down between the tables, as did practically every other man in the room. Laurie didn't disillusion herself it was her small slim figure they were looking at. It was Gayna, of course.

She floated down the room with all the poise and serenity of some well-known celebrity, and took her place amongst a sea of admiring glances. Laurie was rather relieved to hide a little behind the dazzle and take her place in comparative obscurity.

Walking down crowded rooms always unnerved her. It was even more unnerving to find that Ryan's eyes hadn't been following Gayna, as she had thought, but herself. She fumbled for her wine-glass and almost knocked it over, then Bill was talking and everything was all right.

The dinner was slightly less of a strain than she had expected. True Ryan was silent through most of the meal, and Gayna made no secret of the fact that she would have preferred to dine alone with him, but Bill talked happily about life generally in Tanzania and Laurie became so interested she forgot to be nervous. She had a vague recollection of courses coming and going, grapefruit in champagne glasses with cherries on top, hot soup and spicy omelette with several mouth-watering delicacies beaten into it, and white peaches soaked and set fire to in brandy.

Afterwards, Gayna lay back, a cigarette between slender fingers, her head close to Ryan's shoulder. He hadn't lit his pipe, but it could be he was contemplating it, for it lay on the ash tray beside him as he stared absently towards the dancers. Laurie raised her eyes a little to take in tanned, rugged features, and wide shoulders pushing at the grey linen jacket. She noticed he had on now a silk tie and guessed that spares were carried in the cars, for both he and Bill had started out this morning with open-necked shirts. Obviously they travelled well prepared for these evening occasions, and Ryan must have had many in the past with Gayna at his side.

Laurie took a small breath, and tried to concentrate on what Bill was saying, '. . . And you know what I think? The whole lot's going to tumble down on their heads. They got the thing up much too quickly for my liking.'

She found she had lost track of the conversation all together, but steeled herself into not wandering off with her own thoughts again. Thankfully, it wasn't long before Bill had swung round to the subject of animals, and Laurie found herself asking questions, some of which he couldn't answer. He would juggle playfully with one or two of his own theories, and then Ryan would lean forward with a helpful reply and before long the three of them were deep in a discussion about the difference between a white rhino and a black one. After a while, Gayna crossed one slim leg over the other, and let a bored sigh accompany a gust of cigarette smoke.

'Ryan, I thought you brought me here to dance?' she put in a little petulantly.

Bill gave her a metallic smile, and commented evenly, 'That's all you think about, my pet, living it up. You should take more interest in the wild animals that bring us a living.'

'You know I have a horror of anything on four legs.' She allowed him to stub her cigarette out on the ash-tray and he replied with a sly jab, 'Can't for the life of me think what you're doing in Africa, then, old girl. A small cottage in Cornwall is about your weight, where the only things that move are the flowers in the wind and the waves over the beach.'

Ryan got to his feet with a lazy smile and took Gayna's arm.

'Time to dance, Gayna. I don't trust our friend here when he goes poetic,' he said with a grin over his shoulder. 'Haven't you sold that cottage yet, Bill?' he added.

The other man shook his head and stared upwards in dry humour. 'Might come in handy one day, old boy,' he quirked.

Laurie saw Ryan draw Gayna close. She snaked an arm over his shoulder so that her fingers stretched, long and cool-looking, across the back of his collar. The chunky engagement ring flashed a million stars round the room as they danced, the band of gold next to it gleamed quietly on the silver-grey backing of Ryan's jacket. They might have been a married couple, Laurie thought.

Was that the impression Gayna wanted to give? Certainly no one in the room could have missed the rings, and if ever a pair looked perfectly matched these two did. Ryan, big and dark: Gayna, slender to the point of frailty and beautiful beyond words, with her flawless features and smooth fair hair.

As they glided round now, they talked intimately and smiled often, just like a happily married couple, Laurie thought bleakly, unable to stop torturing herself. Everything pointed to their being man and wife quite soon, perhaps within no more than two or three weeks after she herself had left Africa. She tried to shut her mind down over the scene before her and concentrate on her return to England.

Instead of mooning over what wedding was going to take place in Mbinga shortly, she ought to be thinking about the one that was due to take place in London some time in the not too distance future. Her own. Try as she might, Laurie couldn't picture Desmond in her mind. She had photographs of him in her suitcase, but she had never taken one out to look at since her arrival in Tanzania.

She fingered the stem of her wine-glass thoughtfully. Could it be right to have this 'out of sight, out of mind' attitude to a man she was practically engaged to? Would she feel like that if the man was . . .

She didn't get the chance to answer her own questions, for Bill was helping her to her feet.

'Well, Laurie, how about you and me having a bash at the light fantastic?' he joked.

Surprisingly for his small stature, and rather heavy bones, Bill moved superbly across the polished floor. Laurie had never enjoyed a dance so much. The only pity was that he had chosen to partner her almost at the end of the tune, and they were soon retracing their steps back to the table. Gayna walked to her seat within Ryan's encircling arm, but before she had made the chair, Bill had drawn her close and on to dance floor with a mocking, 'Well, since you're twisting my arm, old girl—!'

Ryan had been about to sit down, but now he hesitated. 'Care to try this one with me?' he queried with the slant of a dark eyebrow.

'No, thank you,' Laurie murmured down to the tablecloth. Perhaps if he had been asking her out of anything other than politeness she might have accepted, but she had no desire to play stand-in for Gayna. He would have her back in just a little while anyway, but Ryan didn't seem prepared to wait, nor did he look as though he was going to take no for an answer. She felt herself being drawn to her feet and then she was staring in the region of his jacket lapels while his arm slid around her waist. He was remarking somewhat vibrantly, close to her ear, 'I know the tune went out while you were still sucking your thumb in your cot, and I've seen the way you and Dave writhe to this modern stuff . . .'

'But?' Laurie raised her eyes coolly.

'You're something of a dark horse, young Weldon. You and Bill practically stole the show just now,' he grinned.

'I'm not all that young,' Laurie could barely keep herself from snapping. 'I can actually remember this tune coming out, and why can't you call me Laurie?'

She felt he was holding her closer than he needed to. The green eyes were lit with mocking lights as he smiled down her way:

'Youth is not a think to bristle over, child,' he said softly. 'Enjoy it. It will be over before you know it.'

But too late for me! Laurie's heart cried out, as she leaned momentarily against the muscular chest, and swayed dreamily to the music. Through the misty rainbow valley of this brief happiness, she heard his voice again, 'Laurie? Isn't that an odd name for a girl?'

'It's Laura really,' she explained in weak tones, feeling the beat of his heart next to her own. 'It somehow developed into Laurie with having . . .'

'I know,' he nodded. 'The three brothers again.'

She looked up to meet his thoughtful green gaze. 'In about five years' time, you'll look a Laura,' he smiled, 'when you've learned not to put every uncertain thought into those big grey eyes, and maybe have a couple of fair-haired youngsters stepping at your skirts.'

Laurie turned a pink cheek towards the dance floor. Desmond was fair-haired. Had he guessed that? She wondered what Ryan's children would look like. Long-limbed and dark, probably. Perhaps fair like Gayna. They would be beautiful children, there was no doubt about that. She swallowed painfully, drawing a little away from the wide chest and staring purposefully over one broad shoulder.

She felt his whole physique go slack and then he was saying coolly, 'Had enough? We don't have to prolong the agony, you know.'

His hand was on her arm and she was being guided between the dancing couples and back to their table. Bill and Gayna were already seated. Gayna, drawing on the inevitable cigarette and following Laurie through narrowed eyes, drawled in bored tones, 'Isn't it time we were getting back, Ryan? I've had enough of this place anyway.'

Ryan offered no argument and went off to settle the bill. Laurie and the others went outside. It was then that Bill started up his spasmodic whistling through the teeth again, and as Laurie and Gayna waited in the drive, he bounded away with a jaunty, 'Hang on, girls, and we'll bring the cars round.'

He disappeared into the night, and they waited for what seemed an unusually long time, then Gayna clicked her heels impatiently and eventually went off to see what had happened to the men and their cars.

112

Laurie stood in the shadows. She could see the swimming-pool like an L-shaped sheet of silver under the moon, but thick clouds were gathering on the horizon. The trees lining the drive bowed and swayed as the wind quickened. Laurie was beginning to get a little concerned when, to her relief, she saw the stocky figure of Bill approaching. He was hurrying along the drive towards her.

'Sorry about the hold-up, Laurie,' he apologised cheerfully. 'Fact is the old Chev's come over dicky and refuses to start. Could be serious, I'm afraid. Looks like we'll all have to go back in Ryan's car.'

'Oh dear!' Laurie was gripping her handbag tightly. Another ordeal in store, but at least it would be dark and if she shut her eyes tightly she needn't look at a certain dark head behind the driving wheel. Bill had taken her arm and was pointing in the opposite direction to the way he had come.

'You hurry along to Ryan's car. I'll just have one more go with mine before I give it up as a bad job. You'll find it round to the left,' he called over his shoulder as Laurie wandered off uncertainly into the darkness. She found the car, with Ryan sitting impatiently at the wheel. He looked through the window without opening the door.

'Wrong car, Weldon,' he barked. 'Bill parked his at the other side of the hotel.'

She hesitated at the door, wondering what had happened to Gayna.

'Bill's car has . . . broken down,' she stammered. 'He says we'll all have to go back together.'

A slight frown played above narrowed green eyes as Ryan sat, seemingly digesting this, then he opened the door and stepped out. He leaned across her to open the back door with a curt, 'Get in, I'll go and see if there's anything I can do. In the meantime keep a look out for Gayna and tell her to get a move on. We're in for some rough weather shortly.' As he spoke, a battery of raindrops hammered at the windows. He hurried away, turning up the collar of his jacket against the downpour.

Laurie stared through the raindrops, keeping a sharp eye open for Gayna, but though people were coming along all the time to step into their cars and zoom away there was no sign of the hotel proprietress. After a while, Ryan's car was the only one left on the parking lot. The lights of the hotel started to drop out, window by window, and then there was only the sound of the patter of raindrops on the roof of the car and the thump of Laurie's heart. What had happened to everyone? Surely they weren't working on the car in this weather? And where was Gayna? She couldn't be in the hotel all this time, and in any case she had gone off in the same direction that Bill had gone.

Laurie couldn't sit any longer without trying to find the answers to some of these questions. She climbed out of her seat, but hadn't gone many steps before her blouse was soaked and clinging to her skin. She lowered her head, hoping her skirt would stand up to the rain a little better and collided straight into Ryan coming round the corner. He dropped his arms away from steadying her, as though she was spiked.

'You young fool! Get in! You're soaked,' he ordered.

Laurie couldn't move. She looked up at him, rivulets of rainwater running down from her hair.

'What's wrong? Couldn't you get the car to start? What happened to Bill and Gayna? Shouldn't they be . . .'

Her teeth started to chatter and Ryan swept her impatiently towards the car. There was a pause and then he opened the rear door, saying through tight lips, 'You'd better sit at the back, I think.'

The door was slammed behind her, and then Ryan was sliding into his seat behind the wheel. He turned and, seeing her stricken look, spoke with features taut as leather.

'You wanted to know what happened, Weldon? Well, if my assumption is correct, Bill told Gayna exactly the same story that he told you, only my car would be the one that was out of action, not his. I should say they have a thirty or forty-mile start on us by this time.'

'But I don't understand.' Laurie stared. 'Do you mean Gayna got into Bill's car because he told her yours was broken down and we would all be going back in his?'

Ryan nodded, switching on the headlights and edging the car forward. 'Sounds like Bill,' he replied. 'Now I know why he wanted to park way over the other side of the hotel from me. All he had to do was let enough time elapse to have been able to talk to me, while in actual fact I was attending to the bill, always a lengthy business.'

114

'Why, yes,' Laurie nodded reflectively. 'We had to wait in the drive a long time before Gayna went off to see what had happened.'

'And once she was in the car, Bill being Bill, he wouldn't stick around to answer any questions.'

Laurie saw Ryan's taut white features through the driving mirror, and shrank back. Now she knew the reason for his cold, solid fury. Bill had snatched Gayna from under his nose, and left Laurie in her place. She hung on as the car, driven at speed, crashed over bumps and pools along the way. It would be another eight or ten miles before they reached the blissful tarmac that would take them the best part of their journey, but if Ryan continued at this pace she wouldn't live to see it.

She stole another glance through the driving mirror to see if he had cooled down, and then her heart stopped, for he hadn't been looking at the road in that moment but at her. Before she had time to recover from the jolt, the car was pulling over into the side of the road and Ryan had stopped as suddenly as he had started.

She shivered in her wet clothes. Now what was wrong? Surely they weren't short of petrol, or anything as awful as that? Nothing as awful as that! Something ten times more calamitous, for Ryan was saying in cold, matter-of-fact tones, 'Get those wet things off. You'll freeze to death before we're half way there.'

Laurie turned a look of blushing dismay in his direction.

'I . . . beg your pardon?' she stared.

He hissed a breath through clenched teeth and, swinging his gaze back to the front, growled, 'For pity's sake, Weldon, don't go coy on me now. There's a rug at the back of your seat. Get the blouse and skirt off and turn into that.'

'I couldn't.' The grey eyes were wide orbs of panic. 'I mean . . . I feel perfectly fine as I am.'

She saw the wide shoulders curve forward as he folded his arms. 'Maybe you do, but I don't,' he snapped. 'You picked me for your safari master, that makes me directly responsible for you until you leave. I'm not sending you out with pneumonia, so suit yourself. We don't budge from here till you do as I say.'

'Well, why didn't you say you were worried about your reputation?'

Tears spiking her eyes, she fumbled jerkily for the rug and silently slipped out of her blouse and skirt. She was beginning to despair of ever being able to think straight and normally again. This man did things to her that made all reasoning fly out of the window. She had been angry when she had thought he had been concerned for her, but even angrier when she had found out he hadn't. Huddled beneath the rug, she stretched one bare arm out to hang the wet garments over the door handle. Ryan turned before she had time to retrieve it. She saw his glance coast along it and up to her face and then he was swinging round to crash in the gears with a throaty curse and something that sounded like, 'This is the last thing I wanted to happen!'

Laurie sank further into the rug, feeling she would never know such misery again. Of course, it was the last thing he wanted to happen with *her*, but he wouldn't have minded if she had been Gayna.

The rain seemed to be coming down in sheets and the road in the headlights looked like a river of red mud. The going was becoming steadily more difficult and at times Laurie saw the needle of the speedometer barely touch twenty. At this rate they would never reach the tarmac, she thought. It looked as if they never would, for the estate car suddenly dipped its nose towards a slope in the road and failed to come up the other side.

Ryan revved the engine endlessly, but the car moved not an inch. Laurie felt her heart would pound out of her chest as she saw him drape back in his seat. He rested his hands loosely by his side.

'Are we stuck?' she asked unnecessarily from the confines of the rug.

'We're stuck.' His reply was abrupt. He tacked on as an after-thought, 'Another two or three miles and the worst would have been over.'

'Can't we get help from a passing car?' she suggested hopefully.

He kept his gaze to the front.

'This is Africa, child, not Piccadilly. There may not be another car along this way for a week.'

A week! She was shocked into silence. What if the rain went on and on? Well, of course, they would have to get out and walk, then surely . . .?

The deluge outside battered the car noisily, but inside, the silence became a breathless intangible veil that banded them closer together. Laurie couldn't drag her eyes away from the powerful shoulders and motionless dark head. She saw the tiny curls start at his collar and work up to damp clipped waves, and was reminded with a hysterical rush of that very first day when the zebras had stampeded and he had made her get into his car. He had been forceful and horrible then, and he was forceful and horrible now, except now of course she was in . . .

She slipped down into the rug. There could be no putting it into words, not even behind the curtain of her own mind. There was Desmond and there was Gayna, she told herself repeatedly, but try as she might, the three fluttering words she had held in check for so long broke suddenly free. Free to circle round inside her head, beating out their sweet message, 'I love him . . . I love him . . .'

She wanted it to change. To anything! Even to 'I loathe him.' At least then she would have had the strength to do something about the situation they found themselves in. As it was, all she could do was sink back drugged with the knowledge that Ryan was but an armstretch away. She saw the tiny muscle in his jaw working furiously. Suddenly he turned.

'I'm going out to see what I can do,' he said crisply.

She sat forward, watching him weigh things up in the pouring rain. The back wheels seemed fairly hopeless, and so it seemed did the front ones. Ryan had opened the door again. She saw him standing there, his shirt plastered to his chest, black strands of hair clinging to his face.

'It's no go, I'm afraid . . .' He raised his head and stopped talking. She hadn't realised that in leaning forward the rug had slipped from her shoulders. She couldn't move. The look in the green eyes was somehow hypnotic. She felt locked and drawn into that gaze and then suddenly something seemed to snap inside of him. He lowered his head and swung away, cursing, 'Hell's teeth! I'll get this thing moving if I have to pick it up and carry it!'

In a daze she heard him rattling about with tools in the

117

boot and then the car seemed to rock. Perhaps he was going to carry it, she thought, stifling a gush of hysterical laughter.

Whatever he was doing, he worked like a man possessed. The minutes ticked by. Once he came to the door to mop his face with the handkerchief from his jacket pocket, another time he came to fling off his shirt, and when Laurie went to wring it out and hang it up he almost snarled, 'Keep wrapped up! How many times do I have to tell you?'

'I don't catch pneumonia easily,' Laurie jerked, tears starring her eyes.' And I don't know why you're being so beastly. I didn't choose your wretched car. Things would be different if Gayna was here. I know you wish she was here!'

He swept the sodden strands of hair from his eyes and looked at her for a long moment. His lips were trickling rain-drops. They parted from the grim tight line into an absurdly crooked smile, as he murmured, 'You're darn right I wish Gayna was here!' He turned away to become just a blur in the rain, but before long he was opening the door to swing behind the wheel, with a terse, 'Keep your fingers crossed, Weldon. We might just do it.'

The noise of the racing engine made her head throb, but slowly, miraculously, the car pulled up from its sitting position and jerked and bumped erratically on to level ground. Silently Ryan climbed out to gather whatever he had used under the wheels.

He flung everything into the boot with a terrific jolt, swung back into the seat and started the car. A few minutes more and they were on to the tarmac. After that, Laurie lost track of the time, but it seemed she had dropped her eyelids for no more than a couple of seconds and then Ryan was swinging the car through the gates of Nyumbaya and up the drive.

The rain was easing off as they hurried up the steps of the lawn, Laurie clutching the rug around her, Ryan giving it extra support with an arm about her shoulders. They must have looked quite a pair, for Dave's face when he saw them was a study in amazement.

'For Pete's sake! What happened to you two?'

'Got stuck in the mud.' Ryan grinned. He looked at his watch. 'Nabu gone to bed yet?'

'No, we've been playing records. I'm just off.'

Ryan hurried Laurie across the hall. 'Ask him to see about

some bath-water before he goes, there's a good chap, and perhaps a thermos of hot coffee and sandwiches would be a good idea.'

'Okay.' Dave nodded absently and then turned. 'Where's Bill and Gayna?' he asked.

Ryan shrugged. 'Took the wrong turning and got bogged down, I shouldn't wonder.'

'But *you* dug yourself out okay?' Dave's grin slanted between Laurie and Ryan. 'Maybe Bill didn't want to get his whiskers wet?'

Going by the mischievous light in his eyes, Laurie had an idea Dave was trying to imply that Bill might not be in a hurry to get back. Perhaps Ryan had got that message too, for she heard him saying somewhat gruffly, 'Off to bed, then, Dave. Had a good day fishing?'

'So-so,' Dave grinned. ' 'Night, Ry, 'night, Laurie.' He left them whistling pointedly and Laurie went along to prepare for her bath dejectedly. Whatever slant Dave was trying to put on Bill's and Gayna's absence, Laurie would always know that Ryan had been prepared to move heaven and earth to save himself from a similar situation.

CHAPTER EIGHT

LAURIE saw by her watch that it wasn't as late as she had thought, but just barely midnight. She felt refreshed after her bath and amazingly wide awake – hungry, too. Would Nabu bring the sandwiches to her room, she wondered, or would he have left them in the lounge downstairs? By the time she had slipped into tiny flowered pyjamas and a matching dressing-gown, there was still no sound of a knock on her door. Probably the food was in the lounge. She decided to go down and bring back a little on her tray to her room. She had never seen a fire in the big stone fireplace, though she knew Ryan and Gayna preferred one when the nights were cold. Dave must have had one lit tonight because of the rain.

She could see the glow of the logs on the wall, as she scuffed over the carpet in her slippers towards the tray. She was only half-way across when a figure rose from a chair at the fireplace and proceeded to poke the logs. They crackled into flames, and her heart somersaulted at the sight of Ryan in soft open-necked shirt and silk dressing-gown tied at the waist. The tanned features shone dully after his bath, the dark hair, still wet, gleamed in the glow of the flames.

'Feeling better?' he smiled, apparently relaxed and slightly more even-tempered. 'Come over to the fire, child. I'll get the tray.'

Laurie didn't know why she sank down on to the rug unless it was because she always sat before fires in England this way. Just for a moment she had almost believed they were in a house over there, sitting before a wintry fire.

'Not going to fall asleep on me? I thought you'd want to eat after your adventure,' he drawled.

She dragged her gaze away from the flames towards the plate of sandwiches he held.

'I am rather hungry,' she revealed shyly.

For the next few minutes they ate to the sound of the tick of the clock on the shelf, the gradual collapsing of the logs in the fireplace. Ryan placed his coffee cup down and draped back.

Laurie dreamed in the glow.

'What a difference a fire makes to a room,' she mused. 'You know, I almost believed I was back in England just now.'

'Disappointed to find yourself here?'

'No, I think one would have to go a long way to find a house and a setting as perfect as this.'

She sensed the shrug in the chair.

'Dave doesn't exactly go overboard for it,' she heard him say evenly. She smiled reminiscently. Dave didn't go overboard for anything at the moment except loud music, way out clothes, and mod girls, but Ryan could have been like that once. She replied absently, 'Men like to pick their own castles and settings.'

'And girls?'

'Girls? Well, I suppose . . .' The ground didn't feel too steady beneath her. 'I don't think a girl gives a house too much thought until she's making plans to marry.'

'Which is from about fourteen upwards these days.'

Irritation flickered through her at this cynical comeback. She sat slightly straighter and pointed out: 'Other thoughts do enter our heads sometimes, such as how to earn a decent living and get the best out of life at the same time. We don't see every date as a prospective husband, you know.'

'No!' His voice was heavy with derision. 'Just the first guy you clap eyes on at a party.'

'Desmond was different.' Laurie raised her chin a little, getting his implication. 'He helped me from the start – offered me a job, and found me a place to live in London. Naturally I was drawn to him.'

'And now you can't wait to harness yourself to his kitchen sink. Let's hope he's sold on the camera work,' he added dryly.

'Well, if Desmond does like my pictures,' she replied coolly, 'there won't be much time for kitchen sinks. We'll have to build up the magazine together. It's working on a shoestring at the moment. We'll probably travel. Maybe as far as Australia,' she said hopefully. Surely Ryan and Nyumbaya would be easier to forget halfway across the world?

'Should be quite a honeymoon,' he drawled with undisguised sarcasm. 'Kookaburta down under, and moose in Canada.'

Laurie rose unsteadily to her feet, partly because the thoughts of marriage and a honeymoon with Desmond made her panic slightly, and partly because Ryan seemed to have had enough of her company.

It would be better to go now before the hurt showed. He could hurt her so easily, she thought, just by the tone of his voice. The knowledge made her angry, and as she turned to go she couldn't resist a small thrust in return.

'Maybe dislodging the car took more out of you than you thought. Still, we all get bad-tempered when we're tired,' she said lightly.

Before she had time to turn away an arm snaked out and her wrist was caught in a steel clamp. She saw the glitter of green from the shadows of the chair, a white even smile.

'As you can see, Weldon,' he jerked her towards him, 'I'm far from flaked out. As a matter of fact I was just going to suggest another cup of coffee.'

'Please . . . I think I'd rather go to my room.'

'And leave Desmond's letter till the morning?'

'Desmond's letter?' Laurie echoed the words without really taking in their meaning. She was far more concerned with the pulsing grip on her wrist and whether the tall figure coming up close to her from the chair had any idea of the havoc he was causing inside her. Apparently not, for he was saying flatly, 'Dave remembered it and brought it to my room. I wanted you to eat before the excitement took hold.'

He moved away and vaguely she was aware of the lights coming on and then the airmail letter was being placed into her hands. It was very obviously from Desmond. His name had been scrawled all over the back of the letter. It was addressed to the magazine in London and had been forwarded to the Safaritrek Hotel and then on to Nyumbaya. Laurie opened the letter with slightly trembling hands. Desmond had become a shadowy, misty figure in the back of her mind. It was uncanny to have his words and thoughts here in her hand now.

She started to read the letter and smiled at the opening.

'Dear Laurabelle . . .' – slightly more affectionate, she thought wryly, than the plain 'Weldon' she had been getting lately, 'I've been trying . . .' he went on, '. . . to write this letter for some time . . .'

She read on. The smile faded. Slowly the colour drained from her face. She turned the page over, sinking down into the chair at the same time, her eyes raced over the words and then she dropped the letter into her lap and stared dazedly ahead. She hadn't realised Ryan was beside her until she saw the pattern of his dressing-gown from the corner of her eye.

'Bad news?' he asked.

'Well, I . . .' She raised a white face upwards. 'It seems I'm without a job and a flat. Desmond is going to marry a girl he's met in Canada. He . . . he's closing the magazine down.'

'May I?' Coldly Ryan picked up the letter and skimmed through it. He folded it, slipped it carefully into its envelope and went to pour a drink.

'Here, get this down,' he ordered.

'Oh, I couldn't!' Laurie waved it away in agitation. 'I've got to think.'

'Be damned to thinking. A stiff drink is what you need!'

She had it clapped into her hands and knew he would have held it to her lips if she refused. She sipped it, grimacing, but trying to think. Things were going to be a bit hectic when she got back to England. There would be a new job to look for and a new place to live.

The flat went with the magazine job and Desmond was getting rid of everything anyway. Luckily the rooms had been furnished for her to move into, and she had brought most of her possessions on this trip; but no job! There was no denying that his news had come as a shock, and what of the expense of coming out to Africa to acquire pictures that wouldn't be needed now? It didn't bear thinking about. Still, that had been entirely her own fault, or as Ryan had so aptly put it, her own tin-pot idea. She stared wistfully ahead, certain that the elephant shots would be something special, and the giraffe; Desmond would have liked the birds too . . .

'For heaven's sake, child, take the rest of the drink.' Ryan sounded irritable. 'Tomorrow if you like we'll see about making some kind of contact with him. That's what you want, isn't it?'

'Oh no!' Laurie looked up quickly. She didn't see any point in getting in touch with Desmond except to wish him well. He was going to marry a girl he had obviously known for some time in Canada. That would explain his frequent visits over there. He hadn't wanted to say anything to Laurie for fear of hurting her, knowing that he had been the only person she could turn to in the whirl of London. Laurie knew now that the only emotion she had ever felt for Desmond had been gratitude for his many kindnesses. Maybe he had known it, too. Perhaps that was why they had only toyed with the idea of getting engaged.

'I see.' Ryan was nodding. 'Want to leave things as they are? Well, you're young. You'll survive. Get some sleep and we'll talk about it in the morning.'

He dropped an arm about her trembling shoulders and didn't take it away until they had reached the door of her room.

'Okay now?' He stayed to give her a searching look. 'No good saying save the tears, the guy's not worth it, I suppose?' he offered.

She shot him a querulous smile and opened the door.

'Good night, Ryan . . . and thank you.'

'Don't mention it. Any time—' he shrugged the massive shoulders and turned away.

She watched him stride off, wondering what it was that made him kind to the point of tenderness one minute, brusque and almost brutal the next. With a sigh she decided she would never know the man who was Ryan Holt.

Laurie awoke next morning with the thought that tomorrow would be her last day at Nyumbaya. She had risen, donned a cotton housecoat, and gone to stand on the balcony before Desmond's letter and its contents came back to her. Strangely enough, gazing out on a garden that must have had more colours than a painter's palette, over the flame trees and flamboyants to a sky that was the bluest of blues, things didn't seem half so bad as they had done last night. Of course, she would get another job. There would be someone in London who needed a photographer, and the pictures she had taken out here would help. If the worst came to the worst and there were no opportunities in the city, she could always go up to the provinces or even . . . no! She had been going to say stay on in Africa, but Ryan was here in Tanzania.

He *was* Tanzania! Every plain and every mountain would remind her of him, every flower and every blossoming tree would bring home again the beauty of Nyumbaya. And there was Gayna. There would always be Gayna for Ryan.

She turned into the bedroom, dispensing with the idea of Africa. England was a sounder proposition. Forgetting would come easier over there, after about the first forty years, she told herself wryly.

Mid-morning, Bill and Gayna turned up, bickering as usual as they crossed the lawns, but not looking unduly unhappy. Bill was caked in red mud that looked as if it might have dried on him some five or six hours or more. Gayna was Gayna, encased in perfection like a doll under its plastic cover. No stray hair fluttered up from the smooth blonde head. The make-up was as fresh as it had been before dinner last night. She clicked along the terrace gracefully.

'Ryan darling! I'm so glad you got back safe! This imbecile' – she shot a withering glance in Bill's direction – 'tried to take a short cut and got us stuck. He's been trying to claw us out all night.'

'I wouldn't exactly say *claw*, my sweet.' Bill thrust his hands into his caked pockets and lay back on the breeze. 'Though I did get the Chev halfway out of the slime at one time.'

'Imagine! We had to spend the whole night in the car!' Gayna fumed mildly. 'I hardly got a wink of sleep, what with the rain, and Bill talking—' She raised an expressive eyebrow. 'And you know how Bill talks!'

'I know how Bill swops driving companions too,' Ryan drawled, reaching for his pipe and tossing Bill a chilly smile.

Gayna looked blank for a moment as though she had forgotten Bill's deception of last night and then she rushed on, 'Oh, don't worry! We've had all that out. Wild horses wouldn't get me into his car again.'

Bill twitched an unashamed smile. 'Pure misunderstanding, old boy. I really *did* think you were having trouble with your car.'

Ryan could have disproved this explanation in a minute had he wanted to. Laurie knew it, and so did the others, yet strangely enough, nobody seemed particularly eager to disprove anything, least of all Ryan. He grinned good-naturedly at Bill and ran a glance over his clothes.

'I can't guarantee Nabú will be able to do anything with the suit, but you should be able to chip some of the mud off in the tub,' he said pleasantly.

'If I don't fall asleep on the job—' Bill gave a mock snore as he went towards the house. 'I had to walk about three miles to a farm this morning for help. It's me for kip for a few hours.'

Gayna stretched prettily. 'I'm dead on my feet. Would you ask the servants to go about their duties extra specially quiet for me, Ryan? I'm sure I shall sleep like a baby until three or four o'clock.'

'I'll issue wings for the staff.' Ryan took her arm attentively. He left her at the door with, 'Rest well, my dear.'

Laurie was making her way indoors too in search of Dave. She hadn't seen him since breakfast. It wasn't like him to linger in his room unnecessarily. As though reading her thoughts, Ryan laid a hand on her arm.

'Dave's driven over to Mbinga to fetch the vet,' he explained. 'One of the lion cubs is under the weather this morning.' He looked down at her. 'I'm just off to the enclosures now. Like to come along for the walk?'

Laurie nodded eagerly. She never refused a trip to see the animals. She looked down at Cando, sitting patiently at her feet, and then up again quizzically to Ryan. 'Will you take the two of us?' she asked.

'I don't see how I can refuse.' Dryly he took her arm and the fox was already two yards in front, leading the way to the path as though it was his favourite walk. It certainly was Laurie's.

The magic wonderland of colour and perfumes always sent her off into a dreamy trance, that she never really came out of, until the hard grass of the clearing was beneath her feet, the snuffling and grunting from the enclosures upon her ears. This morning she arrived leaving one dream world to be instantly caught up in another, for her fingers had somehow become entwined with Ryan's along the way, and he was strolling along obviously unaware that they were holding hands. She couldn't imagine how their fingers had become locked, but it must have been the time when she had almost tripped over a loose rock on the path and he had put a hand out to steady her. Laurie felt her cheeks flame. She must have been clinging hold of it ever since.

Quickly she loosened her grip, and dropped her hand, staring shakily ahead and willing the blush to recede. She felt Ryan watching her.

'Decided what you're going to do?' he asked casually.

She knew he was thinking of Desmond's letter. 'Oh, I shall look for another job,' she exclaimed brightly. 'It shouldn't be too difficult. There are plenty of opportunities in London.'

'And photographers,' he came back with dryly. 'Remember the glut you told me about?'

She shrugged and sighed. It was true, of course. There were dozens with twice the skill that she had.

'I might have to move out of London,' she said thoughtfully.

'And back to the three brothers. One at a time, of course.'

She couldn't tell whether his raillery was good-humoured or slightly satirical. With an uncertain smile, she murmured, 'I expect they'll have me in turns until I find somewhere. Rather like an ageing relative.'

'Or an unwanted one.'

'That's hardly fair!' She looked up quickly. 'They've all been kind in their way. I can't expect them to take a special interest in me when they have their own families to think about.'

'I don't see why not,' he replied. 'The only girl in the family ought to rate something. Especially when she's just a kid like you.'

Laurie let her breath out through tight pink lips. Mentally she was counting to ten, not that it would do any good. Ryan would always look on her as a child, never a woman. His next words confirmed this belief, for he was saying casually, 'Of course, you could always stay on here as a pal for Dave.'

She looked up at his face. 'And fly home when he goes back to college, you mean?'

He nodded and then grinned wryly. 'You know how he feels about this place, and he's a few more weeks to go yet. It would help him a lot if you were here. You're both round about the same age, and you seem to like the same kind of things.'

'I suppose so,' Laurie replied dubiously, 'but . . . I mean, shouldn't he be studying or something?'

Ryan shrugged. 'I'm not going to force the issue. If he wants it, he'll go back to it of his own accord. In the meantime I want him to enjoy life, and he never seems to have difficulty in doing that when he's with you.'

'Well, I'd like to help,' Laurie said sincerely, 'but . . .'

'I take it you're staying, then?' His reply came on the heels of her hesitation, and Laurie found herself saying breathlessly, 'I suppose I could stay until Dave is ready to return to England. There's no urgency for me to go home yet.'

As the words left her throat, she felt suddenly twisted up inside. Only someone out of their senses would want to prolong such unhappiness when they could have ended it all by a polite refusal.

Ryan examined the lion cub and had a talk with the man tending him. Laurie wandered amongst the enclosures until they were ready to return to the house. When they were walking back, Ryan asked lazily, 'Think you're going to be able to forget this Desmond guy?'

Laurie's heart took a jolt. Desmond! She hadn't given him a thought. He was going to marry a girl he obviously loved very much, and Laurie hadn't even got around to sending her congratulations. She would write to Desmond as soon as possible. She hadn't realised she had given no answer to Ryan's question until she heard him saying tartly, 'Crying him out of your system every night is one way. Another is to tell yourself what a heel you nearly married.'

Laurie lowered her eyes with a hurt smile.

'I wish you wouldn't, Ryan,' she murmured. 'Desmond is one of the nicest people I know.'

'Sure.' He gave a twisted, begrudging smile. 'But you don't marry a person because he's *nice*. There's supposed to be something a darn sight more to it than that.'

'Supposed to be?' Laurie raised her eyes. 'Can't you speak from experience, then? I should have thought at your venerable age you would know all there was to know about love?'

'I once thought I did.' He smiled crookedly, taking her arm.

Of course it was Gayna that had shaken him, Laurie thought miserably. Who could deny the beautiful Gayna was enough to shake any man?

Dave took the news that Laurie was staying on in Tanzania with a youthful leap over the flower beds to swing her laughingly into his arms. Bill was delighted and Gayna said she was too.

When Ryan and Bill were down at the animal enclosure that evening, she pulled thoughtfully on her cigarette for a while and then drawled teasingly, 'Davey, you're a sly one. Don't think I haven't guessed why you're so delighted that little Laurie is staying on.'

Dave flicking lazily through a magazine, raised his head.

'What's that, Gayna?' he asked absently.

Gayna crossed one slim leg over the other.

'Oh, come now! No need to play dead-pan with me, dear. You children are up to something and I think I know what it is.'

Laurie felt herself colouring slightly. It was painfully obvious what Gayna was trying to imply. She gazed on the two of them like an adoring aunt giving her blessing. Laurie jerked to her feet with a bright smile.

'If you two will excuse me,' she demurred, 'I think I'll go upstairs. I have a couple of letters to write.'

She walked out of the room, feeling Gayna's syrupy smile burning a hole in her back, but what worried her more was that Dave had watched her go, with a strange new light in his eyes. Confound the woman if she was putting romantic notions into his head, Laurie thought with a harassed frown.

But was it just romance with Dave? The next day she learned, with something of a shock, that things were nowhere near as straightforward as that.

She and David were parked in the estate car down by the lake. The transistor had been going full bounce, but now he had switched it off and was gazing at her thoughtfully.

'Laurie—' He drew lines on the knee of his white jeans with a fingernail, 'Ry said you were going to marry a bloke called Desmond, but now it's all off. Is that right?'

Laurie nodded. 'Desmond is going to marry a girl he has met in Canada. We weren't exactly engaged,' she explained.

'No.' Dave grinned, and in the same tone of voice he might have used to ask her to dance, he queried, 'How would you like to marry me?'

Laurie gave him an enigmatic smile.

'I can see you're in one of your joking moods, Dave, though I hardly think marriage is a subject for fun,' she said evenly.

'I'm not joking.' He sat forward, the good-looking features suddenly serious. 'It's an idea I have. Ry doesn't like the thought of me giving up college, because I've got nothing else lined up, but if I told him I wanted to get married and start out on my own he wouldn't stop me. With a wife to support I'd have every excuse to pack in my studies.'

'Well, thank you very much.' Laurie sighed mildly. 'I've always wanted someone to marry me for an excuse.'

Dave grinned, unabashed. 'Well, what do you think?' he asked.

She turned to twinkle at him. 'I suppose you know that thousands of married men carry on with their studies?'

'I know, but I wouldn't. Once a bloke's married he becomes more or less his own boss after that.' He pondered happily on the thought for a while and then with typical male conceit stated, 'You would like to marry me, though!'

Laurie flopped back with an incredulous laugh.

'Dave! You know that marriage is for a lifetime,' she gasped. 'You don't just go in for it to get yourself out of an unpleasant task. You're stuck with your wife for keeps, you know.'

He dropped a pensive frown over her. 'It would be a bit of a drag being tied down ... but so what? There's supposed to be all this talk about marriage being a great something or other.'

'Institution?'

Laurie gave him a tolerant and amused smile.

'And what about my say in the matter?' she asked. 'I've got certain ideas about marriage myself, and the first and foremost ingredient I consider necessary is love ...'

He brushed this aside with the stock reply he used for all the things that amused or embarrassed him, 'Strictly from freaksville.'

Laurie continued pleasantly, 'Now I don't love you, and I know you don't love me, so I think we should forget the whole thing.'

Dave grinned good-naturedly. 'Can't promise. It's the best idea I've had.' He shrugged then, sliding an arm round her shoulder. 'And what is this love business anyway except smooching all the time?'

'I rather think there's a little more to it than that,' Laurie replied, feeling her heart drop like a stone.

'Well, if it's something that comes with practice, I've got plenty of time.'

'Practise away!' she challenged, with a strained laugh as his fingers tightened on her arm. While there was a Ryan Holt, she knew she was quite safe from all other advances.

CHAPTER NINE

LAURIE had no intention of taking Dave's proposal seriously. To her it had all been light-hearted fun that merged in with the day's happenings. If she noticed he held her hand a lot more these days, or deliberately chose a dreamy tune so that he could hold her close, instead of dancing the usual two or three feet apart, she took it all with good-natured tolerance.

As far as she was concerned, Dave was looking for any ruse to escape his studies, but once he really got down to realising the seriousness of marriage he would be only too pleased to forget the whole thing.

In a way she would be glad when the novelty of the idea had worn off. For Ryan was beginning to give them peculiarly piercing glances, and Gayna drawled succinctly one day, 'I'd adore to stay on and watch developments, but more's the pity I have to get back to town. Heaven knows what the boys have done to the hotel!'

Early next morning, a morose-looking Ryan brought the estate car out to drive Gayna back to Mbinga. Tersely he told Dave that he expected to have a full day in town himself and probably wouldn't be back until late in the evening. Bill followed them out of the drive in his shaky Chevrolet, waving to Dave and Laurie on the lawn and shouting, 'Drop in the shop when you're in Mbinga! We'll have a natter.'

'Good old Bill!' Dave grinned, and waved him out of sight, then took Laurie's hand. 'What shall we do today?' he asked. 'I'm sick of the lake.' He considered for a while and then, with a sudden inspiration, 'How about climbing the mountain?'

'The mountain?' Laurie echoed, staring towards the brooding pyramid of inky green forest. 'Dave, we couldn't do that,' she laughed.

'Why not? I've been up with Ryan, and I went up with a game reserve bloke once.' He shrugged confidently. 'There's nothing to it. As mountains go it's only a hill.'

Laurie hesitated and he urged cheerfully, 'Come on, Laurie, I've never known you get cold feet over a walk!'

'A walk?' In her amazement at Dave's suggestion that they

actually climb the mountain, Laurie couldn't help repeating everything he said, but she had to admit the idea intrigued her. There might be a chance of some photography up there and if Dave had been up twice before it must be a fairly easy climb. He wasn't one to go out of his way for exercise other than dancing.

'Well, if you're sure you know the way . . .' she pondered uncertainly.

Dave dragged her across the lawn. 'I can do it with my eyes closed,' he scoffed. 'Now you go and ask Nabu to put us up some food and drink . . . although . . .' he paused for a moment, 'we'd better just make out we're not going too far from the house. If we mention the mountain he might think he ought to come with us, and that would spoil everything.'

Laurie pondered on this. She knew Nabu was supposed to accompany them on any outing, but he tended to be over-careful like Ryan, and he might try and prevent her from getting the kind of pictures she wanted. Yes, she was inclined to agree with Dave. A third party would spoil everything. She went for the sandwiches and drink, and they packed them into a duffle-bag. Dave swung it over his shoulder.

'We can have lunch up there and start on our way back straight after. That way we'll be down long before it gets dark.'

'What do I wear?' Laurie asked.

He looked at her shorts and shirt and soft sandals.

'You're okay as you are, the less we carry the better.' He looked down at his striped hipster trousers. 'I'll put on my shorts and a tee-shirt. Hang on, I'll be down in a sec.'

As Laurie passed the time, strolling in the garden, Nabu hung about on the terrace. Did he suspect something? she wondered.

Perhaps he did, for he came over to say uncertainly, 'Sahib Holt will want to know where you have gone, Mem.'

She couldn't bring herself to lie, but replied with forced lightness, 'Oh, just the usual places, Nabu.' From that, Sahib Holt was not to know they had gone to the mountain, and anyway, they would be back long before he left Gayna.

The sky was the blue wash of early morning as they started out towards the track at the foot of the mountains. They hadn't got very far along it before it petered out into a thickly wooded path, and they were soon climbing up through a tunnel of green.

Dave walked ahead and Laurie followed, but she was soon far too engrossed in her surroundings to hurry. She couldn't resist brushing her hand through the stream at the side of the track.

It was cool and crystal clear, and there were so many different flowers and shrubs she would have liked to inspect them all.

Dave was obviously out for the climb, not the view along the way. He called her impatiently at intervals and she was forced to hurry ahead. Soon they were climbing in earnest, between bracken and stinging nettle, past mixed evergreens, tree ferns and wild bananas and beautiful feathery bamboo that let the sunlight through in dappled patches of gold. Laurie's heart stopped for a moment when she saw huge footprints running across the path they were following, but Dave gave her a relaxed smile.

'Elephant tracks. Don't worry, they usually stay in the tall grass down in the foothills.'

Laurie digested this soberly. The elephants obviously hadn't stayed down there to make these tracks, had they? And what if she or Dave came across one or more? The thought made her wonder if they had been wise to come up here without any weapons of defence. She looked at Dave's slim boyish figure ahead and wished suddenly that it was the tall wide-shouldered physique of his brother she was following.

Not that she had any wish to deprive Ryan of Gayna's company right now, but it would have been quite a comfort to have the experienced safari master along, especially as Dave was adding conversationally, 'About the only two animals to worry about are elephant and leopard. The elephants don't come up high, and leopards don't go out of their way to look for trouble, so we're okay.'

Laurie must have looked doubtful, for Dave came to turn his arm about her waist.

'Don't look so scared, silly,' he grinned. 'I'm not a complete moron, you know. I wouldn't have brought you up here if I hadn't known it was safe.'

Laurie relaxed a little, and later her qualms disappeared completely, for there were animals now that fascinated, not frightened. Black and white monkeys sat amongst the twisted vegetation, just waiting to be photographed. There were tiny buff-coloured antelopes, a small furry animal that Ryan had once told her was a hydrax, and even a chameleon. It jerked erratically along a low branch, swivelling a heavy-lidded eye in a revolving socket distrustfully. Dave forgot to be impatient and became as fascinated as Laurie. He would encourage the animals into clever poses for her camera and actually took five minutes over a shot of Laurie and two soft-eyed antelopes sitting obediently on a rock.

They laughed a lot over the journey, and for once Dave was completely himself, with no thoughts, it seemed, other than reaching the top of the mountain. Once up there, however, he had other ideas.

They ate the sandwiches and drank the coffee that Nabu had prepared, looking out over an expanse of moorland and huge clumps of heather. Stretched out, dozing after the meal, Laurie had difficulty in realising that they were on top of an African mountain, but looking up it was easier. The sky had never been so blue over England. None of the trees over there were hung with brilliantly coloured birds and garlands of silvery lichen.

Dave was lying close to her. His head was turned. She hadn't realised he was looking at her until he spoke.

'I never noticed before, Laurie,' he said without altering his position. 'You're some looker.'

'Well, thank you,' she replied lightly, and then, because he continued to stare, 'Are you seeing me for the first time, then?'

'No, I've been seeing you for some time,' he smiled lazily.

She could see her own reflection in the hazel eyes and considered it wiser to sit up and look at her watch. In matter-of-fact tones, she asked, 'How long did it take to get up here, Dave?'

He looked at his watch. 'About five hours, but we'll make it down in half the time.'

'Still, it's almost two,' Laurie smiled. 'Shouldn't we be starting back?'

With a slow smile he took her arm and drew her down again. 'Relax,' he murmured. 'We've got stacks of time.'

Relax! One of Ryan's favourite expressions, Laurie thought, though he wouldn't be resting so easy now if he knew Dave's train of thought as she did. He had made it clear from the start that he wanted no romantic tangles for Dave.

The inevitable happened before she could stop it. A pair of warm lips came down on her own and lingered for a moment, and in the next she was pushing Dave gently away and rising to her feet.

He was up almost as soon as she was, flicking a curl away from his brow happily.

'You know,' he said reminiscently, 'I could tell on that first day you came to the house there was something different about you. And you know something else?' He took her hand as they started to walk. 'I like that difference. I wouldn't mind being stuck with you for life, Laurie.'

'Even if I *am* strictly from freaksville?'

He let her lighthearted remark drift away on the breeze and swung along smilingly down the path. They walked for some time in silence. Laurie was busy with her own thoughts and she guessed Dave was, too. She wondered what he was thinking. Of that kiss just now? Was he hoping to take it further some time? She might have been reading his thoughts, for he remarked, swinging her hand easily, 'Wouldn't it be great if we made it a double wedding? You and me and Ryan and Gayna.'

Laurie stumbled. At the same moment she heard herself giving a queer, flat-sounding laugh. Dave carried on thoughtfully, 'I might even see what Ryan thinks of the idea.' When Laurie took care to look unimpressed, he said with a hurt smile, 'You still don't believe I love you, do you?'

'No, I don't,' she replied lightly. 'I think you're just looking on me as a way out of your studies.'

He laughed softly, but she noticed he had made no attempt to deny it.

After a few heart-steadying minutes, Laurie felt sure enough of herself to ask casually, 'Will they marry, then? Ryan and Gayna?'

'I don't see why not.' Dave quickened his step after a glance at his watch. 'They've known each other long enough.'

'What was Mrs. Lewis's husband like?' she ventured. 'I mean . . . did you know him?'

136

'Tony?' Dave nodded. 'He was great. Knew all there was to know about big game. He split his time between running the hotel with Gayna, and going on the safaris with Ryan.'

'What happened? How did he die?'

Dave helped her over a fallen tree. 'Somebody took a pot shot at a rhino, apparently, but never bothered to go after it to finish it off. A wounded animal is always dangerous, but a rhino! Man, they're foul-tempered without a bullet in their side.'

'Did it charge?' Laurie looked uncertainly at the undergrowth.

'Straight out of nowhere. Ryan was bringing in the hunters. Tony was up ahead. He stood his ground to give the others time to scatter, but he never really had a chance to get his rifle up. Ryan had to put three shots into the blighter before he could drop him.'

Laurie stared ahead. 'So Tony really saved Ryan's life too?'

Dave nodded. 'He could have shinned up the nearest tree, but he didn't. He stayed where he was long enough for Ryan to get his sights on the brute, and that was that.'

Laurie shuddered. 'What a shock for Mrs. Lewis. Was it very long ago?' she asked.

'Couple of years back. I was over in England, but Ryan told me all about it. Gayna went home to her parents for a while and then she came back to run the hotel.'

They walked for a time in silence, and it occurred to Laurie, then, that the tree Dave had just helped her over hadn't been there on the way up. Stranger still, there were these great tall swaying plants with flowers on top. She was certain she hadn't seen them before.

'Dave,' she asked apprehensively, 'we are on the right path, aren't we?'

'Probably crossed out on to another one, but we're going down all right.' His smile was reassuring, but it disappeared when he looked up at the sky. 'Hey, we'd better get a move on. It's later than I thought.'

After that, they spoke little. Laurie saw several little darting animals, but her mind was now on the patches of sky she could see between the branches of the trees. That deep azure blue was changing by the minute. First it was a paler blue, and then a deep oyster grey, and now the silvery sheen of pearl was laced with ribbons of flame, lilac and puce. The trees arched above looked like the inside of a cathedral in the glow, and lowering her eyes, Laurie was shocked to find that the bushes and rocks were beginning to take on the silhouette of night. Dave had stopped. He was flapping his arms against the ever-increasing cold, and looking at her with an uncertain smile.

'You . . . er . . . don't suppose it's possible to go round in circles on a mountain, do you?' he queried.

'Is it?' Laurie returned the question shakily, gazing over the rolling surf of multi-coloured moss, the lichen hanging like wispy chiffon scarves from the trees. She didn't like the eerie feeling the giant plants gave her. It reminded her of one of those science-fiction thrillers where everything had got out of control.

'This is nothing like the way we came up,' she said worriedly. 'It might almost be another mountain.'

'It's the same one all right. Just looks different in the dark.' He took her hand, but the confidence of his grip belied the uncertain look in his eyes. It was growing steadily colder. All day while the sun had shone they had been comfortable in shorts and thin top. Now, with no heat from above, the ground was a floating carpet of damp misty air. Laurie tried to keep from shivering and longed for the cardigan she had very nearly brought but decided against at the last minute. In the end she became far too tired to care about anything and stumbled blindly on behind Dave in the gathering darkness. The night was alive with cries and scuffles in the bushes, and at one time Dave stopped so abruptly in his tracks that she came up with a painful jolt behind him.

'What is it?' she whispered, her heart hammering at the sight of two luminous eyes floating suspended along the path.

'Nothing much,' he breathed. 'Just a cerval – a kind of cat.' He turned round and gripped her, she suspected, to gain a little comfort from another being, and then he was saying,

'We daren't go on, Laurie. Too risky. We'll have to find somewhere to sit the night out, I'm afraid.'

'Stay up here all night?' Laurie gasped through chattering teeth. 'You *are* joking, aren't you, Dave?'

138

'I wish I were, and I could kick myself for getting you into this mess, but I've just realised – We must be coming down by another route and there's no telling where we shall land. It could be hours before we get back on the road to the house.'

'Couldn't we go back to the top and start all over again?' she suggested hopefully.

'How would we know where to start in the dark? No, I think we must look for a reasonable patch of safe ground and wait for first light. We'll get down as easily as anything, then. It's just a case of spending a few uncomfortable hours, that's all.'

Uncomfortable! Laurie had always considered herself fairly tough when it came to ordinary everyday hardships, but huddled beneath a dripping tree, half-way up an African mountain, with nothing to combat the biting cold but light-weight shorts and a thin cotton shirt, she had serious doubts as to whether her toughness could stand up to this. Surprisingly, though, in spite of the nightmare-like conditions, she must have dozed, for at one time her body seemed almost warm in the haze of sleep, another time she opened her eyes to find herself not propped up against the tree, but huddled round it, the duffle bag under her head as a pillow.

Gradually the stars faded and that same oyster-grey light rushed over the heavens to herald the day. At first Laurie thought she would never walk again, but gradually her legs came back to life, and she hobbled round for a few minutes to get the circulation going. Dave stretched stiffly and scratched his head. He looked, Laurie thought with a rueful smile, just about as good as she felt. His face was drawn and smudged with dirt. The hazel eyes were sunk in deep shadows.

'Gosh, I'm hungry!' He struggled groggily to his feet and fingered distastefully his nightly growth of beard.

Laurie realised now why her legs felt like flower-stalks and her blood pounded uncomfortably in her ears. Neither she nor Dave had eaten since yesterday lunch time. With the gruelling climb and their nocturnal wanderings, it wasn't likely that they would have any surplus energy to fall back on now.

Dave took her arm. 'Let's get going. The sooner we're down the better.'

'I think we would feel fresher if we had a wash,' Laurie suggested. 'We could look for a stream . . .'

'No, thanks.' He gave a weary grin. 'This time we keep going, straight down all the way.'

They followed Dave's plan, but there seemed to be no end to the mountain. True, the slopes were more gradual and they saw much of the open moorland and gigantic heather blooms similar to the patches they had seen on the way up, but as far as actually coming to the bottom of the mountain, they might have been hitch-hiking across Africa. It went on for ever.

Laurie looked down at her sandals. When she had started out, they had been newish and reasonably well kept. Now they were nothing more than frayed strands about scratched and bleeding feet. Every step became more painful than the last, for the looser they got the more they rubbed. Still, she was luckier than Dave. His sandals had given out completely and he was hobbling along in stockinged feet. When they came to an opening fringed with tall bamboos, and saw yet another undulating expanse of open moorland and weird-looking plants, Laurie had to sink down on the spot and beg for a rest. Dave shook his head and helped her gently to her feet.

'We've got to keep moving.' He looked anxiously at his watch and then at the sky. 'There are only a few more hours of daylight left and I'm not sure how far we'll have to go to get to a decent road.'

'You mean, we'll thumb a lift or something?' she asked wearily, a thread of hope in her voice.

'Anything,' he grinned, taking her hand reassuringly, though she didn't miss his anxious glance. No wonder! Laurie smiled wryly to herself; she must look a sight. Her legs and arms were scratched and dirty, and her face couldn't be much better. Her hair felt lank and lifeless, and if the sight of Dave was anything to go by, they looked like a couple of mountain guerillas who hadn't made much of a success at living close to nature. But things were looking slightly better.

The path they had been following for centuries was gradually widening out into a dirt road. There was a cluster of thatched huts in the distance and the blue plume of smoke that suggested possibly an open fire. Laurie kept herself going by thoughts of endless cool crystal water, but on their arrival, the smiling villagers could only offer some strong-smelling liquid that they kept in gourds at the side of the huts. Dave thought it was some local brew derived from the surrounding plants and advised against drinking it. The food situation was a little better, for there was an abundant supply of eggs, but without a drink Laurie didn't feel she could tackle this diet. Dave forced himself to down a couple beaten in goat's milk and then entered into a laboured conversation with a couple of the men. He smiled as he returned to her, walking as he talked.

'From what I can make out, it's not as bad as I thought. We're way off course, but at least we didn't come down on the other side of the mountain. I reckon we're about five or six miles from the house.'

Laurie put a hand on his arm and turned to look back longingly at the village. 'Dave, couldn't we stay for a while? I don't feel I could manage five or six yards at the moment,' she trembled.

He took her arm apologetically. 'We've got to get back. But cheer up, we might be getting some help. One of the men has a bike. He's offered to ride on ahead with a message.'

Laurie saw a figure wobble by on a machine that had seen better days. Bony knees stuck out from the pedals like the wings of an uncertain chicken.

She estimated his speed just a few minutes faster than their own walk, and pressed on with a dejected sigh. So much for their winged messenger! But could it be he just needed time to get into his speed? Either this or Laurie was walking in a dream state where time had no significance and the dusty road was but a testing ground to see how many more steps she could put along its burning surface.

They didn't seem to have been walking very long when a familiar red and cream shape slewed practically on two wheels round the corner and screeched to a halt a little way up the road.

Dave hurried towards the estate car, laughing with relief. Laurie stayed where she was. By the look of things, Ryan wasn't in the best of moods. Of course he would never do such a fool thing as to get lost on a mountain, and it looked as if he had little patience for those who did.

141

She heard the slam of the door as Ryan stepped out and Dave's garbled explanation of all that had befallen them since they had lost their way, but if Ryan was listening he made no comment. She heard him striding towards her, and raised her head, preparing herself for the worst. Even that didn't come up to what she saw. The longish face was pale and taut. Dust had settled in the lines around the grim mouth and red-rimmed eyes. The dark shadow of overnight beard made him look almost violent. Whether it was this, or the molten look he gave her, or just the fact that her energy supply was down to nil, Laurie didn't have time to ponder, for as she crumpled he swept her into his arms and held her roughly and speechlessly against him.

With an anxious look at Laurie's ashen features, Dave rambled nervously.

'I'm telling you, Ry, it was the easiest thing. One minute we were on the path okay coming down, the next . . .'

'Shut up, Dave, and get in.' Ryan was back at the car in a couple of strides. He waited until Dave jerked open the door and then Laurie felt herself being deposited with amazing gentleness on to the seat. She made a feeble attempt to swallow back the hot tears.

Only Ryan could show such superb self-control when it was obvious his temper was longing to take a free hand. He gave it a little of its own way when he entered the car. The door was slammed with such violence that she thought it must surely drop off its hinges.

The engine was whipped into action and the car shot forward as though shunted sharply from behind.

Life at Nyumbaya seemed vaguely unsettled after the mountain incident. Laurie guessed that Dave had taken the brunt of Ryan's fury after he had carried her to her room and ordered her to spend a day in bed, but moving about the house now, pale but none the worse for her experience, she couldn't help feeling that the row between the two brothers had touched on other matters besides the affair of the mountain. She knew that they had talked long into the night after it, but she couldn't imagine what about, nor was there any explaining Dave's sudden decision to stay in his room.

Out in the garden, she endeavoured to put the questions

from her mind, by trying to think up clever photographic poses for Cando. She hadn't been at it long before Ryan strolled over to take a chair nearby. 'Maybe you'd do better if you turned away from the sun,' he drawled lazily.

Laurie hadn't realised the position she had chosen was hopeless for photography. She gave a small smile.

'I suppose my heart isn't really in it today.'

'But it *would* be in holding Dave's hand?'

So he was in one of those moods? Laurie looked up to flick him a cool glance. When he saw she wasn't going to answer he remarked levelly, 'I suppose you know I let him have it over the mountain fiasco?'

'I guessed you would,' Laurie replied sweetly. 'And I've no doubt you told him that *you* have never made a mistake in your life?'

'I wouldn't say that. I've made at least one.'

She ignored the twist of his smile and snapped,

'I know all about the disaster of you taking me on safari and asking me to stay on with Dave!'

The smile faded slightly.

'We were discussing the mountain escapade, I believe,' he said curtly.

Laurie said quietly, 'I think the experience of being lost was punishment enough. You could have passed the whole thing off as a joke.'

'A joke?' She wasn't prepared for the blaze of green that smote her. The look on his face brought back vividly to her mind the moment before she had collapsed in his arms. 'Some joke when the brother of a white hunter takes a girl up an African mountain without so much as a penknife for protection,' he said roughly.

'Your reputation again!' Laurie replied with a light waspishness. She had a feeling she might have gone too far, for he was up to grip her wrist.

'Have you any idea of the dangers you were open to up there?' he snarled. 'Can you have any conception of how I felt not knowing where you were? It was well after one when I returned from Mbinga, yet there was no sign of you or Dave anywhere in the house.'

Well after one! He had been with Gayna, of course. Laurie swallowed the ache in her throat, and felt it wash over her heart like an ice-cold wave. No wonder he had been angry that night. It couldn't have been much of a joke to return mellowed and at peace with the world after an evening spent with the woman you loved, and then to find two tiresome children missing from their beds. Her hurt made her shake from his grasp angrily and retort,

'Dave may not be the world's greatest safari master, but *I* had every confidence in him. I found his company infinitely more acceptable than that of certain others I've been stranded with of late!'

He arranged his face into a thin smile. 'For a kid of eighteen you'll soon be loaded with experience. Marooned twice with me and once with Dave. Pity that was the third time, though. They say things only go in threes, don't they?'

She swung away, hating his tone. 'Believe me, I'm just as relieved as you are.'

He moved unhurriedly to block her way.

'Going already?'

'I've decided to wash my hair.'

'Looks pretty enough to me.' She could hardly suppress the trembling as slim brown fingers flicked through a wave at her ear.

'And Dave will never notice you washed it, anyway. Takes a man of my years to appreciate these little touches.'

She couldn't fathom the tight smile, but his voice sounded ominous. Perhaps she had sensed he was going to take her in his arms, but she couldn't have guessed with what force. She found herself being brought up roughly against the broad chest, and stared up with wide grey eyes and lips slightly parted in her breathlessness.

The face above hers was working with some kind of inner emotion, and then he was rasping throatily,

'You spent a day and a night with Dave. I reckon you can spare me ten minutes to discuss his future.'

'Future?' Laurie looked blank. 'If you mean whether he's decided to go back to his studies or not, I really couldn't tell you.'

'Well, *I* can tell you.' The twisted smile was back. 'He's going back to his studies all right, and just to make sure he picks up on lost time, I'm engaging a tutor.'

'Oh, I see.' Laurie lowered gold-tipped lashes because

she knew he was watching her closely. So Dave would have no further need of a holiday companion. 'When would you want me to go?' she asked quietly.

'We'll have to talk about that, won't we, but the way things are between us I don't somehow think this is the time, do you?'

She looked up to see his bitter smile and murmured heavily,

'I never did shine at solving riddles.'

'Don't let it worry you, Weldon.' The green eyes lingered around her lips. 'You've got other talents.'

He looked for a moment as though he didn't know what to do with her, then she was thrust roughly away from him, and almost before she had regained her balance, he was roaring down the drive in the estate car.

CHAPTER TEN

As Laurie had long since learned, whenever Ryan got on to anything, he usually moved fast, but nothing could compare with the lightning speed with which he produced Dave's tutor. That evening, Paul Valji, born on the island of Zanzibar, educated in England at the same time as Ryan, had recently returned from a lecturing post over there, was merely the subject of a discussion between Ryan and his brother. The next afternoon he was a reality, and the day after he was a working member of the household, taking Dave for two hourly sessions, morning and afternoon.

Nor did Laurie have time to work out where she would fit in to this new picture at Nyumbaya, for barely had Dave been carried off for his first helping of work than Ryan was heading towards her across the lawn with a purposeful stride.

'All set for a day at Lake Shimo?' he asked pleasantly.

Laurie looked blank. 'The hotel, you mean?'

'The hotel, I mean.' He dropped a tight smile. 'The food's good, the company so-so and there's a swimming-pool. You have a swim suit, I take it?'

'Well, yes, I have, but Dave didn't say anything about going out. I thought he was going to be busy?'

'He is for the next couple of weeks.' The curl of his lip was more pronounced. 'That means you're stuck with me.'

'You?' Laurie drew Cando closer in her arms as though he could still the thumping of her heart. 'You mean go to Lake Shimo with you?'

'That *was* the idea.' A flicker of impatience showed itself as he fastened the single-breasted button of his tan lightweight suit. 'You obviously can't hang about the house all day waiting for Dave. As I'm free for some time yet . . .'

'Oh, but . . .' As Laurie looked up, her grey eyes clouded. Of course, she ought to have realised he was just being polite, filling in for Dave when he would much rather be hurrying off to Gayna.

'I really don't mind waiting until Dave has finished his work,' she finished jerkily.

'Maybe you don't, but I have an idea he'll work better with you off the scene.' He took her arm with an intake of breath. 'Now I suggest you put on a dress or something. Shorts won't go down well in the Shimo dining room, and since the place is mainly for tourists taking a breather from animals and cameras, I think we can leave these behind.' He took Cando from her arms, and the camera from the table. 'Be back here in five minutes, and don't forget the swim suit.'

'But Ryan, I don't think . . .'

'Five minutes!' He strode away, leaving her no opportunity to argue. Later, clad in a lilac-patterned dress with a full skirt and tiny cap sleeves, she sat in the car, staring directly ahead, waiting for the authoritative click of a heel along the drive. She must have taken ten minutes or more changing, and she had been sitting in the car another five, before she heard him making his way up towards the back of the car. There was a slight thud as he threw something in the boot and then he was climbing in beside her.

She saw an appraising green glance flicker over her and then he was saying with a mocking smile,

'You put two years on, Weldon, every time you put on a dress. In that one,' – he dropped a grin towards the cool plunging neckline and small waist – 'I'd say the woman was winning over the green kid in the pony-tail.'

But *he* would never think of her as anything else but a green kid in a pony-tail, Laurie thought, with an ache. Even now he was probably replacing her in his mind's eye with the glamorous and mature Gayna. Perhaps that was why he had suggested a visit to Lake Shimo? Because it was his and Gayna's favourite haunt and he could let his imagination wander a little, even though he was stuck with Laurie herself.

The thought was so painful that she swung round to ask unsteadily,

'Ryan, do I *have* to go? I mean . . . I have been to Lake Shimo before.'

The mild smile was being replaced by the all too familiar frown. They were on the road before he replied in clipped tones,

'You'll have to put up with it again, I'm afraid. You may have noticed we're somewhat cut off out here. Lake Shimo is about the only fair-sized entertainment between us and the coast, so we don't grumble too much.'

Laurie sank back in her seat, drained of any reply. Ryan seemed just about tolerant of the fact that they had been thrown together for the day, whereas to Laurie the knowledge was almost unbearable in its sweetness – so much so that she barely noticed the changing panorama. Here, senses were throbbingly alive to the brush of a wide shoulder, the glint of green to the right just above her shoulder, and the firm grip of two strong brown hands on the steering wheel.

There was no stop for refreshments as there had been on the last trip. Ryan kept the car going at a fairly high speed and they were pulling into the drive of the hotel barely two hours after they had started out. Laurie had her swim wear in a straw bag at her side. She picked it up almost eagerly at the sight of the shining blue waters of the pool in the distance, though her eyes didn't linger on it for long. There were too many other things demanding her attention. The hotel, seen for the first time in the daylight, was a luxurious pink block set amongst green sloping lawns and a circle of palm trees. Gay sun-blinds hung from the windows and the terraces were dotted with red-clothed tables, matching chairs and sun umbrellas.

Ryan helped her out of the car and inside towards the reception desk. To her surprise he booked her a single room and one for himself. As he led her away, the keys in one hand, the other under her elbow, she asked somewhat coolly,

'Was that necessary? I'm sure there must be changing facilities down by the pool.'

'Bound to be crowded.' He opened the third door along a green tiled corridor and dropped the key non-committally into her hand. 'See you down at the pool,' he saluted.

Thankfully, she discovered that his room wasn't next to hers or just across the hall. She saw him push his key into a lock four or five doors away and nod to her briefly as he stepped inside. Laurie turned to find that there was luxury inside of the hotel as well as out.

She saw a turquoise-coloured room with gleaming white wood bed and matching furniture. The blue-tiled floor was decorated with white skin rugs, and a single french window opened out on to a view of blossoming trees and distant blue hills. She pondered on the room and the setting. It would be perfect, she thought, for a stay of days or more, but such a waste to be used merely for changing into a swim suit. She went into the small adjoining bathroom, primrose-tiled and neat, and slipped thankfully out of her clothes.

With the peach two-piece bathing suit hugging her form, she found she was almost looking forward to a dip in the pool, providing, of course, she could keep a reasonable distance away from Ryan. But this apparently was going to be difficult, for he was waiting for her on the terrace.

Her knees went weak at the sight of him standing there, big and tanned and muscular in brief pastel blue swim shorts. She would have liked to sidle past him and down the steps of the terrace, but he swung away from the men he had been talking to and stepped to her side. She was far too shy to meet his gaze, and the other men's appraising glances were a little unnerving, but then Ryan had dropped an arm negligently about her shoulders and he was saying easily,

'I thought I'd better wait in case you lost your way again.'

She could tell by the mocking tones that he remembered, as she did, their last visit here, when he had caught her close to him in the sudden influx of people making for the bar. No doubt he was thinking only of the stupidity of her losing sight of Gayna so easily, whereas Laurie was thinking . . .

She drew away from him jerkily. What was the use of thinking or dreaming? There could be nothing in it for her but heartache. She mustn't be lulled into a state of ecstasy just because he had been polite enough to bring her out for a few hours.

Ryan was saying testily,

'If you prefer it, I'll swim at the other end of the pool?'

The reflection of the water seemed to show itself in his eyes, making them appear as hard as pebbles.

She shot him a quick, grey stare.

'You're swimming? I'll only be splashing, I'm afraid. I've never got any further than lifting my feet from the bottom,' she admitted.

'You don't swim? Then obviously you can't go in alone.' He spoke as though the pool was fathoms deep, when in actual fact it only came up to her shoulder and Ryan's chest in the shallow end.

The water felt like cool silk on her hot prickly skin. She closed her eyes at the sheer pleasure of it and opened them to find Ryan still standing close by. She rose to shake the water out of her hair and murmured politely,

'Please don't feel you have to stay here with me. I'm sure you would much rather swim.'

He looked up the length of the pool, frowning against the sun, and then back at her.

'Sure you'll be okay?' he asked. 'Not frightened of the water?'

'Not in the least,' she smiled. 'I only wish I'd taken the trouble to learn how to move in it.'

His glance rested on her for a while and then he was saying under his breath,

'Too busy hopping from brother to brother, I shouldn't wonder!'

She saw the gleam of his smile as he left her to shoot through the water and then the powerful shoulders were moving effortlessly as he sliced his way up the pool. Laurie watched him go and then gazed round at her surroundings with a sudden lightening of heart.

It was a gorgeous day, and there was no denying that the fabulous Lake Shimo was *the* place to spend it. The pool was scintillating in its blueness, the blossom trees fringing it just shouting their colour to a deep turquoise blue sky. Occasionally a gust of laughter would ring out from one of the heads dotted over the pool, and soft music drifted imperceptibly over the tables on the terrace and beneath the trees.

With a sizeable stretch of water all to herself, Laurie was inspired to try out a few arm movements. It wasn't anywhere near as difficult as she had imagined, and soon she had both feet off the tiled bottom for several seconds at a time. Thoroughly enjoying herself, she stood up and then lay back on the water. Her hair was completely wet now, so there was no point in worrying, and it might be fun to see what the sky looked like from this angle.

Definitely turquoise, she decided, taking a wave for a pillow and moving her arms and legs to keep afloat. So engrossed was she in her upside-down world that Laurie didn't notice a ripple of water closer by. She was just pondering on the possibility of staying like this for ever when a hand came up to support her back and she buckled under with a worried flailing of arms and legs.

'Hold on there!'

As the water washed over her face, she felt herself being swept up and steadied against a wide chest. Ryan was smiling down at her and her voice died in her throat as she watched rivulets of water trickle down tanned, rugged features. She saw the dark hair flat against his head, and teeth gleaming white. He must have felt the pounding of her heart, for he queried mockingly,

'I thought you said you weren't frightened in the water?'

'I'm not usually.' She pushed away with a tiny laugh. 'It's just . . . well, I didn't know you were quite so near.'

'My fault,' he nodded. 'I should have warned you. Just the same' – he had taken her arm again – 'you ought to learn how to handle yourself in the water. Could be useful.' He put one hand at the back and one at the front of her waist. 'Let's see how far you've got.'

'Oh, but I don't think I . . .'

Already he had lifted her to float face-down in the water. His smile was reassuring as he held her. 'Don't worry, I won't let you take another ducking. Now relax and move your arms and legs as I saw you doing a few minutes ago.'

Relax! If only she could! If only she could get her crazy heart to understand that the only motive for Ryan's embrace was a lighthearted attempt to get her afloat. Thinking firmly on the lines of swimming instructors and their pupils, she forced the tenseness from her limbs and struck out at the water. With Ryan's hands supporting her, she felt quite buoyant and it was several seconds and a couple of yards later before she realised, to her horror, that the support had vanished. With a surprised gasp she was all prepared to capsize beneath the surface, but already a pair of strong arms were about her and she was laughing up at Ryan in her relief. He was laughing too and holding her, as her heart would have it, a little closer than if he had been her swimming instructor.

'You're a born swimmer,' he commented. 'I reckon that with a lesson a day, we'll have you moving like a fish by the end of the week.'

She drew slowly away and pushed the silver silk hair from

her face. 'Nice thought,' she smiled, 'but I can't imagine making this trip every day just for swimming lessons.'

There was a pause before he remarked, 'Quite a drive, isn't it? Pretty exhausting for you to keep doing this trip both ways.' He ducked under the water and came up to shake his hair and brush a hand over the droplets on his face, adding evenly, 'That's why I booked the rooms.'

Booked the rooms? Laurie wanted to ask him what he meant by that remark, but she was being guided up the steps from the pool towards a table and the chairs that held their towels. She felt hers being draped and patted around her, then Ryan was saying,

'How about something to drink?'

She sank down, nodding abstractedly, pleasantly aware of the sun's warm caress on her limbs. Seeing the copper-tanned bodies stretched out around the pool, she supposed her skin was pale by comparison, but happily, owing to her swim-suited sessions down at the lake with Dave, it was an overall honey gold. After the white-coated waiter had drifted in and away from their table, Laurie fingered her long glass tentatively. She looked across at Ryan and asked,

'What was it you meant about the rooms?' I take it it's all right to go back there to change?'

He sipped his small drink, gazing out over the water with eyes half-closed against the sun. 'I should think so,' she heard him murmur lazily, 'I've booked them for at least a week.'

'A *week*?' She almost dropped her glass. 'That was a bit rash, wasn't it? Just to acquire a couple of changing rooms?'

'I wouldn't say that.' He finished his drink. 'Considering that's just about how long we'll be staying.'

'Staying?' Laurie would have jumped up but for Ryan's steadying gaze as a group of people drifted by. 'I couldn't possibly stay,' she babbled down to her glass. 'For one thing, I haven't brought any clothes, and for another, there's Dave. I told him I . . .'

'Don't concern yourself with Dave, child.' There was a thread of irritation in his voice. 'He knows where we are. As for clothes, I put everything I could find of yours into your bag and alongside mine before we left. They've probably been delivered to our rooms by now.'

So that was what he had been doing while she had sat

waiting in the car this morning? He had cleared everything of hers from Nyumbaya. She took a trembling gulp of the liquid in front of her, but it did nothing to ease the pain in her throat. She raised her eyes slowly to comment,

'I'd much rather go back to Dave and say my goodbyes properly.'

'Time enough,' he drawled. 'Dave's got work to do, so for the time being you'll have to put up with me. Right now,' he frowned at his watch, 'I reckon it's time we went up to change for lunch.'

Laurie lived the next few days poised on the edge of a wonderland that beckoned hypnotisingly with every throbbing second. The touch of Ryan's hand, his smile as they danced, that proprietorial arm about her shoulders as they strolled through the gardens, everything would have her step over to that polished golden world that was love, but she knew how quickly it would tarnish once this interlude was over and Ryan had hurried back to Gayna.

No, Laurie thought bleakly, love was not for her. She had turned her back on it before, and she could do it again. It was only a matter of remembering to keep a cool distance from Ryan. Though her aloofness seemed to rankle him, she found it a useful rock to cling to, except at times when her hold was somewhat precarious.

His smile now, for instance, as he draped back in pearl grey slacks and nylon shirt, made her heart spin. She was thankful for the table between them and for the waiter who was discreetly lowering his tray, but all too soon the white-clad form had disappeared, and she was trying not to let her glance collide too often with a warm green one.

As she gazed resolutely along the terrace she saw him lean forward to take a sip of the amber liquid in his glass; then he was drawling laconically,

'This life agrees with you, Weldon. If you came to ask me now to take you on a safari I'd be too bowled over to refuse.'

Flattery from Ryan! Laurie wanted to dive under the table.

She had lingered a while in front of the mirror after slipping into this straw-coloured dress, and had had to admit that the sun had done her a favour, but surely Ryan couldn't be noticing the peach gold of her skin, the sun-bleached eyebrows and flaxen stranded hair? With an air of flippancy, she replied,

'Then it's just as well I won't be asking, isn't it?'

'Just as well.'

There was a vibrant ring about his voice that reminded her crazily of the night in the tree-platform. With his eyes on her now, his hand touching her own, she didn't think she could survive the moment, and then the ominous sound of clicking heels echoing along the terrace made them both look up. Had the noise reminded Ryan of Gayna, Laurie wondered, or was it that he had been expecting her? Feeling as though her heart was being squeezed, she watched him rise and hold a chair for her. With a gay, 'Ryan darling!' Gayna dropped down daintily, cool in white wild silk. A wide-brimmed hat rested on the ash-blonde hair, and shaded the flawless make-up and a pair of brilliant blue drop ear-rings.

She waited until her drink was on the table, crossed one slim leg over the other and remarked with studied lightness, 'So this is where you two are keeping yourselves?' and then at Laurie, 'Poor Davey, no fun at the end of his working day. Callous little girl,' she admonished with a slim finger, 'leaving him like that!' She turned her attention smilingly to Ryan. 'I came down with half a dozen others from the hotel bar. Mbinga is its usual rip-roaring self. We all felt we needed a break.' She touched her limbs gingerly. 'I missed your driving, darling.'

Ryan downed his drink in one gulp. 'You've been to see Dave, then?' he asked, holding a lighted match to her cigarette.

Gayna nodded. 'Bill and I were over there yesterday. I must say, Ryan, it was rather clever of you fixing him up with a tutor like that, but I *do* think you should let him have his head in some things.' She smiled obliquely towards Laurie.

'Dave gets most of his own way with me.' Ryan dropped a lopsided smile. 'And what do I get?' she pouted prettily, sweeping silken lashes over sultry blue eyes. 'Do you realise . . .'

Laurie rose, forcing a smile. 'Would you excuse me, Mrs. Lewis? There's something I'd . . . like to collect from my room.'

154

'Of course, my dear.' Gayna smiled without taking her eyes from Ryan's face. As Laurie fled she heard a throaty, 'Darling, when you come back to Mbinga, why don't we? . . .' and then, thankfully, she was conscious that other people's conversation made the rest of the sentence a blessed blur.

Closing the door of her room, Laurie was amazed to find she was trembling. Not because of the arrival of the lovely Gayna, nor the fact that Ryan must be the envy of every other man on the terrace. No, the turmoil going on inside her had something to do with Ryan's touch just now, the sound of his voice, the light in his eyes.

Surely, her heart cried out, when a man acted like this, it meant— Her mind calculated coolly that he was missing desperately the woman he loved. Well, Gayna had come to him now, so it wasn't likely that Laurie would have to suffer any more soul-shattering moments. She busied herself washing her hairbrush and comb, and rearranging her clothes in the drawers and on the hangers. This done, she wandered out on the balcony to stare pensively towards the lavender hills.

What would happen now? Probably Ryan would want to drive Gayna back to Mbinga. That meant that his and Laurie's stay at Lake Shimo would be cut short by a couple of days. She drew in a quivering lip, half glad that the sweet agony would soon be ended, half sorry that it couldn't go on. Deep in thought, she wandered back into the room, just as Gayna was slipping in the door and closing it softly behind her. Perhaps it was because Laurie had just stepped in from the bright sunlight that the other woman's face looked paler than usual, the blue eyes over bright. Gayna gazed round the room with a smile drooping at the edges. The usual sultry tones sounded strangely high-pitched, as she exclaimed almost to herself,

'It really is amazing just what lengths you young girls will go to these days!'

'To do what?' Laurie forced herself to sound pleasant.

'Not to *do*, my dear, to get!' A beautifully-lined eyebrow rose cryptically as she turned her smile towards Laurie. 'Oh, come now, I know men are slow to see through these things, but we women know, don't we?'

Laurie felt her insides quiver with sudden emotion. She remarked as evenly as she could manage,

'Mrs. Lewis, I think it would help us both if you came to the point.'

'I agree.' Gayna dropped her half-smoked cigarette on the tiles and tapped a slim foot on it carelessly. She swung her eyes up without warning. 'Yes, I think you and I have fenced around politely long enough. How would it be if I said a straightforward "you're wasting your time"?'

'Well, it would be fine if I knew what . . .'

'You know all right.' The vivid drop ear-rings began to shake slightly. 'And so do I. The way you've cheated and schemed to get this far. Oh, I admit' – she strolled around Laurie leisurely – 'you've made a little headway with Ryan, but then these things are always easy when one doesn't care too much about one's reputation. Thankfully I've never found it necessary to endanger mine.'

'Nor I,' was all Laurie could manage, through clenched teeth. There was a whole ball of heated words rolling around inside her, but nothing could pass this surging tide of anger. She struggled to hold herself rigid against the trembling as Gayna pursued sweetly,

'My dear! You don't expect me to believe that? We all know about the young idea these days, even out here. Everything's free, isn't it? Including love, *and* on the cheap, I believe?'

'Mrs. Lewis,' to Laurie, her voice sounded as though she had just called down a well, 'I think you'd better leave.'

'Oh, I'll leave when I've finished, don't worry.' Gayna's face was pinched and shrunken like that of a wax doll put too close to a fire. The dark eyes flashed like blue gems, and coral lips were drawn back over small white teeth so that her next words seemed to be delivered almost with a smile, 'You've been all out to land the biggest catch in these parts ever since you arrived, but I want to tell you, darling, you're too late by about two years.' She lowered a contemptuous glance over Laurie's small, trembling figure. 'You don't think I've rotted in these parts all this time, struggling with a hotel that doesn't pay, put up with endless gibberish on the whys and wherefores of all four-legged brutes, to lose Ryan at this stage, do you?'

'No, I think you deserve something for your tenacity.'

Laurie felt a little of her composure returning. She trained a steady grey gaze across the room. 'Two years is a long time. Perhaps Ryan was never really sure?'

'He was sure all right,' Gayna flamed, 'until you came along!'

After a long pause, she took a step nearer to Laurie, her face relaxing slightly and soaking up some of its former beauty.

"Any man will tire of *your* kind of games, my dear,' she breathed. 'It's just a question of Ryan naming the day for me.'

'I'm sure it won't be long.' Laurie struggled to sound lighthearted, and as the other woman moved over towards the door she added thoughtfully, 'Mrs. Lewis, disliking Africa as you do, its climate, the animals and everything, how do you expect to make a success of living here with Ryan?'

'I don't intend to live here. We'll be leaving, thank heaven. Nyumbaya will fetch an excellent price, and Ryan has other qualifications, you know. He won't need to bother with this tiresome safari business.'

'I can't see him leaving all this.' Laurie waved a hand towards the view of plains, and trees and distant hills. 'It seems to be almost a part of him.'

'He'll do it for me,' Gayna replied easily. She turned with a hand on the doorknob, coral lips turning upwards into a farewell smile. 'My friends will be waiting, they're in an exploring mood. I told Ryan I'd just pop up to say goodbye.' As though having second thoughts before opening the door, she turned to say levelly, 'Just remember, my dear – I had Ryan before you came, I have him now, and I don't intend to let go.' She stepped out and closed the door silently behind her.

Laurie flopped down on the bed, feeling physically sick. The whole series of exchanges she had found distasteful. It was as though she and Gayna had been through a bout of surreptitious tugging for a rare and unique commodity. Ryan was unique all right, but what on earth made Gayna think that Laurie herself was anywhere in the running for him?

The rest of the day passed in a clouded unreal world of a

dream. She was aware of Ryan close at her side, his occasional conversation and often penetrating gaze, but nothing could push from her mind the scene that had taken place in her room. Gayna's cold, drawn features seemed to be everywhere she looked. Gayna's voice, shrill with emotion, rose like a cry above all the others, so clearly that Laurie was tempted to put her hands to her ears.

Some of her consternation must have shown, for while they were dancing, Ryan lowered a searching look over her face and commented darkly,

'You're looking all in. Feeling okay?'

'Yes, thank you,' she answered briefly.

'Anything wrong?'

'No, except . . .'

'Except what?'

She would have liked to draw a little away from him then, but for some unaccountable reason he held her suffocatingly close.

'Except what?' he demanded.

She took a breath and turned a clouded grey gaze upwards. 'Ryan, could we please go back to . . . to . . .'

'Back to Dave?' he asked, grim-faced.

She hadn't been thinking of Dave, but he was as good an excuse as any. She lowered her head, but nothing happened to make him slacken his hold on her. He asked harshly beneath the tinkling undertones of a popular song.

'You don't like it here, I take it?'

'Oh, it's not that.' Laurie shot him a starry gaze before she had time to realise her folly. Afterwards she could only flounder uncertainly. 'It's just that . . . well, I know this is a hotel for tourists and everything, and . . . there must be dozens of unattached couples, but . . .' Her cheeks were growing hotter by the minute. 'You and I . . . well, we don't know each other awfully well and . . .'

'And what you're trying to say is you think people in Mbinga will talk?'

Laurie felt the blush spreading down to her throat. She was thankful for the subdued lighting and jostling couples hemming them in. Ryan seemed amused. She thought she saw a mocking light in his eye as he murmured close to her ear, 'I think you and I can safely look beyond the word

158

compromise, don't you? But then again . . .' He paused, resting his eyes on her, and then she was gripped against him in a breathtaking whirl. His voice sounded slightly uneven as he finished, 'I could always make an honest woman of you!'

Laurie was still trying to regain her breath, not all of it lost in the whirl of his embrace. She stared up with eyes wide to hear Ryan saying blandly,

'We could get married.'

Her heart, which had been bouncing around ever since the dance had started, suddenly stopped in mid-air. She heard herself saying in a strangled voice,

'Get married?'

'People do, you know.' Ryan's mouth seemed somewhat tight. He looked around at the crowd and muttered impatiently, 'Let's get out of this.' She felt herself being guided around the couples and out into the night. Where they walked she had no idea, but it seemed the night was thick with trees, and the air laden with a thousand sweet perfumes. A sheet of gun-metal grey was the sky, and the figure of the man at her side a huge dark shape against it.

Laurie had no words ready and Ryan seemed preoccupied. He stood a distance away from her now, hands thrust deep in his pockets, pin-points of light giving the green eyes a steely look. She waited for him to pass off his suggestion of marriage as a joke, but he made no move to. His next words were,

'Have you anything against it? Our getting married?'

'Well, I'm not sure . . .' Laurie struggled with herself. She ought to have been drifting into Ryan's arms. And shouldn't he have been holding her close? That *was* the usual practice when a man proposed, wasn't it? Yet here they were standing a world apart, like two strangers who had accidentally met up on an evening stroll. Laurie desperately wanted things to be different.

She gazed across the darkness, trying to inject some lightness into her voice. 'I can't imagine what made you think of it.' She thought she saw him tense in the dim light, and then he was putting on a shrug, and saying,

'Maybe because you're pretty much alone in the world. You've no set way of life or work to go back to in England, and you seem to fit in well out here.'

Laurie digested this bleakly. To him, that was reason enough to get married. She drew on her lower lip and, as if sensing the movement, he started to pace.

'You said just now that you and I don't know each other very well. Well, I think we do. A few weeks can be a lifetime out here, and though I don't know how I rate against Desmond' – she could almost see the downward slant of his smile – 'I think you and I have quite a bit in common. It doesn't seem to worry you living cut off from the outside world, and you've got quite a way with animals.'

Laurie supposed she ought to have felt flattered, but instead she found herself biting back her hurt. In the strangest circumstances imaginable, Ryan was asking her to marry him. She could refuse him and go back to England, for there could be no staying on after this, or she could accept him and continue to 'fit in well with the surroundings' and cultivate her 'way with animals.'

But she would be close to Ryan. Wouldn't that be something? And though there had been no mention of love, perhaps later . . .?

She wrestled with herself and the thousand questions hammering from within, but her heart, eager as ever, wanted no reasoning, and for once its clamouring drowned out anything her mind might be saying on the matter. Before Ryan had stopped pacing she knew she had her answer. As she took a step forward he lifted his gaze a little to take her in, and asked gruffly,

'Well?'

With a firm hold on her voice, she replied unwaveringly, 'Yes, Ryan, I'll marry you.'

The moment hung suspended as though they were both waiting for a balloon with too much air in it to pop, but nothing happened.

Ryan stood perfectly still and Laurie felt her breath coming in uneven spurts. Then it seemed that the rigid black shape relaxed into the bulk of the man she knew and Ryan was saying easily,

'I'll have to cancel the first safari, but that's no problem,' and then, 'There's a mission house some distance north from Nyumbaya. You'll stay there until I can tie up all the formalities, and I'll need the address of your oldest brother. I don't think we'll have too much trouble getting his consent.' She could just make out the wry smile. 'When everything is tied up we'll get married in Mbinga, and after that it's anywhere you like.'

Laurie swayed. Did he mean the honeymoon? She summoned all her strength to reply evenly,

'I liked Dar-es-Salaam when I was there.'

'It will do for a start.'

He moved to her side and she felt his fingers grip hers, but it could have only been to guide her through the trees, for he made no other move to touch her. Silently they walked into the hotel and then he was opening the door of her room and dropping the key into her hand. 'Sleep well, young Weldon,' he murmured, then with a somewhat clipped, 'I could use a drink,' he was gone.

CHAPTER ELEVEN

'So Ryan has finally decided to take the plunge! I always told him some young girl would catch up with him one day.'

Molly Pacer, the missionary's wife, beamed with all the plump cherry-red features at her disposal, and these were considerable, Laurie mused, watching the rounded double-chin wobble with excitement. In her floral smock, and with flour-covered hands, she looked more like a farmer's wife in England than one of Africa's missionary's. John Pacer was a little more true to type. Small and slight of build, with a neat cap of iron grey hair and a tranquil smile, he stood now talking earnestly to Ryan, just a few yards from the house.

Laurie watched them for a while through the open window and then circled her gaze over the scene beyond, giving half her attention to Mrs. Pacer's merry chatter as she busied herself behind the long trestle table, and half to the cluster of buildings and their neat garden plots. When Ryan had mentioned the mission house, Laurie had conjured up in her mind the picture of a stark wooden hut in a desolate waste, but the Ngungua mission was a collection of sturdy buildings and long thatched huts and had all the comings and goings of a fair-sized village.

The square clearing was surrounded on three sides by trees, and an airstrip ran across the bottom. The whole place reverberated with the sound of children's laughter and deep-throated singing, and Laurie felt some of her tension slipping away. It might have disappeared completely if her eyes hadn't come to rest at that moment on two proud hens squabbling over who should have sole rights to a particular pecking patch.

For some ridiculous reason Laurie was reminded of Gayna, and immediately she felt the old familiar knotting up of her senses.

Ever since Ryan's proposal, neither her heart nor her mind had wanted any part of deliberations on the future of Mbinga's beautiful widow, and in a way she was glad. What could be gained from going over Gayna's words at Lake Shimo that day?

She felt a hand on her arm, and Ryan was depositing her suitcase down beside her on the polished wood boards.

'It's all fixed,' he nodded. 'John doesn't think the wait will be too long.' He cast a good-natured smile down the long room with its assortment of wooden furniture and gay mats, and then back to Laurie. 'Reckon you're going to be okay here for a while?' he asked.

'I'm sure I shall,' Laurie smiled, catching Molly Pacer's wink. She looked up at him shyly. 'Will you be coming back again to let me know how things are going?'

'No.' He buttoned his linen jacket purposefully. 'We won't meet again until the wedding ceremony. I'll contact you if there are any hold-ups.'

He said his goodbyes to John and Molly Pacer and, after a pause, and looking back at the couple, he took Laurie in his arms and dropped a light kiss on her cheek. 'Don't stray away from the mission, remember,' he drawled, 'and keep a hat on when you go out in the sun. I don't want you . . .'

'You're beginning to sound like a husband already,' John Pacer remarked humorously. He dropped an arm around Laurie's shoulder and nodded to Ryan. 'We'll deliver your young lady safe and sound. Just mind you don't keep her waiting too long or we mightn't be able to keep her from straying from the mission,' he chuckled.

He must think we're very much in love, Laurie swallowed, looking anywhere but at Ryan. Perhaps she tensed a little in his arms, for she heard him saying in flat tones, 'Well, that's it, then. So long, Laurie.'

Before she could send him a farewell smile he was striding away to the estate car. It shuddered into life and had turned out of sight along the airstrip, almost before Mrs. Pacer had offered to show her to her room.

The days at the mission, though pleasant, were for Laurie a kind of marking time to something she both dreaded and yet ached for. Her wedding day. She supposed all prospective brides must feel this way, and yet wasn't her own position a little odd?

Here she was, helping out at a small African mission, waiting to marry a man she had never known existed until a few weeks ago.

As her safari master he had made no secret of the fact that

163

he had considered her nothing less than a nuisance, and the only kiss that had taken place between them seemed to have caused him irritation rather than delight.

He had invited her to stay at his house because his brother was at a loose end, and then without a word of warning had spirited her away to the luxuries of the Lake Shimo hotel, and his proposal. Laurie could still hear herself saying yes, but the whole idea of marrying Ryan was all so much part of a hazy dream that she couldn't actually believe it would happen. Just how far away she was from believing, she hadn't realised, until she and Mrs. Pacer were unpacking supplies flown in the day before.

'How do you plan to dress for the special day, dear?'

The plump woman paused abstractedly over a pile of books, and Laurie raised her head from the list she had been checking. The shock of knowing that she hadn't even thought of her wedding outfit jerked from her a panicky laugh.

Mrs. Pacer looked up. 'Don't tell me you're just fixing to wear an everyday outfit?' she asked disappointedly.

'Well, I thought out here . . .'

'Oh, but . . .' The little woman was already across the room, holding Laurie at arm's length and smiling over the flushed features. 'It would be such a waste, dear . . . such a waste. Now let me see . . .' She went off into a study. 'I have some pretty material my sister sent me a few weeks back. It's whiter than white. I expect it's got a new-fangled name, but to me it looks similar to a crêpe-de-chine. Make a pretty little dress and hat.' She was already out of the door of the thatched hut. 'It's in a trunk in my room. Come and let's have a look.'

Standing in a room similar to her own, with gleaming wood and gay covers, Laurie had to admit that the material spread out on the bed might have been bought for a wedding outfit. Molly Pacer, thoroughly carried away now, delved into a cardboard box and came out with a handful of paper patterns.

'These are some my girls use in our dressmaking classes,' she smiled. 'Nothing fancy, mind, but you have the basic idea here. A tiny bodice, I thought, and a full knee-length skirt. Short dresses seem to be all the go these days and you would be cool. What do you think, dear?'

'Well!' Laurie's eyes were shining. She was already getting ideas for a small upstanding collar, deep neckline and several covered buttons down the front. 'If you're sure it's all right,' she hesitated.

The older woman put her hands on her hips, gently admonishing.

'Now, which do you think I'd rather see? Myself with three plain blouses or you decked out sweet for your wedding?'

Making the dress brought the day a little nearer reality for Laurie. She found herself thinking of Ryan as she stitched, wondering if things were going smoothly and when she would hear from him. She wondered too with the tiniest flutter if he was thinking of her, and then one day she had a message from him brought by a least expected arrival.

Everyone at the mission station was surprised to see a light plane make an unscheduled landing on the airstrip, but Laurie was too busy to give it much thought until she saw John Pacer walking across the clearing with a lead in his hand, and a tiny red-gold shape trotting by his side. At first Laurie thought she must be dreaming or seeing things, but there was no mistaking those huge white-tipped ears and the gently-swaying tail.

She was soon running out of the hut to sweep up the little fox in her arms. He seemed thinner and looked slightly bewildered at this sudden display of affection, but then the big golden eyes suddenly hazed over as though with a sense of recollection and a pink tongue washed vigorously over her hand.

Laurie smiled fondly and turned to gaze at the ticket on Cando's collar. She slanted her head to take in the large sloping handwriting

Dave and I don't seem to have the touch. I think it's the feminine one he's after. Take care. Yours, Ryan.

Laurie pondered on the message and Cando's means of arrival. As far as she knew there were no airstrips near Nyumbaya. That meant Ryan must have made a special drive and arranged for a diverted plane to stop off here. She rubbed her cheek against the fox's fur, thinking that for a man of steel Ryan could be amazingly gentle-minded when it came to the business of animals, and perhaps . . . just perhaps, he had thought a little of her happiness too?

Molly Pacer had just put the finishing touches to the small close-fitting hat when her husband came in to announce that the date of the wedding had been fixed, Laurie sank down weakly at the table.

'Is it very soon?' she asked.

'The day after tomorrow,' John Pacer beamed.

'The day after tomorrow? I . . . suppose you're quite sure?'

'Why shouldn't he be?' Mrs. Pacer smiled. 'Ryan never was one to make a move unless he was sure. He might have guessed we were all ready and waiting.' She picked up the tiny hat with the white flowers stitched at the sides, and sighed happily. 'I just can't wait to see you on the day!'

'The day' came all too soon. It seemed that Laurie had only just been gazing at the hat in Mrs. Pacer's hand, and now here it was on her own head, set upon silken waves. The flowers framed a face that looked too solemn; lilac shadows were dusted beneath huge grey eyes, and rose pink lips looked uncertain. The white dress hugged her form to the waist, and then cascaded in a swinging flare that stopped at her knees, and then it was sheer-stockinged legs and white slim-heeled shoes. After Mrs. Pacer had rushed round to find a pair of white gloves to balance the neat short sleeves she stood back and quavered,

'You look just lovely, dear, as I knew you would.' She hugged Laurie and allowed a single tear to run down the side of a cherry pink nose. 'I wish I was coming, but I don't know how I'd feel in a helicopter.'

'A helicopter?' Laurie's eyes widened. 'Was that all the noise I heard just now?'

Mrs. Pacer nodded and smiled. 'Trust Ryan to do it in style, but then he's a man who thinks of everything. He'd want to be sure you arrived fresh as paint, and you're bound to, landing practically in the garden of the Safaritrek Hotel.'

'The Safaritrek?' Laurie seemed to be making continued exclamations, but this time her heart froze over as she heard Molly Pacer's remark, 'That's right, dear. You're to be married at the hotel. Mrs. Lewis very kindly offered, and then the helicopter will take you on to the airstrip for the coast.'

Laurie could hear her own heart thumping. She looked drowningly at the missionary's wife, stammering, 'Mrs. Pacer . . . I'm scared.'

'Oh, I expect you'll find the helicopter's fine once you get

166

used to it,' the older woman encouraged, misinterpreting Laurie's fears. She paused reflectively, sending an affectionate twinkle across the room to her husband and then back to Laurie. 'Bit different from the old-style weddings, but none the less romantic now, is it?' She gave Laurie a final hug and finished briskly, 'Now off you go, and mind you tell Ryan to bring you back again to see us.'

'I will.' Laurie smiled at the couple. 'And thank you. Thank you both for everything.'

John Pacer picked up her suitcase, kissed his wife and turned.

'Time we were going, Laurie. They'll all be waiting.'

All? Laurie passed Cando inside and stepped up into the helicopter. Who were 'all'?

The pilot gave her a friendly wink as he secured the doors and put the huge blades in motion. With the comforting presence of the missionary at her side, Laurie watched the ever-changing African bush turning under her window as though it were being wound on a giant roller. They were losing height almost before she had spotted Mbinga, then suddenly the sprawling building of the Safaritrek Hotel was rushing up to meet them.

The helicopter settled itself down unhurriedly on the ground just beyond the rondavels and when the huge blades had finished spinning, Laurie stepped down into the welcoming arms of Bill Alexander. After he had helped John Pacer down and the missionary had hurried ahead, Bill turned to take her in at arm's length.

A twitching smile showed beneath the forest of moustache as he exclaimed,

'Strewth! Wait until Ryan sees this!' With a humorous gleam he asked, 'Happy?' Laurie nodded shyly, and he led her between the rondavels saying cheerfully, 'I'm to take you to the one you used while you were here, for any last-minute touches you might want to make.'

He must have sensed her quivering, for he squeezed her hand encouragingly. 'Now don't be nervous, just lean on me. You'll be Mrs. Ryan Holt before you know it.'

It seemed that half of Mbinga had come to watch the wedding, but when Bill led Laurie into the hotel she had eyes only for one man.

167

Ryan turned as she entered. He looked bigger than ever in a dark grey suit. The copper tanned features, above the white shirt and silk tie, looked slightly worn, but the green eyes that rested on her as she walked towards him glowed strangely beneath drawn brows.

It was as though she stepped out of herself to hear the words of the wedding ceremony and the shuffling of the people in the background, and then she was thinking this couldn't be *her* finger that Ryan was slipping the wide band of gold on, not *her* lips he was brushing lightly with his own. Almost when she had convinced herself that all of this was happening to someone else and not Laurie Weldon, there was a general slackening of tension in the room and people were rushing forward to pump her hand vigorously.

Two town-suited, officious-looking gentlemen with brief-cases seemed to be the only ones not concerned with the occasion, but they stood in the background smiling benevolently over the proceedings. She saw a blurred picture of Dave moving towards her with a grin, and then he was kissing her on the cheek with,

'You look fab, Laurie!'

Someone else was waiting their turn, and at the sight of Gayna's slim figure poured into an emerald green sheath dress, Laurie found herself clinging shakily to Dave. Wide shoulders loomed near and all too soon Dave had moved away and Laurie was staring into those exquisite features that seemed today to have acquired the fine transparency of delicate porcelain and just a little of its ability to crack. After sweeping a gaze over Laurie, she drew Ryan down to kiss his cheek and then Laurie felt herself being enveloped in a perfumed embrace.

'You make a lovely bride, my dear.' Perfect lips turned up attractively. 'And of course you must use my room to change in.'

'Oh, but I laid out the things I would need in the rondavel.'

'No problem,' Gayna smiled. 'I'll pop across and fetch them.'

Ryan nodded and with an encircling arm about Laurie he walked with them as far as Gayna's apartments. 'I'll see to the bags and have a word with the helicopter pilot.' He paused at the door and Laurie felt Gayna's hand on her arm.

'This way, my dear, and please feel free to use anything of mine you wish.'

Her bedroom followed on from the living room. It was shabbily furnished, but the covers and curtains and surrounding accessories were undoubtedly of top quality. Gayna was back within minutes.

She draped the blush pink suit over a chair and waved a hand expansively at the door. 'Anything at all, my dear.' The sultry voice seemed to be somehow laced with bubbling undertones, and Laurie raised her head quickly from unfastening the buttons on her dress. She couldn't be sure, but she thought she saw that 'sucking on a sweet' smile of Gayna's before the smooth head disappeared from the doorway.

Laurie shook her head as though to rid it of imaginative thoughts and continued with the buttons of her dress. She allowed her eyes to roam over the room in a sort of halfhearted interest, over expensive cosmetics, tall-bottled perfumes, and gossamer négligées.

There was a jewelled casket on the dressing table and . . . The dress half over her head, she slipped out of it slowly and methodically, willing herself not to look back at the dressing table, but her eyes were drawn to it, like a magnet. She saw the pipe, similar to the shape and make that she had seen in the rack at Nyumbaya.

It was Ryan's pipe. Laurie had never been so sure of anything in her life, but she hung on to reason. He could have left it in any room of the hotel. It wouldn't be too fanciful to suppose, would it, that a slender fiery-nailed hand had recently placed it in its present position for the purpose of . . .?

Laurie took a deep breath and shivered in her slip, even though the sun blazed in at the windows. She really must get on with the business of changing. She was just about to move across the room when the murmur of voices made her stop. It sounded as though someone had come back into the living room next door. Gayna's voice, slightly higher-pitched now, came across clearly,

'In here, Bill. We can talk in here.'

Oh dear! Laurie drew on her lip worriedly. She had no wish to eavesdrop on a conversation, but Gayna had very carelessly left the door connecting the two rooms ajar. She probably thought Laurie had changed and left. Before she had time to think what to do, Bill was saying,

'Well, that's the excitement over. Leaves you and me now, old girl.'

'*You*, darling,' was Gayna's smooth reply. 'Not me.'

'You're not coming?' Laurie heard Bill say. 'I thought you might be glad of a change from Mbinga now that things are different between you and Ryan?'

Laurie wanted to tip-toe across the room, but to her horror she saw the chair with her suit draped over it was almost in a direct line with the open door. She couldn't possibly go across there in her slip, and worse still she couldn't stay here and listen to . . .

A throaty laughter rippled across her nerves. Gayna was saying,

'But things are no different between Ryan and me. Why should they be? You know he only married the Weldon girl to save his brother's career.'

Laurie felt as though her limbs were dissolving into water as she hung on to the bed for support and at the same time could sense Bill straightening in his seat.

'That's a pretty rotten statement to make, Gayna,' she heard him saying curtly.

Gayna seemed to be blowing out cigarette smoke before she replied lightly,

'It may sound it, my dear, but I can assure you it's perfectly true. Everybody could see that Dave was getting this crazy crush on the Weldon child, and you know what these young people are. They don't bother to think things out. Why, they even went up the mountain together, you know!'

'So?' Bill's voice sounded grim.

'Well, can't you see? Dave has already had one mad year, a wedding now would certainly put paid to his career, and you know Ryan. He's not the kind of man to sit around and let that happen. Dave means everything to him.'

'So Ryan married Laurie himself and when Dave gets some sense and goes back to college they'll be all washed up. Is that it?'

Laurie's fingers felt bruised as she clutched the bed cover tight in her hand. She heard a long heaved-out sigh from the other room. Bill sounded incredulous.

'You women! You never let go, do you? And what do you plan to do now? Stick arouud and pick up the pieces you hope will fall?'

'Pieces!' Gayna laughed. 'There won't be any pieces, darling. These kind of weddings can be annulled quite painlessly. Ryan will be as whole as he's ever been. The Weldou child might be a little put out, but she'll soon realise she made a mistake and pop off quietly back to England.'

There was a pause then and when Bill's voice came, heavy with derision, it sounded as though he had moved to the door,

'So I suppose I should wish you happy scalp-hunting, old girl, or something to that effect?' He sighed. 'Well, it's nice to know where one stands. I thought I'd just tell you it'll take a couple of weeks to run the old store down, and then I'll be off.'

'Well, if you're still in Africa, my dear . . .' Gayna's voice had drifted further away as though she too was getting ready to leave. Her last words, however, came over precise and clear, 'Ryan and I will invite you to a *real* wedding.'

A sharp, underlined satisfaction in the tones brought something home to Laurie with almost the force of a physical blow. She knew now that Gayna hadn't left the adjoining door open by accident.

She had planned it that way. She had known that Laurie was here in the room and had skilfully arranged that she should hear every word of the conversation. Bill, all unsuspecting, had given Gayna the right opening for a perfect speech.

The agony of it was – Laurie sank down and buried her face in her hands – the awful agony of it was that Gayna was right.

Everything she had said was true. It all fitted into place so perfectly. The way Ryan had whipped her away from Nyumbaya and Dave. Those few days sunning and dancing, which he had needed to work himself up to a proposal. How he had hidden her away, out at the mission until today, the day of the wedding.

The wedding! Laurie's body shook in an uncontrollable sob. She could see it now. Ryan hadn't wanted her at all. He had married her simply to protect his brother.

Everything within her wanted to let go and flood the bed with tears, but she raised a white, stricken face, moved across the room and slipped mechanically into the pink suit. Loath to touch Gayna's hairbrushes, she pushed dishevelled waves into position, ignoring the ravaged face that stared back at her through the mirror.

The crowd round the helicopter divided as Bill laughingly, and over-indulgently, Laurie thought miserably, led her through.

Ryan was standing in the doorway ready to help her up, but before she had taken the step, Dave had pushed through with Cando in his arms. He nuzzled his chin in the fur with mock affection, shouting over the babble of voices,

'I'll watch him for you, Laurie. He's getting used to me now.' Laurie shot him a grateful smile and took the bundle from him. She murmured through a tight throat, 'I wish I could take him with me,' and then, as Dave went to haul him back, she found herself clutching tight hold and hanging on. 'Please. I'd like to take him with me.'

'But Laurie, you don't want . . .'

'It's okay, Dave.' Ryan was watching her. 'Let her have him.'

Dave nodded good-naturedly and stepped back with the rest of the crowd. Gayna was the last one to go. With a vivid smile she called out gaily to Laurie, 'Goodbye, my dear. Have a dream of a time.'

The blades sprang into life and Laurie had a good excuse to keep her head down, but in the struggle to hold on to Cando and at the same time attain the high step, she was forced to give herself up to Ryan. He swung her up close beside him, gently tilting her face to meet his gaze. She didn't want to look at him. How could she? She knew she looked terrible, but something within him compelled her to raise her eyes to his and in that moment she thought they would drain her soul. Before he swung his gaze away, something seemed to snap off like a light going out, then he was offering a brief wave to the crowd.

Seated at his side, Laurie watched the people grow small as the helicopter rose. It seemed to her that the last figure to fade from view was the one with the most vigorous wave.

The one dressed in emerald green.

CHAPTER TWELVE

THE delicate feathery tracing of palm fronds hung etched out in breathless perfection against the dull peach glow of the sky.

From her seat on the veranda Laurie watched the strip of silver sand hurriedly match itself to the black silhouette of the trees as though eager to heighten the effect of a molten gold sea.

She was conscious of a movement behind and the white-clad boy who had been here to meet them was asking if anything else would be required before he left. Ryan shook his head and rose from his chair to go with the boy to the door. Laurie knew vaguely that the house they were in, and the sleek car standing in the drive, belonged to a friend of Ryan's. Beyond that she hadn't bothered or dared to enquire, for since leaving the airport, conversation, even small talk, had become impossible between them.

She tensed now as she heard him come back into the living room behind her. The clinking of glasses made her nerves soar. She got up, unsure of where she would go, and as Ryan moved forward to hand her a glass she noticed almost hysterically that Cando was brushing around his legs with the affection he usually reserved for her.

She stared down at the liquid in her glass, then turned her head to watch the dull white shape of the houseboy bobbing away along the drive.

Ryan was saying tersely, 'Drink it. You're shaking like a leaf.'

'I'm all right,' she mumbled.

'Sure you're all right,' Ryan jerked at his drink and then he was saying with icy matter-of-factness, 'but you can't put the thought of Desmond out of your mind . . . or Dave, is that it?'

Laurie didn't bother to control her trembling now. She turned round slowly to whisper,

'I know you only married me because you didn't want your brother to.'

The silence was so long she wondered if he would ever answer. He took another pull at his drink and twisted a smile.

'That's right. It took you some time to work that one out,' he replied.

So it *was* true! There was no need to say any more. She swallowed back a sob, and glanced down wildly at her wedding ring, her voice catching over the words, 'Too long!'

The drink she was holding spun round violently, tipping over the rim of the glass and on the floor in tiny splats. Ryan whipped it away and clapped it down on the table. He didn't immediately raise himself, but stayed head bent and eyes closed over the glass. When he did turn his face seemed drained of life. Dull green eyes and grim smile seemed only part of a mask as he drawled sarcastically,

'I can see how you're placed. After Desmond you were ripe to fall into anybody's arms, but now you find you're not prepared for them to be mine?'

Not without love, Laurie's heart cried out, sane at last. Never, without love. She hadn't known she was shaking her head so wildly until Ryan jerked her to a stop with a rough hand on her wrist. He gazed down on her with sudden menacing calm.

'Well, it's a bit late now,' he snapped.

But not too late! Laurie raised her eyes pleadingly.

'I want to leave you, Ryan. Right now. Please, I promise I won't go back to Dave.'

'And you can't go back to Desmond.'

His constant harping on a man she had almost forgotten about brought a flame of angry colour to her cheeks. 'For heaven's sake leave Desmond out of it!' She tried to whirl out of his grasp, but he jerked her close to him with breathtaking force.

'I intend to,' he sneered, 'for good. And you'd be wise to do the same. Dave too. It's important he stays unhampered.'

'And *you've* seen to that, haven't you?' She stared up at him in distaste. 'Marriage to you wouldn't be too drastic a step.'

'No, I wouldn't say it was drastic.' His eyes blazed above hers. 'I'd say it could be vastly entertaining.'

His mouth came down hard on hers, with such fierceness she almost cried out, but all her resistance was like a small

174

heap of sand against a mighty onrushing tide. When she felt she could strain no more against the frightening demands of his lips, he raised his head and swept her up roughly into his arms.

'Ryan!' Laurie gasped. 'Please put me down!'

'Why?' He strode through the open french windows and across the room. The face was working darkly around a thin white smile. He turned strangely lit green eyes down her way. 'You *are* my wife.'

With his foot he kicked open a door. Laurie stared up wildly and clutching at her last shred of strength, pleaded 'Ryan . . . please!'

She saw in that crazy moment that her weight in his arms had pulled away the second button of his shirt, and the breath he took now seemed to send the wide shoulders tugging even more. The green eyes raked her face, lingered, and then it was as though he knew a need to ration out the inhaled breath. Slowly, almost imperceptibly, it came through clenched teeth as he dropped her on to the bed. He ran a lightning hand through his hair and swung away out of the room.

Almost before he was through the door Laurie struggled up. The droop of his shoulders, the lowered dark head cut a line of compassion deep on her heart.

'Ryan . . .!' She was running almost without knowing it, but he had covered the living room in half a dozen strides. By the time she got to the terrace he was already flinging himself into the car. 'Ryan!' she cried out with a new fear now, for a small dark shape with triangular ears and quivering bushy tail had darted down the steps and was sidling alongside the car.

The headlights blazed and the thunder of the engine drowned her voice. She ran down the steps, arms outstretched, as though she would take hold of the car and pull it to a stop. Ryan saw her through the open window just as he was shooting off. With a searing curse he slammed his foot on the brake and jumped out to pull her roughly away, rasping, 'You young fool! What are you trying to do? Get yourself killed?'

Laurie stood motionless, staring ahead. 'Cando,' she said huskily. 'He was near the wheels.'

Ryan stared hard at her face as though he couldn't quite

soak up the meaning of her words, then he turned to walk quickly back along the drive.

Laurie waited. A whisper of breeze tossed the hem of her skirt. The soulful sigh of the waves that fell on the beach seemed somehow connected with this strange new ache that had settled in her heart. She heard Ryan come up behind her and turned to see his ashen face.

'Better not.' He gripped her shoulders as she would have moved, but she dragged herself free.

'Let me go! You've hit Cando. I know you've hit him!' She ran along the drive, straining her eyes in the shadows yet dreading to see.

Cando was lying on his side in the glow of the house lights. She knelt beside him. One front paw was crossed over the other and the tip of a small pink tongue showed beneath the white-flecked nose. Thankfully his eyes were closed, and but for the glistening dark pool a few inches away she could almost imagine he was stretched out in his favourite position for sleep.

But Laurie knew Cando was dead. She swallowed back the flood of tears. Cando was dead, and tonight something else had died too – the final flicker of hope that she could ever mean anything to Ryan. He had married her, yes, but it was Gayna he loved. She heard a footstep. Firm hands came down on her shoulders and Ryan was saying heavily, 'Come along inside, Laurie.'

She felt incensed by his touch, furious with herself for falling so easily into his scheme of things.

'Don't touch me!' As he would have helped her to her feet she pulled away and ran blindly up the steps and into the house.

She told herself that her tears were only for Cando, and that the stricken look on Ryan's face was nothing more than sympathy.

He didn't go out after all. She heard him moving about the house long after she had bathed her face and sank down on the cool of the bed. She heard a door shut now in another part of the house and then all was silent. Spent of all emotion, she drifted off into a fitful sleep.

Laurie struggled through the days, convinced that hers must be the strangest honeymoon on record. She toured the city of Dar-es-Salaam, its handsome avenues and elegant stores, saw the harbour and the colourful old Arab vessels unloading Persian carpets and exotic eastern goods, sailed above an enchanting world of multi-coloured fish and spiky coral formations in a glass-bottomed boat.

All this with Ryan acting as the perfect guide and nothing more.

With leaden heart Laurie noticed that though he might assist her up an excessively long flight of steps, or offer a hand in the tricky operation of stepping from rocking boat to firm land, he seemed to prefer not to touch her at all. Conversation was cool and kept strictly to the minimum, and when they did find themselves talking at length, it was usually about Laurie's photographic achievements of the day or of some place of interest yet to be visited.

Only once did she become flutteringly aware that he might be something more than just a companion and guide. Stretched out one day after their sail to a nearby coral island, she had imagined him to be still swimming in the sea until a shadow fell across her face.

Before she had time to pay any attention to it a pair of warm lips had descended on her own and she was spiralling down on a dizzy wave of ecstasy. All too soon the lips were drawn away and she stared up at Ryan's lopsided smile. He shrugged easily and glanced around, murmuring, 'Just thought we'd help the old place to live up to its name.'

Laurie searched her mind for the name. Of course! Honeymoon Island! She rose slowly and went to stare out to sea. That would be the reason for the kiss. Ryan must be feeling that some husbandly role was expected of him. He paused before following her. His voice was slightly metallic though mocking.

'I didn't have anything to do with the naming of the island, child.'

She lowered her lashes impatiently. 'You can stop referring to me as a child. I've had my nineteenth birthday!'

She saw the green eyes sweep over her and fasten on a point near her mouth.

'Remind me to celebrate some time,' he sneered, swinging away in the direction of the boat.

The house they were staying in on the outskirts of Dar-es-Salaam was small but impressive. Its white walls were honeycombed with flower entwined arches and led to a cool tiled veranda.

Beyond the french windows were four or five tastefully furnished rooms and fronting the house was a wide flight of stone steps that led down between green lawns and blossoming trees to a private beach. A road ran along the back of the house and a white-gated drive led to steps and a paved terrace.

It was down these steps that Laurie saw a familiar figure bounding, as her taxi slid into the drive. Purely as an experiment she had made an appointment at a hairdressers in town, and today Ryan had driven her in and ordered a taxi to bring her back.

With a somewhat feathery, but she couldn't help feeling attractive hair-do, she stepped gingerly out of the taxi, to be almost bowled over by Dave's embrace.

'I thought you weren't going to make it,' he grinned. 'Do you realise it's less than half an hour to plane time?'

Ryan strolled negligently down the steps, sending a lazy smile of appraisal over the new hair-do.

'What do they do in these places?' he drawled. 'Count the hairs before they wave them?'

'Two hours isn't a long time to be in the hairdressers,' she smiled, walking between the two brothers, but turning to Dave, whom she noticed was dressed rather more conservatively than she was used to seeing him, in a neat brown suit.

'What,' she asked with a puzzled smile, 'did I nearly miss?'

'Me!' he cried. 'I'm going back!'

'To college? So soon?'

Dave nodded. 'Term starts in a week. Paul's going back with me and I think I'm going to be okay.'

The tall African tutor came out on the terrace to give her a smiling nod, and Dave shot him a grateful glance before giving Laurie a wry smile.

'You know, that guy really works you to death, and you know something else? I actually feel keen to get back to the grind – I must be mad!' He looked at his watch. 'Well, it would be a laugh if I missed the plane now, wouldn't it?' He turned to his brother, sending a covetous glance to the sleek car at the foot of the steps. 'Can I drive, Ry?' he begged.

Ryan gave an enigmatic nod. 'If you promise to keep it below ninety.'

'On these city roads?' Dave snorted a laugh. 'I'll be lucky if I make twenty!' He turned to give Laurie a hug and a grin. 'Well, so long, Laurie. For once I'll be looking forward to the holidays, with a sister-in-law like you to come back to!'

Not me. Laurie shrank a little inside at the knowledge of Gayna waiting in Mbinga. It won't be me as a sister-in-law you'll be coming back to, she thought bleakly, avoiding Ryan's sharp glance.

She waved them off with a patent smile, trying to put all thoughts of Mbinga and Gayna out of her mind, but they were brought sharply to the forefront the next morning. The phlegmatic houseboy had come in to serve breakfast as he did every morning, showing no sign that he thought a man and his wife coming out of separate rooms was anything but normal. When he had departed for the kitchen Ryan informed her that they would be leaving for the bush that evening.

So soon! Laurie swallowed a mouthful of coffee to dissolve the lump in her throat. He hadn't let much time elapse after Dave's departure.

'Preparations have been going ahead for a big safari due to start the day after tomorrow,' Ryan was saying. 'A group of American business men and their wives.'

'I thought you didn't take women on safari?' Laurie murmured.

His smile had a wry touch. 'Maybe I've become more acclimatized.' He filled her coffee cup. 'I'll be over at the office most of the time, so you'd better put up at the hotel. You'll be on hand when we move off.'

'Me?' Laurie stared. 'Why do I have to go?'

He pushed his plate away with a touch of irritation. 'I can remember when you were mad keen on safaris.'

She stared out over the peacock blue sea. 'I think I've lost my taste for them,' she muttered.

'Lost your taste or your nerve?'

There was no telling what he meant by that; even so her cheeks flamed with sudden colour. She was grateful for the pause, and then he was saying lazily, 'Never mind, you'll make out. Our guests are pretty high stock. As my wife you would be expected to accompany me in deference to the other wives.'

'What are they like, these business men?' Laurie asked. 'Mr. Cape was an American. Will they be like him?'

Ryan shrugged. 'Who can say? They're oil kings with a yen to see Africa in the raw. Whether they know the front end of a rifle from the back is another matter.'

'Rifles?' Laurie looked his way. 'You're not going to shoot things?'

'*I'm* not going to shoot anything, but it's possible our friends will want to down a couple. I'll have to be there to make sure they land a clean hit.' He looked at her steadily, then added, 'I'm as much against the sport as you are. I'm making this my last safari.'

His last safari! Laurie lowered her head in case he should see her drained features. So Gayna was going to have her way? She and Ryan would be leaving Africa.

As she packed her things ready for the trip, those beautiful porcelain-pale features hovered in front of Laurie's view. She could hear the sultry voice as clear as though it were here in the room:

Just remember, my dear, I had Ryan before you came. I have him now, and I don't intend to let go.

Well, Laurie thought miserably, Gayna needn't worry about losing her grip. Ryan was showing no desire to be free of it.

The bustle outside the Safaritrek hotel reminded Laurie of Mr. Cape's safari preparations except that they were on a much larger scale. Several safari assistants, younger versions of Ryan, with their khaki hunting outfits and leopard-skin banded hats, supervised and checked the long caravan of bulging lorries and Land Rovers that would be needed for the journey.

Inside the hotel the sounds of laughter rose above the clinking of glasses and the shuffling of heavy booted feet. Though there were only six men and their wives in there it sounded like the whole population of Mbinga. They were a gay crowd, Laurie thought, remembering the introductions earlier; middle-aged but eager to get the most out of the trip. As Ryan had led her round their expressions had been of

180

delighted awe that they were actually shaking hands with the safari master's wife.

Looking down at herself now, Laurie supposed she must look the part. Her freshly laundered cream-khaki shirt and slacks were smart, but had a well-worn look about them. She knew thick strands of her hair had been bleached by the sun, and her face, fresh from the sea air and tumult of Dar-es-Salaam, had lost the last of, as Ryan would have put it, 'that green kid look.'

Standing in the shade of the hotel veranda watching the various activities, Laurie pondered on this new-found sophistication she had acquired. Mightn't it be useful in securing a job here in East Africa? Only two or three days ago she had seen an advertisement asking for assistants for a big photographic safari leaving shortly for Uganda. Uganda. She said the name in her mind. It sounded as strange to her ears as Tanzania had done once, but if she could fall in love with one part of Africa, there was no reason to believe she couldn't do it again.

Love! She dug her nails deep into the palms of her hands. So long as she kept her interests strictly confined to the scenery and tried to forget about one certain safari master she might even be a success at her job. But she hadn't got it yet, and the paper she had seen the advertisement in had been the Dar-es-Salaam daily.

The sound of stiletto heels clicking about inside the hotel froze her thoughts momentarily. Gayna! She hadn't seen the hotel proprietress since returning to Mbinga. It had been dark on their arrival and Ryan had taken her straight to the rondavel. As far as she knew he had spent the night working in his office. The click of those heels sounded to be just beneath the open window now.

Laurie shot off the veranda. She had just remembered that all the city newspapers were over in Ryan's office. Now would be as good a time as any to search for the advertisement. She knocked politely on the door and went in almost without thinking, her mind mainly on what she was going to say to Ryan to get the papers.

She raised her head to see him sitting at his desk and two men seated on chairs opposite.

'Oh, I'm sorry!' she blurted. 'I thought . . .'

Ryan was standing. 'It's all right, Laurie. Come on in.' He dropped an arm across her shoulders and drew her forward. 'Gentlemen, this is my wife. Laurie, meet Mr. Makinga and Mr. Ngunu from Dar-es-Salaam. They're just on their way home.'

Shaking hands, Laurie was vaguely aware that she had seen the two distinguished-looking Africans somewhere before. It was only when they were smiling their goodbyes and turning to leave that she remembered them as the two figures in the background at the hotel on the day of the wedding. So they had been in Mbinga all this time! Something must have proved interesting.

Ryan nodded as the long black car slid away from the door, and then closing it, he turned inside.

'Got everything ready you want to take on the trip?' he asked.

Laurie nodded, looking down at herself. 'I thought I'd keep these on to get used to wearing them again.'

'It's been a long time.'

She was aware of him sending a tight smile down the length of her, and afraid that she might find herself compelled to think too deeply on that other occasion when she had come to his office dressed like this, she asked, struggling to sound vague, 'I – er – was wondering if you still had the city newspapers.'

'For about the last three or four days, I think. Why?'

'Oh, I thought I might flick through them. I haven't much to do just now.'

'Seems to me you read them pretty thoroughly while we were there – two or three times a night, in fact,' he said pointedly.

Laurie turned to stare at the map on the wall. Had he guessed that half the time she hadn't been reading them, only hiding behind them? She shrugged. 'Well, the advertisements are always interesting . . . for dresses and things, I mean. Still, if you've thrown them away . . .'

'I've got them.' He went to his desk and turned back to drop the bundle in her hand. He went to open the door for her, but just before she stepped out he added,

'By the way, I'll be spending the evening with Gayna again. She's decided to close the hotel after this safari. I'm giving her a hand to tie things up.'

182

Laurie nodded dumbly and walked out. She would have liked to go on walking, straight along the dusty Mbingan road on and on until she had walked Ryan out of her heart. But she knew that would never be possible even if she carried on for ever. Tears pushing at her lashes, she started to run as though she might escape from his last words.

I'll be spending the evening with Gayna again.

That meant he had been with her last night too. What more evidence did she want that Ryan and Gayna were deeply in love and longed to be together?

CHAPTER THIRTEEN

LAURIE was moving rapidly across the road now, but she had to stop suddenly, for Gayna was standing directly in her path.

'My dear!' the hyacinth blue eyes dipped over her and came to rest on her face with a humorous light. 'You're looking a little pale. I hope you're not going to go down with something?'

'I'm fine, thank you, Mrs. Lewis,' Laurie mumbled. 'If you'll excuse me I – er – have things to do.'

'Well, don't overdo it, child.' With a tiny smile Gayna turned and carried on, the slim, swinging figure making straight for Ryan's office.

Once in the rondavel Laurie scanned the newspapers and found the advertisement she wanted. She scribbled out a hastily worded request to be considered for the job, tacking on a slightly colourful account of her photographic activities and experience to date. She paid the boy from the hotel to take it along to the post office, putting the address of the hotel she had stayed at in Dar-es-Salaam on her arrival from England. She would go there and wait for the reply.

When to go she hadn't decided. It seemed that as the wife of the safari master she was expected to accompany him on this trip, but she needn't necessarily do the whole of it . . .

Her pulses started to race as a plan began to form in her mind.

What if she slipped away after they had made their first camp? She had never driven a Land Rover, but she couldn't imagine it would be much different from driving a car. Ryan would be sure to come up with an answer to cover her disappearance, that she had been taken ill or something and had had to return to Mbinga. No doubt he would view her disappearance with relief.

Once back in Mbinga she could get Mahmoud to drive her to the coast, and the first move then would be to explain the position of her marriage to a good lawyer. Everything clear in her mind now about just what she intended to do, Laurie found the hours dragged by, but at last the tawny-orange light of dawn slid through the open door of her rondavel. She rose and washed and slipped into her safari clothes. As she stepped out towards the hotel Ryan was just coming along the path to meet her. After a brief good morning and a searching look he led her towards the leading Land Rover.

He seemed about to open the door, but turned instead at a commotion from behind and as the road suddenly became alive with dust he pressed her gently back behind him. Bill Alexander pulled up noisily in his battered Chevrolet. The back was piled high with boxes and crates, and on the seat beside him was a bulging leather holdall. He grinned palely from beneath a battered hat, 'Great minds think alike!' As though at a loss for words, he thrust an unsteady hand through the window and looking at Laurie as though the pearly light of dawn was too bright for his eyes he grunted, 'Well, I'm just off. Thought I'd better get some mileage out of the old girl before she caves in.'

Ryan took the hand firmly and smiled, 'She'll make it all right.'

'To the coast?' Bill raised a sceptical eyebrow. 'I doubt it, but one can always hope. Well, cheers, Ryan. I'll drop you a card from Cornwall.'

He stuck his chin towards Laurie as though in a hurry, then apparently having second thoughts, caught her hand and squeezed it tight. 'Goodbye, Laurie. We might run across one another some day.' He contemplated starting the car, and then as though he thought they expected something else, turned a glance towards the hotel. 'I've said my goodbyes to Gayna . . . about a couple of years back, I think.'

The engine coughed into life, and with an overbright eye and an attempt at humour that brought a lump to Laurie's throat he called wryly above the racket, 'Give me half an hour to get out of the way, old man!'

They waved him out of sight, then Ryan turned. 'I've put a couple of flasks behind the seat, but there's some coffee in the hotel if you want it,' he offered.

'No. No, I don't feel like anything just now.'

'Sure?' He gazed down at her. 'Get enough sleep last night? You look rough.'

'I might say the same about you,' she countered, not wanting to admit that she hadn't had any sleep.

Although his khaki drill was immaculate, the clean-shaven features were drawn and scored with deep lines. The green eyes looked red-rimmed and weary. He twisted the handle of the door non-committally.

'I'll go and round the party up and then we'll get moving.' He closed the door behind her. Laurie sat in the Land Rover for some time, listening to the clinking of cups and the dull murmur of conversation coming from the hotel. Eventually the sounds changed to the tramp of heavy boots and excited chatter as the Americans drifted out of the hotel to take their places in the waiting vehicles. Another ten minutes went by, but there was still no sign of Ryan.

Laurie was rather surprised to see Nabu open the door across and step in smilingly behind the driving wheel. Before she had time to comprehend his action the estate car pulled alongside and Ryan was directing a hand forward and called across her, 'Okay, Nabu, I'll meet you at Mborni ridge. Keep the rest in line, and take it easy!'

Before the car shot away Laurie caught a glimpse of a smooth ash-blonde head and faultless profile at Ryan's side. As the rear windows receded she saw a neat pile of suitcases and pigskin handbag on top. She knew what was happening, of course. Ryan wouldn't want Gayna to stay on at the hotel. What better place for her to wait for him than over at Nyumbaya? Devoid of all feeling, Laurie watched the red and cream car streak away out of sight.

Laurie sank down on the edge of the bed. The drive had been a long one, and she wasn't fooling herself for one minute that she could remember the way back to Mbinga. Still, she had one or two landmarks in her head, and since Mborni ridge when the road had finished she had taken careful note of Ryan's handling of the Land Rover; what it could tackle, and what he thought it wiser to drive around.

Of course it would be difficult at night, but for once luck was on her side. A bright full moon shone its benevolent smile obligingly over the camp. It was too soon to think about going yet, the place was seething with activity. This afternoon when the tents had gone up she had thought the clearing resembled a small village. Each couple had quarters to themselves.

Then there were the safari assistants to be catered for, and the safari boys, various trackers and skinners – she shuddered at the title. What it must all be costing didn't bear thinking about, but the Americans wanted nothing spared and seemed to be enjoying every minute of it.

The men, apparently all crack shots, wandered about the camp itching to get their rifles into play. The women, less concerned with the excited talk of this or that trophy to be bagged, waved their movie cameras at just everything that moved. The couples had listened with good-natured patience to Ryan's pep talk about the animals. He said that most of them were tolerant and easy-going, but like people, there was always one that didn't conform. They were warned to stay close to the camp except on actual hunts, and never to under-estimate an indifferent docile stare.

Laurie had listened too, but of course she had heard it all before. Ryan had pounded it into her almost daily on their last safari. She had sat with the others and listened, because it gave her a chance to gaze openly at the rugged tanned features. She could soak up every last detail of the man she loved without him suspecting a thing.

The picture she had in her mind now would stay fresh for years to come. She looked down at the wide band of gold, not hating it as she should have done but twisting it wistfully against the skin of her finger. She hadn't heard the flap of the tent go, until Ryan stood inside the doorway. He dropped a glance to her hand before striding over to the far side of the tent.

'Time you were turning in,' he said brusquely, his back to her. 'You've had a long day. I've got some work to do check-ing the supply list, but I can do it over in the dining tent.' He swept up a sheaf of papers from the opposite bed, and turned at the door to say evenly, 'I won't disturb you when I come in.'

Laurie snatched a last look at fathomless green eyes, power-ful shoulders, then Ryan was gone.

She sat for a moment, heavy-limbed and unable to think about moving, until the idea came to her that it might be better to go now while the camp was still active. That way no one would be likely to pay much attention to one Land Rover being driven out.

187

It could be any one of the safari assistants going out to make a check on the surrounding bush. There was no hope of taking her suitcase. That would attract far too much attention if she walked out of the tent with it now. The best thing would be to go exactly as she was as though she were taking a final stroll before bed.

With a last look round the tent she didn't allow her eyes to linger too long on Ryan's holdall, but swung dizzily out into the night. As she had hoped, nobody paid the slightest attention to her apparently idle stroll past flickering camp fires towards the far belt of trees. The sharp-eyed safari assistants might have questioned her climbing into Ryan's Land Rover, but thankfully they were supervising the positioning of the lorries on the edge of the clearing. What was even better was the noise of revving engines. It completely drowned out the rumbling start of this one.

She let in the clutch clumsily, took off the brake and guided the car out towards the moonlit plain.

Apart from the uneven ground, driving the Land Rover was comparatively easy. The light was good and she could see a fair distance ahead. The only thing that unnerved her was the stationary black shapes dotted along the plain, but she knew she was safe here inside the car, even if one of them, the one that didn't conform . . . she thought wryly of Ryan's words . . . came to investigate further.

She had been driving for half an hour when, to her surprise and dismay, the grassy plain that she had happily expected to go on for ever suddenly gave way to uneven scrubland. Where before there had been just the Land Rover, the black shapes and the moon, now there were huge rocks, sentinel trees, and eerie clouds of thorn bush. She braked for a moment to consider, then carried on. What else was there to think out? She had to get to a town or village and then on to Mbinga, and the simplest way to do that was to keep moving.

It might have been wiser to slacken speed with so many obstacles looming up in the headlights, but Laurie had no wish to linger on any part of the journey where visibility wasn't too good and a punctured tyre imminent. She pressed on, ignoring those weird calls across the night that she had been conscious of since starting out, but never so much as now . . . and another sound. In the moment that she had

188

pulled up to study the terrain, she thought she had heard the hum of another car engine, but of course it was only her taut nerves, and the night playing tricks on her ears.

The wheels bounced and she became almost lulled by the flying dancing shapes of the rocks and bushes – then she blinked as one of them seemed to leap not away from the car but towards it.

In the moment that the headlights caught it Laurie had a clear view of a terrified gazelle struggling to get out of the path of the car. She closed her eyes to the bump, and slammed the brakes on with such force that she came up heavily against the driving wheel and stayed there, momentarily winded. Long after she had regained her breath she sat staring in a hypnotic trance along the column of headlights.

The gazelle had been right in front of her and she had felt the bump, so she must have hit it. But how badly? She knew she wouldn't be able to go on until she had found out. Switching the headlights off as though the action might break her daze, she clutched for the torch she had seen Ryan use and climbed out beside a dark hump of rock. After the glare of the headlights she found it difficult to see anything in the dull grey glow, but the pale beam of the torchlight picked out a sprawled shape directly in front of the bonnet of the Land Rover.

She must have pulled up almost on the moment of impact. But not soon enough. She gulped, watching a dark stain creep up slowly above one small ear, bringing back with startling clarity the fate of Cando. She brushed a hand across her eyes as though to shut out the picture, and with a quivering sigh wondered that she could do for the gazelle. About the only thing she *could* do was move it out of the way, then perhaps . . . She stopped as two sounds came to her ears almost simultaneously – the stirring of the bushes beyond the clearing where she had just driven through and . . . she froze; a rustling from just behind the rock.

Confused and in a daze of indecision, she pondered on whether to move the gazelle or step back into the Land Rover, but in the end the only logical move seemed to be to get away from the rock as quick as possible. Hardly had she thought of it than her legs were flying, but she hadn't got many yards before a glimpse behind rooted her to the spot.

189

She stared horrified as the huge head and mane of a lion appeared round the side of the rock. A second later his long lithe body swayed round to the front of the car to stare back into the clearing where she had retreated. Laurie stood rock still. She couldn't have moved if she had wanted. It was one thing to see the lions, playful as puppies, from the safe confines of a car, and entirely another to be standing face to face with a pair of yellow eyes and a slightly twitching nose. When she thought the lightness in her head would spread to the rigidness of her body and send her sprawling, she heard the sharp sound like the crack of a dry twig near the bushes. She strained. There it was again. This time the lion heard it. Perhaps he was meant to, for in that moment when he turned Laurie saw Ryan with eyes and rifle trained on the huge shape. She could have slumped down in relief, but something more than his lightning glance of encouragement helped to maintain her stillness.

Another shape had appeared from behind the rock and now the pale form of a lioness wandered curiously over to the side of the lion. She followed his gaze towards the tall dark shape in the clearing and padded slowly forward. As the lion followed, Laurie wanted to press a hand to her mouth to stifle a cry. Though Ryan was gazing coolly along the barrel of his rifle she knew one man was no match for two leaping animals. She disciplined her hands to stay down by her sides, and watched as the two huge forms padded around uncertainly.

The lioness seemed to be losing interest in the situation. She sniffed the air, turned back towards the Land Rover, and disappeared round the front. After a moment's consideration the lion followed. There was a slight scuffle, then the sound of full-throated grunts which gradually faded out into the night.

Laurie closed her eyes and let go the breath she seemed to have been holding for ten minutes. She heard Ryan's strides, opened her eyes to see him swaying beside her, the sheen of sweat on his skin, but a laconic light in the green eyes.

'It's coming to something when you prefer the animals to me,' he drawled.

190

CHAPTER FOURTEEN

LAURIE wanted to answer all sorts of sensible things, but, weak from anti-climax, she forgot everything but the sweet knowledge that Ryan was safe. In the moment that she fell into his arms he let the rifle slide and swept her to him with a muffled groan.

'You idiot! You sweet darling little idiot!'

'Ryan!' Laurie felt that if she didn't laugh the tears of relief and love would be bound to take over. 'I was terrified for you,' she choked. 'If anything had happened to you it would have been all . . .'

Things developed rapidly from there. Somehow she felt that words would never be enough to explain what she was feeling at this moment, and Ryan's shoulder was so close at hand. She clung to him as though she would never let go. Several seconds later he raised his head to murmur, 'Say, maybe I should have put myself in front of a couple of lions a lot earlier!'

Laurie drew away from him at last to ask worriedly, 'What if they come back?'

'Probably miles away with their supper by now,' he replied.

'Supper!' Laurie shuddered. 'The gazelle, you mean?'

He held her close. 'That's what attracted them. Lucky for us they considered it the more tempting proposition.'

'Lucky for *you*.' She gazed up at him, soft grey eyes big in the pallor of her face. 'If either of those brutes had . . .' She swallowed and buried her face in his shoulder again. He stroked her hair, his tone slightly humorous. 'I'd have made out. With my rifle and Nabu standing behind with his.'

'Nabu?' She stared up in surprise. 'You mean he was back there too?'

Ryan nodded. 'I suspected you were up to something ever since you asked for the newspapers. I went back to the tent early, and put two and two together.' He smiled down at her. 'It wasn't difficult to follow your erratic trail across the plain, then when Nabu spotted the lion and lioness we decided to investigate on foot.'

'You and Nabu!' She tried to push him away from her in pink embarrassment. 'And all that worrying I did for you!'

He seemed in no hurry to release her, but murmured, 'Why shouldn't a wife worry over her husband, if she loves him?'

'Well, of course I love you, but . . .'

'You've got a funny way of showing it, running away!'

'Well, how could I stay when . . . when Gayna . . .'

'What's Gayna got to do with it?' He brushed his lips along her cheek abstractedly, and Laurie stared up.

'You mean she's not at Nyumbaya? But this morning before we started out . . . I saw you driving her . . .'

'She wanted me to catch Bill up.'

'*Bill?*'

He looked down at her amazed features and explained, 'I advised her to pull out of the hotel because in the scheme of things it would be likely to go under. Over coffee this morning she seemed surprised to hear that I wouldn't be leaving too, and when I told her about my new job she just tore around packing.'

'So that's why you were making this your last safari?' Laurie said softly. 'You're going to do something else?'

He raised his head to gaze out over the bush.

'Mbinga is about to become part of six hundred and thirty-four square miles of game reserve. They want me to stay on in an advisory capacity.'

'They?' And then Laurie asked dawningly, 'Mr. Makinga and Mr. Ngunu?'

Ryan nodded. 'I'll still keep my own office, and with a bit of luck I should be home every night, which—' he dropped his gaze down to hers '—is as it should be when a guy has a wife—' He looked about to say something else, but instead he took her hand abruptly, and calling across the clearing, 'Okay, Nabu, you can head back,' he led her to the Land Rover.

Seeing his purposeful stride, Laurie asked breathlessly, 'Ryan, where are we going?'

'Back to Dar-es-Salaam,' was his reply. 'We've a little matter of a honeymoon to recap on!'

The soft sigh of the waves drifted up from the beach as Ryan came behind Laurie on the veranda and turned his arms about her waist. She laid her head back on his shoulder to stare out over the starlit night and asked dreamily, 'What about the safari? Should you have left it like that?'

'I was in two minds whether to lead it or not. I've had a good man standing by. He'll be there by now,' he brushed his lips along her throat. 'I never did believe in working honeymoons, anyway.'

'Won't your friend mind our coming back here?' she asked softly.

'He's up country for another three or four weeks. I still have the key.'

Laurie spoke to the night. 'We need never have left here if you hadn't said you married me because you didn't want Dave to.'

'What else could I say? It was the truth. I knew Dave was just looking for diversions from his studies, whereas I had a better reason for marrying you.' His arms tightened, and Laurie asked lightly, 'What went on that night after our mountain adventure? Did you two argue?'

'No. Dave told me he wanted to get married and get a job. I said that was fine by me so long as he found his own girl, and in the meantime he'd better try and pass a few exams so that he could support her.'

'That was when you got the tutor in.' She felt Ryan smiling.

'I've known Paul a long time. I knew if anybody could whip Dave into shape he could.'

After a while Laurie turned to gaze up at him innocently.

'And what was this "better reason" you had for marrying me?'

'Just that I was crazily in love with you,' he smiled down at her, 'and have been ever since you swished that ridiculous pony-tail at me.'

'But you never said . . .'

'There was always Desmond, and then it looked as if you were getting tied up with Dave.'

She traced his lips with her finger. 'I've known for a long time it wasn't love between Desmond and me, and I only turned to Dave because you went around so much with Gayna.'

He shrugged. 'Purely routine. Ever since Tony, her husband, got killed I've felt a certain responsibility towards

Gayna. She's had a lonely couple of years. I just wanted to help out where I could.' As Laurie smiled down at his breast pocket he asked, 'What's funny?'

'I was just thinking. All these weeks I've been eating my heart out for something that was purely routine!'

He grinned. 'I wanted to tell myself it was something more, this time when Gayna was up at Nyumbaya, but I never succeeded in putting the thoughts of you out of my mind.'

He lowered his lips, but Laurie hurried, 'What about that night when you didn't leave Mbinga till one o'clock?'

He thought. 'The night you were missing? That was when Messrs. Makinga and Ngunu and myself were ironing out plans for this new job. I spent all day and up to ten in the evening at the office.'

Laurie relaxed completely in his arms; there was nothing more she needed to know. A long time after his kiss he murmured, 'Reckon you're going to like the idea of going home to Nyumbaya?'

'Home!' She breathed the word with shining eyes and watching her Ryan drawled casually, 'By the way, I saw the boy at the vet's the other day. He's got a labrador pup he wants taking out of his hands. Great feet and a face as black as soot. Want him?'

Speechless with pleasure, Laurie could only nod her head.

Ryan put a finger under her chin. 'Funny little kid,' he twinkled.

'Not really,' she gazed up. 'Everybody needs something to love.'

'Well, you've always got me,' and with a slow smile, 'and there might be one or two other small items coming along in the future.'

He drew her hand in his, and as they walked down towards the whispering waves Laurie took her first steps in this new and wonderful world that was love.

A SUMMER TO LOVE

A
SUMMER
TO LOVE

"You'd be well-advised to steer clear of such friendships with Italian men," Mark Lawford said severely. "Don't be fooled."

Stacey was annoyed to think that she had been fooled, but it was even more galling to have this man point it out.

Even if he was her boss, she was not going to let him spoil her summer in Sorrento.

CHAPTER ONE

THE white steamer was called *Napoli* and looked hardly big enough to take the crowd of people milling on the quay. As the barrier went down Stacey had just time to grab her luggage before she was being carried along with the flow of jostling bodies towards the opening.

She almost came to grief handing in her ticket. A hefty travelling bag came up from the rear and caught her squarely behind the knees, making them buckle. The big man holding the bag scowled down at her as though everything was her fault, but he did put out a hand to steady her before the momentum of the crowd took her forward. Before she had time to catch her breath the smooth springy boards of the sailing craft were beneath her feet.

Phew! If this was sea travel to Sorrento in the spring, heaven knew what it would be like making the trip at the height of the season. The rows of seats were packed tight with people all looking as though they had been sitting there since time began, yet they could only have made it seconds before Stacey. Ah well! She lifted her shoulders with a resigned smile. The journey was only about an hour long anyway, and who wanted to sit when the view all but demanded that you stand on tip-toe.

She moved along the deck to a less crowded spot, but hardly had she given herself up to the matchless beauty of the shimmering blue bay of Naples than she was surrounded by a profusion of young men all offering her their seats.

'*S'accomodi, signorina. Prego! Prego!*'

Stacey laughingly refused the offers, partly because she was being encouraged to go off in every direction at once, which was impossible, and partly because she had come to know that the Italian male with his fantastic good looks could be counted on to press for a more lasting relationship even when he was merely offering his seat. As politely as she could she turned towards the rail.

The boat must have filled up in record time, for already it was shuddering into life. She watched the ribbon of water widen as they left the quay, and as though to welcome its release from land, the steamer let out a full-blooded shriek on its siren. The final touch, Stacey thought, laughing along with everyone else, and enjoying every minute of being just a small part of the Italian scene. The scene that was gay-shirted youths, vivacious girls, stocky gesticulating men in crumpled suits and plump dark-eyed women noisily scolding or embracing their dusky-skinned children.

Life along this golden coast, Stacey decided with a twinkle as two small unattended mischiefs circled boisterously around her before disappearing up the length of the deck, looked like being anything but dull.

She caught sight of the big man again. He was standing towards the front of the boat, slightly aloof from the rest of the passengers and staring out to sea. He was English, of course. Stacey didn't know how she could be so sure. Perhaps it was the unmistakable cut of his light-weight suit, the impeccable shirt front and sombre tie. The breeze flicked a thick lock of dark hair just above the line of his frown, and Stacey swung her eyes gaily away. She wanted no part of stern faces today. This was the start of her stay in Sorrento. Nothing was going to please her more than to lapse into the Italian mood of things; that way of life which, from what she had seen so far, seemed to be to enjoy each and every minute as it came.

The group of men who had offered her their seats seemed not in the least perturbed that she had turned them down. In fact they appeared to have lost interest in reclining themselves, and hovered around her flashing their white smiles, and lowering black appraising glances over her.

That was another thing about the Italians, Stacey mused, the men at least. They could make a girl feel that she was something really special, just by looking at her. Not that Stacey had any illusions about her looks. A slim five feet four, she had long since come to accept the fact that the face she saw in the mirror every morning wasn't going to start any fires. Still, she was thankful for a clear complexion, and a pair of wide-set grey-green eyes. The mouth apparently thought that these went well with the smooth bronze hair curling up from her shoulders, for it always smiled back at her, sending the lower lip into a deep full curve, and the upper one towards the laughter dimples at the corners.

She felt these dimples deepen now as her new-found escorts vied playfully for her attention. One, a dark handsome youth, swung up athletically on the rail just behind her. Another in sky-blue trousers and flowered shirt did his version of what Stacey assumed was a local dance. It was impossible not to be amused by their antics, though the smile became slightly tremulous when one of the youths anxious to cut a dash grabbed the smallest of her suitcases and tossed it effortlessly into the air.

'Oh, really! I don't think. . . .' She took a quick step forward. How did one say in Italian that the catches on that particular case were rather shaky, and that too much buffeting might encourage it to open? Something told Stacey that she wouldn't find *that* in her Italian phrase book.

She tried a light *'Basta!'* for 'That will do!' but unfortunately all it did was to show the luggage tosser that he had secured her interest, and now he looked determined to keep it. She saw her case rise to meet the blue sky, again and again, and wondered which moment it would choose to disgorge its contents over the laughing youth. Though little more than an overnight bag, it was packed with all manner of nonentities, enough to make a striking little pile on this open stretch of the deck. Hastily shutting the picture out of her mind, Stacey made a grab for her property, only to see it sail across to another pair of eager hands. So it was going to be like that, was it? A kind of 'piggy in the middle' game. Well, it was one way of whiling away the time, she supposed, putting herself good-humouredly in the path of the next recipient.

Many of the passengers without seats had gone below, and the youths took advantage of the increasing space on the deck to spread out. Stacey's case became a kind of overweighted rugby ball. It was anybody's guess where it would turn up next, and a full-time job trying to intercept it, she decided, becoming slightly over-heated in her cream suit and high-necked blouse.

Not that she had a hope of catching the case if it did come her way. Tossing forty odd pounds of luggage around might be child's play to these husky Italians, but going by its speed Stacey suspected that she might find it something of a blow to come up against.

Perhaps that was why she experienced no little surprise when having successfuly anticipated a throw, the case seemed to float strangely just above her reach. She remembered thinking vaguely that the flower-shirted youth behind her must have shot up in size, but only vaguely, for now the case was almost within her grasp. With another stab at the Italian language *'Finalmente!'* 'At last!' she grabbed it.

Cheeks flushed and the light of gay triumph in her eyes she spun round to come face to face with the big man of the bulky travelling bag. He lowered the case abruptly into her hands. Not that he intended doing any favours. The look on his face was more like one of an irate neighbour who has suddenly put a stop to an annoying ball game.

The young men drifted off good-naturedly, slanting her their white smiles over shrugging shoulders. The man facing her seemed to have changed his mind about letting her have her case back. He dropped it down loosely by his side, and casting a cursory glance over the other two, bent to swing up the lot.

'I take it this is the rest of your stuff?'

What else but deep-pitched tones could come from such a frame? She didn't get time to answer the question, for the man and her cases were already moving off towards a narrow doorway. She hurried after him, slightly open-mouthed, to hear him continue in clipped tones, 'You needn't have dragged these around with you, you know. You could have had them stowed below.'

'I suppose I was too excited at the thought of coming on board,' she laughed, swaying down the narrow stairs and following him along a carpeted corridor. He turned to look at her as though he had never heard of that particular kind of emotion, and then swung off into a long, low-ceilinged room. Stacey noticed the respectful bow of the boat attendant as the man handed over her luggage. He was used to commanding, she could tell. He rattled off something in Italian and then he was turning to ask her in English,

'How far are you going?'

'Sorrento,' she heard herself coming back with smartly. His brisk manner was slightly catching.

After some more clipped Italian he turned again. 'Your luggage will be up on top when you're ready to leave.'

Stacey nodded, feeling that something was expected of her. It wouldn't of course occur to this type of person that he was being in any way high-handed or arrogant. His whole manner was that of a man who thinks and acts to please himself. Still, she considered, he *had* intervened in a game that had been fast losing its sparkle. And he *had* got her case back for her. She ought to say thank you for that at least.

She tried it and immediately wished she hadn't. He nodded the boat attendant on his way, and then procceeded to light up a cigarette as though he hadn't heard. But he would!

'You really shouldn't have bothered, you know,' Stacey stuck at it. 'The trip's half over anyway.'

'Maybe,' he shrugged, flicking a glance towards her receding cases, 'but as far as I see it they're less of a menace to the other passengers down here.'

He was determined to make her feel irresponsible. Stacey knew it. And she was just as determined to remain unruffled. After all, it was going to be part of her job to keep in good humour, to stay pleasant at all costs. The next few moments looked like being a good test of her capabilities.

Viewing it as just another game now, Stacey met his gaze with a decided twinkle in the grey-green eyes. 'It *was* getting a bit hectic up there,' she admitted lightly.

Since her arrival in Naples she had seen many dark eyes, all warmed by the Italian sun. The brown ones she looked into now were as cold as an English river. They tilted down her way beneath straight thick eyebrows and slightly lowered lids. She saw a rather narrow nose, and a mouth that had grown used to being clamped tight, judging by the deep lines at the corners, and two more scored down each lean jaw.

Not a handsome face, Stacey decided. Striking perhaps in a craggy sort of way.

He seemed to be taking his time in choosing a remark. No doubt when it came it would be weighted down with disapproval. It was.

'It doesn't take much encouragement for things to get out of hand out here,' he said shortly, 'especially with the type you were entertaining just now.'

'I thought they were a jolly friendly lot,' Stacey replied, masking her irritation with a smile, 'and anyway,' she added, hoping that her eyes positively sparkled with devilish lights, 'I could have handled them.'

'No doubt you'll have other opportunities.' He dropped a distasteful glance over her. 'I guess it's none of my business . . .' That's right, it isn't, Stacey thought, widening her smile. '. . . but if you're new to the country it might help to know that womanizing is a favourite pastime of the Italians. They'll go to any lengths to get into a conversation.'

'Like swooping down unintroduced and marching off with one's luggage?' she asked with an air of innocence.

He must have seen the humour of the situation, for a slow smile flickered along the line of his lips. Not that any of it reached his eyes, but there was rather a nice, though brief, gleam of white even teeth as he shrugged his reply.

'Fellow-countryman's prerogative.' After a pause he nodded beyond her, and flexing an arm added, 'Might as well extend it to the offer of a drink. Mark Lawford's the name.'

It might have been only an offer, but it seemed refusals weren't in order, for Stacey found herself being propelled firmly through a crowded carpeted lounge.

The table he chose was one at the end of a line, cut off from the main part of the room by a row of pillars. Mandolin music drifted in over speakers above the portholes and many of the passengers had drinks in their hands. Stacey felt a chair being held for her, and then the tall figure draped down opposite. The merest incline of his head brought a waiter rearing up with apparently the right drink first time. For him. Stacey wasn't consulted on *her* choice, but seconds later a glass was placed in front of her. She liked the taste of the light wine the man sitting opposite had ordered for her, but it would have been nice to have been asked.

Still, he was being pleasant in a stony kind of way. It was up to her to keep up her end until the drinks were finished. 'I'm Stacey Roberts,' she smiled. 'I can tell you're from England.'

Her remark evoked no comment apart from a brief nod and a deep draw on the gold-banded cigarette. She turned her attention towards the commotion of people beyond the pillars. 'I'd no idea the boat would be so crowded at this time of the year,' she exclaimed.

Following her gaze, he replied mildly, 'Week-ends are not exactly the ideal time to make this trip.'

'You mean they're mainly local people? Is it some kind of excursion?' she asked with interest.

'Or celebration,' he nodded. 'The Neapolitians can be guaranteed to come up with one for practically any day of the week. You'll see what I mean during your holiday.'

'Oh, I'm not here on holiday!' Stacey explained laughingly. 'I have a job to go to in Sorrento,' and then because there was something of a silence, she asked politely, 'What about you? Are you staying in Italy?'

'I live across the bay.'

Not very revealing, Stacey thought wryly. 'Across the bay' could be anywhere along this side of the Sorrentine peninsula, even Capri. Still, it couldn't matter to her where he lived.

'It must be fun,' she smiled, already caught up in the mood of the laughing, gesticulating people, and then quietly hugging herself and gazing around, she sighed happily, 'I think I'm going to like it out here. I get the feeling that life was made for living.'

'And you intend to live it.'

The dry reply was more of a statement than a question. He drew on his cigarette and gazed idly down the room, giving Stacey an opportunity to study the chiselled features. Mark Lawford. The name suited him anyway.

He looked as though he would be a law unto himself. Probably a recluse of some kind, she decided, noticing the shut-down expression. She had heard there was a whole string of them down the coast. She could just imagine him. High up in his deserted villa – or was it castle? – scowling down on anyone who had the audacity to be within sight of his domain. Probably disapproved of people enjoying their work, too.

Something within her – perhaps an impish desire to champion all the things that face looked as if it was against – prompted her to reply gaily.

'That's right, I intend to live life to the hilt. My boss and I made a pact to enjoy every minute of our season in Sorrento. Swimming, sunbathing, dancing ... night clubs,' she added, ashamed of herself for enjoying the flicker of annoyance that showed in the brown eyes.

He leaned forward to stub out his cigarette. 'Must be an easy-going guy, the boss?' he drawled.

'The best,' Stacey returned, delighting in making the words sound pointed. 'He got me my first job in Switzerland two years ago. Last year we did a season in Malaga.' She finished her wine sweepingly. 'We're looking forward tremendously to this one in Sorrento.'

Her table companion must have had enough. He stood up. 'Order another drink if you want one. I've got things to attend to.' The slant of his smile did nothing to take the bite out of his departing words: 'And good luck with the pact. The work apparently takes care of itself.'

A sudden churning within Stacey was against him having the last word, and especially the manner in which he delivered it. She wouldn't be seeing him again anyway, and there was *something* about him. ... 'There's really nothing to it,' she sparkled light-heartedly, 'Jeremy and I consider we have our jobs as holiday representatives worked down to a fine art.'

In the action of moving off Mark Lawford stopped and swung his head sharply round and down. Stacey felt that the steel-flecked brown eyes were looking at her for the first time, penetrating through the fixed smile on her face as though to get to the bottom of something they would rather not know. Imagination of course, but she

206

blinked up uncertainly. And to rid herself of a tiny uncomfortable feeling she blurted idiotically, 'We ... er ... we work for Sunflair Travel.'

She dropped back in her chair slightly drained as he moved away. Well! It couldn't really be said that she had made a hit with her first acquaintance in Italy, but then the feeling was fairly mutual.

She told herself it was ridiculous to dislike a man she had met and talked to for but a few minutes. How could she possibly know what type he was, up there in his ivory villa? How indeed? She watched the wide shoulders disappear through the doorway. It was written all over him. That particular breed one came across occasionally in England. Cold, autocratic and critical. She stood up weakly. Thank heaven this was Italy, and in her work with carefree, laughter-seeking holidaymakers, she wouldn't be likely to come up against any more of *his* type.

The same commotion that had taken place before the boat sailed occured when it pulled into Sorrento, although Stacey had made sure of being ahead of the crowd this time and was one of the first to leave. She couldn't see anything of the man responsible for the two faint spots of colour in her cheeks, so he must be coming up behind or staying on for Capri. In any case she wasn't going to be tempted to look back. She had no particular desire to set eyes on the man again.

A straw-coloured head of hair caught her attention on the quay and a few seconds later she was falling into the arms of a tall gangling man with light blue eyes and a pink sunburnt complexion. 'Jeremy! You came to meet me! Isn't this wonderful?' She clung to him with slightly more fervour and for considerably longer than she had intended, just for the benefit of a certain pair of frosty eyes, wherever they might be, and then Jeremy was stooping for her cases and Stacey forgot everything but the view.

Everywhere was colour! The sky, a canopy of purest blue, hung over tall cliffs, streaked in the shadow and shade of deep purples and rich browns. Pink and yellow houses, dripping with blossom, hung suspended in the curl of tropical greenery, and below them were multi-coloured boats, striped beach huts and gay sun umbrellas.

The air felt warm as though permanently stocked up with sunshine and the scent of the blossom mingled with the smell of hot sand, and paint and lapping sea water.

Stacey was on her second sigh when Jeremy took her arm and led her to a waiting car. He thrust her cases inside, but she hung back, gazing around. 'Oh, couldn't we walk?' she asked. 'Is it very far to the hotel?'

Jeremy grinned and pointed round the curve of the cliff. 'It's all uphill. We'll have to send your luggage on.'

He paid the taxi and led her along the quay and soon they were making their way up a sun-dappled lane over-hung by pines and slender mimosa trees. Villa gardens bursting with flowers lay on one side, the smooth peacock blue of the sea on the other.

Stacey looked about her and sighed again happily. 'It's everything I expected it to be, Jeremy,' she exuded. 'Can't we stop a while and jubilate? I still haven't got over our luck at landing these jobs.'

'You think it was luck?'

'Well, what else could it be?' she laughed. 'My Italian is practically non-existent and you've never worked for Sunflair before.'

'That's what I've been thinking,' he replied slowly. 'Maybe *we* were the mugs.'

Since meeting him off the boat Stacey had sensed a certain slackness in Jeremy's manner. Now his words made her look at him curiously. There *was* something bothering him. She quickly shook off the feeling of appre-hension that his dull expression gave her. It was ridicu-lous, of course. What could possibly be wrong in a para-dise like this? Probably Jeremy had 'start of the season' nerves.

She hugged his arm lightly and quirked a humorous eyebrow to ask, 'What's wrong, Jeremy? Is it the hotel? Do you think our clients are going to be let down because it's too far from the beach or too small or something?'

Jeremy smiled wryly. 'They're hardly likely to object to living at the Palazzo,' he pointed out. 'It's got just about everything, including its own beach.'

'Well then?' Stacey laughed in relief. 'Why the gloom?'

'You forgot I've been here a fortnight already.'

'All the more reason why some of the gold should have rubbed off on you,' Stacey replied, gazing around.

'Something's rubbed off all right,' Jeremy nodded. 'I'd say it was the shine of this job.' He stopped and led her across the road and through the trees, to where a grassy flower-strewn bank rose in a platform overlooking the bay. As she sank down beside him he asked, staring out to sea, 'You don't know much about the head of Sunflair, do you, Stacey?'

'Only that she's a woman,' Stacey replied, puzzled.

He nodded. 'And a very young one. A bit too young for a business the size of Sunflair.'

Stacey dragged her eyes from the gay red roofs of the town. 'You mean the boss of our firm is only a girl?' she asked.

'And her brother a couple of years younger, I believe. They got it into their heads that they could run things as well as their father had done. He died a while back. Needless to say the business went steadily downhill.'

'Oh dear,' Stacey's mouth tightened in concern. 'What happened?'

Jeremy shrugged. 'What does happen when the core of discipline goes? From what I've heard, it was just a general deterioration in standards. Poor accommodation. Indifferent staff. The customers started going somewhere else.'

'And yet everything seemed so well organized at the other end.'

'Oh, it is! Everything's okay now. A friend of the family stepped in and started tightening things up.' Jeremy's smile had a satirical droop. 'Things have never been tighter. He vets most of the staff himself, and makes spot checks at the other resorts when it suits him.'

'A regular martinet,' Stacey smiled. After a pause she added ponderingly, 'But wouldn't it have been better for the brother and sister to sell out, or whatever it is a family do when they're left with a business?'

'Don't ask me,' Jeremy shrugged morosely. 'I think the

209

girl's got some notion she wants to keep things simmering until kid brother's got the hang of it.'

'And until then they've got this family friend,' Stacey reflected. 'Well, I suppose they need someone like him to keep things up to standard.'

Jeremy nodded deliberately. 'From what I've seen of him he has no intention of letting things slide back into their old groove. I've an idea you and I will be doing this season on our toes.'

'You've met him, then.' Stacey reached out to pick a purple flower. Marvelling on its velvety perfection, she heard Jeremy say matter-of-factly:

'He owns the Palazzo.'

The Palazzo! The hotel where they would be working from. So the friend of the Sunflair family was an Italian business man. Stacey mused on this for a while, and then slipping the flower through the buttonhole of her jacket, she pushed blithely to her feet.

She couldn't help thinking that Jeremy was being unnecessarily pessimistic about a man who was merely looking after the interests of a young brother and sister. If he owned a hotel over here it could be no more than a fatherly eye he was keeping on things, and from what she had seen of the Italians, even the fatherly ones, they were affable, good-natured people, always ready for a joke.

In an effort to disperse Jeremy's gloom she said lightly, 'I think you're looking on the grey side for no reason, Jeremy. Why should any of this affect us? As long as we do our work well, and we've never had any complaints before. And what about us anyway?' she laughed. '*We* weren't vetted, at least I only had an interview with a very nice person in London and you got in just on the strength of your experience with other firms.' She looked at him humorously. 'How do you explain Sunflair engaging us?'

'For Sorrento? The lion's lair?' Jeremy twisted a smile and rose to his feet. 'I've a feeling it was either us or nothing. Who'd want to come back for a second dose of Mark Lawford?'

'Oh, really, Jerry! You've only been here a ...' Stacey

snapped her laughter short to blink up at her companion.

'I though you said . . . you *did* say Mark Lawford,' she swallowed. 'But . . . but . . . he's an Englishman.'

'So he likes Italy.'

'And he . . . well, he can't be more than thirty-five.'

'Slightly younger, I'd say.' Jeremy looked at her. 'Don't tell me you've met him? He's due back from Rome today.' At Stacey's slowly nodding head he added listlessly, 'Well, I hope you made a good impression. He's got the idea that all holiday reps are out for nothing but a good time. That's what I wanted to tell you.'

Taking his outstretched hand dazedly, Stacey gave him a lopsided smile. 'Oh, I made an impression all right,' she gulped.

Just what kind she was due to find out any minute now.

CHAPTER TWO

THE PALAZZO was situated somewhat aloofly from the rest of the town, amongst orange and lemon groves with terraced vineyards rising up to the backcloth of mountains. Ostensibly a hotel, it still retained much of the glamour of the old world Italian villa with its trellised vines, walled terraces, and statues.

Along the drive, rose hedges mingled with creepers of jasmine, and fronting the pillared entrance fountains played to an audience of palms and tall cypresses. The building, dazzling white against sea and sky, was laced with balustraded balconies, many of which were lit with the smouldering glow of bougainvillea.

Stacey could have gone on feasting her eyes indefinitely but for the light tap on her shoulder. A man dressed in a smart olive green uniform smiled. 'The Signore wishes to see you,' he said in accented English.

Stacey turned on the hotel steps, feeling her heart plummet to zero. And the 'Signore', being none other of course than the invincible Mark Lawford, was wasting no time, she thought wryly. He could have given her a chance to catch her breath from the uphill climb.

Jeremy took her arm. 'That will be the big chief himself,' he said unnecessarily. 'He must have seen us coming up the lane.' He squeezed her hand encouragingly. 'Go to it, old girl, and for crikey's sake try to look ... well, you know ...' he smiled flounderingly, 'efficient.'

Stacey doubted if she had ever looked efficient in her life, and flushed cheeks, awry hairstyle, and eyes aglow with the excitement of the trip were not going to help now. The fact that she hadn't been given five minutes to compose herself did not endear the owner of the Palazzo to her.

She followed the uniformed man through the wide impressive doorway and along a thickly carpeted corridor. The rich dark furnishings had a mellow orange glow after the glare of the sunlight. Alcoves along the way opened off into high-ceilinged spacious lounges, showing views of green terraces and the bay.

As Stacey turned her head to look forward, a large dark door loomed up at the end of the corridor. At first her knees quavered, but she quickly shook the nervous sensation away. Why should *she* care? She ought to be grateful to the man for not allowing her time to put on a veneer of angelic reserve. She was Stacey Roberts and nothing could be gained from pretending she wasn't. If Mark Lawford didn't like what he saw, he would know what to do about it.

Perhaps he had already decided, she thought, reflecting on the somewhat wild picture she had painted of herself on the boat, and unable to deny that she had enjoyed every minute of it.

The smile of amusement still playing about her lips, the door was opened, and she found herself face to face with the man from the boat.

'Miss Roberts. Sit down.' He nodded, and the door was closed discreetly behind her.

Stacey didn't sit down immediately. Too late now to give an impression of meekness. She surveyed the room done out in muted greys and greens, and casually furnished with a desk and deep armchairs. Slowly making her way towards one, she saw the brown glance flicker over her. The second time around it latched and fastened disdainfully on the bright flower thrust carelessly through the buttonhole of her suit. Oh dear! Another black mark against her.

Struggling against the odds, she opened lightly with: 'Hello again! I'd no idea we were going to have a local business mind looking after Sunflair time,'

He gave her the benefit of his steel-edged smile. 'You mean if you *had* known you would have taken care not to talk so revealingly on what you meant to do with it?' he replied.

Well, there was nothing like bringing things quickly to a head. She smiled, holding his gaze. 'There wouldn't have been much point since you had already decided we were coming here to abuse it,' she said evenly.

'I see you've been talking to the boy-friend.' He

213

watched her drop into a chair and rearrange herself unhurriedly before he added caustically, 'I make a point of expecting the worst.'

'Let's hope you won't be disappointed.'

It took some effort to keep her gaze fixed on his. As he came round the side of the desk she felt her neck crick.

'I think you'll find it's you who are in for the disappointments, Miss Roberts,' he glinted. 'I don't want to depress you, but I'm here to see that Sunflair gives of its best twenty-four hours a day.'

'What do we do for sleep?'

'We'll fit that in somewhere.' He picked up a slip of paper from his desk. 'You say you started as a holiday rep two years ago?'

Oh, heavens! He hadn't got it written down, had he? All those crazy things she had said to him on the boat. Perhaps she ought to explain that the whole thing had been a joke. What good would it do? Seeing the grim mouth, she sighed inwardly. He was quite determined to think the worst of her. As she nodded in reply to his question he came back vibrantly with:

'Little young then, weren't you? How old are you now?'

'Twenty-one.' She considered for a moment. 'I suppose I was slightly under age then. Most firms prefer a twenty to thirty age group, but I knew this was the kind of work I wanted to do and ...' she tossed him a bright smile, 'I've always been lucky.'

He made no comment, but as the brown eyes held hers she could almost hear him thinking,

'Well, this time it looks as though your luck's run out.'

He went to the window, stared out and turned. 'I suppose on the face of it the job has its glamour? May to September in a continental resort, first class accommodation, swimming, sunbathing, dancing, night clubs. . . .' He was using almost the same words *she* had used. Stacey felt the smile drying on her face. If only she had known the hot seat she had been preparing for herself. '. . . here of course things are slightly different. Our hostess is on call to the clients twenty-four hours a day. . . .' He was certainly pushing the twenty-four-hour bit. Perhaps he enjoyed working his staff into mere shadows of their former selves? '. . . and the only swimming, sunbathing, dancing and visiting night clubs she gets is when the clients are doing the same, and it's up to her to keep the party going. During high season she may have to check on the comfort of holidaymakers in as many as a dozen different hotels. Needless to say . . .' he drooped a hard smile, 'stamina is one of the first requirements.'

Stacey felt her irritation growing at the thread of satisfaction in his tones. He needn't worry, and he could reel off a dozen more duties that his precious holiday hostess would have to perform. She'd cope with it all, or die in the attempt. She said icily, 'I'm quite familiar with my job, Mr. Lawford, and other firms have been satisfied with my work.'

'Maybe, but I think you'll find they fall considerably short of my standards.'

'I don't doubt it for a minute,' she retorted acidly, and then with a slightly raised chin, 'Jeremy has worked for many of the leading firms. He has helped me quite a lot.'

'I can imagine.' The heavy sarcasm in Mark Lawford's voice sent Stacey's mind racing back to this afternoon on the quay when she had thrown herself into Jeremy's arms for *his* benefit. Naturally he was going to make the most out of *that*!

She heard him saying offhandedly. 'Incidentally, you won't have Mr. Farrow to lean on in Sorrento. I'm posting him up to Rome.'

'Rome?' Stacey jumped up, big-eyed. 'But Jeremy hasn't done anything wrong! It's all so ridiculous. Just because I said on the boat that. . . .'

'There isn't enough work for the two of you here,' he drawled, 'so the romance will have to take its course outside Sunflair time.'

Hating his tones and that flint-eyed smile, Stacey swung her head away. What kind of a mess would she be in now, without Jeremy to help her out with the language? And imagining a whole season of Mark Lawford's biting comments, she said quickly, 'I think I'd rather go to Rome.'

'And I think not. Farrow has already proved himself a capable worker, whereas you . . .' the brown eyes flickered over her, 'you're an unknown quantity.'

'Oh no, I'm not!' As Stacey stepped forward the last thread of her control snapped. 'You've already decided that I'm going to fall down on the job. Well, I don't think I want to start with that against me, and I haven't signed anything. I don't *have* to stay.'

She saw the white gleam of a derisive smile as he replied unhurriedly. 'I thought you might want to leave once I made it clear there was some work attached to the job.'

Stacey stood facing those jutting craggy features, her bosom heaving slightly. She had only known the man a few minutes, but she was sorely tempted to hit him. Forcing herself not to linger on the luxury, she said jerkily, 'If you can give me some indication as to the whereabouts of my room I'll get unpacked.' She added icily, 'It might be the only chance I'll get.'

With the same smile he turned away to press the bell. 'Carlo will direct you. And er . . . Miss Roberts. . . .' As she turned to go he thrust a lazy hand into his pocket. 'I should practise a little more self-control if I were you,' he drawled. 'You'll get nowhere if you fly off the handle at the customers.'

Of all the insufferable . . . ! Stacey held on to her breath as he opened the door for her, and then let it go fiercely, not sparing him a backward glance. Perhaps it would have been better if she had let him know just what she thought of him on the boat. It wouldn't have made her life any easier here in his hotel, but at least she would have had the satisfaction of getting it in at the start. Then she had felt only dislike for the man, now she found him positively loathsome.

Once back in the carpeted luxury of the Palazzo, Stacey's anger quickly dispersed. Always more at home on the sunny side of the world, she was far too interested now in the classical decor of the hotel, the scantily clad couples strolling out to the sun, and the smiling Palazzo staff, to give *that man* another thought. She had already placed him on the top shelf of her mind anyway. After all, her job was with the Sunflair tourists. If she did it

216

well where they were concerned what could he possibly find to grumble about? Another thing, he had all this to keep an eye on. It might well be that she would see hardly anything of him at all during the summer. With this blissful thought she followed the man of the green uniform up a wide gently curving staircase.

Her rooms on the first floor came as something of a surprise. She had half expected to be led to some insignificant corner of the hotel, and shown into the usual no-nonsense staff quarters. Instead she found a cream-carpeted lounge and deep lavender bedroom with an adjoining bathroom. Beyond the lounge was a small office with writing bureau and chair, and from all the rooms curtained glass doors led out on to a vine-entwined balcony.

Apart from the armchairs and settee, all the furniture was in a warm deep cherry and the occasional bowl of spring flowers was reflected in its mirror-like shine.

Stacey wandered back into the bedroom, to take in the satin padded headboard of the bed, and the two matching panels running parallel down the pale coverlet.

He, of course, couldn't have had anything to do with the feminine slant of the rooms. She was convinced if he had his way all holiday representatives would be men. Well, being a girl was much more fun than being one of his tight-lipped kind. She unpacked, revelling in the summer frothiness of nylons, chiffons, and silks. And there was more to come – another trunk in fact that she had sent on, filled with gay cottons, sun tops and evening dresses. All that she had collected over the past two years, and was she going to enjoy wearing them *this* summer!

Stacey never thought that she would be donning one of the most expensive items of her wardrobe so soon, or in a gesture of defiance, but later after bathing and brushing the bronze-silk hair she had to admit that the midnight blue dress seemed the perfect reply to one Mark Lawford. Sleeveless with folded silk banding the throat, and dropping low at the back on to a flared panel skirt, it wouldn't conform with his strict ideas on what a holiday hostess should wear, but he had no say in that, thank goodness. Sunflair had no rigid rules about uniforms.

The men usually wore blazers with the name on the pocket and the girls name brooches.

Disliking heavy make-up, she dabbed on powder and lipstick lightly and stepped into slender-heeled shoes. Losing her nerve a little, she moved towards the door. Heaven help her if Jeremy wasn't around somewhere downstairs. She had never needed him as much as she did now.

The lights of Sorrento were just pricking through the rustling trees as Stacey wandered the terraces. There was much to see and the mingling perfume of flowers and may-blossom beckoned from every direction, but her only concern at the moment was to find Jeremy.

She had no idea what the dining arrangements were for the Sunflair staff, and no desire at the moment to go inside and find out for herself. In the half-light she could see the occasional couple, and small groups of people drifting over towards the loggia that flanked the restaurant. Several white-clothed tables were set out along it, but as yet no one had been inclined to sample the warm May evening.

There was no sign of Jeremy in that direction. Uncertainly she turned back along the terrace towards the french windows, and found her way blocked by a striking figure about to step out. Thick set in tight dark suit, and white frilled shirt, the deeply tanned face above it hovered only inches from her own. Stacey could only gulp at its incredible handsomeness. Black waving hair, dark eyes lit with a peculiarly fiery light, and full-shaped lips framing a breathtaking smile. '*Scusi, signorina.*' His murmured apologies were deep-throated and laced with humour as he stepped back to sweep her with a look of undisguised appraisal.

Stacey smiled shyly, about to pass, and then she noticed the guitar swinging negligently from one hand. If this man was employed by the hotel he might know Jeremy.

'Excuse me. I wonder . . .' she blurted in English, and then bit her lip. Oh dear! This was where the language snag came in. As she frowned over the best way to put it, the man turned his head on one side and repeated musically,

'Excuse me, I wonder?'

'Oh, you speak English,' she laughed, feeling quite ridiculous. 'I'm looking for Jeremy Farrow. I wondered if you knew him . . . if you'd seen him?'

'Ah, Jeremy!' he sighed, leading her inside. She felt the long slim fingers brush across the bare surface of her back, and then he was raising a black-clad knee on a chair to support his guitar. 'And you come from England also?' He accompanied the question with a strangely exciting ripple of chords.

Stacey smiled, glad that there was no one else in the room, though she could see people passing by beyond the alcoves. She also had a clearer view of the man now in the light from the chandeliers. He couldn't be much older than Jeremy, perhaps twenty-eight or twenty-nine, yet the face had a lived-in look about it. There were lines of self-indulgence around the yes, a sensuous curl to the full lips.

She heard herself saying a little breathlessly, 'I'm Stacey Roberts. I work with Jeremy for Sunflair Travel.'

'Antonino of the Palazzo,' he replied with a bow. The way he placed the accent on the last syllable but one left her knees weak. 'I know something of this England.' He continued to strum tunefully, turning the dark eyes over her with a lazy smile. 'The streets are filled with horses and dogs and everyone gets lost in the fog.'

'Well, it's a little different from that!' Stacey laughed, trying to imagine horses and dogs in the chaos of traffic. 'We do occasionally get a fog-free day,' she added dryly, aware that the guitar player was looking beyond her.

She turned in time to see a tall figure moving down past the alcoves. Mark Lawford veered in through one of the openings and strolled across the room. She heard him state mildly, 'We're filling up, Tony,' and then he had disappeared through the french windows.

The guitarist dropped his knee with a flourish of rumbling chords. 'And now I must work,' he sighed, 'but we will meet again soon, no?'

He took her hand, held it for too long and then moved off along the terrace. Stacey watched him go, letting out a breath. He hadn't been much help as regards Jeremy's whereabouts.

Luckily her tall loose-limbed colleague turned up just as she was about to explore on her own. The blue eyes took in her dress as he came into the room. 'Gosh, you look terrific! Where's the party?' he asked.

Stacey smiled sheepishly. 'I felt like a first night splurge,' she murmured.

'First and last for us for the time being.' He took her arm as they started to walk. 'You've heard the news, I suppose?'

'That you're going to Rome?' she nodded. 'I think it's terrible.'

He shrugged a smile, leading her towards the restaurant foyer. Stacey hesitated at the sight of a marble staircase leading down to amber carpets and old gold walls. Dark polished wood armchairs circled the wide entrance to the restaurant and in the centre of the room an ornate chandelier hung over a flower-filled table.

Jeremy gave her an encouraging tug. 'It's all yours, silly,' he laughed. 'While you're here you live like one of the customers.'

'So I've noticed,' Stacey smiled wryly, 'and I'm beginning to wish I was one, now I've seen the working side of things.'

'Lawford, you mean?'

She nodded. 'He's everything you said he was and worse.'

As they moved into the restaurant Jeremy made no comment. He seemed occupied with the choice of tables. She was glad when he led her out on to the loggia to a lamplit corner. They were slightly out of the way here and could talk without being distracted.

Once the meal was ordered, a variation of Italian dishes that Jeremy chose, Stacey pursued the subject of his departure for Rome. 'What day do you have to go?' she asked. 'I hope it's not too soon.'

'I'm leaving directly after dinner.'

'Tonight?' Stacey was wide-eyed.

Jeremy grinned. 'Bit of a rush job, apparently,' he explained. 'Our rep in Rome has gone down with a virus and has had to be flown home. Someone will have to be on hand to sort out the new batch of tourists. They're due in tomorrow.'

He refilled his wine glass, and watching him Stacey said with a thoughtful smile, 'You don't seem all that put out about going? Aren't you going to miss ... Sorrento at all?'

'Like the devil.' He seemed to have caught her meaning, for he placed a hand over hers. 'But it's a relief in a way. I'm used to running my own show, and quite frankly this isn't it.'

'Yet you don't mind leaving me in the lion's den,' she twinkled.

'You'll cope. Bigger men than him have been known to bend under that dimpled smile.'

'I don't somehow see Mark Lawford bending even a little finger for anybody,' she said dryly.

'Neither do I,' Jeremy grimaced.

'Who cares anyway? I'll just refer my troubles to head office.'

'My pet,' Jeremy looked up over his fork, 'for you he *is* head office.'

'That's right, cheer me up!'

After that Stacey decided to give her attention to the Italian fare, quite delicious, and the sparkling chianti wine. When the meal was over Jeremy led her down the steps of the loggia and through the gardens towards a cluster of palms.

Swinging his hand, Stacey remarked casually, 'Rome's a fairly cosmopolitan place, isn't it? I don't expect you'll be lonely.'

Jeremy replied offhandedly, 'I know one or two people there. Holiday reps with other firms.'

'Really?' Stacey looked up good-humouredly. 'Male or female?'

'That shouldn't make any difference to you,' he murmured, drawing her into his arms. 'And we'll see each other on our days off.'

'The way it went in the office this afternoon, I don't think I'm in for any such luxuries.'

Jeremy grinned, brushing his lips along her brow. 'Lawford's pretty strong stuff, but he seems a fair-minded bloke,' he said equably.

'It's all right for you to talk now that you're leaving,' she gazed up teasingly. 'My impression of Mark Lawford is that he is considerably less than human.'

'I'd ... er ... hate to have to break anything up, Farrow, but your train leaves in exactly twenty minutes.'

Stacey was suddenly aware of another dark shape beneath the trees. Jerkily she unclasped her hands from around Jeremy's neck and turned away from shadowy craggy features. The vibrant tones, slightly less sarcastic now, added evenly,

'It might save time if I drove you to the station.'

Jeremy ran a self-conscious hand through his hair. 'Right,' he grinned, 'I'll nip up and get my gear.' He disappeared into the night before Stacey had any chance to follow. She took a few steps blindly and then realized that she had no idea which path to take. Nor did she intend asking the man behind.

She felt a wave of relief as a group of laughing guests loomed up from out of the trees, but this quickly dissolved into embarrassment when two men detached themselves from the group and moved in a little too close for comfort. She heard their murmured 'Simpatico' and 'Bellissima', but their flattering remarks were wasted on Stacey. She had but one desire at the moment – to get back to the hotel as quickly as possible.

She said as pleasantly as she could, 'Let me pass, please,' but warm hands were already stealing around her waist.

A sharp comment from behind made the men jerk back with puzzled smiles, and seconds later they were disappearing into the shadows after their friends. The big bulk came up close to one shoulder and she heard Mark Lawford saying tersely, 'It might be a good idea to dress a little more fully for your job out here, Miss Roberts. Otherwise you're likely to find some of the men a little too human for your own good.'

So he *had* heard her last remark to Jeremy! And this was his subtle way of letting her know. She whipped away from the cool fingers steering her on course beneath the trees. 'I'm not a child,' she snapped. 'And I'm not fresh out from England. I can look after myself.'

'You may have hopped around the Continent,' he replied derisively, 'but I doubt if you're on to the guile of the Italian male.'

'Whatever it is I find it rather refreshing,' she said with an acid smile. 'At least it shows they've got something more than ice water in their veins.'

Stacey considered she had put that rather neatly, and coasting along on the success of her retort she added primly, 'And I think you are overstepping your duties, Mr. Lawford. I intend to dress exactly as I please while I'm here.'

'Well, don't forget it depends entirely on me whether you stay.' He took her arm roughly as they came to the steps of the terrace. 'And I certainly don't intend keeping any girl who insists on turning every head in the place.'

The brown glance flickered towards the restaurant and the sound of a guitar. Stacey knew he was referring pointedly to Antonino. She said with fixed coolness, 'I suppose I *am* allowed to make friends.'

'You'd be well advised to steer clear of those kind of friendships.'

'Not more rules and regulations,' she sighed airily. 'And just when I was telling myself the men over here were a vast improvement on ours!'

He smiled above her cutting comment. 'Don't be fooled. Tony might have a cute Italian accent, but nobody knows what part of the world he comes from,' he stated mildly.

Stacey was annoyed to think that she *had* been fooled, but it was even more galling to have this man point it out to her. She had no intention of letting him see it, however, and turned a spirited grey-green gaze upwards to say sweetly, 'Well, thanks for the advice. In any case, I've already decided who I'm going to steer clear of.'

She felt the silk of her hair swish round her face as she swung away, fully expecting her trembling limbs to give out before she reached the safety of her rooms. They held her as far as the small office at least. Here the chair came in handy to flop down on and let out a long breath of exasperation.

Imagine having to spend a whole summer under the same roof as *him*! She smiled wryly at the holiday brochures scattered across the desk. Italy might be all they said it was. But Sorrento was fast losing its charm.

Having slept a good eight hours on that statement Stacey woke up next morning with a complete change of heart. How could anyone fall out with Sorrento, its mountains and flower gardens, pastel-tinted villas, winding roads and lemon groves? Viewing it from her balcony through the pink veil of a jasmine-scented dawn she knew its charm had already taken a firm hold.

Out to sea Capri floated up on a rainbow-coloured mist and beyond, a white nothingness was the edge of the world. As Stacey gazed towards the wide sweep of coast that stretched away to Naples, friendly green lizards whipped back and forth along the balustrade as though they would draw her attention to the view below.

She lowered her eyes to the Palazzo gardens. Apart from the formal area with its smooth lawn, fountains and statues, there were sun loggias and arbors, smothered in pink and white oleanders, and rose walks and terraces shaded by leafy palms and blossoming magnolia. As she gazed towards the trees circling the gardens Stacey's heart gave a peculiar lurch, and this time its behaviour had nothing to do with the view. Somewhere out there last night she had crossed swords again with the man who ruled over all this, and for Sunflair, it seemed. Things had not only started off badly between them, they looked like continuing that way.

She turned inside with a light sigh. Without Jeremy she needed more than ever to be a success at her job, but how could she hope to do anything right when Mark Lawford fully expected her to do everything wrong?

One way of course was to keep clear of him, and happily her work for the coming week would take her well away from the Palazzo. There were all the local tours to go on, a good hairdresser to be located in Sorrento, as well as chemists' shops and places of entertainment. She would need all the facts at her fingertips ready to pass on to the first of the Sunflair holidaymakers, due to arrive a week from today. Working single-handed there wouldn't be a second to lose. She would start immediately after breakfast.

Busy as she was, the days flew by for Stacey. Scarcely had she taken notes on all the advantages and disadvantages of one tour than another was upon her. By the end of the week she considered she knew as much about Sorrento and its immediate surroundings as did any of the residents. Struggling along on half a dozen words of Italian, she had mimed her way on to local buses, horse-drawn fiacres, the odd silver-haired donkey, and an occasional steamer. Now there was only one place on her list to explore – Naples.

She had left it until the last partly because she had seen something of it on her arrival from England and partly because of its size. Nothing less than a day would do to glean all the facts on its museums and palaces and *castellos*. She set off on the last day before the real work began, armed with a street guide and her Italian phrase book just in case.

As Naples was an international seaport Stacey considered it wise to slip her passport into her handbag, also more than enough money to cover the day's outing in case of unforeseen difficulties. The day promised to be another warm one, so there was no worry of carrying a coat.

In a sleeveless peach linen dress with a small envelope handbag clutched in her hand Stacey tripped down the steps of the Palazzo feeling as free as a bird, and almost inspired to sing like one. There was no doubt about it, the butterfly blue of an Italian sky could be guaranteed to put one in a good mood for the day.

She was tempted to take the steamer to Naples, but as she had already done the trip one way it might be wiser to go for the experience of the bus trip. Some of the clients might want to know about the coastal route.

Riding on an Italian bus was always an entertainment in itself, and today's journey was no exception. Everyone going to Naples knew everyone else's business, or was engaged in a passionate attempt to find out. Arms waved, voices were raised and olive-skinned faces drooped or beamed according to the line of conversation. A smiling youth seeing himself as another budding Italian tenor burst forth with the first few bars of *La Mattinata* and the driver, not to be outdone, replied with a bass of *Il Sorrentino*.

Nobody cared about the view outside that thousands came to gape at every year. While they were on the bus it was only the world of the bus that mattered. Food and sweets were passed generously around, and children strutted up and down the aisle to be patted and fondled by adoring adults. The Italians always had time for their own and other people's *bambini*.

One small girl with enormous eyes and a piquant face came to rest a shy hand on Stacey's knee. After smiles were exchanged she scuffled off to clutch round her mother's skirts in an agony of embarrassment. Stacey would have liked more time to strengthen the slender thread of friendship, but already they were pulling into the outskirts of Naples.

Minutes later the people were hurrying down the steps to go their separate ways and the world of the bus disintegrated as though it had never been.

Stacey waved good-bye to the small girl and set her shoulders squarely. After such a gay ride it was difficult to feel even the remotest inclination for work, but work she must if she was to interest her clients in what to see in Naples. Now, where to start? The obvious answer would be to hire a guide. It would certainly save time to be taken around the major sights of the city. After that she could wander along the side streets at her leisure, and make notes of the smaller shops and the picturesque taverns where it might be pleasant to take a glass of wine.

She looked up the local tourist bureau and made her way there with a view to hiring a guide. She was lucky enough to secure one within minutes, and life after that was a dazzle of rare tapestries, varied sculpture and richly ornamented galleries. She saw the famous monuments, toured the antiquarium and ate lunch at a tiny *osteria* perched on a hillside, with a view of the gently smoking Vesuvius on the left and the palm-lined seaside avenues of Naples down below on the right. The latter part of the afternoon impressed Stacey the most. After the guide had gone, she had to admit that though she had seen it all, the two chief attractions of Naples were, for her at any rate, its beautiful views and its people.

It was fun to walk amongst the Neapolitans now, just following her nose along the side streets, which incidentally seemed to wander off in all directions. And it was well worth the detour off the main Via Roma, for here many of the little shops were pure Italian, and dealt in the local cameos, and coral and tortoiseshell articles that the tourists went for.

She noticed that the area grew more closed in as she walked, but to be able to rub elbows with the people, to listen and watch their effervescence as they talked, made up for a slight deterioration in the surroundings. The guide had shown no inclination to take her around this part of the city, and it wasn't likely that any of it would appeal to Sunflair clients; houses with chipped discoloured stucco, and lines of washing hung up high above streets so narrow one could almost touch either side with outstretched arms, but now that she was off duty Stacey found that she rather liked the idea of going in for a little local colour.

Strolling on, she came upon a small *piazza* where several open-fronted stalls seemed to be catering for the local clothing needs. All manner and type of garments swung in the breeze. There was much bartering and shouting, and scowls of angry passion, and radiant smiles, clicked on and off the swarthy faces as though worked by a switch.

Stacey was drawn towards one stall where a silk blouse, embroidered in true Italian style, had caught her eye. She wandered around the garment several times before reaching in to touch it. Should she? She considered and then opened her handbag with a quick excited breath. Why not? All her work was finished for the day. Wasn't that as good a reason as any for buying herself a present?

The stallholder couldn't have agreed more. He had the blouse off the hanger and inside a crumpled piece of paper, barely before she had time to take out the money. Stacey always found the amount of notes one needed to carry in Italian lire slightly overwhelming, and as she had brought far more than she had needed today, the result was a ridiculously fat wad.

She went through the ceremony of counting out the notes, aware that several pairs of fascinated eyes were turned her way, but once the transaction was completed she picked up her purchase with a happy smile. It was a relief to know that she had gauged the price correctly. Perhaps it wouldn't be long before she was counting out Italian lire as unflappably as she did English money.

Though the streets were even closer knit further ahead Stacey had an idea that the waterfront was close by, so she pressed on. She could smell the sea air between wafts of sun-blistered paint-work, and the hot ovens of Italian cooking. As she walked she looked at her watch. How the time had flown! It would have to be just a quick look at the harbour, and then a bus back to Sorrento.

Already the sun was gazing at its reflection in mirrored waters as she turned the last corner and looked up the narrow alleyway to the sea.

She felt a sharp jerk at her hand.

The action was so lightning-swift, so out of the blue that she had walked several steps before anything registered. Even then she could almost believe it had been a trick of the mind, until her own open hand stared up at her. The hand that had, until seconds ago, been curled tight over the small envelope handbag.

A light film of perspiration crept slowly across her brow, and cooled as she spun round and gazed down the empty alley. It was impossible. There wasn't a soul about, and hadn't been for the past ten minutes. Who would have? ... She hurried back to the last corner. Perhaps in turning it her hand had come up against the jut of the wall?

Her heart sank as she reached the spot. She knew it had been too much to hope for to find the handbag lying there on the ground, yet she didn't want to think ... didn't *dare* to think. ... The roll of notes, Sunflair money and a little of her own, and her return bus ticket. If they *had* been stolen, and she might as well face it, the idea was slowly beginning to make itself felt, how on earth was she going to get back to Sorrento?

A knot of dusty-looking children tumbled through an archway and eyed her with puzzled curiosity before resuming their laughter and tearing off towards the sea. Stacey followed almost at the same speed. She had suddenly lost her taste for the small back streets of Naples.

The full view of harbour, mountains, and lilac-dappled sky was there waiting for her at the end of the alley, but Stacey might as well have been gazing at a brick wall. The only picture she could see at the moment was herself trudging along the road that led to Sorrento.

It wouldn't come to that, of course. Crazy to even think of such a thing. There were several places she could go to for help – the tourist bureau, for instance. In fact wouldn't that be the best place to go? She had been there once today. They would be bound to offer some kind of assistance. The only problem was, which way was it from here?

She drew in her lower lip, shivering slightly as a cool breeze rippled across the water. No use pretending she had the remotest idea. The only answer was to ask for directions, and that was going to prove difficult with no phrase book. She cast her mind back to some of the useful words she could remember and tried them out on a couple of dark-haired women who were coming along. The only reply she got was shaking heads, the deep shrug of plump shoulders and backward glances of curiosity.

Well, she wasn't going to get very far at this rate. Perhaps it would be better to walk in what she hoped was the right direction, and see what turned up. She had almost put her best foot forward ready for what might turn out to be quite a trek when something made her heart float a little lighter.

Standing a little way ahead, gazing pensively out to sea, was a uniformed figure, a harbour official by the look of it. She hurried up to him, and as she had hoped he understood her opening sentence. She went on to explain rather jerkily what had happened, and the man listened sympathetically, nodded slowly at intervals. When she had finished he took her arm solicitously and led her along the road.

Stacey felt that some of her troubles were over. She could make up the money to Sunflair from her own account, and the other things would be bound to turn up somewhere. The man was talking now in a mixture of Italian and English. It seemed that she would have to go with him to his office to report the loss and then he would see what could be done. Stacey nodded in relief. Perhaps she wasn't going to have to go wandering round the city of Naples again after all.

Weary of sightseeing, the only thing that interested her now was a seat on the bus back to Sorrento, and the security of her rooms at the Palazzo. When she had mentioned the hotel to the harbour man, he had nodded immediately. It seemed the place was known wherever one went.

In the somewhat sombre room through the doors of an unimpressive building Stacey was given a seat while the man went off to make his report. He was gone such a long time she soon found herself pacing. Half an hour had ticked away before he returned again with a pencil and pad to write down her answers to his questions.

She passed away a further period of waiting by studying the maps on the wall, and the slowly darkening sky through the windows, and then a plump smiling girl came in to ask if she would like a cup of coffee. Stacey would much have preferred something to be happening in the way of getting her back to Sorrento, but she smiled her thanks and sat down again to wait.

Some time later the man came back carrying the coffee. Stacey took it, but she was far more interested in developments to do anything but place it down on the seat beside her. She looked up at the harbour man expectantly and he smiled, apparently pleased with his work. She rose, thinking that she was on her way, but he patted her reassuringly back into a sitting position with, *'Si va bene!'*

Thoughtfully she watched him go. What did he mean things were going well? How could they be? She was still here, wasn't she? Things would be going a whole lot

230

better if he had handed her her bus fare to Sorrento, or put on transport to take her to the tourist bureau. Slightly exasperated, she stared down at the dark syrupy coffee on her lap, and then as something clicked into place she jerked upright, almost spilling the lot. He didn't mean—? ... Oh, good heavens! He wasn't thinking of getting in touch with the Palazzo!

Dumping the cup and saucer, she jumped up and hurried through the door, ready to blurt to the first person that she met, 'Really, I only wanted a few directions. I'm perfectly capable of. ...' But a gloomy corridor flanked by frosted glass doors was all that faced her. She considered for a moment and then hurried outside into the dusk. If she left now the harbour man would probably assume that she had decided on other arrangements for getting back to Sorrento, and leave it at that.

Once outside she breathed a little easier, although the sable shadows laid down by the harbour buildings didn't making walking a particularly exciting prospect. She moved briskly and kept to the waterfront for no other reason than that she lacked the courage to try the side streets. The guide had told her that one could always get one's bearings in Naples by the mountain Vesuvius, so walking towards it seemed as good an idea as any. Some distance ahead, a group of children, the same group Stacey noticed that she had followed earlier, only with increased ranks, stood and stared as she passed and then skipped to her side. They tugged her hands, and then her dress, and blocked her way, dancing in front with impish upturned faces and repeated requests for 'Lire! Lire!'

Stacey smiled wanly and shook her head, but it didn't do any good, not even when she went to patient lengths to explain that what money she *had* possessed had been taken from her. The grubby faces grinned sceptically, small bodies swung on her hands. She was almost being weighted to the ground when for no apparent reason the pressure eased. The children backed off, and with shouts of laughter skipped away into the alleys.

At first Stacey couldn't understand the silence. Or was it silence? She thought she heard a gentle ticking over of a car engine. She turned to see a long open top and ...

Oh no! Mark Lawford sitting at the wheel. In the shadows she couldn't quite see his face, but she had an idea that those leather brown eyes had been raking her for the past five minutes. He leaned across and swung open the door with a swift flick of the wrist. 'Get in,' he said harshly.

Never a wasted word. Stacey twisted a smile inwardly, swallowing back the tears of desperation that had just been about to erupt. Here she was, dust-covered and dishevelled. There were smudges of grubby fingers down her arms, and her hair hadn't seen a comb since lunch time, yet Mark Lawford's only comment was a clipped, 'Get in,' an order as usual.

She slid into the seat and stared miserably ahead, as he started up the engine. The breeze plucked at her bare arms and throat as they sped along the harbour road, and through a maze of gaily lit streets. The car stopped with a jerk at the corner of one and the man at her side dug a hand in his pocket and said something briefly to a woman at a stall who was just closing up business for the day. She stepped forward, handing him something, and beaming her thanks, and then the car was starting up again.

As they swung round a corner Mark Lawford held the wheel with one hand, and reached across with the other. Stacey found a heavy silk scarf being dropped into her lap. She looked nonplussed and he motioned with an impatient hand. 'The women drape them somehow around their shoulders. It's about all I can think of. If I'd have known you were only half dressed,' he drawled, 'I'd have brought you a coat.'

Stacey folded the scarf into a triangle, swung it around her shoulders and knotted it lightly at the throat. It certainly gave her that little extra warmth she needed on an evening when summer hadn't quite made itself felt. They had only been driving for perhaps ten more minutes, when the car stopped again, and this time the man at the wheel got out. Stacey gazed puzzled at the small dimly lit *trattoria*, but one didn't ask someone like Mark Lawford why he had stopped or where he was going.

He strode off inside the building and returned seconds

later to open the door for her. There was nothing she could do but follow him through into an amber-lighted foyer, to where a man, grey and distinguished and probably the owner, was showing her the way to another door. Through this one a woman rose to meet her, and after seeing soap and towel, wash basin and mirror, Stacey proceeded to wash off the day's dust without delay. She was handed a spotless hairbrush and after several brush strokes, the bronze-silk hair was gleaming again.

She held the scarf, noticing its gay colours, loose in her hand, and after thanking the woman, passed through the door again. She was guided by the bowing grey-haired man through a series of arches to a lamp-lit table, where Mark Lawford was sitting back drawing on a cigarette.

Feeling like a freshly-scrubbed schoolgirl, Stacey slid into the seat opposite simply because she was too self-conscious to stand under that sweeping brown gaze.

A glass of golden liquid was placed in front of her. She sipped it slowly, feeling it burn her throat as it went down, and wishing those eyes opposite wouldn't take such an interest in how she was getting on with it.

At last the drink was finished. She placed the glass down on the table carefully. He leaned forward to stub out his cigarette.

'Feeling better?' he asked.

'I was feeling all right before,' she returned primly.

'Sure. You looked it.'

She lifted her gaze from where it had been resting on her hands in her lap, to see the gleam of his disbelieving smile. She noticed his casual attire, lightweight wool shirt and sports slacks, and thought he looked less of an ogre, though there was a thin spear of ice in his eyes. That would be to let her know she had some explaining to do.

Thank goodness she wasn't going to have to start now, for he was already rising from his seat, to what seemed to Stacey, after spending the day amongst diminutive Neapolitans, a tremendous height. He dropped some notes on the table and guided her out to the car. The top was up now, and with the silk scarf, once again knotted at her throat, and a new strength, induced by the drink, flowing through her, Stacey felt as near to herself as she would ever feel with these wide shoulders next to hers.

The car kept up a steady speed now, and thankful that there was to be no conversation she settled herself down to listening to the soothing hum of the tyres on tarmac. Through the open window she caught the occasional perfume of the waxen orange flower, and night-scented blossoms, and gazing towards the sea as the car climbed, it was difficult to make out where the lights of the bay ended, and the stars of the heavens began.

Had the evening been a normal one, and her driving companion anyone other than Mark Lawford, Stacey might even have said she had enjoyed the ride, but things being as they were, she breathed a small sigh of relief when the lights of the Palazzo flamed up out of the darkness. Now slim brown hands were swinging the steering wheel to take in the tree-lined drive, and then the car was pulling up with a jerk below the steps of the main entrance.

A green-uniformed attendant was quickly on hand to park the car, and the tall figure was still behind her as she went up the steps. She turned politely at the top with words hardly likely to suffice, but all she had the courage to come out with was: 'Thank you for coming to Naples to collect me.'

Once inside the chandeliered interior she made a quick retreat.

It took a warm bath, a fresh change of clothes and a touch of her reserve supply of make-up, for her lipstick and compact had gone with the bag, before she felt composed enough to go down to the restaurant for a meal.

Tony was there strumming his guitar as usual. She had become quite used to him smiling and nodding his songs her way, though she would never be used to that nerve-tingling Italian style with which he put them over. Later when he joined the small orchestra of soulful mandolins, accordion and violin, the effect of black eyes watching her beneath half-lowered lids was somehow strangely exciting.

From her own reserved table, she lingered over her wine, gazing around the room, which had the relaxed atmosphere of a favourite meeting place, which in fact it probably was. The Palazzo restaurant seemed to be the haunt of most of the wealthiest residents of Sorrento.

Her glance wandered towards the double doors, to where a laughing group stood in the foyer. Mark Lawford was there, huge in evening dress. There was nothing restricted about his smile tonight. She saw the spark of it hard and white in the tanned features as he moved among his guests. And there was no denying he made a striking figure. The women obviously thought so. They gazed up at him attentively. The men seemed happy to linger in his company.

Stacey swallowed on her irritation and took her last sip of wine. The Palazzo owner might be popular with his guests. *They* didn't have to work for him. She left her table and slipped out past the animated group, catching a slight nod from Mark Lawford as she went. Something in the brown eyes made her feel uneasy – a light that said there was a little matter of some unfinished business to be settled.

Stacey didn't agree. She wanted to forget today and the predicament he had found her in. She would make her own inquiries regarding the lost handbag. As for the suave smiling man back there, she could only hope that his friends in the foyer would steer his thoughts away from business matters for the rest of the evening.

She returned to her rooms not too hopefully. Mark Lawford wasn't the type to forget what was on his mind.

She tidied up the small office abstractedly, considering the possibility of going to bed, yet not really feeling like the concentrated effort of undressing.

The uneasiness was still with her.

It stayed with her as she moved out on to the balcony and strolled for a while. She could hear distant laughter from the scent-laden gardens, and the music and murmur of conversation from where the restaurant tables spilled out on to the loggia.

Saturday night in Sorrento. She took a breath. A week ago she had expected to be spending it with Jeremy. Now he was in Rome, and she was here, and there was only. . . . She took another breath which could have been an inward sigh and wandered off into the bedroom. No sense in brooding over the fact that the job had turned out to be different from anything she had expected. She was here now and there was nothing else for it but to be a success.

Perhaps one way to start off well with the Sunflair holidaymakers would be to get a good night's sleep. She had just spread fingers over the first button of the white nylon dress, when a knock sounded on her door. It was ridiculous to feel a numbness about her limbs as she walked through the lounge to answer it. A perfectly harmless knock, and here she was working herself up into. . . .

The stocky uniformed figure of Carlo was standing outside as she opened the door. 'The Signore wishes to speak with you in his office,' he announced pleasantly.

Oh, heavens! Here we go! She smiled dumbly, closing the door behind her and following him one step behind. Their feet whispered rhythmically over the turf-thick carpets, as they made their way along one of the many upstairs halls and round down the red and white staircase.

There was an air of late night quiet descending over the lounges and alcoves downstairs. A distant thread of music was snapped by the sound of a car engine being sparked into life. Carlo smiled and branched off towards his own station. Stacey carried on, her heartbeats matching her steps, to Mark Lawford's office.

She didn't hesitate at the door but walked straight in, her chin at a nice steady level. He was there, dark-suited and dour, the white of his dress shirt giving only a fine strip of relief, as he stood gazing out of the open french windows, over the garden towards the dimly lit lane that led to the sea.

He didn't turn as she entered, and Stacey didn't sit down this time. She felt far too edgy to be able to keep a seat. After a lengthy silence in which she felt he could have counted every light along the road he said crisply to the night, 'Okay, let's have it. What happened?'

Stacey rested on the other foot stammering, 'I ... thought you knew that. . . .'

He turned and went to pick up a sheet of paper from the desk, flicking it with his finger and thumb. 'I know what I got from the guy at the harbour over the phone. As soon as you reached his office he got in touch with me.' He looked up to train a brown gaze on her. 'Now I want your story.'

Stacey swallowed, thinking of the three facets of the Mark Lawford make-up she had seen tonight. The one where he had dropped a scarf in her lap and sat over her watching her take a reviving drink. The other with his guests in the restaurant; the suave and smiling host in his own domain. And this one – the rigid disciplinarian for Sunflair. This one suited him the most, she thought, fidgeting and starting with, 'Well, you see, I had my handbag stolen . . . and. . . .'

Now it was his turn to rest on the other foot. He did so with a pointedness she wasn't expected to miss. 'Surely you can come up with something a little more original than that,' he said with a barbed smile.

Stacey wanted to lower her eyes, but she wouldn't let herself. She replied somewhat crossly, 'It might not be original, but it's what happened to me. I was exploring the side streets for possible shopping areas, for Sunflair visitors, and then later I saw a . . . well, something I wanted to purchase for myself. . . .'

'An Italian style blouse, I believe?'

She nodded slowly. How did he know about that? And what had happened to it anyway? She hadn't given it a thought after fleeing the harbour offices. She took a breath and continued, 'Well, I bought the blouse and then not long after my bag . . . just went out of my hand.'

'I see.' He leaned over to take a cigarette from a box on the desk and lit it with a heavy lighter. After a long draw he breathed out the words, 'Obviously your experience of the kind of work you fancy yourself at, Miss Roberts, is practically nil. No holiday rep in her right senses would go wandering alone in the kind of area *you* chose.' He flicked a grim brown glance down the length of her. 'It would have occurred to the most feeble-minded amongst them that they were handing someone an opportunity on a plate.'

Stacey lowered her lashes, inwardly seething yet knowing he was right. What could she say? There seemed nothing, yet she couldn't bear to take everything he gave without tossing something back.

The kind of work she fancied herself at indeed! Feeble-minded!

A suitable rejoinder fixed in her mind she raised her eyes to meet his. 'Perhaps no holiday rep would go where I went today, but most of them get time off. I took mine and enjoyed it as I saw fit when my work for Sunflair was finished.' She forced a lightness into her tones. 'I never miss an opportunity to live a little when I can.'

'And you expect to fit the job in between times, I suppose?' He left his cigarette to smoulder in the ashtray. 'You seem to have a penchant for *living*, Miss Roberts, *and* dreaming.'

'I suppose that doesn't make me a good holiday rep?'

'You can't operate with your head in the clouds.'

'I don't see why not. They hide some of the more unpleasant views down here.'

The veiled sneer in his voice had prompted her sharp retort. Unrepentant, she purposely let her eyes rest on him before lightly staring at other objects around the room. When her gaze returned it was in time to see a flicker of humour travel fleetingly across the dark features. He stretched his shoulders up from where he had been draped on the desk and strolled back to the window.

'What was in the handbag?' he asked.

'Money, quite a bit, I'm afraid.' She didn't permit herself the luxury of relaxing. It wasn't over yet. 'My passport, street guides, phrase book and. . . .'

'Phrase book?' He swung round to scowl at her.

She was right. It wasn't over yet. Not by any means.

'Don't tell me you've been wandering over half of Italy for a week and you need a *phrase book*!'

'I'm learning fast,' she said briskly.

He came to stand over her. 'I suppose you know that girls in your line of business should have a thorough knowledge of the language of the country they're working in?' He ran an incredulous hand through the dark

hair. 'It beats me how you got this job,' he said with un-
necessary anger.

'Maybe there were no other takers,' Stacey retorted,
immediately wishing she hadn't. One could only go so far
with a man like Mark Lawford. She had a feeling she
had long since passed her yardage. She was also beginning to feel quite spent trying to match his remarks with
something suitable of her own. All she could hope was
that her weariness didn't show.

In the silence he towered over her, but his face relaxed
before hers did. He said in slightly deeper tones, 'I seem
to be constantly fishing you out of hot water.'

'I hadn't noticed,' she replied with a tremulous tilt of
her head. 'The boys on the boat were merely being
friendly, and I *have* spoken to men in hotel grounds
before.'

'And tonight when you were practically at your wits'
end, on the Naples waterfront?'

Stacey swallowed. He had her there. He knew it, and
she knew it. The knowledge brought tears of defeat rushing to her eyes. 'All right,' she choked. 'It was a stupid
and idiotic thing to do. So now you've found a reason for
dismissing me. You've been looking for one ever since I
arrived. Well,' she flung a drawn smile up at him, 'you
can keep your beastly job. I'm only sorry I had to come
here at all!'

She stormed to the door, but before she reached it he
called her name. She turned, expecting to be helped on
her way with a parting shot, but instead he was bending
towards a drawer in the desk. She saw the silk of the
blouse she had bought that afternoon minus its grubby
wrapping paper. He strode across the room and dropped
it in her hand with a mild, 'You've forgotten something,'
and then watching her, he stated harshly, 'I suppose
that's why you left the harbour offices in such an almighty hurry. To avoid me?'

'That's right,' Stacey explained lifelessly. What was
the use of denying it now? 'I only wanted a few directions. I could have got back on my own,' she mumbled.

'Too bad it had to turn out the way it did.' She
couldn't fathom his tone now. It seemed slightly dry. He

dropped a hand on her arm and led her to the door. 'What you need is sleep. I take it you can find your way to your room.'

For once there was nothing barbed about the comment. In fact if Stacey hadn't been befuddled with weariness she might have said there was something less tense about the hard mouth. His next words, clipped as they were, made her feel lightheaded. 'Let's hope you come off better with the Sunflair crowd tomorrow than you did with the city of Naples.'

Dazedly she made her way back to her room. The twist of his smile stayed with her until her head came down on the pillow, but the coolness of the silk acted like a douse on her brain. She raised herself to stare through the open window into the night.

Was it possible she still had her job, or had she imagined those last deep-toned words? She hugged her knees, picturing again the tight smile, and half-smiling herself in return. There was no accounting for the moods of some men, was there? After such a verbal battle she had hardly expected to get away with her neck, let alone her job.

She studied the stars for a moment and then squared her shoulders slightly. It would be easy enough to imagine it as some act of benevolence on his part, but of course it was nothing of the sort. Oh no! If she went now who would meet the first guests tomorrow? She flopped down, plumping her pillow. She might as well get it into her head from the start that his decision to let her stay had been made purely with Sunflair in mind.

An incompetent holiday hostess was better than no hostess at all. That would be Mark Lawford's view.

CHAPTER THREE

'MISS ROBERTS, you really will have to find me another room, there's this ghastly tree. . . .'

'We're not used to taking so much oil with our food, Miss Roberts, could you have a word with the manager? . . .'

Stacey stretched blissfully on the beach, closing her ears to the echoes of a working day, and listening instead to the laughter of the waves on the shore. It was pleasant here on this quiet half-moon of sand. The Palazzo private beach consisted of two natural coves. One, the largest with all the amenities, was given over to the hotel guests. This one, fenced off by a high rock formation, was used by the staff, and thank heaven for the barrier, Stacey mused, listening to the distant shouts and whoops of Sunflair clients on the other side.

Not that their demands or complaints were anything she couldn't cope with. During her work she had found that holidaymakers on average were always eager to enjoy what was offered, and it didn't usually take long to explain such things as that the 'ghastly tree' was nothing more than climbing bougainvillea and certainly wouldn't attract more insects to the client's room; or that a full English menu was available in the restaurant and it was perfectly in order to ask for it.

Just the same, she wiggled her toes happily, it was nice to be away from it all for a while. And this really was away from it, for though this stretch of beach was available to the hotel staff most of them lived locally and went home on their hours off.

Stacey sat up on one elbow to gaze possessively round her world and then sank back to muse on her first week's work. Had it been a success? She liked to think so. True, she had felt slightly overwhelmed at first, to know that so many people were depending on her, and there was no Jeremy to lean on, but once she had got a routine going things hadn't been too bad.

She had made a point of spending a couple of hours each morning in the office, offering advice on the day's tours, and various local walks. Each night she had arranged some kind of entertainment, and attended herself. The Palazzo offered various forms, from dancing under the stars on an open terrace to watching a display of the tarantella, the local dance. There was also dancing inside, to a sizeable orchestra, and dining and cabaret, in another part of the hotel.

Though she was happy to give herself entirely to her work, there had been moments throughout the week when the band of eager holidaymakers had threatened to engulf her completely, and to make matters worse on these occasions she had been aware of unmistakable wide shoulders hovering in the background. They had stayed there, thank goodness. Mark Lawford was giving her a chance to show her worth. She thanked him for that at least.

Just the same it was possible he didn't think much of her efforts, for towards the end of the week, he had dispatched Maria, plump smiling receptionist's assistant, and wife of the chef, to take over some of her daily duties.

Stacey pondered on this and tried to find an answer in the awning of blue sky, but after a while she relaxed and breathed out a long contented sigh. Why waste time wondering with a man like Mark Lawford? His action had made it possible for her to take the afternoons off each day. Why look any further than that?

Revelling in her own seclusion, she spread her hands in the warmth of the sun, and came into contact with the basket beach bag at her side. She fingered the postcard lying on top thoughtfully. Was Jeremy having similar good fortune in getting time off? She hoped he was, although a few scrawled lines, written hurriedly by the look of it, didn't tell her much. Still, that was Jeremy. She had only heard from him twice during the winter, though they had been fairly close the summer before.

The reminiscent smile drooped slightly at the edges at the sound of scuffing sandals on the flight of worn stone steps, leading from the hotel grounds to the beach. She looked towards the Greek archway, half suspecting yet not fully convinced until a tanned thick-set figure in brief white trunks came into view. Tony again!

She closed her eyes quickly, feigning sleep. Perhaps if she stayed like this, he would spread out somewhere at a distance and leave her in peace, but no – here he was strolling towards her as he had done yesterday and the day before. Stacey bit back a sigh. She certainly hadn't planned to spend the whole afternoon with him again.

She felt his shadow blot out the sun and opened her eyes to find that incredibly handsome face hovering above her own. The shaped lips parted into a white smile.

'Is one permitted to join the fair Inglese who stretches so delectably on our beach?' he asked.

'Please do,' she smiled up, hoping she didn't sound over-polite.

Perhaps it was due to a surfeit of Tony's company these last few days, but Stacey found that her heart didn't swing quite so low at the sound of his voice. Now she was beginning to feel that his words were deliberately soaked in an inner sweetness before they came out.

He spread his towel a little too close to hers, and as he lowered himself, Stacey heard her own quick intake of breath. She might have become slightly hardened to his deep-throated eloquence, but there was no resisting the racy warmth of those dark glowing eyes, the brilliance of his smile.

'I see you like the sun almost as much as I do,' she said drowningly, dragging her eyes away from his.

'A little more, I think,' he smiled, comparing his mahogany tanned limbs with the pale gold of her skin.

'That's hardly fair. I bet you had a head start,' Stacey laughed.

'A head start? What is that?' Tony patted his hair uncertainly as if he thought she doubted the perfection of his dark shining waves.

'I mean you were probably sunbathing while I was shivering in England,' she explained.

'Tell me about sheevering England,' he said absently, his eyes roaming her face.

Stacey knew it was his usual way of opening up a conversation, but she preferred talking to looking at Tony anyway. She readily obliged, knowing he was only half listening, and once or twice his lips came perilously close to hers.

The third time she backed away, half laughing. 'I thought Italy had a law against kissing in public,' she scolded lightly.

Tony looked around the deserted cove and shrugged happily. 'Who is to see?' he asked. Stacey followed his gaze, lost for a reply. A few minutes ago she had been revelling in her own seclusion, now she would have given anything to see the beach littered with holidaymakers.

As muscular arms slid slowly around her she pushed them gently away. 'I ... I'd rather not, if you don't mind,' and then to give her heart a helping hand she added lightly, 'I hardly know you, Tony.'

'Know!' He sighed as though this argument were familiar to him. 'What is there to know, to wait for?' The black eyes were hypnotic as he drew her close. 'This week, next week?' he shrugged. 'In Italia, *ma bellissima*, we live only for the day.'

You certainly do! Stacey felt herself being engulfed in an iron embrace and instantly she knew a wild desire to be free. Why, she couldn't explain. She had been kissed before by men just as devastating, but something about Tony's approach. . . .

A tiny flame of anger flared within her at his persistence, and she had all but brought a hand up to his face, when he pulled abruptly away and flopped back smilingly on his towel. Stacey hadn't time to steady herself before a tall white-robed figure passed across her vision and moved up towards a section of beach near the water's edge. Because she still didn't feel composed enough to look at Tony she watched Mark Lawford throw off his robe and walk off into the sea.

As far as he was concerned, she and Tony might not have been there. Stacey wished ardently that this was so. Heaven knew what slant he was putting on the scene he had just broken in on.

Tony, completely at ease again now, was rubbing himself with sun oil and scanning the magazine at his side. Watching the swift powerful strokes a few yards out, Stacey relaxed a little. By the time the big tanned figure in pale blue shorts was striding out of the waves she had dropped back into her former position of face to the sky, and slim figure encased in a yellow two-piece swimsuit, soaking up the sun.

She knew that the Palazzo owner came down for a daily swim, but she had never seen him down at this time of the day before. No doubt he was here for a quick dip and then it was back to his office again.

Propping her head up negligently on one arm some minutes later, she knew a ridiculous relief at still finding him there, just a few yards up the beach. A towel was thrown round his neck, one muscular knee supported an equally wide arm, as he drew on a cigarette and gazed thoughtfully out to sea.

If Stacey was glad of a third party on the beach just now, Tony obviously didn't share her pleasure. He made one or two attempts at a low conversation, and took it in turns to look at his watch and then at the motionless figure a few yards away. Stacey knew that Tony was due to play in the restaurant very shortly, though he obviously hoped to outstay the other man down here.

Her own time fast dwindling away, she decided to make the most of what was left by abandoning herself to the water. She swam around for a while, averting her gaze from the two figures on the beach. Perhaps when she looked again they would both be gone – but no. Five minutes later as she stepped out from the pull of the waves Tony was still sitting there, watching her move towards him, the black eyes sliding over her limbs in a way that made her feel vaguely unsettled.

Mark Lawford wasn't watching her, thank heaven. His glance was directed more at Tony. After drying off and pulling off her swim cap Stacey draped her towel out slightly more to the side of its original position next to Tony's. Not that it made any difference now, for after a last look at his watch he pushed scowlingly to his feet. He picked up his belongings, flashed a brief smile at Stacey and trudged towards the steps.

Minutes later Stacey felt a shadow fall across her face for the second time that afternoon. The features she looked up into now were a far cry from Tony's. Tight and unbending, and certainly no hint of a smile. Mark Lawford was holding her beach robe. 'No doubt you're eager to sample everything Italy has to offer,' he said with sarcastic undertones, 'but I wouldn't advise too much sun at first. Over-exposure isn't all that good for fair skins.'

Stacey got slowly to her feet only because she felt at a distinct disadvantage stretched horizontal under that dark brown gaze. As the robe was dropped around her shoulders she replied coolly, 'I *have* learnt to gauge it. I don't usually let myself get much darker than this.'

'I'm glad to hear it. The copper over-baked look wouldn't suit you.'

Not that he cared what would suit her individually, Stacey told herself. He was merely stating his ideas on how Sunflair hostesses should look.

He picked up her towel and bag, and Stacey got the obvious message that she was expected to return with him. As they walked he asked casually, 'Heard from the boy-friend?'

As if he didn't know! Stacey felt her irritation growing. The postcard from Rome was there quite plain to see on the top of her bag, but of course he would have to make her feel cheap by asking. She hadn't missed his subtle reference to Tony in that 'sampling everything Italy has to offer' bit.

She returned lightly in answer to his question, 'Just the card. I expect Jeremy's too busy to manage a letter.' Though she couldn't complain of being overworked herself, she found some small satisfaction in implying that Jeremy probably was. There was no comment, however. They climbed between cascading blossoms and flowers, taking the steps slowly in the afternoon heat. Half-way up Mark Lawford remarked idly,

'It's no concern of mine what you do in your free time, but until you get more accustomed to Tony's pace, I suggest you confine your meetings to the garden.'

Meetings! Stacey felt her cheeks flame. So he actually

thought she had been arranging to see Tony. Her anger made her stumble on the steps, and as a steadying hand came out to save her she shook it roughly away. She certainly didn't need *his* helping hand. She took the next step up ahead of him, and turning found a small advantage at being almost on a level with pebble-hard, brown eyes.

'You like to look for the worst in people don't you?' She managed an acid smile. 'Well, for once you're wrong about me. I've no intention of going behind Jeremy's back to meet Tony or anyone else.'

She hadn't intended to watch the effect of her words, but as she turned to swing away, he dropped a hand on her arm. The brown gaze sharpened as he looked at her.

'So Tony's been making a nuisance of himself?' he said evenly.

'Well ... I'm sure he never meant to,' Stacey put in slowly, already regretting her words. She had no wish to make trouble for the guitar player. 'It's just that we both seem to like the beach and. . . .'

'The staff beach has never held much attraction for Tony before,' Mark Lawford said dryly. 'It takes slightly more than sun and sea air to bolster his kind of ego.' The nostrils of the aquiline nose flared slightly as he added, 'Maybe it was a good thing I happened along when I did this afternoon.'

Did he just happen? Stacey would never know. She heard him saying tersely as they walked,

'I'll have a word with him.'

'Oh, really! No,' she looked up, pleading. 'I'm sure Tony meant no harm.'

'He knows my views on dallying with the staff.' The brown eyes swung quickly away, and as he took her arm Stacey let herself be led meekly. He was letting her know that she and Tony, and all the rest of the workers at the Palazzo, were merely his staff.

Around the next bend, the path joined with the one coming up from the guests' beach, and set back under a canopy of trees was a carved wooden seat. Mark Lawford was leading the way to this, and what with the climb, and the tumultous exchange of words between them,

Stacey found that she didn't object to having some support for her knees.

When they were seated he took cigarette case and lighter from the pocket of his robe, and after she had declined his offer, he lit one for himself and drew on it leisurely before stating, 'Handbag turned up, by the way.'

'My handbag?' Stacey looked at him in happy surprise. 'Why, that's marvellous! What about . . . ?'

'No money, I'm afraid,' he shook his head with a half smile. 'Though according to the list you made everything else in the bag is intact.'

'No money,' Stacey echoed, biting on her lip. 'I'll have to make up the loss to Sunflair. Most of it was theirs.'

'We'll leave things as they are for the time being. It may still turn up.'

Stacey didn't think there was much hope of seeing the money again, but she considered it wiser not to argue. A silence descended then in which the warm scented air seemed to envelop them in something like a peaceful moment. The first one, she thought, feeling anything but peaceful inside, since he had rescued her case on the boat.

She didn't know whether to be relieved or disappointed when a party of holidaymakers pushed round the bend of the path and claimed her with shouts of pleasure.

'Miss Roberts! We missed you on the beach! Why didn't you come in for a swim?'

'Hey! Guess where we went this morning, Miss Roberts? Capri! By helicopter too. Gosh, you should have seen. . . .'

Everyone was around her chattering at once, and Stacey, a natural friendliness bubbling up in her, listened and laughed and answered the least difficult of their questions.

Mark Lawford, ignored on the seat, looked on in between lazy draws on his cigarette.

There were several family groups amongst the visitors this week, and Mr. and Mrs. Thompson's two teenage sons were jostling good-naturedly now to get close to Stacey. The taller one having managed to get a hand on her arm led her to the edge of the cliff.

'Look down there, Miss Roberts. You see!' He pointed away to Sorrento and the main beach. 'The third boat from this end. The one with the red stripe.'

Stacey doubted if her eyesight would stand the strain, but she nodded intelligently.

'We went out in that this morning,' he said proudly. 'You should see the colours of the fish they catch out here.'

'I'm glad you enjoyed your morning, Derek,' Stacey smiled up, conscious of freckle-framed eyes gazing down into hers.

'I sure did,' he said absently.

A yell from the others making their way up the path jerked him back to life. He hurried after them, tossing her a grin and a wave.

Stacey was reluctant to return to the seat under the trees. She smiled at her own stupidity. Mark Lawford had probably left for the hotel by now anyway. A deep-timbred voice drawling close behind made her start.

'For a minute I thought he was going to ask you to swim from here.'

In her confusion she stepped back hurriedly almost on to the Palazzo owner's toes. As her hair brushed his beach robe she laughed in jerky embarrassment. 'Derek was just showing me the boat they went fishing in this morning,' she explained, wondering why her heart should go racing crazily by just because she had moved against him.

Without looking up she made carefully for the path again, and when they were climbing more steps he nodded towards the holidaymakers up ahead.

'Going by their conversation I gather it's Ischia to-morrow?'

'That's right,' Stacey replied, keeping strictly to her side of the steps.

'I didn't know it was an overnight stay?'

'Well, it wasn't,' she smiled, 'but I've arranged for us to go up the volcano by moonlight, and watch the dawn over the gulf of Naples.'

'Very original.'

She wasn't prepared for the twist of his smile, but

managed to answer lightly in return, 'Not really. Lots of parties have done it.'

'And this party includes you?'

She nodded. 'As practically all Sunflair are down for the trip, I'll have to go.'

After a pause he breathed, 'And how far do you think you're going to get with some thirty-odd people in tow, and no Italian?'

She looked at him. So that was it! The peaceful interlude was over. They were back to her shortcomings as a holiday hostess.

She raised her chin a little higher to reply coolly, 'I've managed up to now.'

'Only because you've had Maria between you and the obvious language difficulties that would have cropped up around here. I can't spare her for Ischia.'

'You won't have to,' she replied shortly. 'It *is* only across the bay, you know.'

'But still in Italy,' he said annoyingly. 'Or maybe you think everybody is going to speak English for your benefit.'

For some reason that Stacey couldn't explain, his harsh words brought the shine of unhappy tears to her eyes. Staring straight ahead, she said dully, 'Since I'm so completely useless I wonder you don't get someone else to take my place.'

In the pause that followed he swung the brown gaze up to where the holiday group were waving from the top of the steps. 'I'm against making unpopular moves, Miss Roberts.' He drooped a peculiar smile. 'You're such a big hit with everybody else. . . .'

But not with you, she wanted to say, but didn't dare. And what did it matter, anyway, whether Mark Lawford liked her or not? She got on well with everybody else in the world.

He took her arm for the last few steps and stated evenly, 'Since I can't spare Maria tomorrow and we have no one else on hand to make the trip with you to Ischia, it seems there's only one answer.'

'What's that?' Stacey asked dismally. As if she didn't know. He was going to say cancel the trip, of course.

'Me.'

She stopped to swing the grey-green eyes full on him. 'You?' Her heart started to thud in panic. Imagine having to spend two days under *his* eagle eye, knowing that he was watching every wrong move she made! 'I should have thought,' she said unenthusiastically, 'that you had enough to keep you occupied here.'

'Sunflair is my pigeon at the moment,' he returned irritably. 'And what kind of recommendations do you think we're going to get from customers stranded in an alien country, with you and a phrase book for company?'

'You're so sure I'm going to make a mess of things,' she snapped, taking the last of the steps and hurrying through the gardens. 'But then you have been right from the start.'

He strode effortlessly and maddeningly at her side. 'Talking of sure things,' he said crisply, 'Sunflair is out of the red, and I intend to see that it stays that way.'

'In spite of me, of course.' She raised her eyes to give him a grimacing smile and purposely turned off on another route beneath the trees. As the white-robed figure moved off, she slackened her step and after a while walked back despondently towards the hotel.

As a man to work for he was thoroughly unbearable, but ... she watched the muscular frame swing up the steps to disappear indoors ... it must be rather nice to have someone like Mark Lawford pulling for you.

She thought of the head of Sunflair. A girl. Fairly young, Jeremy had said. Twenty-two, twenty-three maybe? And pretty, no doubt. Stacey lowered her gaze to stare wistfully at the blaze of red poppies along the path.

There were bound to be romantic ties, of course. Why else would Mark Lawford put everything he had into getting the girl out of trouble?

The day of the Ischia excursion dawned clear and still and Stacey rose to meet it with mixed emotions. She bathed and dressed in a russet-silk pencil slim affair with no-nonsense cap-sleeves, and a small neat collar. Her hair usually following the curve of her cheek and turning up from her shoulder, she caught back with a slide into a businesslike cloud of bronze curls framing each ear. When she had fastened two small white button ear-clips into position she stood back to view the finished effect critically.

Never let it be said she didn't look the part today!

Everyone was in high spirits during breakfast, and Stacey had to admit that the pleasurable anticipation she was feeling for the trip held only the merest dusting of apprehension. There was no sign yet of Mark Lawford, but no doubt he would time his arrival as faultlessly as he seemed to do everything else.

The hotel bus drew into the drive just after ten, and Stacey stood at the door ticking off the passengers as they climbed in. When everyone was checked off the list she raised her eyes a little unwillingly, but the steps of the hotel were empty. There was just the usual sprinkling of guests strolling the drive and the gardens.

The driver banged impatiently on the side of his bus, and Stacey stepped up into her seat in a haze of specu-lation. So Mark Lawford wasn't coming after all. He had decided against playing the heavy overlord for Sunflair, or perhaps – she turned a downward smile to herself – he'd just got the message that he wasn't wanted.

Watching the vineyards and fruit groves whizz by as they dropped towards the harbour, Stacey tried to tell herself that she was glad the Palazzo owner had changed his mind about coming, but one tiny corner of her heart held out against her relief and nursed its own disappoint-ment.

Everything went smoothly down at the boat, though Stacey had an anxious moment when a uniformed official confronted her with a barrage of Italian just as she was counting the tickets. She stared up wide-eyed, trying to take segments of his conversation slightly slower in her mind, but long before she had a reply ready he just shrugged pleasantly and turned away.

Looking back on the incident as they cast off, Stacey had to smile to herself. Probably the man had only been passing the time of day, but with the Italian language she always felt as if she was being accused of something. The day couldn't come quick enough when she knew a little more about it.

There was no time for further conjecture on her failings as a linguist, for her charges were crowding around wanting to know what route they were taking, and what would be their time of arrival. After the usual light-hearted commentaries on the views and various points of interest, Stacey let the younger holidaymakers take over with their transistors.

She was drawn into conversation with a party of some half dozen couples at the rails, and joined in gaily, laughing at their jokes, and loving the cool fingers of the breeze in her hair. This might be work, she told herself, but it was one of the pleasantest ways she knew of making a living. Especially now with the autocratic Mark Lawford out of the way.

After a couple of smaller islands, Ischia came into view. Stacey saw umbrella pines sprouting from bone-white beaches. There was the ruin of a castle brooding high on a craggy hill, and villages of pink and yellow houses were sprinkled along the coast. The steamer turned in at a narrow entrance and sailed across the mirror-like surface of Porto d'Ischia's harbour.

As her party clustered together ready for the landing, Stacey stepped amongst them to give a rough outline of the rest of the day's programme. Lunch would be at the Hotel Martino, and then a few hours could be spent exploring the island. Rooms were booked so that, alternatively, those who preferred it could have a few hours' rest before the moonlight climb.

Dinner at the hotel in the evening would be followed by dancing and a late night floor show, after which they would make their way to the village at the foot of Monte Epomeo, where small pack donkeys would be available for those who didn't feel up to making the climb on foot.

A murmur of delighted approval preceded the exodus from the boat, and stepping out at the rear Stacey couldn't help congratulating herself on how well things were going, so well in fact that there was a danger of her enjoying this trip almost as much as her clients. She took a deep breath of the warm scented air and came up smiling. A carefree crowd, a sunny day and La Isola

Verde – the green isle of Ischia. Theirs for a day and a night. Why fight it?

Laughingly she prised her release from the young brothers Thompson and moving up ahead, led the way along the waterfront.

If her instructions were correct the first turning up behind the harbour buildings would bring them to the parking lot. There transport would be waiting to take them to one of Ischia's largest hotels, a peach-tinted building set back on a hill across the circle of water. She didn't attach too much importance to the fact that another party was coming up close behind her own. There were other steamers in the harbour, and now that the holiday season was in full swing one could expect to see tourists all over the place.

A lone chocolate-coloured bus shimmered in the heat of the deserted square. Coming upon it, Stacey breathed a small sigh of satisfaction. It was always a relief to know that things were on time. Waiting around encouraged frayed tempers and too many of those could dampen the holiday spirit. Thank heaven it wasn't going to be one of those days.

Happily she made her way towards the driver standing at the door of his machine. The only thing that seemed odd was this feeling she had that the leader of the other party had exactly the same plan in mind.

Perhaps he only wanted to make inquiries. It couldn't be anything else, could it? for this was definitely the Sunflair bus. The name of their hotel, the Martino, was printed quite plainly on the front.

Just the same, the man coming up on a level with her now raised a questioning eyebrow in her direction and hurried forward. This action for some reason prompted Stacey to put a spurt on and consequently the two parties arrived at the entrance to the bus at the same time. Without delay the thick-set black-moustached gentleman thrust a paper at the driver and swept his arm wide for the first of his party to board.

Well, of all the . . .!

Stacey stepped briskly forward, opening her bag for the hotel receipt. She held it up with a smile, although she was hard put to it to find one.

'I think there has been a mistake,' she explained pleasantly. 'This bus was sent to collect the Sunflair party ... and as it's not a very large bus I don't think there would be room enough. ...'

She had been talking for a full minute before she realized that her words were making no sense to the two men watching her. They turned their mouths down and shrugged at one another expressively before shaking their heads at her.

'I'm sorry. You don't understand,' Stacey's smile was growing feeble. She tried again in Italian. Her own special brand, of course. She might have known that every word she had ever learned strung together wouldn't make the right kind of sense.

The other leader threw his glance to the sky impatiently. He burst forth in Italian. Very good Italian. An excellent holiday rep, whichever country he came from, Stacey thought wryly, wincing slightly at the volume of his voice. She argued back staunchly in English, but as the other man swept his arm again, it looked as though there was nothing she could do to prevent his party from boarding the bus.

The driver however had seen fit to place himself squarely in front of the entrance, and though he gazed at both slips of paper nodding and shaking his head alternatively, it was obvious that he was not going to set himself up as arbitrator. From the withdrawn look on his face Stacey gathered that she and the other man were going to have to work it out for themselves.

Moving away, she drew on her lip. What was going to happen? There was only one bus, and two parties waiting to be transported in it. One of the parties was obviously going to be left behind. As Stacey was no match for the volcanic eruption behind, laying down all kinds of law, and waving his arms to prove it, she had a rough idea who was going to come out on top.

Wilting in the hot sun, she cursed her own inefficiency. If only she hadn't been feeling so smug about the smooth way things were going, she might have been a little more prepared for some such difficulty.

As she gazed around Sunflair clients were exchanging worried glances. No doubt the older members of the group were not looking forward to a trek across town, after a morning's journey. On their behalf she made a stand between the crowd and the bus and tried again with Mr. Black Moustache, but her English pleas were lost in his impressive vocabulary. To back him up several members of his party, mouthing his words, began waving their arms impatiently, and apparently this was all the man needed. He drew himself up to his full height, frowned over her, and then pushed her roughly to one side.

Almost in the same second a sharp spate of Italian came across the head of the waiting people. Stacey didn't know what it meant, but it was enough to stop the man in his tracks. He turned and so did she, to see a figure taller than the rest making his way through.

She had thought there had been something vaguely familiar about the clipped tones even in Italian. Now as she gazed on a wide-shouldered physique in pale linen suit, her heart spun in idiotic relief. Imagine being glad to see him!

She watched as Mark Lawford walked over to the driver and entered into what looked like a pleasant conversation. The other man went to put in his piece, but after a while he simmered down, and then nodded and stepped back, shrugging and murmuring something to his party.

Stacey couldn't believe her eyes when a linen-suited arm waved her on.

Before anything else could go wrong, she ushered her perspiring clients forward, assisting the wearier ones up the step. When everyone had seats, the driver climbed up, and Stacey felt a hand on her arm as she moved up into the bus. She had no idea what was happening now, but it looked as though Mark Lawford was here to stay. He dropped down in the seat beside her, and bent his long legs double to fit the space.

In a matter of minutes they were pulling into the grounds of the Hotel Martino, and Stacey wondered what all the fuss had been about. While she and the other man had been arguing like children back there the driver could have done the trip half a dozen times. She sank into the seat miserably. If she had been able to converse coolly and sensibly in the native language, they would probably have settled the matter agreeably in no time.

After a lunch eaten silently opposite Mark Lawford, with the rest of the group scattered happily amongst the white-clothed tables on the dining terrace, she sought the cool of the deserted lounge and a corner armchair. She was followed. Inevitably, of course, but all the fight gone out of her, she said dully to the figure dropping down in the opposite chair, 'I'm beginning to think you're right about me and this job. We just don't seem to go together at all.'

Mark Lawford shrugged and draped back, crossing one finely creased trouser leg over the other. 'These things happen,' he said mildly. 'The Naples ferry made good time today. Apparently it slipped the other fellow's mind that he was ten minutes ahead of schedule.'

So that was how he had settled it? By the steamer time-table. Looking down at her hands she said, slowly,

'It all seems so silly now, and I wish it hadn't developed into an argument. I'm afraid I let the firm down rather badly.'

'No. I think you just gave as good as you got.'

She looked up quickly to see a spark of humour in the brown eyes. Whether she had surprised it there or not she couldn't be sure, but he made no effort to douse it as she said faintly, 'You were there, then? You saw the whole thing?' and then dawningly, 'You've been with us since we left Sorrento!'

'In the background.' He drew lazily on his cigarette. 'I didn't want to interfere in anything you could handle yourself.'

Stacey lowered her lashes. It was a little unnerving to think that those brown eyes had been watching her every move. What had he thought of her performance on the boat? Looking back, it had been anything but subdued. Feeling completely uninhibited, she had let herself fall in with the gay mood of the holidaymakers, but if she had known. . . .

A flicker of annoyance prompted her to return thinly, 'I can't say I care for your spy tactics, but you must be pleased at the results.' She rose from the chair with a fatalistic smile. 'And now that you've proved to yourself just how incapable I am. . . .'

The man opposite didn't speak, as a party of guests gusted through, but she felt compelled to drop back into her seat under the force of the dark gaze.

'You're getting jumpy about your job,' he drawled when all was silent again, 'and tenseness comes over to the customers. As you're bound to be in big demand tonight,' the smile was twisted, 'I suggest you rest up this afternoon.'

Rest! After rising at dawn and completing two hours' office accounts before the day had started, Stacey had to admit that the idea appealed, but she shook her head slowly.

'I couldn't do that. There's far too much work to do,' she murmured.

'I'm the other half of the team. I'll take over.' He met her grey-green stare with a lazy shrug. 'That's what Farrow would have done, isn't it? Since he's helping me out in Rome I might as well return the favour.'

He rose to stretch unhurriedly to his full height. As he turned to leave, his tone brooked no argument. 'I don't want to see you down here again until dinner.'

Stacey rose uncertainly, as he strode away. The bus affair had taken more out of her than she cared to admit, but it hadn't occurred to her that she might be looking as worn as she felt.

Upstairs in her room she slipped the russet dress on a hanger and lay down on the cool of the bed. It was something of a new experience to be ordered to take a break from things, and by Mark Lawford too. After all the hard labour he had threatened her with. Even Jeremy would have expected her to take a half share of the afternoon's paperwork.

Jeremy. Drowsily she tried to conjure up his boyish smiling face in her mind, but tanned craggy features were all she could see, and a white steel-edged smile. . . .

There was a rose glow about the sky when she woke. After a wash and a fresh application of make-up, she felt she could tackle anything. But could she? Mark Lawford in a flexible mood posed quite a question. He held her chair for her at dinner and took his own place opposite her, to let a relaxed gaze drop over the bronze silk hair, brushed smooth to fall behind button-clipped ears, the simple russet dress. 'Chic, I think the word is,' he murmured before removing his attention to the menu.

Later the dancing came as something of a relief, for there was Derek Thompson to lose herself with, in the whirl of the crowd, and after Derek his brother Lance. Though only seventeen Lance had the height of a man, and the same ideas. He held her suffocatingly close, paying almost no attention to his feet, and too much to the tip of her ear.

Middle-aged Mr. Webber proved to be something of a rest cure, for he hardly moved or held her at all, so intent was he on telling her about his bakery business. Stacey listened and smiled. She was used to hearing about the various occupations of her clients.

When an arm came round her for the next dance, she fully expected to be brought up to date with Mr. Popplewell's chicken farm, or it could be that she was due for her next lesson in dentistry.

Looking up ... and up at the face above hers, her limbs suddenly felt as if lead had been poured into them. She wanted to glide serenely on to the floor as though dancing with Mark Lawford was the most ordinary thing in the world, but instead her legs moved awkwardly. She stumbled and was caught up close against him. His smile was reassuring, but there might have been a flicker of irritation in the brown eyes. 'The boy-friend probably has a different technique,' he said suavely, 'but I'm filling in for him, remember.'

He willed her steps to match his own and as they took to the floor he added, 'The pact between you two was to take life to the hilt, I believe. Well, I'll see what I can do.'

Stacey knew he was referring to her speech that first day on the boat, but for the life of her she couldn't make out whether he was being sarcastic or merely bantering. There was no time to question his mood, for as though to give weight to his words he swung her into the serious business of dancing.

The sensation wasn't too unpleasant. In fact there was something a little pulse-stirring about being led so faultlessly over the polished floor. The Ischian music had something of a heady quality about it. As it strummed out its telling rhythm, Stacey relaxed against the muscular frame. The lead in her limbs dissolved considerably and was in danger of becoming water until she steadied herself.

It was really only make-believe, wasn't it? Jeremy was in Rome and Mark Lawford had offered to act as his stand-in.

Whether Jeremy would have taken up the rest of her dances for the evening she very much doubted, but obviously the man holding her believed in living the part.

Stacey's imagination must have been working well too, because she didn't particularly miss not partnering Derek Thompson again, or his brother Lance, or for that matter Mr. Popplewell. . . .

CHAPTER FOUR

As though in answer to the spangling lights of Ischia, an inflated moon climbed disdainfully over crowded stars to make himself the centre-piece of the sky.

He wasn't the only one with confidence. Stacey checked off her list of passengers as they climbed into the bus, without any qualms. This part of the trip could only be plain sailing. The route to the mountain village was a popular one, and donkeys and their drivers were standing by to assist with the ascent. Epomeo was small, as mountains go, and there weren't likely to be any language difficulties in putting one foot in front of the other to get to the top.

Even with Stacey Roberts running things – the soft mouth cradled its smile as she took a step up into the bus – there wasn't much that could go wrong between now and the party's return to Sorrento. Perhaps that was why Mark Lawford had left. She hadn't seen him since the dancing had ended, so it was fairly obvious that he had taken the last boat back.

Through the misty picture in her mind, of a tall figure at the rail on the steamer, she was aware of the driver eyeing her impatiently, and a little impatient of her own rambling thoughts, she took the steps jerkily to wave the all clear.

Being the last one to board the bus, she hadn't expected any assistance from behind. Least of all the kind that made her elbow tingle. It seemed to know before she did that a certain wide-shouldered presence was close by. But shouldn't he have been on the. . . .

Before she had time to ponder on the quirks of men, Mark Lawford had swung up beside her. 'All set?' he asked briskly, and nodded to the driver.

They were on the bumpy road almost before Stacey could take a step, but as a similar commotion was going on inside her she preferred to make for the safety of her seat, without the helping hand of the man behind her.

It wouldn't do for him to know how idiotically her pulses were reacting to his decision to make the mountain trip after all.

It was a relief to find that she wasn't required to make conversation, for once they were seated the man beside her leaned forward to take up a point with the driver who was sitting directly in front. Listening to the pleasant Italian lilt of their exchanges, and watching the flat-roofed oriental-looking houses slide past the window and then the moonlit countryside, Stacey gradually relaxed. It seemed to be all she was ever doing these days, she thought wryly – relaxing one minute, tensing the next. Anyone would think that she was glaringly new to her job as a holiday hostess instead of being a two-year veteran.

This man was responsible for her dithering, of course.

She had been confidently poised when she had thought he had gone back to Sorrento, and in what could only be described as a flap when he had turned up on the bus. But shouldn't she have got over the worst of him by now? Certainly he wasn't the easy-going Jeremy, but she had known other exacting employers before taking up this career.

When was she going to be able to accept the simple fact that Mark Lawford was just another boss? He looked like just another boss. Slightly more massive, of course. She half-turned her head to take in the linen-suited shoulders, the rim of silk circling a tanned neck and contrasting vividly with the thick dark hair. No other man could have quite the same chiselled profile, or the same cool flair for laying down the law, but that's all he was really. Just another boss.

The murmur of voices along the bus suddenly rose to a noticeable babble, as the lamplit road curved outward on to a view. Though Monte Epomeo was a dominant feature of the Ischian landscape, seeing it from the town was nothing like having it lean almost on one's shoulder.

Dusted with the grey of night, its spiral road looking like a grubby ribbon thrown carelessly around it, it displayed its topmost spur proudly against the luminous moon-blue of the sky. Looking at it, Stacey was brushed with the same growing excitement that rippled round the bus. It was quite something to climb an extinct volcano. And how many people got a chance to do it by moonlight?

She was glad now that she had put this trip in the Sunflair itinerary. It looked as if it was going to prove popular with the bulk of the clients. The donkeys waiting at the last village before the climb were the tiniest that Stacey had ever seen, but endearing for all that. They cheerfully carried their loads as if they were bundles of straw instead of buxom and heavy-limbed holidaymakers.

Lucky for the donkeys not everyone wanted to be hoisted to the top. Derek and Lance Thompson scorned a lift, and several of the younger men elected to walk. Soon there was no one left for Mark Lawford to assist into the saddle. He flicked down the list in his hand and turned to check the number with the tattered owner of the team.

As the party moved off Stacey prepared to follow. It didn't take her long to see why the donkeys were one of the local amenities. The track was rocky and loose scree made it difficult to know where to put a firm foot hold. Biting on a smile, she made another attempt. There was bound to be a knack.

If there was she didn't get the chance to acquire it, for a furry body came pushing against her under the clipped directions of . . . who else but Mark Lawford? Before she had time to think about him stepping up close, he had placed his hands about her waist and swung her up lightly on to the back of the animal. As he patted it into action she murmured primly, 'I was going to walk, you know.'

In the moonlight she saw something of his slow smile as he drawled, 'I don't think you need the exercise.'

He meant the dancing, of course. But she had got over that. Or at least she hoped she had. From the position of side saddle she took care not to let her glance rest on the dark shape striding ahead. She hoped too that he would keep on being concerned with the state of the track and not pay too much attention to the heavy silk scarf that she had draped round her shoulders.

Back in Sorrento when she had been preparing for this trip she had taken into account that the night would be cool, and the white cardigan she had put in might not be sufficient to combat a higher altitude. But what on earth had possessed her to pack this particular scarf?

She had brought at least three others out from England.

Ah well! Men didn't usually pay much attention to what they bought in the feminine line. The man up in front had probably never noticed the pattern or the colour of the scarf he had paid for that night in Naples.

They were making good progress, slightly behind the main party, but as it was likely to take some time before they reached the top Stacey felt obliged to make some kind of small talk. It was part of her job to be a good conversationalist, so she might as well keep in practice.

'I thought you'd gone back to Sorrento,' she struck up, simply because it was the first thing that came into her head.

'Disappointed?' He stopped to come level, directing her a quizzical gaze.

'Slightly,' she carped, still searching for her words in the air. 'I thought I was actually going to be trusted to supervise some part of the trip myself.'

'You'd have made out,' he said easily. 'Let's just say I missed the boat.'

He moved up just a little ahead again. Stacey was relieved. Talking hadn't been such a good idea after all. It was too unsettling. Probably because there was something of a bizarre intimacy about going up the side of a mountain on a moonlight night, with a man she had met briefly on her arrival in Italy, and never expected to set eyes on again. Still there had been something just as bizarre about his filling in for Jeremy on the dance floor tonight. To her, of course. Not to him. He was only practising subtle ways of getting her to eat her words about 'living it up'.

She had enjoyed getting under his skin that day. Now he was entitled to get a little of his own back. However, she mused, lulled into a dreamy state by the gentle sway

and clip-clop of the donkey, things hadn't been too difficult to weather so far. A sense of well-being stole over
her. She was almost tempted to test her confidence with
words again, but decided against it just in time.

Talking up here wasn't the same as confronting him
across a desk, or with the space of a room between them.
Far better, Stacey decided, to keep her conversations
with Mark Lawford for more workaday places. And since
that was him off her hands, she gazed round at the ever-
changing scenery, there was nothing for it but to give
herself up to the sheer adventure of this trip.

The palest whisper of saffron spread over the sky, as
the donkey caravan came to a rest a few feet from the
summit. Everyone was out to secure the best position
for viewing the bay, but before they could scatter, Mark
Lawford made it perfectly clear that no one was to
attempt the final narrow spur.

The Thompson brothers looked slightly disgusted on
hearing these firm orders, but it was doubtful if anyone
else had had any thoughts of balancing up there over
the sheer gaping drop all around.

Stacey was quite satisfied with her look-out. She had
wandered a little way round the curve of this last slope
and come upon a wide grassy platform. Resting back
against the tall moss-covered rocks, she saw that the sea
was still under the dominant hold of the moon's silver
glow. But there were signs that his supremacy was about
to be contested. Businesslike tendrils of puce, flame and
burnished copper were pushing up from the rim of the
horizon. Stacey settled herself to watch the battle.

Her seclusion was short-lived, however, for Derek
Thompson and then his brother came pushing round the
jut of the rock.

'So there you are!' The elder of the two spoke almost
accusingly. 'I must say I think it's a bit thick. We come all
this way up and then we're not allowed to go to the top.'

Stacey followed his gaze to the fat finger of the spur
that poked up against the lightening sky. 'It doesn't look
all that safe to me,' she said frankly.

'Rubbish,' Lance snorted. 'It's a piece of cake. Dozens

of people go up there.'

'Perhaps not in this light, though.' As the younger brother continued to pace sulkily she asked lightly, 'Have you spoken to your father about going up there? What did he say?'

'What do *you* think?' Lance returned scathingly. 'Said I'm not insured against diving off a mountain.'

Stacey bit back a smile and turned to wait for the next barrage from the older brother, but Derek's face had smoothed out considerably. As he looked at her, he seemed to have got over his discontent.

'I've got a raincoat, Miss Roberts, if you'd care to sit down?' he offered eagerly.

'I prefer to stand, Derek, thank you,' she smiled. 'I wouldn't want to miss any of the view we came to see.'

'View!' Lance mocked, swinging a baleful glance around. 'Tame stuff, if you ask me. I bet from up there. . . .' His eye came to rest on a small peak slightly lower than the spur. 'What about that?' he pointed. 'Can I climb that one?'

'Well, I'm not sure. . . .' Stacey hesitated.

'Aw, for Pete's sake! Get going,' Derek said impatiently. 'And take it easy.'

As Lance loped off his brother moved in closer.

'Is it okay if I stay and watch with you, Miss Roberts?' he asked, settling in.

'I suppose it will be all right,' Stacey said slowly. She had an idea that Derek had other things on his mind. He had brought his shoulder close to hers against the back rest. She could feel his eyes on her.

'Gosh, you're pretty, Miss Roberts,' he murmured to her ear.

'It was the view we came to see, Derek. Remember?' she said lightly, ignoring his remark and staring pointedly out to sea.

Some minutes passed and then he announced, not moving his gaze, 'I'm going to see if I can make it back for another holiday. On my own next time. You'll be here, won't you?'

'I'll be here, and up to my neck in work, I shouldn't wonder,' she said gently discouraging, and pushing herself away from the rocks. Perhaps this wasn't the ideal spot to watch the dawn after all.

'Yes, but you get time off,' Derek persisted. 'And we could always. . . .' He was just about to move in close again when two figures appeared round the corner – Lance, looking slightly dishevelled, and Mark Lawford at the rear.

'I should keep a closer watch on this idiot brother of yours, Thompson,' the latter barked. 'Unless the two of you are looking for a short cut back home.'

Lance grinned ruefully as his brother's eyes swung up towards the peak and then back to roam over the other's scratched arms, and dusty slacks, ripped at the hip pocket. 'Too steep,' he shrugged. 'I had to come down on my. . . .' he petered off in embarrassment and turned from Stacey.

She saw Derek's face tighten slightly in angry concern as he dropped an arm about his brother's shoulders. 'Leave you a minute and what happens?' He blew his exasperation to the sky and led the other away.

'I was thinking,' Lance grinned as they disappeared, 'it might be better if you told Dad that I. . . .'

Stacey didn't hear what the explanation was to be. Mark Lawford's footsteps scraped on the gravel amongst the grass and drowned out the sound of receding conversation. After settling for a spot a few feet from her, he stood so long gazing out to sea she felt pressured into making some comment.

'So much commotion,' she ventured slightly. 'I'm beginning to wonder if I'll ever get to look at the view!'

'You didn't seem all that interested in it just now,' he returned icily, 'or the fact that as a holiday hostess, you're not supposed to let yourself be monopolized by any one member of the party.'

'I try to avoid it,' Stacey replied, a little taken aback at his foul mood.

'Well, one tip is to stay in with the main party. It helps to discourage advances from hot-head youngsters.' His words made the colour rush to her cheeks. She heard him add with a slight sneer, 'Ideas can get a bit fanciful at that age, or maybe you've noticed?'

'No, I hadn't noticed,' she stepped forward, breathing quickly, 'and since Derek and I were merely having a discussion. . . .'

'Oh, sure! With kid brother playing gooseberry. Is that why you packed him off to break his neck on the rocks?'

'Apparently it's not only *boys* who get wild ideas,' she retorted witheringly. She had taken a step away before a hand came down roughly on her shoulder.

'Lost your taste for the view too?' he vibrated, swinging her towards him.

'It probably looks better from another spot.' Her face, pale now with emotion, was turned upwards defiantly. He gazed down at her for some seconds, and then something seemed to slacken inside of him. He dropped his hand to say with a mild testiness,

'I doubt whether Farrow would care for the idea of you sloping off alone.'

Jeremy! Stacey thought of him with a slight shock. She had almost forgotten that Mark Lawford saw himself as something of a stand-in for the other man. It looked as though he was setting himself up as keeper too.

In slightly deflated tones she murmured, 'I don't think he would object to me watching a perfectly innocent dawn.'

'Maybe not,' Mark sloped a tight smile and Stacey thought he would move off, but he took a position a little behind her. Thankfully the view below was enough to take some of her mind off his presence.

The sea had taken on the molten gold of a new day, and two islands were set like black stepping stones reaching to the rose-tinted mainland. Stacey opened her bag, but before she could get to her guide book, the voice came lazily from behind.

'The smaller island is Vivara. The other is Procida or Isola di Procida, if you want it in Italian.'

Stacey nodded, keeping her attention on the view.

'See the one past the cape?' A linen-suited arm came level with her shoulder. 'That's Nisida. Naples is just round the point.'

She turned her gaze to the ever-lightening bay with its

shot-silk dazzle and edging of misty mountains. The arm dropped lightly across her shoulders.

'We just miss Sorrento here,' he pointed. 'You might be able to pick out Castellamare slightly lower down the coast.'

Feeling the warmth of his fingers beneath the scarf, Stacey said a trifle quickly, 'Capri looks completely different from this angle.'

'You're lucky to get any view,' he smiled. 'She usually hides herself in the mist for visitors.'

Under a sky violent with pinks and lilacs Stacey asked matter-of-factly, 'Have you been up here before?'

'A couple of times. When I first came out here, about fourteen years ago.'

'Fourteen years?' She turned slightly to look up at him. 'And you've been in Italy ever since?'

'Well, I sampled a few other places first.'

'But you settled for Sorrento?'

He nodded. 'I split my time between the Palazzo and England.'

England and the Sunflair girl, of course.

She moved a little away from the encircling arm to gaze intently at the view. 'We couldn't have picked a better day,' she remarked brightly. 'It's all quite breathtaking.'

'I reckon you'll have a few satisfied clients on your hands.'

She turned quickly at his dry comment. 'Does that mean I'll be able to bring another party up?' she asked.

He shrugged under the flicker of a frown. 'I don't know about that. You've got your work cut out in Sorrento. A guide is the usual answer to organized sightseeing groups,' he pointed out casually.

'But think of the money I'd be saving the firm!' Her carefully aimed remark brought a spark of amusement to the brown eyes. He let it go without comment and lowered his gaze to her shoulders.

Stacey had forgotten about the scarf until he came to finger it with a negligent smile. 'Finding it adequate?' he asked.

She lowered her eyes in confusion and pretended to

be examining the colours beneath her chin. 'It's the only one I had to bring with me,' she lied. 'I ... realize I should have returned it to you, but. . . .'

'Keep it.' He dropped his hand abruptly. 'I'm not likely to find a use for it.'

The climbing sun picked out a taut mouth in tanned features, and turning, Stacey realized with a slight jolt that the day was completely launched.

'Well, that's it, I suppose,' she laughed shakily to the sky. 'I bet everybody's thinking about breakfast.'

'I bet,' Mark replied laconically, guiding her round the curve of the rocks.

One shouldn't welcome someone else's misfortune, but when Mrs. Browning, the dentist's wife, developed a slight attack of migraine, Stacey couldn't help jumping in to offer her assistance. Anything to save her from making the journey down with a certain man and a donkey again. And though the attack had almost worn off by boat time Stacey made sure her attention was fully occupied with the lady's indisposition right up to arriving back at the Palazzo.

Life after the Ischian trip settled down into something near to a routine. The June nights were warm and with the holiday season under way there was dancing on the terrace, midnight bathing, and lively discussions in the hotel lounges.

Stacey talked and mingled with the Sunflair guests as though she had known them all her life. Sometimes she felt that she had, but that was only because their holiday exuberance was catching and it was easy to pretend that her days could be lived with the same gay abandon.

Occasionally, in the midst of an animated group, she would turn her laughter outside the circle to come up against a familiar brown gaze. The Palazzo boss, just seeing that she was getting on with her job, of course. She wondered sometimes if he objected to her enjoying her work so much, for often there was the suggestion of a frown drawing the dark eyebrows together.

Or perhaps he was still thinking of the Ischian trip and the muddle she had got herself into over the hotel transport. More than likely this was the explanation, for there had been no more sightseeing tours led by Stacey Roberts. Her only connection with names like Vesuvius, Pompeii and the Amalfi drive was in booking and arranging the trips.

Stacey couldn't really say that she was sorry. Supervising some thirty odd people at a time round a strange country could be quite a strain, even though her knowledge of the Italian language was improving considerably. Thanks to Maria's daily coaching, difficulties in that direction would soon be a thing of the past.

On the whole Stacey considered she wasn't doing too badly without Jeremy's help. Nothing had turned out as drastically as he had forecast, thank heaven. If it had she would have been packed off back to England long ago. As it was she had been given a chance to handle the Sorrento business almost on her own, and was actually making a go of it.

Mark must have an unrock-like streak in him somewhere. She would never have guessed it, confronting him that first afternoon in his office.

One thing worried Stacey about Jeremy. She couldn't make up her mind whether she missed him or not. She wrote to him regularly telling him of the events taking place in Sorrento, and putting her letters in with the outgoing Palazzo mail, but his absence seemed really no worse than it had done all winter. His writing hadn't improved either. So far she had only had two postcards and one letter from him.

At first on slitting the envelope and seeing four closely written pages, she had thought that she was at least going to learn how life was treating him in Rome. But racing over the words she had seen that the letter was filled mainly with descriptions of the city and very little about himself. Something on the lines of her own letters from Sorrento, Stacey had mused with a half-smile.

Maybe he was just as stuck for something to write about as she was. Or too busy to make the effort. Certainly Stacey had plenty to keep her occupied. These were the days when life was full and there were dozens of entertainment-hungry clients to be satisfied with this

271

suggestion or that advice, days when she hardly gave Jeremy a thought.

But there were other occasions when she knew a wistful longing for his company. Times when the evenings were still and heavy with the perfume of jasmine. When the world seemed to be made up of couples and the pulse of all Italy seemed to throb in the music that drifted out from the lamp-lit tables of the restaurant. Even Mark would be paired off then, dining intimately with some enamelled beauty down from Rome.

Stacey learned that most of Italy's celebrities came to Sorrento some time during the summer, and invariably the female contingent made for the Palazzo. She had never seen such elegance in clothes, or such fantastic beauty in figure and bone structure. She had to admit, too, that on the occasions when she had gazed from the darkness of the gardens into the restaurant, Mark looked good with any one of his guests. Big and vital in immaculate evening dress, he always appeared at ease, whether he was partnering a sheath-gowned, sloe-eyed model-type, or a grey-haired, black-velveted dowager.

Young or old, there was always someone. They must think he had something, Stacey decided, wondering why her heart should feel tight. Why should she care if half the women in Sorrento wanted to dine with him? And why should it matter to her that he obviously enjoyed it?

It was on these nights when she was wandering alone in the gardens that Stacey usually came upon Tony. He hadn't been singing to her quite so blatantly in the restaurant lately, and she had noticed on one or two occasions in the hotel when he had been talking to her in that throaty accent of his, how he had turned quickly away at the sight of a certain wide-shouldered figure.

Mark must have said something to him. What, Stacey didn't know, nor did she particularly care. She might be just part of his hotel staff, but she felt she was entitled to do what she liked in her own time. Why should *she* feel restricted?

In any case the handsome Tony always seemed to be on hand when her clients had coupled off, and she was left at a loose end. There was something just a little heady in selecting his company rather than sit out the star-spangled evenings in her room. Heady, because he invariably walked with an arm about her waist, and once or twice in the seclusion of the trees, those shaped lips had brushed her cheek.

Sometimes in her saner moments, Stacey wondered if she was right to encourage his friendship. Other times, usually when he was approaching with that Adonis smile of his, she would ask herself what harm there could be in just walking and talking in the hotel grounds.

What harm? None, perhaps, if she had kept things that way.

It was the night when she was due to escort a party into Sorrento that Tony suggested another way of spending the time. There was over an hour to go to the time of departure and she had been wandering in the half-light through the formal gardens when he caught up with her.

How they got on to the subject of caves she never could remember, but the ones the sea had scooped out along that part of the coast soon became a firm topic of the conversation. At first Stacey was vaguely excited. She had heard a lot about the grottoes and their changing lights, and knew that they were a must for visitors. But when Tony suggested that they explore the ones dotted along the hotel beach she stared.

'Tony! We couldn't go looking at caves at this hour,' she laughed incredulously.

'It is the best hour,' he shrugged with that slow smile of his. 'Most perfect to see the glow of dusk on the waters.'

'Waters?' She looked up, hoping her smile hid her relief. 'Of course, there are boatmen, aren't there, and they will row you around, I believe.' The grey-green eyes were alight with interest now. 'I've heard that some of the openings of the caves are so low that the men can only just manage to get their boats through, but once you're inside. . . .'

'Si, si,' Tony nodded, lowering his gaze. 'But we must hurry.' He took her hand and pulled her gently in the direction of the beach steps.

Stacey hesitated. Something in the way he brushed his fingers along her arm made her clutch at her most valuable excuse. 'I really haven't time to go tonight, Tony,' she smiled. 'I'm due to take a party out in less than an hour from now.'

'So?' he shrugged. 'I too must play again this evening. It is but a short way.'

'But what about the boat ride?' she asked. 'Surely that will take some time?'

'Oh, that.' She wondered if she had imagined the pause. 'Well, a boat ride does not take very long.'

With the time factor out of the way it looked as if Tony was taking it for granted that she had accepted his offer to show her the caves. But though he drew her coaxingly towards the steps, Stacey didn't move. Something was holding her back. She didn't know what.

Perhaps if she hadn't turned at that precise moment to see Mark strolling the terrace with an exquisite vision in lilac tulle, she might have decided against accepting Tony's offer. But something about the way the slim figure raised itself to drop a kiss on a tanned cheek made her want to lose herself for a time. Why not in the cool dimness of Sorrento's caves?

Tony's eyes deepened to a peculiar glow as he led her to the steps. He talked continuously in that low and lilting accent of his, and Stacey listened in fascination. She found that he could take the most ordinary sentence, and make it sound as though it had been set to music.

She smiled to herself as they walked down the dim-lit descent. Wherever he came from Tony certainly favoured the Italian line of approach, and in a way her dress was fitting for the occasion. She was wearing the Italian-style blouse that she had bought in Naples. Perhaps he was a little flattered by her choice of attire.

Perhaps that was why he was holding her so close now. Half-way down to the beach Stacey felt her smile slipping away. Taking its place inside was a faint whisper of apprehension. It was almost dark now. What could they possibly hope to see of the caves?

She relaxed, feeling foolish. They would be artificially lit, of course. How else could the boatmen hope to do business all through the evening? Now that that was cleared up she walked with a lightness in her step, suddenly eager to experience the beauty of the underworld. Her mind happily working on light and colour, the effect of stepping down on to a beach lit only by a strip of night-grey sky and a handful of stars came as something of an eerie shock. The place was not nearly so inviting as when it was flooded with sunshine.

She scanned the deserted stretch of sand for signs of life. Heaven knew where the boatmen were hiding themselves, or what business they hoped to attract leaving it to the customers to search them out. As her eyes grew accustomed to the dark she saw the sea, motionless and dull, as though it had been flattened into sullen submission by the weight of the night. There were no boats.

Something occurred to her then. Strange that none of the Sunflair guests had mentioned anything about picturesque grottoes on this stretch of the beach. And stranger still, how were she and Tony going to be rowed into the caves, when the strip of sand was yards wide as far as the eye could see?

She schooled herself into not jumping to silly conclusions. Ever since she had started out she had had one qualm or another. Perhaps now she was thinking of the last occasion that she had been on a deserted beach with Tony.

But why think of that? Hadn't they walked often alone in the dark since that day? They had. She swallowed. But always in the vicinity of the hotel and its guests.

To harness her soaring nerves she said with an attempt at lightness, 'Where is everybody? Anyone would think we were the only two people down here.'

'Is there anything wrong with that?' Tony's arm tightened about her waist, and something tightened in Stacey's throat.

She pushed her words out jerkily at the same time forcing a smile. 'There's quite a bit wrong with it, Tony. We're looking for a boat, *and* the boatman. Remember?'

'What do we need with a boatman?' The flash of white teeth didn't look all that attractive in this light, or perhaps it was the peculiar slant of his smile.

They had been walking since they had stepped on to the beach, but now Stacey stopped. 'We need a boatman to row us,' she said crossly, and then in reply to his smiling silence, 'Tony, you did say we were coming to see the caves.'

'But we are! Be patient, *bellissima*.' Laughing softly, he led her on. Stacey moved her feet through the soft sand reluctantly. She was certain now that there were no boats down here, or boatmen, or lights. What was Tony up to? She began to get a sickening feeling that it had been unwise to come this far from the hotel with him.

Why hadn't she taken more notice of the tiny warning signal that had sounded in her mind at the start?

They had been veering in towards the cliff. Now she was being led to a yawning black mouth in the base of it.

'You see!' Tony laughed, with a sweep of his arm. 'Did I not say a cave?'

Stacey gazed at the rock-strewn interior and glistening bumpy walls. She turned abruptly. 'You said *caves,* I believe, *and* boatmen and. . . .'

'Oh, come, Stacey. You didn't really think that there would be anyone here but you and I?'

He seemed to take it for granted that her mouth was waiting for his lips. Stacey knew now that she had never wanted anything less in her life. She swung her face away palpitatingly.

'I most certainly did,' she snapped. 'But apparently I was mistaken.' And then in the iciest tones she could manage, 'I'd like to go back, Tony.'

If she was annoyed, it was nothing to Tony's mood. He gripped her tightly, the black eyes smouldering above an angry mouth. 'Why do we go now?' he queried tensely. And then, scowling down at the turned cheek, 'There are some things we men give much time for, but I have given too much already, I think.'

As he held her suffocatingly close Stacey endeavoured to keep up a sensible conversation. 'If you're referring to the walks we've been taking in the evenings, I'm sorry Tony, I thought . . . well, if I'd known they were leading up to this. . . .'

'What else?' he said in subdued tones. Her heart turned over at the message in his eyes. He brought his head down, murmuring, '*Chi la dura la vince.*'

A rigid Stacey, trying to sound flippant, inquired with a weak smile, 'My Italian's improving, but I'm afraid I. . . .'

'*Chi la dura la vince,*' he repeated musically. 'Perseverance brings success.'

The flame of anger that shot through Stacey gave her the strength to push away from the descending lips. 'I don't think I care for your proverbs, Tony,' she said shakily. 'Something on the lines of exploiting a friendship might be more like it.' Her bare arms throbbed from the grip of his fingers as he blocked her path. Defying his smile, she said flatly, 'I think we should go back now.'

He didn't speak, but she knew he had no intention of falling in with her plans. Her senses reeled at the power of his embrace.

Muddled as she had been about her feelings for Tony over the past weeks, there was one thing she was a hundred per cent sure of now. She didn't want his arms about her. Not tonight, or any other night. Summoning all her strength, she shook herself free.

In her confused state it was some seconds before she realized that she had staggered towards the back of the cave instead of the opening. With a deep-throated laugh Tony wasted no time in following. But perhaps hers hadn't been such a disastrous move after all, for as he reached towards her, his foot came into contact with one of the loose rocks scattering the floor of the cave.

What happened after that Stacey didn't wait to find out. Tony might have sprawled headlong, or merely lost his balance, but in the moment that he was temporarily occupied with staying on his feet, she saw her chance and took it.

She didn't stop running until she was in the lights of the hotel grounds. Aware that the silk of her blouse had given way under the grasping branches of trees brushed too closely on her flight, she clutched at her shoulder, and hurried into the hotel. What she must have looked like didn't bear thinking about, but luckily nobody paid much attention to the slightly dishevelled figure making for the staircase.

She had thought she was going to make it unmolested to her room, but as she turned the top of the stairs Carlo came hurrying to her side.

'The Sunflair party have been waiting for some time, *signorina*. They are. . . .' He stopped talking to eye her curiously.

Stacey kept moving with her head down. 'I'll be there in a minute,' she nodded jerkily. In the nightmare of the last half hour she had completely forgotten the scheduled trip into Sorrento.

Carlo, keeping up with her pace, murmured with heavy concern, 'The Signor has asked me to remind you. . . .'

'Just give me a minute, Carlo,' she almost sobbed in her irritation, and then fled to her room. Once inside she lay back on the closed door, swallowing back hot tears, and trying to regain a reasonable composure. Nothing could blot out the picture of a dark face smiling above hers, but she had to somehow keep it at bay for the rest of the evening. They were waiting for her downstairs, and already two or three minutes had elapsed. She must change as quickly as possible.

With an effort she moved across the room, but came up against a chair as a shiver gripped her. So much for her friendship with Tony! How could she have been such a fool as not to know what he had been leading up to? And worse still, how did she stand with him now?

She had made it crystal clear what she thought of his antics, but somehow she couldn't get rid of this feeling that Tony wouldn't be prepared to let it go at that. Paling considerably under these deliberations, she hadn't noticed that the door had opened. Nor did it register for some moments that the Palazzo owner was standing there.

When she did finally become aware of his presence he had closed the door and was striding across the carpet.

'What's wrong? Are you ill?'

The harshness of his tones brought Stacey upright. He

was annoyed about her keeping the guests waiting, no doubt.

'I'm . . . perfectly all right. I was just going to change,' she returned steadily. As his eyes swept over her she saw the mouth tighten slightly.

'What happened?' he snapped.

'Just a slight misunderstanding.'

'About what?'

His rapier-like questions did nothing to ease the turmoil going on inside her. She swung over-bright eyes away to reply chokily, 'If you're going to start on about the correct procedure for a holiday hostess, well, don't bother. I know I'm late . . . I've already told you I. . . .'

'You said something about a misunderstanding.' He stood over her, with no signs of letting up, and Stacey was goaded into replying,

'Tony had the idea that I'd like to see your precious caves, only they weren't lit up and supervised as I thought. . . .'

'I see.' He was silent for so long after that that she wondered what he did see apart from the tear at her shoulder, which his eyes seemed to be riveted upon.

'It's not as bad as it looks,' she said with a shaky wryness. 'I hooked it on a tree making my own way back.'

'It's bad enough.' The brown eyes seemed darker in the taut features as his glance lowered over her bare arms.

The full shock of seeing the ugly marks of Tony's fingers there made Stacey slump against the chair in distaste. She said on a slightly high-pitched note, 'From now on I think I'll stick with the clients to view the Italian scenery,' and then turning blindly, 'I'll have to see if I can find a long-sleeved blouse. They'll be. . . .'

'Stay where you are,' Mark strode across the room. 'I'll get Maria to take over for tonight.'

He was angry, Stacey thought, and for once she couldn't blame him. Her little adventure with Tony had left her in no fit state to take a party into Sorrento. That meant extra work for someone else. But she could go if she made the effort.

'Please,' she turned, 'I don't want any favours, I'd

rather. . . .'

He dropped his glance before turning on his heel. 'I can't risk you going completely to pieces down there,' he barked. 'Do as I say!'

She stared for some moments at the closed door, and then pulled out of the torn blouse, dropping it as though it were hot. In the bedroom she decided to be rid of the patterned skirt too. She bathed her arms and face, shrinking from the ghastly pallor and huge eyes that stared back at her from the mirror.

Slipping into a pale frilled negligée, she wandered slackly out on to the balcony to gaze up at the stars. Out here, at least, everything seemed normal. It was only inside that Stacey felt different. Things were going on there that she found difficult to understand, had been ever since she had set foot in Italy. She had thought that a friendship with Tony might be an answer to some of them, but he had turned out to be the opposite of everything her unsettled heart wanted. She slumped against the balustrade. Nothing had been proved more conclusively than *that*.

'Get this down. You'll feel better.'

She turned to find Mark standing directly behind her. Staring up, she was vaguely aware that he was holding a small glass of yellow liquid. Her heart started to pound at the nearness of his great bulk, as though it had been caught out in something.

She turned quickly back to the night again. 'Why do men always come up with a drink on these occasions?' she asked wryly. 'I really don't need anything. I feel perfectly all right.'

'I'll believe it when you start looking less like death.' He took hold of her fingers and turned them around the glass.

She had no option but to drain the glass, otherwise he might never move away. The liquid induced a deep shudder, but she felt better after it. Better, until she saw that a sun-chair was being placed behind her knees, and Mark was saying, 'I want the whole story.'

So that was why he had come back! He wanted a full explanation so that he could decide whether she was justified in missing a night's work.

'There isn't one.' She sank down listlessly. 'Tony misinterpreted our meetings and walks in the gardens. What happened tonight was as much my fault as his.'

'For pity's sake! Don't try and whitewash the man!'

Pacing the balcony, Mark suddenly swung round on her and Stacey found herself slightly taken aback at his anger. Some of her surprise must have shown for after gazing at the wide grey-green eyes, he jerked a hand through his hair and then reached into his pocket for a cigarette. Drawing on it deeply through the flame of his lighter, he took his time before saying with a grim smile, 'Our Tony has something of a reputation. It's not the first time he's overstepped himself with a woman.'

Stacey turned her burning cheeks down towards her clasped hands. She longed to change the subject and attempted with, 'How did you know I hadn't started out with the party? I suppose Carlo . . .?'

'He rambled on about you being in some kind of state.' There was a pause and then Mark added levelly, 'You could have come to me, you know.'

Of course. Everything around here was *his* business.

She got up and wandered to the balustrade to say shortly, 'I *would* have preferred to keep it to myself.'

'I've no doubt you would.' He let his irritation go through the cigarette smoke. There was the suggestion of derision in his tones as he tacked on, coming up behind her, 'This "living it up" business can sometimes get out of hand.'

She swung round, not caring that he was only an armstretch away. 'You never let a thing drop, do you? I suppose to you it's a crime to want to get the most out of life?'

'You're doing all right,' he replied, dropping her a slightly sour smile. 'I've never seen a hostess go down so well with her clients.'

'I thank my lucky stars I can get on with *most* people.'

'You've got the gift. Too bad Latin lover-boy got the wrong idea, though.'

Her anger stifled any retort she might have wanted to make after that. She could do nothing but leave the way open for him to say bitingly,

'From now on I should stick to the ice-water type to practise your talents on. There should be more of us around somewhere.'

Eyes lit with brittle amusement met and locked with hers. Though he was still an armstretch away Stacey had the feeling that the muscular frame was far too uncomfortably close. She wanted to drag her gaze away, but something in the brown depths held her. The eyes lowered to flicker fleetingly over the frilled negligée and then he turned abruptly.

'Get a good night's rest,' he said tersely over his shoulder.

She watched him move off into the lounge. The blouse that she had pulled off so hastily had slipped to the floor. He picked it up in passing, held it for a second and then tossed it into a chair.

'Never did bring you much luck.' The gleam of his smile was brief and somewhat wintry as he turned out of the door.

Stacey went to bed determined to take orders for once, but it seemed a good night's rest was not for her. It would have been understandable if she had lain awake half the night, and later taken to measuring the length of the balcony with her steps, because of Tony's behaviour down on the beach. But all this because a pair of brown eyes had lingered too long on her. It was almost dawn before she would admit that the look in them had caught on something close to her heart.

And with that shattering thought she hurried back to bed. Sleep had to come now. It wasn't safe to lie awake thinking. . . .

CHAPTER FIVE

DURING the next few days, Stacey threw herself whole-heartedly into her work. Life, she decided, was much less complicated if one left oneself as little time as possible to think about it, and hordes of laughing holiday-makers were the best protection against that.

She swam in their midst, ignoring the staff beach, walked with them on hikes over the peninsula, and toured the taverns and nightclubs of Sorrento untiringly. Life at the Palazzo was crammed too, and she had let herself become so much a part of the scene that it wasn't possible to slip away to her room at the end of the day. She was claimed for endless dances on the terrace, hilarious discussions in the bar, and sometimes a late night meal in the restaurant.

One thing, though, she did sleep quickly and dreamlessly when the gaieties were finally at an end.

The only times Stacey wished she had hurried away to her room were when a firm arm came up behind her, and she was led on to the dance floor in Mark's embrace. She was always careful to keep her conversation at business level on these occasions, as well as telling herself every five seconds that these arms holding her were really no different from those of the other men she had danced with. Just the same, it was a little disconcerting to think that he might feel her pulses racing crazily, and she was always glad to get back to the safety of her holiday clientele.

As for Tony, she saw nothing of him. He wasn't playing in the restaurant these days, and there was no one to step out on her from a dark corner, when she made her way through the gardens in the evenings. She wondered vaguely if he had decided to take a holiday. It wasn't until some time later that she learned that Tony had left the Palazzo for good; and this from a most unexpected source.

The last person that Stacey expected to meet on her return from a beach party was Jeremy. He was looking taller and fairer than ever, and the surprise of coming upon him was so complete she almost fell into his arms. It was not until she drew away from warm lips on her cheek that she noticed that Jeremy had been talking to Mark.

She saw the dark head incline politely her way, and then he was striding off across the terrace.

Jeremy held her at arms' length and let the sky-blue eyes lower over slim sun-tanned limbs and white beach suit. 'Wow!' was his only comment until he thought to add later, 'Sorrento has certainly brought out the best in you. Not that there was any worst.'

He laughed easily, but Stacey fancied she detected a slight sheepishness behind his humour. More so when he took her arm to say, 'Sorry I couldn't get back to see you sooner.'

She laughed then as they started to walk. 'With Rome a hundred and sixty miles away,' she pointed out, 'I didn't expect to see you popping back every few days.'

He looked down at her in mock disappointment to state, 'So you haven't missed me at all.'

'Of course I've missed you,' she hurried, 'but ... well, we both have a job to do, haven't we?'

'Not for the next ...' he looked at his watch, 'twenty-four hours we don't. I don't have to go back until six tomorrow night and you've just been given the same amount of time off.'

'I have?' She stared up wide-eyed. 'But I'm not due for. ...'

'The great master himself has decreed it, my sweet. We have the use of his car for any trip we might want to make.'

'Why, that's marvellous.' Stacey wished she could coax a little more enthusiasm into her voice. Luckily Jeremy didn't seem to notice her slack reaction. He was saying almost on the heels of her words,

'Mind you, I'd rather not do too much tonight. I'm pretty whacked with the travelling. Tomorrow I suppose we could go over to Castellamare. It's not bad there. We

284

could take a look around.'

'Lovely,' Stacey smiled as he let her pass before him into the hotel. An elderly lady came up to inquire about tours for the following day, and while Stacey was discussing them, Jeremy leaned in to say,

'Okay, then? I'll see you out front, about eight in the morning.'

He left her to take the stairs two at a time. Later in her room Stacey felt a little ashamed of her own slightly indifferent feelings for something which a year ago she would have considered the ultimate in happiness. A whole day spent with Jeremy. Laying out her prettiest garments, she resolved to put everything she had into making up for some of her lukewarm enthusiasm.

It was doubtful though if Jeremy noticed her efforts next morning. His gaze went past her floral elegance towards the horizon, as he murmured absently, 'Looks like it's going to be a hot one. You know, the air down here is completely different from the stuff we breathe in Rome.'

He held the car door for her with a smile that seemed as distant as the look in his eyes, and then they were cruising down the drive and out of the hotel grounds.

During the journey Stacey felt her carefully disciplined heart betraying her again. It wouldn't let her forget that though Jeremy's driving was faultless, this was Mark's car, and nobody sat behind the wheel quite like him. Thankfully their destination was only a few miles north of Sorrento, so they weren't in the car for long. From then on the day brightened considerably.

As she and Jeremy walked hand in hand through the thick chestnut woods and mountain pine-trees of Castellamare, Stacey felt some of the old camaraderie returning. They talked lengthily on past summers spent working together, and sang snatches of songs they had learnt in the Austrian inns.

Laughter was very much in evidence, tempered only slightly to take in the cable-car ride to the top of Mount Fiato, a tour of the pockmarked castle, and later the museum down in the cove. When most of the city's sights had been sampled and duly appreciated, the late afternoon found them recuperating good-naturedly in palm-shaded chairs outside a *trattoria*. The whole curve of the bay spread before them.

After about ten minutes of quite pleasurable silence, Stacey placed her glass down on the basket-work table to comment smilingly, 'You haven't said much about your work in Rome, Jeremy.'

He took a long drink and shrugged before replying. 'Not much to say. And anyway, who wants to talk about work? This is supposed to be a holiday.'

'It's practically over,' Stacey sighed, watching a lowering sun. After a while she brought her gaze back to Jeremy to ask pleasantly, 'I just wondered if you were being grossly overworked. You remember how we both thought we were going to be?' She smiled and then went on, 'But I suppose you must have someone to help you, otherwise you wouldn't have been able to make this trip?'

Jeremy finished his drink, and then crossed one trousered leg over the other expansively. 'I get my fair share of time off,' he grinned. 'With two girls under my thumb, I've learnt how to wangle that.'

'Two?' Stacey laughed her incredulity. 'Well, of all the. ... You mean to say I'm struggling along here, and you've got no less than two assistants!'

He raised a quizzical eyebrow to smile, 'You don't look all that bad on the struggle, and don't forget Rome's a big city.'

She picked up her glass to study its contents before querying lightly, 'Are they . . . nice girls?'

Jeremy nodded reflectively. 'Couple of good kids,' he agreed. 'Tessa's married to a pilot doing the London to Ibiza run, and Maureen's practically hitched to one of these computer boffins.'

There was a considerable silence then. Stacey put her glass down and watched the quivering pattern that the contents made on the sunlit table. Jeremy relaxed and lay back to stare at the deep green spears of palm leaves up above. Settling back in her chair, Stacey found the experience restful too, but after a while she lowered her gaze, and let her eyes wander over the tanned boyish features and detached smile of the man opposite.

What prompted her to ask the next question she had no idea. The words were out almost before she knew what they were. 'Is Melanie Davis still working in Rome?' she heard herself inquiring.

Though Jeremy hadn't moved as much as an eyelash at her question, Stacey had a feeling that inwardly he had sprung rigidly to attention. 'What made you ask a question like that?' He sat up slowly.

'I don't know, I just thought of it.'

Was it her imagination or was there just the suggestion of pink creeping up under the handsome tan? Perhaps not imagination, for now the sheepish gleam was back in the blue eyes.

'She's still in Rome,' he grinned. 'As a matter of fact I've seen her once or twice.'

When the colour had subsided he eyed Stacey thoughtfully to add, 'I didn't know you knew Melanie.'

'I don't. It's only what I heard of her that first summer when I came to take over.' Stacey gave him a wry smile. 'The Farrow–Davis partnership took some living down that year, you know. Everyone seemed so surprised that I was working with you instead of Melanie.'

Jeremy lay back reminiscently. 'People get used to the same team, I suppose,' he smiled.

'The rumour was,' Stacey probed teasingly, 'that after three seasons together, you two had had enough of each other's company. Melanie took a permanent job in Rome, I believe?'

Jeremy nodded. Stacey had the feeling that the blue eyes were searching hers as he said with a slight quirk of the lips, 'Ironic, isn't it? We couldn't get far enough away from each other, and then I end up getting posted to Rome.'

'Very,' Stacey twinkled over the top of her glass.

For some reason conversation seemed to come much easier with Jeremy after that. He ordered fresh drinks, and flopped out happily, rattling on about his job in Rome, and the different type of clientele that had passed through his hands up to date. He seemed to be seeing Stacey for the first time too, for he ran an appraising

287

glance over her and commented equably,

'You *did* say you were struggling along down here? Well, stop me if I've said it before, but you're looking pretty good on it. Come to think of it,' he took a long drink and clapped his glass down good-humouredly, 'neither of us seem to have done too badly out of the new boss they sneaked on to us. Maybe he's not such a bad old stick?'

'Old stick!' Stacey raised an eyebrow and smiled. 'Mark Lawford can't be all that much older than you are.'

'I know.' Jeremy grinned boyishly. 'But I get the feeling he knows all there is to know when he's striding around that Palazzo of his.'

Stacey let her gaze roam over towards an alfresco roof of bougainvillea as she asked casually, 'This ... er ... Sunflair girl. You know, the boss. What's she like?'

'Quite gorgeous, I believe.'

'Oh. I suppose she and ... Mark Lawford have been friends for years?'

'I don't know about *friends*,' Jeremy shrugged absently, and then probably because Stacey's gaze was slightly inquiring he quirked, 'Well, he's opened up his place to Sunflair strictly so that he can keep an eye on her interests. You can take it from me, he doesn't need the business. *And* he goes hopping about the Continent on her behalf. Make what you can out of that.'

I've been doing nothing else, Stacey told herself bleakly. Out loud she murmured with apparent disinterest, 'Mm. I see what you mean.'

That subject apparently exhausted, Jeremy struck up blithely and without warning with, 'By the way. What goes with Tony? He got the push, I believe?' Stacey blinked. Her mind on other things, Jeremy's words had knocked her somewhat off balance. 'He got the sack?' She stared numbly, and then quickly lowered her gaze. 'I wondered why I hadn't seen him around lately.'

Jeremy, obviously pleased at being able to come up with such a first-hand piece of information, went on cheerily, 'I got it from the boys in the band. Apparently there was the most almighty row between him and the old man. Tony didn't take too kindly to being kicked out either, from what I hear. Left practically under force.'

Stacey shivered in spite of the warm air. She had always suspected that Tony could be fiery. Looking into those black eyes was sometimes like gazing into the turbulence of one of the active volcanoes. He was a man who liked his own way, and when he couldn't have it. . . .

She was relieved to hear Jeremy talking again. He mustn't have been expecting any comment from her, thank goodness, for he was calmly meditating out loud.

'Funny nobody seems to know what the rumpus was about, but I've got a pretty shrewd idea.'

'You have?'

Stacey swallowed, wondering what was coming next.

Jeremy crossed one leg over the other knowledgeably, to impart, 'Well, Antonino might be the biggest draw musically this side of Rome, but,' he lowered a grin obliquely over his drink, 'the trouble with Tony is he can't keep his mind on his music.'

Though the conversation was trying, Stacey made an effort to sound lighthearted.

'How can *you* talk?' she forced. 'You've only known him two weeks.'

Jeremy shot her a blue offside glance from under a crooked eyebrow. 'It wouldn't take two *hours* to weigh up *his* game,' he grinned.

'I don't know what you mean,' Stacey managed, fighting to hold down the colour in her cheeks.

'Never mind,' came the easy reply. 'It doesn't concern you.'

If only you knew, she thought miserably, staring hard into the bottom of her glass. Apparently everybody was on to Tony's ways, except the simple-minded, featherheaded Stacey Roberts, and because of her naïveté Tony had got the sack.

Was he blaming her?

Stacey's heart quickened slightly. She had never had any intention of leading him on, but there was no telling how Tony was viewing the matter. She could still hear his sharp curse as he had stumbled in the cave, and though everything within her wanted to believe that she had seen the last of him. . . .

She had Jeremy to thank for putting a halt to what she half-smilingly termed to herself later as a too-colourful imagination. The man at her side broke into her thoughts to round off lazily,

'Just the same I can't help thinking it must have been something pretty rugged that led to Tony's exit. His musical flair has been a standing attraction at the Palazzo for quite a while, I believe, and you can bet Lawford knows good box-office when he sees it *and* when he waves it good-bye. Still, that's the way the cookies crumble, I suppose.'

Cheerfully putting an end to the subject, he drew Stacey to her feet with, 'Shall we go?'

As she rose silently he watched her and put forward tentatively, 'I thought I might take an early train back to Rome. That is . . . if you don't mind, of course?'

'I don't mind,' Stacey smiled up. 'It's been quite a day. I'm going to treat myself to a tepid bath when I get back and lounge deliciously with a book.'

'Under the master's eye everything prospers' was a saying that hadn't been too difficult to learn in Italian, since it was one of Maria's favourites. And Stacey had to admit that even when the master's coolly discerning eye was turned further afield, the workings of the Palazzo progressed as smoothly as ever. Although Mark must have flown out a few times already this season on behalf of Sunflair, she had never really thought of him as going off one day and coming back another.

To her he had been a somewhat unsettling presence hovering in the background, and whenever he had been missing she had taken advantage of his absence merely to breathe a little easier.

Now on the days that he wasn't around, she found her gaze lingering on his closed office door as she passed, or across at his apartments just opposite her own. She wondered who was getting the benefit of his dictatorial tongue, or on the other hand that rather heart-stirring white smile. Perhaps he was holding someone in a close embrace on another dance floor or talking suavely across a table in another restaurant.

Constantly Stacey would tell herself that none of this was her concern, and it couldn't matter to her when he returned. But it didn't stop her gazing around expectantly, first thing in the morning when she got downstairs. Often when caught up in the business of arranging the day's pleasures for her clients, she would turn her head, her pulses falling over one another, only to find that the dark shape seen out of the corner of her eye was just another holidaymaker or a member of the staff.

All this was silly, of course, because when Mark was back he always made it his business to be in the picture somewhere anyway.

Bouncing along on these topsy-turvy days, Stacey managed to keep on top of her job with comparative ease. The July holidaymakers came in pale and subdued, and went away tanned and smiling, and looking back to the days of Derek and Lance Thompson, she didn't think it would be too conceited to say that quite a few contented clients had waved her good-bye since then.

Of course there were always the guests who didn't care for the position of their room, or didn't like the food, or couldn't bear the climate, but these kinds of problems could usually be soothed away with a little extra care and attention. When, however, *all* the dislikes, coupled with some half dozen others, were rooted in one man, Stacey's job became slightly impossible.

According to his oaths, Garfield Yates, a big brusque farmer-type, liked nothing he saw, heard, ate or drank, while he was at the Palazzo. Stacey could rather imagine him stumping through the highlands of Scotland, or scowling over a rifle at some English shoot, than trying to blend in with the mellowness of Sorrento.

What made it worse for her, when she had met the new batch of Sunflair guests from the holiday-tour train she had inadvertently left Mr. Yates to make his own way to the hotel. Though it couldn't be considered Stacey's fault that he had gone striding off in the wrong direction the second his feet had come into contact with the platform, he seemed to blame her for his late arrival, and everything that displeased him after that.

At the end of his first week, Stacey was beginning to feel slightly worn. She had become used to having her meals interrupted, being told of her slipshod methods in arranging the guests' entertainment, and accused of sleeping in too late in the mornings, but her nerves didn't take it any the lighter for all that. She gritted her teeth and hung on to her one consolation. Sunflair's most trying client had booked in at the Palazzo for only ten days, so the end was in sight. Though her own patience was in danger of deserting her these days, Mark's seemed solidly intact. He became adept at heading off the scowling figure making for her table in the restaurant, or to where she would be explaining points of interest to a carefree group.

The only time she saw that craggy, urbane, exterior crack slightly was the day when Garfield Yates was at his most disagreeable. The awful part of it was, Stacey really was responsible for his mood this time.

Why was it, she asked herself in exasperation, that the more one realized that all one's efforts would be needed to please someone, the more things seemed to go wrong? Was it some capricious trick of fate that made the dour Yorkshireman always the last to be reminded when some event was about to take place, and always the first to be told when all the day's tickets had been sold?

Why, Stacey asked herself, did her job have to be less successful where Garfield Yates was concerned, when it needed to be two hundred per cent on top? Maybe she was trying too hard?

That could have been why she carefully and reverently set aside from all the others the ticket she had booked for him, for an event he specially wanted to see. Just so that she could hand it promptly to him when he asked.

And what happened?

While the others were lying snugly secure in the bureau drawer, Mr. Yates's must have been wafted gently out of the leaves of the ledger, by what Stacey was convinced was a conspiratorial breeze, and presumably carted off with the rest of the bits and pieces that were swept up daily from the office floor.

She searched all morning before the awful truth caught up with her. Mr. Yates's ticket had flown as surely as if it had had wings. How was she going to tell him of her latest blunder? If he hadn't been feeling it before, he would be fully convinced after this that she had a definite grudge against him.

She muddled along after lunch hoping that the occasion might slip his mind, but of course that was too much to hope for. Mid-afternoon saw him stumping along to her office. His wrath when she broke the news of the lost ticket to him was no less than she had expected. To calm him she offered to go and find out where the rubbish was deposited and make a search, but the man must have thought that she was making light excuses to be rid of him, for he followed and grabbed her roughly by the arm as she turned out of the office and hurried down the hall.

'Now listen here, young lady,' he glared. 'I don't know what you think you're up to. . . .'

Tensing under his grasp, Stacey didn't hear anyone approaching over the thick carpets, nor did the man holding her, for he looked all set to go into a colourful tirade until a vibrant voice broke in over his shoulder to inquire crisply,

'Trouble again, Mr. Yates? What is it this time?'

The scowling man turned outward to bellow, 'This fool girl has deliberately mislaid my ticket for the only decent event likely to take place in this one-eyed town! and what's more I know that she. . . .'

'I think we can get to the bottom of the matter without manhandling the staff.' The answering tones held a kind of harsh humour, but Stacey felt that the hand gripping her arm was being somewhat briskly dislodged. 'We can talk about it in my office,' Mark suggested, gently sweeping the man to one side.

'I want her to come too,' Yates poked a shaking finger at Stacey. 'I'm going to see to it that she doesn't get off scot free this time, and if *you've* got any authority around here. . . .'

'Shall we go?' Mark bit out, nostrils flaring slightly as he guided Stacey to the front.

He listened patiently to the other man's complaints once the office door was closed, and then swung over to the phone. He talked for several minutes in pleasant unhurried Italian, before dropping the receiver lightly on to its hook.

'There you are, Mr. Yates,' he smiled, putting an arm round the man's shoulder. 'It's all fixed up. You're in as a guest of the organizers themselves. How's that?'

'Hrumph ... I don't know why I couldn't just have had a ticket like the rest of them, instead of a lot of fuss and nonsense. Now I'll have to go, I suppose. . . .' The man turned belligerently as the door was opened for him. 'But don't think I intend to let the slapdash methods you seem to condone go unreported. When I get back to England, you mark my words, I'll. . . .'

The door was closed sharply, slicing off his words so that they faded out as a low rumble on the other side.

Mark gave a low sigh of relief. 'When does that guy leave?' he asked mildly.

'He's got another couple of days yet.' Stacey's smile was limp as she rose from the chair. She wished the brown gaze wouldn't linger on the violet smudges she knew were beneath her eyes, the lethargic way she moved across the room.

'You don't look as if you'll last that long,' he drawled perceptively.

'I don't think there's much else that could go wrong for Mr. Yates now.' She smiled a little more firmly this time, making for the door.

After a considerable pause in which she had almost reached it, the words came casually from over by the desk.

'I'm off to Amalfi tomorrow. Care to come along for the break?'

Stacey turned, her pulses flickering into life.

'I don't know,' she hesitated. 'There's so much to do and. . . .'

'*What* is there to do?' he asked irritably. 'Can't these damned people do anything for themselves?'

Stacey blinked. She pondered back into her mind. 'Well, everybody's more or less taken care of tomorrow,' she said slowly. 'Except Mr. Yates. He might be at a loose. . . .'

'To hell with Yates,' Mark cursed lightly. 'And I'll pick you up at the far entrance tomorrow, just in case he's on his usual dawn patrol.'

Stacey digested this and then opened her eyes inquiringly. Had she got it right? 'Dawn?' she asked.

'That's what I said, dawn,' he reiterated. 'And I don't expect we'll be back before dark, and the day after old man crab will be busy packing, so you can reckon you've seen the last of him.'

'Yes, but there's this afternoon. I'll have to. . . .'

'Rest up,' he put in evenly. 'And get an early night. I don't want an invalid on my hands.' He opened the door for her with a downward smile. 'You've still got half a season to go.'

CHAPTER SIX

STACEY felt less like an invalid than she had ever done in her life, preparing for the drive the next morning. There was a sparkle in her eyes that she would have toned down if she had known how to. Her body had recovered its healthy bounce after a solid twelve hours' rest.

She dressed with special care, telling herself repeatedly that there was absolutely no need to. This was just another day in her working life. It was almost certain that Mark was going to Amalfi to see the Sunflair representative of the area. More than likely he would find something for Stacey to do while they were there.

Work or no work, she couldn't resist selecting something slightly less businesslike for her outing today. The cream lace dress, cascading just to her knees from the small nipped-in waist, was a little different from the slim silks and shirtwaisters that she had been wearing around the hotel lately.

Small cap-sleeves balanced the low-cut front which was edged with a tiny round collar, and decorated with a central row of matching covered buttons. Choosing soft kid, slim-heeled sandals, and a similar coloured handbag, she stepped back to weigh up her reflection. Would she pass for a working girl? Only just. The bronze silk hair didn't exactly give her an efficient look. She had piled it so that it fell as a fringe just above the centre of her forehead and continued down along the curve of her cheek to her shoulder. The other side was swept slightly back, showing the full line of her face and one small ear before it fell to curl up level with its twin. In the dawn light her lightly tanned skin glowed gold against the cream of the dress.

The smile playing around the soft mouth was glaringly transparent.

She thought about camouflaging that eager schoolgirl look with a wide-brimmed hat, but decided against it. Mark's car nearly always had its top down. She could carry the hat. It would come in useful for the sun later. She went downstairs and outside.

Much of the bulk of the Palazzo spread back inland, belying its size. The grounds it stood in constituted a walk in itself. Thankfully there was no sign of Garfield Yates. Perhaps he was just grumbling his way through the front lounges, or maybe he was still in his room sleeping peacefully. . . . Well, not peacefully. Erratically was more like it.

Smiling to herself, Stacey turned the corner and took in the tall figure standing by the car. She saw the soft shirt, pale blue sharkskin jacket, and even paler knife-edge slacks as Mark flicked a lighter under his cigarette. Perhaps it was the flame that made the brown eyes dilate slightly as they toured the length of her?

Could have been, for seconds later he was drawing on the cigarette and commenting with a lazy smile, 'That's what I call a quick recovery!'

He held the door for her, closing it with a brisk movement, and then strode round to his side. As the car turned out into the road, the world was only just shaking off the night. Vineyards, lemon groves, and blossoming oleanders were engaged in the business of making themselves seen again, and the sky, still not decided on what colour it would choose for the day, toyed with raiment of lavender, saffron, and flamingo pink.

Swinging his gaze round and lowering it to rest on Stacey's slightly parted lips, as she stared in wonder, Mark said in the same lazy tones, 'Two dawns in one summer. We're doing well.'

Something about the gleam of his smile, the relaxed air with which he swung the wheel, seemed to set the mood for the day. Stacey's natural lilting spirits, previously submerged under the strain of having a broad shoulder so close to hers, suddenly came bubbling to the top. She laughed lightly and settled back to gaze out eagerly on the changing scenery.

Behind them, the ground dropped gently away to the red roofs of Sorrento, and the gulf of Naples. In front was a vista of changing blues and greens that Stacey had seen on the map as the Gulf of Salerno. As the car descended in reverse curves, through groves of ilex, oak, and majestic pines, Mark asked casually,

'Been on the Amalfi drive before?'

'No.' Stacey shook her head smilingly. 'All the tours for this side of the peninsula were listed and sampled before I came.'

He let his gaze rest tolerantly on soft, animated features, and then turned to steer down the road that dropped towards the sea. 'Could be you're in for something of a surprise,' he drawled.

Surprise, delight, and considerable awe were Stacey's main reactions as the road followed the incredible windings of the coast, at a breathtaking height above the water. On the left the mountains rose brown and arid to a now unbelievably blue sky. Further along terraces had been cut in the rock face to support grape-vines and fruit trees. The whitewashed cube houses with their domed roofs gave the scene a peculiarly Arabic look.

Round the next curve Stacey wondered why they were drawing off the road. The car came to a halt beneath a cluster of trees, and then the door was being opened for her. Mark led her towards a railed edge. He dropped an arm negligently across her shoulders and nodded below. Following his gaze, Stacey was caught straight at the heart by what she saw.

The brown rock dropped sheer to a transparent green curve of water, and on the opposite shore pastel-tinted houses rose tier upon tier from a tiny beach that was littered with fishing boats. From up here they looked like multi-coloured splashes of paint. A cluster of small islets lay just out to sea, and as though to balance the effect, the same ochre-coloured mountains rose ever upward, above the town.

'Positano,' Mark explained just above her ear.

'Positano!' Stacey echoed the name almost lyrically, dreamily unaware that she had swung her gaze up to his. 'Couldn't we go?' she asked impulsively, and then lowering her eyes rapidly she stammered, 'I mean . . . have we got time?'

'Everybody should make time for breakfast,' came the dry reply. 'Like to have it down there?'

'Very much.' Stacey smiled, not caring now that her gaze had once again crept up to his.

Back in the car they descended in hairpin bends to a small triangular square. Here there were shops, and cafés, and horse-drawn fiacres; and traders creating a general air of early morning bustle. Parking space was plentiful.

From the *piazza*, Stacey was guided down ramps and stairs, some of them so narrow that the encircling arm about her shoulder occasionally had to draw in breathtakingly close.

'You don't walk in Positano,' Mark remarked easily. 'You either climb up or slide down.'

They ate a breakfast of light rolls, parmesan cheese and coffee, on the balcony of a pink and white hotel, and watched the gathering life on the beach. Gay sun parasols were going up above rows of striped beach chairs. One tanned figure after another came to sample the strip of white surf. Stacey smiled occasionally at the exhibitionist antics of some of the swimmers, and Mark lay back in his chair pulling lazily on a cigarette, and apparently uncaring that the morning was drifting away.

Later, making their way back to the car, Stacey exclaimed wonderingly at the view. 'Nature doesn't seem to be able to go wrong in Italy, does it? I mean, the mountains are just the right shape, the trees always set in a perfect position, even the houses have a kind of grace. Everything's so . . ,' she laughed, 'so harmonious, and yet no one ever looks in the least surprised.'

Mark held the car door for her, gazing down with a bemused smile. 'I guess the Italians have grown used to living with beauty,' he murmured.

Beyond Positano the Amalfi drive began in earnest. The turns were sharper, the coast more precipitous, and around every bend one could expect a new scene of surpassing beauty to snatch the breath away.

Eventually the car entered a sloping dark tunnel cut through the rock, and at the far end signposts announced Amalfi. The drive made one of its rare descents to sea level, and they were soon caught up in a square jammed with carriages, parked cars and olive-skinned Amalfians strolling in the hot sunshine.

Apparently Mark had no intention of stopping in the centre of the town, for he steered the car straight through and up and away again along a road flanked by blossoming trees. At the crest of a slope a mass of even more brilliant colour caught Stacey's eye. Seconds later, the car was stopping beside a high wall, over which a cloud of roses and carnations glowed red and pink against the deep blue of the sky.

Mark guided her through a sweet-scented garden, and from the arched doorway of a scintillatingly white house a grey-haired lady came smiling down the path. Stacey thought that there was something of a Latin darkness about the fine-boned face. The figure was ageing, but the walk was sprightly. The dark eyes were anything but faded. They came to rest on Stacey with a kind of amused wonder and then turned upwards.

'Well now, Mark,' she spoke in English with the merest trace of an accent, 'you didn't tell me you were bringing a visitor.'

Mark stepped up to take the outstretched hand. He drew Stacey forward with a sloping smile. 'Miss Roberts, our Sunflair representative,' he explained. 'Signora Minetto,' he added for Stacey's benefit.

Her hand was taken in a gentle clasp.

'Sunflair? Well, well. I hope this terrible man is not overworking you, Miss Roberts,' the dark eyes twinkled merrily, 'or perhaps we could be a little less formal. . . .'

'Stacey,' Mark put in lazily.

The Signora gave a pleased nod.

'Shall we go in out of the heat?' she suggested. 'I'll have Nicola set another place for lunch.'

Stacey was led through rooms with whitewashed walls and hollow vaulted ceilings. They were blissfully cool after the blazing sun, and furnished in the old world Italian style. Their quiet elegance was somehow fitting to the serene charm of their owner. Over a meal of typically Italian dishes, and a pomegranate-coloured wine, the Signora talked knowledgeably to Mark about business at the Palazzo, and frequently invited Stacey to express an opinion on the popularity of Sunflair tours and what type of customer they attracted.

Later in the sleepy heat of the afternoon Stacey was led along to one of the guest rooms where a white-covered bed looked vaguely inviting.

'Sample it by all means, my dear,' the Signora gestured with a shrewd twinkle. 'Our weather can be a little enervating, and Mark tells me you've been up since dawn.'

Cool water and oatmeal soap stood on a stand near the door, and reaching into a cupboard for towels, the old lady added, 'For freshening up later.'

'You're very kind,' Stacey smiled.

The Signora seemed in no hurry to put the towels down. She ran her fingers through them, gazing across the room to ask, 'And what do you think of the Palazzo?'

'It's a beautiful place,' Stacey replied sincerely. She sat down on the bed, her fingers searching for the buttons on her dress.

'And Mark?'

The question was enough to make her hands drop down in surprise. 'Mark?' she echoed flounderingly, yet liking the feel of the name on her tongue. 'Well . . . I think he runs his hotel admirably.' She breathed again. Thank goodness she had got out of that one!

'Indeed he does,' the Signora agreed, the twinkle back in the dark eyes. 'Mark's an old friend of mine,' she explained. 'I lived at the Palazzo two years before he found me this house.'

'It's a lovely situation,' Stacey smiled, gazing out over a riot of flowers towards a motionless sea.

'It's right for an old woman.' The Signora nodded and turned towards the door. 'Rest well, child,' she smiled. 'I'll see you before you go.'

Stacey draped her dress over a hanger, and lay in her slip on the bed. A warm perfumed breeze drifted in from the window. She wondered where Signora Minetto had learnt such faultless English, and what Mark was doing, and whether they would be going on to see the Amalfi representative later, and then a pleasurable drowsiness made her thoughts jumble meaninglessly and for an hour she slept.

She awoke refreshed, and after washing, applied a light dusting of make-up. The cream lace dress was crisp after its sojourn on the hanger, her hair smooth again with a touch of the comb. She stepped out into the white-washed hall. The house appeared to be empty, but guided by the sound of voices she made her way through the rooms and out on to a shaded veranda.

Mark and the Signora were sat at a small round table. Judging by the empty wine glasses and the used ash tray, they had been talking most of the time that Stacey had slept.

As she stepped out shyly, Mark rose to his feet, to lower a smiling glance over her. 'Just give me a couple of minutes to get cleaned up,' he said nodding, 'and then we'll be on our way.'

As he disappeared the Signora rose and held out a chair.

'And in the meantime, my dear, you can take a cup of tea. You see!' she chuckled, 'I know all of your English customs.' As she turned to go indoors she added in an enlightening tone, 'My husband and I had a business for many years in England.'

Some time later, the Signora waved warmly from the doorway as Mark guided Stacey down the path and out into the car.

The afternoon was still hot, but the air was less sopori-fic. Now that the sun had passed its peak, the languid blossom stirred occasionally, adding its own perfume to an already laden breeze.

As the car nosed its way down the lane Stacey closed her eyes pleasurably, loving the coolness that played about her ears and throat.

'Got any inherent fear of caves?'

The question drifted across almost as leisurely as the breeze. Stacey opened her eyes in time to find the brown gaze just leaving hers. 'No,' she smiled, looking back now on her experience with Tony as no more than an unfortunate misunderstanding.

'Fancy a look at one of the grottoes along this way?' Mark asked casually.

'Oh, could we?' Stacey looked at him eagerly. 'I've been meaning to set aside some time for a visit.'

'We've got all the time in the world,' he grinned, swinging the car down into the Amalfi square, and through the tunnel.

The Grotto di Smeraldo – The Emerald Grotto – was discovered when the nearly tideless Mediterranean dropped low enough to reveal the underwater entrance. A small opening was enlarged on the landward side and the cave was opened shortly afterwards.

Mark explained most of this to Stacey as they descended in a lift through a shaft in the rock. After the glare of the sunlight, she could see nothing when they stopped at the bottom. With Mark holding her she was led blindly until her eyes became accustomed to the semi-darkness, and then she saw that they were on a kind of concrete embankment. At the side was a pool of dark water, and a faint blue light glowed in the distance.

Stacey stood entranced. She felt as though she was exploring the basement of the world. She could hear the water dripping in far off places, smell the eternal damp on the walls. Her mind wandered on to eerie things. What kind of creatures inhabited a place like this? Was it possible to get lost in the dark? Her nerves tightened at the thought and when a voice came straight out of the water, she almost jumped off the embankment.

'Steady,' Mark's arms were reassuring. 'It's only the boatman.'

A flat-bottomed boat glided up to the pier and she was helped into it by a calloused hand from below. Mark stepped down lightly beside her, and then they were being rowed across the still pool. From the high curved ceiling, straw-coloured stalactites reached down for the water. Some even went below the surface. With their circular encrusted drippings, Stacey thought they looked like weirdly carved pillars in a ghostly ballroom.

Over the black mirrored floor the boat glided to where the patch of luminous water glowed a vivid electric blue. As they neared, it changed to a fantastic shade of green, and as the boatman's oars struck the surface, glistening droplets fell back like liquid emeralds. Stacey saw that the beautiful colours were caused by the sunlight reaching through the limpid water.

Looking at Mark's face she saw that it was a ghostly blue, 'and realizing that her own must look exactly the same, and that a dark gaze was resting on it, she gave a low incredulous laugh. The sound pattered around the grotto like the chuckles of a disembodied jester, and gazing up in laughing wonder to the white gleam of a smile above hers, she felt the fingers of the hand resting on her shoulder tighten slightly.

Back in the sunshine, strolling the beach, Stacey saw that the sea had hollowed out dozens of caves along the Amalfi coast. If they were all as beautiful as the Emerald Grotto, she mused, one could go on viewing indefinitely. A few minutes later, she was rather surprised to be beckoned towards one which was no more than a tiny room with its own miniature sandy beach.

The wrinkled-faced fisherman signalled and grinned and constantly repeated, '*Degli inamorati, la grotto degli inamorati.*'

Mark dropped a crooked smile and drew Stacey on. Gazing back, she asked curiously, 'What was he saying? Don't tell me they've got a name for a tiny place like that?'

Mark was still strolling on. He wasn't being very communicative. She smiled up inquiringly. 'I got the first bit. *La grotto*,' she told him, 'but *degli inamorati?*' As he lit up a cigarette she asked laughingly, 'Well, what does it mean? The cave of what?'

With a humorous slant of the mouth Mark pulled slowly on his cigarette and then drawled, 'The old boy was trying to sell us the Cave of the Lovers.'

'The cave of the....' Stacey digested this and then swung her gaze out to sea. She kept it there until the heat had receded from her cheeks. That would teach her not to be persistent! The next time she went chasing Italian names she had better make sure that she found them between the pages of an insensible dictionary.

The light was fading as the car headed for the ribbon of road that hugged the mountain. Now that they were making for the Amalfi drive again, Stacey assumed that they were on their way back to Sorrento, but Mark swung the car in the opposite direction.

Some time later, after travelling constantly upwards through a high-walled narrow valley, they came on to a rocky strip of land, that jutted out and seemed to hang suspended high, so high over Amalfi.

Going by the Palazzo standards the hotel that Mark drew up at was small, but Stacey thought that many people would come just for the view. Gazing down from this height was, in her opinion, the nearest thing to flying. Mark seemed to be on friendly terms with the man who led them out on to an open dining terrace. The short squat figure beamed back at them over his shoulder and when they had been shown to a secluded table, grasped the other man's hand and shook it vigorously.

After a brief conversation in Italian Mark turned.

'Stacey,' he brought her forward in the circle of his arm, 'meet Luigi, the owner. He used to work at the Palazzo.'

The small man with the receding hair bowed and smiled broadly. 'From *maître d'hotel* at the Palazzo,' he said swelling his chest, 'to this.'

Though the shrug of the shoulders was accompanied by a modest lift of the eyebrows. Stacey guessed that 'this' was the ultimate in Luigi's happiness.

He rubbed his hands in eager pleasure as Stacey was helped into her seat. Mark draped down opposite her and cast only a cursory glance over the menu.

'We've been dining Italian-style all day, Luigi,' he remarked. 'I fancy Stacey might like to be reminded of our own shores tonight.'

'But pleasurably.' Luigi kissed his clustered finger tips and spread them out like an opening flower. 'Our English cuisine is the best, *signorina*, as you are about to see.'

Stacey did see. The only thing that puzzled her, after she had sampled Aylesbury duckling with all the trimmings, was why they didn't cook English food so well in England. Perhaps it was the same reason that Chinese food always tasted better in London. Not that she had ever been to China, it might even taste better there. . . . Her thoughts were rambling on idiotically. She didn't know why, unless it was to give herself something to think about during this pulsing silence that had dropped over the night.

Mark had spoken very little during the meal. Now she sensed him watching her as he pulled lazily on a cigarette. She finished the last of her wine and turned to gaze out into the dark void. The feeling of pleasurable restlessness that had been mounting within her during the day was becoming increasingly difficult to stifle, and how could she hope to keep a tight rein on herself when that brown gaze seemed all the time to be willing hers to meet it? It was attempting to even now as he said negligently,

'I don't recall saying anything that needed all that much thought.'

Stacey couldn't turn her eyes. She rose jerkily and walked to where a platform jutted out and was railed like the bow of a ship. Her heart pounded as an arm came up behind her, but keeping her mind firmly on her previous culinary thoughts she said steadily, 'I was just thinking how the Italians seem to do everything so much better than the British.'

'You think so?'

She wasn't aware of turning towards him, yet suddenly her face was very close to his. He lowered his head and as his mouth explored the curve of her cheek, her own slightly parted lips strained to catch the kiss as it went by.

It was the distant clink of a wine bottle that brought Stacey to her senses.

Mark was obviously having his little joke, and yet here she was, preparing to take the cover off her heart. She turned slowly out of his arms, towards the rail, thankful that she hadn't made a complete fool of herself. She heard herself explaining with a shaky laugh,

'I meant the food . . . and the way they run their resorts and everything. . . .'

'Exactly.' Mark stared out over the rail. She couldn't somehow say it was an understanding nod he gave to her faint ramblings, but the jerk of his head, the cool twist of his smile, told her that at least he had heard.

She was thankful for a dramatic view to take her mind off the last few soul-shattering seconds.

Far below, the lights of cars crawled like twin-beamed insects along the edge of a grey scalloped ocean. Just below her feet she could smell the green of the vineyards, the heady sweetness of the lemon groves. It must have been all this that was keeping the world rocking, for minutes later it still hadn't got back on to its steady turn.

She heard Mark saying just above her shoulder, 'We've had quite a day. Reckon you can cope with the hostessing job again now?'

Stacey nodded and tried her quivering voice. 'I think so.'

'Let's hope you won't have old man Yates to contend with when we get back.'

She thought the words, spoken close to her ear, sounded slightly mocking.

'I'll have to look in on the dancing, I suppose,' she jerked. 'But Mr Yates is not a dancer, thank goodness.'

'And tomorrow he'll be gone, and your troubles will be over.'

Troubles! As the warm breath brushed past her throat Stacey had a feeling that they were just beginning. If only Yates's grumbles were all she had to worry about. Struggling to keep the conversation going, she said quickly, 'He goes on to Rome tomorrow.' And then as the thought struck her she mused almost to herself, 'Poor old Jeremy! He's in for a trying time.'

She had a feeling that the wide shoulders had receded. When she looked they had taken a slightly hunched position at the rail. Mark put one foot up while he lit a cigarette. Blowing out the smoke with a tight white smile, he said, 'I take it you've known Farrow a long time?'

Stacey nodded. 'This would have been our third summer together.'

A thousand feet below, fishing lamps cast pools of shimmering light as boatmen prepared to put out to sea. Watching them, Stacey thought the voice came over slightly harsh as Mark asked,

'And what happens in the winter?'

She shrugged with a light sigh. 'Jeremy is always sure of a job at a winter resort. He's been in the business long enough to qualify.' As the silence seemed to go on she added, 'Me, I work in my parents' shop in Richmond.'

'Shop?' He turned to drop a lazy smile over her. 'What kind of shop? Fashions? Hats?'

She shook her head with a twinkle. 'Small sweet and tobacconist near the station,' she explained.

He nodded, still watching her. Stacey wondered if he was trying to put her behind a shop counter in his mind's eye. The thought brought a smile to her lips. But perhaps he didn't care for the softly curving mouth, for he swung his gaze away to say sourly, 'I think I get the idea. Farrow's got himself nicely arranged, I'll say that for him.'

Stacey felt something flutter up into her throat. 'I don't know what that's supposed to mean,' she said coolly. 'Jeremy does arrange these jobs for me, and each year I go out to him somewhere. . . .'

'And don't tell me . . .' Mark moved in close. Before she could do anything to prevent it, a mouth sloping with sarcasm was just above hers. 'Once you're with him you're all set. I've heard how it goes. A summer to love, and a winter to get over it.'

'It's not like that at all.' Stacey held his gaze spiritedly. 'Jeremy always keeps in touch with me in the winter.'

'Seems to me he shouldn't want to let you out of his sight.'

'He *does* have a living to earn, you know.'

'It should be a perfect man-and-wife arrangement.'

Seeing the gleam of his mirthless smile, Stacey told herself that now was the time to turn away and be done with whatever it was that made her want to stay close to him.

All through the slightly disjointed conversation, even now after the somewhat heated exchange of words, she still knew a crazy breathless longing for the half kiss that had started on her cheek, and never quite made its destination. If she was going to move away it had to be now. Had to be . . . and yet. . . . The brown eyes hovered just above hers. They were lit with tiny pinpricks of flame. The tanned face lowered. She willed herself to listen for the clink of a wine bottle that would break the spell, but Mark broke it for her this time. He slackened his frame and muttered in gravel-like tones,

'For Pete's sake let's get back to Sorrento.'

To Stacey the air lightened none at all as the car made its way back along the coast. With every mile, as Mark's shoulders brushed hers, as his hand came out to assist her to drape the net stole that she took from her hand-bag, the air became less breathable. She felt as if she were going up, up into some stifling rarefied air, climbing, just as surely as the car had climbed up from Amalfi to the hotel on the rock. The effect tightened her heart, cut off her speech, so that all she could do when Mark guided her up the steps into the Palazzo was to turn blindly towards her own room.

It ought to have been all right here, but it wasn't. She bathed and slipped into a negligée, and wandered around. The throbbing emptiness of the rooms drove her out on to the balcony. Here in the darkness it was something to be able to listen to the steadying sounds of the sea rolling over the beach, the whisper of the breeze amongst the bushes.

She sank down in a chair and gazed up at the stars, and when she couldn't hold herself back any longer she let her gaze lower to Mark's rooms just across from her own. They were in darkness, but there was the red glow of a cigarette out on the balcony. She saw it burn suddenly bright as though a deep inhalation had drawn it into life, and then it continued to move backwards and forwards in the night.

Stacey closed her eyes and tried to put every single thought out of her mind except what she would wear for the dancing downstairs. Mingling with carefree holidaymakers would be one way of getting the world back into its true perspective, so she had better start thinking about it.

What made her choose black she couldn't have said,

but the rather startling effect of bare shoulders and big strangely glowing eyes told her that at least she looked as if she meant to have a good time. With a dark side she caught her hair up on the top of her head so that it fell in loose coils just to the nape of her neck. With a small diamanté clip fastened in each ear, she made her way downstairs.

The thing to do now, she told herself, was to treat this evening as though it was just like one of the many that had gone before. Thankfully there was no shortage of partners tonight. If she had had to stand in with the crowd and make light-hearted conversation Stacey felt she would have fallen to pieces, but gliding round in the centre of one small world at a time was no effort.

At least it wasn't until she saw a big tuxedo-clad figure talking with a group at the far side of the room. Then it became the biggest effort she had ever known in her life. She ought to have been prepared, of course. Mark always looked in on the dancing at the latter part of the evening, as he did the other entertainments in the hotel. He was merely doing his job, as she was doing hers. And he often asked one of his guests to dance.

She sensed him moving towards her now, and turned her head, but it was only in time to meet him swinging his partner in close on the other side. Easing himself a little away from his dancing companion he leaned in to say mildly, 'Back on the job, Miss Roberts?'

To anyone else it would have sounded like a polite remark. To Stacey in her hypersensitive state it seemed the tones were slightly ironic.

When the tune had finished and her own partner had moved away she wondered wildly if she ought to go back upstairs, but before she could move, the voice that she had just left on the other side of the room came up close to her ear to murmur drily,

'Not thinking of deserting your clients already? It's barely midnight.'

Mark drew her into his arms. He would have swung her out on to the floor as the next tune struck up, but Stacey went rigid against him.

'I don't really want to dance, Mark.' She sent him a

310

steady gaze.

'Okay! We don't dance.'

She couldn't make out if he was angry or not. There was a bitter twist at the mouth as the brown gaze flickered over her bare shoulders. He stood at her side as she watched the couples move across the floor. Watched with her eyes, while her senses were rocked by his nearness.

She thought she might have escaped with another partner, but each one was sent on his way with a slow smile and a shake of the dark head. There was one young man who tried Mark's tactics of swinging straight on to the dance floor, no questions asked, but he only got as far as holding her, when an arm dropped between them, and Mark was saying with flint-eyed humour, 'Sorry, old man. The lady's not for dancing.'

Somehow his other arm had become draped about her shoulders. The next thing she knew, she was being eased through the crowds, out of the room, and into the night. She heard Mark muttering irritably, above her, 'For Pete's sake let's get some air. There ought to be a law against hostesses being pawed by every man loose out of England!' An unreasonable remark, Stacey considered, seeing that the holidaymakers' embraces had never been anything else but friendly.

Mark's arm didn't leave her shoulders until they reached the end of the garden and then it dropped away somewhat abruptly. He turned to stare into the night, and like a sleep-walker just waking up Stacey panicked at her surroundings. She knew her suspended heart could never stand the pitch of being alone with Mark tonight. This warm, scented night, when the trees were gently rustling, and only the stars, it seemed, were there to hang on to for sanity.

But the stars were a long way off, and a certain dark figure was too near, and the soft sigh of the sea blending with the hauntingly-sweet sound of distant mandolin music didn't help.

She turned to say faintly, 'Mark, I think I'd. . . .'

Perhaps it was the sound of Stacey's voice that was her undoing, or the slight step forward she took before speaking. Whatever the cause, the effect was world-shaking, for it made Mark swing round and move in close. In the breathless space he had left between them, she tried to think of what she had been going to say, but the words were never uttered, for she was caught roughly against him, and his mouth had fastened on her own.

To Stacey this was the pinnacle of the day's climb heartwise, but as every particle of her being reached out for Mark's kiss, she knew that the trek had started a long way back. Perhaps even as far back as that first day on the boat. . . .

As hard lips lingered long and searchingly on her own, it seemed that Mark might be trying to make up for lost time too, but then he drew slowly away, and jerking a hand through the dark hair, turned abruptly towards the sea.

The action was enough to shake Stacey back to her senses. Those ordinary everyday senses that should have told her that warm Italian nights, soft music and wine did peculiar things to the mind. Mark had sensed it, but he hadn't done anything to avoid it, and because she couldn't bear to see him standing there cursing his own temporary lack of discipline, Stacey fled.

CHAPTER SEVEN

THE biggest surprise to Stacey the next morning was to see Jeremy stepping into the office, and the first thing she noticed was his Sunflair blazer. As the door closed behind him, she rose wide-eyed from her chair to query, 'Jeremy! What are you doing here?'

'I was hoping *you* might be able to tell me.'

The usual pinkish tan was a shade deeper as he paced. Stacey watched him, and then, as the best part of the office work had been done for the day, she led him through into the lounge.

He flopped down heavily to continue, 'All I know is that I got orders to pack my bags and set up here.'

'You mean you're back in Sorrento for the rest of the season?'

'That would appear to be the idea.' Heavily sarcastic, he got up to pace again, and then went to stare out of the window.

At a complete loss, Stacey offered philosophically, 'Well, you were sent up to Rome without warning, now you're back here. Perhaps that's the way Mark Lawford works?'

'I was sent to Rome because they badly needed an experienced rep up there,' he said shortly. 'And I happen to know that the two kids I left are likely to stay stranded until the firm can dig up another one.'

Stacey drew on her lip and lowered her eyes to the carpet. 'I suppose it's natural that you should want to snap at me, Jeremy,' she said quietly, 'but I'm just as much in the dark as you are.'

Jeremy turned round and thrust his hands jerkily into his pockets. Letting an apologetic sigh go, he groaned, 'Sorry, Stacey. It's just that . . . well, I'm a bit on edge.'

'Because you didn't want to leave Rome?'

As though he got the full point of her question he lowered his eyes from her steady gaze, and then brought them back uncomfortably. 'That's it, I'm afraid,' he sighed. 'I ought to have told you, I suppose, but . . . well, Melanie and I have been going around together quite a bit these last few weeks.'

Across the silence he watched her face and asked frankly, 'Do you mind?'

After a pause Stacey gave him a warm smile. 'I don't mind, Jeremy,' she said softly. 'I used to think there was something between us once, but that was before. . . .' She trampled over her own raw feelings to finish lightly, 'Before I found I could get along quite passably without you.'

Jeremy dropped an arm around her and walked towards the door opening on to the balcony. 'Looks as though you're going to have to get used to having me around again, though,' he pointed out heavily. 'I've got a feeling I'm stuck here till the last day of the season.'

The boyish smile was tinged with bitterness, and Stacey said pensively, 'It certainly seems a funny time to be making changes.'

'Probably Lawford thinks Sorrento could do with a few new faces,' Jeremy sneered. 'Like mine, for instance, and this girl boss of ours, Sharon Kingsbury.'

'The girl from Sunflair?' Stacey turned away from Jeremy's arm. She wandered over to straighten the circle of lace under a vase of flowers. 'You mean she's coming here? To Sorrento?' she asked.

Jeremy nodded. 'Most of the news goes through the Rome channels. Apparently Lawford wants her to fly out today,' he replied.

Stacey's heart dropped down to its lowest ebb as her trembling fingers fiddled with the lace. The dark she had been in was becoming rapidly lighter. Glaringly, dazzlingly lighter. Blinking the tears away, she began to see all too clearly.

Mark wanted Sharon near in case there might be any misunderstandings about last night.

For him the kiss had been a mistake. Not one he'd found unpleasant, but just an experience for all that. Just another experience, she thought bitterly, still feeling those hard demanding lips on hers. Men collected *them*, as

314

girls collected pretty handkerchiefs. The awful part was that the wine and the evening had nothing to do with Stacey's feelings. She knew that now. But while she had been soaring up into the light and rarefied atmosphere of love, Mark had been simply amusing himself.

Now he wanted to forget the whole affair. She could just imagine his relief at being able to come up with an all-round solution. Sharon for Mark, and Jeremy for Stacey.

'You've gone dead quiet. Are you sure you're not upset about Melanie and me?'

Hearing Jeremy's voice close behind, Stacey put on a bright smile and turned. 'No. I was just thinking that things seem to have gone . . . a bit topsy-turvy,' she said steadily.

'All round,' he smiled, giving her a searching look, 'but they'll drop into place, you'll see. Now what about work? I suppose I'd better start?'

Stacey nodded. 'Most of our guests have gone to Pompeii today,' she pointed out, 'but there's still a bit of book work to do.'

'Okay. I'll start there. And, Stacey,' he caught her hand as she led the way back into the office, 'thanks for being a sport about . . . well, you know what.'

For the rest of the morning Jeremy spent his time going through the accounts, while Stacey attended to various queries from the remaining Sunflair contingent. Later seeing all the work finished and a completely free afternoon ahead, it brought home to her even more forcefully that Jeremy's assistance was not needed in Sorrento.

Her partner however seemed to have ceased puzzling over his recall. He had an adaptable nature, and had already settled down to doing the job that was expected of him. No doubt he had worked out some scheme for keeping in touch with Melanie.

Regarding Stacey, he was attentive and considerate, and didn't seem to be able to do enough to make up for the break he had made between them. They lunched together in the restaurant, and shared a special bottle of wine, and later walked hand in hand through the gardens.

Jeremy's solicitude was balm to Stacey's bruised heart, but she knew that she would soon have to take up the awful business of living again.

It started that evening when she and Jeremy were half-way through dinner. The private table that was always specially reserved was only a few feet from their own, and though Stacey kept her eyes carefully averted, she sensed that Mark had someone with him tonight. Once while accidentally turning her head more than she had intended, she caught the blur of a blue dress from the corner of her eye.

For Stacey the meal was the longest she had ever known, but eventually Jeremy was holding her chair and they were leaving the restaurant. Thankfully work started again after that, and she managed to get herself included in one of the moonlight sailing parties about to take place. Later, lost in a world of laughter, hearty singing and plangent slapping waves, she pretended blissfully that she had no part of the life that went on up there, above the steep black cliffs. But all too soon the boats were heading back for the shore.

Her one consolation was the fact that at least it would be late enough when they got back to the Palazzo to justify her slipping away to her room. If only it had been as easy as that! And if only she hadn't decided to go across the sun terrace to reach it.

In the lights overflowing from the hotel she saw several people talking in groups or strolling beyond the open french windows. It wasn't until a pair of broad white dinner-jacketed shoulders loomed up that she wished she could have sprouted wings and flown up to her balcony.

It wouldn't have done any good. She had an idea that Mark had seen her long before she had seen him.

With a slight incline of the dark head he greeted her suavely and drew the person he had been talking to forward. Stacey saw a dusky-skinned girl about her own age with gloriously black silky hair and eyes that in this light looked slightly violet, but in all probability were a pure Wedgwood blue.

'Sharon, meet Stacey Roberts, our girl rep in Sorrento,' Mark was saying. 'Stacey, this is Miss Kingsbury, the head of Sunflair travel.'

'Hello.' There was an attractive huskiness about the voice. The slim hand that was offered was as cool and smooth as silk.

'I'm happy to meet you, Miss Kingsbury,' Stacey smiled, and then demurring politely she added, 'I hope you'll excuse me, but I was just on my way to my room.'

Including both in her pleasant goodnight her glance was caught up for a second with Mark's. As dark brown eyes looked down into hers, she knew that nothing had changed as far as her heart was concerned. Not even though the hard mouth that she remembered so well from last night was tightening now into something like a grim smile.

Stacey had one thing to thank the August rush of holidaymakers for. They provided the overflow to other hotels in Sorrento, and gave her the chance to get away from the Palazzo for longer periods during the working day.

In time she *would* have got used to seeing Sharon and Mark together, but it was a relief not to have to wait around until her senses became numbed to such scenes as black silken hair spilling over a wide shoulder as a familiar car slid out of the drive each day; the table in the restaurant where they dined together nightly, and the soul-shattering perfection of Sharon's dark beauty against Mark's dinner jacket as they danced.

Driving around in the small Fiat provided by the firm also allowed Stacey to step outside herself occasionally and ponder on the strange person that she had become. It seemed funny to think that the smile she had grown up with suddenly didn't seem to belong to her face any more. She wore it as though it had been carefully pinned at the edges. And talking wasn't all that easy these days. Before, she had always found an endless supply of gay conversation on hand for the groups of holidaymakers at the Palazzo. Now the source seemed to have run dry.

No one could have noticed the changes, thank heaven.

Back at the hotel she was always careful to make the smiles and the chatter appear as unlimited as ever, but it was rather like turning the handle of a mechanical toy, and to be alone in the car was to know the relief of being able to let go of the handle for a while.

Another sanctuary she had turned to was the small office adjoining her own apartments. It was useful to be able to sit up there, waiting for would-be inquiries and at the same time avoiding the miseries of life on the lower floor.

But fate, Stacey decided wryly, was not going to let her keep her head in the sand for long.

Going over the accounts for the third time one day she heard a knock on the office door, and looked up to see Sharon Kingsbury stepping inside.

'The tickets have come for the Naples concert,' she said with a smile. 'Mark's out, but I thought you might be waiting for them.'

'Thank you for bringing them up, Miss Kingsbury,' Stacey smiled, rising from her chair.

'Oh, call me Sharon,' the girl insisted. 'It's all right really. And you're Stacey, aren't you? I like first names best, don't you?'

Without waiting for an answer she swung round to examine the interior of the office. Seeing the door ajar leading into the apartment, she asked, 'Are these your rooms?'

Stacey nodded. 'Would you like to see them?' she invited.

'Oh, I expect they're much the same as mine.' The shrug might have appeared to be indifferent, but the smile was eager.

Stacey led the way through and the other girl wandered around gazing at everything with a ligering interest. The figure was sylph-like in the white embroidered dress, the dark hair swept back behind a wide turquoise headband. All sophistication, Stacey pondered, yet she couldn't help feeling, on this closer look, that there was much of the small girl about Sharon Kingsbury.

A commotion outside made the Wedgwood blue eyes turn to gaze out of the open door and down over the balcony to where Jeremy was leading a fairly sizeable group of guests towards the beach steps.

'Our tours really are popular, aren't they?' Sharon said thoughtfully.

'You must be thrilled to be the head of a successful business concern like Sunflair,' Stacey commented pleasantly.

'Oh, I'm not very effective as a boss, I'm afraid,' Sharon turned smilingly, 'though I used to think I was. When my father died, I thought it was just a matter of answering the odd telephone call, signing my name a few times to keep things as they were.' She pulled a wry mouth. 'I soon learned different. Rick and I . . . that's my brother, he's nineteen . . . we got things into the most awful muddle. If it hadn't been for Mark. . . .' She petered off dreamily and then without any warning the words came floating on a sigh. 'What do you think of Mark?'

Stacey ran a tongue around a dry mouth. Everyone wanted to know what she thought of Mark. The trouble was she'd never be able to tell them. 'Oh,' she fumbled around in her mind for a clever answer, 'he seems to be taking care of things very well for you.'

'You know what it was I first fell for?' Sharon swung her hair absently down her back and gazed smilingly heavenwards. 'That deep brown voice.' She laughed and whirled round. 'I remember we were. . . .'

'Anybody at 'ome?'

The sound of broad Lancashire accents calling out for the steamer timetable cut across the rest of Sharon's conversation. Stacey had never been more thankful to return to work.

This however was the start of many visits from Sharon. Whenever Mark flew out, or had business in town, she would come up and watch the comings and goings of the clients with interest. When there was no work to be done, she would rush away for a tray of tea or coffee and serve it with a kind of childish pleasure before the open windows in the lounge.

One afternoon when she came in wearing toreador slacks and loose-fitting blouse, the black hair caught up in a casual pony-tail, Stacey felt she was getting near to the real Sharon Kingsbury.

After tea she flopped on to the bed and watched Stacey prepare for an evening out at another hotel housing Sunflair guests.

'I wish I had your poise and *savoir-faire*,' she said, swinging her legs and resting her chin in her hand.

'My what?' Stacey laughed, fixing a small ear-clip beneath the upsweep of bronze-silk hair.

'You know. Polish . . . confidence. . . . I've watched you downstairs. You're marvellous with the guests. I suppose. . . .' Sharon fingered through the jewellery casket lying on the bed, 'you've got used to relying on yourself to get by?'

'Well,' Stacey pursed her lips into a smile, not sure which way the conversation was going, 'I've been a working girl for quite a while now.'

'The whole business of living is work to me,' Sharon sighed. 'Dad did everything for us, you see. Mother died when Rick was born, and I suppose he wanted to make up where he could. He meant well, of course, but. . . .' She took a deep breath, 'it's an awfully big world when you step out into it.'

'I shouldn't worry,' Stacey said sincerely. 'I don't think anyone suspects you're a newcomer. I certainly didn't.'

Sharon was obviously pleased with the reply. She laughed gaily, and in that moment Stacey had a peculiar feeling that the blue eyes ought to have been a flashing black, something about the tilt of the dusky-skinned chin was fleetingly familiar. Now where. . . .? Before she had a chance to pin down what was floating around in her mind, Sharon's next words came to disperse it completely.

'I like you, Stacey,' she was saying magnanimously. 'You can come to the wedding if you like.'

'Wh . . . what wedding?' Stacey asked weakly. Not that she didn't know, but she had to hear it with her own ears.

'When I marry Mark, of course!'

'Of course.'

Stacey fumbled for a clean handkerchief, feeling her life drain away with those two simple words.

She saw little of Sharon after that. The news was going

around that her business lawyers had arrived from England, so it was possible that she was occupied with Sunflair matters. Jeremy said that there was a big discussion on, but he didn't know what about. Probably planning some kind of merger with the Palazzo, for when Mark and Sharon got married, Stacey thought miserably.

She often wished that there was more to do, to keep her mind from gnawing at the subject of Mark and Sharon, but with Jeremy's adept handling of the Sunflair work, their afternoons were usually free.

It occurred to her on one of these free periods that the summer days were fast slipping away, and there wouldn't be all that many more to soak up, in the tranquillity of the staff beach. She resolved to make much more use of it from now on. Jeremy was with her all the way on this suggestion. He was gay and bouncy these days and his good humour made him especially considerate. In fact if it hadn't been for that distant smile in the blue eyes she might have believed he was the same old Jeremy.

Not that it would have made any difference to her if he had been, Stacey thought dejectedly. Thanks to a pair of penetrating brown eyes, the gleam of a certain smile, nothing would ever be the same again for Stacey Roberts.

Still, the remaining weeks at the Palazzo had to be got through somehow, and she couldn't have had any brighter company than Jeremy's for the afternoons on the beach. The only snag with the staff section as far as her fair-haired companion was concerned was its lack of refreshments. He was constantly padding off towards the hotel beach in search of iced drinks or cigarettes.

Stacey usually took advantage of these occasions, by drowsing luxuriously under the beach umbrella that Mark had provided together with a long padded sunchair. She would revel in the feel of the warm breeze brushing over her limbs, the pure peace of the outside world.

One afternoon when she had almost drifted off to sleep, she sensed a presence standing over her. She opened her eyes with a drowsy smile, thinking that Jeremy had returned sooner than usual. The sleep fled from her senses when she saw who it was.

'Tony!' She sat up quickly. 'Wh ... what are you doing here?'

'Admiring the scenery.' The black eyes roamed over her limbs impudently.

'How did you get here?' she asked, just grasping at anything to say, for it was fairly obvious how he had arrived. His tanned body was dripping with sea water and he wore the local snorkelling equipment.

He must have known that the question was superfluous, for he merely shrugged. The smile playing about the well-defined lips seemed totally without humour, the glint in the dark eyes could have been anything ... suppressed anger, maybe.

Stacey felt her heart racing. This was the first time she had seen Tony since that awful night in the cave. His look seemed to be turning her inside out.

'You lose me my job, you know,' he said eventually and almost lightly.

Stacey swallowed. 'I *was* partly responsible for that, I'm afraid,' she admitted. 'But not,' her tones iced over, 'for the slant you tried to put on our trip to the beach. You were determined to get the wrong idea....'

'So next time we make sure we get the right idea, hah?'

'I wasn't aware there was going to be any next time.'

Tony might only have been joking, yet somehow she didn't like the sound of his tones. She held his gaze for as long as she could manage and then swung her eyes away distastefully. Her heart knocked wildly inside at the vast emptiness of the beach, and the nearness of the dripping figure, but then Jeremy's voice was drifting in blissfully from the rocks.

'Tony, you old devil! What are you doing back?'

To Stacey, Jeremy had never looked so adorable, scuffing over the sand, a can of iced orange juice in each hand, the boyish grin stretching his tanned features.

Tony gave a slow smile. 'I swim down the coast most days,' he explained pleasantly enough now.

'Got a job yet?'

The thick-set shoulders shrugged. 'So far I have not been lucky.'

'Not such a good recommendation, getting fired from

the Palazzo, huh?' Jeremy dropped on to his knees near the beach bag.

As the two men exchanged oblique grins Tony replied, unabashed, 'It is the wrong time of the season to be looking for work.'

'Sure!' With a crooked smile Jeremy reached into the bag for the can opener and pierced the tins. Pouring the liquid into the beakers, he said cheerfully, 'Sorry I can't offer you one, old man. We weren't expecting guests.'

He handed Stacey her drink and threw half of his back in one go before eyeing Tony with renewed interest. 'What do you plan to do?' he asked, pursuing the subject of work.

Tony drew patterns with his toes. 'I think I move on,' he said slowly. 'I think perhaps I try Venice. It is fine there for tourists.'

'Might be a good idea,' Jeremy grinned knowingly, and then perhaps because he had noticed that Stacey was taking no part in the conversation, he rounded off with, 'Well, don't forget to look us up to say goodbye before you go,' and then settled back on his towel.

Tony's smile was very white as he turned it to rest on Stacey. 'I won't forget,' he murmured. 'But I like to play. I will stay in Sorrento, I think, until all my friends go home.'

Jeremy grunted from the towel and Tony bowed briefly, with *'Arrivederci!'*

Stacey nodded, but turned away before the figure had reached the water's edge.

When the dark head had disappeared round the rocks Jeremy raised himself on one elbow to comment humorously, 'You practically talked us to death just now.'

Stacey gave a small smile. 'I suppose I wasn't feeling very convivial,' she said wryly.

Jeremy studied her and grinned. 'Tony's got something,' he observed. 'The women either love him or hate him, but they're certainly not indifferent to him.'

'I don't know anything about that,' Stacey shrugged. 'I'll just feel better when he's gone to wherever he's going.'

If Tony had anything, she was thinking privately, it

was a warped sense of humour. She lay back and tried to recapture the peace of the afternoon, but it was difficult to shake off those smiling innuendoes. What had he meant by that 'Next time' bit? And why was he staying in Sorrento when he hadn't got a job? She sat up again and waited for her nerves to slacken. If Tony hoped to get back at her simply by making her feel uneasy he was doing very well.

Happily the worried mood soon passed. Jeremy's presence was a soothing influence, and it wasn't long before Stacey was reclining and sipping the rest of her drink dreamily. She wondered about Jeremy. Lots of things. But the all-important one was, how were things going with Melanie?

Looking down at his relaxed pose, she was tempted to ask, but knew he preferred not to talk about it. Talk or not, Stacey smiled to herself, it was fairly obvious that something was bubbling up. She sensed it as he lay there whistling to himself with closed eyes, and later as they made their way back up to the hotel when he took the steps two at a time. He was everybody's favourite organizer that night, but though he held Stacey in a kind of joyous embrace, whenever they could snatch a dance together, it wasn't until several evenings later that she learned the reason for Jeremy's elated spirits.

The day started off with a new influx of Sunflair guests, and Stacey was kept busy sorting out accommodation and directing people to various places of interest in Sorrento. Towards evening the pace died down and she was able to snatch a couple of hours in her room.

A leisurely soak in the bath worked wonders and she even found a little pleasure in dressing for the evening. The face that stared back at her from the mirror had hardly changed at all since that calamitous event under the stars.

There were tiny tell-tale smudges under her eyes, but these only seemed to make the pupils look larger and the lashes thicker, so there was nothing catastrophic there, thank goodness. The face had a paleness about it, but since she had been careful not to let the sun give the rest of her skin anything more than a gentle straw-coloured tan, it didn't look unduly so. In fact the lavender sleeveless chiffon she chose, with a halter neckline, seemed if anything to enhance her complexion.

Brushing her hair ready to sweep it back in the style she had adopted for the evenings, Stacey wondered if Jeremy had been as busy as she had. She hadn't seen him all day as he had been out at the other hotels, but they were due to meet for dinner, and with most of the new guests exploring Sorrento, they were fairly sure of a quiet night.

Lightly made up and all ready to go, Stacey gazed at her reflection pensively. It would be useless to say that she hadn't done a good job, in fact she had to admit that the picture she made was just a little breathtaking. But there was no tell-tale racing of the pulses. Why should there be? Jeremy was the nicest person in the world, but she wasn't looking for *his* appreciation.

The restaurant was crowded, as it usually was on a Saturday night, but one had the feeling that each couple or group was concerned only with the small world of their own table.

Stacey concentrated, as she always did, on making this the case with Jeremy and herself. The time they spent in the restaurant was infinitely more bearable that way. As it happened there was enough going on at her own table tonight to keep her attention centred there.

Jeremy was looking like some successful male model, with his tanned boyish features showing just enough lines of life to be interesting, and the up-to-the-minute cut of his dark lounge suit. The fair hair gleamed almost flaxen under the chandeliered lighting, and there was a gleam too, Stacey noticed, in the bright blue eyes.

As they started on the first course Jeremy said as though itching to come out with something, 'I nipped into Sorrento today.'

'I thought,' Stacey said with puzzled amusement, 'that you had been in town all day?'

'Well, I have,' he pointed out. 'What I meant was, I nipped out to buy something.' In the pause that followed he looked at Stacey with a kind of happy impatience to ask, 'Well, have you got any idea what I'm talking about *now?*'

'Not the faintest,' Stacey said genuinely.

With a tantalizing shrug Jeremy continued with his meal. He seemed to enjoy her good-humoured exasperation, and purposely talked on the subject of work to prolong it. It wasn't until the last course was finished that he pushed his plate away to say with a weighty casualness, 'I was on the phone to Melanie the other day.'

'Nice,' Stacey smiled, waiting.

'We had a long talk.'

'It can be so much more satisfying than letters.'

He put his hands across the table to say carefully, 'I'll be going to Rome at the end of the season.'

'To Melanie?' Stacey asked needlessly.

Jeremy nodded. 'I want to spend the rest of my life with her.' He said it so completely unaffectedly and with such a depth of feeling that Stacey was stirred into taking his hand and squeezing it affectionately.

'Lucky Melanie,' she said sincerely.

'Now,' the gleam was back in the blue eyes, 'you must know what I bought?'

'Haven't a clue,' Stacey replied not quite truthfully. He reached into his pocket and pulled out a small leather-covered box. Opening it, he placed it reverently in front of her.

'What do you think of that?' he asked softly. Stacey gazed at the ring, a jewelled cluster of sparkling lights amidst velvet, and gasped.

'Well?' He waited expectantly.

'What can I say, Jeremy, except that ... it's beautiful beyond words,' she breathed.

'You really think so?'

'Fabulous!'

He continued to smile down at the ring absently. 'I suppose I could have bought one in Rome,' he murmured, 'but I couldn't wait. I want to give it to her as soon as I step off the train. There's only one thing. . . . I've just thought. . . .' His face dropped as he took the ring out of the box.' I don't know if it will fit. I'm going to look a prize idiot if it goes spinning round her finger.'

'It looks about average,' Stacey smiled reassuringly.

'It does, doesn't it?' Jeremy looked relieved. 'And Melanie's about your build. Let's see what it looks like on you.'

Still smiling, Stacey kept her hand firmly on the table.

'I couldn't do that, Jeremy,' she demurred. 'These things are sacred to a girl, you know.'

'I suppose so.' He looked thoughtful for a while and then continued to wield the ring eagerly. 'But hang it all! Dozens of people may have tried it on before I bought it, and it'll only take a second.'

He was like a small boy with a new possession, and Stacey didn't have the heart to stifle his pleasure at this stage. She put her hand forward acquiescently and Jeremy slipped on the ring.

'Gosh!' He stared with undisguised delight. 'It was made for a woman's hand all right. And it fits too.' He took both her hands in his and raised his eyes. 'I couldn't have asked for a better model.' And then as the blue glance darkened to roam over her appraisingly he murmured with humorous incredulity, 'I'm actually buying a ring for someone else. I must be mad!'

'I bet Melanie doesn't think so,' Stacey said, twinkling. She slipped the ring off her finger and placed it back in the box. It lay on the table between them until they had finished their wine and then Jeremy dropped it back into his pocket.

They had a look in on the dancing before dinner, but Jeremy seemed too keyed up, and after pleading weariness went off to his room. Stacey didn't really mind. She was ready for an early night herself. After all, she told herself bleakly, it would be one less to endure before the end of the season.

Perhaps a sudden desire to get away from all this gaiety now made her rush rather blindly along the dim carpeted foyer. Had she been walking, she would have taken the corner a little steadier, and so avoided the wide frame coming from the direction of the restaurant. But too late, she came full on to meet a white dinner jacket.

As arms whipped out to steady her, they held her for a moment and then tightened roughly, until she was caught up close and staring up almost under a craggy chin. Steel-flecked brown eyes gazed down into hers. Drawn features resembled chiselled teak, but the hard mouth held something of a twisted smile as Mark commented laconically,

'Looks as though congratulations are in order. I take it you won't be wearing the ring on duty.'

Before his words had a chance to sink in, he had thrust her away from him and disappeared down the deserted hall.

CHAPTER EIGHT

STACEY was still trembling from the impact long after she had reached her room; not the force of the collision, for Mark's arms were steel and his weight had taken the shock, but the upsurge of everything she had been trying to live down since his kiss.

She waited for her flying pulses to settle and decided that from now on she would have to watch her step. Any more brushes like that with Mark and she would be liable to fall apart. Thank heaven there was only a short while to go before the end of the season, and she wasn't likely to be seeing much of him in the meantime.

That was what Stacey assumed, but she had reckoned without Sunflair's youngest visitor to date, little Yvette Taylor.

Children didn't make up a very high contingent of the Palazzo guests, probably because much of the local coast was rocky, and parents usually favoured wide spacious beaches for their offspring.

It was doubtful though if Yvette would have been tearing around on miles of sand even if she had had the opportunity. A tiny-boned creature, with big cloud-grey eyes and an immaculate pigtail, she could usually be found sitting motionless on the wall flanking the hotel steps, or scuffing her shoes absently over the lawns.

She had arrived with a Mrs. Lander, a middle-aged woman whom she called Aunt Margaret, and that for Yvette seemed to be that. Aunt Margaret kept mainly to her room and balcony, and Yvette sat or walked disconsolately in the sun.

Stacey had made several attempts to be friendly, but without much success. Aunt Margaret, it seemed, wasn't the only one who preferred her own company.

Taking all this into account, Stacey might have thought it strange when, one morning, a tiny pigtailed figure boarded the hotel bus, bound for a day trip to Capri. She might have done, but for the fact that Aunt

Margaret had made one of her rare appearances to wave her off, and Yvette had settled down nicely next to Miss Pinder, the young schoolteacher. It looked as though the two ladies had come to some arrangement, so what was there to question about that?

For Stacey it was one of those hectic days when nothing really went well. Jeremy had arranged the Capri outing some days before and then found he was needed in Naples.

'One of our crowd has got into a mix-up about passports,' he explained to Stacey in the office that morning. 'I'd better go. The old man's acid these days.'

Not entirely to help Jeremy out, Stacey had willingly volunteered to take his place for the trip to Capri. Anything, she thought, to get away from the Palazzo for a day. She hadn't reckoned for a tiny island crowded to the edges with late holidaymakers; hot airless weather, and a certain irritability amongst her clients, triggered off no doubt by the claustrophobic conditions of a packed boat to start with.

One of the men in her party lost his wallet, containing a considerable amount of Italian lire, over the side when he tried to do a bargain with one of the floating gift shops. Another client had his hat knocked off by an over-exuberant hand.

Late afternoon there was an argument amongst the crowd at the bus stop for Anacapri, when it was found that some people were trying to jump the queue, and when Stacey and her party did eventually arrive, practically everyone complained of the shortage of amenities in the tiny hill town.

All in all, Stacey wasn't sorry to see the Palazzo again, much as it was the root of her unhappiness. Jeremy still wasn't back from Naples. She got through most of the office work that had accumulated during the day, cleared up, and was having visions of dining alone on her balcony, when a light knock came on the door. She was a little surprised to see the matronly figure of Mrs. Lander gazing expectantly round the room.

'Hello,' Stacey greeted encouragingly. 'Don't tell me you're thinking of trying a tour yourself now that ...?'

'I saw the bus arrive back, some time ago,' Mrs. Lander broke in, the smile battling with a somewhat furrowed frown. 'I thought I ought to pop along and say thank you for your kind offer today. Most of the guests will have gone down to dinner now, I should think.'

'I expect so,' Stacey nodded with a weary smile, wondering what offer the woman was talking about. Perhaps it was some service Jeremy had performed? 'It's been a bit of a hectic day,' she added with an intake of breath. 'I think we're all glad to be back.'

Mrs. Lander looked around. 'I expect Yvette is tired,' and then in slightly injured tones, 'I *had* hoped she would come straight along to her room, but if she's with you I suppose. . . .'

Stacey rose from her chair to take the other woman more into her view. 'Yvette isn't with me,' she said wonderingly. 'Why should she be?'

'Well, since you were so kind as to offer to take her along with you today I thought. . . .'

Stacey looked blank. 'Nothing would have pleased me more,' she laughed, puzzled, 'but I'm afraid I've never been able to get close enough to Yvette to suggest even a walk.'

'You mean you didn't arrange to take her along with you today?' Mrs. Lander's features paled slightly. 'But you saw her get on the bus. I was there. I waved you off.'

'Yes, that's right.' Stacey cast her mind back. 'But weren't you waving at Miss Pinder? I thought you two had settled something between you?'

'Oh dear!' Mrs. Lander groped for a chair and dropped down. 'I don't like the sound of this at all.'

Not liking the look of the other woman's colour, Stacey said cheerily, 'Don't worry. We'll sort it out. It looks as if Yvette thumbed herself a free ride, but there's no harm done.'

'I'm not so sure.' The tones sounded so strained that Stacey found herself looking at the other woman hard. She heard her ask worriedly, 'Well, where is she?'

'Oh, she'll be around somewhere,' Stacey smiled.

'She isn't.' Mrs. Lander looked up. 'I've been looking and asking since the bus came in. Yvette is nowhere in the hotel.'

Experiencing the first tug of uneasiness, Stacey heard herself saying distantly, while searching for an answer, 'I think we're worrying unnecessarily. She's bound to be here somewhere. I know!' Her next thought strengthened her a little. 'What about Miss Pinder? Yvette's been with her all day. I wouldn't be surprised if she isn't in her room at this moment.'

'I hope you're right.' Mrs. Lander didn't brighten much, but Stacey was feeling confident.

'You wait here, and I'll go and rout her out,' she smiled. 'She probably hasn't any idea of the time.'

Stacey's hopes dropped, when she met Miss Pinder hurrying down to dinner. 'Why, yes,' the schoolteacher recollected pleasantly, 'I had Yvette with me right up to Anacapri. I could see how busy you were, and I rather enjoyed the child's company. . . .'

'You mean she told you that I. . . .' Stacey held the breath she wanted to let go, and asked steadily, 'And what about after Anacapri?'

'Well, I really couldn't say,' Miss Pinder went on. 'I met this young lady who was from the same part of England as myself. We sat together coming back.'

'I see,' Stacey swallowed. 'And you didn't see where Yvette was sitting?'

'I can't say that I noticed her on any of the other seats, but I must confess I didn't give it much thought at the time.'

Stacey nodded, turning to go. 'Thank you, Miss Pinder,' she said faintly. 'I hope I haven't held you up?'

The other woman inclined her head and moved on. 'Sorry I couldn't have been more help,' she smiled.

Mrs. Lander didn't look in the least surprised at the news, but she was visibly more shaken. She clutched the back of the chair and rested her head on her hands with a moan. 'It's only what I expected,' she quavered, 'and just like Yvette. She isn't nine yet, but she knew enough to get herself on your bus *and* to disappear over there on the other side.'

'But it's crazy!' Stacey pushed her hair back worriedly. 'Why would Yvette want to run away? And why Anacapri of all places?'

'To her small mind it's far enough away, I suppose.' Mrs. Lander raised her head and gazed long and steadily at Stacey. 'Perhaps there's something you should know, Miss Roberts,' she said slowly. 'My niece isn't really here on a holiday, nor am I for that matter, although goodness knows . . .' She broke off and then went on with a sigh, 'Her parents are going through a difficult time at home. There's talk of a separation . . . and what with the endless arguments . . . and Yvette's a sensitive child . . . well, I thought she was best out of it for a while. As her aunt I wanted to do what I could, but it hasn't helped much, I'm afraid.'

'I see what you mean,' Stacey nodded, feeling some of her colour drain away. She did see, all too well. A desperately unhappy child, living with the uncertainty of a floundering marriage, and the right to both parents, and coping with a well-meaning but somewhat indifferent aunt. No wonder Yvette had forgotten how to play, and no wonder. . . .

Stacey cut off her thoughts abruptly and moved quickly to the door. 'I'd better go downstairs now, and explain that I have to go back to Capri,' she hurried. She patted Mrs. Lander's shoulder as the woman rose to follow, and forcing a reassuring smile, stated with a cheerful matter-of-factness, 'And don't worry. If your niece managed to dupe both you and me into making the trip, she's probably taking care of herself with the same shrewdness. I'll have her back here before you've had time to miss her.'

Mrs. Lander went off to her room with an inconsolable bright eye. Stacey made her way to the downstairs office and though outwardly calm, she felt something near to panic rising within her. Yvette was only eight years old, and the precipitous cliffs of the island yawned clear over the sea. What if she felt unwanted? What if . . . ?

By the time she had reached the office door, Stacey could feel the perspiration pricking coldly at her temples. She knocked and went in and blurted to the man who was scowling over papers on his desk,

'Mark, I'm going to have to go back to Capri.'

Eyeing her sharply, he stood up and came round the side of the desk. 'What's wrong?' he asked.

'Oh, some small matter I should have attended to,' she hedged, wishing those brown eyes wouldn't rake her so.

'This . . . small matter seems to have taken quite a swipe at you,' he said with grim perceptiveness, and then in even tones, 'All right, let's have it.'

Feeling that precious time was slipping away, Stacey took a breath. 'Little Yvette Taylor . . . I don't know whether you know her. . . .'

'The pigtailed nipper,' he nodded. 'We've made one or two tours of the hotel together.'

Stacey bit back an hysterical laugh. 'You got further with her than I did,' she said, pacing, 'but perhaps I haven't been doing my job very well, in fact,' she wrung her hands, 'I'm sure I haven't, otherwise I would have seen that she was alone on the bus this morning, and I had only to check the list that Jeremy left to see quite clearly. . . .'

She was aware of firm hands pulling her up. 'You're rambling, Stacey,' Mark said quietly, turning her towards him. 'Now let's try it a little slower. What's this about young Yvette?'

'She didn't come back with us from Capri,' Stacey confessed. 'I've only just found out that her aunt thought I was supervising her on the trip . . . and there's something else I've just learned. . . .' She raised a drained face. 'Yvette's mother and father are splitting up. That's why she's been brought out here.'

Mark kept his eyes on her while he took this in, and then he asked levelly, 'Have you eaten?'

'Oh, good heavens!' Stacey pulled away impatiently. 'Who can think of eating at a time like this?'

'I can,' he snapped. 'I'll order you a tray in here.'

'I suppose you know the whole thing is my fault,' she said, fighting back frustrated tears. 'The first thing I should have done was check with Yvette's aunt.'

'None of us is infallible.' His eyes made a play for hers and with something of a twisted smile he reached for the phone. After a lengthy conversation in brisk Italian, he lowered it to state, 'The authorities have been alerted. They'll pick her up in no time. Relax!' He phoned again briefly for a meal and lowering the receiver added, 'When you've eaten we'll go.'

'We?' Stacey's heart stumbled out of time. 'Why you?' she asked. 'Why can't I be allowed to straighten things out my own way?'

'Because you're a woman and you think like one, and you've probably got the kid into untold scrapes in your mind already.'

'Whereas you—?' she queried coolly.

'I think I have a pretty shrewd idea of what she's up to.'

While Stacey was battling with the food brought promptly after the phone call Mark lowered a glance over her sleeveless lime-coloured dress. 'You'll need something a little warmer,' he pointed out. 'We don't know how long this is going to take.'

'I have a matching duster coat.' She lowered her fork. 'I'll go up and....'

'Keep going,' Mark nodded, moving towards the door. 'I'll fetch it.'

With the cleansing pads from the handbag that she had brought with her, Stacey was able to wipe away some of the weariness of the day. Strengthened after the meal and with a light dusting of fresh make-up, she felt in slightly higher spirits.

Mark came back with the coat. She slipped into it with lowered lashes as he held it, trying to shut out the picture of slim brown hands flicking coolly through her wardrobe.

As they went out towards the car she had to remind herself that the light grip on her arm was nothing more than a continuation of the politeness he had shown in holding her coat. It wasn't too difficult, seeing that Sharon's perfume hung unmistakably over the seat he was helping her into now. She drew her arm quickly away, and as he slammed the door shut with a slight testiness and strode round to his side, she supposed miserably that all this must be a frightful nuisance to him.

Obviously he could think of better things to do with his time.

Down at the harbour he helped her out of the car to say tersely, 'We'll take a motor launch. It should get us there in about twenty minutes.'

As the small boat sliced purposefully through the waves, Stacey found herself hugging her coat round her. Even in the small cabin it was possible to feel the gentle evening breeze being whipped colder by the speed of the boat.

Mark stood by the rail. He seemed oblivious to anything but the wash of the waves.

Capri drew rapidly nearer with each second, but it was almost dusk when the island loomed up before the boat, like some large lounging sea creature, lazily indifferent to the mass of life crawling over it.

Mark led her towards a funicular which they took up to a building in the Piazza. As she waited on the steps he was striding back out to her within seconds.

'Nothing's turned up yet,' he informed her. 'Any ideas where we might start?'

'Well, she was with us at Anacapri,' Stacey replied dejectedly.

'That's something.' He guided her through the straggling crowds in the square, towards the first line of taxis. Minutes later they were climbing the road, past vineyards and villas and tall cypresses. A dying sun had cast a copper glow over the world, but Stacey was too strung up to appreciate the beauty of the evening. Her mind was on a tiny cotton-frocked figure that should have been tucked up by now in one of the Palazzo bedrooms. *Would* have been but for her own carelessness.

Stacey bit back a worried tremor as the car came on to a view of sheer cliffs and a dark sea some thousand feet below. If anything had happened to Yvette Taylor, she alone would be responsible.

They came into the old town of Anacapri and Mark instructed the driver to tour the streets, but though they went around for some time there was no sign of Yvette.

'Just making sure,' Mark remarked as he paid off the taxi. He took Stacey's arm and turned towards the sea.

'I've an idea she'll be more off the beaten track,' he added.

'Wherever that might be,' Stacey said tightly.

He looked at her and remarked abruptly, 'She's only been missing a couple of hours. Give the imagination a rest.'

'A couple of hours since I found out,' Stacey snapped agitatedly. 'But it's ages since we were up this way. Yvette must have been on her own since we left to go back to Capri for the boat.'

'So we'll have a slight case of malnutrition on our hands.'

'And apart from that she'll be perfectly safe, I suppose,' Stacey flamed, annoyed at his easy tones. 'Then how is it nobody's seen her? It's only a small island, you know.'

'She's only a small kid.'

'And when it comes to *small* things,' she dragged free angrily, 'men have no hearts.'

As she stumbled over the uneven ground he caught her up roughly and swung her towards him. 'And women are *all* heart, I suppose?' For a second the brown eyes blazed down into hers, and then his gaze was drawn past it to a point over the cliffs.

Fleetingly Stacey felt her pulses race, but all too soon he had drawn away to get something below into perspective. She followed his gaze to the beach and saw a tiny cove of sand with one rock taking the first frill of the waves. Sitting on the rock, a small figure was swinging bare feet idly through the waves. In the dwindling light it was impossible to see the colour or style of the hair, but there was no mistaking the flash of primrose cotton that Stacey had seen on the bus this morning.

'It is! It's Yvette!' she exclaimed breathlessly. 'How on earth did she get down there?'

As she hurried forward to the edge of the cliff Mark took her arm. 'Take it easy,' he said drily. 'That's the quickest way to find out.'

Further along they found a gentler sloping descent, and with Mark leading the way in the gathering shadows, they made their way down to the sand. The small head turned as they approached, but the legs continued to trail in the water. When Mark and Stacey reached the rock, Yvette stared blandly and said, 'Hello.'

Her greeting had all the aplomb of a child swinging on her own garden gate. Stacey could have slumped down with relief. Instead she smiled and said shakily,

'Yvette! Your aunt has been very worried about you, you know.'

'Has she?' The swing of the legs was indifferent, but Stacey fancied she saw an interested light in the big grey eyes.

'Hadn't we better get going?' she coaxed.

'S'pose so.' Yvette drew one foot up, and pulling a handkerchief from her pocket proceeded to dry off methodically. As though she suspected that some assistance might be offered, she promptly picked up the sandals and socks that had been lying on the rock beside her, and placed them squarely in the primrose lap. Slowly one sock was pulled on, and then a sandal. The buckle took time.

Mark lit a cigarette and rested a foot up leisurely on the rock. Stacey gazed out to sea. The air was warm down here. The waves threw themselves playfully at her feet, and in the distance she could see the lights of another shore. The sheer peace of the moment was overwhelming, until she remembered the reason for being here.

Yvette was fiddling with the buckle of the other sandal.

'Ready to go?' Stacey asked lightly.

Yvette finished fumbling and stood up. As Mark put an arm out she balanced aloofly. 'I can walk, thank you,' she said primly.

'I'm glad to hear it.' Mark shrugged with a grin. 'I wouldn't want to carry a heavy weight up those cliffs.'

He let her jump down on the sand unattended and lead the way up the cliff. Stacey didn't feel that Yvette was by nature a slow child, yet she took her time up the narrow path. With Mark bringing up the rear, it was stifling to feel his nearness coming up close by her shoulder. Occasionally she would lose her footing and drop back against him, but there was no hurrying Yvette. She kept up her snail's pace to the very top.

They walked back towards Anacapri in silence, but when a *pensione* appeared with chairs and tables laid out on a terrace, Mark looked down to the petite figure some distance below him to ask, 'Hungry?'

'A little.' Yvette stared straight ahead.

'You'll have lots to eat when we get back,' Stacey smiled.

Yvette pondered on this and then took hold of Mark's hand. 'Couldn't we have something now?' she asked, lifting a serious gaze.

'Not now, darling,' Stacey encouraged. 'We might be able to get you a snack on the steamer.'

'Why not?' Mark turned a gaze down thoughtfully on Yvette as though the conversation was strictly between the two of them. 'It's been a long day, hasn't it, pigtail? And I could do with a drink myself.'

He turned towards the *pensione* and Stacey followed without a word. She was all for seeing to Yvette's needs, but what about getting back?

Once sat at a flower-decked table, a glass of the *pensione*'s own wine at her fingertips, and the duster coat discarded over the back of a chair, Stacey changed her mind about rushing away from Capri. For the first time today she felt as though she could relax a little under its magic. Its scented air, tumbling blossoms, soaring peaks and winding lanes, above all its spellbinding calm.

She took a deep and satisfied breath. Perhaps the evening was the best time to soak it all in. Around her, fig trees and pepper trees looked a pale emerald in the concealed lighting. The white bulk of the *pensione* was silhouetted against the night sky.

Yvette, for once, was moving at speed and making short work of the meal that Mark had ordered for her. It was only when she came to the Neapolitan ice cream that some of her previous languor returned, and with it this time an inclination to talk. Twisting her spoon in the ice cream, she gazed with interest at the row of french windows in the *pensione*.

'Are those the rooms where people stay?' she asked.

'Might well be,' Mark drawled, watching the ice cream.

Yvette considered. 'I expect it's fun living on an island,' she jerked with a small laugh.

Hoping to encourage the brighter mood, Stacey asked pleasantly, 'Was it fun today?'

'Sort of.' Yvette trailed a pink tongue over her spoon. 'I played with some children. We had a good time,' she emphasized with a straight stare, 'but then they went home and I paddled.'

'Didn't you find it a nuisance not being able to talk ... in their language, I mean?' Stacey asked.

Yvette shrugged as though her mind had already wandered from the subject. Perhaps it had, for her gaze returned to the french windows. 'Are those the rooms where people stay?' she repeated.

'You've already asked that, pigtail.' Mark hitched the trousers of his lightweight suit and crossed one leg over the other good naturedly. After a long hard stare at the building, Yvette looked at her watch pointedly to sigh,

'I expect we've missed the steamer?'

'Half an hour to go,' Mark checked.

'That's a long time, isn't it?' dejectedly.

'Enough.'

She tightened her lips over the small blob of ice cream, and then turned a beseeching look towards the *pensione*, and then back to Mark.

'Couldn't we stay?' she asked quickly. 'We could easily get the steamer in the morning.'

Stacey bit back an incredulous laugh at the bizarre request, but much to her surprise Mark didn't flinch. He lowered a glance over the small figure to enquire lazily, 'What about your aunt?'

'She'll just think we've missed the boat.' Yvette traced a finger carefully over the tablecloth.

Stacey felt compelled to offer evenly, 'She expects us to bring you back tonight, Yvette.'

'But how can you if there isn't a boat?'

The steamer wouldn't have left yet, and there were still the speed launches, but with wide-eyed innocence Yvette had conveniently dispensed with all means of leaving the island.

Instead of questioning this Mark murmured easily,

340

'You've got a point there, nipper.'

In the silence that followed Stacey felt her heart knocking. She raised her eyes in time to see a brown glance lower over her and then Mark was pulling on his cigarette and rising to his feet. 'It's been a rough trip,' he commented mildly. 'I reckon we could all do with a break. I'll go and see what the room situation is.' Minutes later he was back with two keys and as Yvette looked up bright-eyed he grinned, 'You bunk in with Stacey, the third from the end. I'm on the next floor.'

Yvette didn't allow herself any childish whoops of delight, but she did lapse into quite unstoppable chatter after that. Bowling along, she turned to Stacey to say proudly, 'And I *can* talk in Italian, you know. With my hands anyway!' As Stacey blinked Yvette laughed gaily. 'I'll tell you what,' she chattered on, 'you ask me what I think about . . . well, right now, f'rinstance.'

'All right, I'm asking.' Stacey slanted her a gaze with a bemused smile.

'Now I put the knuckle of this finger, the first one, into the side of my cheek like that. You see?' she demonstrated. 'That means "Things are good".'

A highly debatable point, Stacey thought wryly, conscious of wide shoulders opposite, but she managed to rest her chin in her hand with a light, 'Ingenious!'

'And if I put my finger and thumb together, and wave it about like this, it means "Why?" and if I put my hands towards my throat, that means "Nothing doing".'

The slang expression spoken with full authenticity brought a bubble of laughter from Stacey. Obviously Yvette had picked something up from her wandering around the Palazzo, and was making the most of this opportunity of showing it off.

As her laughter rippled in with Stacey's Mark drawled from his relaxed position. 'I thought eight-year-olds needed lots of beauty sleep?'

Yvette was suddenly intrigued by this new track. 'I wonder what the beds are like?' She jumped up from her chair. 'I think I'll go and look at mine.'

'I should sample it too,' Mark returned drily, 'until about seven o'clock tomorrow morning.'

Stacey found that none of the bedrooms of the *pensione* had doors. To gain entry one used the french windows. She turned the key into a room that was pure white with plain wooden furniture. The single beds on either side of the wall had mosquito nets draped over them.

'Can I have this one?' Yvette lifted the cover to flop down. She made a thorough job of testing the bed-springs, before falling back with a yawn. 'Gosh, I'm tired,' she murmured absently.

'Well, don't fall asleep like that,' Stacey smiled. 'There's a wash basin in the corner. We'll probably be able to buy toothbrushes in the *pensione*.'

As she helped with the buttons of the primrose dress, Yvette looked up with a grin. 'It's fun, isn't it?' she chuckled. 'We haven't brought any luggage. We'll have to sleep in our slips.'

'We'll manage for one night,' Stacey nodded, keeping her face straight. She wasn't at all sure that Yvette ought to be encouraged into congratulating herself on her escapade. Tucked up beneath the sheets, she gazed up to ask,

'Do you suppose that someone could get lost for a very long time on Capri?'

'Doubtful,' Stacey shook her head. 'It's not a very big place.'

'Still, a day and a night is quite long, isn't it? A whole day and now a whole night,' Yvette added, rolling the words pleasurably over the small tongue. Before Stacey could sort out her suspicions Yvette had turned on her side with a drowsily satisfied smile and a serene 'Good-night, Stacey.'

Mark was draped against the vine-entwined loggia when Stacey came out. With no light from the french windows, she couldn't see his face, but there was no mistaking that physique. The cigarette he had raised glowed a sudden deep red as she approached.

'Room okay?' he asked lazily.

She nodded, feeling a sudden tightness in her throat at all this darkness, and Mark only a handstretch away. She found strength against a wooden pillar, and groping for a light remark came up with, 'I don't think we'll be hearing much from Yvette for the next few hours.'

'For an eight-year-old, she's an enterprising kid,' Mark breathed.

'Enterprising?' Stacey slanted him a hypercritical gaze. 'To you, maybe. To me she's just an unpredictable handful.'

'Something to get worked up about?'

She lowered her gaze humorously. 'I admit I imagined the worst,' she murmured. 'But someone else's child is quite a responsibility.'

'You'll get into the same flap over your own youngsters.'

The deep-toned words drifted into the night, and were contested only by the chirping of the crickets. Stacey resisted the desire to meet his gaze, and in the pause that followed, Mark drew deeply on his cigarette and dropped it. He spun his foot to add sneeringly, 'You'll have to with the old man away for the best part of the year.'

So they were back to Jeremy! To Stacey it was something of a relief to be able to cling to the thought of him. Out here it would be dangerously easy to forget that Sharon existed. There was none of her perfume to intervene, only the scent of the flowers. Sorrento was an ocean away, and here was the witchery of Capri.

It would have been easy to create a situation where none existed, she told herself, turning bleakly towards the night.

When the ache had subsided, she asked conversationally, 'When does the season end?'

'Around October.'

'As late as that?' Stacey's heart sank. Another month at the Palazzo was unthinkable.

'You mean you want to go sooner?' The voice came harsh from behind. 'Most of the reps like to hang on till the last.'

'Only because they want to stretch out their employment,' she said evenly. 'To me it doesn't make any difference. I'm finishing with the travel business.'

'Settling for good old England?'

Slightly ruffled by his sarcasm, she retorted, 'I seem to

recall you saying *you* settled for it, for part of the year.'

'Not any more. There's nothing to take me there, apart from the odd holiday.'

Not with Sharon at the Palazzo and a wedding in the offing, Stacey thought with an ache in her throat. That was the reason, of course, but just to make sure that her heart got the message she asked carefully, 'I suppose Sharon will be going back to England soon?'

'Sharon? No, she's staying on in Italy.'

Now that her misery was complete Stacey felt drained of words. She draped back against the pillar, gazing out into the night. Perhaps the silence had been overlong while she had been examining her own bruised thoughts, but she hadn't realized its palpitating quality until Mark moved in from the shadows.

'Taking any special memories of Italy back with you?' he asked lazily.

Gazing up at the sloping smile, Stacey felt her senses whirl. She knew what he meant, of course. Being typically male he wanted to remind himself of the stray kiss he had captured. To him it had been a temporary indulgence to look back upon with amusement. To Stacey it had been the last step into the bitter-sweet world of love.

Afraid that the memory of that shattering embrace might be written in her eyes, she turned away, and made a pretence of peering at her watch.

'It must be getting late,' she said jerkily. 'I suppose I ought to be getting back to Yvette.'

She half expected a guiding hand, as they moved through the gloom towards the french windows, but though Mark was close at her side, he made no effort to touch her.

He waited until she was inside the room, saluted briefly and with a drawn smile strode off.

CHAPTER NINE

In the dazzling light of the morning, the turmoil of the night before seemed far distant. They ate breakfast on the terrace, Yvette bright-eyed and spruce with her freshly plaited pigtail, Mark clean-shaven and relaxed, the damp tendrils of recently combed hair at his brow.

The view now was of *pensiones* and villas, olive groves and flowers, and out to sea fishing smacks bobbed like moths on the water.

They took the bus back to Capri, but Mark didn't seem in any particular hurry to get down to the harbour. Strolling through the *piazza*, he asked lazily, 'What's it to be? The steamer or the speed launch?'

'Oh, the steamer!' Yvette looked up, big-eyed.

'That means another hour,' Stacey calculated, meeting a brown gaze. 'I thought you'd want to get back?'

'Do you?' He put an arm out as she was jostled against him, and amidst the crowds – Neapolitans in showy shirts, Capri dwellers with baskets on their heads, the holiday exhibitionists in their bright silk pyjamas, and the staid in their white tropical suits – Stacey laughed lightly.

'Well, all this looks vaguely exciting,' she mused, 'but....'

'We'll take the steamer,' Mark said drily.

With Yvette holding a hand on either side, they wandered along winding streets and whitewashed alleyways, through the heart of the old town which was littered with tiny shops, and alfresco cafés. They drank fresh orange juice at a wayside table, and later when Yvette and Stacey became intrigued with an array of gaily coloured straw hats, Mark lazily dug his hand in his pocket to pay for one each of their choice.

To Stacey the hour was precious, something she would want to hang on to, long after the rest of the memories of Italy had faded.

She walked down to the steamer, dreading every footstep that would take them that much nearer reality – back to Sorrento, and Sharon, the Palazzo, and eventually a plane home to England.

Apparently Stacey wasn't the only one reluctant to leave the enchantment of Capri. The outgoing steamer had few passengers, and despite the brilliant sunshine there was a forlorn look about the empty seats on deck. Yvette had slipped back into something of the mood of the serious-eyed elf on the rock. She watched Sorrento grow nearer, and seemed to become more doleful with every minute that passed.

Stacey felt that she ought to try a little cheerful conversation. 'You'll be seeing your aunt soon,' she smiled.

The pigtailed head nodded, with, 'Aunt Margaret's nice.'

Well, that was something, Stacey considered. Yvette obviously didn't hold anything against her guardian at the Palazzo. Conversation seemed hard to find and while Stacey was searching around in her mind for another track, Yvette flopped back on the seat, and scuffed her feet disconsolately on the rail.

She said suddenly out of the blue, 'I bet you and Mark don't argue.'

'All the time,' Mark dropped a dry glance over Stacey.

Yvette pondered on this and asked gravely, 'Are you going to have children?'

Stacey fought back the colour to say lightly, 'You have to get married first, Yvette.'

'I know, but you're going to. I can tell.' Yvette looked round.

Stacey remembered that Mark had draped her duster coat at the back of her seat, but she hadn't realized that his arm had stayed along the length of it. She wanted to jump over the side in embarrassment now, but Mark was saying easily,

'Like all women you talk too much, pigtail. Maybe you'd better be thinking what you're going to say when we get back to the Palazzo.'

The hotel seemed a world away, balancing up there along the cliff, but it didn't remain far distant for long.

The steamer made good time, and with Mark's car still parked from last night, they were soon leaving the town behind, and cruising towards its numerous square red roofs.

On arrival at the Palazzo, Stacey had anticipated going straight to Mrs. Lander's room with Yvette, to make the explanations. She hadn't reckoned with anything untoward happening on the way. But happen it did, almost as soon as Yvette had stepped from the car.

Just as they were about to take in the hotel steps, she suddenly tugged her hand from Stacey's and skipped somewhat coyly towards a couple who were pacing and talking together on the lawn. After that everything seemed to happen at once. The woman crumpled over Yvette, and the man scowled and laughed and thrust his hands into his pockets alternately. Words tumbled forth, and there were snatches of 'almost out of our minds . . .' 'such a long way from home . . .' 'just the three of us, darling, as soon as you like. . . .'

While Stacey was adjusting her dazed mind to the scene, and working out step by step that the two people falling over Yvette could only be her parents, Mrs. Lander came out of the hotel. She looked harassed at first, but then she saw the performance going on a few yards away, and put her hand out in a gesture of relief.

'Thank heaven! I got in touch with Yvette's mother and father right after you left,' she explained to Stacey. 'I couldn't bear the responsibility. They arranged to fly straight out.' Stacey drew on her lip, wondering how she was going to explain. 'Yes, about last night. You see, what happened, Mrs. Lander. . . .' She made a start, but Mark had taken her arm and was saying in strictly businesslike tones,

'Better skip the details, Miss Roberts. The work's piling up.' He nodded towards the chattering threesome on the lawn. 'Yvette took off for a while, but by the looks of it, it's all straightened out now.'

Mrs. Lander clasped her hands happily.

'I expect they'll be over shortly to thank you,' she smiled.

'No need,' Mark bowed pleasantly. 'It's all part of the hotel service.'

He guided Stacey inside, and as they passed through the lounges she looked up wonderingly to ask, 'Do I take it you never sent any message out from Capri last night?'

He nodded. 'I got in touch with Mrs. Lander when I went to book in at the *pensione*, but by that time Yvette's parents were on their way here.'

'But you didn't consider it worth mentioning?' She continued to watch his face. There seemed to be a decided gleam in the brown eyes as he shrugged,

'I had a rough idea of what Yvette was up to. I don't think it did any harm to play along with her little game.'

As he left her at the foot of the stairs his parting words were, 'Who knows? It might have done some good.'

It might at that, Stacey considered, the scene in the garden still clear in her mind. She climbed the stairs to her room with a slight frown playing over her brow. What a puzzling man Mark was! She had practically accused him of having no heart out there on Capri, but it seemed he had a lot more than she realized.

All Stacey could say to that revelation during the next few days was, lucky Sharon!

With the season winding up, people inevitably had more time on their hands, and more time for Mark meant more time spent with the Sunflair girl.

Shutting her heart off from the view of two dark heads together, dancing, dining or driving off to some secluded spot, no doubt, Stacey sought to lose herself in her work, and almost succeeded.

With less than a dozen Sunflair guests to entertain, it seemed that she and Jeremy were just another couple in the party, a very gay one at that. There was moonlight bathing, and midnight parties, and visits to night clubs and cafés. Blissfully benumbed by all the action, Stacey willed the pace to continue until the time came for her to leave the Palazzo. But as the days passed, her clientele gradually dwindled to two elderly couples, who wanted nothing more than to wander along the main street of Sorrento, or snooze in the hotel grounds.

Jeremy took advantage of the quiet periods to see to some of his packing, and Stacey, not caring for the loneliness of the staff beach since the day that Tony had popped up unannounced, resorted to life in and around the Palazzo.

Though the hotel guests were down to a minimum, there was an animated air about the place. It was as though the staff, having given of their best throughout the summer, were now coming into a little of their own. Tenor voices soared to top notes in the kitchens, and plump room attendants tossed sheets and pillowcases about the corridors with uninhibited merriment.

With Stacey wandering around pretty much on her own, it was inevitable that she should run into Sharon. It happened one day, when she was taking a sun-chair to the far reaches of the garden, and though she would have liked to keep the conversation brief, it looked as though Sharon was in the mood for talking.

'I'll get a chair and come and sit with you for a while,' she said cheerily.

She did sit, for about two seconds, when they reached a secluded spot, but after that the slim supple body, in rose-coloured slacks, bare midriff, and tiny black lace top, seemed happier moving erratically beneath the trees.

'Gosh, I feel good!' She stretched her arms to the sky with a tiny laugh, and Stacey, hoping to digress from what was obviously the main source of Sharon's pleasure, said past the lump in her throat,

'I suppose Sunflair have had a fairly good season?'

'One of the best,' Sharon nodded, 'but it's not that.' She plucked a flower sweepingly. 'Ever since Father died, I've been tied up fairly tight with the business, even though half the time I didn't know what was going on. Now with Mark nudging me, I find I'm actually going to get a chance to live a little. I had hoped . . .' she raised a humorous eyebrow, 'in my usual ham-handed way, of course, to keep a hold on the business until Ricky could take over. But he never was keen on the idea, and as Mark said, why push it?'

'Why indeed?' Stacey tried to sound brightly intelligent, while inside she was slowly disintegrating. Why push it when Mark could run a hundred businesses and still find time to get married?

As though Sharon thought the conversation was becoming one-sided, she asked, flopping down at Stacey's feet, 'What will you do when the season finishes?'

'Oh, go back to England.' Stacey heaved a smile up from an aching heart. 'My parents have a shop and there's always the Christmas rush to think about.'

'Will you be coming back here next year?' Sharon asked chattily.

'I don't think so.' Stacey kept her eyes on the rejected flower, wilting in the sun. 'This is my third summer abroad. I think it's about time I settled down.'

Sharon nodded with an absent smile. 'It's nice to find out where you belong, isn't it?' she murmured. She took a second look at her watch and jumped up. 'Heavens, I must go and change. Mark's taking me to Amalfi this afternoon.'

Amalfi! Stacey swallowed. You'll like it there, she said to herself, trying to keep her smile from twisting. I did. Too much for my own good.

'Well,' Sharon stretched out a hand smilingly, 'if I don't see you again before you go. . . .' Did she have some idea that Stacey had been avoiding her? 'I'll say good-bye and thank you for all you've done for Sunflair this year.'

As her hand was taken shyly, Stacey thought it was the strangest farewell she had ever had from an employer. A girl no older than herself, with an almost puppy-like friendliness, shaking her hand warmly.

'I hope you'll come back for a holiday at least,' Sharon was saying.

'Perhaps.' Stacey watched the slim figure recede, knowing that as far as her future holidays were concerned, Italy was just not on the map.

One thing the conversation with Sharon did for Stacey. It infused in her the strength to see about leaving the Palazzo as soon as possible. She resolved to speak to Mark that same night about returning to England.

Though her crazy heart should have known by now, it

had her hanging around his office door, hoping to see him arrive back from Amalfi at some reasonable hour, but by twelve o'clock, she gave up and climbed despondently to her room.

Emotionally ironed out after a night spent wrestling with unhappiness, she went down to the office with a slightly raised chin and a straight gaze – a gaze that only wavered slightly as it met a dark brown one.

'Mark, I'd like to see about clearing up what's left of the Sunflair work, if it's all right with you?' She got it out quickly. As he rose from the desk she thought the features looked slightly drawn. Amalfi must have been quite a drive, she considered bitterly. His mood seemed hardly better than his looks, for he clipped sourly,

'To spell out the words in plain and simple language, you mean you want to go? When?'

'Well, I thought tomorrow. The last of the Sunflair guests go then. . . . I could do my packing and. . . .'

Mark was shaking his head. 'Sorry, Stacey, no can do. If I let you go before the staff gathering, I'll have the lot of them on my neck.'

'The staff . . . ?' Stacey looked blank, and he draped down on the desk to explain.

'Something we lay on at the end of the season for the Palazzo employees, though practically half of Sorrento muscles in too. They get the complete run of the hotel, coupled with a barbecue on the beach, fireworks and a midnight sail to view. Oh, it's quite an occasion. You and the boy-friend should lap it up.'

Ignoring the slight sneer, she asked, 'Do I have to stay?'

'Well, you've been a wow with the clients, and everything's on the house for the staff that night.'

'My company included?'

'Precisely.'

Only the staff to contend with wouldn't be so bad, Stacey contemplated, she had made friends with most of them during the summer, but. . . . 'I suppose you'll be there?' she asked, knowing no way to put it other than bluntly.

'Sorry to disappoint you,' he nodded with a twisted

smile. 'It's my show, but the staff are a volatile lot. You and I are not likely to get time to tangle.'

Tangle! That was a funny way of putting it. Stacey lowered her eyes from a peculiar burnt out brown gaze. Did he mean argumentatively, or . . . ? To steady her galloping senses, she asked matter-of-factly, 'When are they? The festivities?'

'Saturday night.'

And today was only Sunday.

'With no guests to entertain, I don't know what I'm going to do for another week,' she pointed out, walking to the door.

'You'll find something.' Mark stood in the centre of the room flexing his shoulders. The tones were slightly mocking as he added, 'If you get stumped let me know. We could have another go at the Amalfi drive.'

She looked up to give him a candid grey-green stare. 'The Amalfi drive seems to be a very popular run out here,' she said coolly.

In spite of her composure she felt herself turn and close the door with a light slam.

CHAPTER TEN

As it happened the week wasn't as much of an ordeal as Stacey had expected. Jeremy expressed a desire to do a round of all the local resorts before leaving, and borrowing the small Fiat, they more or less roamed at will.

It seemed peculiar to wander around Ischia again. To see coloured shutters going up at some of the cafés, and life continuing in the pink and yellow houses, as it would do all winter. Naples looked much the same, crowded, gay and faintly cosmopolitan. Castellamare, with its vivid umbrellas fairly sparse on the beach now, its chestnut woods, yellow with fading leaves, and green with the prickle of the fruit.

Capri Stacey couldn't bring herself to visit again. She made the excuse of not feeling particularly like another steamer trip, and Jeremy, easy-going as ever, settled for Vesuvius. It was quite an experience to go up in the little cage and gaze down into the commotion going on inside the mountain.

By Friday they were both slightly travel-weary and spent the day on the staff beach. Stacey was glad of the interval. It was a kind of unwinding before the tensing up for tomorrow. She felt it was going to take everything she had to get through the day, but at least she would have Jeremy. He had been marvellous for leaning on these past few weeks.

Mark had been so sure and probably relieved that she was going to marry her working partner that she had almost believed it herself at times. And she could believe it devoutly tomorrow, if only to take her up to taxi time and her departure from the Palazzo.

After all these comforting thoughts it came as something of a shock to learn that Jeremy wouldn't be staying.

Gazing up at the patterned colours of the beach umbrella, she was aware of the lean tanned figure pushing up from his towel, and dropping down to recline on one elbow at her side.

353

'Well, old girl, it's here,' he grinned. 'Curtain down on our last season together. How do you feel?'

'Terrible,' she smiled. 'But don't rush things. We've got right up until tomorrow night, remember.'

'Afraid not. I'll be leaving about three tomorrow afternoon. I've sent most of my stuff on.'

'Oh, must you?' Stacey jerked up, paling a little. 'I mean ... what about the festivities tomorrow night? Mark expects you to stay.'

'I know he does,' Jeremy nodded. 'But from what I've heard of the size of the gathering he'll never miss me, and you can cover for me.'

'I suppose so,' Stacey lowered her eyes, feeling her heart sink like a stone.

Who was going to cover for her? All she could do now was hope that the crowd would be sufficient to lose herself in until the time came for her to leave. A faint wryness took hold of her at the thought that she had been doing this for most of the summer. One more night wouldn't make any difference.

'You don't mind, do you, Stacey?' Jeremy looked up suddenly with a searching gaze. 'I want to make good time to Rome. These last few weeks have been the longest I've known.' He gave her a sheepish grin. 'And without you they'd have been hell. It's the waiting, I suppose, but I feel I'll just burst if I don't get to Melanie.'

'For goodness' sake stay intact!' Stacey put a hand on his shoulder humorously. She looked at her watch. 'You've got about twenty-four hours to go.'

Jeremy drew the hand down and kissed it lightly. 'You're a great girl, Stacey,' he murmured. 'Some day, some bloke's going to bless me for walking out on you.'

It won't do him any good, Stacey thought, swallowing back the ache behind her smile. She retrieved her hand gently to ask, 'Are there any last-minute jobs to be cleared up for Sunflair? What about the books and receipts?'

'I took the lot down to the hotel office the other day,' Jeremy replied. 'Thought it would be a good time to say my official goodbyes to the chief.'

'Oh, you've done that!' Stacey looked down at the fair head. 'What was he like?' she asked curiously.

'Bit short, but then I never was exactly his blue-eyed boy. Still,' Jeremy shrugged easily, 'you can't please 'em all.'

'You pleased the holidaymakers,' Stacey smiled. 'That was the important thing.'

'Not too difficult with you around,' he grinned, and then frowning in concern, 'You're sure you're going to be all right? What about getting home? Are you flying?'

'From Naples on Sunday morning,' Stacey nodded, 'though I'll be leaving the Palazzo directly after the gaieties tomorrow night.'

'Might be too late for a steamer,' Jeremy pondered.

'No, I'll get a taxi, I think. I'll be sure of getting straight to the hotel in Naples.'

Jeremy looked up. 'Of course you could always stay on at the Palazzo until Sunday morning,' he suggested.

Stacey fingered her straw hat, Mark's gift from Capri. 'I'm like you,' she replied evenly. 'I want to get away.'

'What's this?' Jeremy raised twinkling blue eyes to gaze at her perceptively. And then because there was no reply he went on playfully, 'Here's me rattling on about Melanie all the time. I didn't know the world had its sunniest spot for you too, let alone that you'd be rushing off to it.'

'I'm not,' Stacey returned lightly, jumping to her feet. 'Rushing away from' would be more apt. 'Race you for our last swim!' she challenged, swinging away.

'You're on,' Jeremy pushed laughingly to his feet. 'And if the orchestra's still playing tonight we'll probably have the dance floor to ourselves.'

It wasn't quite as sparse as that, as they learned later. The Palazzo guests were still reasonably numerous and probably would be throughout the winter. Some Stacey had come to recognize as residents, and these seemed to expand in the new roominess of the hotel.

She danced with elderly business men, retired no doubt, and gossiped with the ladies at the tables, but Jeremy, obviously wanting to give of his best for his last night, was never far away, and whenever possible they talked or danced together.

To Stacey, the evening was comparatively bearable;

even so, she wasn't sorry when Jeremy decided he had had enough, and she was soon making for her own room. There were endless jobs to be done before tomorrow night, but slackly she wandered about the rooms, unable to tackle anything.

Bed was the best place for a mood like this, of course. Things always looked better the next day. Maybe they wouldn't look any better for Stacey Roberts, but at least there would be no alternative then but to get down to the business of packing.

She wandered out on to the balcony and dropped down into a chair. There was something soothing about the breeze on her face, the distant strum of a mandolin. The odd guest still strolled in the grounds below, but most of the rooms of the hotel were in darkness.

She raised her gaze to the ones opposite. They would be unlit, of course. Mark rarely turned in before midnight. Gazing at the netted windows, she wondered what it was like behind. What kind of furniture was in there? What blend of colour? Would it be gay and contemporary like a modern house? No. She could imagine it being slightly old-world Italian like the rest of the hotel, with big arm-chairs, pale carpets, and bordered squares of rich deep-coloured wallpaper.

Strange to think that she had never seen inside Mark's apartments, wouldn't even have known they were over there if she hadn't seen him out on the balcony occasionally, sometimes flicking through a newspaper, or pulling on a cigarette and apparently gazing into space.

Still – she heaved up from her chair and turned inside, suddenly weary. No point in letting the mind linger too long on past views. Those kinds of memories could be fatal anyway. From Mark on the balcony, she might be tempted into thinking of Mark in other places. Ischia and Epomeo, for instance. Positano, the Emerald Grotto, Capri. . . .

Capri. Weakly Stacey moved towards the bedroom, still feeling the queer pent-up magic of that night. Mark had seemed different there too. It was the island, of course. Everybody said it did queer things to one.

She busied herself with her evening toilet, and the

chores of bathing and donning a nightdress helped to get her mind back on to its steady swinging pendulum of rational thinking. By the time her head touched the pillow, she was mentally filling her suitcases, and arranging to book a taxi from Sorrento.

The taxi booking idea had seemed a good one in the darkness of the bedroom. It was an even better one in the pure golden light of day, for it gave Stacey an excuse to go into Sorrento. She could easily ring up, of course, and with her knowledge of Italian now that wouldn't be difficult, but as far as anyone else was concerned there was nothing like having a personal talk to the driver. After all, Naples was forty-odd kilometres away, and that was quite a taxi ride. She wouldn't be able to give an exact time for the booking, but she could arrange to ring directly her duties were finished at the Palazzo. That would mean only a few minutes' wait.

All these thoughts were passing through Stacey's mind as she dressed. The Fiat would probably be still available. She could have breakfast in Sorrento and say her goodbyes to the friends she had made down there. With a bit of luck she needn't return to the Palazzo until round about three. There wouldn't be much point in looking Jeremy up before then. If she knew anything about his past departures he would be chasing around until the last minute.

The day was washed in sunshine. Only in the shadows did one feel a slight coolness. Instead of the usual cotton or silk, Stacey chose a lightweight oatmeal dress, with small sleeves and a wide buckle belt. She hurried downstairs and outside. It was a relief to see the Fiat still parked in its usual place. Lingeringly she drove down familiar lanes, still vivid with late summer flowers and shrubs; past villas and gardens and laden orange groves and eventually into Sorrento.

From the main *piazza* she wandered at leisure. The large amount of Sunflair business that she had transacted over the summer had brought her into close contact with many of the cafés and businesses in Sorrento. She spent most of the morning accepting a handshake from the owners, or returning a wave. There was always an invitation to come back next year.

'*Ritorni l'anno prossimo!*'

They all thought she would come back. Their laughter and smiles and shrugging plump shoulders all said, 'How could anyone not want to come back to Sorrento?' They had something there. Stacey swallowed painfully and turned towards the harbour.

Looking for something different, she decided to try lunch at a restaurant built out over the water. It was a pleasant half hour, and though a lot of the tables were empty, a smiling accordion player tinkled and sang lazily in a patch of sunshine at the door. All too soon, the time came to climb back up to the *piazza*. Stacey turned to take a last look at the view. The beaches and fishing boats, the steamers and the piers, and the rows of bathing tents. Along the cliff the greenery had faded. Even here in sunny Italy the golden veil of autumn was in evidence.

She could have taken a fiacre up to the square, but she wanted to prolong every step, to take in every sound and scent and view along the way.

The taxis were parked in the shade in the square. Ordering one proved a lengthy business, because of the distance she wished to go, and the various explanations involved at not being able to give a definite time. Eventually it was sorted out and there was nothing left to do but take the Fiat back to the Palazzo for the last time.

She parked it in its usual place, locked it and gave the key to an attendant. Slowly everything was being wound up. Though it was barely two-fifteen, she was surprised when she turned into the drive to see Jeremy stepping out along it towards the gate.

She called as she ran, and he turned lazily and lowered his canvas hold-all. 'I thought I was going to miss you.' He looked at his watch.

'And I thought you said three o'clock,' she chided, catching her breath.

'Oh, that was only a rough estimate,' Jeremy shrugged. 'I'm catching the two-thirty bus to the station. No sense in hanging around.'

'And you were going to leave without saying goodbye?'

She looked up with over-bright eyes.

He stooped to drop an arm around her. 'Oh, I suppose I'd have hung on until you showed up,' he said with an apologetic grin. As his lips brushed her cheek Stacey knew his mind was already in Rome. She clung to him briefly, because not seeing Jeremy again was another wrench she was going to have to take and eventually get used to. He stooped to pick up his hold-all. 'I'd better get going or I'll miss the bus.' He waved briefly. 'So long, Stacey. I'll drop you a card some time.'

'Goodbye, Jeremy.' Stacey blinked away a dampness at her lashes, and waved him to the gate. He turned out of it without a backward glance.

She nursed her aching throat within the privacy of the trees, and wandered slowly to the farthest corner of the garden. If this was what it was like saying goodbye to Jeremy, how was it going to feel to . . .

The sound of a soft footfall over the grass made her turn. Because she thought it was one of the hotel guests out to engage her in a friendly conversation she moved slowly, almost absently, still clinging to the picture of Jeremy moving down the drive.

It was only when she saw who was approaching that her pulses rocketed into life.

She willed herself to keep her gaze steadily on Mark until he stopped a short distance away, then she lowered it to ask, 'Am I needed in the hotel?'

'No. Just checking to see that you're all ready for the ram-jam tonight,' came the reply.

'More or less.' She looked up and nodded, and looked away again. The silence felt solid. After a while she raised her eyes to the deep blue sky to offer conversationally, 'Looks as if it's going to be a perfect evening.'

'We're usually lucky,' Mark returned in dry tones. After another silence he asked casually, 'Where's Farrow shooting off to?'

Stacey brought her gaze round to his quickly. He enlarged with a slightly sarcastic shrug, 'I saw the tender farewell just now.'

So that was it. He had seen Jeremy leaving before he was supposed to. Perhaps that was why the white smile had a definite twist about it. As he kept his eyes on her, coolly inquiring, she felt obliged to say non-committally, 'Jeremy's gone to Rome.'

'Oh? Can't wait to get lined up for the winter, eh?'

Stacey held the brown gaze. So he *was* in a mood! Well, if covering for Jeremy meant defending him, she could do that too. Hating the smiling way that Mark thrust his hands in his pockets, she returned evenly, 'I suppose what he does now is his own business.'

'Too true!' The sarcasm was back. The muscular frame swayed gently. 'What is it, a ring this summer, and a wedding the next? If you're lucky.'

His sneering remark scorched Stacey. She retorted swiftly, 'You never have been able to get along with Jeremy, have you? Well, I can tell you, he's everything a girl could wish for.'

'Sure! So long as she's the kind willing to settle for a half-baked love affair.'

Flame-lit brown eyes held on to hers, and for a moment Stacey felt almost overpowered. She lowered her eyes to rush jerkily, 'I haven't time to stand here listening to your derogatory remarks. I've still got all my packing to do.'

'Well, go ahead.' He swept an arm wide. 'And happy wintering.'

Stacey swung her back to him and gulped at his biting farewell. What a way to end things! Wasn't there going to be anything to take away? Not even a friendly hand-shake? She turned back slowly.

'I've got one big travelling case. Could you see about having it sent on for me?' she asked. 'I can take my bags with me.'

Mark was a lot closer than she expected when she made the turn round, but he looked as hard as rock and just as unbending. 'Left you with everything, hasn't he?' he stated flatly.

Feeling her blood heat up again, Stacey snapped, 'One travelling case isn't exactly everything, and besides . . .'

'Save it.' He put a hand up sourly. 'Consider it attended to.'

'Thank you.'

The silence that followed dropped like an end curtain

on the stormy interlude. It should have been easy to leave after that, yet Stacey wouldn't bring herself to be the first one to move away. She said slowly, 'When will you want me tonight? Do I go straight down to the hotel beach?'

Mark nodded. 'Everything's set up down there,' he pointed out. 'I'll pick you up about eight.'

'I can easily find my own way.'

'You'll go down with me,' he said roughly. 'This is Italy's night out, and anything can happen.' He had made no mention of Sharon, but as this was a working night for Mark he had probably decided not to take her. With that familiar 'No arguing' grip on her arm Stacey was led back towards the hotel.

Packing was not as big a job as she had envisaged, but it was slightly more heartrending. To see the wardrobes and drawers empty, and the rooms devoid of all personal touches, was something that cut low on her already fast dwindling self-control. But at least, in this case, she could console herself with the fact that she had felt exactly the same last year, and the year before. Departures from actual living quarters, where one had put up for the whole of the summer, were always sad.

Tomorrow night at this time she would be in her own small bedroom in Richmond, and life would have to start all over again.

She had left one or two garments out of the travelling case in an effort to decide what to wear for the beach tonight. It would undoubtedly be cooler, so the sleeveless, scooped-neckline type of thing was out. On the other hand it was something of a party for the staff, so anything heavy was out too.

She chose in the end a white linen suit, with pencil-slim skirt, and three-quarter-sleeved, waist-hugging jacket. A white blouse, with its froth of lace down the front, and a small diamanté flower at her shoulder, added the touch of glamour she felt was needed for the occasion. Faintly tinted lilac sandals and handbag balanced the all-white effect just right, and standing back from the mirror, Stacey realized that she need only slip a light coat on top for the journey to Naples. That was something anyway. Everything except the coat could now be packed away. All she had to do when she returned from the beach was have the suitcases taken downstairs to the taxi. She was just on the point of carrying the last one into the lounge when a light knock came on the door and Mark walked in.

'All set?' The brown eyes flickered along the line of luggage, and came up glinting above a hard smile. 'I see you are,' he added succinctly.

'I was just finishing the last of my packing,' Stacey blurted unnecessarily. Mark calling up here for her was a shock in itself, but added to this was the picture of him standing just inside the door now – big, devastatingly masculine in dark dinner suit, crisp shirt, with a small tracing of black tie beneath the collar. The tanned jawline looked leaner in this light, the face more lined, but the smile gleamed as white as ever. The dark hair had its usual light touch of hair oil to keep it in order.

All this Stacey took in, in a lightning glance. Her heart couldn't have stood the strain of lingering over it. She swung her eyes away and made a pretence of looking round the room for possible left-over garments. 'I think that's about everything,' she murmured lightly.

It was then that something else happened to send her pulses flying, for as she brought her gaze back, the brown eyes were still resting on her. The look in them left her slightly breathless. But it was a passing luxury. All too soon Mark had dropped his gaze and strolled into the room, and by that time Stacey had regained her common sense.

No need to get carried away with a look like that, she told herself bleakly. Tonight was party night. Mark had said that anything could happen, and of course he would expect her to know that appraising glances were all part of the mood.

He wandered about the room now, eyeing its bareness with a flexing jaw, and the tight white smile. 'Stripped clean,' he nodded, flicking a chair sharply into place with his foot. 'By tomorrow we'll never know you were here.'

'I hope I've left everything exactly as I found it,' Stacey said politely over her hurt.

'Not exactly.' He dropped a fathomless glance over her and turned out on to the balcony.

'Well, I did rearrange the furniture slightly,' Stacey pondered, 'but that will only take a . . .'

'Skip it.' Mark had his back to her near the balustrade. She could see the wide shoulders silhouetted against the luminescent blue of a fast darkening sky, but she couldn't trust herself to move from her position near the door.

After a while she asked tentatively, 'Mark, are we going?'

It seemed an even longer while before he turned, and then he was moving back into the room with a nod. She thought the grip on her arm was a trifle too tight. It was accompanied by words of icy humour, 'I almost forgot you were waiting to finish the job. Let's go.'

The hotel was strangely quiet as they went down the stairs. There was the odd elderly person in the lounge armchairs, and an occasional attendant at his post, but it seemed that the life core of the Palazzo had been lifted and transported to the area of the evening's festivities.

The sky was strung with stars as Mark guided her across the gardens towards the beach steps. Stacey gave a tiny delighted gasp at the lantern-lit trees flanking the downward route. The sight was entirely unexpected, and she wondered a little breathlessly what else was in store for her down on the beach.

Watching the delicate shades of lilac, pink and green pass by over her head, she took one of the steps too quickly, and Mark caught her close as she stumbled.

'Still walking with your head in the clouds?' he drawled just above her ear.

Stacey could make no reply. Close contact with that hard frame was enough to stifle any. She had to admit, too, that as this would probably be her last few moments alone with Mark, she hadn't the strength to draw away.

A laughing couple came bounding up the steps, and Mark drew her to one side as they passed. With his arms about her, it seemed strange to think that there were other people in the world, but she felt steadier for the knowledge and made the first move to continue down the steps.

There was no doubt of the world's populace now, for

by the sound of the noise drifting up half of it seemed to be on the beach. Even so Stacey wasn't prepared for the scene when it came.

The gaily lit lanterns continued to pick out the night all along the base of the cliffs, and to the front of these a succession of fires cast their dancing lights on the sea and the myriad tiny boats bobbing at the jetties. The people were formally dressed: the men in dark lounge suits or roll-collared dinner jackets, the women in typical Italian coloured silks, of rich ruby reds, deep greens and blues. In the copper glow their faces looked darkly attractive. Black eyes flashed and white smiles gleamed in contrast.

It was all very much a party picture and the bowl of black sky and soft sand underfoot added rather than detracted from the glamour.

Mark guided her past beach chairs and tables, cases of supplies, firework stands, and a mini-orchestra whose gentle Italian-style music vied with the laughter and the clinking of glasses and the sounds of the waves falling on the beach. From then on Stacey had no time to take in anything except the mad gay whirl of the night.

The Palazzo staff were as high-spirited as any holiday crowd, and though Stacey had an occasional difficulty in placing a face without its familiar olive-green uniform, she managed to hide the fact until the strangeness of a dark suit or a frilled dress disappeared and she was seeing perhaps Angelo of the bar or Carmella from the stationery counter.

There were other guests too, some residents of Sorrento, and some, it transpired, from as far away as Ischia and Naples.

Previously dreading this night, Stacey had hoped that she and Mark would be too busy to see much of each other. The surprising thing was, he hardly ever left her side. With his hand on her elbow and his suave smiling introductions to guests and friends, she tended to lose sight of the fact, dangerously so at times, that for her this was just a job.

And very soon now it would be at an end. She stood with Mark at the central fire, handing out to the queue the plates that the tall-hatted chefs had filled with steaming skewers of meat, and later she did the same with dozens of glasses of bubbling champagne.

Laughingly taken unawares when Mark clinked his glass with hers, Stacey felt her heart begin to accelerate wildly. The air seemed to be growing more and more alive with a peculiar exciting quality that plucked at her senses, making them quiver slightly. It was as though something within her was urging her to take everything that this last Italian night had to offer. Sharon was waiting for Mark in his apartment, no doubt, but there couldn't be anything wrong, could there, in gathering a few last-minute memories for the years to come?

With Mark draped in a chair at her side, Stacey watched a thrilling display of the tarantella, and later they walked together on the edge of the lacy waves, slightly aloof from the crowd and its glowing, colourful setting.

The biggest shock of the evening came when Mark was called away to attend to some matter concerning a firework stand. Stacey, lulled into a dreamy sense of well-being, stood in the glow of the lanterns. For once she was alone, but she made no effort to join a group, and was glad that nobody seemed to notice her. It was enough just to stand here, soaking up the beauty of the night.

The arm that suddenly curved around her waist seemed to come from nowhere, and for the first few seconds Stacey was too stunned to take in its owner. As a dark handsome face came down close to hers, something within her contracted.

'Tony!' She struggled to sound not too surprised. 'I didn't know you were coming tonight.'

'I am here,' he smiled. 'In the flesh, as you say.' Before she could do anything to stop it, his lips had brushed her cheek. She could smell the wine on his breath, as he murmured, 'It is a good party, no?'

'Terrific.' Stacey drew away with a small smile.

She was just wondering how she could manoeuvre herself away from Tony without hurting his feelings, when he suddenly moved off again, taking his leave of her with a slight impudent bow.

Mark was holding her arm almost before she knew he was back. His face looked mask-like in the dull glow of the lanterns. The brown eyes glinted as they followed the receding figure. She heard him saying harshly almost to himself, 'This is one gate-crasher I think we can do without.' As he moved forward Stacey put a restraining hand on his arm.

'Let him stay, Mark,' she begged. 'He is ... or was ... one of the staff. He must think he's entitled to something.'

'That's the story of his life,' Mark replied drily, but he turned back and Stacey was relieved when an animated group pushed by, and he guided her back towards the fires.

Almost at once they were engaged in conversation with Mario, the elderly car-park attendant, and Stacey thankfully put the business of Tony out of her mind. He would probably enjoy himself as much as anyone, now that he found he wasn't to be turned away. It wasn't likely that she would see any more of him tonight.

Mario was almost perfect in English, having learned the language during his working life in a London hotel, and to Stacey it was a relief to give her laboured Italian a rest. She listened to snippets of the old man's experiences of London life, drawn on endearingly for her benefit, and then he expanded on to the night's festivities with something of an air of happy bewilderment.

Shrugging deeply and bringing the palms of his hands up expressively on the last word, he exclaimed, 'This year things are really *happening*!'

Thinking that he meant the general revelry, Stacey laughed agreeably, but then she thought she saw a sly twinkle as the faded charcoal eyes turned sideways to Mark and then roamed around the scene again.

'The lanterns are something new,' Mario nodded, rubbing his chin. 'And this year we have champagne.'

Mark pulled unhurriedly on his cigarette and dropped a negligent arm around Stacey's waist. 'Always trying to improve, Mario,' he said with something of a dry gleam.

A few minutes later after the old man had moved off to join his friends, the first of the fireworks hissed into life. Mark grinned down at her.

'All set for the water?' he asked.

'Do we go out there?' Stacey looked towards the black void beyond the golden sheen of the firelight's glow.

'It's the best place to view,' Mark pointed out.

All was activity at the jetties. Couples and groups were climbing into small boats and one by one the craft chugged out gently over a glass-like sea.

Mark was making his way towards a powerful-looking white four-seater – his own boat, by the look of the hotel crest on the side. He held it with his foot, for it seemed already impatient to drift off, and taking Stacey's hand, steadied her down to a level area ahead of the padded seats. She thought he stooped then as though to untie the rope before joining her, but things happened so fast after that, nothing really registered.

It seemed that her feet had only just come into contact with the boat when the engine suddenly roared into life, and she was thrown back, startled, against the seat. Down near the cockpit where all had been shadowy darkness, a figure reared up. She saw Tony's wide smile, his swaggering salute as he called above the noise of the engine, 'So glad you could come, Stacey!'

The next thing she knew, she and the seat she clung to were being catapulted forward into the black night.

At first Stacey could do nothing but slump back, stunned with surprise.

Later when her senses returned she was horrified at the speed they were going. It seemed that they were already well out from the beach, but judging by Tony's haphazard route he had no set course.

He swung the boat in sharp crazy circles, and one minute they were slicing the black expanse of sea, the next they were shooting past anchored boats, jetties and buoys with only inches to spare.

Ashen-faced, Stacey struggled up. With the bounce of the boat, it was no easy matter making her way to the cockpit, but she hung on, and once there managed to find a hand-hold on the polished wood. Calling Tony's name above the din took what was left of her strength, and when he didn't answer, she tapped him sharply on the shoulder.

After another wide circle he turned and it seemed to

Stacey then that all the pent-up anger of the passing weeks glowed there in the dark eyes.

Trying to sound unconcerned, she called firmly, 'I don't think I care for your jokes, Tony. You can take me back now.'

'Jokes?' He shrugged smilingly. 'This is not a joke. Don't you care for our farewell trip?'

'Not at all,' Stacey said coolly. 'I'd like you to take me back.'

His smile and stance behind the wheel were solidly uncompromising. He laughed throatily. 'But I like it out here.'

'Well, when you've finished playing childish games let me know.'

Stacey went back to her seat with a steady shrug, but she was far from feeling serene inside. There was nothing childish about Tony's mood. If he carried on at this speed in the dark, he would be bound to hit something. Yet if she showed her fear she would only be playing into his hands.

It took all her will power to drape back leisurely in her seat when all she wanted to do was huddle down in fright, but as she had hoped, her apparent nonchalance paid off. Tony became bored with his one-man circus and gradually slackened speed. At least that made for easier breathing.

Stacey sat forward and tried to make out where they were. She could see the lights of the beach not far distant. It seemed they were following the curve of the bay. After a few seconds her heart began to thump again. Whereas before she had been alarmed at the speed in which they had been moving, now she began to feel considerable concern at the lack of it.

The boat was cruising now at barely a walking pace, and Tony appeared to be making no effort to return to the hotel beach. She wondered what he was up to, but didn't dare speak again in case he felt tempted to rev up the motor. He turned to look at her, and then, clicking something on the wheel, came to sit down at her side. Stacey felt chilled. She said as lightly as she could, 'Isn't it time we were getting back, Tony?'

He merely pushed his elbows over the back of the seat and looked at the stars. 'It's a beautiful night,' he sighed contentedly.

It would look a lot more beautiful from land. Stacey drew on her lip, and racked her brains for the right words. She said as tactfully as she knew how, 'It is a lovely night. But this really isn't our boat, is it? And what about the fireworks? We're missing them.'

'Fireworks?' Tony shook his head, pouting his lips into a slow smile. 'Too noisy. I think I know of somewhere a little quieter.'

Stacey stood up in case he should sense her going rigid. As the lights of a beach came nearer she asked faintly, 'Where's that?'

'I have a friend who has a boat,' he nodded towards the opulent-looking launches anchored amidst tiny fishing craft. 'I'm sure he won't mind if we borrow it for a while.'

'What do we want with another boat? We already have one.' She tried to put her reply over as humorously as possible, hoping he wouldn't notice her shaking tones.

'This boat . . .?' he shrugged, and looked around it.

'Well, what's wrong with it?' Nerves taut, Stacey could barely keep herself from snapping.

The shaped lips were pulling into a slow smile, 'No wine, no cigarettes, no . . . cushions.' He swung the wheel jauntily.

Stacey felt the last thread of her control snap. 'Hasn't this gone far enough, Tony?' she said acidly. 'I certainly have no inclination to drink wine at this hour. I don't smoke, and the only cushions I'm interested in are the ones in my own room tonight.'

'Wait until you've seen my friend's boat,' he gazed over the bow towards the rocking shapes.

'I'm not interested,' she snapped, dropping back on the seat. 'And I'm not getting out of this one until I step back on to the hotel beach.'

'And I think you would like to do that in one piece, no?'

The dark eyes flashed ominously as he clutched the wheel.

It was an empty threat, Stacey knew, for Tony valued

his own neck too highly to do anything foolish. Yet there *was* the awful thought that he had come perilously close to hitting something last time. He might not be so lucky in his judgement going back. Compared to the thoughts of that, the anchored launches looked a haven of safety. Stacey sat mute as Tony guided the boat in amongst them. All she could do now was hope that he would see sense, after his glass of wine, and at least take her to the nearest beach.

He pulled alongside the last boat in the line and Stacey felt heartened. The lights didn't look all that far away.

Though the rope ladder on to the launch felt inadequate, she preferred its scant stability to the boat below. Nothing would induce her to go back into that, with Tony at the wheel. She began to wonder if he really did know the owner of the launch, for once on deck he seemed uncertain of his way and tried two doors before drawing her into what looked like a spacious lounge. When he didn't make any move towards putting on a light, she knew her suspicions were correct.

She also began to feel a new and sickening fear. Standing rigidly in the centre of the room with nothing but the faint glow of the harbour lights for comfort, she heard Tony rummaging in lockers and cupboards. With a bottle and glasses in his hands he came towards her. He had removed his jacket, but the whiteness of his shirt was no match for his smile.

'You see? It is good here,' he commented, taking her arm. 'Shall we drink?'

'I've told you,' Stacey didn't move, 'I don't want any.'

'Okay!' Cheerfully he went to spread himself out on the padded seat under the portholes. He made an elaborate show of pouring out the wine leisurely, and Stacey was hard put to it not to give way to the angry words rising in her throat. Her nerves, stretched almost to breaking point with the events of the last half hour, were not going to weather much more of Tony's behaviour. Perhaps high speed sailing would have been preferable to this.

When she thought his glass was empty she said coldly, 'Isn't there a law against trespassing on other people's boats?'

'Law?' She saw the glass swinging below the smile. 'There are laws for everything . . . and everyone.'

'People have to protect their property, I suppose,' she said, not really knowing what he was talking about.

There was a silence. She shivered to think he might be filling his glass again, but the bottle had been placed down. He came over to circle round her, raising his gaze slowly. ' "Hands off" I think is the way they say it in England,' he said in smooth tones.

'We don't put it quite as bluntly as that.' She wanted to keep her tones light, but Tony's smile put her teeth on edge.

'Marco has his laws too,' he nodded, lowering his gaze over her.

Stacey took a quick impatient breath. 'Look, I know I was responsible for you losing your job at the Palazzo, but you've had your fun tonight. I think we can call it even, don't you?' When he didn't reply she said firmly, 'I'd like you to take me back, Tony.'

'So impatient!' He looked amused. 'We have only just arrived.'

'Well, I want to go.'

'You have the boat.'

She looked at him. 'You know I can't go back on my own.'

'Too bad,' he sighed, lifting his hands.

'What do you mean?' Stacey queried over her thumping heart.

He shrugged deeply. 'Well, I like it here. I think I will stay the night,' he replied.

Stacey swayed slightly on her feet. 'You . . . can't be serious? What about the people who own the boat, they . . .' She felt numb to the point of not being able to think clearly, but Tony's laughter jerked from her a sudden burst of action that took her a few steps in the right direction. 'I've had enough of this,' she said shakily. 'I'll get the boat started somehow.'

'Why bother, Stacey?' He had hold of her wrist in a flash. 'We have such a pleasant arrangement here. And you know I like company.'

'There were lots of people on the beach that you left,'

she said witheringly.

'Who said anything about people?' As he drew her close Stacey tensed. She was only a short distance from the door, but it might as well have been miles away.

Her relief when he made no effort to hold her was short-lived, for he was saying throatily, 'You see now why I chose a boat, Stacey. It is but a small island. This time there is no Palazzo to run to.'

He was right, but Stacey didn't stay to congratulate him. She hurried out on deck, gulping in the night air. Tony, sure of himself, sauntered up behind. He didn't think she would try for the rope ladder, but he was in for a surprise. She had almost reached it before he started forward.

With her heart beating in her throat, she completed the last few feet with a red haze in front of her eyes. There wouldn't be time to take in the ladder. She would just have to. . . . As she swung out wildly towards the gap a figure suddenly came up to block it.

For a moment she stared uncomprehendingly. Mark looked almost unrecognizable in the shadows. The drawn features were pale. A thick lock of hair had fallen forward over a glistening brow, and narrowed brown eyes blazed as they turned to gaze beyond her.

She knew a rush of almost choking relief as the familiar bulk stepped up unhurriedly on to the deck.

'I think,' deep tones rasped over her head, 'you've caused enough trouble for one night, Tony.'

It was difficult to know what Tony would do, for he stood rock still by the rail. As far as Stacey could see in the darkness, the smile was still there, but there was an uncertainty in the shuffle of the feet.

Perhaps he too had found Mark's mood a pretty frightening spectacle.

She was just asking herself what would happen next, when Tony answered the question for her. Almost quicker than she could take it in, he had kicked off his shoes, and jumped up lithely on to the rail. With something of an impudent bow, the brief flash of white teeth, and he had dived clean and straight into the water.

Stacey went to take hold of the rail, but either she misjudged, or Mark was nearer than she thought. As he caught hold of her he said gruffly, 'You're shaking like a leaf. Are you all right?'

She nodded with a wan smile. 'I just don't think I'm cut out for night-time speedboat racing.' How she came to be leaning against a wide chest, she never really knew, but it was nice to have a hand stroking her hair as she tried to make light of her experience.

'I was sure Tony was going to hit something. It was a relief to get out. When we got on to this boat, I thought he would just have a drink and then take me back, but . . .'

'You needn't go on.' She was gripped tightly. 'I know something of Tony's methods. I was on to another boat within seconds,' Mark explained, 'but it was impossible to keep track of the fool's crazy antics. All I could do was keep close to the shore. I saw him making for the launches, but I didn't fancy coming in too close in case he belted off again.'

Stacey turned her gaze on to the water. 'Will he be all right?' she asked, watching the bobbing head moving inshore.

Mark nodded. 'Our Tony can swim like a fish. He'll make it.'

'I imagine Sorrento has seen the last of him,' Stacey said, studying.

'That's for sure. He's broken about every law in the book tonight. I ought to have kicked him out when I saw him hanging around.' As Mark turned his head to follow her gaze, his fingers gripped her almost painfully. He said darkly, 'The guy's lucky to get away with no more than a ducking.'

Stacey couldn't suppress a wry smile. 'I was all ready to take an evening swim myself,' she said against the dark dinner jacket. He held her close.

'It took me a while to locate where the boat was tied up, and then I wanted to make sure I wasn't going to have another chase on my hands.' His lips brushed her cheek. 'I had one or two bad moments when I saw Tony shaving the jetties.'

Bad moments for what? Stacey wondered. The boat, of course, she told herself dejectedly. It was obviously worth a lot of money. Naturally Mark would want to know what was happening to it.

Suddenly and embarrassingly aware that she had fallen straight into Mark's arms after Tony's exit, ·that even now her head was nestled on a wide chest, she pushed herself away, and made a pretence of looking at her watch.

'Good heavens! Is that the time?' she jerked shakily. 'I'd better be getting back.'

She sensed a stiffening in Mark, but he stepped aside as she moved towards the opening. 'Reckon you can manage the ladder?' he asked shortly. As she nodded he added, 'I'll go first and give you a hand.'

She saw him disappearing over the side, and then she turned to make her own way down. Halfway, he caught her lightly by the waist and helped her into the front of the four-seater. He went to tie the other small boat at the rear.

On the way back Stacey found herself wishing that the journey would go on for ever. The white boat cruised over black silken water. As the lights on the shore dropped out one by one, it seemed that the whole world was hers and Mark's.

In the dim light of the stars, she could see the big dark-clad figure at the wheel. The only movement there was a flexing muscle in the jaw, the slight flick of a finger on the wheel. Mark obviously didn't feel like talking, and in a way Stacey was glad.

For a little while, she wanted to imagine that this was only one of an eternity of nights she would be spending with him. That they could go anywhere in the world in this boat and never meet another person. She swallowed back the ache, looking at the dark head.

What was the use of make-believe? Mark had Sharon to go back to, and Stacey was on her way to a plane that would take her back to England. There wouldn't be any more nights alone with Mark, and soon precious few minutes.

The boat glided into the jetty, and she gazed on a beach eerie with the ghost of the festivities. Discarded crates and containers looked like live things in the shadows. Scattered pieces of paper rose up at the beckoning of the breeze.

As Mark led her past tables and chairs, the last embers of a dying fire caved in, and when a silk scarf fluttered suddenly from one of the poles of the doused lanterns, she stumbled with relief into his encircling arm. He held her as they climbed the steps, but Stacey was past caring. She doubted whether she would have had the strength to make this last move away from the Palazzo without assistance.

Most of the hotel was in darkness, but the subdued lighting in the entrance and the foyer cast a golden half-circle of light over the hotel steps. As they walked towards it their footsteps were like tiny droplets of sound sprinkled on the dark pool of night. Stacey looked up to Mark to ask in a whisper,

'Will it be all right if I phone for a taxi?'

'A taxi?' He turned granite features down her way. 'For Pete's sake, what for?'

'To take me to Naples,' she blinked, and then added, 'It's all right, I told them I might be late.'

'Late!' He took her arm roughly. 'That's an understatement, if ever I heard one. You'd better hang on here for tonight.' As she drew away he added tartly, 'It's okay. It's on the house.'

'Well, that's very kind of you, Mark, but ...' Stacey mumbled, trying to sound polite. He was merely being considerate, but if she leaned on that too much she would be lost.

She tried again with an attempt at firmer tones. 'I don't think I want to start unpacking again. And I *do* have a hotel to go to in Naples.'

She was slightly appalled at the etched lines on the face that loomed over hers.

'Eager to get going, aren't we?' he sneered. 'Quite the dutiful little fiancée.' As he swung away he bit out, 'I bet you just can't wait to become the dutiful little wife!'

Stacey felt too far gone to cope with his jibes. As they reached the steps she said wearily, 'I'll go up and get my luggage.'

'Save your legs,' he snapped. 'I'll get it. And you can skip the phone call. I'll drive you in myself.'

CHAPTER ELEVEN

'You?' Stacey stopped. 'Haven't you got ... other things to attend to?'

'Nothing that can't wait until morning.'

She couldn't see whether the lights were on in his apartment, but it was possible that he hadn't expected Sharon to wait up for him.

Minutes later he came back out to the steps with her cases, and the coat she had laid out thrown over his shoulder. He dumped the lot at her feet and strode off into the darkness. She waited meekly as he drew the car up quickly opposite the steps and got out to drop her cases into the back.

He held the coat to ask briskly, 'Cold?'

Stacey shook her head and stepped into her seat. Words were becoming more and more difficult. He moved in beside her and closed the door quietly. She turned to take her last view of the Palazzo. She was still looking when the car moved out of the drive, and Mark said testily,

'Maybe you should have bought a postcard of the place.'

He seemed moody and foul-tempered, and Stacey's heart sank to think that he was already regretting his offer to drive her into Naples.

He took the roads at less than moderate speed, and Stacey couldn't help feeling that they could have made the city in half the time, had he kept his usual pace. She made no comment, because she was caught in the bitter-sweet torment that is wanting something to continue, yet longing for it to end.

She had taken care to sit well over in her seat, so that there was no danger of his shoulder brushing against hers, but the temptation to drop her hand over the firm brown one on the wheel was at times overwhelming.

Whenever they turned a corner, she wanted to rest her head against him, feel the smooth cloth of his dinner jacket beneath her cheek.

Thankfully his terse questions at intervals helped her to keep her head. 'Plane seat all fixed? Okay for small change? Don't forget to get someone to see to your luggage. . . .'

It only took a nod to answer his questions, and though the tones were gravel-harsh she wanted to hang on to the last of his words.

Though at first she had been longing for the buildings of Naples to appear, now she shrank from the sight of their jagged peaks along the skyline. She could only whisper the name of the hotel in answer to Mark's clipped question.

All too soon, he was drawing alongside the pink-washed, dimly lit building, with its two heavy brass lamps lighting the way into the foyer. Mark opened the car door for her and dipped into the back for her cases. With one in each hand and the other under his arm, he led the way into the hotel. Stacey followed carrying her coat.

There was no one in evidence at the desk, but no doubt a ring on the bell would bring someone on the scene.

Mark dropped her cases in the centre of the patterned carpet. He stood for a second. Stacey stood too.

He paced a few steps and then thrust his hands into his pocket. 'Well,' he gave her the twist of a smile, 'I guess this is it?'

Stacey nodded, unable to conjure up anything resembling a smile.

In the pause that followed he took his hands out of his pockets abruptly. She thought he might be going to shake her hand, but the arms stayed stiffly at his sides.

As she looked up at him, he looked at her for a long moment, and then nodded briefly. 'So long, Stacey. Have a good trip.'

His voice sounded strangely far away. As she whispered faintly in return, 'Goodbye, Mark,' he swung on his heel and strode out of the hotel.

She heard the car start up and move off, and blinked away the glitter of a tear.

'A summer to love, and a winter to get over it,' Mark had once said jokingly. There wasn't a winter coming that would get her over him. She dropped her coat on the island of suitcases and was tempted to slump down with it, but there was a room waiting for her. She might as well let the tears go in style.

As she moved over towards the reception desk, she wasn't aware of a figure coming in at the door. Nor did she hear the firm footsteps over the carpet. It was only when a steel clamp fastened around her wrist that she swung round with a gasp of surprise. 'Mark! What are you doing here? I thought you'd. . . .'

With a grim line for a mouth he tugged her away from the desk and across the foyer. 'We're getting married,' he said roughly.

'We're . . .?' Stacey's mouth fell slightly apart.

For a second the world shone in rainbow colours, and then she knew what had happened.

She *had* pressed the bell on the reception desk, *and* she had been shown to her room. Now she was sleeping in the bed, and this was the dream she was having. Her wildest!

In a daze she felt herself being thrust roughly into the car. Her cases were flung into the back.

Almost before she had caught her breath they were racing away from the city of Naples.

The buildings receded quickly behind, and as they came on to the familiar orange groves and vineyards, the car swung down a narrow lane and came to a crunching halt on a palm-lined platform above the sea.

Though Stacey's heart had wings, it fluttered around uncertainly.

No dream could be as real as this, and if it *was* actually happening, what . . .? Her door was swung open and she was being helped out on to the springy turf. Here the cliff fell away at their feet, and the sea spread like an endless apron of grey silk, beneath the lightening sky.

With Mark towering over her Stacey stammered over her thundering heartbeats, 'I didn't really think there was . . . enough between us to think about . . . marriage.'

She wasn't prepared for his rough embrace, nor the force with which his mouth came down on hers, but long before the fierceness had receded and only a gentleness sought the warmth of her lips, she was spinning round and down in the life-draining quality of his kiss.

A world later, when it seemed that she would have nothing left to give, he raised his head and with strangely lit brown eyes murmured, 'That's what's between us, and you're stuck with it.' He dropped his lips into her hair and brushed them along her throat, adding in blurred tones, 'You know you can't settle for anything less.'

'I never wanted to,' Stacey looked up with shining eyes, 'but what about. . . .' She couldn't bring herself to mention any names and petered out faintly with '. . . the others?'

'Farrow?' Mark grinned. 'He'll understand. We'll demonstrate if necesssary.' He found her mouth and brushed it with his own, murmuring, 'I felt all kinds of a heel last time, that's why I had him whipped back from Rome. But any guy who goes off and leaves . . .'

'I seem to recall, too,' Stacey pushed away from the wide chest slightly, 'that you had Sharon brought out here rather quickly after that . . . that other night.'

'That's right.' He looked down at her with non-committal humour.

Stacey couldn't bring herself to ask the questions that she so badly needed to know the answers to. Even now she couldn't be sure of happiness. After a pause she stumbled in with, 'Well, for a man who's done as much as you've done for Sharon. . . .'

'Not just Sharon,' he drew her close again, 'Rick and Signora Minetto too.'

'Signora Minetto of Amalfi?' Stacey looked up for a long moment at Mark's face. 'Has she got something to do with Sunflair?' she asked.

'Well, as grandmother of the firm she didn't have much say in the running of the business, but . . .'

'You mean,' Stacey's grey-green eyes opened wide, 'the Signora is Sharon's grandmother?'

'Maternal,' Mark nodded with a smile. 'She was staying at the Palazzo when all the trouble blew up concerning the Sunflair business. She asked me to get the Kingsbury kids out of trouble, and I've been doing it ever since.'

Signora Minetto. Of course! Stacey nodded dawningly. *That* was who Sharon had reminded her of, that afternoon when they were chatting in the bedroom of the Palazzo.

And come to think of it, going back to that afternoon . . .

'Signora Minetto . . . is a very old friend, isn't she?' Stacey fingered a shirt button pensively.

'More than that,' Mark dropped his arms round her waist humorously, 'She helped finance the early days of the Palazzo.'

'Yet it was Sharon who you sent for in such a hurry, and . . . you spent an awful lot of time with her?'

He drew Stacey close. 'It was a blow knowing what you could do to me. I wanted to throw myself into any kind of work.'

'Work?' Stacey raised a cryptic eyebrow, steering clear of his lips.

Mark grinned. 'It was quite a job getting Sharon tuned to the idea of letting Sunflair go. Rick was all for it, but his sister didn't care for the idea of seeing all her dad had worked for going to one of the big tour operators.'

'So it was another travel firm that wanted Sunflair?' Stacey gazed up wonderingly.

Mark nodded. 'Signora Minetto, like me, reckoned it was the best move for Sharon. That's what we discussed that day I took you to Amalfi. We had to get Sharon to see it, so . . .' he smiled darkly, 'it was decided that I might try a little friendly persuasion.'

'Are you sure that's *all* it was?' Stacey asked after a long pause, slowly tracing his lips with her finger. 'Sharon told me that she was going to marry you.'

Mark shrugged easily. 'Probably I was current favourite at the time. I think I lost out, though, to one of the young lawyer types who came out from England. She's invited him to her grandmother's home.'

Stacey digested this, but not being able to let go she asked seriously,

'Mark, what do you really think of Sharon?'

'A sweet kid who's had to grow up overnight.' He drew Stacey close with a roguish gleam. 'But not my type.'

Stacey relaxed against him, drinking in the words. She looked up to ask, 'Do you think anything will come of it?

You know, what you said about Sharon and this lawyer?'

'Judging by the way he looks at her, I wouldn't be at all surprised,' Mark reflected.

Stacey slid her hands up and around his neck, and she gazed up to ask innocently, 'How *does* he look at her?'

With a sloping smile, Mark dropped his face in her hair. 'The way I've been trying not to look at you,' he murmured. 'But now the game's up. You'll have to give Farrow his ring back.'

There was a silence. Stacey's grey-green eyes twinkled as she replied in low tones, 'I would if I had it.'

In answer to Mark's quizzical grin she smiled, 'Jeremy's going to marry a girl he met in Rome. He bought the ring in Sorrento and asked me to try it on for size.'

'Well, of all the crazy . . .!'

The arms about her became steel. They gripped almost painfully, as he vibrated in her ear, 'You really wanted to put me through the mill, didn't you?'

'You were seeing so much of Sharon, there didn't seem much point in explaining,' Stacey laughed breathlessly. 'And anyway, you were so quick to rush me into marriage. I thought you were just trying to ease your conscience.'

'The only conscience I had,' Mark said with the gleam of a smile, bringing his face down close to hers, 'was in letting you go to Farrow. You see, I knew what you'd be missing.'

'Pretty sure of yourself, weren't you?' She raised starry eyes.

'You forget,' he drawled, finding her mouth, 'you gave me something to be sure of.'

After a long moment his arm slackened. 'We'll go to England in a couple of days,' he murmured, 'and see about the wedding. I might let you do half an hour in the shop while I'm meeting these folks of yours. But no more,' he grinned. 'We've got a lot of time to make up for. From about two minutes after I met you on the boat.'

'That first day,' Stacey mused, 'I thought you were some kind of a recluse living in a remote villa. Later on at the hotel I thought you were thoroughly detestable.'

'And what do you think of me now?'

'Oh, much the same,' Stacey said, airily teasing.

'We might be able to change that.' As his lips brushed her throat he said softly, 'I rather fancy the idea of being a recluse with you. We'd better start looking for a remote villa.'

'What about the Palazzo?' Stacey laughed incredulously.

'It runs okay,' Mark grinned. 'And I've no intention of sharing my wife with half of next season's clientele.'

He took her arm, and as they turned, the sky over the bay was shot with the wild colours of a new day.

Dawn over Sorrento.

As Stacey walked with her hand in Mark's, she knew it was the start, too, of a long and everlasting love.

SEA OF ZANJ

Their meeting in Mombasa was accidental: Lee had missed the ship taking her to her new job as governess in the Seychelles. When their paths parted abruptly, Lee was left with haunting memories of Nick Reynolds, a man who had attracted her very strongly.

Their second meeting was equally accidental, but potentially disastrous—because, this time, Lee was pretending to be another man's wife!

CHAPTER ONE

'I wish I had your nerve. Straight from Little Ashby to a spot in the Indian Ocean!'

The pale fringed eyes that gazed at Lee were wide with admiring disbelief. They lowered as their owner took a deep sigh and went on to lament drily, 'You know what's going to happen to me? The primary at Tingleton. Sixty-five babes in all, and I'll be lucky if the school doesn't fold up like this one through shortage of customers.'

The games teacher went back to stuffing the books into the case with wry humour, and Lee smiled, continuing to pile the things up out of her desk.

'Little Ashby only closed down because most of the parents have moved into the towns to be nearer their work,' she pointed out. 'And you know you're going to love every minute of looking after your new brood at Tingleton.'

'True,' Grace Pennyweather grinned goodnaturedly, 'but look at me! The high spot in my week is Saturday night in town, and in my year, a fortnight on the Isle of Man. Why couldn't I have struck out for something more exciting like you? Don't tell me!' She put up a plump square-nailed hand in a kind of happy resignation. 'I know. I'm a confirmed rustic, who can only see as far as the next village, and only that because I've been turfed out of this one.'

Lee lowered the lid on the empty desk and pulled in her lip diffidently. 'A couple of weeks from now I might be wishing that *I* had gone no further than the next village,' she said uneasily.

As though she were inclined to agree Grace asked in sympathetic tones, 'What is it you're going to do out there? Did you say there are three children?'

Lee nodded. 'Twin five-year-olds and their brother aged seven,' she returned meditatively.

'Well, you can't make up a school out of three!' the

387

games teacher scoffed lightly. 'Not even a class!'

'No,' Lee smiled, dropping a handful of pens and pencils into the space at the side of the case. She looked around to make sure that there was nothing else and then snapped it shut, adding reflectively, 'I don't think it's so much a teacher the children need as someone to keep them occupied generally. Apparently this is the first time they haven't accompanied their parents on one of their trips, and the oldest is somewhat resentful at being farmed out. Then there are only a handful of labourers on the island and the uncle that the children are staying with. He has some sort of plantation to attend to, so he probably doesn't get much time.'

'All madly romantic,' Grace twinkled, folding her arms knowingly. 'The bachelor uncle, the remote island...'

'I don't think so,' Lee laughed, stepping down from the dais where for the past year she had looked out on a sea of shining chubby faces and small bodies writhing and squirming in the strict confines of chair and desk. 'From what I can make out,' she continued, her heart catching slightly at the sight of the empty, haphazard chairs, 'Alec Hayward seems a nice enough person, but apart from offering to take on the children, his main interests seem to be his job and the girl he hopes to marry. I think the most I can hope for,' her soft amber eyes twinkled back as her colleague's well-built shoulders sagged deflatively, 'is a few months with a change of scenery and a little more sun.'

'Maybe.' With a disbelieving smile Grace swung the case down loosely into her hand and added pointedly as Lee took a last look around the classroom, 'I've been looking up facts about the Seychelles, since you broke the news. I didn't find many, but everybody waxes poetic about them. "The last of the island paradises ... the original Garden of Eden ..." Coconuts are said to be twice as big as anywhere else and...'

As though she were describing another planet Grace's eyes opened slightly in awe again. 'How on earth did you get on to it? The job, I mean?' she asked.

'Well, in one of my wilder moments I ordered a London paper.' Lee forced a smile as she moved towards the door.

She was glad Grace was giving her the excuse to prattle on this way. It was ridiculous to feel a tight throat at leaving an untidy room with chipped green paintwork and gaudy daubs of pictures on the walls. 'And then in one of my crazier moments,' she laughed brightly as they moved out into the corridor, 'I answered an advert, and things just snowballed from there. The parents, both archaeologists, were looking for someone with my kind of qualifications to go out to their children. The father was over here to equip for a dig they're going to in Africa. After exchanging letters I went up to see him. End of term here seemed to fit in perfectly with when his wife would be joining him out there, and that was it.'

'And tomorrow you're on your way to the island to take over. Talk about a quick change!' As they moved out into the sunshine Grace rested a long look on Lee to add, 'But then you've got nothing to keep you here, really, have you?'

'Family, you mean?' Lee smiled and shook her head. After a pause she inhaled a light sigh. 'My aunt had high hopes of my obtaining a headmistresship, as *she* did before she was thirty. I'm cheating a little, but I can always come back to that.' Her laughter was a little anxious as she added, 'One has to get the adventure out of one's system first.'

'Of course,' Grace nodded, looking unconvinced. She went on to say, poker-faced, 'And you're not doing it by halves, are you? Travelling thousands of miles to this place ... this ...'

'Half-Moon Island.'

The remote-sounding name seemed to invoke in Grace a kind of suppressed shudder. She lowered her lashes and then raised them again, apparently relieved to find herself still in the school playground, then she said briskly, 'Are you sure you wouldn't like to come home with me tonight and think it over?'

Shaking her head, Lee swallowed her amusement. Grace spoke as though she had suddenly had this new job thrust upon her instead of going all out to get it. But then Grace had made no secret of the fact that she wouldn't dream of taking such a plunge, and it was obvious that she couldn't believe anybody else would.

Lee thanked her for her offer and turned to take a last look around. No building had ever struck her as being more without life, yet bursting with the echoes of it, than an empty school. She was glad in a way to be going from the village now that this one was to remain empty. Perhaps when she returned it would be thriving as a village institute or something.

She took her case as Grace went to push her bicycle from the shed. Later, at the gates, they parted with cheerful goodbyes and promises to write, and Lee watched the other girl pedal off stolidly along the lane. Not exactly a friend— for with Aunt Ruth life had been a round of teachers' conferences and committees and unions, and there had never been much time to make friends—but a close colleague. And one, Lee mused, gazing after the slowly receding figure, who preferred to stay firmly embedded in the core of the countryside, where there was no danger of the outside world inflicting its pace.

Off she would go now to her scones and jam for tea, and her knitting on the back porch if the evening was warm enough. Yet she was content and wanted nothing more.

Lee took a deep and fluttering breath as she looked out over the meadows. She couldn't say the same for herself. Though country-bred with no more than the experience of living in at a training college up north, and the odd trip with her aunt to the coast, she had always been eager to know what lay over the next hill.

She was going to find out tomorrow in no uncertain manner. Her heart lurched at the thought of the journey she was about to make. All those miles by plane and boat! Suddenly the cottages along the lane looked very homely, the trees with their new speckle of spring green, the daffodils swinging low in the gardens to the rhythm of the breeze.

Every sight and sound took on a magnetic quality that seemed to drain her of all fight. She was seized with a desire to run after Grace Pennyweather, to apply for a position at Tingleton and cling to the security of an unchanged routine.

But the moment passed. Security and the urge to see over the next hill just didn't go together somehow.

As she walked along the lane to her rooms in the village, her mind moved on to the time when the last of her cases would be packed and her tickets safely in her bag, and later when she would be stepping down from the airport bus. She turned in at the green gate, wondering with a new kind of trepidation just how she would cope on her first flight ever tomorrow.

Fortunately, or unfortunately, as it turned out for Lee, the worry of flying for the first time was completely obliterated by a growing agitation that the plane she had taken for Mombasa wasn't going to land in time.

According to her instructions and information, the boat leaving for the Seychelles sailed on Tuesday the fifteenth. She had left Little Ashby with ample time to spare, yet here it was, the fifteenth, and down below was nothing but the dragging endless grey of the sea.

Nowhere near as seasoned a traveller as most of the other passengers appeared to be, she hadn't understood why everyone had got up from their seats on that other plane at the airport and calmly filed back into the waiting lounges. Some sort of explanation had been given, but she had been too tensed up to take anything in. Then there had been a trip to the restaurant for a meal, and then more waiting. Heaven knew how many hours had been lost before they had finally boarded a plane, but it was obvious from the acquiescent smiles that nobody had to get to a remote island with only the odd boat stopping off there, as she had to.

She leaned to look down again over the water as though this might have some magical effect of drawing the African coast nearer, and caught the light of an amused twinkle in the eyes of the woman sitting in the next seat.

'It's still there,' the woman remarked waggishly, looking down at the sea.

Lee smiled, drawing her gaze back to the inside of the plane. At least she had been lucky enough to secure a pleasant travelling companion. Mrs. Deighton, neat in navy blue polka-dots, with short cropped blue-rinsed hair, had kept things bright from the outset. Quick to sense that her neighbour was new to the business of flying, she had opened up a friendly conversation, helping Lee over the first few unsteady moments without fuss, and without being tediously sympathetic. She had none of that formidableness that tall elderly women often had, but rather a gentleness of manner and speech that put one immediately at one's ease.

Smiling at Lee now as her gaze wandered around the interior of the plane, Mrs. Deighton quipped, 'Are you wishing the infernal thing would hurry up and touch down on to something solid?'

Lee inclined her head to return the smile.

'No, I find I'm quite enjoying it,' she said truthfully. 'I'm just a little concerned about our time of arrival.'

'I see,' Mrs. Deighton gave an understanding nod. 'You're travelling on from Mombasa. Well, I shouldn't worry, my dear, there's plenty of transport.'

'I'm not going overland,' Lee explained, turning the corners of her mouth down ruefully. 'I'm due to catch the boat leaving for the Seychelles and I've got a horrible feeling I'm going to miss it. I believe they only sail fortnightly, or once a month or something.'

'My dear!' Mrs. Deighton laid a hand on her arm in sudden concern. 'Why didn't you say back at the airport? In your case they would certainly have squeezed you in on an earlier flight. You ought to have applied to the stewardess.'

'I didn't know I could,' Lee said simply, knowing that Mrs. Deighton wasn't the type to look on in amusement at another person's inexperience.

Firm fingers tightened on her arm as the older woman leaned in close.

'Now don't you worry,' she said again reassuringly. 'I live in Mombasa, and I'm sure if your boat has sailed there will be something else to take you.' The blue-grey hair quivered round leather-brown cheeks as she added sternly, 'Now just you be sure to badger the authorities into doing something for you when you get there.'

'Oh, I will!' Lee spoke up weakly. She failed to see what

good badgering anybody would do if the boat had already sailed.

Later when a lump of land appeared and gradually shaped itself into a surf-edged coast, Lee sat a little straighter in her seat and mentally crossed her fingers. It was going to be all right. Of course it was. Unused to travel on this scale, she was getting herself worked up for no reason. It was rather like worrying if the Little Ashby bus would make it for the connecting service into town, only on a much grander scale, of course.

She smiled to herself now. How many times had she sat biting her lip on the edge of the seat as the bus had careered down the lanes, and then found she had an interminable wait before the other one was even in sight?

This line of thinking made her feel much better. As the plane circled and the passengers were instructed to fasten their safety belts she breathed considerably easier. Of course there had been no need to worry! The boat would be in, and probably wouldn't sail for hours after she had embarked.

She only wished that Mrs. Deighton's smile had been a little more encouraging as they left the plane together.

'Now don't forget. Don't be afraid to speak up when you get to the docks,' she said kindly. 'There's nothing the young men out here like better than helping a stranded young lady.'

The lavender eyes took on a whimsical light as they rested for a moment on the slender trim-suited figure; a face not beautiful but interesting if only for the fact that the dark hair was drawn back from a kind of gentle vulnerability at the temples.

'I'm sure you're going to be all right,' Mrs. Deighton smiled thoughtfully.

They parted in the customs shed.

'Bye-bye, my dear!' the older woman called from up ahead. 'And a safe journey.' She disappeared in the crowd and Lee felt as though a kindly relative had suddenly let go of her hand.

She was aware of dark-skinned smiling faces ushering her on. Her cases were whisked back and forth, people were pushing behind and ahead of her, and then she was out in the open. With a gulp of the warm breeze she was tempted to stop and take in Africa, but a sense of urgency made her hurry towards the next stage of her journey.

Once inside the speeding hired car, however, she drank in views of brilliant skies, pencil-slim palms, red-roofed villas, and vivid blossoming trees. The sea was bluer than anything she had ever seen in her life, the beaches purest white. If she hadn't let herself get so carried away with scenery, she might have been preparing herself for the blow that all along she had half suspected would fall.

As it was, she dreamily paid off the driver of the car, drifted trance-like into the shipping offices and was told that the liner for Bombay, calling at the Seychelles, had sailed two hours before.

Aghast, she spoke freely of her troubles, but there was no gallant young man eager to fashion a boat for her with his own bare hands, just a lot of harassed officials, sympathetic but detached. It was unfortunate, they said, but what could be done? Very few boats called at the Seychelles, they said. The next one sailing from Mombasa was two weeks from today and nobody could make it any sooner than that. Of course they understood the young lady's disappointment, but...

Disappointment! Lee stood on the dock, her luggage scattered around her, the warm wind cooling as the sky took on a violet glow. It was a disaster! Here she was with a one-way ticket to an island that was virtually unreachable. The money she had wouldn't stand up to a fortnight in a Mombasa hotel, nor would it buy her a ticket back home.

She let go a worried sigh. There hadn't been anything like this in the careful instructions mapped out for her by Bruce Pasmore, the father of the children she was going out to. According to his notes, everything was plain sailing. She winced at the cliché. She was to catch the plane to Mombasa, hire a car to the docks and embark on the boat for the Seychelles. Everything had been arranged for her and it all ought to have been very simple. Of course losing all that time at one of the airports on the way probably only happened once in a dozen times. But it had to happen to her, she thought wryly. The one person who wouldn't have a clue what to do next. She knew she ought to be making some cool, constructive plans right now, but the fact of the matter was, she couldn't think of a thing.

Several moments had dragged by before she took to clustering her luggage close. One thing was obvious. She couldn't stand here for two weeks. She was just considering which direction to make for when a familiar voice floated out from a long maroon car that was cruising some distance away.

She saw an arm extend from the open window and a pointing finger wagged impatiently at the end of it.

'There she is, Paul. Over there!' The voice urged, 'Do be a good fellow and get a move on.'

Lee was conscious of the chauffeur-driven car drawing alongside, and then Mrs. Deighton's head came through the open window.

'*There* you are, Miss Travers!' she called, turning the handle of the door and stepping out almost before the car had stopped. 'I'm so glad I found you!' She glanced down sympathetically at the suitcases. 'My husband told me your boat had sailed,' and with a humorous light, 'I pestered him to make enquiries when I got home.'

Lee smiled ruefully. 'If we had arrived on time I would have had several hours to spare. As it was I missed it by two.'

'It's awful luck, I know,' Mrs. Deighton nodded. 'Have you any idea what you'll do now?'

'Not much,' Lee drooped. 'I didn't come intending to spend two weeks in a hotel.'

'Then of course you must come home with me.'

The suggestion made Lee step back a little. 'Oh, but I didn't mean . . .' she stammered.

'I know you didn't.' Mrs. Deighton patted her kindly. 'But I've talked it over with my husband. We're both agreed that if you have to wait in Mombasa, you must do it with us.' She twinkled at Lee's hesitant smile. 'You won't be intruding, my dear. I have young stewardesses coming and going all the time. My husband's connected with the airline and I suppose I'm just as tied up with it as he is.' As

Lee's smile changed to one of gratitude, the older woman said briskly, 'Now into the car with you, and Paul will put your bags in the back.'

The chauffeur came round and with a slight bow and a smile at Lee he took her luggage and proceeded to stow it in the boot. Lee stepped aside for the other woman to enter the car, stooped herself and then hesitated.

'You're very kind, Mrs. Deighton,' she blurted, 'but I can't imagine what I'm going to do for two whole weeks.'

The woman inside the car smiled.

'You must go out and see the town. Enjoy yourself. You'll be amazed at how quickly the time will go.'

'But what will my employer think?' Lee looked dubious. 'I have a job to go to in the Seychelles.'

'I'll get Bob to put a message through to be relayed by radio phone. Your island should have one. He'll explain that you've been delayed.' Mrs. Deighton looked consoling. It could happen to anyone,' she smiled, patting the seat beside her.

As the car left the docks behind and made its way along wide tree-lined avenues, Lee made an effort to relax in her seat. It seemed strange to think that in this day and age she should be stranded like this a thousand miles from her destination. Back in Little Ashby she had assumed that there wasn't a spot left on earth that couldn't be reached by some method or other.

She thought of Grace's words, 'The last of the island paradises.' Perhaps that was why the Seychelles were so-called. Until they got an airport they were reasonably secure from the outside world. She experienced a tiny thrill of excitement at the thought of journeying somewhere so awesomely inaccessible, but it did nothing to ease her frustration. For the next two weeks, she thought glumly, the islands were quite safe from one Lee Travers.

The car turned along a road flanked with green tropical growth, colourful houses and rolling lawns. Mrs. Deighton, taking in Lee's serious features, chuckled encouragingly, 'The girls will look after you. They come to me when they have a few hours off and they certainly don't seem to get stuck for places to go or ...' the waggish gleam was back in the faded lavender eyes as the car stopped and she finished softly, 'for young men to take them.'

To Lee, the Deighton household was the merriest she had ever been in. Music and laughter drifted from the upstairs rooms, and cars were constantly calling and pulling away again, loaded with riotous groups.

Apologetically Mrs. Deighton had put her in with Cheryl Kenton, but Lee had liked the dark-haired, laughing-eyed girl on sight, and they had talked long into the night.

It was the next morning when Cheryl was prattling on about what to wear for the beach that Lee found there was more to this 'making the most of Mombasa' than met the eye. She pulled out her swimsuit to hear a horrified yelp as the other girl asked, 'What on earth is that?'

Lee held up the black cotton doubtfully. 'I know it's regulation school issue, but I thought...'

Cheryl heaved a deep sigh.

'Lee, how old are you?' she asked gently.

'Twenty-two.'

'And you've never owned a slinky swimsuit?'

'Well, I...' Lee bit back a smile, lost for words and wide-eyed as Cheryl stepped up and unclipped the slide from the back of her head.

'All this glorious hair shouldn't be strapped down,' the girl said, frothing it out admiringly, 'and this shirt. Open it at the neck and roll the sleeves up high to show your arms. You've got a gorgeous figure and those slim skirts suit you, but you need a little more heel.'

Standing back, she took a long look at Lee to ask thoughtfully, 'What did you do for entertainment back home?'

'Entertainment?' Lee looked vague. 'I was nearly always busy with work connected with the school,' she replied, taking in this new picture of herself through the mirror. 'But Saturdays were quite pleasant in Little Ashby.'

'Well, this is little big Mombasa!' Cheryl bubbled suddenly into laughter, 'and every day is Saturday. Too bad I can only spend two of them with you,' she flicked briskly through Lee's garments in the wardrobe, 'but before I drop out of your life again you're going to know what heaven meant teachers to do out of school. Now apart from the swimsuit, what else can you afford?' She looked back towards the wardrobe.

'Your dresses are quite good—simple, but they're the best. I'd say a couple of good evening ones, a *kikoi*, that's a kind of Arab-style sarong we wear on the beach, and some shoes. Can you run to that?'

'Well, yes, I think so, but ...'

Cheryl lived in a world of no buts, and Lee was soon a neighbour. She shopped recklessly, loving the huge stores in town, the bustle of the cosmopolitan people.

That night Cheryl took her by the hand as a car full of laughing air crew came honking up to the house. Before she knew it she was being squeezed into a ridiculously small place and speeding towards the airline club in Mombasa.

Initiated into the world of blue serge and gold braid and openly appraising smiles as first one uniformed arm and then another encircled her with a proprietorial air, Lee soon lost track of the invitations she received from young men eager to make the most of their off-duty hours, though she laughingly accepted every one.

Somewhere in the whirl of the days that followed, Cheryl disappeared as though she had never been, but for Lee life continued to turn in a round of beach parties, nightclubs and sightseeing, and she couldn't say she disliked it.

Her skin took on the glow of a peach-gold tan. The colour of her eyes seemed strangely enhanced by its warmth on her cheeks, her smile whiter and somehow attractive. She had discarded the flat shoes in favour of slender heels, and her hair, free from its tortoiseshell slide, hung in soft coils about her shoulders.

Her shyness was the last to go. In fact, it didn't, not altogether, but with often a handsome crew member on either side of her, she could pretend she had all the confidence in the world.

She got to know the popular spots for beach activities, the neon glitter of Mombasa at night and most of all the Butterfly Club, catering for air personnel and most of the English contingent of the town.

She liked the club. She liked its name. It reminded her of herself—the village green caterpillar sloughing its skin for colours befitting Mombasa. Of course she wasn't fooling herself that this was the real Lee Travers, but the butterfly life was rather fun in a way, and worth living up to, if only to help the time pass.

Her one regret was that she didn't see more of the Deightons, although they had assured her, Mr. Deighton being a tall genial man, that her message to the island had been received and acknowledged, and that there was nothing for it at the moment but for her to make the most of her stay.

There was no doubt she was doing that, Lee thought sometimes a little guiltily. She wondered what use she would find for frothy evening dresses on a remote lonely island. Perhaps she could swish around under the palm trees pretending that she was still in the company of a good-looking air crew.

One item of wear she felt she would never regret buying was the dusky rose swimsuit. In one piece and completely plain except for a rose of matching material stitched at the base of the low-cut front, its perfection was in its fit. Lee always wore it with supreme confidence, and the afternoons on the beach were some of her happiest. It was difficult not to feel you were something special when constantly in the company of over-attentive young men.

Tossing a gay coloured beach ball among a group of them one afternoon, Lee had to smile to herself. If only Grace could see her now! Miss Travers of Class B—not exactly wined, dined and fêted in Mombasa, but caught up in the high-powered living of holidaying air crews it could amount to something like that.

Lost in her own humorous thoughts, she tossed the ball over her head abstractedly and stepped back into a solid wall of movement that had suddenly rose up from behind. The collision was enough to snap her head back, jerking out a breath, and then a rough grip was steadying her and a matching voice with a touch of mockery about it suggested, 'Try looking where you're going. It helps.'

Lee would have murmured some apology, but she was slow to react from the shock of a wet muscular frame against her. She looked down at the splodges of deeper colour on her swimsuit where the water had caught her and the voice from the dripping frame drawled, 'Sorry to spoil the pretty picture. The suit should dry okay. They're supposed to stand up to water.'

A steely white smile showed briefly through dripping features and then the figure had moved on.

Lee ran after the bouncing ball as though nothing had happened. Well, nothing had, had it? Why her heart should suddenly behave as though she were whirling down a helter-skelter ride, she had no idea.

Unless it was because she had seen the man several times in the Butterfly Club and had grown used to watching him. Invariably in the midst of smart-suited men and elegantly dressed women, he had in contrast a kind of rugged hardness that seemed to suggest the outdoors, though his own lounge suits were always immaculate.

He was a man who seemed to draw one's gaze. Lee remembered that there had been more than one disconcerting moment, when as she looked out from the laughter of her own group, her glance had collided with his.

Of course she would have to go and step back just now, the very moment he was passing. She threw the ball up vigorously, laughing to disperse her irritation. What was so special about him anyway? He was big and muscular and tanned, but so were several of her escorts today. And *they* were handsome too, which was more than could be said of a longish craggy face and lean square jaw.

She continued to play feverishly for a while, aware of the figure swathed in a brilliant white robe some distance away.

For some ridiculous reason she hoped he wouldn't stay after his swim, but he draped down and leisurely lit up a cigarette, and Lee hastily sought the security of her chair.

Later though, ostensibly enjoying the fun conjured up by her male companions, she found herself going over those few words spoken to her in vibrant tones. It was difficult to work out just in what frame of mind they had been delivered. Had he been merely commenting lightly on her damp swimsuit to tide them both over an awkward moment, or did he see her as some kind of enamelled bathing belle who, loth to spoil the picture she made, declined to get wet?

A small flame of annoyance flared up within her as she remembered his mocking drawl. Well, too bad he hadn't been down here when she had spent most of the afternoon in the water. If he thought she was going to do the same today, just to satisfy his... She caught herself up with a small smile. What *was* she going on about? He had probably never noticed her before the bump, and would have promptly forgotten all about her immediately after it.

Roger, a flight engineer, dropped a tanned arm about her shoulders to show her the intricacies of a huge shell he had found.

Head down, fingering its pearly finish, Lee could just see the white-robed figure out of the corner of her eye. She knew he was drawing leisurely on his cigarette, but she couldn't be sure where his gaze was directed. Not, she told herself, smiling hard at the shell, that she was particularly interested.

CHAPTER TWO

LEE was never really sure how Nick Reynolds came to be one of her party, but the following evening at the Butterfly Club her hand was being taken in one of the firm brown ones that had steadied her on the beach, and someone was making polite introductions.

She gathered that the captain of a flight that had flown in only that night was a friend of his, for the two men spent most of the evening in conversation, and Lee had to admit it was a relief. More at home with junior officers, she was comparatively relaxed in their company. The senior officers were much more mature and worldly, and she sometimes felt out of her depth with them, as she would undoubtedly if she was left alone with Nick Reynolds. She supposed he must be about thirty-five, and she was quite happy for him to stay slightly aloof, talking to the captain about whatever men do talk about for hours on end.

When the group occasionally merged for a drink, or some general topic of conversation, her eyes encountered in passing a pair of steely grey ones. She noticed they were deep set and gave nothing away except perhaps a kind of flinty humour.

She never expected to come into any closer contact with Nick Reynolds than that first introduction. But then ever since leaving Little Ashby events seemed to have developed this capricious knack of landing her with the unexpected.

A little weary of the social round, she had by the next day, her tenth in Mombasa, learned how to decline some of the offers of the carefree air officers with time on their hands. She spent the morning in Mrs. Deighton's airy kitchen, helping her to prepare lunch, and discussing the grandchildren she had recently visited in England. In the afternoon she dozed luxuriously on a shady terrace at the rear of the house.

Towards evening when the harsh metallic blue of the sky softened to a pale lilac she started to prepare reluctantly for a visit to the Butterfly Club. Though her latest escorts were three of the nicest young men, and she had got to know them fairly well during their stay in town, nothing would have induced her to go tonight if she hadn't promised to join them for their last evening. They were due to fly out at dawn, and there was no reason to believe that she would see them again, but she had given her word. And if she didn't go to meet them as arranged they would surely come up to the house to fetch her.

Shaking off her lethargy, she bathed and slipped into a dress of soft green, with slender waist and full skirt. It had a low embroidered neckline and small cap sleeves, and was one that she had fallen instantly in love with on that first shopping spree, when Cheryl had raved that it 'fitted like a dream.'

Mr. and Mrs. Deighton had arranged to drop her off at the Butterfly on their way to some evening's entertainment. Amidst neon lights and honking traffic she waved them off along the road, and then walked through the wide doors of the club.

A little unsure at having to make her own way for once, she ventured among the chattering groups, feeling small and insignificant beside prosperous-looking business men and prima-donna-gowned ladies. There were several uniformed men dotted about the bars and chandeliered restaurant, but none in the familiar blue and gold braid of Cheryl's airline.

After scanning the rooms again, Lee realised with a tiny nervous jolt that her air crew friends were nowhere to be seen. She was wondering if she ought to wait, and whether she could survive the agony of standing so obviously alone in the crowded foyer, when a hand dropped lightly on her arm.

She jerked round to find Nick Reynolds, huge in light-weight suit and white shirt, immediately behind.

'Your pals asked me to tell you they've been roped in for an earlier flight,' he said lazily. 'They just about had time to leave their apologies with me to pass on.'

Pals! She looked up at him not quite sure whether she liked the way he said that or not. He seemed to have the habit of talking in tones that could lean either way, flippant or biting. Right now though she was concerned with his message.

Reluctant as she had been to make her way out tonight, the knowledge that she had missed the three effervescent young officers filled her with a deep disappointment. They had been generous and kind to her during their stay, and she would have liked to have seen them off, if only to wish them good flying.

Realising that the disappointment was probably showing, she lowered her lashes and murmured politely, 'Thank you for giving me the message.'

As she turned towards the door those two-way tones came over her shoulder to drawl, 'Don't tell me you're going? There's plenty more of your guys around.'

Puzzled but determined not to show it, Lee turned back to follow his gaze over the uniformed figures.

'I don't know any of these men,' she said simply.

'That shouldn't stop you.'

Perhaps his reply was meant to mean something, but she couldn't think what. She raised her gaze to try to fathom his look, but searching the depths of the cool grey eyes was a hazardous business and she was glad to give it up.

'I don't think I'll be staying,' she said, feeling that she should force some sort of smile of thanks. She went towards the way she had come in and was surprised to see the grey-suited arm holding the door for her.

'Which way are you heading?' Nick Reynolds asked evenly. 'I'll flag you a taxi.'

Lee had a nervous desire to be quickly rid of the man towering over her. She said lightly, draping the net stole about her shoulders, 'I think I'd prefer to walk, thank you.'

Moving off, Lee realised with a tiny thrill that this was the first time since her arrival in Mombasa that she was absolutely free to do as she pleased. Not that she hadn't enjoyed being whisked around in hired cars and open carriages, but she had often gazed out at the colourful city and known a longing to take it all in at walking pace. Now she had the opportunity.

Taking a deep breath of the warm African night, she stepped into the throng of cheerful inhabitants jostling their way beneath the tinsel lighting of coffee houses and cafés and gaily lit shops, and then a hand came down on her arm again, and Nick Reynolds was saying, as though the conversation had never ended, 'Walk where?'

Lee turned with a small gesture of impatience. 'Wherever the mood takes me,' she said, trying not to sound too short.

As she hurried on ahead the tall figure strolled up alongside. He pulled out cigarettes, lit one and drew on it slowly before saying, 'Might be okay when you're with your airline pals, but I wouldn't recommend walking alone at this hour.'

Lee looked up, genuinely apologetic.

'I hope you don't feel that you're under any obligation to...'

'I don't.'

Lee swallowed and stared ahead. Well, that was clear enough anyway! She jerked forward uncertainly. Now she was hampered again. She wasn't going to be allowed to roam at will after all. But why shouldn't she? She only had to pretend that she was still on her own.

This proved a little difficult when a hand came up to take her arm and she was steered somewhat firmly through the shouting crowds and blaring traffic.

'Working for the airline company?' he asked casually.

'No. I'll be leaving Mombasa in three or four days,' Lee replied.

'Enjoyed your stay?' The question had a laconic ring about it, and Lee was goaded into replying with throaty fervour, 'Tremendously!'

Surprisingly she caught the white gleam of his smile for a second, and then as they turned a corner and a long gaudily-lit alley came into view, she said eagerly, 'I'd like to go down this way.'

He shrugged, 'You'll find nothing down there but the usual tourist merchandise.'

'But that's marvellous!' she laughed, starting off along

the alley.

For once the enquiring glance was on his side, not hers, for he raised a mocking eyebrow at her words. She wondered why. Perhaps he thought her only interests were nightclubs and parties. Just as he had thought on the beach that her swimsuit had been bought for posing in, not for swimming.

She knew that now and the thought rankled, but there was too much to see to remain ruffled for long. Starry-eyed, she examined silks and saris and gold and silver threadwork; wandered slightly breathless through coloured mosaic archways, past piles of camphorwood chests, lacquerware and Chinese and Indian novelties. All quite uncaring of an occasional mocking gleam from the man at her side. Let him think what he liked! She hadn't asked him along anyway.

It was quite late when they came out on the brightly-lit harbour road, and feeling satiated with crooning imploring voices, wailing music and flashing souvenirs and jewellery, Lee said on a sigh, 'I think I'll take that taxi now.'

Nick Reynolds snapped one to a stop and held the door for her. He seemed to be waiting to give the driver her address, but Lee said primly, 'I can manage now ... and thank you for giving me your time tonight.'

'Think nothing of it.' With a brief mocking salute, he stepped back, turned and strode off. Watching him, head and shoulders above the robed pedestrians, Lee found herself wondering about him. Did he work in Mombasa? Or was he in transit like herself?

It was only after several seconds she realised that the driver was still waiting patiently to be told where to go.

The next afternoon she strolled leisurely down to the now familiar stretch of beach. With none of the company's air personnel in town at the moment, she was more or less a free agent. And after so much high-pressured living it was going to feel good just to soak up the peace of her own small area of sand.

She chose a chair beneath a gay umbrella and blinked at the sapphire blue of the sea.

This was the kind of life she liked, and yet... It was crazy to feel so unsettled, and even crazier to let her eyes have their way in roaming over the other people on the beach.

Just supposing she did see a brilliant white robe? What then? Wouldn't she feel more inclined to leave than to stay, knowing that he would be sure to think? ...

Impatient at her own topsy-turvy thoughts, she pulled on the petalled swimming cap and strolled down to the waves. The water was choppy but invigorating after the enervating heat on the beach. She struck out, glad of the concentration of aiming for a swimming float anchored a short distance out. It would be something to do, and when she got back she would dry off and make her way back to the Deightons'.

At one point she thought of abandoning the idea of the float. It looked as far away as ever. But so, now, did the beach! It was only her puny strokes, of course. In the school swimming pool in England one could zoom from one side to the other with no effort. But the sea was quite different. And what a sea! There seemed to be miles of it all around now.

It occurred to her, as the water pushed up against her face before she could take a breath, that she might have taken on more than she was capable of. Only the odd burly crew member had attempted the float, and that ought to have told her something. That it was a whole lot further out than it looked! she thought wryly, wondering what kind of commotion there would be if she were to throw up her hands and cry for help.

Perhaps no one would hear?

The thought sobered her and she swam seriously for several seconds. The float bobbed ever out of reach. She knew it was only yards away now, but her limbs were beginning to feel as though they were dragging a heavy load. Thank heavens she was almost there.

So intent was she in making the last few feet that she didn't notice tanned shoulders slicing the water a short distance away. Only when a dark head came into view did her heart do a somersault, taking with it the last store of strength that she had reserved for getting to the float.

For a second the water closed in over her head, and then a hand came under her arm and she was practically catapulted the last two or three feet up to the float. As she hung there panting for dear life but trying desperately not to show it, she saw the familiar gleam of a hard white smile and Nick Reynolds was saying in his best sardonic tones, 'I take it you found life too tame on the beach today?'

Though fully occupied with the business of inhaling sweet air again, Lee couldn't resist saying lightly between breaths, 'Now why would I do that?'

'You seem to have quite an appetite for being noticed.' The wide shoulders shrugged in the water. She saw glistening droplets fall away from the deep bronzed skin, as he finished in dry tones, 'Though with the boy-friends noticeably absent today, it's beyond me who you expected to fish you out.'

Lee felt a sudden spear of anger. He actually thought she had made an attempt at the float simply to draw attention to herself, to induce someone to come to her aid! Well, of all the cheap——!

She was on the point of giving him the benefit of a very sharp retort, when she was struck by the humour of the situation. She might as well admit it now. She had taken to the sea to shake off all thoughts of Nick Reynolds, and then it had turned out that he was the one man she should meet at the float. At least she assumed she had just met him here until she heard him drawling, 'I saw you dithering about, half way out. You were taking one hell of a risk, carrying on when you saw you couldn't make it.'

She felt a pair of hands come up to rest impersonally on her waist and then she was being thrust up roughly on to the float. Feeling capable of doing nothing but lying exactly where she was, Lee made a pretence of stretching in the sun. The reply she had planned to deliver smoothly came out a little shaky. 'I was quite aware of what I was doing, you know,' she managed.

'Oh, sure!' He swung up lightly beside her. 'But I can't imagine it doing much for the ego being found floating face downwards.'

Lee made no reply. She didn't know why his words

should cut so deep. She hardly knew the man, anyway. She said steadily, gazing up towards the awning of blue sky, 'You don't like me very much, do you?'

She hadn't expected the width of muscular chest to lean in quite so close, and she wished now that her bosom wouldn't heave so much from her exertions in the water. It was impossible to keep her gaze fixed on the sky, for her view was being blocked by a half-smiling streaming tanned face and eyes lit with supercilious lights.

'Peeved because you can't win them all?' he asked in gravel-deep tones.

She was becoming used to his obscure remarks, but this one suddenly clicked everything into place. So that was what he thought!

Caught up with the Deightons' hospitality and Cheryl's introductions at the airline club, she had simply been falling in with everybody else's plans to have a good time. To her, the company of the handsome uniformed air crews, the nightclubs and days on the beach had been just one way of passing it, but to Nick Reynolds she was a girl out to make the most of her stay in Mombasa; someone who basked in the bright lights and popularity of an all-male entourage until the time came to move on to the next gay pitch.

Looking up into the mocking features just above her own, she knew it shouldn't have mattered what he thought, but for some ridiculous reason it did. And because it did she knew a strong determination not to show it. He had been quick enough to form his own opinions of her, so she might as well live up to them.

Holding his gaze, she said sweetly, 'If *all* includes *you* I'm not particularly worried.'

'What a pity. I thought you were going to work at it.' His tones were pitched to match her own, and Lee's heart, busily pounding from her foolhardy swim, showed no signs of slowing down. She was beginning to wonder if she had started something she might regret, for the dark head lowered ominously.

She heard him murmur drily, 'Well, here goes. We might as well know what we'd have missed,' and before she could do anything about it, hard damp lips had descended on her own.

For Lee the experience was one of anger, tinged with a lethargic vow to do something about it, later. Of course he was going the full length of making her feel cheap in the one way a man could.

But then again, if she jumped up now and reeled on about what she thought of him, it wouldn't be in keeping with what he thought of *her*, and nothing was going to induce her to let him see different at this stage.

Determined to carry the pose, she lay passive under his kiss, but when its lingering quality sparked off something like a minor explosion inside her she pushed away, to say as lightly as she could manage, 'So you see, we needn't have bothered, need we?'

Apparently he agreed, for the mocking smile was practically non-existent. Abruptly he dropped a hand towards the zipped pocket of his swim shorts and drew out cigarettes and lighter. After she had refused his offer, he lit one up and pulled on it deeply.

'You say your stay in Mombasa is almost up?' he asked, frowning, probably against the brightness of the sky.

Lee nodded. 'Three more days.' And then, remembering her part, she said with a gay laugh, 'I don't know if I'll survive without the air crew boys. There's not likely to be any more in town this week.'

'I'll be around.'

He dropped her an obscure smile and Lee swung her glance in the opposite direction. Never at ease under that mocking, penetrating gaze, she found it harder than ever now to meet it. Not because he saw her as a girl who thrived on shallow affairs, but because he had chosen to put her in her place with a kiss that had meant nothing at all to him.

Of course it had meant nothing to her either, but . . . Annoyed with herself at not being able to meet his gaze squarely, she pushed to her feet and moved towards the edge of the float.

'I think I'll be getting back,' she said, putting on her best carefree tones.

'Think you can make it?' He was by her side in a succession of lazy strides.

'I made it out here, didn't I?' she said chirpily, not caring for the strip of choppy waves between her and the beach. The muscular frame beside her was a little disconcerting too.

'You mean you only *just* made it,' he was saying sternly. 'And don't get any ideas about doing it again. This is strictly crack swimming stuff.'

'And *you* can do it with your arms folded, I suppose?' she purred.

'I might have to do it with them full if you do the disappearing act again.'

Not caring for the glint in his eye, she slipped down into the water. It dragged on her more than she would care to admit, but she struck out boldly, trying to ignore the smooth, effortless rhythm of the wide shoulders at her side.

As before, the haven of solidity looked far distant, no matter how much she struggled towards it. The water wasn't at all friendly. It hung dead weights along her limbs and sent wicked little waves up just when she was about to scoop up a breath.

At one point she had to stop to take a rest from the skirmish. Swiftly a hand came under her arm.

'Okay?'

'I could swim for miles,' she lied breathlessly. The ocean wasn't exactly a good place to get a sinking feeling at Nick Reynolds' concern.

Something about his touch made her swim stronger after that. Perhaps a desire to get away from it, she mused, casting her mind back to a certain disturbing moment on the float.

Before she knew it her feet were hitting the sand, and then she was walking serenely—well, she hoped it looked that way—back to her sun chair. Hardly caring that she was streaming sea water, she hurried to flop down in its blissful support, but before she could make it, her towel was being draped around her shoulders and Nick Reynolds was saying casually, 'I should rub down if I were you. Advisable after a swim like that.'

Cursing her tottering frame, she was even more annoyed at finding she needed to lean against the support of his hands on her shoulders. Thankfully he made no comment, but obligingly kept his arms about her until she could summon up enough strength to step away.

She pulled off her bathing cap and after a half-hearted attempt at swinging the towel away, sank into the chair under a stranded disarray of cloudy dark hair.

How long she lay there she had no idea, but when she opened her eyes, the world looked a much more acceptable place. The people on the beach were laughing and enjoying life, and gossiping in groups. The sea looked its usual docile self, and her heart had stopped banging from the difference of opinion she had recently had with it.

Nick Reynolds was draped in the sand in his beach robe. He had obviously dried off and the dark hair gleamed, damp and freshly combed and curling slightly against the teak tan of his neck.

He looked up as though he sensed her gaze on him.

'How's it going?'

'I always have a snooze in the sun,' she replied airily. 'As a matter of fact I feel quite fresh now.'

Aware that she didn't look it, she took a comb out of her handbag and proceeded to tidy her hair. It was a little unnerving to feel the grey eyes on her as she worked, and occasionally her fingers trembled through the strands.

As he watched the movements of the comb Nick Reynolds said lazily, 'I'll drop you off at your hotel when you're ready. Save you having to go chasing up transport.'

Terrified at the thought of having to sit next to him in a car, Lee said impulsively, 'Thanks, but I'm not going back for ages yet.'

It was true in a way. Mrs. Deighton had gone up to the airport to help her husband with some work in his office. They didn't expect to be back until later on this evening, so there was really no hurry for Lee to return.

Nick Reynolds was still watching her through the drift of his cigarette smoke.

'I thought you'd be at a loose end,' he smiled lazily.

He was harping again on her having no aircrew friends to take her around. She knew that, but for once she had no answer ready.

After a considerable silence he said, changing his position in the sand, 'Fancy a run up the coast? A friend of mine is getting himself tied up for life to a girl. There's dinner and dancing lined up for the evening.' When she hesitated he added casually, 'Nobody worries about formal dress out here.'

Lee still couldn't give a reply, one way or the other. She knew she wasn't running true to form. As Nick Reynolds saw her she ought to be jumping at his invitation. That was just the trouble. She had to stop herself from doing just that.

She was experiencing a sensation now that she had never known in her life before—that of wanting to rush away from someone yet crazily wanting to stay. The trip he was suggesting would obviously involve a car journey, yet somehow the idea of sitting beside him in the close confines of one didn't seem all that bad now. Perhaps because something about his smile, sloping and gently mocking yet...

Well what would she do if she stayed in Mombasa anyway? There was no one to tour the island with today, and she didn't somehow care for the idea of sticking to her own company. Having settled it fairly neatly in her mind, she nodded, hoping her reply didn't sound too demure, 'It might be rather nice.'

Nick Reynolds rose unhurriedly.

'Right, I'll go and get changed,' he replied negligently. 'See you on the road in about twenty minutes.'

Later, pulling the broad belt in to fit the waist of her full-skirted lilac cotton dress, Lee told herself that this was just another one of those jolly outings she had been going on since her arrival in Mombasa. The only difference was that Nick Reynolds was a deal more austere than the gay airline officers she had grown used to. Even with that half smile and sardonic gleam in his eye, he still had a rock-like appearance and probably unbent very little.

Her hair, smooth again now and curling up slightly from her shoulders, she added a touch of pink to her lips and then gathering her belongings into the gay beach bag, she stepped out of the changing cubicle. A long dark car turned the corner on to the beach road almost at the same time, and hardly before she had realised it, it had slid to a stop at her side.

'All set?' Nick Reynolds, looking cool in cream shirt and linen slacks, leaned to open the door at her side. As she stepped in he stretched a tanned arm across her to close it, and Lee found herself tied up in a bout of shyness that kept her staring rigidly ahead long after the car had made its way through the traffic of the town.

As they cruised towards the bridge of the old harbour, Lee found herself gradually relaxing, and soon she was turning in her seat to gaze at the red and brown-sailed dhows that Mr. Deighton had told her came from as far as Persia and India with their wares.

Once on to the mainland the traffic thinned out and the car leapt ahead along a wide dusty road flanked with blossoming trees. Occasionally an impressive-looking villa rose up above the deep green of tropical foliage and to the right, in the distance, showing every now and then was the azure blue of the sea, and silver sand of palm-lined beaches.

The road must have been gradually veering towards the coast, for some twenty minutes later they were pulling into the grounds of a house with its gardens practically on the beach. An assortment of cars lined the drive, and the music and laughter drifting from the open windows of the veranda-fronted villa suggested that the festivities were already under way.

With her shyness rearing up again as Nick Reynolds parked the car and helped her out, Lee wondered in sudden panic how she was going to get through the evening. She was guided inside and introduced to a dusky-skinned couple who held each other's hands and smiled at one another adoringly, and then all at once everything was all right.

The guests mostly around her own age were friendly and talkative, and she didn't find it too difficult to get herself drawn into first one group and then another down the room. No one talked much sense, but it was a relief to be away from the big cream-shirted figure in the doorway. And he was fully occupied with a knot of smiling females anyway.

Lee began to laugh along with the other guests. Music boomed in the background and glasses clinked. The younger men became more and more attentive, and as first one and then another plied her with sparkling champagne Lee decided it was all vaguely enjoyable. When the time came to sit down to the wedding feast in a room suitably decked out for the occasion she was aware that her cheeks were flushed from the heat and the excitement of it all.

Nick Reynolds, whom she had seen hovering occasionally in the background, gave her one of his specialities in cynical smiles as he held her chair, but Brad Sanderson, fair-haired and boyish, who had swung eagerly into the one on the other side of her, was far too talkative for her to ponder on what was behind that smile.

Later the long french-windowed room was cleared of tables and rugs and the general mood seemed to be to take to the floor and move to the music of the records.

More accustomed to the formality that went with the organised school dances, Lee had only just learned this new way of swaying uninhibitedly opposite one's partner, since her arrival in Mombasa. But she was at ease with it, and felt she could hold her own with the rest of the youthful guests on the floor tonight.

Because it *was* strictly the younger ones who were indulging in the modern-style shaking, Lee was slightly surprised to see Nick Reynolds approach and calmly tap her partner on the shoulder. There was no question of her having to separate herself from the hold of the lively young man, for they were already dancing two or three feet apart, but as she started to move tentatively opposite Nick Reynolds, he drew her swiftly into his arms with a sloping smile.

'I'm too old to be cutting that kind of caper,' he said drily. 'This is all you'll get from me.'

This, Lee told herself as she found herself being piloted expertly around the room, wasn't bad! The man holding her moved impeccably with a polished rhythm that belied his somewhat rugged outdoor appearance, and Lee breathed in her pleasant surprise.

Heartened by the sight of the more formal dancing being

executed, other mature couples took to the floor, and gradually overran the youngsters. As space became limited Lee found herself being steered towards the open french windows. Though he could move with the best of them apparently her partner was not really a dancing man.

As they strolled along the veranda Lee found herself without a word to open up a conversation. She had been chatting gaily all evening with everyone she had met, now talking seemed to be the hardest thing in the world.

The veranda came to an abrupt end and Lee felt compelled to gaze at the sky pale with stars. There was no mistaking the mocking intonation in his voice, as Nick Reynolds drawled deeply, 'Missing the boys?'

'The boys' being her air crew friends, of course, Lee thought, wincing at the jibe.

'I've hardly had the time,' she replied, reaching for her most unflappable smile.

'Hardly.' He gazed down at her briefly and then thrusting his hands into his pockets said lazily, 'Tomorrow I think we'll settle for something midway between floundering out at sea and flopping around on a dance floor.'

'Tomorrow?' Lee found difficulty in breathing naturally. She flung her gaze to the stars again to say lightly, 'I hope you don't feel that you have to ... I mean, I haven't got much longer in Mombasa and ...'

'So? You might as well see it out in style.' The derisive smile was back. 'And with the airline boys being unavailable ...' He shrugged, dropping his gaze over her with acid humour. 'I can spare the time.'

'Well, thank you, that's very ... kind,' was about all Lee could manage.

Perhaps he thought she had uttered the words flippantly, for he came back drily with, 'Don't mention it.' After a pause he said evenly, 'I'll be tied up out of town until noon tomorrow, but if you can arrange to be at the Butterfly I'll pick you up just after.' As Lee nodded he asked with a thread of sarcasm, 'Any ideas where you'd like to go to continue the racy living?'

Lee felt a sudden flicker of irritation. Forgetting for a moment to be anything other than herself, she raised amber

416

eyes with a decided sparkle in them to say coolly, 'You seem to have got the idea that that's all I'm interested in!'

He shrugged annoyingly.

'You could practise being a little less transparent.'

Transparent! Lee inhaled her anger. 'Because I've enjoyed the company of the aircrews, I suppose,' she retorted. Raising her chin a little, she added disparagingly, 'You're so certain you know what I want from life, aren't you?'

'Stop me if I'm wrong.' He was a lot closer than she had realised, and before she knew it she had been pulled roughly against him and his lips had clamped down on her own.

Lee felt her entire senses flame in humiliation. She wanted to push away and release some of it in a well-aimed blow at that mocking smile, but her anger was being displaced by another sensation. It brought her hand up all right, only slowly with the other to turn around that muscular neck. Had she wanted to she couldn't pull away now, for an arm that had started off in a negligent hold suddenly tightened drawing her in suffocatingly close.

For one long sweet moment Lee became quite attached to playing the part as Nick Reynolds saw her. At least that was what she told herself she was doing.

No sense in pushing away and spoiling the image at this point!

She had an idea the embrace had gone on longer than intended, for he dropped his hands abruptly, and flicking the dark head, tossed an overhanging lock of hair from eyes a slightly darker shade of grey.

Though inside her heart was banging, Lee willed herself to keep her gaze on his and said with a bright shakiness, 'You keep on doing that.'

'Habit-forming, I guess.'

It was difficult to put a finger on what was behind the tightness of his smile, for his head lowered as a hand jerked up to push the unruly lock of hair into place.

Lee was just wondering where they would go from there when a group pushed out noisily on to the veranda. She recognised them as the younger element of the guests, that

417

she had made friends with during the evening.

In the darkness of the night she was still acutely conscious of the man standing close to her; the bated sigh of the sea as their glances held, but with the indelicacy of youth, the laughing group rushed up to grab her hand.

'We're all going into town, Lee!' they chorused. 'It's getting deadly dull inside. Brad wants you to sit next to him.'

There were some delighted giggles as the fair-haired young man stepped shyly forward. Lee hesitated and turned to look back along the veranda. As she might have expected, the cream-shirted shoulders were lifting in a derisive shrug.

'So long.' Nick Reynolds saluted briefly, adding in lazy tones, 'See you tomorrow.'

As she stopped off to collect her beach bag from the open-topped car in the drive, Lee was somehow grateful for those last three words 'See you tomorrow.' She had a feeling that she was being dragged away from something that was bordering on the exciting, and though it it was probable that Nick Reynolds was continuing his policy to show her just what he thought of her, she was glad he hadn't gone back on their date tomorrow.

Once back in town she laughingly extracted herself from the gay group, and caught a taxi back to the Deightons'. Her mind lingering dreamily on what she would wear the next day, she stepped up to the house, quite unprepared for the shock that was waiting for her inside.

Going by Mr. and Mrs. Deighton's beaming features, the news shouldn't have been a shock at all, but when Lee heard their words her floating spirits dropped as though shot through the heart.

'Such news, my dear!' Mrs. Deighton took her arm happily. 'You're going to the Seychelles at once! As soon as we heard about the schooner we knew you would want to be on it.'

'Schooner?' Lee tried to sound pleasantly enquiring.

'It's been fitted out for service in the islands,' Mr. Deighton explained readily. 'We heard about it at the airport today. I got in touch with the people concerned and explained your position. They've offered to give you a passage *and* drop you off at your own island!' He almost slapped her on the back in his enthusiasm. 'The liner only calls at the main island and you would have had to sail on from there, but this one's taking you direct—now! What do you think of that?'

Lee gulped. What were her thoughts? She had to admit she was ashamed of them. The Deightons had obviously gone to a great deal of trouble to arrange her passage. The Pasmore children had been left stranded without supervision, and the uncle of the trio must be just about at his wits' end by this time, waiting for her. Yet all she could feel was acute disappointment at having to leave Mombasa.

Perhaps taking her silence as a kind of overwhelmed delight, Mrs Deighton squeezed her shoulders understandingly to smile, 'I know how you've been fretting to be away.'

With an effort Lee pushed her disappointment aside, and said on a bright laugh, 'Absolutely marvellous! When do I sail?'

'You'll have an early rise, I'm afraid.' Mr. Deighton frowned his concern. 'The boat sails at dawn. But if you can manage to get your things packed tonight I'll run you down at first light myself.'

'I'll come and give you a hand, my dear.' The older woman led her away.

Convinced that they were doing their guest a good turn, the couple spared no effort to see that she got away in good time the next day. Shaking them by the hand down at the harbour, and thanking them for all they had done, Lee began to feel that they *were* doing her a good turn.

Three more days in Mombasa could only mean for her, at the most, more mocking overtures from Nick Reynolds, more demonstrations of his slow smiling determination to put her in her place.

Because he had seen her constantly in the company of men, he had jumped to his own stuffy conclusions, and for that reason alone she was well rid of him. And even if she did want to get in touch with him to tell him that she wouldn't be able to make it today, she wouldn't know where to start looking.

Heavily she climbed the gangplank, seeing nothing but a tanned craggy face in her steps.

It ought to have been hilarious, of course, the fact that she had been kissed twice by a man she knew nothing at all about. Ought to have been. Yet she couldn't laugh, not even smile.

It wasn't likely that he would give her another thought, of course, but even if he did want to find out why she hadn't turned up today, he would have the same difficulty in locating *her*. She hadn't told him anything about herself, and as far as she knew, he knew nothing of where she had been staying in Mombasa, or where she was going. That severed the association fairly neatly.

With those rugged outdoor looks, he was probably an engineer or something preparing to move off to some distant part of Africa, while she was about to sail a thousand miles in the opposite direction.

With the knowledge that she would never see that sloping derogatory smile again Lee waved rather limply from the rail of the ship as it sailed. The pale light of dawn spread like a saffron wash over the beaches and palms of the island. Wistfully she watched the black rooftops of the town flame into red as the sun caught them. It was crazy to want to stay on and take the kind of treatment that Nick Reynolds doled out. Crazy, and yet . . .

CHAPTER THREE

As the schooner sailed out of the harbour Lee turned her back determinedly on Mombasa and the memories it invoked. She had let her gaze linger too long already on its shores; now it was time to realise that all that was behind her. She had come out from England with the specific intention of caring for three young children on a remote island in the Seychelles group. Anything that had happened in between could only be by the way. *This* was the real Lee Travers, she told herself. The one with the businesslike hairstyle, the plain clothes and the no-nonsense shoes. Half-Moon Island was waiting for her and the sooner she got down to some serious work the better.

How long it took the liner to complete this trip she had never thought to find out, but it was three days before the schooner came within sight of land. Of those days Lee never knew a dull moment. Once out to sea, it was as though the fresh winds rising on all sides conspired to blow away all small thoughts of herself. She suddenly became wondrously aware of her romantic mode of travel, and spent most her time gazing up at the billowing sails and sturdy masts of the schooner.

Though the crew were pure twentieth century in their white T-shirts and blue denims she amused herself by imagining yells of 'splice the mainbrace!' and other old-world seafaring expressions, as the boom rose and fell in a mountain of spray. One day when the water resembled green glass and the ship's engines were rumbling, she saw a disturbance in the distance as though a lot of splashing was going on, on the surface. Minutes later, veering off at a sudden sharp angle away from the schooner, were hundreds of fish leaping into the air and soaring on gauzy metallic blue wings that glinted with iridescent patterns of orange and flame.

As Lee watched the colourful passage with an unbelieving gasp, one of the crew nearby pointed out to her something in the water below. Her pleasure dissolved into a mild sadness as she saw the long silver shapes of the attackers racing just below the surface. Another day the skipper lent her a pair of binoculars to follow in the distance the antics of what he informed her were young whales.

It was an exciting trip, and basking in the hot sunshine, or sipping a cool drink in the shade, Lee enjoyed it to the full. So much so that on the third day when the thin smudge of a line showed on the horizon, *her* line, or her island, as she was told it would be in less than two hours, she knew a tiny whisper of regret.

At least she had thought that was what it was—regret that the long lazy days of sunning and sailing were at an end; but as the schooner sped on its way and the island began to take shape, the feeling became more one of apprehension.

What was waiting for her out there? she wondered. Was she going to regret that she had ever left Little Ashby? Grace and the school and the long leafy lanes seemed to be part of another world now; a very safe and secure world, she thought, knowing a sudden querulous desire to be back there.

The mood didn't last, however. How could it when her heart and mind were slowly being bewitched by the view; the overwhelming beauty of white unbroken beaches, curtsying feathery palms and brilliant blossoming undergrowth. A lagoon, bluer than the bluest of tropical skies, was embraced by arms of white booming surf, and as the schooner hove to, a small boat filled with a handful of occupants, sped skilfully through the narrow opening at its centre.

Lee saw her luggage being handed over the side, and as she prepared to follow, the skipper, a cheerful bearded man, clasped her hand warmly and explained in his halting English that the satchel of mail going down into the small boat had missed the normal consignment for the islands, and should be delivered at once.

Waved off from the schooner, Lee realised that there was

another performance going on, on the strip of white beach in the distance. A reception to end all receptions, by the sound of it. It wasn't entirely in her honour, of course, Lee smiled to herself. She had heard that a boat was a rare occurrence in these parts, and to see one was a high spot in the islanders' lives. It certainly looked like it! They danced and jigged on the edge of the waves, banging hollow tins and waving anything that might be available. Sticks and branches and wide-brimmed hats were being thrown into the air, and dogs barked and tore around wildly, smitten with the excitement. The noise must have frightened every fish for miles.

Moving inland amidst the curious smiling glances of the men rowing the boat, Lee spotted three miniature figures jumping and cavorting around more energetically than the rest. Small arms were going like Catherine wheels and she could just make out now, blond thatches rising and falling in rhythm to some very inelegant jumps.

Beside them a long lean figure stood with his hands in his pockets. Lee swallowed. She hoped there wasn't anything in the fact that he wasn't waving too. She was relieved to find, as the boat crunched up on the beach, that the man's smile made up for his lack of gyrations. It was just about the friendliest she had ever seen.

He was thinnish with very light blue eyes and pale sandy hair. His colouring probably had a lot to do with his freckles, for they spread across his nose and up into his hair and down the front of his open-necked shirt. Raising her eyes again, Lee decided after a second look that it was a nice face. There didn't seem to be much of the heavy uncle about its owner. He looked far too boyish for that, although with the faint lines across his brow, and finely etched around his mouth, she put him at about twenty-eight.

The boat was pulled up from the waves by some of the helpers on the beach, and as Lee stepped out on to the sand she felt her hand grasped warmly and the man was saying humorously, 'Miss Travers, I presume?' He swung her cases well away from the water, and came back smiling to add, 'I'm Alec Hayward. Glad to have you with us.'

'I'm glad to be here.' Lee laughed suddenly, finding that

she meant it.

A setting as idyllic as this was enough to lift the lowest of spirits, to say nothing of having your hand taken and held and being beamed upon as if you were a long-lost friend.

The islanders, or labourers as they were, who worked the plantation filed slowly by until she had been greeted enthusiastically by each one. Apparently the sighting of a ship meant a complete turn-out, so in all Lee calculated that there were about twenty men on the island, plus Alec Hayward, and now also herself.

And of course the three small reasons why she was here at all.

She hadn't flattered herself that all the commotion on the beach had been just for her, but at least the others had torn themselves away from the view of the schooner to come and greet her.

That was more than could be said for the three figures still gazing rapturously out to sea.

Following her gaze, Alec laughed throatily on a groan.

'Correction—I'm not just glad to see you. I'm practically prostrate with relief!' He grinned woefully. 'If you hadn't come today I'd have shinned up a palm tree and stayed there!'

'In that case I'm glad I managed to thumb a lift.' Lee smiled at the schooner.

She lowered her gaze again to the three small boys on the beach. They couldn't be as bad as all that. In fact from behind they looked almost endearing.

Three sets of baggy, grubby trousers dropped well below small sunburnt knees. One set was filled out with slightly sturdier longer limbs and there was something of an arrogant straightness about the cotton-shirted back.

All three had identical mops of hair—dead straight, corn-coloured and swishing, probably the same length over their eyes as it did at the collars of their shirts.

As none made a move to turn but continued to stare at the slowly departing schooner Alec said easily, 'Kids, come and say hello to our new guest.'

The two five-year-olds turned and gave Lee the benefit of two big hazel-brown stares. Their mouths were smeared with a dark red sticky-looking substance which they explored absently with the tip of their tongues as they watched her. Within seconds they had turned back to the sea.

The elder boy didn't bother to turn. He was making private incantations, mouthing low-toned sea terms, and living every moment of the schooner's departure. Alec breathed a light sigh of impatience and went to round the threesome up.

'Show's over, boys,' he said good-naturedly. 'We're off back to the house.' As he ushered them forward he smiled up to say, 'Meet the Pasmore gang.' He knocked the head of the tallest and in spite of himself the boy grinned. 'This one's Jeffrey, or Jeff to his friends. These two, Tim and Pete, look harmless enough, but don't be taken in by their innocent look. They're in league to turn both you and me grey!'

The twins stared up gravely as though they had no argument with this, and pushed back against the legs of their uncle in an agony of shyness, pink tongues still going at the jam or whatever it was round their mouths. Jeff, with the confidence of a seven-year-old, faced Lee and casually looked her over. Lee looked back.

He was bitterly disappointed at being, for the first time, excluded from a trip with his parents, and scathingly resentful of the idea of a schoolteacher nanny. Lee had been forewarned that her job with the oldest Pasmore boy wouldn't be easy. Without altering her smile now, she resigned herself to the fact that she had a minor battle on her hands. She had often seen that swinging nonchalance in rebellious pupils, and recognised the bland, 'Well, go on. Make me!' challenge in every inch of Jeff's stance.

His words, however, were normal for a seven-year-old, if a little blunt.

'Are you going to stay here all the time?' he asked.

'I expect so. Until your mother and father come to collect you,' she nodded brightly.

'You'll spoil everything,' he said, meeting her gaze with a dark brown distrustful one. 'You're a girl, and girls always want to change things.'

Alec quirked her a humorous eyebrow and muttered

under his breath. 'Out of the mouths of babes! ...' and then ushering the trio forward said breezily, 'Such as making the orders stick, for instance? Now, march!'

The smaller boys giggled and straggled up the beach, but Jeff scuffed around, pleasing himself, and eyeing Lee as she walked. After a while he came alongside her in a series of hops, twisting the bark from the stick he held in his hand. As they came to a wide earth road winding through the trees, he turned to look back at the sea.

With a sudden twist at the stick and a scowling look in her direction, he said airily, and with a great show of indifference, 'What was it like on the schooner?'

'Fantastic!' Lee smiled. 'All creaks and groans. I kept thinking of pirates and sailors swinging from the masts.'

It was the truth, and it just came out, but Lee couldn't have hoped for a more promising reaction if she had chosen her words carefully.

The dark eyes glowed visibly as the young mind must have conjured up its own colouful pictures of her words. He threw the stick away and fell into step beside her.

'We came here on a ship,' he said not quite so aloofly. 'Not as big as that, but it had sails and everything. We had fish for dinner.'

The twins gazed up and almost fell over themselves as they listened to big brother calmly conversing with the newest arrival, and then not to be outdone Pete made a jerky grab for one of the large veiny leaves growing at the side of the road.

'We make hats out of these,' he said, thrusting it at her, and then squirming in pink embarrassment.

Lee received the leaf gravely, and examined it with interest, and Tim, struggling to catch her eye, pointed up the road.

'That's our house,' he said, showing two neat rows of milk teeth. As she followed his gaze, and then smiled down at him, he tore ahead ostentatiously, and yelled to the sky, 'We've got a tamperling!'

'He means a trampoline,' Jeff said with a superior smile. 'My dad bought it for us. We've got lots of stuff, because we're ... going to be here a long time.'

426

He lapsed into a tight-lipped silence, but Pete skipped alongside, quite happy to cast Lee an occasional awestruck glance.

Alec walked alongside with an indolent stride, and Tim, his embarrassment forgotten, came back to walk backwards on tip-toe. This apparently didn't attract the attention he desired, so strutting on ahead he chorused his own important little ditty, 'And the coconuts come fumping down, boom, boom, boom!'

Ceremoniously he led the group up to the clearing ahead.

The house was a lot more luxurious than Lee had expected to find on a remote coral island. Seeing her rather surprised gaze roaming over the long low solid-looking bungalow, with flower-decked veranda, Alec grinned.

'The company like to look after us,' he explained. 'We're stuck out in these places for years at a stretch. Copra is our commodity. I suppose you know?'

Lee nodded. 'Mr. Pasmore told me something about it.'

As they walked up the wide steps at the centre of the front veranda and through open double doors Alec went on, 'Beth—you know, Mrs. Pasmore—thought you could more or less live with the boys during the day.'

He led her through rooms sparsely furnished, but neat and clean and smelling faintly of polish.

'The boys sleep in here.' He nodded into a room with the modern-type double decker bed and a single one under the window. All had neat chequered coverlets, and just like the rest of the house, there was an orderly preciseness about each item in the room. There wasn't a toy to be seen.

'You'll sort out what time you want them to go to bed,' Alec ran a hand through his hair sheepishly. 'They've been running slightly wild, I'm afraid.'

Wild seemed to be the operative word, Lee thought listening to the brothers whooping around the clearing and letting off the steam her arrival must have bottled up.

As they walked along the passage that seemed to cut and weave through the house, Alec said, 'There's a garden at the back. Well,' he grinned wryly, 'space!'

Coming out on to the back veranda Lee saw a mangle of

toys, pedal-cars and bikes, bats and balls and innumerable books and pencils scattered around. The trampoline she had heard about was down at the far end to the left of a precarious looking lean-to shed. There was no fence, just a beaten path running the full square of the garden, and then dense green foliage and the straggle of blossom.

The chaotic state of things out here didn't somehow fit, Lee thought, with the scrupulously trim show indoors. She saw that the veranda continued right round the house, and each side had its own wide flight of steps.

As they passed back through the house the way they had come, one of the doors swung outwards and a plump white-coated figure emerged.

'Fidele, meet Miss Travers,' Alec grinned. 'She's come to take the youngsters out of your hair!'

Lee saw a coffee-coloured face, twinkling bright eyes, and a wide grin. The grin seemed to be tinged with relief.

'Not so much in hair as all over house.' He spoke a disjointed kind of English with a French accent. His eyes rolled expressively as he turned an ear to the commotion outside.

Even as they listened there was the crash of metal and sound of bells and horns as the boys transferred their energies to the litter of the back garden.

'We fight at first,' Fidele shrugged still listening, 'then,' he gave a sly smile, 'we come to some arrangement. They get island, I get house.'

Lee laughed, liking Fidele's humour. She also admired the stand he had made and hoped she would have the same success when her work started.

Going back out into the sunshine she saw several small huts scattered about the clearing, and gathered that these were used for stores. Alec pointed to a smaller edition of the bungalow, set back under the trees.

'Beth fixed you up with your own pad,' he grinned. 'I suppose you could call it the guest house. It hasn't been used in ages, but I think my sister made it reasonably okay.'

Walking across the clearing Lee became aware for the first time of the birds. Brightly coloured, and oddly shaped, they soared on the breeze, or flapped through the trees each serenading the late afternoon in its own fashion, with an unmusical squawk, high-pitched whistle, or blissfully sweet trilling song.

The smaller house looked as though it had been intended as guests' quarters, as Alec had pointed out, but with the roominess she had just seen at the bungalow, Lee could understand why this one was seldom used.

Though it was strictly a man's island, she was pleasantly surprised to find that Beth Pasmore had endeavoured to put a feminine slant on the rooms. There were curtains up at the bedroom windows, and matching coverlets on the two small beds. In the room adjoining, sprigs of blossom and greenery stood around in an assortment of containers. As in the bungalow all the furniture had a utilitarian look about it, but with the rattan mats on the floors the place looked surprisingly comfortable.

'There's a shower next to the bedroom.' Alec pointed out, and at Lee's surprised raised eyebrows he grinned, 'It's a bit improvised, but it works. Fidele and I rigged one up for both houses. We punched holes in a big metal container and slotted it in the roof. When you want water you just push back the sliding door above you, and hey presto... !'

'Sounds intriguing,' Lee laughed, 'but where does the water come from?'

'Pumped in from an island stream and stored in tanks at the back of the house.' He smiled down at her. 'Don't worry, we've never gone short yet. Just let Fidele know what time you want to shower in the mornings, he'll see you get enough of the stuff.'

As he brought her cases inside Alec stretched up to say good-naturedly, 'I'm out for most of the day, but if you get sick of my company in the evenings, this place is all yours.'

Lee smiled up at him. 'I don't think I'm likely to do that,' she said pleasantly. 'And thank you for showing me around and making me feel ...' she shrugged, searching for the right words, 'at home.'

'My motives,' he tossed a wicked glance in the direction of the general pandemonium at the back of the house, 'are not entirely unselfish.' He nodded and turned towards the door. 'I expect you'll want to unpack. Fidele usually rustles up a meal about seven.'

Watching him go, Lee found her smile lingering. Thank heavens he had turned out to be so nice. She couldn't have wished for a more affable colleague. The children were still something of an unknown quantity, but it looked as though she could dispense with the worry of trouble from the uncle.

Her clothes unpacked and spread in the drawers of a rough wood dressing table, Lee explored the adjoining bathroom. Despite Alec's modest talk it all looked surprisingly civilised.

She washed in cool water and slipped into a plain white blouse. Her hair, drawn back from her face, needed no attention. She changed her shoes for a pair of brown leather sandals, that had seen much service along the lanes of Little Ashby, and folded a clean handkerchief through the strap of her watch. It was about five to seven when she walked over to the bungalow.

In the room flanking the front veranda, a long table was laid out with raffia mats and an assortment of crockery. The boys were wriggling around straight-backed chairs and Alec, sitting at the head of the table, said tolerantly, 'We'll eat this way tonight, kids. From tomorrow it's up to Miss Travers how she arranges things.'

Taking her chair, Lee smiled. 'I don't mind the boys calling me Lee,' she said. 'It's less of a mouthful.'

As Fidele brought in dishes filled with vegetables, rice and fish, she watched the boys scramble for their seats, making no comment on their smudged faces, and the way they jolted the table and rocked the chairs. Though she was itching to do something about the grubby clothing, and uncombed hair that hung in their eyes, she knew better than to rush in with orders and reprimands at this stage. From the look of Alec's handling the boys had been enjoying a blissfully unrestricted life these last two weeks. The quickest way to make herself unpopular, or more so with Jeff, she thought wryly, would be to put a sudden and abrupt stop to it all.

No, Jeff and his brothers could stay dirty tonight, and topple into bed when it suited them. Tomorrow, gradually, very gradually she would start on the de-urchinising.

The meal continued noisily, but Lee was too absorbed in putting names to the variety of vegetables and fruit to pay much attention.

Leaning back afterwards in the softened light of the evening, she was suddenly struck with a sense of well-being. The boys had long since torn off into the clearing, and Alec, draped at the other end of the table, pulled lazily on a cigarette. Watching her dreamy gaze trail over the railed veranda, and up into the inky green of the night-shrouded trees, he said good-humouredly, 'Think you'll take to island life?'

Lee swung her gaze on to him with a twinkle. 'It seems to agree with *you*,' she commented.

'No end!' he grinned, stretching his legs expansively. 'Well, why not? This is the original paradise island. Weather's good, temperature stays between seventy-five and eighty all the year round. We get rain, but not too much. Swimming is safe, and the company keep me well stocked with supplies.'

'And what about the work?' Lee didn't know why she asked that, unless it was something about the indolent way that Alec crossed his feet up on the table.

'I delegate that where I can,' he smiled, unabashed.

After a thoughtful silence Lee asked, 'Aren't you frightened of falling ill?'

Alec shook his head. 'Believe it or not, Fidele was a medical orderly in the British Army. He's pretty good with the first aid. For anything serious I've got the radio-telephone, and contact with immediate help. Beth wouldn't have left the boys otherwise. Nope,' he sloped a smile and lifted his shoulders, 'I've got no complaints.' As his glance came to rest on the unopened satchel lying carelessly in the chair he added, 'I even get my mail delivered.'

'Sounds like the reflections of a very satisfied man,' Lee commented humorously.

She couldn't be sure, but she thought the light blue eyes dulled over slightly as he pondered on her words. Though the smile was still there and he hadn't altered his relaxed position, she felt tempted to suggest, 'But not a hundred per cent satisfied?'

Meeting her glance, he asked on the lightest of sighs, 'Who is?'

It was the kind of question that brought on a thoughtful silence, and though Lee was content to sit and listen to the splutter of the kerosene lamps and watch their golden light vie with the sable shadows on the veranda, Alec seemed restless. He crossed and recrossed his legs, tapped the tip of his cigarette several times and then asked abruptly, 'Would *you* be against spending married life on an island like this?'

It was a question straight out of the blue and it took Lee completely by surprise, but thankfully Alec was gazing out into space and didn't see the sharp turn of her head.

After gaining a moment to consider she said slowly, 'I don't think I would. No.' Her mind suddenly looped back over time to a certain dark night in Mombasa. She heard herself saying almost dreamily, 'With the right man I'd probably find it quite idyllic.'

She must have said the right thing, for Alec gave her an appreciative smile, but it gradually turned down at the edges as he said in dry jocular tones, 'You wouldn't fancy making the return trip and putting your point of view over to a certain girl in Nairobi, would you?'

Aware at last of what the conversation was all about, Lee said with interest, '*Your* girl? Mr. Pasmore said you were practically engaged.' She gave him a sympathetic smile to add, 'I take it she's not having any of this?'

Alec nodded and took in a good-natured breath. 'I've known Philippa for over a year, almost as long as I've been out here. I take a couple of weeks off now and again to see her in Nairobi. We'd have been engaged ages ago, but like you said,' he shrugged looking round, 'she's not having any.'

'Has she been here?' Lee asked.

'No. I think she'd be sold on the life, just like I am, if she came, but so far I haven't managed to persuade her.'

'Does she write?'

'Not very often.'

The silence fell again, because although in sympathy with Alec, Lee couldn't think of any way of putting it. She saw his gaze roam idly towards the mailbag, and happy to change the subject she said mindfully, 'I think I pointed out to you that the skipper thought the mail might be urgent.'

Alec shrugged easily, not moving from his seat. 'Nothing's urgent on Half-Moon,' he grinned. 'I'll look at it later.' The conversation exhausted, he stood up and thrust his hands into his pockets lazily. 'It's warm enough to sit outside if you want to. I'll get Fidele to bring us some drinks.'

In the light of the stars and the copper glow of a small hanging lamp they listened to music relayed from East Africa. The sound of the boys romping in the bedroom gradually subsided until all was quiet in that direction. Lee lay back, drinking in the warm perfumed night for a while, then she rose and bade Alec goodnight. She watched him stroll casually across the room to pick up the mail bag and then turned towards her own quarters.

Later she lay listening to the whisper of the sea on the beach, and the faint whirring of the birds in the trees, and musing on what a perfect spot this was. Perfect, and yet... Restlessly she turned in her bed. Though she had been over every good point at least a dozen times—perfect island, pleasant uncle, a job she liked doing; working with children —her mind still wandered back wistfully to those last days and nights in Mombasa.

With an effort she willed herself to see only the swaying palms and white beaches of Half-Moon Island in her dreams, but in a relaxed moment before sleep, she wondered what Nick Reynolds was doing now, and if he had ever given another thought to that night on a dark veranda, and a certain world-rocking kiss.

CHAPTER FOUR

As Alec had pointed out the temperature in the islands hung around eighty, and in a nylon overall, Lee decided, life could get uncomfortable. However, as she donned the bluebell button-through, just as a dress with a silk slip underneath, and the short sleeves folded over to come just to her armpits, the effect, if she said it herself, was one of efficiency and coolness. The shower had proved moderately successful, and hair shining and nestling neatly in its slide, she walked over to the house next morning for breakfast.

She had heard the boys whooping their way round the clearing since dawn, and had risen with the firm intention of appealing for a little law and order, but once outside in the sun-drenched world of coconut palms, brilliant birds, and blue sky, she had to admit that it was a pretty whoop-inducing atmosphere. She was almost tempted to let go with one or two herself, until she remembered that she was here to tone down the caveman stuff, not encourage it.

The boys flung themselves down the steps as she arrived at the wide veranda, but for all the notice they took of her she might have been invisible. Lee carried on, smiling to herself. To three small minds her presence on the island was nothing more than a nuisance, and the best way to put up with a nuisance was to pretend it wasn't there. At least that would be Jeff's way of looking at it, and he had undoubtedly stressed his views to the younger boys.

But not, perhaps, with complete success, Lee thought, catching a quick golden-brown glance darted in her direction and the glimmer of Tim's shy, impish grin.

Inside she found the table set with varieties of fruit and cereal, much of the latter scattered across the table, among used dishes and half-eaten biscuits. Fidele was stoically clearing a place for her and Alec was sitting at the head of the table as he had done last night. Lee sat down, privately musing on the mysteries of men and how they could live completely blind to disorder and mess, then she raised her head and noticed with a mild shock Alec's unkempt appearance. White-faced and unshaven, he looked vastly different from the clean-cut man she had met yesterday. The blue eyes were red-rimmed, and even as she looked, he rose scowling from the table and went to stare out moodily on to the veranda.

Well! Not much of a greeting for such a gorgeous day. Lee started on her breakfast humorously. Perhaps Alec was one of those people who didn't really come alive from a night's sleep until about mid-morning.

As though he had suddenly become aware of her presence he turned back into the room, but it seemed to her that his previous thoughts were still uppermost in his mind. With a brow drawn in lines above the fair eyebrows he said absently, 'Oh ... er ... good morning, Miss Travers ... Lee.'

Before she had time to return the greeting he had dropped scowlingly down the steps of the veranda and vanished through the trees.

Hmmm! Lee watched him go with a tilted eyebrow. Definitely not the early morning gabby type, she decided with a smile.

After a leisurely meal, she helped Fidele clear the table and swept the much-littered floor. Some plan would have to be devised for tidier eating—tidier everything, she mused, conjuring up the picture in her mind of three slightly scruffy little boys. But where to start?

Walking out into the sunshine, she suddenly found herself unbuttoning the nylon overall. It wasn't a uniform, but it had only just occurred to her that it might be seen as such. Far better to meet the boys on their own level.

Back in her bedroom, she slipped into a soft checked shirt and narrow linen slacks. The overall folded and away in a drawer, she strolled out into the clearing. There was no difficulty in discovering the whereabouts of her charges, for a hot-blooded argument was going full tilt at the back of the house. She gave it a couple of minutes to subside, then wandered around the side and in just beyond the back veranda.

Jeff was standing supreme atop a conglomeration of small vehicles, all balanced at precarious angles. The twins were sulkily engaged in trying to gain less exalted positions, having obviously lost out to Jeff's authority.

Seeing the pile leaning at a sickening angle, Lee had to bite back the cry that had risen in her throat. Keeping her fingers crossed that the whole lot wouldn't come down with a crash, she strolled around, fingering one discarded toy after another with apparent interest. When she was at a point not far from the pile, Tim, bloated with the success of the position he had reached almost as high as Jeff, looked down to pipe cheekily, 'This is *our* garden!'

'I know it is,' Lee smiled. 'I was just looking at all the things you've got.' After pottering around a little longer, she said casually, 'It looks like a good game. I suppose you'll be playing it for ages yet?'

The angle of the question was perhaps beyond the younger two. They clambered around, nodding a little uncomprehendingly. Jeff, though, stood with his hands on his hips, a look of deep distrust in the brown eyes.

Lee shrugged idly, holding his gaze.

'I thought you might show me the island?' she said as though it didn't really matter. 'Everyone else seems to be busy.'

The younger boys, their chests swelling with importance, looked to Jeff for guidance, while his eyes were slowly taking in her shirt and slacks and open-toed sandals. When he had satisfied himself that there were no devious plans afoot for soap and water, he jumped down, and as the twins followed suit and scuffed up eagerly he stepped to the front to say imperiously, '*I'll* lead the way!'

'And I'll have two escorts,' Lee smiled, putting herself between the twins, 'in case we come across any snakes or horrible creepy-crawlies.'

'There *aren't* any snakes!' Pete giggled and squirmed shyly.

'Oh, and what about creepy-crawlies?' There was a silence as though each was trying to sort out what category this title came under, and then Jeff said loftily, 'I saw a spider once. It had . . .'

'I saw a crab,' Pete chipped in.

'And I saw a . . .'

As the conversation gathered its usual momentum of one trying to top the other, they walked along the road and turned off on to another one that she had seen coming up from the beach yesterday. This one seemed to cut through the centre of the island, and soon they came within the sound of men's voices.

Lee had no idea how big the plantation was, but it seemed that a fair portion of the land was given over to the gathering and preparation of copra. She saw the long trays of the white meat, set out in the sun to dry, and the men in various stages of gathering it. Some chopped at the husks with gleaming machetes, others wheeled the loads in from outlying lands. There were several huge open-sided sheds and Alec was in a small office near the road, shouting at a group of men. He saw the boys approaching and ran a hand impatiently through his hair.

To Lee, the lines around his mouth that were only a whisper yesterday seemed deeply etched today. She had thought in her ignorance that she might pass the time of day with him, that he might feel pleasantly disposed to showing her around, but his look now was anything but pleasant. As the men scattered from his wrath, he strode out and said exasperatedly to his nephews, 'Not *now*, kids!'

To Lee he raised a frowning glance to say briskly, 'You've got the whole island, you know. The idea is to keep the boys from under my feet.'

'Oh, I'm sorry!' Lee ushered Jeff and the twins away and along the road. She thought they looked back in a kind of wounded bewilderment. Obviously they weren't used to that kind of treatment from their uncle. Perhaps he was feeling the heat or something?

They came out on to the beach and Lee suggested that the boys take her on a circular tour of the island, therefore keeping well out of the way of the workers. It was quite a walk, following the beach, and sometimes having to scramble over rocks and around headlands.

She was almost constantly open-mouthed at the beauty

of the place—the fruit-laden palms, the myriad of sea-birds, the brilliant darting shapes in the hot still pools—but the boys were mainly concerned with the highest climbs and the deepest drops and who could stay up the longest on the narrow stretches of taut trailing vine.

It didn't need much imagination to arrive at how the island had got its name. The deep inner circle of the half-moon was the lagoon where the schooner had come in. Its tips were coral rock formations, jutting at unearthly angles, and the wide sweep of the outer curve was mainly coconut groves, edging on to more broad white beaches.

They passed the settlement with its thatched Robinson Crusoe huts where the labourers lived, and scaled the furthest tip of rock formation. When they were almost back at the house, Lee flopped down on a stretch of grass and stared contentedly at the sky. After a while she saw Jeff's face lean into her vision as he asked disdainfully, 'What are you stopping for?'

'I thought we'd have a rest,' Lee suggested. She sat up to hug her knees, and the twins knelt down uncertainly. After scuffing around for some time, a short distance away, Jeff said beneath lowered lids, 'You're a teacher, aren't you? I bet you've come to give us lessons and stuff.'

'It's a horrible thought, isn't it?' Lee twinkled in his direction. 'Especially in a place like this.'

Jeff's answer was a slow smile and a sharp kick at the grass. Tim was inspired to say boldly, 'We like to play!'

'So do I!' Lee laughed, then jumping up, she added, 'Do you know what my class used to do when we had an outing to the beach?' She looked down at the slightly animated faces, and walking towards the white sand went on cheerfully, 'I expect you've done it lots of times. Build a pyramid of pebbles and see how many times you can hit it.'

It was the simplest form of entertainment, but the mere mention of a game set three pairs of eyes blinking with interest. She started to gather rocks and pieces of driftwood and soon small figures were dashing about the beach and eagerly handing in their donations. When a fair-sized pile was erected, Lee instructed, 'Now we want lots of smaller pebbles for aiming, and we'll each have to draw a circle.'

She drew one carefully for herself in the sand and put her initials in the middle. Out of the corner of her eye she saw the boys doing likewise.

'Each time you get a strike ... when you hit the pile ...' Lee explained for the twins' benefit, 'you drop a pebble into your own circle.'

Eager to take up the challenge, the boys hopped about as Lee drew a line and then another one slightly to the front of it.

'The twins will have to be a little bit nearer, because they're smaller than us,' she pointed out to Jeff. 'Right, who's going first?' she asked.

The game commenced and soon each initialled circle in the sand had a small show of pebbles. To keep up the interest Lee said, 'The one who gets the most pebbles can choose what we will do this afternoon.'

Three flushed faces glowed, and brown eyes darted in excited thought. The pitching continued with renewed vigour.

By continuing to search out the biggest pebbles, so that he could hardly miss, and often putting a foot well over the measured lines, Jeff won the contest. All unsuspecting, the twins beamed up with brotherly admiration and waited for him to state his choice.

'I'd like to have a picnic,' Jeff said unhesitatingly as though he had long made up his mind. 'And a swim. We always have to wait until Uncle Alec can take us, and I like to swim all the time.'

'Suits me,' Lee shrugged with more than a little truth. Sea water was the next best thing to soap and water, anyway. As they all began to prance around with delight Lee said purposefully, 'Jeff, you run on ahead and ask Fidele if he has time to pack us a picnic basket. The boys and I will follow and they can show me where their swimming things are kept.'

Visibly pleased, Jeff streaked away, and Tim and Pete scuffed happily along, unaware that they were each holding a hand of the girl between them.

The afternoon passed in a riot of fun, for although Tim and Pete were non-swimmers, they moved on the edge of

439

the lagoon with complete confidence, and taking advantage of Lee's good humour, were constantly up to tricks to give her a ducking.

Jeff went to great pains to show off his rather laboured crawl, and then seeing he was missing all the fun joined in with the rest.

After most of the afternoon spent in the water, three shining, almost angelic faces stared back at her from clean pyjamas that evening. Venturing in with a hairbrush, she knew also the sneaking satisfaction of three smooth, if over-long, heads of corn-blond hair.

It had been a fairly hectic day, and after having a meal set out for the four of them on the back veranda, neither Jeff nor his brothers seemed averse to going to bed at a decent hour. She bade the boys a cheerful goodnight now, and left them climbing uncomplainingly between the sheets.

Alec was stretched in a chair when she went into the living room. It didn't look as though the day had helped his mood at all. He looked up and nodded vaguely, and went on pulling deeply at his cigarette.

Lee sat down to thumb through a magazine with apparent interest, but her mind was mainly taken up with the behaviour of the man sitting across the room. Of course one couldn't expect to sum up a person completely in a few hours, but for the length of time she had known Alec, she would have been ready to believe that he was a light-hearted, easy-going person with not much on his mind. Had she been wrong? Had he simply put on a polite front to welcome her to the island? No, she didn't think so. Without noticeably looking up from the magazine she took in the slightly turned down mouth, the unruly hair. He might be morose in the mornings, even bad-tempered at work, but he hadn't struck her as being a rude or bad-mannered in-dividual, yet he had barely acknowledged her appearance just now, let alone asked her how she had fared on her first day with his nephews.

She wondered what could have happened to douse that easy going charm; why it had suddenly been replaced by a sullen, frowning thoughtfulness.

Without consciously thinking about it, her glance wandered to the chair that had held the leather satchel. Could it have been something in the mail? He had gone to it immediately after she left last night.

Lee pondered on this for a while, then closed the magazine and laid it down. Whatever the reason for the change in Alec it was no concern of hers, and bearing that in mind, mightn't it be a good idea to make herself scarce? Nobody wanted to be bothered with company when they had problems on their mind.

She rose and walked quietly across the room, stopping almost opposite Alec.

'The boys are in bed,' she said pleasantly. 'I've sorted out some fresh outfits for them tomorrow, so if there's nothing else I'll ...'

As she spoke Alec jerked his head up. His eyes seemed to focus in from a long way off, and then he jumped up pink with contrition.

'Hell! I'm sorry!' He ran a hand through the upstanding hair and grinned wanly. 'A rotten host I turned out to be. Would you like a drink?'

'No. Really!' Lee smiled at his polite offer. 'I've got some odds and ends of mending to do for the boys.'

'Had enough of my company first night, eh?' He took her arm as she walked out on to the veranda. 'Well, I can't blame you. I'm not exactly laughing boy. Just the same ...' the blue eyes were boyishly pleading, 'I'd like you to stay for a drink.'

'All right.'

A tray was brought on to the veranda and then, bidding them goodnight, Fidele left for his own hut at the settlement.

Sitting there under the stars, Lee knew Alec had only asked her to stay on, to try to make up for his neglect, so she made no attempt at conversation. Nevertheless she couldn't help feeling the weightiness of the atmosphere, as he swung back on two legs of his chair, gazing into space.

She made a point of not lingering over her drink and soon after rose to go with, 'Well, I'll say goodnight, Alec.'

He stood up lethargically, and sensing complete dejection in the frame Lee felt compelled to add softly, 'Let's hope tomorrow will be a better day.'

'I doubt it.'

The harsh reply apparently needed no thought, and looking up with questioning sympathy, Lee heard herself offering, 'Well, if there's anything I can do . . . if I can help in any way?'

For a second the blue eyes lingered on her, and then he was saying with a pale smile, 'Thanks, Lee, but there's nothing you can do. There's nothing anyone can do, I'm afraid.'

He swung away, and Lee walked over to the guest house pensively. Once inside she knew a strange reluctance to tackle any of the jobs she had been determined to do. It was as though Alec's troubles were pressing themselves in on her too, instilling in her a niggling apprehension. She wondered if she had been too optimistic in her first impressions of life on Half-Moon Island. Something told her that, Jeff's antagonism aside, things weren't going to be quite as smooth-running as she had hoped.

After an hour of drifting aimlessly between the two rooms and along the small front veranda, she tumbled into bed.

It seemed that she had only just dropped off to sleep when she heard a light tapping on the lowered latanier blind. Imagining it to be a rising breeze pushing through the window aperture, she turned over, but the sound came firm and insistent, through the padding of the pillow about her ears.

Oh dear! If the blind had worked loose in some way it looked as though it was going to have to be attended to. With a sigh she thrust a wrist out of the sheet to gaze sleepily at her watch, and that was when the voice whispering urgently in the night made her start up wide-eyed and tense.

'Lee, wake up! I want to talk to you!' She saw Alec's shape through the blind and hastily flung on a dressing gown.

'Alec! You gave me a fright. What is it?' she asked.

He came to stand in the doorway, fully dressed and smiling. Lee was struck immediately by the turnabout change in him. Now he looked almost debonair! If it went on like this, she thought irritably, she was never going to work out what kind of man the boys had for an uncle.

'Come on over to the house, Lee,' he invited blithely. 'I want to talk to you.'

'So you said,' she murmured reticently. 'But couldn't it wait until morning? I mean ... well, it's almost the middle of the night.'

'I know! I know!' He lifted his feet up and down impatiently. 'But I've been thinking, and I've only just hit on it.' As she continued to stare up sleepily he said encouragingly, 'Look, I'll make you some coffee and put a fire on if you like. Please, Lee,' he leaned over cajolingly. 'It really is important.'

'Well ... all right.' She gave a resigned smile. 'I'll go and get dressed.'

'Oh, come on!' He took her arm impatiently and lowered a quick glance over her. 'I won't eat you.'

As they walked towards the dim lights of the house, Lee, wide awake now, had to twinkle a little at the bizarre situation she found herself in. Though she had fully expected island life to be different, she hadn't quite pictured herself walking in the dead of night with a man she had known less than forty-eight hours.

Though she knew romance was the furthest thing from Alec's mind—she hadn't missed that uninspired glance just now over her worn red dressing gown, and leather mules— she had to admit the situation looked questionable. Perhaps it was as well it *was* an island, she thought with a smile.

Once inside the house Alec went to great lengths to make her comfortable. Though the night could hardly be described as chilly he soon had a log crackling in the hearth, and with steaming coffee at her side and cushions at her back Lee was beginning to feel thoroughly pampered.

It occurred to her that Alec moved with a kind of nervous cheerfulness, occasionally darting her a quick searching glance. She found herself wondering uneasily what he had on his mind. When at last he sat down on the other side of the fire she said as brightly as she could, 'What was it you wanted to talk to me about, Alec?'

443

He looked at her and drooping a kind of deflated smile replied, 'I don't quite know where to start.'

Lee lifted her shoulders. 'You know what they say. What about trying the beginning?' she smiled.

'I suppose that was when I opened the the mail last night,' he said, considering, then on a quick breath, 'You know a bit about the copra business, I take it? The big companies, and how they expect to make a certain margin of profit and all that jazz?'

Lee nodded. 'You mean you have to keep up a certain output.'

'You've got it.' He smiled dryly, and then clasped his hands. 'Well, Half-Moon's output has been well below the figure for some time.' He let a silence fall, then with a twisted smile added, 'You can guess what was in the mail?'

'Well, no, not really.' Lee looked puzzled.

Alec stood up to deliver the words slowly and precisely. 'Notice to quit the island.'

At the bombshell Lee jumped up. 'Why, that's terrible!' she gasped, facing him.

'I'm glad you agree.' He looked down at her somewhat lazily. She thought she detected that searching glance again.

'Well, I mean . . .' she stammered uncertainly. 'How long have you got?'

He shrugged. 'If the company decide that an island is not paying off, they can have it vacated at a minute's notice.'

'Good heavens! That *is* terrible.'

Alec gazed down into the wide amber eyes, and said on a slightly whimsical note, '*Again* she agrees with me.' After a pause he turned lazily away to say down to his feet. 'On the other hand, the company rules are that all married personnel get six months' grace to sort out their domestic arrangements and do their packing.'

Lee looked at him blankly for a second, then the worries started to crowd in. What about the boys? Where could she take them? There was no hope of getting in touch with the parents, who were somewhere in the Rift Valley in Africa at this moment.

Her mind weighted down with anxiety, she wandered dazedly to the door, saying over her shoulder, 'Thank you for telling me, Alec. I'll have to work out the best plan for the boys.'

'Lee!' Alec was beside her, his hand on her arm. 'I haven't finished yet.' He drew her carefully back into the room to say, 'You heard what I said just now about married personnel?'

'Yes. That they don't have to leave immediately like the single men.' She looked up, puzzled. 'But how can that help you?' Thinking back over last night's conversation, she rushed on, 'You'll get Philippa to come! You'll get married!'

'No.' He shook his head. 'She wouldn't come, and there isn't time anyway. The company official is coming here tomorrow on the copra boat.' As she continued to stare up he said jerkily, 'Come and sit down.'

When she was back in her seat, he paced and then swung round on her to say with enthusiastic intensity, 'Look, I know these company wallahs. About twenty years past their prime and jogging along till they get their pensions. He'll come and dodder his way round the island, and I'll say all the right things, and then he'll go, and that will be the last we'll hear of him.'

'We?' Lee felt that old apprehension gnawing again. Watching his working features, she asked carefully, 'And what are all these right things you're going to say to him?'

'That you're my wife and . . .'

'Your wife!' Lee jumped up horrified. When she had let the thought sink in she gasped, 'Alec, you can't be serious . . .?'

'Take it easy!' He confronted her smiling. 'The bloke will only be here a few hours till the copra's loaded. I'll just introduce you and then you can disappear. The thing is . . .' he went on quickly as she continued to stare thunderstruck, 'I'll get the extra six months I need. I might be able to get this place back on its feet. Don't you see?' He gave a quick impatient sigh and tempered it with a drawn smile. 'If I can produce a wife for just one afternoon, I get to stay.'

'But it won't work!' Lee shook her head. 'What about the boys and Fidele? They know we're not married. And your plantation workers.' She looked up. 'What if they were to...'

Alec was shaking his head too, but with an easy smile.

'Forget the boys,' he said. 'It's way over their heads anyway. Fidele? He'll do as I say. He and his buddies want to stay here as much as I do. You'll find the Seychellois are grateful for any kind of existence. Work's pretty hard to come by in these parts, you know.'

Lee considered for a while and then said pensively, 'If your output in the past has been as low as you say, wouldn't it have been wiser to anticipate something like this happening?'

Alec shrugged. 'One tends to forget the mercenary side of it in a place like this.'

Rather an irresponsible attitude, Lee felt, for a man whose entire world depended on what he produced.

'If things have been bad all this time,' she watched him, 'how can you hope to improve now?'

He looked slightly irritated at her questions and as his mouth drooped pettishly, he snapped, 'Look, I'll work that out later. Right now is the time to worry about, *and* tomorrow,' he said ominously. 'There'll be a boat in then, and you and I and the whole caboodle can expect to find ourselves on it, unless we do something. Now what do you say?'

Lee considered wildly. What *could* she say? What could she *do*? The boys were her responsibility. Alec had obviously kept the disastrous economic state of the island to himself, otherwise the Pasmores wouldn't have gone off so confidently.

She drew on her lower lip worriedly. If telling a white lie for just a few hours could keep things as they were, could there be much harm in it? Perhaps she owed it to the Pasmores anyway, for arriving two weeks late at her job.

Taking a deep breath, she said, letting it out slowly, 'Well, all right. But I'll be glad when it's over.'

'He'll have been and gone before you know it.' Alec stepped quickly to her side.

She found the hug of gratitude from a man she hardly knew slightly embarrassing, but Alec was too full of his own affairs to notice the pink in her cheeks.

'We'll treat it as a normal day tomorrow,' he was saying eagerly, 'until we spot the boat. I'll bring the old boy up to the house and get it over with, and then you can relax.'

One arm about her shoulders, he led her to the door. Just before they got outside Lee stopped dead.

'Oh dear!' She raised her left hand questioningly.

'I've thought of that,' Alec grinned. He pulled off the gold signet ring from his little finger and dropped it into her hand. 'Try that for size. The other way round, of course.'

He crooked a devious eyebrow as she put the ring on her third finger. It was slightly too big and slipped around, but worn for only a short time it wouldn't present too much of a problem.

Lee looked at it for a moment, removed it and hastily dropped it into her dressing gown pocket.

'I'll put it on tomorrow when the boat comes,' she said with a pale smile.

'That's my girl!'

With another hug Alec led her down the steps and over to the guest house. Facing her as she stood in the open doorway, the good-looking face relaxed and boyishly content again now, he smiled.

'Goodnight, Lee, and thanks. Tomorrow night we'll celebrate.'

Tomorrow night seemed an eternity away to Lee as she lay wide awake on her bed, resisting the temptation to pace. Of course it was little more than a joke pretending to be some man's wife for the afternoon, but somehow she couldn't bring herself to smile about it.

The ring in the pocket of her dressing gown seemed to be burning its way through to her skin. So real was the feeling at times, she wanted to rush back to the house with it and call the whole thing off. At other times through the night she thought of Jeff and his brothers, and their parents, miles away and content.

What were a few hours, anyway? Alec would have his six

months, and she probably wouldn't be here to get caught up in what he would do after that.

Finally convinced that she was doing the best for everybody, Lee drifted off into an uneasy sleep.

The arrival of the copra boat the following afternoon caused the same pandemonium that Lee had experienced on her arrival, but while Alec raced his nephews to the beach, and the plantation workers gave out with their noisy renderings on tins and sticks, Lee stayed quietly in the house.

She sat in an armchair facing the door, and hoping she looked the picture of wifely sophistication. Her hair was drawn back under its usual tortoiseshell slide. She had chosen a plain oatmeal linen dress and green low-heeled shoes.

Though the air was heavy with the heat of the afternoon she felt cold. The shine of the ring on her finger seemed to outblaze everything else in the room.

Ten minutes ticked away, and when she could sit no longer Lee took to pacing the room. She straightened a calendar on the wall, re-set the chairs at the table, and fidgeted generally with books and magazines. When another ten minutes had passed, she took to straightening the chairs and tables along the veranda, her nerves feeling as though they were being tugged tighter with every second. Why was it, she thought wryly, that the fates always seemed to prolong the things you wanted to get over quickly?

She listened for sounds from the beach, but all was silent now. As the afternoon drifted on undisturbed, Lee was seized with a panic-stricken fear that everyone had indeed been hustled on to the boat. Just when she was about to hurry off to investigate, Jeff and the twins came prancing into the clearing, and then thumping and clumping up the steps.

Tim lifted a sticky flushed face to say, 'We've been running. We're thirsty.'

Lee smiled over them absently.

'Where's Uncle Alec?' she asked. 'I thought he was going to bring the man from the boat up to the house?'

Jeff shrugged offhandedly.

'He wanted to look round the plantation. Can we have some orange juice?' He wiped a grubby hand across a glistening brow to add with a pulled-in smile, 'Please.'

As Lee went off to fetch the drinks she found herself smiling too. So it was going to be all right after all. Alec had told his story and the official had got straight down to business. She wasn't going to have to show herself to uphold the claim of marriage status. It had all been taken for granted.

A long pent-up breath escaped her as she went back through the living room and out on to the veranda. Pete, directly in front of the door, and delighted at the display of brimming glasses, pushed eagerly against the tray. The jolt made the orange juice splash up and as it caught him on the cheek he fell back with a peal of laughter. Because she was bubbling over with relief at the way things had turned out Lee laughed too.

It was only when she had made the full turn out of the door that the laughter caught as something like a gasp in her throat, for there, standing on the steps, bigger, broader, and more implacable than ever, was Nick Reynolds.

CHAPTER FIVE

FOR one awful moment Lee thought her hands would lose their grip on the tray. The clinking sound of the glasses as they trembled against one another seemed to her louder than the most deafening rattle.

She dragged her eyes away from the glinting steel-like gaze and came upon Alec's, scowling her into action. He took the steps two at a time and said lightly, 'Good-oh! Drinks all round,' and then heartily, 'Darling, meet Nick Reynolds. He keeps an eye on the company's business in these parts.'

The dark head inclined deeply. There was even a smile, but the razor-edged gleam in the eyes above hers labelled it as a smile of icy contempt.

Because she was so long in putting the tray down, Jeff and the twins jigged around impatiently, and thankfully their clamourings were enough to rally her floundering senses. She moved along the veranda to the table, and after carefully serving the boys, said in a voice that sounded strangely unlike her own, 'I suppose Mr. Reynolds would prefer something a little stronger?'

As the two men draped down in chairs, she saw the wide shoulders lift indifferently; heard crisp tones state flatly, 'What everybody else is having is okay with me.'

She looked at the tray and murmured, 'I'll ... er ... just go and get some more glasses.'

Walking through the house, Lee felt she was moving in a grey blinding mist. It couldn't be true, could it? Nick Reynolds here! *Nick Reynolds of Mombasa! And all the things Alec must have said to him!* She passed a hand over her eyes, as though to shut out the pictures travelling across her mind. Pictures of herself in Mombasa amid the laughing air crews. The gay nights at the Butterfly Club and the sun-splashed days on the beach, and a certain pair of hard,

450

mocking grey eyes watching her every smile. And worst of all, an embrace one starlit evening . . .

She searched out the glasses with difficulty, knowing a flicker of irritation. Doddering company official indeed! Twenty years past his prime! Her lips still throbbed at the memories.

She wished fervently that Fidele were here to serve the drinks, but he was down at the boat loading the copra. Much as she would have liked to hide away, she wasn't going to be given the chance.

With banging heart she made her way back through the house, still dazedly disbelieving at the twist of fate. Of all the people in the world to come out to Half-Moon Island, it had to be *him*. Thank heaven the tour of the island had taken place, and presumably with it the business talk. Now all that remained was the courtesy visit, and somehow, for the sake of Alec's job, she had to get through that.

The men were talking generally when she got back to the table. She poured the drinks as decorously as she could manage, Alec's signet ring on her third finger feeling like a lead weight. She took a drink herself and sat in the only vacant chair—the one opposite the two men. Just when she thought she was going to be able to cling for support to the twins, swinging their legs and guzzling on their glasses, and Jeff staring up at the newcomer with grave interest, they shot up from their seats and raced off with the spasmodic energy of the young.

'My sister's children,' Alec grinned easily. 'We're watching out for them a while.'

The boys' shouts and tuneless whistles drifting in from the back of the house ought to have been just the thing for creating a relaxed atmosphere, but Lee found herself sitting rigidly clutching her glass, and wishing she were the other side of the world.

Since taking her seat those grey eyes had never left her face. The inevitable question came now, casual, yet somehow abrupt, 'How long have you been married?'

'About six months,' Alec put in hastily, catching her eye with a careful nod.

'Find enough to do around here?'

Again Alec rushed in.

'Oh, I'm pretty much tied to the place, but Lee takes the odd holiday back in civilisation. She looks forward to it.'

'I can imagine.'

The ice-cool sarcasm was carefully veiled, and meant only for her ears, Lee knew. She wanted to look anywhere but at the man who had delivered the words, but as though her torment had to be complete she found herself raising her eyes to meet the rapier-like glint of his gaze.

There was a long pause, and then in decidedly pointed tones that implied he wanted no outside interference he aimed at her, 'Your husband tells me he wants to stay on and try to make a go of it here. How do you feel about it?'

With Alec's gaze urgently willing her on Lee heard herself saying in strangled tones, 'Well, I ... I think he should, I mean ... I think ...'

'To my mind,' he clipped across her gibberish, 'the groves are in a pretty bad way and we'd be well to cut our losses, but ...' he rose and turned to Alec, 'if you can pull yourselves out of the red before your six months are up, the company might well have second thoughts.'

The wintry mask had disappeared and the smile he gave Alec had an easy friendliness about it. There was also a flicker of sympathy there, as he swung a brief glance over Lee.

As he made to go Alec sprung up, slightly triumphant. 'Don't worry,' he said jauntily, 'I'll get things under way, you'll see. It only needs ...'

He was talking too fast and too much, Lee thought, but the other man paused to listen patiently to the string of schemes and ideas poured forth. She wondered if all of them were wise ones, for occasionally a frown flickered across the grey gaze that rested on the wooden slats of the veranda.

When Alec's tall talk had finally petered out Nick Reynolds said somewhat tersely, 'The quickest way to end up with no coconuts, Hayward, is to put those kind of plans into operation. Half your trees are diseased. I would have thought your best bet would be to clear the ground on the south side and put in new seedlings while you still have time to wait. '

'I suppose you're right.' Alec looked down at his shoes with a deflated droop to his mouth.

'It's a big job, but it's the only way if you and your wife want to make a life out here.' Nick Reynolds clipped, slightly impatient of the other man's slackness. He flickered a gaze over the bent head and then turned it without warning on to Lee. It stayed on her for some considerable time before he said in slightly moderated tones, 'That *is* what you want?'

It was a question and it needed an answer, but for the life of her Lee daren't try her voice again. She simply nodded her head and hoped that would suffice.

It must have done, for after turning a thoughtful look over Alec, and then slewing his gaze back to her, he inhaled slightly and swung off down the steps.

Seeing him move off, Lee started to draw in the first sweet breath of relief, but it stuck like a pebble in her throat when she heard him say to Alec, 'I'll go and collect my gear from the boat.'

The words hung suspended on the thunderstruck silence and then others came lazily to join them.

'You're going to need help to map out the lines for full production again, and I might be able to give you a few pointers on how to start clearing that south side.'

Lee watched him nod a glance towards the guest house. 'I'll bed down in that,' he stated uncompromisingly, and then with something like irony in his tones he added with a taut smile, 'You won't even know I'm here.'

He bowed slightly, up towards the veranda, and then strode off through the clearing. Almost before he was out of sight, Lee sprang up from her chair. White-faced, she waited for Alec's reaction, but rather surprisingly it showed as nothing more than the casual thrust of his hands into his trouser pockets.

'Well, that's put the lid on it,' he said calmly. 'Looks like we're going to have to drag the thing on until he leaves.'

'Alec! Do you know what you're saying?' Horrified, Lee stepped up to confront him. 'Didn't you hear what he said?

He's going to take over the guest house, and he thinks that you and I are . . .'

'I know, but we can get round that.' Alec swung on his heels easily. 'There's a room adjoining mine. With him over there he won't be any the wiser.'

'No, but *I* will,' she said angrily. 'You're surely not going to ask me to . . .'

'Just to move in with me and the boys for a while,' Alec nodded. Seeing her flaming cheeks, he drew her towards him, and lowered a worried gaze over her. 'Don't back out on me now, Lee,' he begged. 'Don't you see? My whole future's at stake here. If I lose Half-Moon I'm finished. I'm not kidding myself the company will offer me anything else.'

'But there's other copra business,' Lee pointed out.

'I know,' he nodded grimly, 'scratching along as someone else's assistant. No, thanks, I've tried it. I make a lousy second-in-command—and anyway, I like my own pitch.'

'There'll be other islands.' Lee tried to turn out of his grasp, but he held her shoulders and kept his pleading gaze on her to reply, 'Not like this there won't. Here I can do what I like without any interference from the outside world. A place like Half-Moon happens only once in a fellow's lifetime.'

Her irritation soaring, Lee snapped, 'Pity you didn't do something about trying to hang on to it!'

The freckled brow gathered in a frown, and seeing the droop of the rather weak mouth, Lee instantly regretted her harsh words. Poor Alec! He was all for living the life of an idle castaway, but instead he had a job to do, with which he couldn't cope. Now he was in danger of losing both. Her heart catching at the dejectedness of his frame, she said gently, 'You *did* come out here to do a job for your firm.'

Alec shrugged, muttering, 'How did *I* know they were going to get mercenary?'

'That's what business is all about, isn't it?'

At her calm rejoinder Alec dropped his hands from her shoulders and then flung one up into his hair. 'Oh, for heaven's sake, Lee, let's stop going round in circles,' he urged. 'Look, it's strictly between the two of us. We've almost swung the thing anyway. As far as the company is concerned I'm a married man. All it means is that you agree to play my wife until their bloke leaves.' He cast her an exasperated blue gaze to ask, 'What difference can it make to you?'

What difference? None really, Lee supposed, reviewing the situation. Even if she went straight to Nick Reynolds now, and told him the whole story, what would he say? Probably give her one of those faintly derogatory smiles of his, shrug the whole thing off as a joke, and put the wheels in motion for clearing the island. Alec would be out of a job, the Pasmores would be out of their minds and the company official would sail indifferently on.

On the other hand, the man behind those steely grey eyes already regarded her as the lowest form of life, so things couldn't get any worse in that direction anyway. What had she to lose in helping Alec?

She breathed a resigned sigh and meeting the anxious blue gaze asked, 'Do you think he'll stay long?'

Alec relaxed visibly and grinned.

'A couple of days at the most, I'd say. He won't want to hold the copra boat up much longer than that.'

'I ... suppose it will be all right, only ...' Lee, having second thoughts already, wondered why she was trembling slightly. She drew on her lower lip and staring towards the clearing where the road turned in, finished agitatedly, '... these kind of deceptions are apt to get out of control.'

'This one won't.' Alec took hold of her shoulders reassuringly. 'All our friend is interested in is copra. I bet he never sees anything but coconut palms. Now...' he lowered his head in thought, 'we've got to move fast. He'll be coming back to the guest house, so you'd better clear your things out.'

Lee's eyes widening at the thought, she would have torn off down the steps, but Alec held on to her to say in low tones, 'Do it without attracting too much attention. The less the kids know the better. You can get to your room round the side of the house. It's the second door along the veranda.'

Her pulses hammering, Lee schooled herself into walking leisurely across the clearing. She looked along the road wildly. If he came back now, just when she was about to . . . ?

Almost falling in the door, she stumbled around, flinging everything she could lay her hands on into her cases. Every sound outside sent her heart flying to her throat, but soon the rooms were cleared, and she was standing at the door a case in each hand.

Thankfully, the boys were still playing at the back of the house. The clearing was deserted, but it seemed to stretch to twice its size as she moved across it. The door that Alec had mentioned seemed to draw back tantalisingly, out of her reach, but eventually the blissful sound of the wooden veranda was beneath her feet, and the next second she had turned the knob of the door and moved quickly inside.

She saw a room similar to the boys' bedroom, pale-washed and sparsely furnished. There was a white-clad bed, a small chest of drawers, and a luxury she hadn't possessed in the guest house, a wardrobe. Quickly she proceeded to lift the jumble of clothes from the cases, and transfer them to the hangers. Once, in passing the door at the rear end of the room, she turned the key briskly in the lock. Might as well have that clear from the start.

As the clothes and her personal possessions were gradually rearranged in their new home, Lee found herself relaxing considerably. That was one task over with anyway, and though she said it herself, she had managed it rather well. If everything went as smoothly as this there wasn't going to be much to worry about.

In no time at all Mr. Nick Reynolds would be on his way, and things would be back to normal, and as Alec had pointed out, all the man probably ever saw was palm trees. . . .

Before her mind could dwell too long on this track, she swung her empty suitcases away to the far corner of the room, and turned a satisfied glance along the neat row of garments hanging in the wardrobe.

It was then that the awful thought struck her.

The pale wispy negligée that she had bought in a mad moment in Mombasa—it was still hanging behind the bedroom door in the guest house! It had been there since that first night when she had shook it out of its folds.

Lee closed her eyes and opened them again. She fumbled wildly through the line of garments in the wardrobe. Perhaps without thinking she had thrown it in with the rest of her things. Her heart accelerated back to its old pounding rhythm, as she thumbed along the line without success. Of all the things to leave behind!

All thoughts of furtiveness flying from her mind, she raced out of the room and across the clearing. A good job she had come back too, she told herself breathlessly. She hadn't realised that she had left the guest house door open.

On the point of rushing straight inside, she was stopped dead in her tracks by a figure moving up into the doorway. Nick Reynolds stood facing her, the frilled chiffon looking ridiculously incongruous against his khaki shirt and drill slacks.

As he held the negligée up, he said with a tight sloping smile, 'Not exactly my line in casual wear.'

Lee took it from him with one quick snatch. 'A friend of mine left it,' she mumbled.

He nodded unquestioning and went back to unpacking his holdall. In the long silence that gaped between them Lee struggled to find a natural note. Hoping she looked reasonably composed, she asked politely, 'I hope you have everything you want?'

'Everything, thank you.'

His tones were brisk, but his gaze a shade too searching for her peace of mind. She turned quickly in the doorway to say tremulously, 'Right, I'll get back to the house, then.' With the negligée clutched in her hands she left with a feeling that the next two days were going to be the worst she had ever known.

CHAPTER SIX

IT was an accurate forecast. The meal alone that evening was enough to test her beyond endurance. In assuming that neither they nor the house would see much of Nick Reynolds, Alec had blithely overlooked the important item of dining arrangements.

In a way the man was a guest, and realising that in the part she was supposed to be playing she couldn't very well do anything else, Lee asked Fidele to lay another place at the table. Whatever Alec had told the gentle-mannered Seychellois she had no idea, but Fidele moved around with a nervous clumsiness that told all too clearly he wasn't used to subterfuge.

Jeff and the twins had become quite attuned to the idea of having their meals in the unrestricted area of the back veranda. Here they could rock in their seats, argue, and scatter crumbs to their hearts' content, and with Lee hovering in the background to see that things didn't get too much out of control, they ate as only boys can.

By the time the meal in the living room was about to be served, the twins were having serious thoughts of rolling into bed, and after the wash and brushing of teeth that Lee gently but firmly authorised they padded off to their room with some relief.

Jeff, keeping well clear of any similar arrangements for himself, scuffed idly around the back garden, but without his brothers to boss or to rope in for his games, he soon became bored. After a tight-lipped look at Lee he made a lightning visit to the bathroom, emerged slightly less dusty, and trudged off to his room with a comic book under his arm.

The dishes that Fidele served that evening might have been sawdust for all Lee cared. She was too acutely conscious of the wide shoulders opposite to notice what she was

458

eating. Not that she need have worried. As far as Nick Reynolds was concerned she just wasn't there. All conversation he directed towards Alec at the head of the table, and between the two of them, they kept up a fairly pleasant interchange of topics.

Whenever Alec tried to draw her into what she suspected was intended to be a husband-and-wifely bonhomie, she seized up with an almost hysterical realisation that she knew as little about Alec as she did Nick Reynolds.

The only thing that saved her, probably, was the fact that the man opposite seemed to prefer to centre his attentions away from her, and thankfully things stayed that way for most of the evening. When the two men eventually got on to the subject of copra, she shakily smiled her goodnight and fled.

Avoiding the living room the next morning, Lee ate her breakfast with the boys. There had been no problem in coming round the side of the veranda from her room, and if the men were going to the plantation, it wasn't likely that she would run into Nick Reynolds before nightfall. At least that was what she fervently hoped. She might have known things wouldn't have been as simple as that.

Halfway through the morning, her arms full of blossoming frangipani and wild orchids that she had been in ecstasy over down by the beach, and the boys had joyfully helped her to gather, she ventured into the house to look for vases. As she might have guessed, in a masculine household there wasn't *one*. Still, there were plenty of glass water jugs, and with the blossom trailing over the sides amid deep-coloured orchids and spears of green, they made a pleasing picture around the rooms.

It was when she was arranging the last one in the centre of the living room table that the shadow fell across the doorway. She had heard the footsteps along the veranda, but had been too deep in her task to give them much thought.

As she glanced up from the aura of blossom Nick Reynolds was just stepping into the room.

'Excuse *me*,' he said, dropping a twisted, derogatory

smile over her. 'I believe your husband keeps the production sheets in his desk,' and then in mildly authoritative tones, 'If you wouldn't mind.'

Once again Lee found herself floundering over something she knew nothing about. Where in Heaven's name was Alec's desk? Certainly not in here. Her hands trembling around the jug, she said with a forced lightness, 'I don't take much notice of those kind of things. Help yourself.'

For one awful moment she thought he was going to ask her which way to go, but he strode off and returned seconds later with a sheaf of papers in his hand.

Still clutching the jug, Lee waited, head bent, for him to leave the house, but there was no sound of retreating footsteps. When she looked up it was to find Nick Reynolds eyeing her through the thin blue haze of cigarette smoke.

He stepped closer to lower a glinting steel gaze over her plain print dress and leather sandals.

'Bit different from Mombasa,' he drawled in coolly sarcastic tones. She saw the grey eyes resting on the tortoiseshell slide as he nodded accommodatingly, 'Nice housewifely hair-do and...' the gaze dropped pointedly to her left hand, 'what do you know! Something else that wasn't there in Mombasa!'

Lee's eyes flew to the ring. Thank heavens it was the right way round! She felt goaded into replying, and had retorted, 'That's only because...' before she caught herself up on a quick intake of breath. She was saved the trouble of racking her brain for a suitable way to end the sentence, for Nick Reynolds put up a hand and with the sardonic lift of an eyebrow said, 'Don't bother to explain. Mombasa must have been great, and back on your private little island I can understand you thinking the chances of your being rumbled were pretty remote.'

Though lightly delivered, the words hit Lee like a whiplash. As she fought to keep the blaze of humiliation from her cheeks he lowered a smile of icy loathing down the length of her, and turning on his heel, swung out of the door.

Lee watched him go with tear-starred eyes. She had expected those kind of biting comments, but she hadn't realised how much they would hurt. She turned abruptly in the opposite direction and stumbled blindly through towards the back of the house. Served her right for clinging to memories that should have been abandoned long ago! Now perhaps she could get down to the business in hand. She had promised to help Alec to keep his job, and the only way she could do that was to play the part of his wife convincingly. It ought to have been as easy as falling off a log now that she knew where she stood with Nick Reynolds.

It ought to have been, but it wasn't. The minutes on that first day dragged on with agonising slowness, as did those on the second. On the third day the copra boat sailed, and at the end of the week Nick Reynolds was still on Half-Moon Island.

Lee was beginning to feel the strain of his presence in the heaviness of her limbs, the violet shadows under her eyes. She was constantly on edge and had an irritated feeling that the man saw a lot without apparently looking.

Fidele was apprehensive and flustered in his presence and narrowly missed addressing her as 'Mam'selle Travers' on one occasion. Alec was becoming fidgety too. He surprised her one night by trying the knob of their connecting doors, and when he couldn't get through, he called to her softly to let him in. Lee opened the door to meet him enquiringly.

'It's okay,' he nodded. 'Reynolds has turned in.' He strode into the room and flung himself scowlingly into a chair. 'Thing is, what do we do to get rid of him?' he grumbled.

'He's not exactly the get-rid-of type,' Lee said, lowering the book she had been trying to read. 'I don't see him leaving until he's ready.'

'And in the meantime I'll be dead from overwork.' Alec groaned. 'The bloke's a stickler for keeping things moving, *me* included. And he knows how to get the most out of the men too!'

'I should imagine he would,' Lee nodded with a wry smile.

'It's not funny.' Alec gave her a hurt look. 'I'm not used to this pace. You might be a little more sympathetic.'

Lee thought *she* could do with a little of that, plus one or

461

two other things. She heard herself saying shortly, 'Believe me, Alec, *I* find it no funnier than you!'

He shifted his gaze uncomfortably and hurriedly switched to asking her how she was faring with the boys. After one or two exchanges, a silence fell over the room. There was a moment when Alec's eyes lowered over her dressing-gowned form, then he was pushing to his feet.

'Well, one thing I'll have is a prosperous copra business.' he said, reverting to the previous subject. 'Reynolds seems determined to leave me with that.'

He paused in the doorway and Lee pointedly picked up her book. She heard the connecting door close with a click, and went to turn the key back again in the lock.

If Alec and Lee found Nick Reynolds' company trying, Jeff and his brothers were in an entirely opposite frame of mind. Much to Lee's irritation they couldn't get enough of it. When work at the plantation was finished for the day, they would trudge happily along after him, whether he was going for a swim in the lagoon or a stroll along the beach.

With Alec always ready to put his feet up after the day's work, a drink in his hand, the veranda shading his slumped-out form, it was left to Lee to go along after the boys. There was always small limbs to be rubbed down, wet clothes to be changed or drinks to be handed round. To say nothing of the constant worry that they might suddenly start to chatter on about her real reason for being on the island.

She needn't have worried. Jeff least of all wanted to be reminded of that, and the twins always followed his line. To the three of them her presence was just something to be tolerated. Which about summed it up for Nick Reynolds too. He kept his conversation for the boys.

There couldn't be any law against listening, though, Lee thought, eagerly soaking up his lazy words on the trips. She learnt the names of the birds, terns, and noddies and petrels; the fruit that weighted the trees—breadfruit, mangoes and paw-paws. She saw where the birds' eggs were nestled in the pink rocks, and the foot-long lizards trying to search them out.

Though she sometimes cursed Nick's popularity with the boys, Lee had to admit that life on these afternoon excursions was reasonably good. Once down at the beach there was nothing for it but to take to the water like the rest of them. She always made sure to stay on the edge of the lagoon with the twins, while Nick and Jeff swam further afield, yet somehow she was conscious only of muscular shoulders slicing the waves.

Games often developed after the swimming, and the periods away from the house grew more prolonged. Jeff was fond of cricket, and everyone was expected to give of their best. With Lee and the twins against Nick and Jeff the scoring was a bit one-sided, but as long as Lee could keep the length of the sandy pitch between herself and that big tanned frame, she didn't much care.

Not sparing much regret for the black cotton swimsuit that had disappeared without trace, she wore the rose pink, secretly happy that it looked so good with her tan.

Sometimes when, pink-cheeked, she had just managed a run, or when she and the twins were scrabbling laughingly for the ball, she thought she saw the dark glint of something in the grey eyes that were quickly lowered. Pure imagination, of course, Lee told herself. Nick Reynolds was never anything but flint-eyed with her. Just the same she found the hours spent away from the house heady, to say the least.

It was towards the end of the second week, when Nick's presence was in danger of making her lose the slender hold she had on the part she was playing, that Lee thought it wiser to give the beach a miss. The following afternoon she coaxed the twins into staying behind by promising exciting things in the garden. Jeff, casting a sceptical glance over his shoulder, went off in search of Nick.

For a while things went quite well among the litter of toys and books. Lee, neat in white linen slacks and cotton blouse, devised several games that were contrived to get the place tidied up at the same time. She missed Jeff's help with some of the heavier wheeled articles, but with Tim and Pete puffing out their chests importantly, they soon had everything neatly lined up in the thatched lean-to under the trees.

With all the space at their disposal the twins ran madly in circles for a while, but the novelty soon wore off. After a while their glances started wandering around the side of the house in the direction that Jeff had gone. Afraid that their interest was flagging, Lee wondered what else she could suggest. She had often watched Jeff jumping about quite skilfully on the trampoline, but his younger brothers were only just learning the art. They careered about drunkenly, managing only to get their feet up once or twice before falling down.

Strolling towards it now, Lee pondered on whether she could give them any useful advice. It turned out to be quite different from what she had intended.

When the boys saw what she was making for, they leapt ahead and showily swung themselves up on the trampoline, dancing giddily about on landing. Lee couldn't hide her amusement at their contortions, but they only laughed with her and called, 'Lee! Lee! Come on up! Come and jump!'

'Good heavens!' she looked humorously at the wide, taut canvas. 'You don't expect me to get up there! I'll be worse than you are!'

'You'll like it. You will! You will!' they chorused, rolling about and tugging her hand.

'All right. But you'd better watch out,' she said with an uncertain smile. 'Now, when I come up we'll all hold hands and jump, one, two, three. Ready? Here I come!'

She slipped off her sandals and swung up, but the minute her slim weight touched the canvas, the two small boys shot up like peas on a drum. There followed a hilarious moment when all three struggled to stay poised long enough to make the synchronised jump, but the laughter was weakening, and only made them stumble about more, and after a very wobbly attempt they all collapsed in a heap, doubled up with mirth.

A tousled corn-coloured head on either side of hers, Lee let her laughter go to the blue sky above. And then all at once it wasn't just blue sky. A tanned lean-lined face was moving in to block it.

Lying there under the dark grey gaze, Lee knew a peculiar reluctance to move. In a bitter-sweet drugged state she felt herself being dreamily transported back to a swimming float that rocked gently under the blue skies of Mombasa. A hard mocking mouth was lowering to shut out the view and. . . .

The twins giggled and having regained their breath, began to clamber over her, and the spell broken Lee gasped up smilingly to the face above hers. 'I'm sorry. Did you want me for something?'

Nick seemed to be out of humour. With a sour look lingering over her and the twins, he swung away, and striding off, clipped, 'It'll keep.'

After the trampoline incident Lee knew she would have to tread very carefully. Not only was she finding it practically impossible to feel anything like Alec's wife, she was in danger of tripping herself up over her feelings for Nick. For try as she might she couldn't deny to herself that what had happened between them in Mombasa would go on happening with her.

With the burden of this extra knowledge, she spoke very little around the house, and only with apprehension to Alec. Each evening meal became an agony of survival, with Lee fidgety and incoherent, the flush of healthy colour draining away under the pale gold of her skin as the meal progressed. To make matters worse a certain hooded grey gaze was often turned in her direction.

Though Alec carried things along coolly enough, Fidele was always glad to hurry off to his hut down at the settlement. Whenever she could Lee made a hasty exit too, and breathed a little easier in her own room. One night she didn't succeed in obtaining even that scant peace of mind.

As she was politely reciting her goodnights and preparing to make her departure one of the plantation workers came in to say that something had gone wrong with the water supply at the settlement. With a worn-out sigh Alec shrugged up from his seat and went off with the agitated Seychellois. Casting only a sideways glance at Nick draped back with company papers spread out before him, Lee darted out and round the side of the house. The night was stifling and weighted down with all the scents and fragrances of the island, and detectable too was the occasional salty tang of the sea. It was on evenings like this that Lee often felt tempted to wander off under the stars, and roam at will, but as usual she confined herself to her chair on the veranda in case the boys should need her.

Lying back now, she pondered on her progress with them. By this time it might be safe to say that she had been accepted by the twins. They were pliable and enjoyed her attentions, but Jeff was hardened to her advances. He still hadn't forgiven her for coming to wreck his self-styled way of life, and he missed his parents a lot more than he cared to show. She would just have to try a little harder with him in the future. Alec had told her that the mail boat called every once in a while, so she might soon be able to give the boys some news of their parents.

She had liked Bruce Pasmore on sight when she had met him in London, and it was reasonable to suppose that Mrs. Pasmore was of a similar caste. Deep in thought in trying to picture what kind of a woman the boys had for a mother, Lee almost sprang out of her chair at the sound of footsteps beyond the veranda. As her fingers tensed around the arms, she could just about make out pale drill slacks and shirt in the darkness below, and then Nick was taking the steps almost opposite her door. He stopped in the light of her room and thrusting his hands lazily into his pockets he drawled, 'I wondered why you always came round this way.'

She saw his eyes take in the oddments of furniture in the room, the small bed and connecting door, and in her desperation to preserve the lie she almost blurted, 'Alec comes round this way too,' but she thought better of it. Instead she murmured coolly, 'No reason, except it's quicker and I don't disturb the boys.'

He nodded, but she had a feeling that his attention was divided between her and the room behind. Afraid of his thoughts, she pushed up from her chair and said jerkily, 'I ... er ... was just going to turn in.'

'Don't let *me* keep you.' The familiar mocking glint was

466

back, but there was something else behind the gaze, something that seemed to want to find its way beyond her own crumbling façade. The look sent her panicking into her room.

As she turned to close the door Nick was dropping down the steps, but before she could quite shut him out he turned to say casually, 'By the way, I'll be going over to the east side of the island tomorrow.' There was a pause before he went on, 'I've an idea we might be able to use some of the land out there. Reckon you'll be able to make the trip?'

Weary at the thought of having to spend any more time with Nick under these circumstances, Lee said, pale-faced, 'Do I have to?'

' 'Fraid so,' Nick replied easily. 'I've already told Jeff and he's let the youngsters in on it. They'll expect you to be bringing up the rear as usual.' As though he expected her to fumble for an excuse he said somewhat abruptly over his shoulder, 'Be ready when I get back, about two.'

Lee shut the door with a slight slam. Carrying his company officialdom a bit far, wasn't he? He must think he had the right to order her around as he did everyone else on the island!

She was ready the next afternoon at two, but not, she told herself, because of Nick's order. It was simply that the boys were excited about the trip and unlike her were eager to be off. Unsure of what to wear, she had settled for a simple sleeveless cotton and pale kid sandals. Her hair was caught back as usual and she wished, if the mirror was anything to go by, that the light dusting of make-up had camouflaged a little more successfully her drawn look.

She took a deep and steadying breath as the two men turned the curve of the road. What she mustn't do was to go to pieces at this stage. Nick couldn't stay much longer now on Half-Moon, and as long as she held out Alec's position here was assured. Once it was just the boys and their uncle again, life would at last get back on to an even keel, and she could forget the nightmare of the first few weeks. There would be a permanently vacant site where her heart had been, of course, but she would learn to live with it in time. And Nick Reynolds would only ever think of her as someone else's perfidious wife, so that should make it easier.

Easier! From her seat on the veranda she watched the tanned khaki-clad figure draw nearer and, gulping, swung her glance up and over the palm trees. Once Nick had left the island things would be much, much better.

Impatient, the boys had bounded along the road to meet the men, and as Lee stepped down from the veranda Nick nodded a gruff 'All set?'

Though the question was directed down at Jeff and the twins Lee felt somehow that it was meant mainly for her.

Alec looked at her and then at Nick and then snapped his fingers dawningly.

'Of course, it's today you're going over to the east side.' He rubbed his chin thoughtfully. 'I might come over with you. It's a long time since I saw that part of the world.'

Lee thought Nick's glance flickered towards her and then lowered, but he replied evenly with a shrug, 'Suit yourself.'

Lee, on the other hand, was all eagerness at Alec's suggestion. She said quickly, 'In that case you can take over from me. It doesn't need two of us to watch the boys.'

Alec considered this, then with a slow smile shook his head. 'On second thoughts I think I'll give you the pleasure,' he murmured. 'A cool shower and a drink might be more what I'm after.' He strolled up towards the steps of the veranda waving lazily as he went. 'So long, kids. Have a good time.'

A good time! It was all right for him! Frowning, Lee felt her eyes drawn up to a pair of expressionless grey ones, and with the boys dancing around Nick suggested easily, 'Shall we go?'

He looked fresh in open-necked shirt as though he might have cleaned up before leaving the plantation, and swinging up the bag of refreshments that she had packed for the boys he stated, 'I'll take this.'

Lee was careful to keep the group split up on the walk. She found the twins' effervescence a boon to hide behind, and fell in with anything they asked, just to keep herself in their midst. Jeff strode along manfully at Nick's side, and with neither party coming much into contact it was the perfect arrangements as far as Lee was concerned, one worth while hanging on to until she got back to the house, she decided.

Her plan worked for most of the afternoon and then something happened to disrupt it. She wasn't sure what. She didn't know how it turned out that the twins were some distance away busily examining shells on the beach, or how Jeff came to be down at the water's edge when he had never left Nick's side since they had moved off from the house. Just the same, kneeling on a grassy patch to put the empty beakers back in the bag, Lee tensed as a shadow fell across her. After only a cursory glance over the land they had trekked far for him to inspect, Nick lit up a cigarette and draped down to pull on it lazily.

As the muscular arm supporting him was only inches away from her, Lee said in strangled tones, 'Isn't it time we were getting back?'

Nick tossed a glance towards the figures on the beach and replied evenly, 'We'll go when the rest are ready.' Which would be conveniently when *he* was ready, Lee suspected, feeling her pulses pacing her heartbeats.

She dawdled as long as she could over re-packing the bag, but soon everything was stowed away and there was nothing else for it but to sit and wait. She would have liked to have found a spot some distance away, but the angle of the khaki-clad figure was so set that with the circle of undergrowth behind she would have had to step over it. And with the steely grey eyes never leaving her face, such a move was unthinkable. She settled down, determined to remain aloof, yet finding herself overwhelmingly conscious of a dark head close by, a tanned slightly flexing jaw.

The sun cast its dappled warmth down through the palms, and the sea moved with barely a whisper over the bone-white sand. Just as Lee was beginning to relax in the tranquillity of her surroundings, the question came. Though delivered lazily, there was something of a business-like quality about the tones.

'Why did you go to Mombasa? Was it to get a breather from...' Nick nodded meaningly in the direction of the house.

Giving him a startled glance, Lee stammered, 'I ... I

don't know what you mean.'

He studied the end of his cigarette with a grim smile, and then when she least expected it swung his glance up to meet and hold on to hers. After what seemed an eternity, he drawled, 'You two don't exactly make a picture of rosy domestic bliss.'

Lee took a quick breath to steady herself. Better go careful here. There was no doubt in her mind now that Nick had conspired to get her alone on this trip. But why? And worse still, what did he know?

As she fumbled for words he watched her face and began casually, 'If you two don't hit it off . . .'

Lee felt her tenseness recede, leaving behind a certain heaviness. So that was it! He had found something lacking in Alec's method of working and was looking for an excuse to ease him out of his job. An unsuccessful marriage might give him that excuse. Her dejectedness left her with a desire to rally round Alec.

She gave a small forced laugh and explained brightly, 'Why, that's ridiculous! Alec and I are . . .'

She was totally unprepared for what happened next. A hand snaked out and fasted like a steel clamp on her wrist. She was forced to meet Nick's gaze as he snapped, 'Don't come the loyal little wife act with me. You're finding it hell, and you know it!'

Did it show as badly as that? As the narrowed grey eyes roamed her face, Lee was all too conscious of the violet smudges and drained features she had seen in the mirror.

The hard fingers relaxed almost as soon as they had touched her wrist, and pulling her hand free, Lee dropped it in her lap and kept her over-bright gaze steadily trained there. She didn't know whether it was the pain of Nick's hold or the knowledge that his only concern seemed to be for his firm that brought the sudden rush of tears to her eyes. As she was swallowing them back she heard him say harshly, 'I've seen the way you bolt to that room of yours every night, and clenched hands don't exactly give a picture of the contented . . .'

Before she could anticipate his move he had picked up her hand, displaying Alec's ring. Perhaps something of her inner panic showed, for as she made a wild attempt to pull her hand away, the strong brown one held on to it. The grey gaze lifted slowly from her clenched fist, and though she tried desperately to avoid it by lowering her lashes something of its piercing quality went home.

She felt her hand go suddenly free, but the words that accompanied the action were somewhat different in tone from the kind she had come to expect from Nick Reynolds.

'Something's bothering you,' he said quietly. 'What is it?' And after a pause, 'You can tell me.'

Feeling herself dangerously near to succumbing to this strange new gentleness in him, Lee sprang up and moved away.

'I've got nothing to tell,' she said tremulously, and then because he too had pushed to his feet and moved close she snapped hysterically, 'For heaven's sake leave me alone!'

'Okay.' His tones were no less gentle, but his eyes, still narrowed, watched her closely. After a long moment he shrugged as though the subject was closed, and called to Jeff and the twins.

As the five of them made their way back to the house Lee told herself that the worst was over, but somehow she couldn't bring herself to relax.

She wouldn't be able to do that until Nick had left Half-Moon Island for good.

CHAPTER SEVEN

IT occurred to Lee that her time would be better spent in getting on with her job instead of worrying about Nick, especially as she had heard that he planned to leave on the mailboat.

Alec had casually dropped the news at breakfast the next morning before Nick's arrival, and Lee had found herself biting back her annoyance. Just because he had been little affected by the deception, and he had grown used to having someone else to do his work for him, Alec hadn't thought it necessary to give her the vital piece of information he had obviously known for days.

Still she knew now, and it was a relief to see the end in sight. For it *was* in sight. At the worst Nick only suspected that her marriage to Alec wasn't a complete success, and there was nothing he could do about that.

For the first time since her arrival on the island she felt free to map out some kind of routine for the boys. They were young, and there were no hard and fast rules for their education, but Bruce Pasmore had requested that she inject a little learning into their daily programme. She decided to draw up a chart of lessons, mainly picture book studies for the twins with something a little more advanced for Jeff.

The shady back veranda made an ideal schoolroom for a couple of hours' learning each day, but though the twins settled down uncomplainingly over the colourful books she had set out on the table, Jeff obviously resented this encroachment on his time.

Most of his discontent was probably due to the fact that Lee had arranged the time of the lesson to coincide with Nick's arrival back from the plantation. She was ashamed of this act of cowardice, and realised it wasn't going to help her popularity rating with Jeff, but she had to have something to do while the big khaki-clad figure moved around in the close vicinity of the house. Once Nick had left the island, she would let the boys choose their lesson time.

When the men were at the plantation and the boys content to scrabble in the back garden Lee took to helping Fidele in the house. Both drawn against their will into Alec's scheme of things, an affinity had grown up between herself and the Seychellois, one that they both found comfort in. They could relax in each other's company, and Lee often found herself humming a tune beneath her breath as they worked.

Fidele showed her how to polish the floors with a coconut husk and the way to prepare some of the dishes she had been intrigued over at the dinner table. She learnt to use the charcoal iron on the clothes she washed for herself and the boys.

As the days progressed towards Nick's departure Lee told herself that she had almost made it. Alec's job was secure and she could soon leave the unpleasant episode of playing a bogus wife behind. Nothing had developed since Nick's questions that afternoon on the east side of the island, and apart from the steely grey eyes resting thoughtfully on Fidele's fidgety presence in the living room, the evening had passed serene and uneventful.

All considerably cheering thoughts, Lee told herself, yet for some reason she couldn't feel safe. To her an uneasy calm had settled over the household, one that she didn't care for the feel of. She told herself that the tightness inside her was nothing more than the results of living tensed up for so long, but she couldn't smile it away.

As the minutes ticked by, through the lazy somnolent heat of the day to the breathless stillness of the evening, she began to nurse a gnawing apprehension that something was about to erupt.

The first rumbles of it came the day before the mailboat was due.

The men usually stayed at the plantation from dawn to about two in the afternoon, therefore Lee was surprised to see Nick come striding out of the house midway through the morning. The fact that he had come from the direction of Fidele in the kitchen left her a trifle uneasy, but he gave

473

her no more than a flint-eyed nod as they passed on the veranda.

Just the same, there was something about that look that made her uneasiness gather momentum during the afternoon, and by the evening her nerves were strung to snapping point. To her the air in the living room seemed to have taken on the brittle quality of glass that would shatter with the first words uttered.

Only Alec seemed unaffected. He sat detached and faintly amused at the book he was reading. Nick appeared relaxed enough, draped back in an arm chair, but that hooded gaze was still on her as it had been all evening. Once or twice she tried to fathom the look there, but a certain gleam in the grey eyes put her on edge—so much so that she left earlier than usual without even the politely murmured goodnights.

Once outside she moved briskly along the veranda, straining for the sanctuary of her own room. There would be no sitting under the stars tonight. As soon as she had passed inside she would turn and lock the door and then . . .

Even as her mind was racing over these thoughts, she heard footsteps starting along the front of the veranda. The sound sent her nerves soaring. It could be Alec, of course, but just to be on the safe side, she had better try to appear cool and nonchalant. To hurry into her room now and spin the key in the lock would only invite suspicion.

She opened the door of her room leisurely, lit the lamp and then lowered herself into the chair outside. Her heart banged in rhythm to the approaching footsteps, but unlike its racing motion the caller seemed in no hurry. Though she was gazing with apparent unconcern into the night, she knew without a doubt that it was Nick who was coming towards her.

He stopped in the light of the room, and thrusting his hands deep into his pockets, rocked gently back on his heels. The look in his eyes was disguised beneath the half-lowered lids, only his smile seemed sharp and white in the glow of the lamp.

Lee was wondering agitatedly if she ought to try for a casual conversation when the khaki-clad figure moved up and without warning Nick stepped into the room. Forgetting her serene pose, Lee sprang up, but as she stood in the doorway Nick strolled unheedingly about the room, tilting a dark eyebrow over its contents. His hands were still in his pockets, and the same hard white smile played about his mouth.

Unable to do anything, Lee waited, her breath fluttering in her throat. She thought she saw the old mocking gleam back in the grey eyes, but it was difficult to tell because there was too much of something else overshadowing it, something that looked like a quiet anger. Trailing a last, long and unhurried look around the room, he strolled back to the door. As she stepped hastily to one side he bowed low and murmured lazily, 'Goodnight, Mrs. Hayward.'

All caution flying, Lee swung the door closed, and turning the key, heaved her strangled breaths against it.

What was all that about?

He had never called her Mrs. Hayward before, and it seemed to her that the accent had been on the *Mrs.* She lay back on the door and let out a long low sigh. Thank heavens he was leaving tomorrow. Another day of this and she would be a complete wreck!

The mailboat arrived almost at first light the next morning, but quite unawares Lee slept on. Having spent half the night pacing the room and fretting over Nick's nerve-racking behaviour, she lay drugged until the sun was well up in the sky and casting its dazzling light on her pillow.

Usually her awakenings coincided with the rising of the boys, but this morning there were no hearty shouts in the garden, or the clattering of small feet along the veranda. Everything was quiet—too quiet, Lee thought looking at her watch and racing to wash and slip into a white shirt and linen slacks.

She brushed her hair and clipped it back from her face, then went along the veranda towards the back of the house. As she might have known, the garden was empty, and so was the boys' bedroom. There was no one in the kitchen either, though a faint aroma of cooking hung over the stove. She went into the living room last of all, and found her place set out at the table, while still sitting in his was Nick.

He was reading an old newspaper, but lowered it with a brief smile as she came in. He rose and held her chair, and as she sank into it he said lazily, 'Good morning. I take it you slept well?'

Lee nodded absently, looking behind the veranda.

'I can't see the boys anywhere,' she commented, 'and Fidele isn't in the kitchen. Where is everybody?'

Nick shrugged, pouring her coffee.

'Where else, when the boat's in?' he replied.

'Good heavens!' said Lee, tensing at the muscular brown arm so near to her own. 'Is it here already?'

Nick nodded, draping back into his seat. 'Someone had to hang on until you had completed your beauty sleep,' he drawled, and then with that tight white smile, '*I* volunteered.'

Afraid that it was going to be a repetition of last night, Lee took a few quick gulps of coffee and rose.

'Shouldn't you ... er ... be leaving for the boat?' she said as pointedly as she dare.

'Oh, I don't know!' He rose to tower over her, and lifted the wide shoulders in a lazy gesture. 'There's plenty of time.'

Not for me there isn't, Lee gulped, moving out on to the veranda. Not knowing where she was going or what she was doing, she made for a chair and picked up a magazine.

Nick came out to lean up against a wooden pillar. He lit up a cigarette and pulled on it lazily, then said out of the blue,

'I thought we'd take a walk.'

'A walk?' Lee flung up her head, wide-eyed. 'You mean ... down to the boat?'

'Not especially. I thought we'd try the other way.'

'The other way? A kind of farewell walk?'

He made no comment, and not liking the glint in his eye as he drew her to her feet, Lee gazed up wildly to stammer, 'Nick, I ...'

'Well, come on! What's a walk?' With almost no space between them he sloped a queer smile and added succinctly '... after Mombasa?'

Would he never get on that confounded boat?

Through the palms and tall grass Lee walked along at his side, wondering if her legs would hold her the full distance. For once she was unconcerned with the beauty around her. The brilliance of the birds, the sun-dappled clearings and endless trailing blossom were lost on her. What she was acutely conscious of was the silence.

She didn't know whether to feel relieved or not when Nick lowered himself down on to a grassy embankment, and held his hand for her to do the same. The ground would support her shaking limbs, yes, but to sit so close to . . .

She had no choice in the matter, for Nick's grip was rough and demanding and within seconds she found herself leaning against the grassy bank and staring with a fixed gaze out to sea.

How long they sat there Lee had no idea, but it seemed to her that with every fall of a wave on the beach, the air became more difficult to breathe. The fluttering of a leaf as the breeze drifted by, the call of a bird, every sound seemed to twist the tension tighter until nothing stirred.

Choked by the intensity of the silence, Lee turned a wild amber gaze sideways. A steely grey one was just coming in to meet it. It met and held hers as ruthlessly as a magnet and reading something there Lee backed off again with, 'Nick, I . . .'

The words trailed away on a gasp as in one movement his hand shot up and flicked the slide from her hair. In wide eyed bewilderment Lee tossed her head back, and as the cloudy hair came cascading around her face, Nick leaned in menacingly to growl, 'That's more like it. Now we're back on the same old footing.'

Before she could do anything to prevent it, the hard mouth had dropped down on her own and she was pulled against the muscular chest. There was nothing gentle in the hold, and stifled against him, she almost cried out at the roughness of his lips.

A long moment afterwards he raised his head only slightly to give her the full force of his blazing grey gaze. His tones were somewhat unsteady, but the sarcasm was all too much in evidence as he twisted a smile to say, 'And now we get the bit about kissing another man's wife.'

Searching the face too close to her own, Lee gasped from a heaving bosom, 'You know!' And then recalling the scene as he strode from the direction of the kitchen yesterday she whispered 'Fidele!'

'Fidele,' Nick nodded, holding her relentlessly. 'I guessed he knew something. I told him I'd break his neck if he didn't give.'

'What are you going to do?' she asked faintly.

'Take Hayward apart piece by piece, I think, and then . . .'

'Nick,' she took a breath, 'would it matter all that much to you if Alec kept his job?'

'Would it to you?'

As he held her close, she could feel his heartbeat thudding against her own. The faintly smiling mouth was lowering dangerously near to her own, but Lee had already tasted his anger, she couldn't bear his contempt, and wasn't this always the way he got that across?

Straining away from him, she said coolly, 'You think that's the answer to everything, don't you?'

'I thought it was with you.' The white smile hardened slightly. 'In Mombasa, anyway. Here you've got me licked. Just what species are you, anyway?'

'There's no mystery about me,' she said evenly, feeling an emptiness as the encircling arms slackened and fell away. 'I'm a schoolteacher, and I came out here to keep an eye on the boys. And Mombasa?' She shrugged. 'I missed the boat. A friend, a stewardess with the airline, told me I ought to try and look a little more . . . unschoolteacherish, so I did for a while, but now . . .'

As she reached her hand out for the tortoiseshell slide lying in the grass, Nick picked it up and threw it into a distant bush.

'It doesn't fit,' he drawled. 'And no one goes in for that schoolmarm stuff these days.'

In spite of his words he looked, for a moment, as though the sudden abundance of silken hair annoyed him. With an abrupt movement he was on his feet and holding his hand out for her.

'We'd better get moving,' he said roughly. 'We've got a big day ahead of us if everyone is going to be on the boat by nightfall.'

'Nick,' as he strode off Lee hurried along at his side, matching her two steps to his one. 'Couldn't we leave things as they are?' she pleaded. 'The firm needn't know that Alec isn't married. It's a ridiculous rule anyway. Off in a minute if you're single, a whole six months if you're not.'

'I'm inclined to agree with you, now I've seen what guys like him will try to swing.'

'It's understandable,' she defended. 'You know what Half-Moon means to Alec?'

'The lush living, you mean, not the work.'

Ignoring his sarcastic tones, she said quickly, 'But he *has* been working hard lately, and it wouldn't hurt to let him stay, would it?' And then because Nick looked just about as unyielding as a rock, she laid a hand on his arm to beg, 'I wish you'd do it for me.'

'And you were doing it for him, all that man and wife business.' He stopped to flicker a gaze over her. 'And you'd only been on the island, what ... a couple of days?' The white smile was slightly taut as he watched her. 'He must be an even faster worker than I am!'

'I don't think you've ever been sorry for anyone in your whole life!' Lee snapped, swinging away from him.

She was surprised at that moment to see Fidele running from the house towards her. He seemed agitated and stopped breathlessly in front of her.

'I've been looking for you,' he said between gulps. 'M'sieur Hayward sent me on with a message, a ...' he cast a flinching glance in Nick's direction, 'a very important message.'

With a slow smile Nick bowed and swept an arm mockingly towards Lee. 'Don't mind me,' he commented drily.

Fidele looked as though he couldn't wait to be rid of the information he was nursing.

'The owners of the company are on the island,' he said round-eyed. 'Their boat is anchored beyond the lagoon. They have much luggage, snorkelling equipment and such, and there is talk of a holiday!'

As Lee took a quick intake of breath, she felt Nick step up close behind her.

'Blair Newman and André Sauvier,' he said thoughtfully. 'I knew they were in the vicinity, but I hardly expected them to pay us a call.'

'M'sieur Hayward wanted me to come ahead to prepare you,' Fidele explained with a sheepish glance up beyond Lee's shoulder. 'He is showing the men the plantation. I had to help with the unloading of the supplies from the mailboat, but I slipped away as soon as I could.'

So Alec didn't know that his scheme had collapsed, Lee pondered. She and Fidele had held out as long as they could, but now Nick knew, and if he wanted to he could bring the whole thing out into the open.

As Fidele hurried back to the house Lee turned to the tall figure at her side.

'Nick, please!' she looked up urgently. 'Couldn't we give Alec a chance?'

The grey eyes searched her face. A small frown flickered over one dark eyebrow, and then as his gaze went beyond her, he tensed slightly and muttered, 'Don't look now, but we've got visitors.'

Stepping apart from her, he led the way towards the front of the house, where the group were just making for, from the road.

As the boys leapt excitedly around her Lee saw two men, elderly but active looking in gay casual shirts and sailing slacks. One was fairly thickset, with a square jaw and short cropped hair. The other, of similar build, had a round puckish face, with fly-away eyebrows and a big smile.

The latter was saying to Alec, 'You're doing a good job here, Hayward,' and then, turning, he strode forward with hand outstretched.

'Nick, you old dog! So this is where you holed up for your leave. We thought you'd have headed straight back for the coast.'

The other man eyed Nick with a sly smile to say in heavily accented English, 'Ah, Neeck! Don't tell us you've grown tired of the amenities of the beeg ceety!'

Nick gripped the hands, a lazy grin his only reply.

Lee had been aware of Alec eyeing her with open appraisal. Obviously he approved of her hair hanging shoulder-length, though she hoped his turning an arm about her waist and drawing her close was only done to impress the visitors.

As though they noticed the movement, the men turned and stepped towards her.

'So this is the little lady!' The puckish one beamed over her and Alec made the introductions.

'Lee, meet the owners of the copra company, Blair Newman and André Sauvier.'

Lee had her hand taken in two firm grasps. The French-accented man with the quixotic dark eyes said in his deep tones, 'You are a lucky man, M'sieur.'

And slightly over-zealous, Lee thought, conscious only of a narrowed grey gaze as Alec drew her against him. As his hand caressed her shoulder she saw Nick's mouth clamped tight. She tensed herself waiting for the onslaught that looked about to break.

Poor Alec! Little did he know it, but any moment now he was going to find himself out of a job. Nick's tones were just about as keyed up as she would have expected for what he had to say. Only his words as he addressed the two men made her lower her lashes in confusion.

'Well, it looks like the welcome mat should be out. Did you have a good trip?' Nick lit up a cigarette briskly.

'Lots of 'em!' Blair Newman grinned. 'We've left our wives shopping in Zanzibar. André here and myself are looking for a little peace and quiet, and a chance to look at some underwater life. We reckon Half-Moon is just the place. That is . . .' he sent an enquiring smile towards Lee, 'if we're not putting Mrs. Hayward out.'

Lee held her breath, thankful that the boys were playing some distance away. She put on a bright smile, but could manage no more than a shake of her head to the question.

Nick said unhurriedly, 'You can take over my spot. There's two beds in the guest house. I'll move over to the house. Shouldn't be much of a shake-up.'

'That's fine!' Blair Newman exclaimed. 'Save us cluttering the house with our gear. We're still goggles and flipper men, Nick, but we've got an awful lot of gadgets to make it worth while.'

As two plantation workers came along the road, carrying luggage and equipment, the two men and Nick went to meet them. Lee turned herself out of Alec's hold and gathering the boys together, fled to the back of the house.

The rest of the day passed in a whirl with everyone in or around the house. At one point she saw Nick striding purposefully along the veranda with his bags in his hands. Without asking anyone's opinion, he flung open the door of the room next to hers and dumped his things inside.

Meals were eaten communally at the long table in the living room. The company owners were in holiday mood, and talked underwater fishing endlessly to Nick and Alec, while Lee endeavoured to keep the twins and Jeff's spirits simmering at a decently low level.

The boys were conscious of the importance of the new arrivals, and did everything possible to be noticed, but apart from the odd wink and a joking word, the men were too wrapped up in their hobby to give much attention to anything else. Luckily they had taken to calling her Lee, so there was no danger of that 'Mrs. Hayward' cropping up again.

Lee noticed with some relief that Fidele performed his duties with an unruffled smile. It was as though having confessed his guilt, he had passed the load on to Nick's shoulders, and was quite happy to let it stay there.

Lee too found she wasn't anywhere near as keyed up, with the big khaki-clad figure carrying things along for her at the far end of the table. Watching him, she had to admit that with Nick in the know, much of the strain had left her.

Just the same, she felt far from contented. Re-living the morning's shattering events, her mind toyed endlessly with Nick's derisive remark—the one that had compared his pace with Alec's.

The idea, Lee decided lingeringly, of Nick being a fast worker would be heaven if there was anything in it, but there never was. True, she had known his kisses. Her limbs still trembled from the furore of his latest angry embrace. But that was just it. Never slow to put it *that* way, to let her know what he thought of her, it seemed she was destined to know all Nick's moods but the one she wanted.

CHAPTER EIGHT

LEE felt strangely restless in her room that evening, and gazed long at her reflection in the mirror. It wouldn't be difficult to get another hair slide, of course, but come to think of it—she shook her head and the dark silken hair made a pleasing swish about her ears. There was something satisfyingly feminine about wearing it this way.

Feminine! She had never considered herself as anything else, but now suddenly there seemed so many other things that could be done. Slipping into one of her new dresses, she experimented with a light brush of the lipstick that Cheryl had chosen, a touch of the honey-gold powder. Sherry-dark eyes glowed back at her. It was Mombasa all over again, but what did that matter? Jeff and the twins didn't see her as much of a schoolteacher anyway, and they might prefer it, if she gave them lessons looking like this.

If her less formal appearance after that evening had any effect on the boys, she didn't notice. They were still full of the chatter for the letter that had arrived on the mailboat. Lee had read the closely written pages describing, for the boys' benefit, the Pasmores' travels up the Rift Valley, and the various items of interest on the way. She had thought she sensed a certain nostalgia in Mrs. Pasmore's words to her sons, and gathered that the idea of leaving them behind had been even more unpopular with her than it had with her husband.

Her own letter from Bruce Pasmore had been short and to the point, though the fatherly concern was much in evidence. He wanted a complete report on his sons' progress, how they were taking to island life, and particularly how she was faring with Jeff.

In the short space of time before the mailboat sailed Lee had been at a loss what to write, but in the end she had filled three pages. Her letter, admitting that she was no nearer to Jeff now than she had been on her arrival, would be well on its way by this time, but Bruce Pasmore was a straight-talking man who liked straight answers and she knew she had been right to give him the truth. In any case she had tempered it with a certain amount of hope for the future.

The boys seemed quite immune to this certain softening in her appearance. There was, however, a noticeable reaction from Alec. Lee was conscious of his eyes resting on her for long moments at a time these days. She couldn't help musing that if it hadn't been for Philippa in Nairobi, she might have made a conquest there. As for Nick, it was difficult to know what he was thinking. Most of his time was spent down at the beach with the company owners. When he was in the house he seldom looked her way, though she did see him eyeing Alec thoughtfully from time to time.

Lee didn't spare more than a fleeting thought for Alec's new appraisal of her. Then something happened to make her view the change in him with a slight feeling of uneasiness.

For two men probably approaching their sixties, Blair Newman and André Sauvier had abounding energy. They were up at dawn, and always the last to retire in the evenings, lingering over their drinks in the living room, and discussing their plans for the following day.

Since Alec was compelled to put all his time in at the plantation and only arrived back when the house was full he and Lee had little chance to talk. That was why she didn't hesitate when late one night he knocked softly on her door and asked to be let in.

Scarcely aware that the flimsy folds of the frilled negligée were drawn none too tightly around her, she hurried to the door and turned the key in the lock. Alec stepped in and closed the door surreptitiously, and hating the clandestine situation, Lee said irritably, 'How much longer are we going to have to carry on like this? When I came out to Half-Moon Island I certainly didn't expect to . . .'

'Sssh!' Alec put a finger to his lips. 'Not so loud! We're supposed to be a loving couple, remember?'

As he grinned down at her Lee gave him the benefit of a cool stare.

'You mean it's going to go on?' she said thinly. 'I thought you were coming to tell me some good news—that the men were leaving or something.'

'Stop worrying!' Alec strolled happily. 'It's going great. The old boys love the idea of us making a go of it out here, and André has got romance in his soul. Haven't you seen the way he looks at us?'

Lee had seen, but she saw no reason why she should admit it. In the pause that followed, Alec stopped and turned. She noticed the blue eyes flicker slowly down the length of her, and then he stepped up smilingly to murmur, 'What I really came to say was, thanks ... well ... for the way you've let yourself blossom out for the part.' He trailed his fingers through the hair on her shoulders and moved in close to say softly, 'I didn't do too badly, for myself after all, did I?'

Deliberately misinterpreting his meaning, Lee moved towards the door opening on to the night, and said lightly, 'Lucky for you I was on the island when your troubles started, otherwise ...'

'Troubles?' Even as she stepped out on to the veranda Alec was behind her. She felt his arms slide round her waist, as he added, 'I'd almost forgotten I had any. In fact, come to think of it,' he turned her slowly towards him, 'I don't think I have.'

The night was a solid black and apart from the faint golden glow of the lamp falling across the doorway Lee could see nothing. Alec's face, however, with the light behind it, she could see all too clearly. As it lowered towards her own she tensed and said in annoyed tones, 'To refresh your memory, Alec, you were on the point of being turfed off the island, remember!'

'Is that so!' As his lips brushed her cheek she turned out of his hold to say pointedly, 'And I agreed to try to help you to keep your job. Nothing more.'

She stepped back into the doorway and Alec moved into the lamplight to bow indolently. 'Point taken,' he smiled.

But was it? Lee didn't miss the peculiar light in his eyes,

nor the fact that he was waiting for her to move back inside the room.

She stood her ground, and after a while he shrugged idly.

'Okay, I'll go the long way round if you prefer it. 'Night blossom!'

The smiling emphasis he put on the last word put Lee's teeth on edge. She moved out to make sure he had gone round the side of the house, then paused a moment to cling to the veranda rail.

The night air helped to steady her shaking insides. She took several deep breaths of it, and turned back towards the door. After the turmoil of the last few minutes, she couldn't have been sure of anything, but it seemed to her as she looked in the other direction along the veranda that the dull glow of a cigarette burned suddenly brighter, as though being drawn on deeply.

Lee was in bed the following night when Alec knocked on her door. She pretended to be asleep, and after a while the whispered calls trailed off.

Lee wondered if she was ever going to be free of the intrigue she had let herself in for, since arriving on the island. *One afternoon*, Alec had said, and here it was trailing into months. Every evening she listened attentively to the men's conversation on the veranda, hoping to hear something that would tell her the company owners were thinking of leaving, but nothing ever came.

Blair Newman and his partner showed no signs of wanting to give up the carefree leisurely life they had found on Half-Moon Island. If anything they were inclined to want to embody the rest of the household in ideas for enjoying it. Lee was already becoming adept with goggles and flippers, and she and the boys and the rest of the men had made several circular cruises of the island in the partners' ketch *Sea Wind*.

One night the conversation was centred round Montage, an uninhabited island, reputed to be very beautiful, several miles to the south. Nick and Alec were pointing out to the two older men the best way for getting there, when Blair Newman suddenly smacked his knee.

'Hell, why don't we all go?' he said with his usual hearty eagerness. 'There's enough space on *Sea Wind,* and they tell me there's nothing in this world to come up to the place for colour.'

André nodded his head vigorously. Alec, always reluctant to give up his chair on the veranda, gave an indifferent shrug and Blair, ever encouraging, said, 'Aw, come on, Alec! Drag yourself away. You've got the plantation out of the rough. You can afford to take a break.'

As the older man turned an eager enquiring look in Lee's direction, she said with a forced lightness, ashamed of Alec's lack of enthusiasm, 'I think it's a lovely idea.'

'What do you say, Nick?'

The khaki-clad figure draped against the veranda rail changed position at Blair's words. Nick trailed a gaze over Lee and Alec and took it on to the two older men.

'It's okay by me,' he said lazily.

Jeff was agog with excitement the next morning and as usual the twins were smitten with his mood. They could hardly keep still as the pirogue, one of the island's fishing boats, took them out to the anchored ketch.

Alec showed little interest for the stretch of sea on all sides on the journey, and sat in the cockpit pulling idly on a cigarette. Lee had her work cut out keeping the boys away from the rail. Later, though, when Blair took the boys to look round below, Alec drifted over to her side and turned an arm round her waist.

'Maybe this wasn't such a bad idea after all,' he said.

Lee would have liked to turn straight out of his arm, but André was nodding to them, smiling from where he swung the wheel. Tensing inwardly but unable to do anything visibly, she took a breath and caught Nick's eye further down the rail. Before she could read anything in his glance he had lowered it to pull on the rope he was holding.

The beauty of Montage, in Lee's opinion, was not so much in the island as its surrounding waters. The glare of the white beaches dazzled the eye, and the birds rose up in clouds at the merest blink of an eyelid, but the warm waters inside the shallow lagoon were enough to induce a person to float gazing downwards for ever.

While the boys chased fiddler crabs back into the sand, Lee flipped languidly over outcrops of glittering coral and swaying sea grass. Jewelled reef fish darted in and out of colonies of spined sea-eggs, and giant anemones burned like flaming torches from the shadows. Out near the necklace of reef she saw brilliant yellow and blue feelers waving eerily from cracks and crevices, and patches of translucent grey undulating gently on the sea-bed.

The water was so buoyant she could lie almost without moving on the surface, but when a piece of coral moved to reveal itself as a small octopus, Lee decided the beach might be a better place to take an afternoon snooze.

Nick was lazily slicing the water a short distance away. Jeff and the twins were stacking a pile of cowrie shells on the beach. She found on arrival that the two older men were just as excited about a pearl shell they had found. André said it belonged to something called a green snail and was very rare.

The search was on for more, and Lee was dragged in on it, not much, she had to confess, against her will. There was something vaguely exciting about looking for something that there were only a few of in the world.

There was not much shade on the island, but Alec had found himself a patch near a cluster of undergrowth and was stretched out with a straw hat over his face. Occasionally he would wander down to the water's edge, flick a pebble or two, then wander back.

There was no luck in finding another pearl shell, but nobody wanted to give up. The lilac sky was deepening to purple when Nick strolled up in slacks and shirt, the dark hair damp from his recent swim, to say with lazy good humour, 'I don't want to break up anything exciting, but shouldn't we be getting back?'

'No hurry, Nick.' Blair looked up from where he was kneeling. 'Got a whole pile of shells to sort through.'

Nick nodded at the sky.

'Not going to stay light much longer.'

'We can stay the night.' The older man brushed a leopard cowrie shell lovingly. 'We've got tents.'

'Oh, can we, Nick? Can we? *Please* can we?' Jeff danced

around, his thatch of corn-coloured hair rising and falling over big brilliant brown eyes.

'Sure we can, young feller!' Blair rose good-naturedly. 'Not much fun in sailing in the dark anyway. André, go out and get the gear from the boat. There's coffee and soup in the flasks, and a blanket apiece is about all we'll need.'

André moved off, laughing throatily as the boys leapt excitedly around him. They stopped off at Alec to tell him the news and after a few moments he pushed lethargically to his feet.

Lee, with her beach robe around her, went off to get changed, not daring to think of anything beyond that. She eked out the time as the tents were going up, by brushing the sand off the twins and changing their swimming trunks for T-shirts and shorts, but when the coffee came round and André handed her a mug with a beaming wink, she could barely get it past the nervous tightness in her throat.

There were two tents, fair-sized, but only two. Probably Blair and André used one each, but the question was *who* was going *where* tonight. In the darkness she steadied her coffee with slightly shaking hands.

It seemed an eternity before the boys quietened down in one of the black shapes against the skyline, and even longer before the men were ready to move. At last Blair pushed to his feet, and the others followed suit. Lee's skin crept as André clasped Alec around the shoulders and chuckled throatily towards the vacant tent, 'The old men weel take care of the cheeldren tonight. A man and hees wife need to be together, hah?'

Alec, who had been eyeing the other tent for some time, said with a slow smile at the darkness, 'I'm all for it myself.'

'Of course you are, you old dog!' André's dark eyes gleamed in the shadow. 'What more could you ask for? A carpet of sand, the wheeper of the sea.' He pushed Alec playfully. 'Maybe the rest of us should go back to the sheep, hah, and then you could ...'

'For pity's sake, André, cut the guitars and moonlight stuff!'

Nick's voice cut across the gently crooning words

like a circular saw blazing through wood. He swung round to go on in only slightly moderate tones, 'It's impractical out here, anyway. Lee goes in with the boys.'

Slightly surprised, André turned down his lips and shrugged his shoulders with, 'Neeck has sore head tonight.' But Blair slapped his partner on the shoulder good-naturedly and chuckled, 'He's right, André. You know what youngsters are like in the night!'

Without waiting to hear any more Lee stumbled off thankfully into the darkness. That was the last time she would leave herself open to anything like that, she told herself furiously, once settled beside the sleeping boys. If Alec wanted to jeopardise his job by pushing her into impossible situations, he could jolly well stay away from her in future. Not for anything would she let herself be included in any more 'family' outings!

The decision taken, she was always careful to have her excuses at the ready when Blair and his partner were preparing for a sail, after that. Some of the excuses were quite legitimate. One days the boys' hair needed cutting. And didn't it? It was nearly down to their noses. Another day the twins had run out of clean shirts.

Alec was learning to cry off too. He had been more or less ordered to have a holiday, but exploring pools and lagoons was not much in his line. Whenever he could he got out of the trips. One morning when the older men had the map out, he told them he was going to see how work was progressing on the south side of the island. He said he was taking Fidele, and they would probably camp out the night.

Very neat! Lee couldn't help smiling as she saw him hastily stuff books and magazines into his haversack.

Having heard the conversation the night before she had made sure to have the lesson books out and the boys at their seats on the back veranda. Nick ruffled Jeff's hair as he went off, and the two partners waved and followed, quite happy to be starting out on another of their fishing and shell collecting adventures.

One person who was far from happy was Jeff. He watched the men go, scowled darkly over his books and then flung her an angry look.

'It's not fair!' he said hotly. 'You never let us do anything we want to.'

'You know that's not true, Jeff,' Lee said gently, but as the small mouth pulled into a tight line she felt a brush of concern. She seemed destined to cross Jeff whatever decisions she took. If only she could get closer to him! She had started off on the wrong foot, of course, but she had only herself to blame for that. Against her coming in the first place, she had given him the opportunity of living a totally undisciplined existence for two weeks by missing the boat in Mombasa. She could only expect that he would resent her intrusion when it came. He had had a taste of living the life he pleased, with only an indolent uncle in the background. Naturally he had wanted it to continue. Nick's coming had softened things for a while, but she had been instrument in splitting them up by introducing lessons, and now she had defaulted again by banning the sailing trips.

Though in effect Lee was only doing her job in keeping the boys to a set routine each day, she did feel a tiny tug of guilt that the routine was designed to avoid the crises that were continually cropping up on the island. But even if things had been smooth-running, she doubted whether the situation would have been different between her and Jeff. In his view she was the one obstacle that prevented him from living in a man's world, and he didn't intend to forget it.

She had grown used to him swinging away moodily when she approached, now he was openly rebellious to anything she suggested. Inhaling a silent sigh, Lee gazed over the three bent heads. What she would have to do was work really hard to make their days together as interesting and exciting as possible. With another sigh, a lighter one this time, she said on the spur of the moment, 'All right, then, what about a holiday?'

The twins raised their heads to give her a vague look, and then went back to the combined picture they were colouring. Jeff who had been rolling the corner of his book, shuffled in his seat, and Lee pursued, 'I thought we'd have a picnic, go somewhere where we've never been before. What do you think, Jeff? A good idea?'

'S'all right.' Jeff fiddled indifferently with his pencil. Hmmm! Perhaps it didn't sound all that exciting, but there wasn't much you could do on a small island. Just when Lee was beginning to think that here was another idea rebuffed, Jeff looked up with something like an interested gleam in his eyes, and then writing deliberately with his pencil he asked, 'Can I choose the way?'

'If you like,' Lee smiled. 'We'll take enough food for the whole day and stay out just as long as we like,' she added, hoping to instil some piquancy into the plans. Her words had some effect, for the twins were off their seats and whooping in circles. Jeff too had something of a smile about his tight features.

'Go and change into old jeans and shirts,' she instructed, 'and I'll see about the sandwiches.'

She watched Jeff pull a brother close on either side and smirk something under his breath as they went indoors.

Knowing the boys' appetites, Lee prepared plenty of food and drink and to save struggling with a heavy load she packed four individual canvas bags. Later, putting the straps of the bags over each boy's shoulder in turn, she thought she saw tittering conspiratorial glances pass between them, but then decided it was nothing more than a natural effervescence at the thought of going off for the day.

She had to admit she was a little disappointed at Jeff's choice of route, for he was making his way along an insect-infested, overgrown path that looked as though it hadn't been used for years. When they had been walking for half an hour with still no sign of a break in the dense green foliage, Lee called up ahead.

'Are you sure you're going the right way, Jeff?'

'Nearly there!' he called back jauntily.

There to what? Lee wondered vaguely. According to the direction they were nowhere near the beach, and equally far from the more attractive slopes of the island, so what did Jeff have in mind? The next minute there was a break in the trees and she saw for herself. Her heart sank at the view. It was unimpressive, to say the least.

There was an open clearing, that looked as though it had

been used for working purposes at one time; probably years ago, as the plantation was not in this vicinity. The barren ground was hard and dry and dusty, as though lots of heavy feet had flattened it at one time, and rusty tools and implements were scattered around. One bleached wooden hut creaked in the heat, and huge insects swooped and droned around angrily, as though they resented this intrusion on their privacy.

Lee took a long deep breath, and slipping the bag from her shoulders, lowered it and sank down on the rotting log of a tree.

'Well!' she said, trying to infuse a brightness into her tone, 'I can't say I'm tickled pink with the view, but if this is what you want . . .'

The twins balanced on one foot and then the other, looking wide-eyed and expectant. Jeff scuffed around watching his feet. Lee, striving to quell her irritation, asked, 'Well, now we're here, what are you going to do?'

'We . . . we . . .' The twins squirmed and then looked to their brother for assistance.

'They want their ball,' Jeff said clearly, staring hard at a palm tree.

'Ball?' Lee looked blank and then laughed her relief. 'Oh, I see! You mean we've come all this way to collect a lost ball?' She didn't add 'thank heavens', but rose from her seat to suggest cheerily, 'Well, let's get looking, shall we, and then we can move on.'

'We *know* where it is,' Jeff said arrogantly.

'You do?' As Lee raised a puzzled eyebrow, he lifted a rigid brown arm and pointed towards the hut.

'It's in there,' he said levelly.

'Well, then?'

As Lee shrugged Pete stuck a finger in his mouth and chewed on it, watching her, but Tim, apparently losing interest, stomped around the clearing and piped importantly, 'Nick told us not to come here 'cos . . .'

'Shut up!' Mike scowled at his younger brother, and Lee, feeling that this wasn't much of a start to their day out, said briskly,

'Look, I'll get the ball and then we'll move on, shall we?

Perhaps a little nearer the beach. We might find a cove that we've never explored before, and I've packed our swimming things, so we can ...'

It occurred to Lee that the boys were not paying much attention to what she was saying. All eyes were fixed on the hut, and Mike, a small smile showing through his shut-down expression, was moving in that direction.

Lee looked around and followed him quickly. She would be glad to be out of this place. There was something about it that put one's nerves on edge. Even the boys were acting peculiar. The twins' eyes were as big as pennies as she opened the door of the hut. Pete said, twisting his hands, 'When I lost my ball in here once I ...' and then catching his brother's glance, collapsed behind an embarrassed display of milk teeth. Lee smiled and stepped inside.

There was only the light from the door to see in the small space inside, and just as she was getting accustomed to the gloom in the corners, where there didn't seem to be a ball, or anything else for that matter, the light started diminishing.

She realised vaguely that the door was closing, but it was only the final click as it slotted into place that made her go to it urgently. She pushed and knocked on it and called, 'Jeff! The door has swung to. Open it, please!'

Instead of giving, the door seemed to be settling firmly into place, assisted by considerable weight from the other side. There was the sound of muffled laughter and then as feet scuffed away, she heard urgent conspiratorial whispers, 'Let's get going.'

'Where shall we go?'

'I know a place. Come on!'

As the sound of running footsteps receded, Lee called out authoritatively, 'Jeff! Come back at once. Jeff ...!'

But the only reply was the drone and crash of insects as they hit the outside of the hut. Lee tried all her strength against the door, but it was always the oldest and least used that had the most effective locks.

She stepped back into the dimness and moved around. She was seeing again the glances exchanged this morning; the twins' fidgety behaviour, and Jeff's peculiar smiles. So this was what they were up to? A plan to get rid of her. Not very ingenious, but effective. She hoped she wasn't going to find out just how effective.

The hut was in the direct path of the sun and the heat inside was unbearable. Thankfully the surrounding board had warped so that the cracks were considerably widened. In some cases she could see a strip of the green undergrowth, but the air drifting through was not enough to prevent the blood pounding in her head.

Without the sun, the few feet of space might have been reasonably bearable, but how did one cope in a veritable oven? She chose a corner where a sizeable knot had dropped out and sank down to wait. The less energy she used the better, and sooner or later the boys would be back if only to . . .

A sudden thought made the perspiration well up around her temples. The boys' actions were usually ruled by their stomachs, but this time they wouldn't have to come back to her. She had given them all enough food and drink to last the day.

Something else made her throat thump wildly. There was no doubt in her mind now that Jeff had engineered this situation. He wanted his freedom, and he wasn't averse to shutting her away to get it, and that being the case it was reasonable to suppose, wasn't it, that he wouldn't be in any hurry to come back?

The thought made her jump to her feet and try all her force on the door, but she only succeeded in whipping up the heat and the thump of her pulses. She thought of shouting, but the boys would probably be miles away by this time, and there was little use in trying to attract anybody else's attention. This spot was well away from the normal routes of activity.

Careful not to let the situation overwhelm her into a state of panic, Lee put on a wry smile and went back to her corner. She had heard of teachers being unpopular with their pupils, but this was ridiculous!

The humour died out of the situation as the minutes dragged by, and the air became more difficult to breathe. At one time she went to the front of the hut and stared through a crack to where her canvas bag was lying against the tree stump. How could she have been such an idiot as to drop it down there! She thought standing there gazing at it might help, but instead of alleviating her thirst, it only served to increase it.

If the sun hadn't relented in the afternoon and travelled on beyond her tiny prison Lee doubted if she would have been able to keep from passing out, but as the hut slid gradually into the cool shade, the heat of the interior subsided and the air began to circulate sluggishly.

Tired of sitting, she lay on her back, heedless of the dust on her dress. What was a little dirt compared to comfort? Comparative comfort anyway. About the same as sleeping on the floor, she thought, pulling her mouth down. It was difficult to smile, and not wishing to dwell on the subject of a painfully dry throat, and aching limbs, she tried to concentrate on other things.

The twins would be playing somewhere in that carefree abstract little world of theirs. They would probably have forgotten all about the predicament they had left her in, and would probably be expecting her to come along any time to collect them. As for Jeff, he had simply shut her up in a hut. In his mind the mechanics didn't come into it. Lee felt sure that he hadn't noticed that she had slipped her bag off, but even if he had, it wouldn't have made any difference. He wasn't of the age yet to realise that one needed sustenance to survive. He might even hope to leave her here indefinitely.

Lee shuddered. Thank goodness it didn't rest entirely with Jeff.

Just the same, as the knots and cracks darkened and the dim interior of the hut changed from a pale blur of light, to a dense black, she swallowed on a sandpaper throat. Alec wasn't due back at the house until some time tomorrow afternoon, and Fidele had gone with him.

Nick and the company men had gone sailing. There had been talk for days of revisiting Montage, and if they had stayed the night last time, they would probably do the same again.

Lee closed her eyes, not caring for the pictures her mind

was painting in the dark corners of the hut. It was going to be all right. Of course it was. One just didn't disappear without being missed. She didn't dare to dwell too long on the fact that the only ones who knew she *had* disappeared were three very small boys who were in no hurry to alter the situation.

Another thing that didn't bear thinking about, too, was what was going to happen in the morning when the sun rose, and the hut came once again in its path of blazing heat. . . .

It was the wooden floor boring into her head and her limbs crying out against it that woke Lee. How long she had slept she had no idea, but it was still pitch-black, and the smell of acrid sun-bleached wood and dust was overpowering. She rose and moved stiffly about the hut, blinking the tears away at the wretchedness of her position. How long would a night last in a place like this? Too long, she decided, resisting the temptation to throw herself sobbing against the door. It was doubtful if she would have made much more than a croak anyway, and walking about was becoming an effort.

She did try the door again though. It was still its old unyielding self. She sank down and rested her forehead against it. The wood still retained the heat of the sun, but its roughness was somehow soothing, and Lee turned her head from side to side wearily.

At first she thought the sound was the rasping of the wood against her skin, but when she lifted her head it was still there. Something like a rustling through the undergrowth. Afraid to breathe, she listened. The sound increased and as it grew nearer she heard something else.

Voices! Or at least one voice. It was abrupt to the point of being staccato and only faintly recognisable.

'So you came this way, and then what?' There was a pause and then a rough demand, 'I want to know, Jeff.' The words seemed to be coming from tight lips. Only their vibrant quality told her it was Nick. Jeff's voice sounded strangely high-pitched in contrast.

'I've told you it was only a joke. I was coming back. Really I was!'

'Coming back where? So help me, Jeff, if you don't ...'

Lee didn't wait to hear any more. She pushed to her feet and knocked weakly on the door. As the beam of the torch swung on to it she heard a sharp intake of breath and then Jeff was saying in tearful tones, 'We was going to let her out! Really we was!'

He sounded penitent right up to the moment when Nick flung open the door, and then at the sight of her swaying there his tones dropped petulantly and he went on, 'And anyway, she's a ... she ... and ...' with an adult air, 'she gets on my nerves!'

Lee realised that she must look something of a sight in the merciless beam of the torch. Her dress was grubby from the dust of the hut, and her arms and legs no better. What her face must look like with the day's perspiration and the tears, she didn't dare think about, but it was no use bemoaning the fact that it had to be Nick who should find her like this.

Putting on a wan smile, she said brightly, 'Hi!' and then forgot that there was a step down from the doorway. The torch beam spun crazily as Nick caught her. Even without its light she could see his searching gaze. As he held her close he said, presumably to Mike, 'You can't just dispense with a woman simply because she gets on your nerves!'

The moment seemed to last for ever, and then his mouth tightened back into its grim line. He turned his head in the darkness towards the nervous scuffing of feet and growled, 'I ought to beat the pants off you!'

The threat was enough to send Jeff bolting across the clearing. As the beam of the torch picked him out, disappearing through the foliage, Lee made to go after him, but Nick held her in an iron grip.

'Let him go,' he snapped.

'But it's dark and ..'

'He knows his way all right, and he probably prefers the dark to me at the moment.'

Seeing his thunderous look, Lee persisted, 'Yes, but *I* ought to ...'

She was held roughly.

'Stop worrying. He'll be back between the sheets before

you've learned to stand on your feet again. How long have you been cooped up in there?'

'Since about ten this morning, I think.'

He let out a low whistle between his teeth. 'It's a wonder you were able to walk out!'

Lee was beginning to feel it had all been worth it. She could feel the smoothness of his shirt beneath her cheek as she leaned against him. One hand was gently stroking her hair. She heard herself saying shyly, 'It wouldn't have been too bad if I'd taken some refreshments along.' She turned in his arms to point. 'I left my bag over there. Could I get a drink, please?'

Nick shone the torch towards the fallen tree and with an arm around her he moved towards it. As she looked in the direction that Jeff had gone he said mildly, 'He'll be okay. I posted a couple of men along the path. They'll see he gets back.' He put the torch out while he drew the flask from the bag, and thankfully Lee sank down on the log. After a while her eyes grew accustomed to the darkness. She could see slivers of deep indigo sky through the black silhouette of the palm fronds and a faint sprinkling of stars. Against their light she could make out Nick's bulk and even the gleam of the flask as he poured her a drink.

The orange juice tasted bitter and warm from its long sojourn in the sun, but to Lee it was heaven-sent. When she had got rid of the parched feeling in her mouth and throat she looked up to say, 'I thought you were going over to Montage.'

'We did,' Nick nodded non-committally.

Lee took another drink and asked, 'What happened? Between you and Jeff, I mean.'

'Very little.' Nick put up a foot on the log and leaned towards her. 'He was in bed when I got back. Blair and André were having trouble anchoring the boat. I came on ahead. It was fairly late. I gathered you were in your room, but something about the state of the house set me wondering.'

Lee smiled in the darkness, picturing three small boys revelling in the freedom of an empty house.

'As though a light hurricane had passed through?' she asked, twinkling.

'Something like that,' Nick nodded. 'When I couldn't find you I looked in on the boys, and Jeff looked pretty sick. I knew he had something on his mind.'

'Did he tell you what happened?' Lee asked.

'I dragged some of it out of him on the way here,' Nick said grimly, 'but he was cagey. He knew I'd warned him off this place.'

'I thought I was going to collect a lost ball,' Lee explained. 'When I got inside the hut the door closed and that was it.'

Nick inhaled slowly.

'It happened to Pete accidentally when we were up here one day. I suppose that's where they got the idea.' After a silence he added, 'I think Jeff was having second thoughts about leaving you here the night.'

'I'm glad to hear it,' Lee laughed softly. 'I wasn't looking forward to it one bit.'

'You can cut out the humour,' Nick snapped harshly. 'The idea of you being at the mercy of a seven-year-old kid doesn't strike me as funny.'

'He hasn't made a habit of it,' Lee said staunchly. 'And it's my fault if I can't handle him.'

She heard Nick's deep breath and then he was saying in soft, menacing tones, 'Maybe you should have let me know sooner.'

'Nick!' Lee looked up worriedly and put a hand on his arm. 'What are you going to do?'

With a tight grin he took her hand and drew her to her feet. 'Nothing except try a little straight talk,' he drawled. 'If he were yours ... or mine ... the position might be different.'

Coming up close to the muscular frame, Lee felt strangely breathless. For some reason Nick seemed to want to keep her gazing up at him, and it was with some difficulty that she turned in his arms to stammer, 'I expect Jeff's parents find him a handful at times.'

'No doubt,' Nick replied vibrantly, reaching for her bag. She noticed as they moved off that the torch stayed where it was on the ground.

'Feel up to making the trip back?' he asked, his arm about her. He must have seen her nod, for he went on in dry harsh tones, 'Let's hope the old boys will have turned in by this time. It's not going to look so good, me rolling up with another guy's wife.'

Lee looked up. 'Couldn't we go back along the beach?' she asked. 'It would take us longer and I could get rid of some of this ghastly grime.' As he continued to walk she pleaded, 'Please, Nick. I've got my swim-suit.'

'But I haven't got mine.' She sensed his mocking smile. 'And I may have to fish you out. You haven't eaten all day, remember?'

It was true, and the sandwiches would be a write-off by this time, but Lee said, blushing lightly in the darkness, 'The drink has worked wonders. I'll be perfectly all right.'

She stopped to make her point, and Nick looked down at her. After a pause he nodded slowly.

'It's not a bad idea. The house is bound to be in darkness by the time we get back.' He turned with her in the circle of his arm. 'We'll take the short cut across.'

The sea was a strip of black silk, smoothed taut under the night sky. Only its edges re-ruffled occasionally to display the odd lace wave. After the oven-like confines of the hut, Lee couldn't wait to sample its glistening coolness. She chose a rock some distance from where Nick had stretched out with a cigarette, and quickly stripped out of her grubby dress.

The white sand that stretched away in both directions was an eerie grey in the darkness of the night, but blissfully soft to her bare feet. She padded across it, pulling on her bathing cap and keeping her eyes trained on the sea. She swam around for some time, enjoying the soothing motion of the swell. The water was as buoyant as ever. Perhaps she had expected its permanent support, for when she returned to the beach her legs suddenly felt like grass stalks. The strip of sand, the silhouetted palm trees and the sky all started to wheel about her like a spinning propeller, and then she was being swung up roughly and Nick was growling, 'I ought to have my head examined, letting you swim when you can't even stand!'

The grip of his arms left Lee with little breath. She dropped a wet face against him and blinked back a weak tear. What a nuisance he must be finding her! First the trek to the hut and now this! Miserably she found her mind latching on to his words to Jeff. *You can't just dispense with a woman simply because she gets on your nerves.* Perhaps he meant she got on *his* nerves too?

Convinced that he was holding her only because he thought she couldn't walk, Lee pushed away from him and struggled down.

'I'm perfectly all right,' she gulped between tears. 'And I was going to see if the fruit in my bag was worth eating anyway.'

As she lowered to where he had dropped the bag on the sand Nick rasped, 'Save it. I'll go and get you something fresh.'

She saw the dark stain of sea-water on his shirt and slacks as he swung away. She sat staring ahead at the black drape of sea, feeling utterly dejected. Maybe it *was* because she hadn't eaten all day, but right now she felt she could have wept her own private ocean.

Nick was back within minutes. He was holding her towel and a small pineapple. As she pulled off her bathing cap slackly, he bent down and dropped the towel around her shoulders, then taking a small knife from his back pocket, he proceeded to trim and slice the pineapple deftly.

To Lee nothing had ever tasted better. The sweet juice trickling down her throat was like liquid life. She lay back, loving the solidness of the sand beneath her back, the velvety black nothingness of the sky above. Soon she would be fit to move on, but right now . . .

She must have sensed Nick's turn of head, for her eyes came down automatically from the stars to meet his.

'Feeling better?' he asked in deep-pitched tones.

'Considerably,' Lee smiled up, preferring not to analyse whether it was the pineapple or the soft words that had done the trick. She couldn't be sure, but she thought the dark head had lowered slightly as he said vibratingly, 'You could have had a shower and a meal back at the house. Why choose this way?'

Why indeed? Lee knew the reason, but it wouldn't do to let Nick know that she had simply wanted to prolong every moment with him. No sense in giving him another opportunity to reach for that mocking smile. As the shadowy tanned features came down breathlessly close she said hurriedly, 'It's just what you said. We couldn't very well go back to the house and let the company owners see us together. After all, there's Alec's job and...'

'And you wouldn't want to jeopardise *that*?' The low tones had suddenly taken on a sour note, but still the craggy face came down.

'Well, of course I wouldn't!' Lee babbled on. 'That's the whole idea, isn't it? Me pretending to be his wife and...'

'Pretending?' The sloping mouth curled slightly. 'That's for want of a better word, I take it?'

'What do you mean?' Lee stared up, trying to read something in the chiselled face above hers.

The glinting grey gaze held hers, as he said slowly, spelling out the words, 'I mean the midnight meetings in your room, the friendly tussles on the veranda and the partnership in a tent you two nearly ended up with.'

Lee could do nothing but fight back the colour rushing to her cheeks, and Nick leaned in to finish with a derisive twist to his mouth, 'I'm just wondering how far you're willing to go, to make this man and wife thing look convincing?'

His sneering implication sent a bolt of hot anger shooting through Lee. It brought her hand up, and sent it swinging on its way towards that granite jaw. She was looking forward to bringing it down with the greatest satisfaction when it was stopped in mid-air.

Nick's fingers gripped her wrist and for an eternity she lay there, nursing her fury in a heaving bosom and fixing her smouldering gaze squarely on the glinting grey one above.

When it seemed that she would be held like this for ever, Nick's frame suddenly relaxed. He drawled down at her with a ghost of a smile, 'All right, I only wanted to know.'

Though his hand had slackened from her wrist he made no effort to let go, and after the tumult of the last few moments Lee could only gaze up with palpitating heart. She felt transfixed by something she couldn't quite fathom now, in Nick's gaze. The steely glints were fading behind a kind of charcoal darkening that . . .

It was his sudden turning away that brought her to her senses. As he reached jerkily for a cigarette she heard him growl, 'For crying out loud! Go and get dressed.'

Lee hurried off, feeling the old dejection envelop her at his irritated tones. No need to ask now if he was finding her a nuisance.

CHAPTER NINE

AFTER the night of the hut incident, Lee took care to keep a comfortable distance between herself and Nick. She had a feeling she had given far too much away in those moments on the beach, and needed time to live it down. The men were spending a lot more time around the house these days, but with a little skill she found she need hardly bump into him at all.

Of course, avoiding Nick threw her more into Alec's company, but this only added lustre to the part she was playing as his wife, and anyway, nothing could be as trying as finding herself caught alone with the man who had brought her breath fluttering to her throat that night on the beach.

What had taken place between Nick and Jeff concerning the hut business she never found out, but her work these days with the seven-year-old was considerably easier. He fell in uncomplainingly with her plans, though he never lost the tightness about his mouth in doing so.

With the twins making frequent references to their parents in their conversation, and a subdued Jeff on her hands, Lee found herself looking ahead to the arrival of the mailboat. Bruce Pasmore had promised to try to make every sailing, so no doubt there would be news for the boys. Remembering their delight last time, Lee couldn't wait to cheer them up again, but though she counted the days, something happened when the mailboat arrived to make her forget completely the letter she had been waiting for.

Usually when a boat arrived at Half-Moon Island everyone turned out to greet it, but for once the boys were far too interested in the figure that Nick was carving to tear themselves away, and Lee was engaged in dressing a small cut on Alec's wrist. The wound was little more than a scratch, but he had asked Lee to attend to it, and he stood over her smiling now, as she turned the bandage.

Further along the veranda the sound of Nick chipping at the piece of wood speeded up slightly. His tones as he told the boys to stand back were somewhat abrupt.

Lee tied a knot in the bandage, and lowered her hands with a smile, but Alec kept the swathed wrist up and gazed at it happily.

'Finished so soon? I'm beginning to wish I'd broken it now,' he grinned, turning the sky-blue gaze down her way.

'I wouldn't know the first thing to do if you had,' Lee laughed lightly.

Before she knew what was happening, the bandaged wrist had turned about her waist and Alec was drawing her close to murmur throatily, 'You'd think of something for *me*, though, wouldn't you?'

There was a commotion along the road. Blair and André had rushed off to meet the boat like a couple of schoolboys. They were back now, laughing and calling out heartily, 'You boys are going to kick yourselves when you see what we found along with the mail!'

Lee was curious. As the steps grew nearer she hoped that Alec would slacken his hold on her, but sure of himself these days, he continued to hold her in close embrace, letting his eyes roam her face, and listening with absent smile to the approaching voices. Only a name dropped lightly in the air made his head turn somewhat jerkily, and it was then that Lee saw a slim dark-eyed girl staring up at the veranda.

'Philippa, my girl, meet Mr. and Mrs. Hayward.' Blair was happily ushering the girl forward. 'These two lovebirds run the plantation.' He tilted a fly-away eyebrow over Alec's ardent embrace and added roguishly, 'Don't ask me how!'

The girl seemed to lose what little colour she had at Blair's words. She stepped back, stumbling as she went and stammering jerkily, 'I'm sorry, I think I've made a mistake ... I must have got the wrong island.'

Lee stood transfixed. She knew now that this was Alec's Philippa! She had plucked up the courage to come and meet him on his own ground, and this was what she had found. No wonder she looked as though she had just been struck a sharp blow. What must it feel like to have the man you were going to marry introduced as someone else's husband?

She waited for Alec to do something and then ralised with an ice-cold tremor that his arm about her waist had slackened not at all. As far as she could tell he was smiling straight ahead. Unable to believe that he could just stand there, Lee stepped forward to put up a hand.

'Please . . .'

But the girl had already turned.

Nick, who had left the boys chattering over the wooden figure at the end of the veranda, stood by the steps. He must have caught something of Lee's stricken feelings, for after a glance in her direction he stepped down to say evenly, 'I'll see you back to the boat.'

The girl shook her lowered head.

'No, really, I'll be all right.' Without raising her eyes she stumbled back to the road and disappeared round the bend.

'Well!' Blair looked at his partner with a puzzled smile. 'I reckon that was the shortest visit on record.'

Alec shrugged and strolled into the house, and Nick, lowering a quick glance over Lee, went back to the boys along the veranda. Lee was sorely tempted to go after Alec and give him a piece of her mind, but she held on to herself. The subject of Philippa was, after all, his own affair.

Just the same, the thought of the unhappy girl being allowed to leave without any form of explanation, surreptitiously or otherwise, kept her fuming for the rest of the day.

When the gentle knock came on her door late that night, she was only too ready to have it out with Alec. Though she had been on the point of blowing out the light and stepping into bed, she didn't hesitate in turning the key in the lock. Only for the fraction of a second as Alec flickered a slightly darker blue gaze over her did she wish that she had thought to slip into something less revealing than the flimsy negligée, and then she was seeing Philippa stumbling along the road, and her mind swung straight into the business of letting Alec know what she thought of him.

As he closed the door she faced him with folded arms to snap, 'I find it positively sickening, the lengths you're willing to go to hang on to this wretched job of yours!'

Alec shrugged. 'Philippa, you mean?' With an introspective smile he strolled indolently into the room and added, 'She'll laugh when I tell her.'

'I can assure you that wouldn't be *my* reaction,' Lee said, breathing quickly.

Alec turned to rest his gaze on her and murmured with an absent grin, 'She'll get over it. She must have been coming round to my way of thinking and decided to come out and take a look at the place.'

'And what a reception she got!' Lee retorted.

Alec sighed lightly and moved closer.

'It was rotten luck, wasn't it?'

As he came to stand over her Lee raised a furious gaze. 'Is that all you can say?' she asked witheringly.

'Well, what *can* I say?' He dropped an arm about her with a light, incredulous laugh. 'If I gave the game away now, she wouldn't have an island to come to.'

'Is it *that* important?' Lee asked scathingly.

'It is to me,' Alec replied with an unabashed grin. 'I don't give up this way of life easily.' He squeezed her rigid shoulders, saying softly, 'Relax. I'll make it up to her.'

Lee looked up, unable to believe that he could brush it aside so lightly. She saw the dark blue gaze trailing across her throat and as it came upwards to meet her eyes he said hoarsely, 'You make quite a picture when you're angry, Lee.' Before she knew what was happening he had brought his mouth down on her slightly parted lips, and she was being held in a suffocating embrace.

'For heaven's sake, Alec!' She tore herself free, knocking a chair sideways in the struggle. 'We were talking about Philippa. And I think you told me once that you two are practically engaged.'

'So we are,' Alec laughed shakily, 'and we'll probably get married and live happy ever after, but...'

'But what?' Lee asked scorchingly.

'Well,' Alec lifted his shoulders, looming up close again, 'you're here now. You've been around for sometime, playing along for the benefit of the others, I've often thought...' she saw his smiling glance lower towards his ring on her finger, and then flicker pointedly over her low-cut negligée '...it was a pity to waste such a situation.'

Lee felt her face drain of colour. In words barely audible she said, 'Alec, you'd better leave now before I throw something.'

'Oh, come on, Lee. This is the twentieth century. The days of the prudish schoolteacher went out with...'

In her struggle to stay clear of Alec's descending lips Lee strained wildly in his grasp. In the commotion of scraping furniture and shaking ornaments, neither heard the door from the veranda open.

It was the voice, icily sarcastic, that brought things to a halt.

'Fun and games!'

Lee turned to see Nick's bulk filling the doorway. His face was a pale mask of immobility, his glance slightly flame-lit as it flickered for a second over her lightly clad appearance, and then swung with narrowed accuracy on to Alec's flushed features.

Alec lowered his hands from Lee's shoulders and brushed one erratically through his hair.

'Nothing that concerns you, Reynolds,' he said with a drawn grin. 'Just a friendly husband-and-wife...' As he petered off into an embarrassed silence Nick lifted a dark eyebrow to query laconically, 'Without a licence?'

He lowered his glance distastefully and strode into the room, and in the centre he turned and clipped, 'You can skip the pat lines, Hayward. I've known for some time about the pseudo-marriage.' As Alec paled visibly Nick went over to whip the key from the connecting door. 'How you hang on to your job is your own affair,' he drawled, and then, pulling the door open, pointedly added, 'And I think from now on we'll see that it stays that way.'

After a slight pause Alec moved across the room with his usual indolent air. 'It's okay by me,' he shrugged. He turned to look back at Lee and then sent his gaze through the open door to his own room. As he came level with Nick he said with a crooked smile, 'Don't tell me you'd have played it any different if you'd been in my shoes.'

Nick's features tightened, leaving only a small muscle flexing rapidly in his jaw. Meeting the derisive blue gaze, he said with menacing calm, 'Move!'

'Just as you say, old man,' Alec shrugged again, but stepped quickly into his own room. He could barely have got through before the door was slammed at his back. Nick swung the key in the lock and then dropped it unceremoniously into his pocket.

Lee had been watching the scene rigid and white-faced, but the slamming of the door snapped the tension that had been holding her in one piece. Crumpling, she came to rest against the open door of the veranda.

She looked up quickly as a pair of hands dropped roughly on her shoulders. Nick's face as he swung her round was drawn and working. She saw his sneering glance lower over the awry fastening on her negligée as he rasped, 'For a girl who wants to keep things platonic, I'd say you were pushing your luck!'

Straining in his grasp, Lee retorted angrily, 'Don't *you* start!'

'Why?' The steely fingers gripped her painfully. 'Have you had enough entertainment for one evening?'

· She tore away from the blaze of his gaze, and swayed into the centre of the room. Hands trembling over her dishevelled appearance, she jerked, 'You can think what you like!'

Through the shine of her tears she could see him watching her, and then it seemed that the huge frame slackened, and he was moving into the room.

He went to where her heavy dressing gown was hanging in the wardrobe and draping it round her shoulders he asked quietly, 'What happened?'

The action was enough to send her searching for a chair, but arming herself against his sudden gentleness, she said in high-pitched tones, 'Don't tell me I'm going to be allowed a defence!'

'You can cut out the witty remarks.' As she sank down,

he came over to drape himself along the arm of her chair and repeated forcefully, 'What happened?'

'Hardly anything at all,' she said with a thin smile, meeting his gaze. 'Alec asked to come in here, and I thought it would be as good a time as any to have it out with him over Philippa. He let her go off without any explanation and...' She paused and then went on to explain, 'The girl who came here today. She and Alec are practically engaged.'

Nick nodded. 'I gathered it was something like that.'

In the silence Lee shrugged and looking down at her hands said, 'That's all. We'd just about concluded the argument when you came in.' Nick reached for cigarettes and drawing on one, he rose and paced for several minutes, then as though the thought had just occurred to him he thrust a hand into his shirt pocket.

'Incidentally, you left this in with the company mail.' He handed her an envelope, and taking a quick breath she gasped, 'Good heavens! The Pasmores' letter! I'd forgotten all about it.'

She ripped the flap and found folded pages for the boys, and one with her own name on it. She read the contents raising a ponderous eyebrow as she went.

'Good news?' Nick asked lazily.

'I'm not sure,' Lee said absently, casting her eyes slowly over the written page. 'The boys' parents think their mixing with other children might help to pass the time. They say it might be a good idea to put them in at a day school on the main island.'

Nick looked for an ashtray, toured round and finally flung his cigarette outside to reply briskly, 'So do I. You'd better start packing.'

Lee blinked up. 'But I haven't even had time to think about it yet,' she said in dazed tones.

'Okay. You've got five minutes.' Nick swung her cases on to the bed. 'Then fill these. We're leaving in the morning. I'll get on to the radio-phone right now for a boat.'

Watching him trance-like, Lee said faintly, 'But I can't! ... Wh ... what about ...'

'Forget the others,' he snapped. 'You're simply doing what you've been asked to do, taking the boys to school.

The story will stand up to your leaving the island for a while.'

As he turned towards the door Lee rose slowly to say, 'But...' She hesitated as he swung round and then blurted querulously, 'You said "we". Did you mean...'

He lifted his shoulders and thrust his hands in pockets to say lazily, 'I'm pretty familiar with the island of Mahé. You'll need fixing up with accommodation. I might be able to give you a few tips.' For a long moment he let his gaze rest on her and then turning briskly out of the door he clipped, 'Don't forget the packing.'

Later, the wardrobe and drawers empty and her cases bulging, Lee lay gazing at the stars and musing on this sudden turn of events. To comply with the Pasmores' wishes she and the boys were about to sample life on the island of Mahé.

Had she been obliged to undertake alone the task of re-housing herself and the children in so strange a part of the world she might have viewed the situation with certain nervous misgivings. As it was she had one small happiness to cradle. Nick had offered to accompany her.

CHAPTER TEN

IT was an odd turn-out that waved them off the next morning—Alec unshaven and smiling lopsidedly, and Fidele still clutching his night wear about him. André and Blair, unkempt but jovial as ever, waded out to push the pirogue through the waves, and let it be known that they wouldn't let Alec get bored, while the plantation workers stood along the beach, tossing their arms with bleary-eyed smiles.

Lee waved and the boys waved, and the pirogue passed through the opening in the necklace of reef and came to rest against the waiting schooner. As the steps were lowered, Nick helped her up and then the chattering boys, and saw to the loading of the luggage.

Within minutes the water was swirling into action, and the waving men became faint smudges in the distance. Lee watched the island grow smaller with mixed feelings. Though her stay there had been anything but perfect there were some moments she would always want to remember. As she gazed mistily into the distance Nick came down close to her at the rail. He followed her gaze and then commented, 'We should be pulling into Mahé about noon. In the meantime how about some breakfast?'

With the twins skipping at her side and Jeff striding manfully ahead, they made their way along the deck. The boat must have been diverted on its route from other islands, as there were several passengers on board. Their admiring glances over her and the boys and the big man at her side brought a tinge of colour to Lee's cheeks, but Nick smiled, unconcerned, and guided her within the circle of his arm to the steps below.

The five hours passed all too quickly for her. True, it was a small boat with little to do except stroll or look at the view, but blissfully close to Nick, she could have gone on for ever. She had secret hopes of the skipper missing his way and having to sail on indefinitely, but all too soon the island of Mahé was rising up in the distance. In no time at all they were able to distinguish its craggy lines against the background of blue.

There was a huge white liner lying about a mile out from the island, and judging by the general scurry of small boats around her, she was about to sail.

The boys jumped around excitedly, but Lee viewed their arrival as an interruption of something that had been slightly intoxicating. As Nick turned an arm about her waist and drew her gently against him, she wondered with a tiny glow if his thoughts were anything like her own.

The schooner anchored not far out from a long pier and a launch came out to take the passengers off. With the boys around her, and Nick behind, Lee gazed ahead as they prepared to land at Port Victoria.

A tall green mountain gleaming in the sun, with a halo of rainbow-shot clouds, Mahé was breathtaking. Clusters of red and white houses with corrugated iron roofs nestled among palm trees, and luxurious greenery; other tiny abodes hung a thousand feet or more, up in the hills.

'Like it?' Nick said close to her ear. In her delight at the view she turned quickly and almost brushed her cheek against his lips. On a light laugh she exclaimed, 'It's unbelievable!'

'But real.' He grinned, seemingly in no hurry to pull up to his own height. Along the pier, white-clad islanders strolled, and small cars nosed their way in between. The launch pulled in near a shallow flight of steps, and the passengers began to file out. With the boys leading the way, Lee floated dreamily in their wake. The happiness of the last few moments had left a soft smile playing about her lips. She felt oblivious to everything but Nick's presence, sensed him coming up behind as they stepped on to the pier, and then he had moved out and a fair-haired woman stepped forward to throw slender arms around his neck.

'Nick! It's wonderful to see you! I got your message.'

Lee's smile quivered and became difficult to hold in place, as she saw exquisitely shaped lips brush his cheek.

The slender form in coffee silk was held in the circle of tanned muscular arms, and then Nick drew away with a grin and drawled, 'Lee, meet Janine Feuillère. She runs a tea estate just outside Victoria.'

The woman turned a quizzical gaze over Lee and murmured, 'I'm very pleased to meet you.'

She spoke with an attractive husky accent, and Lee thought she had never seen a lovelier pair of dark-fringed eyes. As the slender tapered fingers rested on Nick's arm he added, looking down at them, 'Janine's an old friend.'

'Friend?' A silken eyebrow arched playfully over him as she pouted. 'A long time now he wriggle on hook, but one day!—You see!'

Feeling her smile twisting into a grimace, Lee bent to usher the boys in a group. She wanted to run away and die. How could she have been such a fool as to think that Nick would be even remotely interested in *her*? Those gay nights in Mombasa. The times she had seen him in the midst of beautiful women. She might have known he'd have one of his own.

The suitcases that she had packed in a frenzy this morning for the boys were being dumped down along with her own and Nick's. Raising her head, the smile once again stitched into place, Lee looked expectantly towards the island. There was that at least, and the boys to think of and their schooling, thank heaven.

Nick must have been explaining something of the situation to the woman standing close to him, for she nodded a cool smile over the four of them to say, 'Well, they're welcome at Beauvais.' But Nick was shaking his head.

'Thanks, Janine,' he drawled, 'but the school I have in mind is over at Tailliez. I'd better fix something up where Lee can be on hand.'

And where she'll be well away from Janine, Lee said to herself, hating her own bitter thoughts, but unable to stop thinking them just the same. On a map of Mahé she had seen that Tailliez was well down the coast from Victoria.

Janine was smiling up again at Nick.

'You can take my car,' she offered. 'I'll be in town for most of the day.' She turned an arm through his to say huskily, 'You'll be staying at Beauvais, of course, Nick?'

At his smiling assent, the thick fringed lashes dropped and lifted sweepingly over the tilted gaze. Lee turned quickly away from the pleasurable light she saw reflected there.

Dark-skinned islanders were milling around asking to carry passengers' luggage, and Nick paid two to dispatch the small pile to the end of the pier. Lee only wished she could have acknowledged with feeling the wide split smile of the straw-hatted boy who bent to swing up her bags.

The uniformed Customs officials were almost as glad to see Nick as Janine had been, Lee thought wryly, noticing the smiles and affable conversation. Janine stood by him, letting a tinkle of laughter ring out occasionally at the men's jokes.

To Lee the five minutes since landing from the boat were the longest she had ever known, but at last they were walking to Janine's car along the road. It was a small model, though there was ample space in the boot. Lee noticed that Nick stowed all the luggage but his own.

She murmured her polite thanks to the other woman and went to where the door was being held for her. Once inside she found her shoulder crammed against Nick's. The boys were packed wriggle-proof on the back seat. Janine was waving and supervising the removal of Nick's luggage at the same time. He nodded a smile across to her and then starting the car, swung off along the road.

They drove through the outskirts of Victoria, past wooden houses with rickety wooden porches. These soon gave way to a road winding between huge granite boulders interspersed with leafy palms.

With all the windows of the car open to cool a rather enervating day, Lee had one or two misgivings at leaving the boys alone on the back seat, but the occasional glance round told her they were too concerned with the view to think about what mischief they could get up to.

For her the scenery was misted by her own unhappiness. There might have been gentle mountain slopes with blue seas and beautiful bays dotted with jewelled islands, but these were sights to be enjoyed by people who knew what it was to have what they wanted in life. People like Janine who were lucky enough to have someone like Nick.

Desolately Lee turned her eyes around the view and came up briefly against Nick's gaze. She didn't miss the slight tightening of his mouth, nor the impatient flick of his hand on the wheel as he turned his eyes to the front again.

Lee swallowed back the ache in her throat. Did he have to make it so obvious that he couldn't wait to get back to Janine? Had she had the strength or even cared, she would have asked Nick to stop the car there and then, but disillusionment had brought with it a state of apathy, and she could only sit and gaze dejectedly at the ribbon of road ahead.

The mood continued through the afternoon as Nick went ahead with plans to settle her and the boys in at Tailliez. They stopped for a meal at a beach hotel, a series of thatched huts beneath coconut palms, and while Lee was helping the twins decide whether or not they liked a species of fish on their plate, Nick went off to talk to the owner. He came back later followed by a big thick-set woman with a wide smile. She nodded at what he was saying and then went trudging off along the beach.

Back in the car, Nick drove along the road for a few minutes to a similar setting as the hotel except that there was just one thatched hut beneath the trees. It was set in a strip of lawned garden with a small pebbled wall surrounding it. There was a gate leading up to the door at the side of the hut, a small veranda at the front and a gate set in the wall at the bottom of the garden leading on to the beach. The rooms of the beach cottage were small with cool stone floors, latanier mats and what looked like the island's own furniture, hand-made and solid.

Lee met the big smiling woman again, who was introduced as Angelina. She had donned an apron and was bustling happily around the whitewashed kitchen.

The position of their accommodation couldn't have been better, Lee had to admit, for the school, a surprisingly solid-looking structure compared to all the other buildings she had seen on Mahé, was little more than a ten-minute walk through the palms, and along the road to a small settlement just around the curve.

Walking through the bricked building, Lee experienced a tiny jolt of nostalgia. Schools were schools, be they set on the corner of a village lane or beneath the palms in the Indian Ocean. Nick's interview with the headmistress, when they found her out at the back of the school, was brief but pleasant. Lee never found out what was said because all the children, from eight-year-olds down to some possibly as young as three, were careering about the clearing, noisily airing their lungs. Later she watched as Jeff and the twins moved shyly forward to merge in with the general mêlée.

Nick took her arm and led her away, but before they had gone far through the trees, she heard herself commenting coldly, 'There can't be much more of the afternoon session to go. It was hardly worth leaving them.'

'No time like the present for getting the boys into the swing of things,' Nick said pleasantly. He turned a glance over his shoulder. 'They look okay to me.'

Following his gaze, Lee had to admit that they did. Jeff had gone swaggering off with some boys bigger than himself, and the twins had dropped down to watch with fascination some coloured chips being hammered lustily into place by a heavyweight toddler. None of the three had noticed that she and Nick were leaving.

As they walked, Lee felt the dejection envelop her. Everything was set now for her to take up her routine with the boys, and the cottage and the school. Nick had arranged it all smoothly and competently. Now he could leave. He seemed in no hurry. With his hand on her elbow he pointed out a small stream trickling through a tunnel of breadfruit trees at the roadside, a tall bird with a ribbon-like tail just about to take off.

Back at the cottage, Angelina had set a tray of white china and a teapot on the veranda. Lee poured, feeling Nick watching her every move. She sat down to sip silently from her cup, gazing to where the shimmering blue waves fell over on to the lip of white beach.

After a while Nick said lazily, 'Reckon you've got every thing you want?'

'Everything, thank you,' Lee said evenly.

'Some of the Government officials' offspring go to the school up the road,' he pointed out. 'I thought they'd be company for Jeff and the twins.'

'I expect they will be,' Lee nodded.

He cast a glance towards the sound of singing at the back of the house. 'Angelina has just come back from looking after a group of English ornithologists and their wives over at Frigate Island. She's well schooled to your way of life.'

'I can see she is.' Lee passed a small smile over the tray of white china.

Nick seemed intent on making conversation. After several seconds had elapsed he said, 'There's plenty of books inside if you find you've got too much time on your hands.'

Something *you're* not going to have in the future, Lee thought, dragging her eyes away from the sea, and gazing down bleakly into her cup. She was surprised to feel both it and the saucer being prised out of her hands. They landed on the table with a slight clap, and Nick was towering over her to clip, 'Shall we take a stroll?'

A stroll? Lee rose reluctantly. Why didn't he just go, instead of trying to be polite? They walked out of the gate at the bottom of the garden and along the beach to where a rocky inlet cradled the water in clear still pools. Lee gazed down at the jewelled fish mechanically.

She heard Nick say evenly, 'Lost your tongue?' And then when she didn't reply he swung her round to snap, 'What's eating you, anyway? You've been looking like a sick pup ever since we left the boat!'

Lee swallowed back her misery, hating Nick for what he could do to her, and loathing herself for not being able to hide it.

'Well, *you* wouldn't know,' she retorted, trying to turn away, but Nick held her roughly and as his narrowed gaze searched her face, Lee floundered. Afraid that she had said too much, she forced herself to meet his gaze coolly and lied, 'If you want to know, it's all this being carried about. You may be used to managing everyone else's affairs, Nick, but I prefer to do things for myself.'

He dropped his hands abruptly and thrusting them into his pockets strolled around her to sneer, 'Are you sure that's *all* it is? I thought perhaps you were wishing I'd left you with Hayward.'

Alec was the furthest thing from her mind at this moment, but the thought of Nick hurrying off to Janine made her flash back, 'Perhaps I am!'

She wasn't prepared for his sudden step forward. Trembling, she saw the taut tanned features drain slightly of colour. Blazing grey eyes held hers for a moment, then he swung on his heel, and strode off towards the car.

Lee stood where she was, gazing out to sea and drawing a quivering breath. Well, that was that. Nick had gone, and in a few minutes she would have to go and pick up the boys. Pick them up today, and take them back tomorrow. Life from now on was as simple as that.

Blinking back the tears, she turned towards the house. Was it only a few hours ago that she had foolishly imagined there was something for her in Nick's smile? Thank heavens she hadn't made a complete fool of herself by letting him know. He would probably have nursed his amusement all the way to Janine's.

A big figure staggering up the beach from the other direction turned out to be Angelina, with what looked like her bed and belongings gripped in her arms. As Lee opened the gate, the dark-skinned face split into a huge white smile, and in those light tones that didn't seem to go at all with the big frame she said, 'Always I go back to hotel for night, but M'sieur would like me to sleep here.' With that liquid rolling glance that reminded Lee a lot of Fidele, she strutted up the path to say cheerily, 'I take back room.'

Lee made her way through the palms and up the road to the school. The boys were agog with what they had done in the past hour, and for once Jeff chattered as much as his brothers. Looking at the three sets of animated features, Lee realised that something good had come from the move to Mahé. Well, what had she expected? Determinedly she told herself that her job was with the boys, and it was up to her to see that they remained in a contented state

521

Though the boys settled happily into their new environment, the days at Tailliez for Lee dragged heavily by. There was nothing to do in the house, so she busied herself washing and mending the boys' clothes and delivering the threesome to school as spruce as new pins each day. But though they came home blissfully dusty and in pieces again in the afternoon, the work wasn't enough to keep her mind off Nick and the woman he had gone to.

She could still see the slender form in coffee silk held close in Nick's arms, the petal-pink lips brushing his cheek. She pictured them now, standing together talking somewhere with friends; accepted as a couple, as they had been by the Customs men at the pier.

Towards the end of the week the pictures were as vivid as ever, but given a couple of years, Lee told herself wryly, they might start to dim at the edges.

The boys had taken to splashing in the pools after school, and one afternoon just before tea, Lee was gathering the towels they had left scattered over the rocks. She could hear the shouts as Jeff and the twins rolled in the garden. Her only thoughts as she turned back, sandals in hand, were whether they should eat indoors or out. Raising her head at the gate, her eyes were drawn to another figure crouched near the twins on the lawn. It stretched as she entered, and in spite of her ragged attempts to forget Nick, Lee found herself soaking up the picture he made, big and tanned and casually attired in lightweight wool shirt and slacks. The lean face looked slightly more lined, but the smile was as white as ever, if a little taut.

In her eagerness to take the sight of him in, Lee hadn't noticed that she herself was being held in an absorbing gaze. Then she saw the grey eyes drop over her pink cotton dress, and down towards her bare feet as he drawled, 'Catch any fish?'

'I wasn't fishing,' Lee returned coolly, wondering where he had left Janine. As the twins started to wind themselves laughingly around Nick's legs he said, tousling their heads, 'Thought I'd drop in and have a look at the brood.'

'Help yourself,' Lee smiled thinly, and went indoors. She put a bowl of cool water on the stone floor and rinsing the grit from her feet, dried them off ready to slip back into the sandals. She was just on the point of doing them up when a shadow darkened the doorway. Before she could anticipate the move Nick had dropped down to casually fasten the buckles.

Carefully averting her gaze from the dark head, Lee waited until he had finished, then rose quickly. She busied herself removing the bowl and then the towel, and in between trips asked pointedly, 'How's Janine?'

'Blooming.' Nick gave her a sloping smile. It twisted slightly as he asked, 'Still pining for Hayward?'

Lee swung away and made the task of hanging the towel back on its hook last as long as possible. When she turned she was alone again, and a few seconds later she heard a car engine start.

There was no time to linger over the ache growing inside her, for Angelina came in at that moment with letters for her and the boys. Lee had sent the address of the hotel to the Pasmores on that first day and already here were replies.

With the attractions of an improved mail service she found herself catching up on long-overdue letters. Besides her weekly report to the boys' parents, she wrote to Mr. and Mrs. Deighton in Mombasa and Grace. Poor Grace, who must have wondered what had become of her after all this time.

It was taking the letters down to the mail bag at the hotel that led to the widening of Lee's horizons in Mahé. She met the manageress, Mrs. Baumann, a portly, genial lady who spent her time singing the praises of the islands, though heaven knew they needed none, and arming guests with brochures and island data. It occurred to Lee after one of her visits that apart from the civilised amenities of a flying boat mail service, and schools, Mahé had much to recommend it for the boys' stay. She decided to make the most of out of school hours from now on by organising various outings.

Of course there was always the other reason to be admitted too, that she needed something to take her mind off the all-consuming unhappiness that dogged her, but at least she would be doing her job thoroughly this time—entertaining and perhaps educating the boys at the same time.

Whether it was an education to sit in a pirogue beyond the coral reef and watch five men battle to land what she was told was a manta, she couldn't have said, but there was no doubt about the entertainment. Jeff and the twins goggled along with the other spectators, as the fish, a great slab of grey with bat-like wings that stretched almost the length of the boat, hung half in the water and half out.

One day they went in a Government launch to a neighbouring island, where rare birds hid themselves away at the sound of a footstep and exotic plants spread thick under canopies of pandanus. On another island there were flying foxes with bright orange tufts of hair, and giant land tortoises snoozing under the takamaka trees.

Lee never tired of the Seychelles' magic scent—wood smoke and drying copra and the sweet smell of cinnamon blending with the salt air.

They saw the museum at the shore end of the Long Pier in Victoria and the town itself, with its main streets of wooden buildings and shops set back under railed verandas. The excursions into Victoria became a popular pastime. The twins were intrigued by the rickety buses, with patched sailcloth-covered seats, and fascinated by the silver-painted clock in the square, which strikes the hour twice, for the benefit of those who didn't hear it the first time.

Lee found the trips into town useful for buying her own oddments of shopping, and one day she hit on the luxury of hiring a barber's services to cut the boys' hair. It might have been a regular fortnightly occasion if she hadn't seen Nick walking with Janine while she was waiting for the boys.

They were well up on the other side of the road, walking along the wooden platform that was raised in front of a row of offices, but there was no mistaking those wide shoulders, or Janine's slender shape in pastel blue at his side. With Nick's hand on her elbow they turned into one of the doors along the row and disappeared.

That was the end of trips into town for Lee. Any items

she wanted after that she bought at the hotel. Her excursions with the boys she made sure touched no part of Victoria, and the excitement for these eventually petered out. As it became more and more difficult to coax them away from the rock pools along the beach, Lee had to admit that though she might need a round of constant changing scenery to ease her heartache, the boys were perfectly content to stay around the house.

Another reason perhaps for their sudden love of the local life was the fact that they could run down to the hotel at all hours of the day and enquire about the mail. The twins had a birthday coming up and there were high hopes of parcels arriving. To Lee, the special day had always been somewhere mistily in the distance, now with it looming up she found herself enjoying the preparations that had to be made.

She had promised a party for half a dozen of the boys' closest friends at school, and there was bound to be a run on food and sweetmeats for the occasion. Angelina was queen in the kitchen, but Lee was allowed to cut out the biscuits, and decorate the paper band for the cake.

Mrs. Baumann sent a long trestle table up from the hotel and two big shady umbrellas. On the afternoon of the birthday, the table was draped with a huge white cloth, and with Angelina's cake in the middle, and the rest of the space packed with sandwiches and biscuits and various delicacies concocted from local fruit, the garden looked very festive.

To comply with the occasion Lee changed into a pencil-slim sleeveless silk dress in emerald green and touched a dab of lilac skin perfume behind her ears.

The parcels from parents and relatives had duly arrived and the twins spent the first half hour frenziedly tearing away the brown paper, watched by seven pairs of covetous eyes.

At her wits' end what to get for a couple of six-year-old boys from the limited display of goods in the shops, Lee had settled for two of the big floppy straw hats that the islanders made themselves, then on second thoughts she had purchased three. The boys with their corn thatches and scantily clad suntanned bodies looked like young Huckleberry Finns strutting around the garden.

The headmistress paid a call during the afternoon, and later on Mrs. Baumann and her husband. It was while Lee was talking to the couple about the manageress's speciality, hot doughnuts, that she heard a car pull up along the road. Though her heart missed a beat at the sight of Nick coming through the trees, she continued to gossip as though the sight of the nylon-shirted muscular frame was a regular occurrence about the place. Mrs. Baumann drew him into the chatter for a while and then with a brief smile he moved down to where the twins were trying to play with all their presents at once.

Lee was intrigued to know what was in the long boxes under his arm, but she didn't hang around to find out. As soon as the Baumanns had drifted off, she retreated to the house and stayed there sorting out the chaos in the kitchen, and being on hand to serve drinks to the thirsty young guests.

Eventually the garden quietened down as one by one the children left for home. Angelina cleared the trestle table and hoisted it into the arms of the waiting men, then trudged off beside them with an umbrella under each arm.

Lee cleared up the paper that had got scattered around the rooms, then realised that there was no sound of the boys playing anywhere. The sky was taking on a tinge of purple, and as the nights dropped suddenly out here in the tropics, she hurried outside to see where they had got to. She had only just stepped out of the door leading on to the veranda when she was met by a figure coming in. Because she was hurrying it was impossible to avoid Nick. It was debatable whether he had time to sidestep, but he made no effort to. As she brushed against him, he caught her close, and held her with a trace of the old mocking smile playing about his lips.

Gazing up, Lee hoped the sweet aching pleasure of his nearness didn't show in her eyes. Hidden too, she hoped, was the torment she endured wondering how many times he had held Janine like this. She said as levelly as she could, 'I was just going to get the boys in for bed.'

Nick nodded, lowering his arms slowly. 'They're down at the rocks.' And then as she made to move past him he stopped her. 'I'll go.'

Watching him walk out of the gate, Lee told herself firmly that he had only come because of the twins' birthday. They had been talking about it for weeks, so obviously he had been prepared. As the shadowy shapes approached along the beach, she got some idea of what Nick had brought in the boxes, and when the boys stepped up proudly on to the veranda she smiled.

'Fishing rods! Now why didn't I think of that?'

Nick grinned down at the flushed, upturned faces. 'Takes a man to know a man's mind, eh, fellers?'

Jeff and the boys romped off inside, and Lee followed them with her eyes thoughtfully.

'Something wrong?' Nick asked.

'No.' Lee shook her head slowly. 'Only ... well, did you bring anything for Jeff?'

'No.' Nick arrowed an eyebrow. 'It's not his birthday, is it?'

'No, it isn't,' Lee shrugged. 'But ... well, I'm glad I didn't see his face when you handed out the fishing rods.' At Nick's quizzical gaze she smiled awkwardly, 'I always think a child feels so terribly left out when it's someone else who's getting all the presents and fuss.'

'What's the point in having birthdays if you make them all alike?' Nick said lazily. 'Jeff knows his turn will come for the limelight.'

'The cold logic of men!' Lee smiled to the sea.

'Necessary,' Nick grinned, 'to offset the feminine fancy that children should have everything handed to them on a plate.'

Lee raised an eyebrow at him to return, 'Yours are going to have a tough time.'

'Just tough enough.' The grin sloped as he held her gaze.

Bedlam ensuing from inside made her turn. 'I'd better go and see what's going on,' she said on a slightly fluttering breath.

'Angelina can handle it,' Nick drawled.

'She went down to the hotel with the table and things,' Lee explained, snapping herself out of the dreamy state that was threatening to engulf her. All this because Nick had thought to call in on the twins' birthday!

Bearing that firmly in mind, she hurried inside. Later, with the boys pyjamaed and bedded down, she came out on to the veranda to find Nick lounging in a chair pulling on a cigarette. He rose as the dim figure of Angelina pushed in at the beach gate. 'Goodnight, Lee.' He stubbed out his cigarette and left by the side path.

Lee heard herself calling as he strode off through the palms, 'Goodnight, Nick!'

She was down at the rocks helping Jeff untangle Tim's fishing line the next afternoon when the sound of a car came along the road. She kept her head down and held her breath as a familiar step sounded along the path. Two visits in two days!

Nick came up to run an eye over the snagged line. 'Trouble already?'

'Not really,' Lee smiled up. 'Tim's line has got caught under a lip of rock here and . . .'

'Watch your fingers on those coral tips.' Nick lowered down beside her to reach into the water, and stifled by his nearness, Lee was compelled to keep her position on the rock until he had edged out the line. As it swung free he called, 'Okay, Tim, reel her in!'

Lee rose as soon as she could and brushed off her dress to say lightly, 'Well, if that's everything under control again I'll get back to sorting out the clean shirts for morning.'

She felt Nick's hand on her elbow as she wobbled over the rocks to the sand, then he turned back to the boys.

The discussion on the rudiments of how to hold a rod and line was eventually transferred to the garden, and while four heads talked close, Lee kept herself busy in the house. Only when the boys came in to ask for drinks and Nick looked like following did she decide that there was more air to breathe outside. She poured the drinks from a tray resting on a small table down the garden and handed Nick his, trying not to notice the bronzed hardness of his physique in short-sleeved open-necked shirt.

As the boys romped and slopped the drink over themselves, Nick stood sipping from his glass watching her. At one time when she brought her gaze in from the sea he asked casually, 'Heard from Hayward?'

'No. Why should I?'

She turned to put her empty glass down and collected the rest on the tray. Nick made no reply, but as she moved to go past him he rocked back on his heels with a slightly hooded glance.

That was the pattern of Nick's visits after that. He spent his time with Jeff and the twins, and Lee always made sure she was engaged in some task or other. She didn't join in in the games that took place in the garden and on the beach, and only came close to Nick when he stayed for a meal, or threw the laughing boys into bed at night.

She had never admitted it, but having Nick around was something of a relief where Jeff and the twins were concerned. Though they attended the school, the hours were short and she was left with long periods when they were a drain on her energy. She had never regretted taking on the job, but coping single-handed with three boisterous boys, though satisfying, was also a little wearing.

Fate must have heard her small grumblings, for one morning when she was crossing the clearing outside the school, the headmistress informed her that a local holiday was coming up, and as was customary an outing had been arranged for the school. Buses would take the pupils on a scenic tour through the hills to the beach at Belle Anse. Lee was assured that all the children would be carefully supervised.

She woke up on the day of the trip with rosy pictures of herself stretched blissfully in the sun, with nothing to do but listen to the sound of the waves falling on the deserted beach.

Up at the school, she watched the boys climb excitedly into the bus, Jeff slightly arrogant as usual, choosing his seat, the twins clutching their lunch bags happily against them. The sun was only just coming up into the sky, and with a full day ahead of them, the children laughed and bounced in their seats. They waved vigorously as the buses trundled off, and Lee waved back to anyone and everyone.

No one else had turned out to see the buses off, but Lee had heard that most of the children came great distances to the school and had to stay the week. As she was in no particular hurry, she stood and watched the procession fade from view.

It was only in the silence left behind that she heard the purr of an engine and the soft whoosh of tyres along the road. Almost before she could turn, a long car had slid in beside her and Nick was skilfully drawing it to a stop.

'I heard about the trip,' he said laconically, a furrowed brow shading the brightness of the day from fathomless grey eyes. He relaxed back in his seat to ask lazily, 'Fancy one yourself?'

Lee looked down at the bronze bodywork of the car, the spacious leather-seated interior. At least it wasn't Janine's.

'It won't bite,' Nick grinned, leaning over to open the door.

She lowered her eyes over her lilac cotton dress and open-worked sandals.

'Hadn't I better go back and change?' she asked.

'What for?' Nick hung on to the door purposefully. 'You look cute to me.'

Hmmm! Lee stepped in and took her seat sedately. Was that meant to be a compliment or what?

The breeze whipped her hair back as the car slid forward and turning to flicker a glance over it, Nick asked, 'Ever been big game fishing?'

Lee looked at him. 'We watched a manta or something being pulled in one day.'

'A manta ray,' Nick nodded, and then smilingly, 'One fish hardly qualifies!'

Poinsettias, oleanders and bougainvillea blazed the way along the road he took to a small rocky cove. From soft white sands and palm trees a jetty stretched, and attached to this a white yacht rode majestically on the blue satin sea.

There were other cars parked under the trees and Lee was introduced to two men who were members of the big game fishing association and another who owned an island not far distant. As she was guided along the jetty the crew of the boat were already preparing to sail. Within minutes of casting off, the cove had faded in the distance, and a flat stretch of sun-spangled sea spread out on all sides.

From her position at the rail Lee revelled in the warm breezes brushing her bare arms and throat. She was just musing on the tan she would get from the sea air and salt spray when Nick came to drape an oilskin about her shoulders.

'Better put this on,' he smiled. 'Things might get rough.'

Just what he meant Lee had no idea, but she soon became infected with the excitement as the men with the rods at the back of the boat, prepared to do battle. Nick explained, as he lowered himself on to the rail beside her, that fish in these waters could weigh up to three thousand pounds. She didn't see anything as big as that, thank heaven, but the next two hours were enough to keep her clutching tensely at the rail, and tugging as the men tugged at barracuda, kingfish, tuna and shark. She wouldn't have been so well up on the names, of course, if Nick hadn't pointed them out to her as they came up.

As the deck dipped and lurched at the weight of the leaping fish, he gripped her tightly, and catching his downward smile it seemed to Lee that her heart was having a far rougher voyage than the bobbing yacht.

The men obviously did themselves proud on these trips, for later when Nick led her below, Lee was pleasantly surprised to find a white-clothed table laid out and all the amenities of a miniature restaurant. She ate venison in red wine and listened to the men's talk on the sport of fishing and, inevitably, 'the one that got away'.

When it looked as if the conversation might go on indefinitely she slipped off to bathe the salt spray from her face and add a touch of fresh make-up. Refreshed, she climbed back up on deck to find the sky a hot cloudless blue, and the sea a molten silver where the sun smote it, a pale fluorescent green, where it lapped against the boat.

Now that the fishing was over and the anglers below relaxing behind their cigars, there was a lazy air about the deserted deck, a dreamy gentleness, in the way the bow lifted between sea and sky. Basking in the warmth of the sun, Lee lifted her face to the breeze and smiled thoughtfully at the endless expanse of shimmering water. She was reminded of the lovely ancient map that Mrs. Baumann had hanging up in the hotel, showing an expanse of water dotted with islands of various sizes, all with exotic-sounding names. One of the islands had painted on it a huge bird carrying an elephant in its talons. She had seen that picture before in a book in the school library at Little Ashby. Her smile curved deeply. *The Arabian Nights*! How often had she had pleas to read from it in class? The magic the stories conjured up was never failing. Though she knew every one off by heart, she had never dreamed that one day . . .

Nick strolled up to drop an arm negligently across her shoulders. He followed her gaze to the far horizons to say with a lazy smile, 'What's the attraction?'

'All this!' Lee sighed lightly. She spread a hand around the panorama to murmur in dreamy wonder, 'The Sea of Zanj!'

'Where Sinbad found a magnetic mountain,' Nick put in, crooking his smile.

'And the birds fed their young on baby elephants,' she laughed up, feeling her heartbeats stumble out of step at his downward glance. Endeavouring to keep the moments normal, she twinkled, 'How long is it since you were reading fairy tales?'

'Long enough.'

The mocking lights in his eyes sent her gaze winging back to the ocean.

He dropped down on the rail beside her to say casually, 'Like this part of the world?'

'Story book land?' Lee nodded a soft smile over the view. 'Who wouldn't?'

'How long before your job folds up with the boys?'

Lee lifted her shoulders lightly. 'No set time. The boys' parents have settled in on this dig in the Rift Valley. I think they plan to stay there for about nine months.'

'So you've got quite a while to go yet before you leave Mahé?' At her nod, Nick looked along the skyline to ask unhurriedly, 'And what then?'

What then? Lee looked up quickly, hoping her face was showing nothing of the shadow drifting over her heart. She feigned a philosophical shrug to reply lightly, 'Back to Little Ashby, I suppose.'

'Little Ashby?'

'A small village in Sussex,' Lee smiled, pushing her hair back from her face. 'As remote from everyday life as the islands out here.'

'And what about family? Are they in Little Ashby?'

'I had an aunt,' Lee looked pensive, 'but she died a few months back.' Staring out to seat she said, the smile returning to play about her lips, 'I suppose I'm what you men would call a loner.'

Nick looked down at her to drawl, 'Women don't make very good loners.'

She found herself meeting his gaze to twinkle, 'And men do, I suppose?'

His arm had found its way back across her shoulders. He drew her close to grin with mocking deliberation, 'Some of them.'

Drowning in those fathomless grey depths, Lee suddenly became too breathless for words. Chin tilted, heart hopelessly out of time, she waited, then Nick said with a dry smile, 'Wishing Hayward was here?'

It was like being rudely awakened from the perfect dream just when the best part was coming. Pulling in a quick sigh, she replied irritably, 'Hang Alec! Why does he always have to come into the conversation?'

She was all for swinging out of Nick's arms, but quite unexpectedly his grip became steel. She felt her head being forced back to meet the grey gaze, saw it searching her face, and then he was saying deeply, on a sloping smile, 'Maybe he doesn't.'

Caught against him this way Lee felt a sweet flutter of excitement. She wanted to ask him what he meant, wouldn't have minded if his explanation had lasted beyond eternity as he held her like this, but once again the perfect dream was snipped off at the end, by the sound of the men stumping up from below.

Nick turned to the rail and reached lazily for cigarettes as the heads appeared. Lee continued to investigate the view not too far from those wide shoulders.

Though the dream had been terminated abruptly she drifted through the afternoon still in the aftermath of its rosy glow. Close to Nick, she visited the cool spacious house of Henri Laval, the man who owned an island not far from Mahé, saw the production of cinnamon oil and vanilla, and was handed a glass with lemon juice in it, several other ingredients and a scoop of the local honey famous for its flavour.

If the drink had had the potency of a high-powered liquor, it couldn't have left her as heady as when she walked with Nick along the white scimitar-shaped beach with no sound between them but the lap of the waves, the warm zephyr breezes rustling through the palms.

Walking back along the tiny wooden jetty she felt his hand search for hers, and as the yacht sailed serenely on its way back to Mahé it seemed that the brilliant blue sky would never be marred by a cloud again.

But they were there, fanning outwards from the horizon.

CHAPTER ELEVEN

SEATED in the car again, Lee had expected to be taken straight back to the beach cottage, but Nick surprised her by turning away from the direction of Tailliez. The blaze of blossom and flowers along the road gave way to green craggy-topped hills and fat banana palms, and following her curious glance, Nick said with one of his sloping smiles, 'I want you to see Janine's place. Her plantation is a couple of miles outside Victoria.'

Though Lee returned the smile, her heart shed its wings and plummeted down like a stone. Janine again! Why couldn't she get it into her head that Nick had already decided on the woman he wanted in his life?

Just because he had been polite enough to offer her a few hours' break from her job she had gone rolling along pell-mell, reading all kinds of things in his smile and touch, and really there hadn't been anything there at all. All the time she had been foolishly drifting and dreaming on the boat Nick had been thinking of Janine.

Lee bit back her bitter disillusionment and kept herself steeped in a carefree air. She might as well face it—the dream had really come to an end.

The car wound its way up a smooth road, past tier upon tier of lush green tea bushes. They turned in along a white coral-lined drive, and devastated as she was, Lee couldn't keep back a tiny gasp of pleasure at the picture ahead.

The house stood back in a circle of trees, looking down over elevated lawns. Its entire length was fronted by a two-tier veranda, and these were supported by brilliant white pillars. There were no windows, just latanier blinds drawn up in the space between each pillar, and through these spaces one could see pictures and pieces of furniture in the rooms beyond.

The drive finished up beneath the trees at the side of the

house, and almost before Nick had stopped the car, a white-coated figure stepped out of the big door opposite. With his hand on her elbow Nick was saying easily as they approached, 'Lee, meet Marcel. He's been at Beauvais since he was twelve years old.'

The man with a leather-dark face and grizzled grey hair gave her a gentle smile and led the way inside. When he saw that Nick was already drawing Lee forward, he discreetly disappeared.

With trailing heart Lee allowed herself to be guided through rooms, pale and cool and tastefully laid out. She smiled around as though she was being led on a two-and-sixpenny tour of a stately home, for actually there was something of the stately about Beauvais, with its old-world French style furniture and carpets.

Occasionally Nick would draw her forward within the circle of his arm and show her some distant view from a balcony or the particular colouring of a room, and Lee would nod dutifully, keeping a tight hold on her smile.

The house was achingly beautiful and yet sufficiently mellowed as to be a joy to live in. A joy for Janine ... and perhaps Nick some day?

Bleakly she kept her gaze lowered to the pot of trailing plants beyond the veranda, then she raised them again. Come to think of it, where *was* the lady of the house? Nick must have read her thoughts, for as they came out on to the twin-sided flight of stone steps fronting the pillars he drawled, 'Janine had to go into town. She might be back before we go.' As they went out into the brilliant sunshine, he turned to take in the house and Lee. 'Beauvais,' he shrugged pleasantly. 'What do you think of it?'

Lee looked around and breathed in a sigh. What was the use of denying it?

'It's perfect,' she said simply.

'Fancy a look over the grounds?'

Not if Janine's due back at any time, Lee thought. She looked at her watch as an excuse and got a genuine shock at the time.

'Good heavens! I'll have to fly!' she gasped. 'I'll never make it back in time to pick up the boys.'

536

She fled along the veranda and round the side of the house. She was almost at the car when Nick pulled her up.

'Don't get into a panic,' he said evenly. 'What time are they due back?'

'Six o'clock. It's almost that now.' She looked up in agitation. 'They'll wonder where I've got to!'

'What about Angelina?'

'She's taken the day off. So has Mrs. Baumann. Practically everybody's gone off to some celebration or other at Cascade.'

As Lee made to swing away impatiently to the car, Nick held her. He considered for a moment, then clipped, 'There's a local line down at the plantation office. I might be able to get through to the hotel. There should be somebody capable there.'

Much relieved, Lee watched him lope off along a path through the trees. She only realised her mistake when a few seconds later the little yellow car came cruising up the drive and she was left without any means of escape.

If anything, Janine looked even lovelier than she had done that first day on the pier. Her hair waved smooth and soft about delicately pale features. The ice-blue dress was a perfect cut for the slim, girlish form. Only the heavy gold sunglasses and something in the way she stepped unhurriedly from the car suggested the sophistication of a woman in her late twenties.

Tempted to run like the gawkish schoolgirl she felt, in her simple dress and sandals, Lee held on to herself and watched with a calm air as Janine approached. She didn't miss the tiny flicker of annoyance that sped across the smooth features, the arctic coolness behind the smile.

'Miss Travers, isn't it?' The husky accent was slightly more pronounced. 'What brings you up this way?'

'I came with Nick,' Lee smiled, knocking violently inside. 'He's gone down to the plantation to make a phone call.'

'Well, for heaven's sake don't stand out here in the sun. There are chairs along the veranda.'

It might have been an invitation, but it sounded more

like a command. Janine waited for her to move, and then followed quickly up from behind. As Lee sat down facing the lawns, Janine went to put a cigarette in a slender gold holder.

Turning her head slightly, Lee noticed for the first time that the delicate beauty was marred by a certain business-like briskness, an unnerving efficiency that showed in the precise movements of the manicured hands, the level set of the shoulders.

She was beginning to feel as though she had come to apply for a job, as Janine turned and paced some distance away, pulling on her cigarette and regarding her closely from behind the thick-fringed lashes.

Trying to counter whatever was coming, Lee said brightly, 'I've been admiring your house and grounds. It really is a beautiful estate.'

Janine sent a glance around the surrounding tea terraces. 'My father died believing all this would continue.' The slim shoulders lifted. 'It continues.' The pacing was back again, so was the thoughtful look in the violet blue eyes. 'You're out from England, aren't you, Miss Travers?' Janine asked.

'Well, yes, I am.'

'This work you do with the little boys—is that your occupation?'

'I'm a schoolteacher by profession.'

'In England?'

'Well, we had a school in Little Ashby, but ...' At the raised enquiring eyebrow Lee smiled, 'That's the village where I live.'

Though she was trying hard to forget her simple cotton dress and well worn sandals Janine's coolly amused glance seemed determined to pick them out. After deftly flicking her cigarette she asked smoothly, 'Nick is English, isn't he?'

'Well, I've never actually asked him ...'

'But not homespun, I wouldn't say, would you?'

Lee met Janine's gaze to reply evenly, 'I'm not sure I follow your point.'

Janine tilted her head with a curled smile. 'Was there one?'

Lee couldn't have cared less if the conversation had ended there and then, but Janine was all for talk.

'Nick uses this house like his own,' she said, folding her arms and swaying gently.

'The hook he wriggles on?' Lee heard herself saying sweetly.

'Exactly,' Janine said, returning the sweetness. She turned again to sweep her gaze over the view. 'I need a man like Nick. The difficulty has always been in getting him to settle down.'

'But you're working on it?' said Lee, hating her own waspish tones.

'Incessantly!' Janine's smile curved deeply. 'And you know? I think I'm going to get what I want.'

I'm sure of it, Lee said to herself. She was suddenly swamped in dejection at the thought of how Nick hadn't been able to resist showing even her what he was contemplating.

Wondering how she could have been such a fool to come here knowing how he felt, Lee wanted only to get away. Almost without realising it she had risen from her chair and was backing off along the veranda. As Janine advanced with the slightly supercilious lift of an eyebrow Lee mumbled, 'I'm sorry to ... to have to rush away. Would you tell Nick I couldn't wait?'

'Of course.' Out on the drive Janine asked smoothly, 'Would you like me to drive you back into town?'

'No ... no, thank you. I can manage.'

Realising that she was making a complete fool of herself, she started off blindly along the drive. With an amused violet-blue gaze following her, Lee had the feeling that her sandalled footsteps drowned out every other sound in the world.

The road through the tea estate was hot and dusty, and she was wondering what day of the week she would finally come to the end of it, when a squat green bus rattled by, filled with labourers. She waved it down and climbed aboard, to the surprise of the occupants, and sat primly in her seat until they reached Victoria.

A warm tangerine glow was staining the sky over the sea

when she got back to Tailliez. She could see the black silhouettes of Jeff and the twins down at the water's edge. Claude, a curly-headed boy who helped around the hotel, was showing them how to cast a line on the waves. She was met with the chatter of all that had happened during the day, and added to this was the excitement that Mr. Baumann had offered to buy any fish they could catch for the hotel.

Lee was grateful for the commotion. She smiled her thanks to Claude and led the boys along the beach, soaking herself in the animated conversation that flowed. As long as she could give her mind to the small things, such as how many fruit ices Pete had eaten, and the way Jeff had tried his hand at surfing, there was no danger of it slipping back to brood over those moments at Beauvais.

But slip back it did, later that night, as she lay listening to the birds rustling in the palms. No matter how many times she went over the day it always seemed to her that Nick had been particularly attentive. And crazy as it was, she wanted to believe it. Well, what was life without a little bit of fantasy? Grimacing, she gazed wide-eyed at the sky, waiting for it to pale into dawn. There was Janine, but Nick would come to visit the boys. She had that small comfort at least.

The heat was particularly trying the next day. Lee was glad of the shade of the trees as she went along the road to pick up the boys from school. Their only thoughts voiced as they trudged back with her, was to strip off and make for the rock pools. Lee found the water refreshing too. It was cool where it curved back under the shade of the palms.

The boys favoured the sunlit stretches where it was possible to scoop up the multi-coloured fish with a net. Lee admired the scarlet, turquoise, saffron and blue bodies as they came up, keeping an ear tuned for the sound of a car. She was as mystified as the twins to see the vivid colours fade into a dull matt grey the minute they were turned out on the beach.

The fishing petered out in favour of building a dam with driftwood, and this was forgotten when a white ship sailed majestically by. Waving to the boats was a favourite pastime with the boys, but they leapt about more enthusiastically when it was a liner. Perhaps they saw themselves on one one day, Lee mused, smilingly waving her own hand to the sliver of white in the distance.

She decided after flicking her feet lethargically in the warm pools that tea could wait no longer. She helped Angelina prepare it, looking down the garden every few minutes. Any time now a tall figure would be stooping to hoist a twin on one shoulder or bending to listen to something that Jeff had to say.

Though Lee intended as usual to have some task to keep her occupied, there could be no dulling the glow that came with the sound of those footsteps on the path beneath the palms. During the meal, she found herself poised, listening with every mouthful, and after it, stilling her breathing as Jeff asked her to participate in a new ball game he had devised. Later he and the twins took to making occasional trips along the path to watch the road, but each time they returned alone. As the sun came down to meet the sea, they scuffed off disconsolately to bed.

Lee went briskly about her chores, stitching buttons on and brushing wet sand from small sandals. It had been crazy anyway thinking that Nick would continue to make his visits indefinitely. Obviously he had better things to do with his time.

She climbed into bed thinking of the brilliantly coloured fish that faded into grey as soon as they left the water. That was the difference between rosy-hued dreams and reality.

The days drifted by uneventfully. Though Lee understood the reason for Nick's protracted absence, it was difficult to get it across to the boys. She explained that he was staying at a house some miles away and that his interests must be centred around there. This was silently digested and the matter dropped, but Lee had a feeling that the explanation had not been accepted.

She found it hard to take herself, but it made sense. Nick had obviously taken her hurried departure from Beauvais as a final break in their relationship. Perhaps he had been looking for one? There was nothing to keep him tied to her and the boys. They weren't on a tiny one-house island now.

Admittedly, it wasn't like Nick to break off his friendship with the boys, but perhaps he thought a clean break was preferable to what he had decided could be an embarrassing situation. Heaven knows, she had given enough away on the fishing trip!

Looking back now, she realised too, that Nick had always been around to handle the affairs of the cottage and the school. Sometimes she could have almost fooled herself into believing that he had wanted to do these services, but that was before she would admit to herself how deep things were between him and Janine.

Though she never really gave up listening for footsteps on the path Lee threw herself into organising her days fully. The headmistress at the school had told her more than once that the island was desperately short of teachers, so she offered her services for the same time that the boys were in the class. It had long since occurred to her that she was doing nothing of the work she had been trained to do, and looking back to her interview in London, Lee guessed rather wryly that her appearance had helped more for the job than her qualifications. Recalling her tightly drawn-back hair and plain clothes, she couldn't blame Bruce Pasmore for thinking she was the ideal type for posting on an island with a practically engaged brother-in-law.

Of course it wasn't the thing to wear her hair swishing on her shoulders at the school at Tailliez, so she stitched a wide headband of black velvet, and this kept her hair smoothed back from her face.

She found the pupils fascinating. Though the official language of Mahé is English many of the children also spoke Creole, and if anything *she* was the one who was getting the education. Like children everywhere with a new teacher, they derived great amusement in finding out what she was made of, and it wasn't uncommon to have her questions answered in a gibberish of which she had not the slightest meaning. At the end of a fortnight she was well on her way to learning Creole.

542

Though outwardly serene at her rearranged existence, Lee never failed to make the journey back to the beach cottage with slightly racing heart. The boys, however, leapt along the road, concerned only with thoughts on what to do for the rest of the afternoon. They hadn't mentioned Nick in days, and it looked as though they had resigned themselves to the fact that he wouldn't be around any more.

That was what Lee was ready to believe until his name cropped up one afternoon on the veranda. She was writing her weekly report to the Pasmores and the twins were laboriously scribbling a few words to put in the envelope. Jeff's letter was already written and sealed as usual. She had no idea what he wrote to his parents, but he made no secret of the fact that life had been infinitely better before they had abandoned him.

He tried to shin abstractedly up a beam supporting the veranda, and Tim placed his pencil down to say suddenly, 'Why can't we go and see Nick?'

Lee looked up and blinked. 'I think he would have come here if he had wanted to see us, don't you?' she asked.

Jeff dropped down from his perch with a thud. 'His car might have broken down,' he said, facing her.

'He might have forgotten the way.' Pete slid off his chair to stand by Jeff.

He's forgotten the way all right, Lee told herself bleakly. She went back to penning the letter, and the boys stood over her expectantly. When he saw that she was prepared to make no further comment on the subject Jeff said authoritatively, 'I think we should all go and see Nick.'

The twins leapt in with, 'Let's go and see Nick!'

Lee shook her head over her writing. 'I don't really think we should make a nuisance of ourselves,' she said, trying to find a smile. In an effort to change the subject she looked across at the pages of paper. 'Are you boys all finished? I'm ready to seal the envelope.' When the letters were in her hand she went on pleasantly, 'We'll stroll along to the hotel, shall we, and put these in the mail bag. Mrs. Baumann was telling me about some colour slides she's just had developed at the coast.'

The boys shuffled morosely down the steps of the

veranda and Jeff went to move ahead of her. She didn't miss that 'You never let us do anything we want to' look. They walked slowly in the heat of the afternoon, and as the boys idly tossed pebbles over the sea Lee's thoughts began to tumble over themselves.

Go and see Nick? If only she could! If only there weren't a thousand and one reasons why she shouldn't.

Try as she might she couldn't see beyond that kiss on a dark veranda in Mombasa; a certain light in the grey eyes that had gazed down into hers, that night on the beach on Half-Moon Island.

As she walked, more tinsel-gold memories flew in. They started to snowball inside her until it was like a small sun shining, its brilliance blotting out the rocky landscape.

She didn't go out of her way to find Mrs. Baumann at the hotel, simply dropped the letters in the bag and turned back towards the cottage. When they were almost there she said as casually as her pounding heart would let her, 'How long would it take you to change into clean shirts and shorts?'

The boys looked at her and then leapt into the air. 'Yippee!'

With much the same expression, only under her breath, of course, Lee went inside to wash. Without knowing why she slipped into the soft green dress purchased in Mombasa, and slim-heeled shoes. A touch of powder on the slightly flushed cheeks, the black headband in position, she saw no reason to grumble at the picture she made.

The boys were spruce in white shirts and grey shorts. Angelina was busy knotting red ties under their chins. Calling over her shoulder that she didn't know when they would be back, Lee led the way along the path.

Transport was a tricky business on the island and Tailliez was lucky if it saw one bus a day. There was, however, a converted lorry coming down the road, and as it was going into Victoria, Lee didn't demur. Happily the seats were free from dust and the suspension passable, so everyone arrived in good spirits.

Unable to wait for the dawdling bus service, Lee splurged on a taxi for the second leg of the journey, and they were soon trundling along the road that cut through the plantation. The boys gazed around with interest at the rising tiers of tea bushes, but Lee had eyes only for the lawns fronting Beauvais. Nick might be out there somewhere. She paid the driver off under a belt of trees, and took hold of a twin in each hand, Jeff leading the way up the drive. The trees hung a limp welcome. The house was a pool of shade in a world of shimmering heat. As they came up the gradual slope of the drive, Lee's heart somersaulted at the sight of Nick's car. It was parked back under the cloud of camphor trees, just as it had been that day when he had driven her in from the fishing trip.

They were approaching the big brown door now, and Lee looked eagerly along the veranda fronting the house. Nick would have seen them coming up the drive, and any minute now he would come striding along from one of the rooms. She schooled her heart into not going completely haywire at the sight of him. Heaven knew what she was going to say to him. She had a perfectly legitimate excuse for being here, of course, the boys simply wanted to renew a friendship. As for herself . . . her lips curved into a soft smile. Well, right now she didn't care if . . .

The big door opened and, still in her rosy reverie, Lee smiled absently at the figure standing there. She would much rather just wait here for Nick, instead of being formal about it. They could stroll along the veranda, and later the boys would probably romp around the lawns. . . .

Tim's voice cut across her thoughts, bringing her back to the moment. Apparently tired of waiting for her to speak, he piped up 'We've come to see Nick!'

Marcel lifted a grey eyebrow, and after turning a smile over the boys, he raised it to Lee to say, 'Mr. Reynolds and Miss Feuillière left for Mombasa some time ago.'

Lee felt herself eddying down a deep well of darkness, her voice seemed to come from the very bottom of it as she echoed, 'Mombasa?'

Marcel nodded. 'It must be two weeks since the liner sailed.' After a pause he offered, 'It's a hot afternoon. Can I get you something to drink?'

Lee wanted to shake her head wildly, but there were the

545

boys to think of. She smiled her thanks and led them round on to the veranda. Jeff kicked at the slats to say more in envy than surprise, 'Mombasa!' The twins shrugged at one another philosophically, and went to climb on the parapet flanking the stone steps.

Within seconds Marcel was padding out of a room with a tray of tall drinks. Lee didn't take her glass until he had retired. He might wonder at her trembling hands.

So Janine had finally got what she wanted. Nick had proposed. Two weeks ago, Marcel had said. Two weeks, and there hadn't been a ship in port since.... She closed her eyes on the thought. Nick and Janine had gone off to get married in the very liner that she and the boys had waved so gaily on its way that afternoon on the beach.

The tears wanted to push from under her lashes, but she blinked them away. What was the use of pretending she didn't know it was going to turn out like this? She had known about Janine from that very first day on the pier, and if that wasn't enough, there was that brief but turbulent encounter here on this veranda. Janine had been sure of herself then, but Lee had tried to brush her aside where Nick was concerned, pretend she didn't exist.

Well, she existed for Nick all right. Just enough for him to make her his wife.

Lee pushed the drink down past the ache in her throat. It was no use thinking that Nick might have told her of his plans. Why should he? She was just someone he had helped out on his way to Janine. There was no reason for him to think of her again.

The boys came to clamp their glasses down and as Lee rose from her seat Marcel reappeared. He walked with them back along the veranda, asking in soft tones, 'Have you transport back into town?'

'Well, no,' Lee found a smile, 'but we'll manage.'

'I drive a car,' Marcel offered. He was moving towards the one under the trees. 'Perhaps you would wish me to ...'

'No, thanks all the same, Marcel.' Lee turned quickly away. 'We'll be fine.'

The boys looked dumbfounded that they were to be shunted along the drive when there was a car at their disposal, but for once Lee didn't care. To sit in Nick's car now would reduce her to the tears she had told herself she wouldn't shed.

Round the corner at the bottom of the drive, she thanked heaven for the leisure-loving Seychellois. She hadn't told the taxi man to wait, but he had taken advantage of the cool shade of the trees, and was sat dozing gently. He looked surprised that someone should expect him to work again so quickly, but once the sleep had left him he was as good-tempered as ever. They made a quick and uneventful journey back into town.

The same couldn't be said for the ride back to Tailliez. Lee had long since come to accept that though the buses on the island had a vague set route, they were inclined to go off at a tangent at any customer's request. She wasn't surprised that nobody blinked an eyelid as it cruised along the jetty to pick up a man's trunks, and bucked through a settlement to deliver a couple almost to their door.

The boys giggled under their breath at the constant change of direction. Lee couldn't have cared if the journey had gone on for ever; with all this commotion she could stifle her thoughts. But they had to come out into the open some time, and they did—frequently, in the days that followed.

And with them came a certain rising panic. If Nick and Janine had been gone over two weeks they could come back any time. They would honeymoon in Africa, perhaps Mombasa, she swallowed bleakly, and then return to Beauvais to become the island's most perfect couple—Nick big and virile, Janine exquisitely feminine. They would cause a stir wherever they went, and Lee didn't want to be around to see it. True, Tailliez was some miles from Beauvais, but what if Nick took up visiting the boys again, and brought Janine? She couldn't just sit here and wait for that.

She didn't expect her release to come in the form that it did.

One afternoon when she was listlessly watching the boys playing leapfrog on the edge of the waves, her attention was attracted by a waving figure running up the beach. As it neared, she saw it was Claude and it looked as though he had a letter or a piece of paper in his hand.

Lee didn't get up from her chair. She wasn't expecting any mail. The Pasmores' routine letter wasn't due for some time yet, and nobody else wrote. It was probably an invitation from Mrs. Baumann. She was always arranging some function or another.

As Claude puffed up the garden, she didn't attach any particular importance to the fact that the paper fluttering in his hand was a pale pink, but something in his relished display of urgency brought her forward on her chair.

He came up the steps of the veranda and thrust the paper at her with a triumphant smile. It was his words that brought her to her feet.

'Radio telephone message come to hotel from Victoria!'

Radio telephone! Who would want to contact her as urgently as that? She thanked Claude for his quick delivery, and watched him trot happily back down the path. Before he had reached the gate she saw Lamu, the name of an African coastal town, where the message had come from. By the time he was out of it she learned that her job in the Seychelles was finished.

Her eyes flying for a second time over the printed words, Lee reached dazedly for a chair.

It seemed the Pasmores had decided that conditions at the dig were favourable enough to have their children with them. The *Kajana*, a liner making the round trip from South Africa, was due in Victoria in three days' time, and everything had been arranged for her and the boys to be on it. The Pasmores were in Lamu to purchase supplies. From Mombasa, Lee was to travel there to hand over the children.

The message was short, but she could read a volume in every word. The Pasmores were essentially a family unit, travelling the world together. This was the first time they had ever been split up, and neither side had taken happily to the arrangement. Since Bruce Pasmore and his wife were trained professors, there was no worry of schooling for the boys, so who could blame them for wanting to be complete again?

Looking to where Jeff and the twins were tussling in the

548

sand, Lee knew their views. Once they knew they were on their way, they wouldn't give a second thought to the Seychelles, famed paradise islands.

Packing for the impending journey, Lee wished she could have been just as blissfully detached, but every moment seemed to bring with it some new ache of what she was leaving. The little thatched beach cottage—for some ridiculous reason she had grown attached to it, the children at the school, the crazy buses, Angelina....

After a while, of course they would all settle down in the notches of her memory. But the all-embracing ache! What about that?

Well, you could learn to live with anything in time, Lee told herself, turning a tear-starred gaze away from the fishing rods that were waiting to go in their covers.

Once the boys knew they were to be reunited with their parents it was difficult to keep them in check, but in a way Lee was thankful for their high spirits, in fact where she could she encouraged them. It was important to keep things at boiling point, until it was time to leave. Once she was on the boat it wouldn't matter if she broke up a little inside.

Her determination to appear nonchalant about leaving slipped a little when she and the boys went to the school to say goodbye. The headmistress, herself the daughter of a Government official who had stayed, asked Lee to come back and teach permanently at the school once she had delivered the boys.

Over tea and a very English display of scones and sandwiches, she listened to the extensive plans and schemes that the Government had in mind for education on the island, and the challenge it could offer to young teachers, but smilingly refused at the end of it all.

Half of her wanted to stay desperately. The other half knew she couldn't. Not in the same world as Nick and Janine.

Down at the hotel Mrs. Baumann both surprised and touched her by offering as a parting gift the colour slides she had painstakingly taken of scenes around the island. One couldn't say beauty spots, for every cove, and hill and palm, was beauty in itself, but there they were—twelve colourful reminders of what life had been like in the Seychelles.

When the goodbyes had been said, and Jeff and the twins had galloped impatiently back to the beach, Lee lingered for a while beside the framed map on the wall. The lump in her throat didn't show, thank goodness, so she could absorb the picture at her leisure, and re-live that one magic day when she had sailed its wavy lines. Not that it helped in the least, but what did help these days?

Slackly she moved outside, knowing that in less than a week, she would be back in Little Ashby, and all this, the swaying palms, the Sea of Zanj and Nick, would be no more than another fairy tale in her mind. One that didn't have a happy ending.

The boys were well up the beach by this time, going like the wind, for some unknown reason. As her spiritless gaze followed their progress, she became vaguely aware of a certain purpose behind their speed. The next second she was stepping along quickly herself.

A tall lean figure had moved out from the gate. There was no mistaking that sandy blond hair, the lounging indolent stride. Alec! What on earth was he doing here? She saw one twin and then the other swung high in his arms, and then Jeff was having a friendly wrestle.

As Lee approached Alec dropped her one of his lazy grins and a whimsical, 'Long time no see.'

'It has been quite a while, hasn't it?' Lee smiled diffidently as he held the gate for her. She was just about to ask the reason for his visit when another figure up near the veranda caught her eye. Well, this *was* the day for surprises!

'I don't think you two have met,' Alec led her forward, tacking on with a humorous gleam, 'officially!'

As Philippa came down the steps, Lee steeled herself against what was bound to be a hostile reception. Surprisingly there wasn't one. If anything she felt enveloped in the warmth of the other girl's approach.

Alec, turning an arm about her waist, commented blithely, 'We're off to get married!'

Seems to be the fashion around here, Lee thought, glazing her misery with a smile. 'That's really wonderful,' she said sincerely.

Alec undoubtedly couldn't have agreed more.

'Phil decided to come back and have another look at the island,' he said happily, and then, grimacing, 'and while she was about it she let me have it straight between the eyes about that little dodge of ours. Don't ask me how she found out. I suppose we couldn't have looked very convincing.' Before an awkward pause had time to creep in, he went on with a satisfied sigh, 'Still, all's well that ends well, to murder an old cliché. The company wallahs are not likely to come holidaying our way again for years, and I don't see them dropping in for any other reason, with the copra business as healthy as it is at the moment.'

'We'll tell them the truth, of course.' Philippa's small frame seemed to straighten slightly and then she was stepping forward to add smilingly, 'I can't tell you how grateful I am for what you did to help Alec keep his job, and I'm going to see to it,' she turned to give him a menacing twinkle, 'that he makes more than a success of it in the future!'

'Which means she's going to be a worse slavedriver than Nick,' Alec grinned wryly. He thrust his hands in his pockets to comment lazily, 'He's left, by the way, so I heard?'

'Yes.' Lee kept her gaze on the boys rolling nearby. 'He's left.'

'With some gorgeous piece he's been keeping tucked away in these parts.' Alec swung back goodhumouredly on his heels. 'Well, I suppose even Nick has to tie it up for keeps some time.'

Lee nodded and then veered off the subject hurriedly with, 'By the way, you know that Jeff and the twins are going back to their parents, I suppose?'

Alec lifted his hands in an expressive gesture.' The very reason we're here,' he smiled. As Lee stared up blankly, he went on to explain, 'I got a call through from Bruce. We had quite a natter on the old box. He told me Beth wants the boys with her on the dig and I told him Phil and I were getting married. Bruce has promised to be my best man.'

as we're making for Lamu, the logical thing seemed to be to take the boys back with us.' While Lee was digesting this he added, 'As Bruce pointed out, it will save you making the trip up country, and you'll get back to England all the quicker.'

'All the quicker,' Lee echoed, realising that as the minutes ticked by she was becoming more and more reluctant to leave the islands. She said with a resolute intake of breath, 'Well, it looks as though we'll all be sailing together tomorrow, as far as Mombasa at least.'

Alec was shaking his head and Philippa put in, 'I got my father to charter a boat and crew to bring me out here. It's waiting for us in Victoria. We'll be sailing straight up to Lamu.'

'Does that mean,' Lee felt a heaviness dragging at her, 'that you want to take the boys right now?'

'Uh-huh.' Alec shook his head and grinned. 'We'll let you have them one more night. We're sailing about nine in the morning. It'll be okay if you bring them along then.'

Lee nodded, breathing in a small inward sigh of relief. She had wanted things to start moving, now they were threatening to run away with her. She certainly hadn't prepared herself for saying goodbye to the boys in a matter of minutes.

Alec was saying 'Our boat's the *Sybilla* by the way. You'll see it moored at the jetty reserved for smaller craft. I expect I'll be up to my neck in last-minute jobs, so . . .' With the tiniest flicker of a sheepish light in the sky blue eyes, he put out a hand. 'I'd better make this goodbye, Lee. No chance of seeing you in these parts again, I suppose?'

'It's hardly likely.' Lee took the outstretched hand with a bright smile. 'The Seychelles are a little too remote, I think, for one to just happen along.'

'I'm glad you did once, though,' he grinned. 'I wouldn't have missed it for the world!'

Philippa stepped forward to take over where Alec left off. 'Goodbye, Lee. I hope things go well for you.'

The grip of her hand had a certain strength about it, and Lee felt then that Alec's plantation had seen the last of its run-down days.

As they turned out of the side gate and along the path, Alec said, 'Incidentally, Bruce asked me to thank you for the work you've put in with the boys. I expect he and Beth will be writing to you some time. I haven't said anything to the little perishers about tomorrow.' He cast an affectionate gleam to where Jeff and the twins were bounding along in front. 'I'll leave it to you to prepare them for their prospective sea trip.'

Prepare them! Lee let out a good-natured sigh as she scooped breakfast into them the next morning and made sure they were dressed correctly for the journey. If they were excited before, there was positively no holding them now.

As her sailing coincided almost with their own, there was also no excuse for Lee to hang on in Tailliez. Making sure that every last item had been packed, she supervised the luggage into the waiting taxi and bade a damp-eyed goodbye to Angelina. The big woman hugged her in return, and then went off sniffing to start cleaning through the cottage before closing it up.

Lee didn't permit herself a backward glance as she stumbled along the path to the taxi. If she had stopped and lingered too long, she might have been reminded of a big wide-shouldered frame moving down the garden; the sound of deep tones drifting up from the beach.

Thank goodness the taxi driver was the flamboyant and talkative type. He kept the boys on the edge of their seats with his jollity, and Lee's mind off the views trailing by.

The first thing that hit her, and with considerable impact, as they dropped down into the harbour, was the sight of the white liner, the *Kajana*, anchored out at sea. Not because of its size dwarfing everything around it, but because in no time at all now she herself would be gazing out of one of those portholes, watching Mahé grow smaller and feeling her heart contract tighter with every swish of a wave.

The taxi turned to make its way slowly along the jetty, and Lee saw Philippa waving gaily from one of the boats. She looked radiant in pale jeans and sweater, and that glow that comes only with contentment. In contrast Lee felt limp and restrained in her tailored linen dress. She was glad when the other girl disappeared below after their greeting, leaving her to say her goodbyes to the boys unwatched. Goodbyes! If she had that in mind obviously Jeff hadn't. Allowing no time for a pause, he shrugged her a quick smile and jumped down into the boat.

Watching him rush off to inspect the various things on the deck, Lee wished she could have got a little closer to him during their association. But even though the twins clung to her round-eyed and serious, as she dropped a kiss on each sunburnt cheek, she knew she could never hope to be anything more than a shadowy presence in the pale memories they would have of their days in the Seychelles.

Smiling over the painful ache in her throat, she didn't wait to see the *Sybilla* set sail. As it shuddered into life she hurried off towards her own point of departure.

She had been told that the *Kajana* made a fairly quick turnabout at Victoria, and sailed again within the hour. Of course it had only just docked, so there was time if she wanted to take a last look around the town. But what was the point? She would still have to leave in the end.

No, Lee took a quivering breath, she would go straight out to the liner, find her cabin, shut herself in and forget the whole sorry episode of these islands and ... Well, forget it anyway. She had instructed the taxi driver to take her cases on ahead, so there was nothing to do except follow them. Nothing to do except ... Afraid that her churned-up emotions might be showing in her face, she lowered her head and moved with the sound of the voices, as the other passengers made their way along the pier.

Though she told herself she wouldn't lift her eyes again until she was in the pilot boat, something made her go back on her decision. Something she didn't know what, but her gaze was being drawn up ... upwards and onwards to the car just ahead....

Nick's car!

Lee's heart spun giddily as she saw it. She stepped quickly into the doorway of a shipping office to steady herself.

Though she had guessed that Nick might be returning on

the *Kajana*, it came as something of a shock to know that she was so close to him at this moment. He was probably just coming in on the pilot boat.

He would have ordered the car—bronze and shining and waiting, with its top up now, and Marcel standing dutifully by its side—so that he could drive his bride straight back to Beauvais.

Lee turned abruptly away. She couldn't bear to see Nick and Janine together, even though they probably made the most striking couple on the pier. She willed herself to stay inside the doorway, but at the sound of the car engine sparking into life, she was back on the edge of it, gazing wistfully at the wide shoulders framed in the open window just across from her; the firm brown hands on the wheel, and the sloping white smile as he spoke briefly to Marcel standing nearby. With tear-bright eyes she followed the dark head and lean profile as the car moved forward and past the doorway. She stepped out to see it swing off the pier and speed away up the coast road.

Well, who could blame him for being in a hurry? He had Janine, and he had all this.

Lee took a last look at the green island, the white houses nestling among the hills, and then fled to lose herself in the group making for the pilot boat.

She didn't look back again. Once on board the liner she went straight to her cabin. But she couldn't keep still. Though she knew the *Kajana* was only in Mahé to pick up and deliver passengers, the waiting seemed interminable. She paced in time to the minutes ticking by from a clock on the wall, and paced to the gentle whispering drip of the tape over the washbasin, and all the while the view of Victoria stayed at her porthole to taunt her, keeping her eyes misted with tears.

If only they could *move*!

Then she could start to put her life in order. Start by unpacking; making the best of a three-day voyage. There would be things to do, people to meet, and it would all be training for the years to come. The time when she would have learnt to say, smilingly and detached, 'I knew a man once . . .'

CHAPTER TWELVE

SHE looked again to the portholes. Surely all the passengers must be aboard by this time? Yes, wasn't that the rumble of the engines starting? And at last she could hear the activity outside as preparations were being made to sail. Within minutes it was possible to feel the imperceptible rolling motion of sea travel.

Only when the island began to grow smaller in the distance did she allow herself the luxury of gazing long and steadily at its shape; searching out the point where the cottage would be, the cove where she and Nick had sailed from that day, and where Beauvais looked out from its position on the hill.

The sound of laughter echoed along the corridor outside. The passengers were already attuned to their life at sea. Lee blinked the damp from her lashes. She would have to go out some time, but not yet. And it was useless to attempt unpacking in this state. It would have to wait until her head or her heart was clear.

The latter was a closed book, of course, but in a way the three days at sea helped her to achieve a more passive state of mind. By the time the liner was steaming into the harbour at Mombasa she had learned to hold her chin level, and pretend that the world had never been brighter. She had made friends among the passengers, laughed with her table companions, and even danced with members of the crew, and to them all she was just another tourist, a little wooden, perhaps, but adaptable.

It had crossed her mind to visit the Deightons while she was in Mombasa, but once in among the broad avenues and white buildings she decided against it. There wasn't a doubt they would ask her to stay, and then she would spend her time wondering which places Nick and Janine had visited; if they had gone to the Butterfly Club, or if they had stayed on some secluded beach and . . . well, anyway, it just wasn't practical. She hired a car to take her straight to the airport.

As she expected, her airline ticket was made out for any flight, and walking across to the terminal she was tempted once again to stay on in this world of brilliant colour and warm scented breezes. To counteract the melting mood, she booked on a flight due to leave in half an hour, and went to sit the time out over a cup of coffee.

As soon as it was reasonably near take-off time, she went to take her seat on the plane. Though she glanced around with a disinterested air it was impossible not to be intrigued by the assortment of people making the trip to London. How many of them wanted to go, she wondered, and how many would have preferred to stay behind? There was no way of telling. Faces could hide so much. She saw her own reflection in the window as the plane taxied to a start and sped along the runway.

Then came the gradual process of changing down from vivid peacock blues, tropical greens and splashes of scarlet, to varying shades of grey, and more grey. Or so it seemed.

London in November wasn't a very prepossessing sight. People were hurrying by with pinched faces and pink noses, and Lee felt the keenness of the breezes through her summer coat. The first thing she would have to do when she got back to Little Ashby, she told herself, boarding the train, was to search out a warmer coat.

Dusk was falling over the meadows and leafless trees as she stepped down at the village station. She was the only one to do so, and with a suitcase in each hand she turned and watched as the train rattled off and was sucked away into the night.

The lamps along the lane where she walked were drops of pearly light in a circle of mist, the stars merest pinpricks now in the haze.

She knocked on the door of the house that had been her aunt's home, and where Lee had been privileged to rent a room after its resale. She could hear the television going just as she had always known it, the voices talking above it.

The door opened and the woman stepped back a pace. 'Good heavens, you're back! And there's me here renting your room. . . .' She looked at the suitcases and then straightened her lips. 'Still, you never said when you would be coming or if, and I can't afford to . . .'

Lee picked up her cases. 'Of course I couldn't expect you to keep the room vacant indefinitely,' she smiled, 'but the two trunks I left . . . ?'

The woman nodded. 'That friend of yours—Miss Pennyweather, is it? She's got 'em.'

She waited until Lee had got herself off by the light of the door and then closed it.

Things were much quieter at Grace's house, further along the lane near the school. Chintz curtains were drawn over the tiny windows, the lights within projecting the pattern of flowers and leaves into the darkness. The only sound that Lee heard as she went up the path was the gentle clink of crockery. She knocked on the door and waited.

There was no mistaking the shape looming up behind the frosted glass door. Grace, plump and comfortable and pinafored, stood there, a slight gape on the flushed features, as she exclaimed, 'Good heavens!'

'That's the second time tonight I've induced that comment,' Lee said wryly. 'I've just heard that my trunks are with you.'

'Well, for goodness' sake come in! I always meant to answer your letter, but what with one thing and another . . . Let me have these and this,' Grace swung the suitcases in and took Lee's coat, chattering on fussily as they went along the passage.

Entering a small room with a white-clothed table and blazing fire, she called into a smaller one adjoining, 'Lee's back, Mother! Remember Lee Travers? She went abroad to look after some children.'

Mrs. Pennyweather came into the doorway swishing a tea-towel around a dinner plate. 'Enjoyed your travels?' she asked with a smile.

Grace's father turned his face out of the newspaper he was reading to give her a friendly nod, then went back to what he had been concentrating on.

'I'll go and see if there's a cup of tea left in the pot,' the plump girl beamed, 'and then you can tell me all the news.'

When the steaming liquid was before her and Grace seated opposite, Lee said with an attempt at a lighthearted shrug, 'Well, at the moment I'm mainly concerned with where I'm going to put my head tonight.'

'Upstairs, of course,' Grace came back. 'We've got a spare room. You can have it for as long as you like. Isn't that so, Mother?'

The cheerful affirmative came above the rattle of the dishes in the kitchen, and, relaxing, Lee took several sips of tea.

After a slight silence Grace said apologetically, 'Well, I've got a whole stack of marking up to do, so . . .'

'Oh, don't let me keep you!' Lee was rising to her feet. 'I'd like to go upstairs and get settled in anyway. And if the bed has to be made up I can see to it.'

'Nonsense!' Grace led the way. 'I'll come up and give you a hand.' Later, in a small room at the end of the landing, she patted the bed into shape and stood back with a satisfied sigh. 'There you are! All aired and ready for sampling.' She looked to where Lee was gazing into space and gave a light laugh. 'Well, cheer up! Aren't you glad to be back?'

Lee forced herself to move about the room. 'Just travel-weary, I suppose,' she said with a wan smile.

'What you need is a good night's sleep.' Grace went out of the door and closed it quietly behind her.

Lee gazed after her, pressing her lips together to still their trembling. She was being ungrateful, of course, but all her life she had known sloping ceilings, flowered wallpaper and views of the lane. Some people might think there was nothing like it, but Lee had more in mind, thatched huts and palm-fringed beaches and . . .

She slumped on to the bed and buried her face in the embroidered pillow. If ever the torrent had felt too much to hold, it was now.

'I've been thinking.' Grace spread the marmalade on her toast thoughtfully the next morning and looked at Lee. 'You'd get in like a shot at Tingleton. Half the staff are away with 'flu. Miss Worth's a bit of a dragon, but I know she'd jump at the chance of getting a relief.'

Lee considered, staring out over the dew-drenched garden. Well, why not? Why not get straight into the business of work? They said it was the finest thing, didn't they? She nodded her head and smiled, 'I'll be glad to help out if I can.'

'Right. I'll ask today.' Grace jumped up and grabbed her bag and coat. 'And now I'll have to fly. The bus will be along any minute. 'Bye!'

After a day spent drifting around her room and wandering the mist-laden paths across the fields, Lee heard with some relief that she had been accepted on a temporary basis at Tingleton. There was just the week-end to be got through and then life would be almost back to normal.

On Monday morning she dressed with care in a neat grey suit and white blouse. She thought she looked reasonably fitting for her work, until Grace came in shaking her head at the shoulder-length hair and headband.

'I wouldn't start off like that, not with Margaret Worth. Hang on. I think I've got a slide you can borrow.'

Things really were back to normal! Lee clipped her hair into position, thinking as she gazed into the mirror that if anything the style made her eyes look bigger, her face more solemn, but that was all to the good.

Out at the bus stop she was glad of the collar of her tweed coat about her ears. May Belman, an elderly woman who helped out at the village hotel and delivered the morning papers, was puffing out the frosty air. She nodded to Lee and Grace at the bus stop, and hastily stuffed a paper through a letter box to get back to them.

'Such excitement at the Crown last night!' She drew herself up. The pale eyes were lit with the satisfaction of being the bringer of village news as well as the national. 'Someone booking a room, indeed! And late too! We'd just got shot of the regulars and I was all for shutting the doors when this...'

'Sorry, May, this is our bus!' Grace, who had been listening eagerly, swung round at the sound of an engine, and ushering Lee forward into the shuddering shape that had pulled up, she twinkled shamefacedly, 'We never alter, do we? Some new face in the village and we go completely ga-ga. I bet it wasn't like that where you've been?'

'I suppose you get a little of that wherever you go,' Lee smiled, dropping down into a seat as the bus rattled on its way.

The ride was the same as she had always known it. They tore along the narrow lanes, brushing hedgerows, skimming grass verges and watching the scenery whizz by. With little or no traffic to impede the driver's capriciousness it was a case of hang on to your seat, or rock with it.

'Now don't forget,' Grace said reassuringly as the red-bricked school came into view, 'the Head won't eat you, though she may make out she's going to. Just let her rattle on,' the plump girl smiled as they stepped down from the bus, 'and she'll eventually get round to letting you know which form she's going to land you with.'

They walked across the deserted playground and into a parquet-floored hall. Grace took her coat and left her outside one of the doors with 'Good luck!' and hurried away, and Lee found herself knocking and drawing a deep breath at the same time.

'Come in.'

A small woman, but one emanating great strength, Lee felt almost before she had entered the room, was hanging a felt hat on a clothes stand.

'Ah, Miss Travers, isn't it? Lee Travers?' She nodded in reply to her own question, running a wintry eye over the grey suit and neat hairstyle. 'Been travelling abroad, so I hear. Got it out of your system?'

'Yes, I think so, Miss Worth.'

'My dear child, what do you mean—you think so? Your aunt was a headmistress at twenty-eight and she had great hopes for you. You can't possibly imagine these whimsical fancies are going to do your career any good?'

'No, Miss Worth.'

The older woman looked at her hard. 'Let's hope you can recover the ground you've lost. I'll put you in charge of Three B for the time being. They're a good-natured group, but that doesn't mean you can afford to be too lenient. It's the third door down on the right. I should go along there now and get your bearings before class starts.'

Lee backed out, nodding meekly, and closing the door behind her. Whew! Thank goodness that was over with.

She found her classroom and went to work with a will, but somehow the results were not quite what they should have been. The pupils of Three B were a good-natured crowd all right. Good-natured and noisy!

Halfway through the morning a small knock came on the door and a girl with a serious face informed Lee that she was wanted immediately in the headmistress's office.

'Oh, heavens! Here we go! She could hear the crisp voice already. Miss Travers, I must ask you to exercise stricter control...

Bracing herself Lee picked a level-headed girl to sit at the front of the class and then went quietly out of the door. She walked up the hall, listening to the comparative quiet from the other classrooms, and wondering what excuses she was going to be able to muster for the apparent lack of it in her own. She didn't have a single one on hand, but perhaps...

She had fixed her eyes on the door knob ready to make the last half dozen steps to grasp it, when suddenly it twisted and the door was flung open. She could hear Miss Worth's voice, crisper than ever and slightly irate. 'Very well! But I *will* say it again. It's most irregular! Most...'

The Headmistress was still holding forth as she came out into the hall, But Lee didn't hear another word. She stopped where she was, swaying slightly and facing the figure that had come to fill the doorway.

Nick! Her knees went weak at the sight of him, immense in dark overcoat, pale shirt and tie. She saw the deeply etched lines on his face, the ghost of the sloping smile. There was a look in his eyes that brought a mist to her own. She wasn't sure whether she had run up to take his hand, or whether he had come forward to take hers, but as they stood there looking at each other the door behind swung to with a slight slam.

Lee found herself being propelled along the hall and looking up, she asked dreamily, 'Nick, what's going on?'

'Nothing yet, but in about two minutes from now . . .'

Those deeply vibrating tones left her with no resistance as he opened a door marked Staff Room and drew her inside. Not that she would have wanted to resist the arms gripping her almost roughly now. As his lips dropped to her cheek and throat, he muttered against her, 'Do you realise I've been trailing you half across the world?'

She would have replied that she didn't, but her lips were caught against his in a kiss that was gently lingering.

After a long moment, Lee looked up with shining eyes to exclaim, 'I still don't know what's going on! Where's Janine?'

'Giving out the orders in one of her Paris salons by this time, I should think.'

As the smiling mouth came menacingly down again, Lee said with a light, incredulous laugh, 'Nick, I wish you'd explain!'

'If you had stayed where I left you,' he said, exploring her ear, 'you'd have got your explanations in Beauvais instead of . . .'

He raised his head, and Lee followed his gaze over cardboard models, potted plants, cups and saucers and the general conglomeration that was a teachers' staff room. As their eyes met in amusement he led her towards the door.

'Let's get going. Have you got a coat?' Lee saw it where Grace had hung it, and Nick held it while she slipped into it. Drawing her back against him, he dropped his face in her hair, and almost before she had realised it, he was tossing the slide on to a nearby table. 'I just don't see my wife wearing one of these,' he drawled, edging her out of the door.

On a cloud Lee felt herself being escorted down the hall and out into the chill morning, but one never so beautiful. The cold grey sky was brushed with a pearly sheen, the trees bejewelled with raiments of mist. As she walked with Nick across the playground, their footsteps seemed to echo across the furthest hill, sending the birds swooping and curving in a melody of song.

The little brown bus was just climbing the hill as they came out of the gate. Nick flagged it down and waited for her to climb the steps. He guided her into a seat amidst the curious stares of the occupants. The conductor, equally curious, hovered around tentatively for his fare, and Nick had to swing the flap of his overcoat back and dig deep into his trouser pocket for small change. With a grin he booked to the Crown Hotel in Little Ashby.

Lee watched the countryside spin by, conscious only of Nick's shoulder close against her own.

They stepped down from the bus at the village hotel and he led her inside to a long low-ceilinged room, with lattice windows and faded patterned carpet. The furniture was a heavy dark oak, and looking around at the hanging copper-ware and toby jugs, Lee realised that in all her years in the village, this was the first time she had been in the Crown Hotel.

An aproned woman scuttled in after them and turned a coy glance upwards, before setting an armful of logs in the grate of the huge fireplace, and lighting a match under the wood shavings. When she was satisfied that things were really ablaze, she gave them another coy smile, then hurried out and closed the door with the merest whisper of a click.

Nick took off his overcoat and hung it on the hook of a supporting beam. As Lee stood gazing into the licking flames, he came to slip hers from her shoulders and went to hang it with his own. She didn't hear him return over the carpet, but sensed him behind her. His arms turned around her waist. She was drawn back to lean against him. For a long moment he followed her gaze into the firelight, then turned her slowly towards him.

As she brought her eyes up to his, Lee murmured with a dreamy smile, 'I still can't believe it.'

'Can you believe this?'

Nick's face was darkly serious as he brought his lips down on her own. Whereas before they had been lightly brushing, now they were almost roughly demanding, but caught close against him, Lee found she had much to give.

The yearnings after those heady nights in Mombasa, the ache of loving on Half-Moon Island, the poignancy of leaving on the liner that day; it was all there in her kiss, and it was some time before Nick could raise his head.

When he did it was to say with charcoal dark eyes and a lopsided grin, 'We make quite a team!'

'There was a time,' Lee said, tracing his lips with her finger and watching him, 'when I thought the team was going to be you and Janine. You did get in touch with her to meet you that day, when we landed at Mahé, didn't you?'

'That's right,' Nick nodded. 'Janine has been after me for some time to manage her plantation.' At Lee's tilted eyebrow, he smiled, 'It looked as though you were going to be on Mahé for some time, and I wanted to be around, so I told her I was interested.'

'Just in running her plantation?'

'That was going to be the idea until that day I took you on the big game fishing trip, then I decided that one woman was enough in my life. I knew Janine was itching to get back to Paris, so . . .'

Lee gave a puzzled laugh. 'I always thought Janine lived on Mahé?'

Nick shook his head. 'She was born in the Seychelles, but she's been accumulating business interests in France ever since she was old enough to press the keys on a cash register.'

At his grin Lee asked, 'Beauvais belonged to her father, didn't it?'

Nick nodded. 'And she thought enough of him to try and hold things together there after he died, but all the key men had left to get other jobs. I think she was finding it tough going alone.'

'So that was why she was so desperate to have you? And I thought . . .'

Lee lowered her lashes and pulled in a small breath, then looking up at Nick she twinkled, 'You could have told me it was only a job!'

'I was going to,' Nick brushed her cheek with his lips, 'but then you looked as if you were mooning for Hayward, so I went and took it out of the tea bushes for a while.'

'You mean you were working all that time at Beauvais?'

He nodded with a dry smile. 'Janine spent all her time at the Seychelles club, keeping in touch with her empire in

Europe. We met occasionally in town to thresh out some problem at Beauvais.'

'That day when you took me there,' Lee said, looking up, 'was it to . . .'

Nick drew her close. 'I knew I was going to buy it then, but I didn't know how long it was going to take to talk Janine into selling.'

'How long did it take?'

'About five minutes,' he grinned. 'I think she realised it was the best solution all round. Probably the liner being in Victoria at the time helped too. She was on it almost before the ink was dry on the papers.'

'And you went with her,' Lee said, giving him a sideways glance.

'Necessary,' he sloped her a smile. 'I wanted to make sure the company would take my resignation just as quick. I also had a small matter to attend to in Nairobi.'

'Nairobi?' Lee echoed the name and then, searching his face, she marvelled, 'You went to see Philippa!'

'All in the line of duty before I finished with the firm.' The grey eyes were humorous. 'I found out what boat she left Mahé on. She wasn't difficult to trace.'

'What did you say?'

Nick gave a lazy shrug. 'Just that I'd heard that Hayward was trying to hang on to his job by making out he was married, and that if she thought she fitted the bill, she'd better get out there and make it legal.'

'She's going to do just that,' Lee smiled. 'She and Alec came to Tailliez before they left.' After a moment's silence she said, leaning against him, 'You missed the boys.'

'We'll have them at Beauvais for a holiday some time,' he said, and then, crooking a smile, 'If we've got the room!'

Blushing slightly, Lee drew away to say, 'Nick, is it true that Janine didn't actually live at the house while she was in Mahé?'

'Not that I know of,' Nick grinned, 'but we can have the whole place re-furnished if you want to.'

'I wouldn't want to change a thing,' Lee smiled.

As the logs crackled in the hearth he said, gazing down at

566

her, 'Fancy a sailing honeymoon? There's a ship in London due to leave for the Seychelles a week from today. It's cargo, but I believe the cabins are pretty luxurious.'

'I wouldn't mind if it was a raft,' Lee sighed happily.

'I think I would.' With that old sloping smile Nick drew her close and dropped his lips on hers.

A ship's siren blew gustily in the distance as Lee stepped down from the taxi. The wharf was a clangorous hustle-bustle of activity, but she didn't see much of it.

Three days of being Mrs. Nick Reynolds and it was difficult to keep her head out of the stars.

Nick was holding her arm now, guiding her on through the commotion, and supervising the loading of their baggage. She could see the gangway of their ship just ahead, and an officer at the top waiting to welcome passengers aboard. After a few minutes' easy conversation with uniformed officials gathered at the foot of it, Nick led her up.

She waited only long enough to see their cases delivered to the spacious panelled cabin, then went out on deck towards the rail. Even as she watched, the ship's engines were rumbling into life, and the men running to unwind the ropes.

As they slid away from the side and out into the river Nick came up behind her to murmur, 'Sorry to see it go?'

'In a way.' Lee watched the receding buildings. 'It's funny how you're loath to return to a place, and then you don't want to leave.'

Nick nodded. 'We'll be back for a holiday some day.'

Dreaming against him, Lee asked, 'I wonder what would have happened if we hadn't bumped into one another again after Mombasa?'

'I'd have spent all my spare time following the leads, and probably still ended up tracking you down at some school or other.'

'I suppose you know,' she said lightly, turning towards him, 'that you've put a stop to a very promising career? Although come to think of it ...' twinkling, she tilted her head thoughtfully to one side, 'there's a shortage of school staff on Mahé. And the headmistress did say ...'

'Forget it.' Nick pulled her close.

'But the children!' Lee gazed up innocently. 'They desperately need trained teachers ...'

'They're going to have to get by without this one,' he said drily, and then, brushing her teasing smile with his lips, he drawled, 'I guess you know you've got a full-time job just being my wife?'

And a lifetime's! Lee sighed happily against him. As she gazed ahead, the weak sun was valiantly laying a carpet of pale gold in the path of the ship.

Harlequin Collection Editions

*Please note: The number in brackets indicates the
original Harlequin Romance number.*

Please note: The number in brackets indicates the original Harlequin Romance number.

Harlequin Collection Editions

Please note: The number in brackets indicates the original Harlequin Romance number.

Harlequin Collection Editions

Please note: The number in brackets indicates the original Harlequin Romance number.

Complete and mail this coupon today!

Harlequin Presents...

By popular demand...

36 original novels from this series—by 3 of the world's greatest romance authors.

These back issues by Anne Hampson, Anne Mather and Violet Winspear have been out of print for some time. So don't miss out; order your copies now!

All the above titles are available at 95¢ each. Please use the attached order form to indicate your requirements.

Harlequin Reader Service
ORDER FORM

Please send me by return mail the books that I have checked.
I am enclosing 95¢ for each book ordered.

Please check volumes requested:

☐ 1	☐ 11	☐ 20	☐ 29
☐ 2	☐ 12	☐ 21	☐ 30
☐ 3	☐ 13	☐ 22	☐ 31
☐ 4	☐ 14	☐ 23	☐ 32
☐ 5	☐ 15	☐ 24	☐ 33
☐ 7	☐ 16	☐ 25	☐ 34
☐ 8	☐ 17	☐ 26	☐ 35
☐ 9	☐ 18	☐ 27	☐ 36
☐ 10	☐ 19	☐ 28	☐ 37

Number of books ordered _____ @ 95¢ each = $ _____

Postage and handling = $ _____ .25

TOTAL = $ _____

NAME _____
(please print)

ADDRESS _____

CITY _____

PROV. _____ ZIP/POSTAL CODE _____

NMO 22